For This Land

H.O. Fischer

AuthorHouse™
1663 Liberty Drive, Suite 200
Bloomington, IN 47403
www.authorhouse.com
Phone: 1-800-839-8640

First published by AuthorHouse 5/8/2009

ISBN: 978-1-4389-3559-1 (sc)

Printed in the United States of America
Bloomington, Indiana

This book is printed on acid-free paper.

One

So far, 1928 had proved to be a disappointing year for Albert. It was late summer and he was half a year past his twenty-first birthday. That galled him bitterly, because it meant that he had missed the one goal that could make a difference in his life. In disgust he kicked at the sun-hardened dirt road, raising a puff of white dust that quickly dissipated in the afternoon breeze. Just last year he had made up his mind that he would be married by the time he was twenty-one. Now, six months after the deadline, he was bitter and he knew who to blame. It was her fault. He was sure of that!

Albert wasn't in love; his reason for wanting to marry was very practical. Marriage, more than anything else, would establish his manhood. That was what made it so overwhelmingly important to him. To be twenty-one and not be considered a man was a catastrophe. It blocked his way to success and happiness. Without being recognized as a man he couldn't claim his inheritance and without that he knew he couldn't ever be happy.

His concept of happiness may have been simplistic, but in recent years life had been anything but simple for Albert. Already, at twenty-one years, he could divide his life into two parts. The first fourteen years had been good. They had been wonderful years, full of brilliantly green summers and crisp white winters. He remembered fondly working beside his father in their fields when he was a boy, and the time he spent in Prussia going to school during the war. Even now he could savor those memories as if they were carried by the same fragrant steppe breezes that accompanied him on his way home. They were wonderful recollections of what life ought to be like for a boy. But they existed in sharp contrast to the past seven years of anguish. That's why he held those memories of simple pleasures so dear. They were all that he had to mute the seven years of pure evil that followed. So in his heart, Albert was sure that claiming his inheritance would bring those good days back and get her out of his hair once and for all.

The evil had started when his father had suddenly died, unforgivably altering Albert's life. His brother had become the head of the house then and brought his wife back to the family farm. Since then, everything had slipped away. All that was Albert's, or he had imagined or hoped for, seemed to have been buried with his father. So it was natural that he was anxious to be on his own and the master of his own destiny. But he would not give up his inheritance for that freedom. Without his land he could never be at peace.

Albert's need to establish himself as a man had become an obsession. Where he lived, tucked away in a remote eastern corner of Poland, in the backwater province of Volhynia, a young man knew exactly what he had to do to become a man. He had to get married.

In the community where Albert lived, age was a secondary factor in determining manhood. It was not enough to be as old as a man, as big as a man, or earn the wages of a man. You had to be married to really be considered grown up. At twenty-one, Albert was certainly a grown man. Though he was only 160 centimeters tall and looked rather scrawny, he did a man's work. His muscles had already hardened and he earned his own way. So, in all but the one thing that mattered the most, he was a man. Albert thought of himself as a grown-up and longed to be independent. But there was only one thing that kept him from the ownership of the land that he loved so much. He was unmarried.

This common understanding that a boy was not a man until he married was not something that Albert resented, but it was something that he did not fully understand. He knew that even unmarried boys eventually became men, but where the transition came, he couldn't tell. Was it the age, the attitude, or the size? He couldn't say and no one could explain it. It seemed that a boy became a man when his community accepted him as such, and for most boys that came when they got married.

The more he brooded about it the angrier he became. Yet Albert could easily have been married a dozen times if all he wanted was to satisfy his need for a wife. If he had been willing to settle for one of those silly young girls who wanted only to escape her parents' home, he could have had his choice of several girls. But he wanted more than that. He wanted a real wife, and even though he could not explain what that meant, he was sure he deserved no less. So it was Albert's aim to follow the traditions and customs of the German-Lutheran community he lived in, and find a respectable girl, one that would be an asset. He had faith that if he followed this plan everything would go all right for him. Yet he saw one problem. Without the cooperation of his family he didn't seem to stand a chance of finding a respectable young woman. That was the frustrating part, but he had no alternative so he was willing to be patient. He did not want to repeat the mistake of his brother by impulsively marrying a woman who was unworthy.

And there was still one more reason Albert was not married. How could he take a wife when he had no home to bring her to? But that was what the wages in his pocket and the savings he had secreted away were for. There was some satisfaction in that. It was the one part of his plan that was fulfilling itself. Now, finally, he believed he had enough saved to execute his plan. It even brought him some pleasure to think what the witch's reaction might be if he were to show her the money. It would be wonderful to watch her face contort in pain. But he knew better. It would be dangerous to show her that he had money. It was ironic; his dream was her nightmare.

Albert shook himself and started walking again. He was dawdling and he hated standing still. It was the heat, he told himself, that agitated his thoughts so much that he lingered on the road. It had been hot all day and he had worked feverishly to finish his week's work. Even now, in the late afternoon of a September Saturday as he was returning home, it was still unseasonably hot. So it was easy to blame the heat but he knew it wasn't true. It was hate that fevered his emotions. But that was all right, because it kept him incredibly focused.

The truth was that when he wasn't working, Albert was consumed with thoughts of revenge. The pattern was always the same. All he had to do was to look at the land and then the anger would well up from the pit of his stomach. He loved the land, particularly the land his father had farmed and he hated that it was not his. When he felt like this, he knew whom to blame. In front of him, blocking his way, were Johann and the Witch. They always stood in his way.

He was beginning to wonder if things would ever change. Yet it should have been so easy for him to change his life and at the same time extract the most excruciating revenge on the pair. All he had to do to get his share of his inheritance from his brother and the witch was to get married. It was so simple, and yet he had missed his deadline. It wasn't fair. It had to change. It had to change for him and for his mother too.

It was only when Albert thought of his mother that he softened. After all, much of what she had endured in the last few years she had suffered for him. He could not have survived those years without her. She had allowed her daughter-in-law to badger, humiliate and starve her to death for his sake. That was no exaggeration, not in Albert's mind anyway. She deserved better. It was obvious to him that the end of his torment was the end of hers too. She would come and live with him and his brother would be shamed.

His brother Johann was sixteen years older than Albert and there were ambiguous feelings attached to their relationship. He knew that Johann thought of himself as some kind of brother/father, yet Albert could not think of Johann in that way. No one could be his father, except his father, and he was dead. Only grudgingly could Albert concede that for the past seven years Johann had taken care of their mother and him. Even though legally and morally he had no other option than to let them live with him, he deserved some credit for carrying out that responsibility. Still, it seemed to Albert, that through his wife, Johann had betrayed his mother. It was only fitting that when Albert planned his revenge, he included Johann. Without him, his wife could have done nothing.

Suddenly he caught himself again. Seething in the anguish that kept his hate alive, he found himself stopped in the middle of the road. He needed to find some relief from those frustrating thoughts and so he turned his attention to the fields. They could stir his emotions but they could also soothe them. The wheat was ripe and waiting for the harvest. The heavy heads of grain swayed back and forth in the wind like an amber-green ocean. This was the kind of sight that his eyes could feast upon to bring him out of the depths of despair. Like his father, Albert was basically a farmer whose heart always swelled at the prospect of a rich field of grain, even if it wasn't his. His father had taught him that a farmer needed to draw courage from such sights, fields bursting with thick heads of ripe grain in the fall; whereas the spring that inspired most other people held uncertainty for men of the land. It seemed to be true for Albert. Never had such a sight failed to stir his dreams. From where he stood on the road his view of the land was unobstructed, revealing a field stretching toward the horizon, ready to fulfill its destiny. It was crying for someone to pluck its overflowing harvest. This was the ultimate and best possible use of land.

He knew that not all land was as good as this Volhynian soil, but what he could not know was that there was no other land like it in the world. Even if he had known, it wouldn't have mattered, because he had no intention of going anywhere else. He loved the land, this land where he was born, and his passion, and his schemes, and his hopes rested on his ability to own some of this black gold of Volhynia, even if it was just the small piece his father had intended for him. He was proud to be a German-Volhynian and for a piece of this land he would do anything. For this land, he would even consider selling his soul.

Yet Albert knew virtually nothing about the land of Volhynia. He did not even know the meaning of the name that his people now used so casually and had even adopted. He and his people were Volhynians, albeit German-Volhynians. That the name was older than the land that belonged to it, having taken the name of the ancient Russian tribe that had once lived there, did not cross their minds. Even though through the years of its turbulent history the territory routinely shifted from one flag to another, that name had persisted. Now, in 1928, it was Polish territory once again, so decreed by international treaty after the Great War. Even with its ownership still bitterly contested by the predominantly Ukrainian population, all its inhabitants called this little corner of the world Volhynia. In its history it had been Russian, Ukrainian, Lithuanian, once part of Galicia to the south and for a short time it had been the independent Kingdom of Volhynia. But that was in the past, and few of the Germans who lived there knew of the land's volatile history. In 1928 it mattered little to Albert that his land was a part of Poland. He was, however, glad that it was no longer a part of Russia, as it had been when he was born. Other than that, he cared little what flag flew over the land of his birth as long as he could live there in peace.

Albert didn't care about history. Since he had first understood its significance, his mind had been captivated by the land. Everything about it stirred his interest. It seemed to him that it was the one thing that endured when everything else changed, and so it was the one thing he could believe in. Though its beauty was magnificent, he knew it was insignificant when compared to its power. And even to an uneducated boy it was self-evident that the land's power came from its timeless fertility. That was why the fall was Albert's season of hope and why he stood transfixed by a field of grain.

Full and ripe heads of grain swaying in the breeze had turned the field into a hypnotic ocean. It was so full and rich that Albert wanted to reach out with his arms and take it all. He stood so quietly that he could feel his heart beating in his chest. This was what made him feel alive.

As he stood there wishing that the field was his, he noticed how immense this grain field really was. There were no fences partitioning it into the tiny fields of two or three hectares like his community farmed. "You have to be rich," he said to himself, "to own a large field like this." It was bigger than any field of the German farmers of his village and it stretched across the hills and out of sight, interrupted only by a tree lined lane that met the road some fifty meters ahead. Now he recognized where he was. This was the field of the Countess Viteranno. If he strained he could see the sun glinting off the upper windows of her manor at the end of the road and surrounded by trees. It was her grain field that he admired and was astonished to recall that people said that she was poor. He shook his head. It was not possible to have so much land and be poor.

Albert knew that it was from the Countess's father and grandfather that almost all the Germans in the territory had bought or leased their land. Now it was to her that mortgages and rents were being paid. It was a mystery to him how so much revenue and land could add up to poverty. He could only shrug his shoulders at the contradiction.

As he was admiring the Viteranno fields, he noticed an automobile kicking up dust on the lane. It moved so quickly that

Albert stood amazed as it rocketed past the tall, ancient oaks that lined the road. The countess owned the only car in the district and to the locals it was a marvel. Even he was excited at the prospect of seeing it from up close. But since he knew absolutely nothing about cars he did not realize that the vehicle was approaching the road too quickly. It swerved wildly as it turned onto the Zeperow road, fish-tailing and screeching before it came to a stop. A distinct bang that sounded like a gun shot made Albert shudder. The black automobile stopped suddenly and even he could tell that there was something not right. The vehicle sat in the middle of the road, slightly tilted. Something had broken.

The door opened on squeaking hinges and a slim woman in a very broad-rimmed yellow hat, and bright yellow and white striped dress got out. It had to be the countess, no one else dressed like that. She walked around the vehicle and Albert saw her kicking at something under the car, then she looked up and down the road and spotted Albert. "Young man, come here!" she shouted in Polish, with authority, as if giving orders came naturally for her. Albert approached her cautiously. He had no idea what she wanted from him. He knew nothing about cars. "Do you know how to replace a wheel?" she asked as he came close. Albert shook his head. "Of course not," she said disappointed. It was strange to Albert that this woman could command so much authority in her voice. It was not a raspy voice like the witch's, it was pleasant, yet firm and in control. Dressed so brightly with a flowing white silk scarf around her neck it seemed as if she had stepped out of another world. She carried an air of authority that let him know she was in control even if she had asked for his help. "Are you from around here?" she asked.

"Zeperow," Albert replied.

"What is your name?" she asked switching from Polish to German with such ease that Albert was amazed. She had understood as soon as he said Zeperow that he was German.

"Albert Fischer."

"Oh, you must be Johann's brother?"

"Yes."

"Wonderful! Your brother is a good man. Do you know who I am?"

Albert nodded, "I think so. You're the Countess."

"Yes. Well, Albert Fischer, today you are going to learn something new. I'm going to show you how to replace that wheel. I don't have time to wait for Hermann." She made it sound as if she was doing him a favor and Albert never even thought to object. She opened the trunk and said, "You will have to remove the spare and you will need a jack." Albert looked in the trunk. He was puzzled. It took the countess a second to realize his ignorance. "Of course, you have no idea what I'm talking about." She pointed to the worn looking wheel in her trunk and said, "this is the spare tire and you can remove it by undoing that nut, see. Now the jack is lying in here somewhere and you have to fit it under the frame. Don't worry I'll show you."

She talked almost continuously, but she never laid a finger on the tires or the jack, she just hovered over Albert giving him directions and offering suggestions to help him place the jack in the correct position to raise the car so that the punctured tire could be removed and the spare put on.

"Look at that wheel," she said, "the rubber is almost gone. No wonder it burst. And the spare is not much better. These automobiles are so damned expensive to maintain. You are doing a good job, young man, you obviously have some mechanical ability. Father always said that when it comes to mechanical ability the Germans are unsurpassed. He trusted the Germans, that's why he preferred to lease his lands to them."

Except from a distance, Albert had never seen the Countess Viteranno before. He was amazed by her youthful appearance. She couldn't have been more than a few years older than him and yet it seemed that people had been whispering about her all his life. There were the tales of the precocious teenager who scandalized her father at every turn. Then there was the marriage to a German nobleman that was highly controversial. Even more notorious was her hasty divorce and return to Poland. It seemed that someone with such a past ought to be much older. But then he reminded himself that she didn't have to work like the women of his community. Perhaps she was much older than she looked; her manner seemed to indicate that. Her directions were crisp and confident and although he felt awkward being ordered around by a woman, he was impressed by her. She made him feel like she was teaching him, so he was relaxed and enjoyed the experience. He liked her even though she talked constantly.

When the job was done, she pointed up the tree-lined lane to her estate and said, "Oh, see now, there comes Hermann. As usual, too late to be any help." Albert looked up the lane and saw a wagon loaded with fall hay being pulled by two horses. It was still too distant for him to recognize the driver but he supposed that it was one of her servants. It didn't matter anyway, the job was done and her attention was off somewhere else.

As she opened the trunk of her car for Albert to replace the punctured wheel, she was talking again, but he could barely relate to what she was saying. "Well I'll just have to find the money to buy new ones. If I'm going to do without a chauffeur, I can't afford to have punctures. My man left me so I no longer have a driver. He went off to Krakow to find work. All the young people are moving to the big city, except you German boys, you stay home to work the farms. There, that's good. Now be sure to fasten it onto the bracket again, I don't want it bouncing around while I'm driving."

When everything was packed in the trunk, she thanked Albert, but not in any way he expected. She didn't shake his hand nor did she offer him a gratuity. She just smiled and said, "Good," and drove off leaving him staring at the dust she churned up.

For much too long Albert stood watching the automobile winding away, wondering if his friends at the tavern would believe him when he told them of his encounter with the beautiful countess.

While he stood there, he paid little attention to the clopping of horse hooves as they came closer and closer. A few minutes ago the wagon still seemed to be far off and innocuous, merely a load of late hay on the way to the barn. Now, however, a noise like a whip exploded almost in his ear. That woke Albert from his daydreaming. In a matter of seconds the horses were so close he could hear their strained panting. His escape to the other side of the road was already cut off. Desperate to get away, he leaped over the road-bank, rolling into the wheat that was planted close to the edge of the road. Behind him Albert heard a loud crack like seasoned wood breaking and he supposed that something on the wagon had broken. But that was small satisfaction for almost being run over.

As the wagon passed by he scrambled back onto the road in a burst of self-righteous anger, climbing the two-meter embankment almost without effort. "You idiot," he shouted after the wagon. "What's the idea of running me over?" A large man stood up and glared back at him. Albert recognized him immediately. "Oh, was that you, Fischer," the man called back smiling all the time. "I didn't see you! Maybe when you grow up you'll be taller." Albert's face turned red. It was like Hermann Martin to run him over and then insult him. But now Hermann was pointing tauntingly to the ground beside Albert, "Is that your bag on the road? Sorry! You should be more careful."

Albert looked where he had laid his bag of tools while he worked on the countess's flat tire. Now he understood the loud crack he had heard. It wasn't the wagon breaking but its wheels running over his tools. When he looked inside it dismayed him to see the cracked and mangled handles. Luckily, it was only the handles.

Had Albert known that it was Hermann Martin that the countess was referring to, he would have been more careful. You always had to be on your toes with him. The more pain he could cause the happier he was, and if he made it happen to a member of the Fischer family, that made him gloat. It was hard to believe he was part of the German community since he spent his whole life working against it. Albert knew a lot about hate but he couldn't understand what it was that Martin carried for him. After all, it was Martin who had wronged his family and not the other way around. Perhaps it was true what his mother had said, that Martin just hated everyone.

Albert gathered up his bag, angrily throwing away the pieces of his broken handles and hurried home. As he overcame his disappointment about the tools he began to wonder what Martin was doing with the Countess's hay. He assumed that he had bought it from her, but she had talked about him like he was a servant, not a customer. He was puzzled. He supposed no one would be foolish enough to hire Martin and he was even more sure that Martin did not need a job. Then he remembered that the Countess Viteranno had treated him the same way. All the time he was changing her tire she talked as if she had been ordering him around for years. It was her way. He shrugged it off.

Once more he looked at the sun, now almost sitting on the horizon, and knew that he was in trouble. The witch did not tolerate lateness. No excuse was good enough, not from him. Most likely he would have to do without supper. But it was all right, he knew how to get even. If she did not feed him then he had no money for her. He had a better purpose for it anyway.

Albert was sure that his brother's wife was cruel and hateful because she enjoyed it. He had learned early on that it was not wise to openly offend the witch, so he had found more subtle ways to get back at her. That's why he called her "the Witch." At least that was his secret name for her. But in public he called her "Johann's wife" or "my brother's wife," never "Hedwig" or "my sister-in-law." It kept her more remote, more his brother's wife than his sister-in-law, and therefore hardly related at all. It also kept his hatred for her on the edge of his tongue, more palpable, more urgent.

It had not taken Albert long to discover the real source of the tension between them. It was the farm. Even now that their mutual dislike had taken on a life of its own, he knew that the farm would always be there at the root of their hatred. The land that she was so afraid of losing and the inheritance that he so much wanted to claim had stood between them from the first day she moved in. Right from the beginning, she had pushed intensely for her husband to find Albert an apprenticeship or other work that would take his interest away from the farm. She did not even try to understand how important his father's land was to him and she did not see that the more she wanted to push him off the farm, the more he clung to it.

The insignificant piece of land that created the tension between Albert and his sister-in-law consisted of merely nine hectares. Originally, the family farm had not been much larger, only twelve hectares. But after the War they lost one quarter of their land to the trickery of a neighbor. Even in this extremely productive region of the world, nine hectares could not support Johann Fischer, his wife, two sons, his mother and his brother. Still, it stood at the center of their dreams. For the same truth ruled their lives that ruled the lives of peasants all across the world; owning land was not just the means to success but the definition of it. So even if you had to work outside your farm to support your family, ownership of the land was still the crowning achievement of life. For a Volhynian farmer, the ultimate goal was to have enough of this fine land to support his family. At that point he had achieved everything that he might reasonably expect of life.

Lately, as Albert had been approaching manhood, Hedwig had become almost frantic in her need to find a way to deny him his inheritance. Faced with such intense opposition, Albert, for the first time, was forced to consider his options. He had even begun to wonder why the land meant so much to him and his family and the community. He supposed that the entire German population of Volhynia had come here to find land. The question had never before been important enough to ask. At least that's what Albert told himself, when he knew he was actually afraid of the answer. The only person in Zeperow who knew anything about history was his brother. Unfortunately, asking Johann was risky. It required a strong stomach and much patience because his brother could never use two words when a hundred were so much better. Albert would rather leave the question unanswered than face one of Johann's history lessons.

The sun was long gone by the time Albert turned up the lane to his farmyard. The dog barked his greeting and Albert shouted back to him, "Hold on Wasser, I'll be right there." Even he thought that Wasser, simply translated as Water and spoken Vasser, was a strange name, but he could never bring himself to ask where she had got it. He searched through his pocket but couldn't find a treat to give the starving animal. Then Albert chided himself. If he had anything to eat, he would have eaten it himself. As he opened the gate, the dog waited anxiously, panting and wagging his tail. Albert squatted down and stroked his black fur. "Sorry, I have nothing for you, Wasser. If I get anything I'll bring you some," he promised. He felt sorry for the witch's dog but was pleased that the animal liked him better than he liked her. But why not, when Wasser came begging for food and she would send him running with a swat of her broom, Albert would make sure that he got something, even if he had to steal it. It was another way to get back at her. Right now he didn't even have a crumb, nevertheless, the dog followed him to the door wagging his tail excitedly.

As Albert opened the front door the kitchen table stood right in front of him. His brother Johann sat at the table smoking his after-dinner pipe and supervising his two young boys as they did their nightly reading from the bible. His mother and the witch were busy washing and putting away pots and pans. But all eyes turned to Albert as he came in the door. For a second no one said anything. Albert couldn't help but notice that the table had been cleared. It was disappointing but he held in his anger despite his hunger. At least he had been right and he took what consolation he could in knowing that she could no longer surprise him. He knew her too well. That satisfaction would not outlast his hunger but for now it would have to do.

Gustav, Albert's youngest nephew, a sharp-witted boy of seven, had understood what was developing since supper. "Father works so hard!" his mother had excused once again as she divided Albert's supper between herself and his father. Even at his tender age, Gustav knew it was unfair and he knew that he should have kept quiet right now. But the boy had tired of reading and was hoping for a distraction. "Hello Albert," he blurted out, "there is no supper left! Mama and Papa ate yours."

Johann and his wife stared at their son with a look of consternation that told him he was in trouble. The boy made himself as small as possible in his chair and pretended to read. But then Hedwig turned to Albert, her voice cold and unsympathetic. "You're late, there wasn't much," she said curtly, as she returned to her work.

Albert didn't reply to Hedwig. He didn't even acknowledge that she was there. If he couldn't eat he had to move on to his next concern. There were tools to repair before he went to bed. But before he could move his mother came and kissed him on the cheek and whispered in his ear, "I've saved something for you." Now Albert gritted his teeth. He found his mother's humiliation harder to endure than his own hunger. In her own house Julianna Fischer had to steal food for her son, and his older brother did nothing about it.

It made Albert's head spin. His brother's callous indifference to their mother was his most unforgivable failing. Any good feeling Albert had for Johann disappeared when saw his brother ignore his mother's plight. He was filled with contempt as he stared at him.'He's considered a man, and I'm not,' Albert thought resentfully. 'He's content to let his wife run the house however she wants while he hides in his books.' He knew he had to get out of the house before it made him sick.

"I need a lamp," Albert said abruptly.

"What for?" Hedwig asked sharply. She was the guardian of the household expenses too.

Albert continued to ignore her. His left hand was in his pocket fumbling with the coins that he had earned when a half smile came to his lips. He took two zlotys out of his pocket and smacked them down in front of Johann. The sound drew Hedwig like a magnet. She was there even before Albert took his hand off them. "Two! Why only two?" she fumed. Albert looked her straight in the eyes, "If I have to feed myself I can't afford more." He knew the rebuke hit her where it hurt most and she started to say something but her husband interrupted her. "Then it will have to do," he said as he picked up the coins.

"I need a lamp," Albert said again, "two handles broke today and I need to fix them."

"Careless!" Hedwig accused angrily. "A good workman takes care of his tools."

"It wasn't my fault," Albert snapped back still looking at his brother who had stopped reading to find out about the broken tools. "Martin ran me off the road."

At the mention of Hermann Martin, Albert's mother gasped out loud and Johann looked up in concern. Hedwig's brow wrinkled too. She may have looked on Albert as a threat but she knew Martin was dangerous. For a minute, she softened and became almost conciliatory. "Go fix your shovels," she snapped, "I'll make you something to eat." He couldn't understand it when she changed so quickly. It only served to make him angrier.

Two

The shed where the Fischers' kept their farm implements was small but efficient. There was no big machinery on the farm. They were too poor and the farm was too small to make it practical to buy threshing machines and seed planting drills. Luckily there was a farmers' cooperative in town where those things could be rented. But ploughs, shovels, scythes, pick-axes and hand-tools, including wood working tools of all kinds were neatly hung and well maintained. Albert enjoyed being there. It was almost exactly as his father had left it.

This had often been Albert's refuge. It was where he went when he needed to escape; where he could spend hours in solitude and where the memory of his father was the strongest. When he was younger, Hedwig had often sent him out there as punishment until she found out how much he enjoyed it. He loved working with tools, especially the wood working type. Now he was looking through the stacks of lumber that he had organized himself under the work bench. He was looking for a piece that he could shape into a new shovel handle. It was not a challenge for him, shovel handles were easy, hardly any shaping required, just rounding off a long piece of wood. Almost immediately he found a suitable piece of hard Volhynian-oak that would make a sturdy handle and he attacked the job. With his whittling knife, a plane and a rasp he fashioned an appropriate handle very quickly. He turned the piece of oak in his vice every few minutes to make sure that every side was finished to a consistent width so that it felt right in his hand and he could work with it comfortably all day. His father's words came to mind as he worked, 'When you make it yourself then you know exactly how you want it to feel.'

He hummed and sang as he worked, now a hymn and then a rowdy rhyme someone at the tavern had adapted from the Russian. 'Johann would never approve of that one,' he said to himself, and then sang it again. It wasn't long before all his concerns drifted away and he even forgot about his hunger. It was hard to think about the witch and worry about retribution while he worked with the wood. It was too special to Albert, and he took too much pleasure in the feel and the smell of the oak.

When the handle was done and fixed onto the shovel he stood back and admired it, especially the way he had tapered it from the working end to the butt where he left a slight knob. That made it hard for the shovel to slip out of his hands even when they were sweaty from digging all day. Albert was not an innovator and he knew it. What he was good at was recognizing advantages of changes he had seen others make and incorporating them quickly into his work. His father had told him that he was talented in that way and had praised him for his abilities with wood. That's what he enjoyed most about doing it now; it was the echo of his father's praise that made him feel safe there. And it was his father's praise that he had missed most of all for the past seven years. That almost brought a tear to his eye, but he wouldn't allow it. Tears were not for men.

He was just looking for a second piece of lumber when his mother opened the shed door. From under her apron she pulled a cloth and unwrapped the morsels she had been able to rescue for him, two small sausages and a boiled potato.

"She said she was going to make me something," Albert protested.

"Take this too, Albert. It's not much."

"I hate the way she treats you Mama," he complained between bites, "and I hate Johann for allowing her."

"Never mind Albert. Your brother is a good man. It is your brother's job to cleave to his wife. I know it makes him sad that his wife is so...so unkind to us, but what good would it do him or us if he argued with her all day. She would only be more bitter."

"Maybe she would leave."

"It's not easy for a husband to take sides against his wife, especially with her in-laws. It bothers him as much as it bothers you, but he is a man of faith and the Bible says that a man should leave his mother and father and cleave unto his wife. Once you are married then you will understand."

"I would never marry a woman like that!" Albert said sternly and then he realized how glad he was that his mother had broached this subject. "Mama, I've been thinking that I should marry soon."

"Yes, I know you have. You are at the age. Your friends are marrying and I imagine that soon your friend August will be marrying. It is logical that you should be thinking that way." She smiled and continued, "I've seen you looking at the girls at church."

Albert was grateful for the darkness now as he could feel himself blushing. He changed the subject quickly. "But how can I marry, mother, when my brother will not help me? What father would allow me to marry his daughter if I don't have my family's blessing?"

"What makes you think Johann will hold back his blessing?"

"She does not want me to marry. She won't allow him to help me and he never goes against her will!"

"He cannot deny you your right. But you will have to ask him."

"And if he does deny it? If he lets his wife get in the way?"

Julianna became adamant. "Then he will have to deal with me! I've tried to keep the peace hoping that we could get along but I will not sit by and watch her deny you your rights. If Johann will not do his duty then he is not my son anymore and he is not worthy of being his father's son." It was a rare thing for Albert to see his mother voicing her opinion so strongly, yet it sounded familiar. He could faintly remember that that was what it was like before the witch came. He liked it.

"But you must ask him, Albert," his mother repeated, "and don't think that you know the answer before you ask."

Albert spent another hour finishing up his work after his mother returned to the house. Though he appreciated the quiet of the work shop and the opportunity to brood in solitude, he was tired when he finished. Though his mother's counsel kept ringing in his ears until he almost believed it, what he really wanted now was to sleep.

When he finally walked in the front door of the house, he found Wasser up on the table licking out his bowl. It was the supper Hedwig had grudgingly made for Albert that her dog had just devoured. Surprisingly, he felt no anger. He understood. His first thought was to get the dog off the table before anyone else saw him. It was already too late. As Albert grabbed Wasser by the collar Johann came in from the barn after his nightly check of the livestock.

Johann grit his teeth but Albert couldn't tell that it was out of concern rather than anger. "He's hungry! He's always hungry!" Albert complained. There was a terse quality to his voice that made Johann realize that his brother was not just complaining. It was an accusation.

Johann grabbed Wasser by his collar and pulled him outside. As he slammed the door he sternly pronounced the creature's punishment, "You stay out there tonight!" Albert was relieved that the sentence wasn't more harsh.

Within a few seconds, however, Wasser was back at the door whining and scratching. Johann ignored him. Even Albert understood that some kind of punishment was needed. Johann's action was appropriate. He had expected worse and was thankful that his brother was not angrier. But the dog persisted at the door, scratching and yelping. When that did not work, he began to whine loudly. He wanted to sleep in his place by the stove.

When he began to bark, Hedwig woke and stormed into the kitchen in her nightshirt. "Why is that dog out there?" she demanded. "Let him in!"

"He ate Albert's supper," Johann explained quietly.

"What?"

"He got up on the table and cleaned the bowl," Johann clarified, remaining calm despite his wife's incredulity.

Albert watched his brother intently as he dealt with his wife. The pattern, as he saw it, was that she screamed and he groveled. He suspected that Johann was afraid of her though he couldn't understand why. Deep down he wanted his brother to lose his temper with her but it didn't happen. It never happened. People said he was gentle but Albert believed he was a coward. The proof was there in his refusal to put his wife in her place. Though it bothered Albert it was no surprise. Hadn't the war proved what Johann was.

"No! I don't believe it," Hedwig said gruffly.

Johann shrugged and shook his head. "Hedwig, I saw him."

The witch turned red. Whatever emotions her husband lacked, she made up for. But it always seemed that her emotions were exaggerated, so it was no surprise to Albert that she flew into a rage. She retrieved her broom from the corner and started for the door seething. "I'll teach him!"

"No, Hedwig," Johann pleaded, "what good will that do?"

But she was at the door without responding. Wasser, reacted immediately to the broom in his mistress's hand. He bolted the instant he saw her. "Come back here you worthless dog," she yelled after him, but Johann and Albert heard the clamor as the dog jumped the fence to get away from her. The dog knew her too well.

Albert couldn't help smiling. He almost broke into a chuckle before he caught himself. Even Johann had a wisp of a smile on his lips. They both knew that the dog would come slinking back in the morning after she had settled down. He would allow his worried mistress to entice him back into the house. Wasser might even hold out until she offered him treats of food. That was the difference, Albert thought, between himself and the animal, he would not grovel. He was not so sure about his brother.

"What are you two laughing at?" Hedwig shot out angrily as she turned and looked at the two brothers, her face still red. "Go to bed, both of you!" she ordered as she stomped off.

Tired as he was, Albert would rather have slept, but her order irked him and his spine tingled with resentment. He would not, could not, go to bed on her order. If she wanted him to go to bed he would stay up a little longer. He looked across the table to where his brother was sitting and hoped to see the same defiance in his eyes. He saw nothing!

It seemed strange to Albert that two people so different were brothers. Even when people remarked how much alike they looked he took exception. Eyes, ears, nose, mouth, hair; what did they matter? He could only see the differences between himself and Johann. His brother was unfeeling and unimaginative, more concerned with religion and politics than reality. His brother was hopelessly flawed.

If Albert had really thought about it, he would have conceded that the only unforgivable thing Johann had done was to bring the witch into his life. But because he couldn't see how hate had twisted his perceptions he had transferred the sins of the wife to the husband. His reasoning was simple. If Johann insisted on being the head of the household then he had to be responsible for everything his wife did too.

Albert was sure that under the same circumstances he would have behaved differently. He would have been more diligent and loyal. Most of all he would never have allowed his wife to treat his mother the way his sister-in-law did. No, his brother didn't deserve his respect.

Unfortunately, right now, he needed his brother's help. Time and time again his mother had told him,"Talk to Johann. Explain how you feel. He will do the right thing." He had to try.

He sat down at the table and tried to broach the subject. But he was tired, he told himself, and he didn't know where or how to start. What if Johann refused to help him?

It was Johann who broke the silence first. "Tell me about your run in with Martin. What happened?"

Relieved that Johann had diverted his focus, Albert was eager to relate his encounter with the Countess and Martin. But as he was finished explaining about his thin escape from under Martin's horses he began to wonder about Hermann Martin's unexpected appearance on the road again. "I still don't understand what he was doing there," he began to speculate, "it almost seemed as if Martin was working for the countess."

"Martin works for no one but himself," Johann corrected and Albert nodded.

"Then maybe he's just buying feed from the estate."

"Perhaps, but it's more likely that he's up to something. His appetite for land is unquenchable."

"Everyone wants more land. There is nothing wrong with that."

"Except when you steal it."

Albert knew where that was going and he knew the story inside-out. He searched for someway to lead Johann in another direction. "Is it the land that brought the Germans to Volhynia?" he quickly asked.

"Yes, free land from the Tzarina Catherine brought Germans here and throughout the Ukraine," Johann answered with new enthusiasm. This was a subject that pleased him a lot more than Hermann Martin.

Johann was sixteen years older than Albert and had been educated in a time when the Russians still tolerated the presence of a German School system. As Albert had grown up, that privilege had been rescinded and his parents, like so many others, could not find schools for their other children. There weren't enough Russian schools to take the German children and even if there had been, most of the Germans did not want their children educated in Russian. But Johann had been taught well and come to appreciate history most of all. He didn't just know the history of the German immigration to Russia, he lived it. To him the story of the Germans in eastern Europe was not finished, it was ongoing. There was much more to come and he was as fascinated as he was afraid. The future did not look good but he never passed up a chance to talk about German accomplishments in the swamp that was Volhynia.

"Of course we came for the land," Johann repeated, "we are farmers and to farmers the land is everything. However, our family didn't come from Germany, but from Poland."

"Poland?" Albert questioned.

"Our Opa, Martin Fischer, came here from Middle-Poland after the insurrections there in the 1860's," Johann clarified. "Our father was just a baby." As he talked, Albert tried to convince himself that he only listened to his brother not to be rude, yet he couldn't deny his curiosity about the Polish connection. He had supposed that it was only after the Great War that his family had been connected to Poland. "There were many Germans here already when our grandparents came and the free land was all gone," Johann continued. "Opa leased land from the Countess's grandfather. When he grew up our father married and bought this piece of land. By then there was so much talk of land reform in Russia that he didn't want to chance leasing. There were rumors that the Tzar was not going to allow the Germans to buy land much longer. And it soon became the law. Germans coming from Poland could no longer buy land."

"Why wouldn't the Tzar allow us to buy land?" Albert asked. It was more than curiosity that prompted this question. He knew that this crucial difference between leasing and buying land was one of the points of dispute between the Germans and the Poles. It was also the root of the family's dispute with Hermann Martin.

"The Russians were beginning to feel that there were too many Germans here on their western border. For a hundred years Germans had been moving into Russia, especially the Ukraine. We spoke German, we had better schools than they, better agriculture and we had a different religion. When we first came the Russian newspapers called us an inspiration. A generation later they called us an infestation and an insult to Russia. It's hard to understand what changed. Probably only our numbers."

Albert already had enough information to satisfy his interest but Johann wove an intricate tale. He explained it as if he had witnessed every event. Albert knew that the longer he allowed his brother to talk the harder it would be to leave, but he couldn't stop him now. As he continued Johann explained how the Tzarina Catherine, herself a German, had enticed the German farmers to come to Russia more than a century ago. His tale was basically true but laced with the prejudices of his own heritage. Yet the German account of that story was something Johann believed in strongly and his passion came out as he talked. He loved the history of his people and could go on for hours. Now, as if he was a captive, Albert listened, strangely aware that for the first time in his life, history was interesting. It intrigued him as his brother explained that the Fischers were relative newcomers within the German community of Volhynia.

The facts of their arrival were true, as Johann had detailed. Young Joseph Fischer had come with his parents during the last great wave of German settlement in Russia in the 1860's. His family fled the troubled Russian territory known as Congress-

Poland, named after the Congress of Vienna that established boundaries after the defeat of Napoleon. The Germans, however, insisted on referring to the area they lived in as Middle-Poland. That description was geographically accurate. They had plunked themselves down in the heart of Poland.

There, the Poles were weary of Russian oppression. But the constant struggle of the people to free themselves had made the Germans in that land fear for their safety. They were well aware that they were there at the Russians' invitation, and that the Poles resented their presence.

The Polish-Germans had lived under Russian rule for several generations and were happy to remain under the Russian flag as long as it signified peace and stability. Indeed, they had little sympathy for the constant Polish grumbling about Russian oppression. They were sure that if Poles had not been so rebellious, the Russians would have treated them better. They also reasoned that if the Poles were a more intelligent people, then the Russians would not have invited the Germans to Poland. There would have been no need to improve the agriculture. So when the Russians characterized the Polish as stupid and backward, the Germans not only accepted it as true but embellished the perception. They believed they had seen with their own eyes the evidence of Polish unworthiness.

As the Polish agitation for independence reached a frenzy and armed rebellion began, the Germans began to leave. During the 1860's a major uprising in Poland motivated Martin Fischer and his wife to leave. In 1863 after much of his community had already abandoned their town, Martin packed up his belongings and his infant son Joseph, and drove a horse and wagon east across the Bug River into Russia.

If you asked the Germans of the 1860's why they were heading eastward, instead of west like the rest of Europe's surplus population, they would have told you that they were invited. Most would have known that Catherine the Great, the Empress of Russia, had invited the Germans to Poland and Russia. That Catherine had been dead for almost seventy years when the last great wave of immigration came was irrelevant to them. Even the late arrivals of the 1860's considered that the invitation of Catherine included them.

The reason for Catherine's invitation to the Germans was simple, she needed them. In the latter part of the eighteenth century, with the defeat of the Turks in the Ukraine and the partition of Poland, the Tzarina now had vast stretches of new territory. The land was underpopulated and underdeveloped. Germany, on the other hand, was still divided into small bickering principalities and self-ruling free cities, and their populations were bulging. There was little land remaining to develop in Germany for a second or third son of a farmer. A life of destitution faced most of the landless sons of German farmers. Few had the resources to sail across the ocean and escape to the west. The Russian Empress's call was timely.

Catherine repeated her invitation to the Germans several times, each time sweetening the offer. She offered interest free loans to buy land, thirty years of freedom from taxes, and shorter terms of military obligation. But the clinching offer was the ethnic freedom that she promised the Germans. They were free to keep their own language and their Protestant or Catholic religion. They would also be allowed to have their own schools and a high degree of civic autonomy. Even after her death in 1795 the offer was repeated by her son and once again by her grandson.

The choice was easy for many. They fled east like geese before winter. Even though their own governments tried to stop them they kept coming. In some states the authorities confiscated the possessions of anyone seeking to leave the country. But farmers will risk almost any danger for a chance to possess land of their own. Those who made it to Russia looked on Catherine as their benefactress. Whenever their descendants were asked why they had come to Russia they pointed to the queen.

The first Germans to pass through Volhynia were pleased by the magnificent beauty of the Polesje forest that towered over them as they walked and pushed handcarts under its cathedral-like canopy. The forest was dense with age-old oaks that ascended almost to the clouds and gave the murky woods a primeval quality. The rivers and marshes teemed with fish and deer. The German women were awe-struck by the proliferation of wild-flowers, azaleas and rhododendron, that colored and perfumed the forest glades. Even those who stopped long enough to turn over a shovel full of earth were pleased to find the soil rich and black. Yet, of the thousands of Germans who saw it, almost none stayed. As if drawn there by the fragrant steppe breezes, they continued on to the Ukrainian Steppes.

The reason for this lack of interest in Volhynia was perfectly understandable. A little farther to the south and east, on the fertile plains of the Ukraine there was a farmers' paradise. All that a man had to do was harness his horse to a plough, turn the sod, and reap a bountiful harvest. It was almost effortless. The soil was so easy to turn that before the Germans arrived, local farmers were still using wooden ploughs. On the other hand, stopping in Volhynia would mean that most of a generation would spend their lives in the back breaking toil of clearing the gigantic trees. But even that wouldn't have deterred all the land-starved farmers. The real killer was the swamp. A great part of this extremely fertile land was under water. It was an expansive, almost impenetrable swamp. While there was an abundant supply of land on the steppes, it made no practical sense for a farmer to stop in Volhynia.

Yet by the 1820's there were small communities of German farmers growing in the great Polesje forest. A few hardy souls had fallen in love with the place. They lived in tiny villages scattered in the woods and were not particularly prosperous. It was not until the 1830's and the first great uprising in Poland that large numbers of Germans settled in Volhynia. It was then that farmers with experience in draining the swamps of Poland started to arrive.

Still, a generation spent their lives in this back-breaking toil. The local Polish and Ukrainians, who had laughed as the Germans wore themselves out and died of swamp fever, later marveled as prosperous farms emerged from the swamps and forests.

By the 1860's when another wave of immigration came out of strife ridden Middle-Poland, there were numerous German communities in Volhynia. With their distinctive German houses and villages surrounding their neat Lutheran Churches, they considered themselves to be German colonies, distinct and separate from the rest of the population. They clung stubbornly to the rights that the long dead Catherine had granted them. They remained German, generation after generation. Teaching in German in their schools, often with teachers imported directly from Germany, they knew that education was the key to keeping their children unpolluted. Though their rights of interest free loans and tax relief were long lapsed, they still clung to the promise of cultural freedom. The new immigrants of the 1860's accepted as matter of fact the assertion that they too were invited there by Catherine the Great. They continued to claim many of the privileges granted to those first immigrants.

The truth, however, was that their invitation came not from the Tzar but from Volhynian land owners like Count Viteranno. The Polish and Russian nobility of Volhynia had a crisis in the 1860's and needed the German farmers. In the first years of that decade the Tzar had freed the serfs of Russia. Without their free labor the land owners could not hope to produce anything from these vast tracts of forest and swamps. They realized they needed to lease their lands to people who had the ability to turn forests and swampland into productive farms. Viteranno himself went to Poland to solicit emigrants. He and other noblemen did not trust their own countrymen, who had labored for them for generations, but were glad to grant long term leases to German farmers. The settlers who came east in the 1860's and 1870's did not come at the bidding of the Tzars but were enlisted by the large Russian estates.

By the time Martin Fischer reached Volhynia the only lands available for settlement were in the western parts of the province. He took up land near the Russian city of Lutzk. It was one of the last areas of the region to be cleared and cultivated. Further east, the German communities had been entrenched for several generations and were enjoying the success which now inspired the Russian noblemen to import more hardworking Germans. Martin Fischer built on their success.

In the succeeding years, however, the Russians began to get nervous about the number of German settlements so close to their western borders. The change in attitude came almost overnight with the worsening of Russian relations with Germany. The Germans who had transformed the land were now themselves transformed. No longer looked on as colonizers and developers, they were maligned by the Russian press as usurpers and invaders. Forgetting the promises of the Empress, the Russians were now angry that after several generations these people had not become Russian and showed no inclination that they ever would. This foreign attitude was an affront to their pride.

Though they found the Russian attitude unsettling, the Fischers had survived wars and persecution and never thought that the Russians would do more than complain. As late as 1885, Martin's son, Joseph was still able to buy a piece of land. He was confident that the anti-German feelings would disappear as quickly as they had started.

Joseph was still farming the piece of land he had bought when he died at fifty-four. While working in his beloved fields he chipped his scythe on a rock. A piece of dirty metal lodged in his knee and the wound became infected. Without medical help he died painfully of gangrene.

His younger son, Albert, was only fourteen when his father died and found it hard to cope with the pain. When his older brother moved into the house with his wife and took over the running of their farm Albert felt betrayed. But unlike Germany, the laws of Volhynia did not exclude Albert forever from claiming a piece of his father's lands.

The German colonies had set their own rules for the inheritance of lands in Volhynia. The original German-Volhynians had come to Russia as the disinherited second and third sons of German landowners. They had all the skills required to run successful farms, but had been excluded from ever owning the fields they grew up on. While they understood that land could not be partitioned forever, they felt the need to provide for all their sons, not just the firstborn.

As they prospered in their new homelands, they bought up huge tracts of land so as to enable their second and third sons to share in their prosperity. When a land owner died and left no will, which most often was the case, the surviving sons shared equally. The only condition was that the son had to be grown up before he could claim his share. Unfortunately for Albert and Johann, their father had only seen the tail end of the Volhynian prosperity. He had died poor.

Johann, of course, gave a very Volhynian-German version of this history. He honestly could not see a single point where the Germans could be condemned. This one thing he knew with all his heart, that the Germans did not deserve the mistreatment the Russians had heaped on them.

As Johann finally finished giving his brother his very partisan lesson, Albert noticed that his own thoughts had drifted. Just the same, he now understood more about the German settlement of Volhynia than he ever thought anyone could know. He did not have the intense interest in it that his brother had but at least his curiosity had been satisfied. It was late and he still hadn't broached the subject of marriage. He thought he would give it one more try but his tired lips could only form the words, "Good-night."

Johann smiled. It had been a while since Albert had been so civil with him.

Privacy was hard to find in a poor Volhynian house. In most households the family slept together in one room. The Fischer's were lucky enough to have a large room, partitioned by pieces of furniture that offered some basic privacy. Johann and Hedwig slept in one corner, Julianna in another, but the only corner left for Albert was close to where his nephews lay squirming in their bed. It seemed as if the boys were as active in their sleep as they were awake, wriggling like a ball of worms with arms and legs entangled and flailing constantly. It could be annoying at times but he was consoled by the fact that during the day they annoyed their mother more than they could ever bother him. It was just something to be tolerated in a crowded little farm house.

But despite his weariness, Albert found it hard to fall asleep. He listened as his nephews Otto and Gustav rolled in their bed almost punching and kicking. Every so often they would bump into each other and someone would be awake for a second. Sometimes one would let out a mild yelp, like a puppy whose tail had been stepped on, and then just as quickly be asleep again. It puzzled their uncle how he could feel so close and enjoy two little boys so much. They were the sons of that witch, but he loved them. The boys were one of the few joys he had of living in his brother's home.

It was an amusement to listen to their antics in the night, but it was not what kept Albert awake. The day had been a disappointment and the more he dwelt on that disappointment the more incensed he became. His two worst enemies had gotten the best of him. Martin had run him off the road and even though it made him angry, Albert could only blame himself for allowing it to happen. Worse than that was that Hedwig had gone another day secure in her role as mistress of the house. That had to end. The day had not gone as it should have and now the night gave no relief.

But then Albert remembered. He got off his bed, shoved it ever so slightly aside and lifted a board out of the floor. It was tight but years of practice had taught him how to do it quickly and silently. There was his secret hiding place, a wooden box covered by a short floor board. He pulled a bag out of the box and added his earnings to it. As usual he counted every coin in the bag, silently slipping them from one hand to the other. It reassured him that he was making progress. There was his hope. Now he could sleep.

Three

Alwine Frey hacked at the soil with her hoe. Again and again her arms crashed down like she was fighting with the ground. The sweat poured off her forehead and across her cheeks before it splattered on the black earth. Her face was twisted and intense. This garden was her life.

There was no need to cultivate her garden any more. She had harvested so much that she and her mother had to spend most of their evenings canning. Most everything else in the garden had matured to the point where additional attention was unnecessary. What plants were left she would allow to go to seed for next year's planting. She didn't need to be hoeing, but then she wasn't really hoeing. She was attacking those memories that hung on so stubbornly. Didn't they know that they weren't wanted? If only she could have rooted them out like she had rooted out the weeds, maybe then she could be happy.

But Alwine (pronounced Ahl-ween-eh), the daughter of Johann and Emilie Frey remembered everything, and that was her problem. Her father had ordered her to forget and because she was a good daughter she tried. Once in while they wouldn't bother her for days or even months. But inevitably, there was always another trigger for her memories; a train whistle, a hot summer day, the pure white of a snow-fall, the crying of a child, or the shouting of a bully. Anything and everything restarted her memories and all the orders in the world could not deny them their place in her life.

For thirteen years now, the memory of that day in 1915 had been creeping back into Alwine's life. Even now as she hacked at them with her hoe they wouldn't give up. How had her mother and her brothers been able to do it? She had no idea. No matter how hard she tried to suppressed them, they always came back.

The death of those memories was ordained by nothing more than superstition. No wonder their burial was superficial. The terror of those days was not talked about in the Frey household because their father required that everything be forgotten. And it was not because Johann Frey was uncaring that he imposed this harsh stoicism on his wife and children. He just thought it would protect his family to hide the pain. And yet it was not just the pain that he hoped to shelter them from with this misguided counsel; he just believed it to be a sin to dwell on the past.

He considered pride and vanity to be the chief tools of the world for destroying character. Johann Frey could recite the Bible and its endless injunctions against those allied evils as justification for his sternness. Or he could point to traditional Lutheran wisdom which confirmed through folklore and proverb that pride was the great tool of the devil in bringing people to disaster. With all his heart Johann wanted to avoid that kind of disaster.

It was obvious to him why it was important to forget the torment and struggles his family faced during the war. He saw his duty so clearly that he never realized how convoluted and twisted his logic had become. His culture had put so much emphasis on teaching about the pitfalls of pride and vanity that Johann couldn't help but be terrified of them. His understanding was that they were subtle sins which invaded the human heart almost unnoticed, but were so pernicious that they could easily destroy the soul.

The problem that Johann Frey saw with people who talked about themselves too much, and in particular, about their sorrows, was that they were self-centered. It was self-indulgent to dwell on tragedy until it festered into hatred and self-pity. Or worse, until you thought that it was by your own devices that you overcame problems, instead of recognizing His help. Johann would not allow his family to recall their wartime experiences on the mere superstition that it would make them vain.

The trauma and the upheaval of the War had effected the lives of the Frey children deeply. But their father's reaction did not help them to deal with those feelings. Their fears and anxieties would have been better resolved if the children and adults could have talked about them, but Johann knew a great deal about religion and farming and nothing at all about psychology. He did what he thought was best and even suppressed his own experiences of fighting in the Caucuses. He sincerely believed that such self-indulgence would damage him and his family.

Alwine's dilemma came about not because she dwelt on those memories all the time, but because she was simply unable to blot them out of her mind. She had taken her father's admonition to forget literally, and thought there was something wrong with her when those memories just wouldn't go away. Her hard work at home was in part to make up for that deficiency. But the image of that towering, brutal policeman, twice the size of her mother, barging into the house and screaming that she had one hour to get her family ready to leave, never left Alwine. Her life had changed so suddenly in the summer of 1915, and she could so easily see back to that day when the change started, even though she had only been six years old.

Everything that Alwine saw confirmed to her that her father was right. In her village just a few kilometers south and west of the historic but small city of Vladimir Volhynski, Alwine's father was a respected man. No one every questioned his piety nor his dedication to his family. He was respected not because he was rich. He wasn't. And not because he was a community leader. He didn't like politics. He was respected in the village of Dombrowa because he was a survivor. Her father was respected so much that Alwine was sure that he was always right. She never questioned him.

As a result of the fears that she was never allowed to voice, Alwine became even more shy than was her natural inclination. She felt awkward and stupid and no longer knew what she could discuss with her parents and what she couldn't. And even though Alwine had no one to talk with to keep her recollection alive, the memories wouldn't go away. They seemed as clear in 1928, at the age of nineteen, as the day they started and it bothered her that she could not forget.

Alwine knew well the old wisdom and ancient sayings that her father repeated so often about the evil of vanity and accepted them without question. That these teachings were mere superstitions that had developed out of simple but misleading oral traditions, never entered her mind. It had become self-evident to her as it was obvious to her father that pride always led to punishment.

Superstition, in the disguise of wisdom, had a pervasive hold on the Volhynians. The folklore and myths abounded with tales of folly and God's almost immediate retribution. The example that made the biggest impression on Alwine was one her mother had showed her when she was very young. She had witnessed some boys teasing a crippled little girl, and her mother taught her that such insensitive cruelty came from the pride the boys had in their own good health. Since it was God that gave them their good health then they were taking credit for what God had given them. That was wrong and God would surely punish those boys. Somewhere down the road, Alwine's mother assured her, they would lose their health, or worse, they might even have a child that was crippled or blind or unhealthy. The thought made the girl shudder but she understood that no matter what she might think, God's judgements were always just.

It was hard in that world of superstition to distinguish between what was God's punishment and what was merely the hardships of life. Was God really so unfair to punish a child for its parents' mistake? And yet, who was she to judge what was fair and unfair? She hardly knew her own mind and she couldn't presume to judge God. Still, it seemed to Alwine that a life free of sin ought to go very smoothly, and yet her life was not very smooth at all. Perhaps there was a higher purpose that she did not understand? She supposed that she was being punished for disobeying her father's advice to forget. The fault, most likely, was hers.

Alwine's refuge from these thoughts was her vegetable garden. It was her economic contribution to the family but it was also her passion and her retreat. Though the rest of the family helped her with the ploughing and the planting, her siblings did not relish it the way she did. So it became Alwine's garden, even her parents accepted that fact and were grateful for it. She was the one who planned it in every detail, even preserving the seeds for planting from the previous harvest. She tended it daily through the growing season right up to the harvest.

Only her mother even suspected that it was more than gardening that she did there. She went there when she needed to be alone with her thoughts and bent her back into her hoeing, churning up row after row, when she needed to get rid of unwanted feelings. Neighbors who passed by complimented her on the care she gave her garden and praised her parents for having such a diligent daughter. But Alwine felt awkward about the compliments, because she knew how often her hoe came down in frustration. And yet, row after row, the memories only vexed her more.

Johann Frey would have been surprised how clearly his daughter remembered that day in 1915 when he left to join the Russian army. Even at six years, Alwine knew that her father was making a sacrifice for his family that might cost his life. She had cried inconsolably at his leaving, and her mother had not known the extent of the little girl's understanding. Alwine knew even then that he had saved not only his family by this act, but his land too. She never pondered which had motivated him more, his family's safety, or his love of the land, because in any Volhynian farmer's terms, they were the same thing.

At about the same time as Johann Fischer of the village of Zeperow, sixty kilometers to the east, joined the Russian army, so did Johann Frey, and for the same reason. For a time, while he was in the trenches, even after the evacuation of most of the Germans close to the western front, Johann thought that he had succeeded in keeping his family safe. He continued to receive news from home regularly and knew that they had been permitted to remain in Dombrowa even though thousands of Germans had been exiled to Siberia. He felt warm that his sacrifice in joining the army had saved their lives and their lands. It made him feel a kinship to the family heroes of the past. He had not joined the army out of patriotism or duty, but on the promise that Russia would treat his family well. Every day he gave thanks to his God for the blessing of knowing where his family was.

It was only in late June of that year that he wavered in his hope. They were just rumors at first, but even then they made the Germans in Russian uniform shudder. German-Volhynians, the rumor said, had deserted en-masse and gone over to fight for the Austrians. Johann did not want to believe it at first. The rumors were vague on detail. Some said that it was an entire division of German-Russians, but Johann doubted that there was a division of German soldiers in all the armies of Russia, so he did not believe it. And since that could not be true, maybe the whole thing was a lie. The consequences for the remaining Germans would be disastrous. He could not imagine that German soldiers would so thoughtlessly endanger the lives of other Germans.

The rumors, however, persisted and their confirmation came in the way that the Russian officers began to abuse their German troops and even spat in their faces. They punished every minor infraction. There were also glaring stares and intimidating curses of their Russian comrades that confirmed that something was wrong. Johann stayed close to his unit. All the German soldiers had to be vigilant.

A few days after the rumors began, the German units were gathered together and an officer screamed their new orders at them. He yelled so loudly at first that all the Germans could understand was that they were being sent to the Caucuses to fight the Turks. When he finished reading, the officer was a little more coherent. In control now, he told them that because of the many cowardly desertions by the German soldiers it had become clear that they could not to be trusted in the war with Austria and Germany. In the Caucuses, if they wanted to desert, they would be running into the arms of the dreaded Muslim Turks, who loved to cut the throats of Christians, especially cowards. The transport was to take place immediately.

Hurriedly Johann Frey wrote a note to his wife that she never received. He tried to warn her to run away, that the word of the Tzar could no longer be trusted. He wanted her to run before they came to put her and their children on a train to Siberia. But Johann was himself on a train to the Caucuses before the day was through, with Russian soldiers standing guard over him and his companions to make sure they did not desert.

Emilie Frey was not aware of what was happening on the front or she might have been even more afraid when she did not hear from her husband. As it was, she was saddened by what she had already seen that spring. So many of her neighbors had been routed out of their homes and dragged off to Siberia that she thought Dombrowa would become a ghost town. But instead of being deserted, something even worse happened to her village. Emilie was astounded when a hoard of Polish and Ukrainian peasants swept into the village and occupied the empty farms and houses of Dombrowa. Her indignation at this blatant thievery was only slightly moderated by her fear. She wanted to tell the interlopers what she thought of them, but she was prudent enough to keep her mouth shut. When she realized that they were not thieves, but that the Russian Government had given them the confiscated homes and land, she was relieved that she had remained silent. Officially, those who had been exiled had been declared traitors, by virtue of being German and having no one to fight in the Russian army, and therefore had forfeited their land. Dombrowa now took on an eerie aspect as Emilie encountered her new neighbors whose eyes were full of hate and seemed to say to her, you are the enemy.

She tried to function as best she could under the new circumstances, but since her biggest helper was her six-year-old daughter, she could not handle the farm and the house. There was no one reliable to hire to work the farm so she did as much as she could and left the rest. For the first time she found herself wishing that she and Johann had at least had the foresight to move to East Prussia when the war broke out. Better yet, they should have moved to America as Johann's father had done years earlier. But now it was too late. Soon, besides four-year-old Edmund and two-year-old Rudolf, there would be another baby to take care of, and no man to help Emilie, just a six-year-old girl. But Emilie was not one to wallow in what should have been, she would have to make the best of it. She had enough resources, she thought, to make it through the next winter if only the Russians and her new neighbors would leave her alone.

When at the end of June she hadn't heard from her husband for what seemed a long time, she became worried. There were a few German families like hers still in Dombrowa whose men had joined the army to keep their families safe. When Emilie asked around, however, she found that they had not heard from their men either. Some of them advised her to do the same thing they were doing, preparing to leave quickly. One neighbor confided, "My wagon is packed, I am leaving soon." When Emilie asked where she would go, the woman said, "Why west of course, to Germany. If we wait, they will put us all on the trains to Siberia and we will die." Emilie didn't really know about such things but she suspected that it was too late to go west, that was where all the fighting was. She was at a loss.

There were rumors that German families were hiding in the great Pripjet swamp, moving from place to place so as not to be discovered by the patrols. She considered it only for an instant. A woman with small children and expecting another child, could only meet tragedy in the swamp. Emilie was sure of that. It was best to stay put and wait for word from Johann.

Still, she could not just let the time pass and do nothing but hope and pray for the best. That was not her husband's way and it would not be Emilie's either. She warned her little daughter that they must be prepared for anything, and most important of all they must be together at all times. Into the lining of their coats she sewed what money she could gather, and carefully put together a traveling bag of food that they could grab at a moment's notice to take with them. It seemed to be the best she could do.

Only a few days later, on a clear July morning, the Russian policemen showed up in Dombrowa again.

It was the hatred and cruelty that stayed particularly fresh in Alwine's senses when she recalled how it all began. She remembered how her mother had protested to that brutal policeman many years ago, "My husband is fighting for the Tzar. We were promised...! The Tzar promised we could stay!"

"It doesn't matter," the big brute had yelled at her, frightening Alwine and her brothers to tears, "you Germans are all traitors. Make yourselves ready! I'll be back in one hour."

She could recall too how pale and terrified her mother had looked and how insecure it made her feel to see her mother that way. Yet Emilie had recovered quickly to take control of herself. As soon as it became evident that no protest would dissuade the police, Emilie knew that her children's lives depended on the decisions she now made. Pausing only a few seconds to collect herself, she stooped and wiped the tears from Alwine's cheeks, saying, "Liebling, I know you are frightened but we don't have time to be sad now. I want you to make sure your brothers are dressed. We are going to a place that is very cold, we must pack warm things and be sure to take all of our coats." Then she turned and comforted Edmund and Rudolf and asked them to pay attention to their sister. The renewed calmness in her mother's voice reassured Alwine, but it did not take away her fear. She knew something bad was happening.

While Alwine dressed and assisted her brothers, Emilie grabbed the bag she had prepared. It was hard to decide how much she should take, because she did not know how long the trip would take. She only knew that Siberia was a cold place, a long journey away. She decided that what she had, was not enough, so she packed another bag and filled it with edibles from her pantry. "Food and clothing," she kept repeating, "that is all we can afford to carry. Nothing else matters." When she had two leather traveling bags full of food, she lifted them and found them heavy but she would not remove anything. She reasoned that she would only be sorry later.

As she packed, the hour passed quickly. When the policeman returned her family was ready. Standing at the front door with her children when the Russian yelled insults at her, Emilie was sick with grief at leaving her home and sicker still with the anticipation of what her little family might have to face. Softly, she encouraged the little ones to ignore the screams and told them how brave they were to be so patient, but their tears streamed as they clung to their mother in fear. Now as the policeman ordered them to leave, she fully realized that her bags were too heavy to carry very far, certainly not all the way to Siberia, but what was she to do? In them was only what was necessary to save her children's lives. She had to ask her six-year-old daughter to manage her younger brothers and help them to keep up, while she carried the heavy bags.

Before they reached the farm gate the big policeman pushed himself in front of Emilie and glared at her. "Do you have any money?" he asked.

"No, will we need money? I have no money." She let out a despairing sob, hoping he would not search too closely.

"Let me see your hands then," he said.

He pulled off the thin band of gold that was her wedding ring, twisting her finger painfully as he took it. Emilie made no protest. She knew that if that was all she lost, she would count herself lucky.

Before they had marched even a few feet out of the gate, her new neighbors, those who had already taken possession of the other German houses in Dombrowa, rushed her door. "What are they doing?" Emilie asked, as they swept by her. "There is nothing there that is yours any more," the policeman barked.

They were led to the center of town where the few remaining German families of Dombrowa were being gathered together. It was only a few hundred meters but by the time they got there, Emilie's muscles ached from the weight of her bags. It was clear to her that she would need help or she had to lighten the load. It seemed ludicrous to throw away food.

Silently she prayed for help. Emilie was not timid in her prayers like someone with little experience. She had both understanding and hope. Emilie did not talk to God only out of desperation and fear as some people did. And neither was she unrealistic in her expectations. Even as a desperate mother, Emilie would not ask for some grand miracle to remove her and her children from this trial. Rather she prayed with confidence and purpose, for the strength to carry her precious bags, so she could keep her children alive. It was not that she doubted that God could produce a miracle. It was just that she assumed that it was vanity to ask for one. When so many good people had been asked to endure so much, Emilie felt she was not more worthy of a miracle than the rest. She prayed only for what she needed.

There were only twenty-one Germans left in all of Dombrowa and now they were gathered in the center of town. In the middle of the dusty street they were made to stand with the sun beating down on them, surrounded by four armed policemen, including the brute. Five other women, their children and an elderly couple, the Steins, were already there as Emilie and her children arrived. It was not difficult to recognize the anxiety in the faces of this helpless group. A neighbor who looked particularly distressed, reached out to Emilie as she arrived and held her hand tightly. It was not clear whether she was offering or looking for support. Their only comfort was not being alone.

An hour passed by and nothing happened. They could only speculate why the guards were waiting. Gunther Stein, the only man in the group, suggested that the Russians were probably making a thorough search of the town in case any Germans were hiding. As the exiles waited, the sun beat down on them, yet they were not even allowed to sit.

The children were soon bored and began to whine. The white-haired Gunther Stein, looking very grandfatherly, tried to amuse the children. They warmed to his smile quickly and the children were cheered up as he joked with them and began to do simple slight-of-hand tricks with a coin.

As she watched him, Emilie realized too that she hadn't seen the elderly couple in weeks. She had supposed that they had been dragged off in the first weeks of the evacuation. After all, hadn't their only son run off to East Prussia when the war began? She shook her head. It didn't matter, right now she was just glad to have Gunther Stein there. Besides entertaining the children, he was a leader in their community and a man her husband had always respected.

Yet Emilie had to feel sorry for Marta Stein, who seemed to be wilting as she stood in the heat. Her hair was almost as white as her husband's, but she looked so much more frail. She was barely able to stand. At least one of the other women had noticed too, and she stood beside the pale, elderly woman and helped to support her as her husband played with the children. Emilie wanted to cry. How could they expect such old people to make that journey? It was obvious that the Russians didn't care whether the Steins lived or died. But with that thought she also realized they probably didn't care about her little family either. She shuddered with the coldness of it. But she saved her tears. There was no time now to be weak.

Despite the amusement provided by the kind old man, Alwine and her brothers grew tired very quickly. Before too long, all three children lay on the dusty road, at Emilie's feet, trying to sleep. Fortunately, the guards made no effort to make the children stand. That was a relief, since Emilie knew the little ones would need a rest before they had to march to the train station. It was ten kilometers. Her children were younger than the rest and she was sure that her small family would fall behind quickly. If that happened, she would have to choose between carrying them and the food. As she stood in the heat, Emilie's imagination played out many scenarios. Over and over again, all she could think of was that the brute would shoot them if they could not keep up. Her eyes became wet at the thought, but then she chided herself for her lack of faith. She considered it sinful to ask God for help and not believe.

It was while Emilie was pondering how she could bring her children safely to thc rail station that she heard the scuffle and then the piercing cry of the elderly Marta Stein. In the few seconds it took Emilie to turn around, Gunther Stein was on the ground and guns were pointed at his head. The old man was trying to say something but the guards were shouting at him to shut up.

"What happened, Mama?" little Alwine asked. Her mother only shook her head.

"He just wanted to get his wagon and drive the children to the train," the woman standing beside Emilie explained.

Emilie could see that Herr Stein's mouth was bleeding and his wife was trying to get to him but the other women were holding her back. The anger on the guards' faces was unmistakable. They wanted to shoot the old man.

Emilie did not know where her courage came from. She wouldn't even have called it courage; it was just that she had the impression that she had to do it. She stepped toward the irate policemen, holding her hands out to her sides, submissively. She only wanted to help. With the few Russian words that she knew, she asked, "May I help him, he's bleeding?" Her question broke the guards' concentration. One of them, a sergeant by the stripes on his sleeve, nodded and turned away as if he had become disinterested in the old man.

With a handkerchief she wiped the blood from Gunther Stein's lips and helped him to stand. Emilie wanted to help him back to the safety of their little group, but he held fast where he stood. "Thank-you, Emilie," he said, almost seeming to brush her off. His voice was gentle and yet so controlled that it surprised Emilie. He showed no fear, and he would not allow himself to be lead back to the group of terrified women and children. For a second she thought it was just his pride. She was wrong. Gunther Stein turned to the guard who had hit him and began to plead with him again. It was the same brute who had taken Emilie's ring.

"What would be the harm in allowing these children to ride to the station?" Gunther asked in Russian.

"You are traitors!" the policeman shouted and again showed the old man the fist that had knocked him to the ground.

"They are women and children. What have they done to betray Russia? What crimes are they guilty off?" Stein asked.

Emilie understood much more of the language than she could speak and wondered if Gunther Stein was trying to get himself killed. The guard was so big and intimidating and the old man was so thin and more than twice his age. She could not understand where his confidence came from, but it sounded so heroic that even in this precarious situation she was buoyed by him.

"Crimes?" the brute puzzled. The sergeant stepped in, "Your crime is that you are German," he stated coldly, "there is no greater crime in Russia these days."

"These women can't carry their bags all that way. I just want to get a wagon to help them."

"Then they'll have to leave the bags behind," he said coldly.

"They'll starve."

"Would you prefer that we shoot you all here?"

"If you will let me get my wagon and a horse, it could be worth something to you."

The sergeant smiled at the attempted bribe. "Anything you have we can just take," he said, shoving the old man back toward the terrified group and turning his back. But the big brute stopped his comrade and whispered something. They stood looking at old Gunther, as if they were evaluating his worth.

"I have money hidden away," the old man said as he took a coin from out of his pocket and showed it to the policemen. Then, just as quickly he made the coin disappear. "I have more. Hidden."

The brute didn't like the tease. He came at the old man with his fists clenched. But Gunther pointed to the fist and said firmly and confidently, "Open it!" As the big man stopped Gunther touched his big hand and made the coin appear in his palm. "There is more," he said again.

"He's lying," the sergeant said coldly.

"How much?" the big one asked.

"Enough. Why would I lie? You have the guns. You have the power."

The policemen conferred for a moment and the leader said, "We'll get a wagon but if you're lying, you're dead."

When Gunther Stein returned to his wife, she wrapped her arms around him and cried, but her sobs would not stop. "What have you done old man?" she demanded so woefully that the other women knew something was wrong. "They'll shoot you!" she cried tearfully.

"I'm a dead man anyway. I'll never survive Siberia."

"What do you mean?" asked Emilie, "Did you lie to them?"

"No," Gunther Stein confided, "but there may not be as much as they expect. I gave most our money to our son when he took his family to Prussia. I only have a few coins left where my wife hid them in our luggage. Perhaps that will be enough to satisfy them."

It was about half an hour before the wagon arrived with an old nag to pull it. "Now show us where the money is," the policemen demanded of Stein. All four vultures circled around him now, forgetting their duty to watch their prisoners.

He took the coins that he and his wife had hidden in their bags and held them out, "This is all I have."

A fist shot into the old man's face and bloodied his nose this time. Emilie could hear the cocking of the police revolvers. Frau Stein cried out, "No, no, please, no!" The other women turned their children's faces away. But the shot never came.

"Not here, not in front of so many people," the sergeant ordered. "Take him into the woods."

Emilie didn't think about what she did next. It didn't matter any more that she might need it later. She picked up her coat and tore at the lining. The sound of the tearing attracted the attention of one of the guards. "Here," she said, and then in short, half Russian sentences she sputtered, "I have some money, you can have it. Just don't shoot the old man. He just wanted to help the children."

It was only a few more coins and it did not appease the disappointed guards. The big brute grabbed Gunther Stein by the collar with his massive arms and threw him onto the road. He wanted revenge for the deception. His face showed how much he relished the idea of abusing the old man. It was the look on the brute's face that started the other women searching their bags and ripping into their coats to find the precious coins they had hidden. It didn't amount to much, but at least the sergeant seemed impressed and to everyone's surprise, he let the old man go.

The children and the bags rode on the wagon all the way to the Vladimir train station with the women walking behind. Gunther Stein put his wife Marta on the wagon too but he insisted on walking.

There was no train waiting in Vladimir and they were not told when one was expected. The group of Germans stood on the platform, from which they had made many peaceful journeys. They were now in terrible dread of this one. Slowly, as the day passed, more German families trickled in from the surrounding communities until the group numbered more than a hundred people. Most of them had a father or son fighting somewhere in the Russian army. They were stunned by this betrayal. They stood together on the platform waiting and listening to the local residents ridicule them and spit on them as they passed by. The children found it unbearable and cried to go home. The mothers just prayed for the train to come quickly. It didn't. The train did not come that day, nor during the night.

Emilie put her coat on the boards and watched as her children snuggled up to her and fell asleep during the clear, warm, early-June night. But her emotions were so uneasy that she herself found it difficult to sleep. In the quiet, with her children sleeping she allowed herself to cry. It was only while her babies slept that she could permit herself this weakness.

Suddenly she felt an arm around her shoulders, and although it startled her, it rested there gently. Gunther Stein was comforting her. She looked into his eyes and felt his hope and his strength. But when the old man started to move his lips she was afraid that he was going to tell her that everything was going to be all right. How thankful she was that he said nothing so inane. Instead, he thanked Emilie for her help earlier. She shrugged it off. She knew who had really shown courage.

"I didn't even know that you were still in Dombrowa," she said, changing the subject.

"Our son left for East Prussia months ago. He wanted us to go with him but we are old and we didn't want to slow him down so we stayed behind. I remember telling him that the Russians wouldn't hurt an old couple like us. I didn't believe it even when I said it. When the police passed us over in those first raids we stayed in our home and kept quiet. When they finally came for us, it was only what we expected."

"What you did in Dombrowa was very brave."

"I had to do it for the children. My wife and I are old. When it doesn't matter anymore what happens to you, it's easy to have courage. Emilie Frey you have courage, but you must be careful for your children's sake."

"Oh no, not I. You saved us, my children..."

"It doesn't matter. No one is saved yet, I'm afraid our trouble is only beginning."

The train finally arrived midmorning. An old engine that should have been retired years ago pulled a coal car followed by three freight cars. It belched black smoke and labored to move its load. The cars were old too. Two of them were wooden but the end car, the one that came to a stop directly in front of Emilie, was clad in steel. Emilie thought it looked safer than the other older cars so she picked up her bags and started toward it. "Come, Alwine," she said, "bring the boys." At that moment Gunther Stein saw what she was about to do and barged through the crowd to Emilie's side. He grabbed one of the bags out of her hand saying, "Come with me Emilie, don't get on that car." She had no opportunity to ask why but followed him obediently.

When they were aboard, sitting on the strawed floor, he explained, "That car is almost air tight. In a few hours it will be unbearably hot in there."

Emilie was shocked when she realized what she had almost done. "They want us to die don't they?" she asked.

Gunther Stein replied thoughtfully, "They are full of hate right now. People who hate don't think rationally. Why else would they destroy their best agriculture in the midst of a war? Not just here in Volhynia, but all across the Ukraine they are deporting the farmers that feed their armies."

The children were so happy with the freedom they were allowed on the train that they couldn't contain themselves. They ran back and forth across the length of the car despite their mothers' cautions. Joyfully, they threw handfuls of straw into the air as though they were playing in their barns at home. It was hard to stop their frolicking but Emilie noticed that Alwine did not participate. She stayed close to her mother while Edmund and Rudolf ran around.

In a corner of the car, right beside Gunther Stein and his wife, and away from the rolling door, Emilie made a place for her family. In those first few moments it didn't seem to be so bad lying on the straw in a freight car. It seemed like a respite from the way they had been treated so far.

When the train finally began to roll Emilie felt it was safe to fall asleep. But less than two hours later the engine screeched to a halt. In a matter of moments the space in the car was cut in half as more Volhynian-Germans climbed aboard. Then the train labored on again to the next stop. Emilie lost track of the number of times they stopped that day, each time picking up more exiles. By evening she made a less than casual comment to Marta Stein that soon there would no more room to lie down.

But even through the night the train kept stopping to pick up even more of the frightened exiles. By morning the wagons were all crowded. Emilie encouraged Alwine and the boys to sleep, hoping they would rest while there was still room to lie down. But they were not sleepy. Nothing their mother could say could convince them to rest.

That afternoon the heat was so great that the sweat came pouring off Emilie's face. Each labored breath seemed to bring in less and less oxygen. People found it hard to look in each other's face; they could only find pain and desperation there. Fortunately, there were small cracks and holes in the shrinking boards that allowed marginally cooler air into the car. With each breath Alwine was grateful that Gunther Stein had saved her from her ignorance.

Eventually, when Emilie realized that the train hadn't stopped for several hours she felt a little more hopeful. Perhaps there would be no more stops now that the train was full. She feared the consequences if the Russians tried to put more people on this train. It would be a sure death sentence.

Emilie had barely finished her wishful thinking when the train pulled into Novrograd Volhynski, the center of the German community in Volhynia. As the door of the car was rolled open, Emilie could not believe her eyes. A mass of people stood on the train platform. She could not guess whether it was hundreds or thousands. It was obvious that there were more people than could possibly fit onto the already overcrowded train. It seemed like a cruel joke.

Yet as the train stopped, not a soul moved. For hours the people on the platform and those on the train stood quietly looking at each other, wondering what was going to happen. Finally, as night came, the train lurched forward a few feet and settled again. For a moment Emilie and her children thought that another train had run into them. She turned to Herr Stein who explained, "They're adding more cars." Emilie breathed a sigh of relief.

Word spread quickly, however, that only three more cars had been added to hold this mass. It still seemed unreal when the Russian police ordered them all into the cars. The crowd hesitated to move and the guards shouted louder. They pushed and pushed until each car was packed so tightly that the bodies crushed against each other. It was impossible to move or even just to turn. Children began to wail and even the adults cried. As the door closed and the engine slowly pulled away with its terrible cargo, the wailing of the children could still be heard.

That first night was too much for some. Unable to bear the stress three elderly women and two children died, When the train stopped their bodies were dragged off by guards and thrown unceremoniously beside the tracks.

As the day heated up the car became unbearably hot. Emilie kept her children close to a crack in the siding of the car where a little fresh air kept them from fainting. But the wailing of children oppressed by the lack of air was excruciating to listen to. They begged to go home and cried to be allowed to lie down but there was nothing that their mothers could do. It was hard enough even to maneuver around to comfort them. At the end of the day ten more bodies were removed; five of them were children. One woman watching attentively at the door cried with horror that she had counted two dozen bodies being removed from the steel clad car. Almost an equal number died the next day and more the day after. It was now several days into July and each morning was clear and bright and full of the threat of more heat.

As ominous and wrenching as the daily deaths were, they had a beneficial effect. Each one freed more space. Unfortunately, the extra space became the center of contention as mothers struggled to find space for their little ones to sleep. Emilie was shocked when a woman slapped Alwine as her tired body leaned over the space where she had laid her child. As her daughter cried, Emilie could only comfort her and assure the little girl that she had not done anything wrong. She knew it would be fruitless to get angry or retaliate.

Gunther Stein, observed what was happening with horror. He was sure that unless tempers were kept under control they would be doing the Russians' work for them. He was desperate to avert that. He persuaded everyone that the fair thing to do was to organize the car. Spaces were cleared at either end and by drawing straws each person was given a turn to lie down and rest. His plan worked, but was aided each day as the elderly and children succumbed to the heat and fatigue.

As it made its way east the old engine progressed only ploddingly. Sometimes it stopped inexplicably for hours on a side track or it waited while military traffic rolled west. While they were stopped a woman who kept vigil by the sliding door seemed intent on reporting the number of bodies that were removed from the metal car. Some of the women begged her to stop with her morbid fascination but Emilie sensed something more in her voice. She assumed that the woman had someone she loved in that car.

"They must have plenty of room in that car now," one person ventured as the woman made another of the dreadful announcements. "Yes, plenty of room to die," Herr Stein answered quickly, "those metal freight cars are like furnaces in this heat. Don't envy them, pray for them." The car fell quiet at this explanation except for the woman at the door who began to wail.

In the following days, those who prayed for the unfortunates of the steel clad death-car found reasons to pray for themselves. The train pulled over to a side-rail in a remote area where they were surrounded by a thick pine forest. Hour after hour they stood still while the sun beat down strongly and the temperature of the car rose all day. The dense trees seemed to prevent any breeze from reaching the train and Emilie could not feel any fresh air coming through the otherwise reliable crack. All day the train was stopped and the car only began to cool long after the sun had set. Little children and elderly people fainted and died and Emilie kept a close watch on Rudolf and Edmund. She listened to their breathing and watched diligently for any change.

The next day the train still did not move. As the sun rose high, people began to plead with the guards to open the doors. At first they refused. But in the afternoon, as the guards walked beside the cars, they could feel the heat emanating from them and relented. However, they set up machine guns so that their prisoners would not bolt. Still, the small act of humanity saved many lives that day.

On the third day the train began to move in the early morning, but it moved dreadfully slowly and only for a few kilometers before it was sidetracked again. Over the next few days it became apparent that this would be the new pattern of their journey east; the train would move slowly for a few hours then stop for a long period, even days. It became rare that the train moved forward for an entire day. The trip to Siberia was destined to take a long time.

The passengers began to be very sensitive to any variation of speed in the train. By the vibrations under them they sensed whenever it slowed down. Anxiety gripped the whole car each time the train stopped. Alwine cried to her mother, "I get so sick when the train stops Mama!"

Through all this, the death toll steadily rose. Weakened from lack of food and fresh water people became sick and each day their only consolation was that there was more room for them to lie down.

Marta Stein died. Emilie wondered how she had hung on so long. She died standing up, held in her husband's comforting arms, and it was hours before he told even Emilie. Emilie had sensed that there was something wrong when she noticed that Marta had not moved a muscle in a long time. She said nothing, however. It was only when her eyes met Gunther's that he confirmed her death with a nod. Emilie wanted to comfort her friend but found herself being comforted by him instead. When the guards pulled her body out, she could not watch, but Gunther could not take his eyes away even as they threw his wife's corpse onto the ground like a sack of potatoes. "I only wish I could have buried her," he said to Emilie, but that made her burst into tears.

Emilie's bags of food lasted longer than anyone else's but after all this time her supply too had run out. When she saw the sickly complexions and the languid eyes of the other children, she was pained, but grateful that she had not wavered in carrying those heavy bags. She gave thanks to God. She knew that He had sent Gunther and Marta as an answer to prayer. Still, her supplies were now gone and the only food that the Russians gave them was stale bread and a little water. If they did not reach Siberia soon, she feared that none of the children would survive. Her boys were weak and only Alwine had the strength to complain anymore. But Emilie refused to be discouraged; God had not sent her help in order to abandon her now.

A slow train to Tashkent in peace time could take two weeks, but this trip turned into a three-month ordeal. Later, the survivors would learn that other trains had taken up to four months to deliver their cargoes. One train that had left three weeks earlier from central Volhynia arrived a full two weeks later, with only a handful of survivors. On Emilie's train six out of ten died. Over all, fifty percent of the Volhynians who were expelled died on the trains. Emilie counted it a miracle that all of her children were alive.

Gunther Stein died during the last leg of the ordeal. He had begun to share his ration of bread and water with Emilie's children. He rebuffed her mild protests by explaining that he needed little. Death had become a daily event but Gunther Stein's death almost made Emilie give up hope. His kindness had been so instrumental in helping them to get to this point. Yet for her children's sake Emilie could not let herself show how discouraged she was. She comforted Alwine by referring to the old man as their guardian angel. It was a wonderful thought and Alwine fell in love with the idea.

Emilie decided that it was important to remember the place and date of his death. About the place, unfortunately, she could not be more specific than somewhere on the railway to Siberia. Still she thought that his son, if she ever saw him again, would appreciate knowing the date. The problem was she had lost track of time. She knew it was weeks since the train had left Dombrowa but it could have been three weeks or twice that.

No one else had any better idea than she did, except for the woman obsessed with the metal freight car. "September 27, 1915," she said so positively that Emilie dared not ask if she was sure. Yet Emilie was at a loss to understand how she had kept track. She stood there for a few seconds staring in amazement at this enigmatic woman who seemed so fixated on death. Her stare was improper and she knew it as soon as the woman sneered, "I don't care if you don't believe me."

"I'm sorry," Emilie answered, kneeling beside the woman who was propped up beside the door, "I do believe you. But can it really be three months?"

"I know every day since we left Swehl. I counted the dead each day." She pointed back to the metal car. "10 on June 30, 24 the next day, then 20, 12, 14. If you add up the days then today is September 27. Do you want me to tell you how many people died?"

"No," Emilie shook her head, "I don't want to know."

"Neither do I, but I can't stop counting." Now the woman who had said little to anyone to this point, would not stop talking. "When they shoved us onto the train they made my parents get into that iron monster. I tried to go with them but there were so many people and everyone was pushing and pushing. I know how many dead they took out of that car each day, but I never saw them. You would think that you could recognize your parents, wouldn't you? So I think maybe they are still alive. There were so many deaths it's hard to believe there is anyone alive over there. Maybe I missed them but I don't think so. It would be terrible to have missed seeing them for the last time." She stopped as her eyes began to fill with tears.

"If you didn't see them," Emilie said as persuasively as she could, "then they are probably alive."

"Maybe," was all the woman could respond.

"What is your name, I'm Emilie Frey."

"Hedwig," she said. "I shouldn't be here. My husband is in the army." Her eyes were full of tears now. "They promised to leave us alone. They shouldn't do this to the men who fight for them." She began to sob pitifully. "They took my husband and God knows here he is. Now maybe my parents are dead. I have no one left."

Emilie put her arms around Hedwig to comfort her. There was nothing she could say. Hedwig's frustration was nothing unusual, but it was all too familiar. Still, she seemed to find some relief in talking to Emilie.

As Alwine watched her mother talking to the strange woman she found herself wishing that her mother would come back quickly and sit with her and her brothers. She didn't like it at all that her mother was talking to the crazy woman. Even when Edmund and Rudolf joined their mother on the other side of the car, Alwine would not sit with them. She had grown leery of the woman as she had listened to her daily reports of deaths.

The nights began to grow cold more quickly now. Emilie didn't know much about Siberia except for its reputation as the Tzars' favorite prison camp. She truly believed that the colder nights were because they were approaching Siberia, which she supposed had no summer at all. But in fact, summer was over. Some nights were so cold now that it was hard to remember how they had been so afraid of the heat. She wrapped her children up in their coats and they huddled close together for warmth when they slept. There was plenty of room now to lie down. The crack that let in fresh air and had saved her children from asphyxiation was now plugged with a rag. Even though some days were still warm, those who were left were too weak to enjoy them and few expected to reach Siberia alive.

It was early October when the train arrived in Tashkent in Western Siberia. The men, women and children who staggered off the train were not sure what survival meant for them. It didn't matter. Anything was better than that train.

Emilie carefully lifted her boys down from the car. She was so weak that she had to be careful herself not to fall over. She was eight months pregnant now and had lost a lot of weight. As she prepared to lead her family away she saw Hedwig, her stare fixed on the infamous metal clad freight car. The door had not been opened and the guards were making no motion as if they intended to open it. Emilie told her sons to stay with Alwine and stood by the despondent woman.

"They're all dead," she turned and said with tears streaming down her face, "that's why they won't open the door." Emilie took her by the hand and led her to the freight car. Whatever the truth was, it was better to know for sure. In halting Russian she told the guard that Hedwig was looking for her parents.

"What were their names?" the guard asked.

"Gisela and Eduard Kleindienst."

"Were they in this car?" he asked pointing to the closed one.

"Yes."

"They're dead!" he said coldly.

Hedwig fell to her knees sobbing and would not be comforted. Emilie would have stayed with the despondent woman but she could hear her children crying. Finally, Emilie had to leave her to take care of her children. Later, after she had helped her daughter to gain control she looked back but Hedwig was gone. For a few weeks Emilie looked for her in the camp but could not find her. No one knew of a Hedwig Kleindienst and Emilie had not asked for her married name. She began to fear the worst.

Siberia and its prison camps were hardly a problem after the anguish of the train. A month after she arrived, Emilie gave birth to a tiny little girl whom she named Adele. Consequently, she was given fairly light work in the kitchen of the barracks where the prisoners were housed. Alwine, however, had to be the primary care giver for the baby and even she did not complain. She loved her sister and she loved that the work helped to take away the memories of the train. Only Edmund now sometimes had nightmares.

A year and a half later, in 1917, something happened that Alwine could not make heads nor tails of. She only noted it because everyone became excited and expected great change. Her mother told her that the Tzar had abdicated. The little girl didn't know what it meant. "Have the Germans won the war then?" she asked. But it made no difference in her life nor in the lives of the other prisoners so she ignored it. In the fall they heard that the Bolsheviks had taken over the government in St. Petersburg, but that seemed to make no difference either. At least not in their lives, except that many of the German exiles were leaving Tashkent. "The Tzar is in prison," they said, "we're going home."

"Can we go home too?" Alwine asked her mother.

But Emilie had no idea how to go about getting her family home nor did she know what she would find there. She had seen the Polish and Ukrainian peasants take her house and could not conceive how she could kick them out. She decided to stay. To a neighbor who was returning she said, "If you see my Johann, tell him where we are. We'll wait for him here."

It was the summer of 1918 when Johann Frey in his threadbare and dirty Russian uniform arrived in Tashkent. It had been three years. Alwine did not even recognize her father and looked on in amazement as her mother embraced a stranger. But then he knelt with his family, holding the toddler he had never seen and they prayed together. As her father prayed, Alwine began to sense a familiar quality in his voice. As he spoke with God his wording and his intonations were recognizable and made her feel safe and warm. It was really her father and when he finished praying she sprang toward him and wrapped herself around him and would not let him go.

Johann was pale and gaunt and his face was so hollow that it was no wonder his daughter found it hard to recognize her father.

The fighting in the Caucuses against the Turks had been the most horrific of the war. Men came back changed.

The casualties had been atrocious partly because Russia had reserved its best officers for the western front, sending what was left to the Caucuses. Adding to the problems of the Southern front, there was practically no medical attention. The wounded rarely survived their gross infections and often died horribly painful deaths. The food, when there was any, was disgusting. When it arrived at front after great difficulty and much corruption and incompetence, it was infested with rats and maggots. Sanitation was practically unknown, and typhus and dysentery hampered every military unit. No wonder the survivors were thin and unrecognizable.

Johann Frey was sure that it was by the grace of God that he had been spared. He never presumed to take any credit for it himself. But so many good men had died beside him he was almost ashamed that he had survived. He resolved quietly that if God had seen fit to allow him to live that he wanted to show his gratitude by never letting himself become proud. There was nothing to be proud of.

To Johann the war became a bad dream that had nothing to do with his real life. There was only one thing to be done with these awful memories; he needed to forget them. He never talked about his war experiences, not even with Emilie. His children could only guess at what had happened to him and why he had come back so changed. But in Tashkent, once they recognized him, they were just glad that he had come.

By the time that the Frey family was reunited the exodus from Siberia was almost over. Johann and Emilie and their family were among the last Germans going home. Even though they were uncertain what they would find, they were drawn back to western Volhynia. It was their home.

As they approached the train in Tashkent, however, Alwine began to draw back. A look of horror came over her face that only her mother understood. Her father, holding her hand, looked puzzled as the nine year old pulled him away from the train so forcefully that he almost fell over. "It's the train Johann," Emilie explained. "On such a monstrosity we came from Volhynia. So many people died!" Johann Frey could have tried harder to understand but he had already determined that the war should be left behind. He meant for his children to do the same. He picked his daughter up and put her on the train, saying, "We have no time for such foolishness!"

Four

To Albert, Sunday was the best day of the week. It wasn't because he was particularly religious, he just liked the day. Though he believed in God, to him church was more of a tradition than a commitment. Even on those occasions when he could feel the warmth and fervor of the congregation it didn't stir him as it did his brother. On his own he rarely even stopped to say a prayer. If he were honest, he would admit that he thought prayer was mostly a waste of time, except on those occasions when you really needed help and there was no other way out. But still, Sundays were made for him.

Everything changed on Sunday. Things that were so consumingly important during the week were not as important on Sunday. He got up a few minutes later, went about the morning chores at a leisurely pace, and dressed for church without haste. He didn't even move slowly with the purpose of annoying the witch, that was merely a satisfying by product. Albert just enjoyed the change of pace. Even going to church was a pleasant change. He didn't have to enjoy the preaching, which was difficult enough to follow with their current preacher. It was the company of friends and making plans to be together that made it special.

The only anxious part of the day for him was dealing with Johann and Hedwig. For some reason Sunday did not bring them the same kind of joy. Albert thought he knew why.

Johann became puffed up on Sunday, wearing a dark suit with a heavily starched white collar that his wife ironed to perfection. Johann was every bit as stiff on Sunday as the clothes he wore. A serious frown would be his trademark for the day as if to underline his pious attitude. Hedwig, however, rushed around frantically each Sunday to make sure that she and her husband looked immaculate. She went about all morning preening him as if she were his valet rather than his wife. Yet both were tense all morning, as if judgement day itself had come. To Albert is seemed as if the joy of the day had totally evaded them.

Albert was never sure what the witch's running around and Johann's fretting accomplished. He determined that they did it just because they were snobs. Hedwig, the worse of the two, was filled with pride because of her husband's position. As the wife of a prominent member of the Kantorrat, the community council, she felt important. Even now Albert was embarrassed to think how she beamed when she marched into the church on her husband's arm.

While Johann and Hedwig performed their Sunday morning ritual, Albert retreated to the stable with the boys. As he helped with the chores, he was impressed how his nephews Otto and Gustav jumped into the work. This was his favorite time with them. He joked with them as they fed the animals and cleaned out the pens together. Frequently, a competition erupted between the boys and himself to see who would finish first. It was Otto and Gustav who always started it off. They would try to hide it as they found themselves close to the end of their chores and anticipated being finished before their grown-up uncle. However, their excitement always gave them away and Albert would speed up almost by reflex. Mostly Albert won, but once in a while he would slow down and let them finish just ahead of him. Gustav and Otto exulted in their infrequent victories, but Albert was even happier than they were. He hoped to encourage them and he could see by their smiles that they loved to be challenged.

By the time Albert and his nephews were ready, Johann had already harnessed the horse to the wagon and was waiting impatiently for his family. By then, Hedwig was ready to fly apart. She shuffled from one member of her family to another to hurry them along. Finally, she gave in to her frustration and began to yell. "It is a disgrace," she shouted, "for you to make a member of the Kantorrat late!" She did not, however, offer to help.

Johann's frown deepened when Otto finally came out of the house with the news that his Oma was staying home. He looked to his wife for an explanation and she gave the standard answer, "Her back is bothering her again."

"Her back always waits until Sunday," Johann replied stiffly.

"She works too hard!" Albert shot out tersely. He didn't like his brother questioning their mother's integrity.

"We all work hard," Hedwig answered coldly, "your mother is just getting old!"

"My Mother is not old!" protested Albert. He hated that word. It implied too many things he didn't like. Hedwig might as well have said she was useless or worthless.

"We'll be late," Johann interrupted. "Let's go."

The family transportation was a plain farm-wagon with weathered boards that creaked from age and heavy work. In front was a strong but plodding, brown plough horse that looked as old as the wagon it was expected to pull. But while the horse and wagon matched, Johann looked out of place in his dark suit and gleaming white collar. Hedwig cringed when she saw him beside the wagon. She longed for a proper carriage, even a plain one, to take her family to church, but she knew there was no money for such luxuries. This humiliation had to be endured.

The horse trudged slowly down the road. He knew the route by heart and Johann did little but hold the reins as they passed by the small collection of houses that was called Zeperow. It was barely a town and couldn't be found on most maps. The Germans had adopted the name when they bought the land from the Viteranno estate. No one remembered anymore what it meant. Like the neighboring villages in the region, the town was poor. Yet Albert was always glad that no matter how poor a German village was, it never looked uncared for. At least not in the same way similar Polish and Ukrainian villages looked beleaguered. Those others allowed their fences to lean and the boards to fall off their barns and never seemed to paint anything, while even the poorest Germans maintained their properties.

In the center of the diminutive town, without prompting, the horse turned sharply right. This was the main road but it was no better than a country route. Still, it stretched all the way to the city of Lutzk. But today the Fischers traveled only another kilometer to the town of Antonufka, slightly larger than Zeperow, where their Lutheran congregation met in a typical Volhynian church.

While the church was still a half kilometer or so off, Albert looked behind and saw a team of horses and a carriage quickly catching up with their wagon. He recognized it immediately and turned his back so that he would not be staring as it rolled by. Young Otto, however, yelled out the moment he understood who was going to pass them by. "Speed up, Father, it's Martin!" But Johann shrugged off his young son's request and pulled the wagon as close to the edge of the road as the steep banks could safely allow. It was a courtesy that any traveler on the road extended to both neighbors or strangers with faster transport.

Johann touched the brim of his hat as the Martins' carriage sped by, but his gesture was not acknowledged. Martin stared straight ahead, as did his wife, but their two sons, sitting behind their parents, gave Otto & Gustav a dirty look they thought was uncalled for. It was an automatic reflex for Otto and Gustav to stick out their tongues at the impudent children who were several years younger than they. Albert, however, just kept his back turned and watched the wheat fields go by. Martin sped up once he passed the Fischers, kicking up dust on the road as he drove right past the Lutheran prayer-house.

"If Martin is German then why doesn't he go to our church?" Otto asked.

"I don't know," their father replied, but that was not true and Hedwig was not about to let him get away with that answer. "Of course we know," she said curtly.

"Is it because he hates us?" Gustav asked.

"No," Johann explained to his son, "a long time ago Herr Martin found out that life would be much easier for him in Russia if he belonged to the Russian church. Now it is better to belong to the Polish church. Herr Martin believes that religion is supposed to make life easier."

"Isn't it, Papa?" Gustav asked, puzzled.

"No, religion is supposed to make us better people."

"He's a traitor," Albert interrupted, "and a thief, he'll end up in hell."

"Amen," Hedwig added. She and Albert shared one opinion.

"That is not for us to decide," Johann reprimanded sternly.

It was not a real church. At least it was not like the large and spacious brick churches that could be found in Lutzk and other big centers around Volhynia. It was just what had passed for a church in the smaller German communities. In their straightforward fashion they called it a Bet-Haus, which meant Prayer-House. When he was a small boy, Johann had watched his father as he helped to build the wooden Bet-Haus. There was, for him, a sense of satisfaction that his father had served the community in this way, and an even greater satisfaction that he was now following in that tradition.

The building where the German's met for church was the center of their community. The residents had come together some thirty years earlier to build it as their first and only public building.

It was a simple one-story structure clad with pine boards harvested from the extensive forests that had once dominated the area. A large room served as church on Sunday and as school during the week. It had an office at the back that served the kantor and school master, who were one and the same.

Johann, Hedwig and their sons strolled proudly into the church. Hedwig treasured the respect that her husband garnered as a member of the Kantorrat. Secretly, she loved it when they arrived last. It was such a great gratification to her to find their seats still empty and waiting for them. His wife's pride embarrassed and disturbed Johann. He wanted to hurry to his seat but she clutched his arm tightly, forcing him to stroll. He indulged her. There was so little that he could give her that it seemed such a small thing to indulge her vanity in this.

When he got to the church doors, Albert quietly slipped into the back where he knew that his friend August would be with his family. August Weiss was Albert's best friend. They lived on neighboring farms and they had grown up together. In their lifetime they could only remember one long separation from 1915 to 1918 when they hadn't been together. That was when Albert and his family had fled to East Prussia during the Great War and August and his family had stayed in Volhynia to their eternal regret. Now as young men they were inseparable to the point that they spent all of their leisure time together. Albert sat down quickly and quietly beside his friend and with a nod of his head acknowledged August's parents. They smiled back. They approved of the friendship.

August turned to Albert and whispered, "Are you coming over after church?"Albert nodded. That was where he usually wound up on Sunday. "I want to introduce you to someone."

Albert wanted to ask who, but the Kantor had started and August sat back as if he was preparing to listen. Albert was puzzled at his friend's enigmatic behavior. What was he trying to prove? He never listened in church, not to this Kantor.

The Lutheran congregation of Zeperow and Antonufka was a devout but a small group. As such they did not merit an ordained minister but a Kantor, who was actually a school teacher trained to act in some limited pastoral duties. The biggest part of those duties was conducting services on Sunday. This Kantor system had been worked out by the early German settlers more than a hundred years earlier.

The current Kantor, whose last name was Himmel, German for Heaven, was boring. Sometime ago Albert had begun the joke that now circulated among the younger members of the congregation by whispering in August's ear, "Why do I always feel like I'm in hell when I listen to Himmel?" Rarely did a Sunday pass without the tired joke being repeated by someone.

Even though Himmel was not a particularly dynamic person, he was an adequate teacher. But he was a pompous preacher. His sermons were full of hackneyed phrases and oozed with self-indulgent praise of Germanic ways. It seemed that Himmel believed the world consisted of two spheres, one German, the other non-German. The first was infinitely better than the second. He was sure that this congregation shared his feelings and he was right. Most of his listeners suspected, however, that when the Kantor spoke of German ways, he referred to the true Germany, where he was from, and not this backward outpost. His listeners were often amused at his declarations but he never offended them, so they tolerated him. To them Church was more important than the preacher whose main fault was that he was proud of being more German than his flock.

Today there was something different in his sermon. He began by reading an article from the German language newspaper of Augsburg. It was about a law being considered by the Polish parliament that would require all Church services to be conducted in Polish, even where the majority of the congregation spoke another language. The usually quiet assembly began to murmur. The preacher had struck a cord that resonated through the Volhynian soul and made it shiver.Johann Fischer had paid closer attention than most people. He had felt this coming for some time. It had become clear very early in the decade that the newly-resurrected state of Poland was not pleased to have the Germans there. This was eerily similar to what had happened at the beginning of the century. Russia too, had grown tired of the Germans living in their borders. Was it all beginning again?

He remembered how it had started. It was like a breeze that turned into a wind and the wind into a storm. But the storm was only a storm of words, it was just criticism and innuendo. When in a few short years it evolved into threats and then into discriminatory legislation it caught them all off guard. But the full rage of the Russians did not appear until the Great War. Johann left Volhynia shortly after, under circumstances that even he considered embarrassing. He did not return until western Volhynia became part of the restored nation of Poland. But now the Poles were feeling threatened. Somewhere in history, Johann was sure there was a clue. There had to be something there to show the Poles the mistake they were about to make.

Johann remember how the Russians had attacked their school system. The frustrated Russians enacted legislation which closed down the German school system. Initially, they halted the construction of German secondary schools and then revoked charters for existing schools. Next they changed the qualifications for teachers so that only those who were trained in Russia could teach. Within ten years they brought to a halt the sixty year old German school system. Johann was one of the last to receive a fully German education. He could still remember it all like it had happened yesterday.

Event the loss of the school system had not discouraged the Germans. Then, in a strange turn of events, Russia entered into a disastrous war with Japan. The loss of that war nearly caused a revolution and gave the Bolsheviks grounds to criticize the monarchy and stir up the rabble. To distract the irate populace's attention from that failure, the Tzar threw the Russian peasants a bone. It was the land reform act of 1905. One of its measures was to cancel many land leases held by foreigners. To the Germans it meant that any farmer who had not purchased the land he lived on was about to forfeit everything he had. Leases were arbitrarily canceled and the land was given to Russian peasants. The Germans were devastated.

Although Joseph Fischer had purchased his land, he had also inherited the lease on his father's farm. Together those two pieces of property represented a holding that could do better than just support a family. The prospect of losing more than half of their land was terrifying. Johann could remember how worried his father had been. But the Germans of Zeperow and Antonufka had a friend. Back then, Count Viteranno was still rich and powerful. He interceded on behalf of his German tenants and was able to get an exemption for them. The speculation was that he had bribed some high bureaucrat to get that stay. Many believed he had gone right to Tzar Nicholas to make his case. Still, it was only a temporary reprieve.

For many other communities, however, land reform meant an immediate end to their farming. The land they had leased and cleared, the houses and barns they had built were all forfeited. Thousands of Germans left Russia, following their brothers and sisters who had left in the pervious decades. Before long, those who stayed behind knew they had made a mistake.

The next decade brought an even worse terror for the Germans. In 1914, the war with Germany exacerbated the Russian opinion of their foreign citizens and gave them their best reason to remove the enemy from their territory. The terror did not come until 1915, when Russian paranoia was ripe. With the war turning against them, the army saw with horror that on their western borders, right in front of the advancing German and Austrian armies, sat thousands and thousands of potential German soldiers. They envisioned that the German-Volhynian men were just waiting to greet and even join the Kaiser's army. Some of the newspapers incited public opinion by making the ridiculous claim that the German settlements had been planned generations ago by the Germans just for this eventuality. The western borders were full of spies and traitors.

In June of that year the order was given for the local police to remove the Germans from their houses and put them on trains to Siberia immediately. Because this infamous manifesto called 'The Expulsion Order,' was hastily written and even more hastily carried out, there were great inconsistencies in its execution. In some districts the police were on friendly terms with their German residents and treated them fairly and humanely. However, more often than not, the prisoners were brutalized and even robbed. In the west, where the military perceived the greatest threat to exist, the orders were carried out immediately. In the east, the Germans sometimes were given a few days to dispose of their possessions.

The police invaded the western villages in the middle of the night. It may have been an attempt to decrease the possibility of resistance but the Germans were sure the midnight raids were just to increase the terror. The residents were dragged out of their houses to the nearest train station for deportation.

The horrified villagers were caught by surprise. There was no resistance, except for the protestations of those who had husbands and sons in the Russian army. These families were supposed to be spared this exile. It was one of the tragedies of the hasty implementation of the expulsion order. Except in isolated instances the local police ignored that exemption. Moving swiftly and indiscriminately, the police rounded up some 200,000 Germans from Volhynia alone and hundreds of thousands more in the rest of the Russian territories.

Johann had married in 1914. But only a few months into 1915, he had sent his wife home to live with her parents while he joined the Russian army. They had promised him that his wife and his parents would not be harmed if he served, and he believed it. His father, now in his late forties, was too old to fight, but Johann was only twenty-four. It was up to him to save his family. He told them not to worry, "It would be insane for them to hurt the families of their fighting men." With those last words he was gone.

Johann was just the kind of man the Russians wanted. Besides being young and strong, he was well educated, speaking both Russian and German. They made him a corporal and put him in charge of a platoon of German farm boys. These young men found that the western front was not far from their homes.

They were so close that news from home reached them quickly. In June the rumors abounded about the expulsion of the Germans. At first the soldiers reassured themselves that their own families were exempt. But slowly information trickled in that the Russians had broken their promise again. All the Germans in Volhynia were being sent to Siberia.

Johann did not know what to believe. Were his wife and parents safe or were they being deported to the east? He wanted to believe they were safe. But by the end of June, he and his platoon were demoralized. They had been told by mocking and spiteful Russian soldiers that their families would soon all be freezing in Siberia.

During that period Johann watched his men carefully. He had been warned to watch for desertions and been bluntly told that the consequences would be severe. So when Johann noticed members of his command acting suspiciously he thought he knew what they were up to. Even though he understood and sympathized with them, he could not allow it. He hid and waited until he was sure of their intention. As they quietly left their posts he knew he had to stop them.

"Halt," he cried. They stopped in their tracks. Even fourteen years later Johann could still remember their faces frozen in fear. Only when he came out of the shadows did they relax. "Ernst, Willy," he had all but whispered, afraid to be overheard, "don't do this."

"They have betrayed us. Our families could be dead and they want us to fight for them."

"I know! All the men in our company have families. But what do you think they will do to the rest of us if you desert? They will punish us all!"

"What should we do?"

"Return to your post. In the morning we will all decide together what to do."

Early the next morning Johann laid it before his men. With little discussion they settled the matter. They voted unanimously to follow Johann and to do it quickly so that they would not lose courage. Before the sun was fully up, they marched as they had been ordered to relieve another platoon on the front line. But as they approached, instead of stopping, they ran right over the trenches. The bewildered Russians didn't know what to make of it. Some thought that an attack had been ordered and were ready to follow. But when they jumped up out of the trenches they could see no sign of a general advance, just this single platoon heading for the Austrian lines with a white flag leading them. A Russian officer realized too late what was happening and wildly and vainly emptied his pistol at them. By the time he ordered the machine guns to cut them down it was too late.

The officer who had witnessed this cowardice called a sergeant to his side. "Who were they?"

"Germans sir."

"They had better never return to Russia!"

All of the deserters exchanged their Russian uniforms for Austrian grey. It seemed the practical thing to do since none of them had anywhere else to go. "We'll fight," Willy, the deserter had said to the Austrian officer who accepted their surrender, "all the way to Siberia if necessary, to find our families." His comrades all agreed with him but the Austrians thought it prudent to split them up in case they had another change of heart.

What Johann had not know at the time was that despite the rumors, his parents and young brother were still in Zeperow and his wife was still with her parents in their home. The Ukrainian constable of Antonufka had allowed the Fischers to remain on their land since their son Johann had enlisted in the army. He knew the German farmers and did not particularly care about the dispute between them and the Russians. As far as he was concerned they were all interlopers in his country. It was left to his discretion to make such decisions and his only concern was making sure that his superiors had nothing to criticize him for. He did not want to end up at the front himself.

It was only a few weeks after he had deported the rest of the spies and traitors in his district that the constable learned of his mistake. He was shocked and frightened to hear of Johann Fischer's blatant and cowardly desertion. Luckily for the Fischers, he feared his superiors more than he regretted his decision to let them stay.

The same day that he learned about Johann he rode the long way home. It was an exceptionally lengthy route that took him around Zeperow, reaching the Fischer's farm by a back road.

He explained the situation to a shocked Joseph Fischer, who had no idea what his son had done. Dumbfounded by this turn of events, Joseph Fischer, was uncertain what was to happen next. He stared at the policeman in bewilderment.

"I've come here," the constable explained, "to ask you to leave. Quickly! Right now! I will even help you to load your wagon. Don't even talk to your neighbors. If you are here in the morning I will have to arrest you and it will not go well with you."

"Why are you telling us this?" Joseph asked in amazement. By now he was recovered enough to suspect this was some kind of trick.

"If you are found here tomorrow I will have to explain why you weren't sent to Tashkent. I don't want even your neighbors to know what really happened here tonight. Go! Leave! You might make it to Prussia, but if you stay here you are all dead."

At noon the next day Hermann Martin came by and found the Fischers gone and the house half empty. He assumed that they were among those families who were disappearing every day. Perhaps they had gone into the vast Pripjet swamp, hoping to avoid both the war and the Russian patrols. Or else they had set out for Prussia. Even at this late date many Germans were still trekking to the north, fearing for their lives. He himself never considered it. He had no fear of being expelled from Volhynia. Long ago he had decided to appease the Russians and become one of them. He had married a Russian woman and converted to the Orthodox faith though more often than not he attended Lutheran services. He considered himself to be a practical man, willing to make his bed wherever he found himself.

Hermann was not only practical, he was an opportunist. Even though he had known Joseph Fischer for many years he felt no compunction about taking advantage of this opportunity. Quickly he went home and brought back his wagon and a helper. Everything that was valuable or useful they hauled away. It was so easy that he decided to come back for the livestock later. But then, having gained so much with so little effort, he became even more greedy. He began to wonder what would happen to the land. Before the next morning he was already including the Fischer fields in his plans for crop rotation for next year. All he had to do was to find a way to get the land into his own name.

He puzzled over it for only a few days. When he heard of Johann Fischer's desertion, he smiled. Now he felt sure that no Fischer would ever return. Hastily he wrote out a receipt and signed the name Joseph Fischer to it and presented it to the constable in Antonufka. "He sold me the farm before he left."

The constable almost laughed. He knew better, but it was in his interest to be discrete. "Herr Martin, what do I have to do with this? You must give it to the Count. He is the landlord."

"You know the Count and his family are in St. Petersburg. In his absence you have to witness it."

"If Joseph Fischer were here, I could witness his signature, but he's not here. This is not an official receipt. It would never stand up in court. If Fischer comes back, this paper will be worthless." Hermann Martin, however felt secure that it would never be contested and as much as the Constable hated the idea of this thievery he had no intention of doing anything about it. The fewer questions there were about these particular Germans, the better the Constable slept.

Joseph Fischer, his wife and son traveled 300 kilometers north, eventually reaching East Prussia. There, labor was in short supply because of the war and Joseph found shelter and work on one of the huge state owned estates. There too, young Albert received the three years of schooling that was all of his formal education.

Now, as Johann Fischer sat listening to the Kantor, and the pain of those years came flooding in, he trembled at the thought of the persecution starting again. Unfortunately, the signs were there that the Polish government was only going to get more aggressive and that the new Poland would be every bit as narrow minded as the Tzar's Russia.

What Kantor Himmel had read terrified the Germans. They felt that Poland was determined to put an end to German language rights and this was just one more tightening of the noose. But if they thought they were being clever by manipulating them through their religion they thought wrong. It was inconceivable for the Germans to think of worshiping in any other language. This was like denying them the very air they breathed. The communities of Antonufka and Zeperow were alarmed and some people were glad that they had been aroused.

But Albert was not stirred. He had listened to the Kantor but the point was lost to him. He was more concerned about who it was that August wanted him to meet. Whatever it was that had stirred the meeting he was sure his brother would represent his family's interest and there was no need for him to bother. He had other concerns.

Anxiously he ushered his friend out the front door so they could talk privately. To his dismay August seemed reluctant and stopped abruptly a few feet past the door. "Who is it," Albert demanded, "that you want me to meet?"

"Mother is anxious to get home. We're expecting company."

"Who?"

"Come by this afternoon," was all that August would say as he tore himself away leaving Albert shaking his head.

It was difficult for Albert to tear his brother away from church. Johann was already in deep conversation with several men. It was an hour before Johann Fischer finally relented. By then he had issued numerous invitations to friends to spend the afternoon at his home discussing this latest threat. Albert was glad to have some place to go. The sooner he got away the better.

As they rode home, Johann was animated. "If a man cannot worship in his own language you might as well forbid him to worship at all," he repeated several times as if each repetition made it more true. It made no difference to him that Albert didn't care and Hedwig was more concerned about all the invitations Johann had issued. She was not opposed to her husband's politics, on the contrary, she believed he was very correct in his opinions. What she did not look forward to was being a hostess for the whole of her Sunday. "I hope your mother is feeling better," she said wistfully. Albert cringed.

By the time the horse had passed through Zeperow, Otto and Gustav were trying to fall asleep on the hard boards. Even using their Sunday coats as pillows they bounced up and down but stubbornly refused to wake. When the wagon passed the lane to the Weiss farm they were well past noticing anything.

Albert timed it perfectly. He calculated the gait of the horse and the irksome yet reliable creaking of the wagon bed as it bounced on the axles. Then, with the same agility and quickness that had saved him from being trampled under Martin's horses, he placed both hands on the end board of the wagon and vaulted himself effortlessly onto the road, landing solidly on his feet. He smiled to himself, thinking that with luck they'd be in their lane before they would find him missing.

It was the cow that gave him away. She was lying in the Weiss pasture and was totally surprised when Albert jumped the fence. Quickly the small red milk-cow sprang to her feet and bellowed loudly.

Albert looked to the wagon. Hedwig had heard the animal. "Albert," she shouted, "what on earth are you doing?"

He ignored her and walked away.

"That is not proper behavior for a Sunday!" she crowed at him.

Albert smiled. He had got her goat again. Now he turned and ran across the cow pasture while the Weiss cows watched him as if they too were disturbed by this Sabbath-breaker. He loved to run even if it was considered improper to do so on Sunday. He was excited and happy to be free. His last strides across the field were actually leaps and for a moment he thought that he could leap the farmyard fence in one wonderful culminating stride. He stopped. Even for him it wouldn't be proper to come to their door panting and out of breath. Quietly he opened the yard gate like a proper Sunday visitor.

Five

As soon as Albert came through August's door it was as if he was at home, or as he often told himself, "Better than home." August's mother was busy cooking and preparing for company but she didn't even think of sending Albert home. She knew it was pointless to keep this afternoon closed to her son's best friend. They shared everything.

There were several reasons that the boys had grown so close. The initial reason was that August was an only child and Albert had grown up alone. From almost as soon as they could walk, they had been as close as brothers and had fought as many fights as any set of siblings. The only difference was that they forgave each other more easily than brothers might and so their friendship had lasted. Their attitudes and visions of the future were shaped as much by that friendship as by any other influence, including families. One thing bonded them more than any other; they dreamed together.

As they grew, their parents had been amazed that even in their contrasts they complimented each other. Karl Weiss, August's father, liked the influence that Albert had on August because he was more precocious and gregarious. Whereas Maria was sure that their son's introspective and careful disposition was settling for Albert. Their friendship suited them. Even Julianna remarked that such friendship was a gift.

They were both hard workers and tireless at games. They were always wrestling, kicking a ball or just running. August was a few centimeters taller, but Albert was stronger and faster. He was also more competitive and so it was fortunate that August gave in more easily. It was another aspect of what made their friendship work. But even August didn't like to lose every time they wrestled. If Albert used some unfair hold to win then it was August's size that made up for Albert's strength. But never, not even with his long legs, could August run as fast as Albert, no one could.

Albert and August were bright young men, with great enthusiasm for life. Had they not been born in a backwater community of a backward province that was more tied to the nineteenth century than the twentieth, they might have had more ambition than just becoming subsistence farmers. Here in Volhynia, unfortunately, they didn't even have a chance at a decent education. They lived in houses without any of the innovations of the twentieth century that stirred other boys' imaginations all over the world. There was no electricity in their houses, no motor vehicles on their roads, no magazines, and no radios in their kitchens. They also had an inept and even hostile government that did not want to include them in its future, at least not as Germans. Still, the two friends exuded enthusiasm, especially when they were together.

They were both good looking young men and many girls who were approaching the age of marriage speculated what life with them would be like. August could have married almost any of the young women in Zeperow and Antonufka if the young women had only found some way to attract his attention. And though they found the shorter Albert attractive too, their families always pointed out that there were problems in that household. Luckily, the young women that had grown up with the two friends did not interest them. They would always be just little girls.

Albert relaxed as soon as the door closed behind him. The Weiss home was almost exactly identical to his; the floor plan was the same, so were the materials it was made of, and each had a

Volhynian style chimney, but none of that was the source of his ease. It wasn't the similarities at all that allowed him to relax in the Weiss house. It was the differences.

Karl and Maria Weiss were as poor as any of the farmers around them and struggled to keep themselves and their farm going, but they were solid people, without pretensions. Without the refuge of their kindness, Albert was sure his life would have been unbearable. Frau Weiss was congenial but she was not a doting person. She was full of common sense and liked it when people made themselves at home in her house. She didn't like waiting on anyone because she was most often consumed with taking care of her husband. She was a typical German-Volhynian 'Haus-Frau,' with more than the typical workload.

Karl Weiss was not well. Like most of his neighbors he kept his family from starvation by his hard work, but whereas his neighbors were thin, he always looked hollow. Fighting in the Caucuses during the Great War had left him incredibly sick. Typhus and dysentery combined with negligible medical attention had nearly cost him his life. Though he survived the war, his body had never fully recovered. Now in his late forties, he was already an old man with white hair. His sickness aged him so acutely that it seemed to his family that he actually added two or three years for every calendar year that went by. That was why Maria waited on him, to the exclusion of everyone else. With quiet, loving desperation, she was working to keep him from dying. It was a struggle she would not admit even to herself that she was losing. Yet they both were happy and Albert couldn't help but wonder, when he looked at the couple, how different his life might have been if his father were still alive.

Today, however, even in the Weiss household things were different. Even before Albert sat down at the kitchen table he could sense it. He knew them all so well that he could feel it in their voices and see it in the smiles that beamed from their faces. Something terribly exciting was going on. August was obviously anxious and there was a grin on his face that only got bigger when he looked at his friend.

"So what's going on?" Albert blurted out with unmasked curiosity.

Frau Weiss laughed at her son, "You haven't told him yet?"

"You told August not to tell anyone," her husband replied from his comfortable seat at the head of the table, "Why do you act so surprised?"

"I didn't mean Albert. I never expect him to keep anything from Albert."

"So what is it?" Albert asked, growing more anxious.

August's smile got bigger. "I'm going to be married."

Albert felt his jaw drop. He was stunned. He had always assumed he would be the first to marry, if just for the simple reason that he felt the greater need. It was unfair, grossly unfair. A sinking feeling was forming in the pit of his stomach. For a moment he thought the anger would overwhelm him but he knew it wasn't right to feel this way. He fought it down and told himself that it was not really jealousy that he felt. That was something he could not allow himself to feel for his best friend. When he finally smiled, it was forced.

"How...when...who is she?" Albert fell over his words when he was finally over the initial shock. The smile on August's face became wider and wider as Albert became more and more flustered. He and his parents were happy that Albert shared their excitement.

"It was a surprise to August too," Maria Weiss explained. "We didn't tell him what we were doing. But it certainly is time. Young men of your age did not wait so long to be married when we were young. When he showed no interest in any of the local girls I wrote to my brother in Dombrowa and asked him if he knew of any suitable young women there."

Albert was fascinated and discouraged at the same time. The futility of his own situation had just been laid bare. He had no one to take the kind of initiative that August's parents made for him.

That hurt because he knew that young men were rejected as suitors unless the proper protocol was followed. Suddenly, he realized he wasn't even listening to August's mother any more. He was just making himself more miserable.

"It's time that August took over the running of this farm," he finally heard Frau Weiss say. "We have scrimped and saved enough to put an addition on the house. It will work out well."

"They arranged it all without my knowledge," August explained. "Last week when Mother and I took the train to Vladimir I thought it was just to visit my uncle. Almost as soon as we arrived my uncle said, 'Let's go meet your bride.' I thought he was joking."

Albert wanted to laugh but all he could do was sit there and smile benignly.

"Her name is Irene, Irene Stein," August continued, "and she's beautiful."

"She's beautiful, she's beautiful," Maria Weiss said mockingly. "Is that all you want in a wife? It's not beauty that will do the work."

The boys had no answer for her and could only smile sheepishly. But Karl Weiss, who hadn't said much, gave them a wink when his wife wasn't looking that put them at ease again.

"You'll like her Albert," August said, "she's wonderful."

"So when are you getting married?" Albert forced himself to ask. He felt he had sat long enough without saying anything.

"Irene and her Father are coming here this afternoon," Frau Weiss explained. "They took the train to Lutzk and stayed with relatives last night. Today they are coming here. If all goes well, we will set the date today."

"I should get out of your way then. So you can get ready," Albert offered, but he wasn't quite sure why he said it.

"Why?" August smiled, "I want you to meet her."

"And you might as well stay for dinner," Herr Weiss agreed. "She should meet you, you are August's best friend."

The prospective bride and her father arrived in the early afternoon. Albert stood back as August, clearly apprehensive and flustered, introduced the young lady and her father to his parents. His friend was so distracted that he completely forgot about Albert until they were about to sit down to their meal. When he was finally introduced, Albert looked into Irene's eyes and knew he liked her. He also knew that he was jealous.

August's awkwardness went away as soon as they all sat down to eat Maria's delicious meal. It was simple and unpretentious: cabbage rolls, vegetables from her garden and the Volhynian staple, potatoes. Dessert was a fruit-covered coffee cake served with a coffee-like drink made of barley. The meal helped everyone to relax, except for Herr Stein who seemed to remain aloof.

At first, Albert didn't like Irene's father. He looked dour and stiff, almost like his brother Johann. The man didn't smile throughout the meal. Irene's father acted more like an inspector who for the moment seemed unimpressed.

After the meal, when they got down to the business of the visit, Herr Stein seemed more at ease. Albert guessed correctly that he was acting aloof because he had not totally made up his mind. Unlike a lot of fathers, he didn't want to marry his daughter off. She was much too precious to him to just hand her over to the first young man who presented himself at his door. Irene's father wanted to evaluate August in his own home. He had discovered long ago that one of the best ways to tell the character of a young man was to observe him in his own home with his parents. If he treated them with respect he would, most likely, treat his wife the same way. And of course, even though he accepted that the Volhynians were poor, he did not want his daughter to fall into an unlivable situation. But having assessed all of this in August's favor, he left the rest up to his daughter. She had something else in mind.

While they talked, Albert watched Irene. She was certainly beautiful, yet there was something different about her. He couldn't fix it at first but it became more evident as the afternoon went on. She didn't look like the typical German-Volhynian farm girl. Her clothes were a little more stylish and her dark-brown hair was fixed up in a way that framed her face. Most of the Volhynian girls he knew dressed very plainly. They wore shapeless dresses that hid their figures, while their hair was pulled back into tight unflattering buns. But even though Irene was dressed with flair, it was neither immodest nor inappropriate. She spoke with flair too, proving with each statement that she was knowledgeable about the affairs of the day and even about farming. She was clever, yet not intrusive or overbearing. Albert couldn't help comparing her to the girls he had grown up with. She was so much more exciting.

Throughout the afternoon Irene commented freely and showed both confidence and a sense of humor. Yet her intent was very specific too. She was not content to sit back and let the others make the most important decisions of her life. She might not have phrased it so coldly but this was her test for August. She wanted to let him know that she had interests beyond cooking and washing. If August's intent was to shove her into the background of his life like so many German-Volhynian men did to their wives, she would not allow it. If he couldn't cope with that, then they could not be married even though he was good looking. She was firm that not even her father could make her marry a man she didn't like.

The effect of listening to this vibrant young woman was exhilarating both to August and Albert. They both decided they wanted a girl as charming, personable and intelligent as Irene. This young lady had more personality than either one of them could ever have imagined. They both fell in love. Albert, unfortunately, had to hide his excitement. He and August sat across from this self-confident young woman and felt her humor and sensitivity so much that they longed to get closer to her.

In the face of such unexpected charm Albert was as defenseless as August. The more he looked and listened, the more he was carried away into improper thoughts. He let himself drift into daydreaming what life would be like with this wonderful woman at his side. He would be the envy of everyone. Yet even as his aspirations soared he kept coming back to the reality that she was August's fiancee. It hurt to think that what August was about to get was what he dreamed of; to be the master of his own home with a wife that was beautiful and personable. It did not even concern him whether she had all the skills a young woman needed to be the wife of a farmer. More than ever the status quo was becoming less acceptable to Albert.

All was going so well that it surprised Albert when the afternoon hit a snag. He couldn't understand where it had come from. Albert had thought that everyone was pleased, but now it was obvious that Herr Stein was uncomfortable about something. It seemed unbelievable that something had happened to damage such a congenial afternoon. Had Irene's father found something that displeased him? Was everything falling apart for August? With only a little guilt Albert let his own disheartened feelings rise as he seized on the idea of winning the beautiful Irene for himself. It was only logical, if August couldn't have her then she ought to be his. As fast as the thought had occurred to him, he dismissed it. If her father could find fault with August's prospects, then his own didn't stand a chance. He continued to listen to the conversation, hunting for some clue to what was wrong.

The discomfort lasted only a few minutes until Herr Stein asked to speak to August's parents. The girl's father suggested that the three young people go for a walk. From the look on their faces, he could tell that the young men were surprised. "From what I have seen you are both honorable young men and I expect you to take good care of my daughter's reputation," he explained. "I do not object to young people being in each other's company when properly chaperoned." Then he addressed Albert and said bluntly, "Herr Fischer, I expect you to protect my daughter."

As soon as they got out into the cool evening, Irene revealed the secret of his father's unease, "They want to discuss the dowry," she said with a wisp of a smile that made her seem impish. Then she confidently took each young man by the arm and led them down the path to the road.

"I have been assigned to protect your reputation," Albert declared as he maneuvered between the couple. But Irene protested, "I'm positive that with the two of you I am in no danger." Albert could not object.

From the moment she was alone with these two young men she was in charge. They were like two affectionate tail-wagging puppies, panting with delight to be able to walk with her. Though Irene neither savored nor sought such flattering attention, she handled it wonderfully. She accepted their compliments with ease and made no insincere denials. It was as if she was perfectly in tune with these two young men and knew them well. With every step they took August and Albert were more entranced. Yet, she too was happy for the opportunity to talk to these young men. She had an idea that would only remain an idea if she couldn't talk to these men alone.

As cool as Irene was, she also liked the idea that her future husband was tall and good-looking. It was not on her list of requirements, but it was in her dreams. Walking with these two young men gave her a more intimate feeling about them than most girls in her position ever were given a chance to see. As they walked, with her hanging onto their arms, she could feel their strength and even if she sensed that they were not as educated as she was, she could also see that thy were thoughtful and bright. And when she had a sense of the depth of their friendship her idea came to life.

"It will be very nice to live here," she said as the three made their way down the lane to the road, "the countryside is beautiful and the farms are well kept."

"We are poor people here in Zeperow," August explained, "you won't find many large landowners, but we can make a living because the land is good."

“It’s no different in Dombrowa,” she assured August, “we are poor also.” Her voice was steady without the least hint of disappointment. She wanted to convey to her fiancee that poverty was no drawback. “With hard work a man and a woman can accomplish much,” she reassured August. Then she turned to Albert and with all the sincerity she could muster, asked, “Herr Fischer, are you married?” She already knew the answer.

“No, not yet.”

“Engaged?”

“I will have to find someone to marry first. In Zeperow there is no one.” It was true, there was no one like Irene.

“That’s a pity, but I know several young women in Dombrowa that I’m sure a bright young man like you would find acceptable.” As Albert smiled she became bolder. “It would be nice to have friends close by of our own age.”

“That would be splendid,” August spoke hopefully. He had noticed Albert’s interest in Irene too.

“Perhaps at our wedding you can be introduced and if you wish, something can be arranged.”

Albert almost couldn’t breathe. Over the course of those few words that Irene had spoken, without feeling even the least bit fickle, Albert abandoned his hopeless feelings for the young woman who held his arm. It was a new and better hope that he had now and it was somehow appropriate that it came from the woman that only a few breaths before, he had imagined he was falling in love with. “I would like that,” he replied, hiding his excitement as best he could.

Six

As Alwine Frey grew up no one could blame her for thinking that life was a litany of hard work and disappointment. Beginning with the trauma of 1915, it seemed that life was conspiring to teach her the most ugly and brutal realities. Even when her father scooped her up while she tearfully resisted being put on that train in Tashkent, it was more proof that her life was not hers to control. Since that day the lesson had been reinforced many times. It was not with resentment but resolution that the girl, now a young woman of eighteen, absorbed these harsh lessons. She took her mother's example. If life took control out of her hands then the only thing left was to make the best of it. She had seen her mother do it, time and time again, especially in 1918.

After Siberia, Emilie Frey, was sure there was nothing that could shock and surprise her. She was wrong. When she saw her home in the early summer of 1918, her heart sank. The war had torn right through the middle of everything she loved and left nothing standing. Right there in Dombrowa the Russians had staged one of their bloodiest counter offensives. The entire area around the village had been a part of the battlefield. Everywhere stood burnt out ruins and piles of charred lumber. The grain fields and pasture were torn up with miles and miles of trenches and barbed wire. As Emilie cried for the land, she began to realize the disastrous implications. "If we had stayed, we would all be dead," she said in amazement. "They saved us by putting us on the train." But the land looked scarred beyond repair. "What shall we do?" she asked her husband, thinking there was nothing to be salvaged here.

"Rebuild," Johann said with a casualness that shocked his wife. He had already seen the destruction when he returned from the war and had resolved to stay. "It's a blessing, really," he explained. "No one wants this land now except those who really know its worth."

"How can we rebuild?" Emilie responded incredulously. What was her husband thinking? "Do you have money to build a new house?"

"Somehow, we will rebuild."

"No," Emilie said firmly. It was the first time that Alwine ever saw her mother argue with her father. "We should follow your father to America or at least we should go to Germany."

"This is our land," Johann answered firmly. "It is all we have. We have no money to travel to America, not even as far as Prussia."

"Where shall we live?"

Behind the place where the house had stood, on the other side of the orchard, which had miraculously survived the maelstrom, there was a hill that Johann had always thought of as a nuisance. Even though it overlooked his farm and provided a pleasant and panoramic view of the village, the practical Johann thought of it as merely an inconvenience. It was hard to plough and it stood like an island of rock in a sea of fertility. During the war the Austrians had built a bunker at the top of it from which they could guard a stretch of several miles. Into this bunker Johann moved his unbelieving and protesting wife.

Yet once Emilie realized that the decision was final no one worked harder than she to restore their land and home to its former beauty and productivity.

In time, more and more families returned. Some of the people returning from Siberia were discouraged at the destruction they now saw. When Johann pointed out to them that they were very fortunate they stared back in disbelief. "All over Volhynia," he pointed out to them, "returning German-Volhynians are finding Poles and Ukrainians in their houses. There is no hope of getting them out. This is their country now. In Dombrowa we are lucky. Torn up like this, no one wants our land." It made sense. Most of the returning residents of Dombrowa were able to reclaim their farms, even those drifting back from Prussia. Among them was the son of Gunther Stein.

As always, Alwine followed her mother's lead. Her mother knew that the key to survival was hard work. The work was unavoidable as the farm and fields needed intensive labor to restore them. With her parents and her brothers she worked at filling in the trenches that had made their fields almost useless. It was grueling labor for a child and the only respite for Alwine was when she was needed in the garden. There, growing vegetables that kept her family alive, she found the only excuse her father would accept for not working in the fields. Unfortunately, that work kept her isolated too. And when she wasn't in the garden or the fields she was looking after her little brothers and sisters now that her mother had begun to have children again. She had little time for herself and only one person outside her family whom she considered a friend. She grew up with work as her constant companion, but she grew up a shy, almost an introverted young woman.

Her brother, Edmund, worked equally hard as he grew up. When their community rebuilt the Bet-Haus he was still young enough to go to school and he excelled there. He loved to learn and wanted to understand everything in the world. Even the civil war that went on until 1921 fascinated him and he would not stop asking questions about the reasons for it. Consequently he understood the history of the area and the historical dispute between the Poles, Ukrainians and Russians better than the natives. It was a bitter disappointment to him when his father stopped his schooling only a couple of years after it started. He was needed at home. But ending his formal schooling did not stop Edmund from asking questions and learning. It had become part of his nature.

In 1925, when Alwine Frey reached her sixteenth birthday without the prospect of a marriage, she shrugged it off. At seventeen she was concerned, because other young women her age were finding husbands, but there was still time. A year later she cried in her garden as she turned eighteen. Alone and away from her father's vigilance, the fear came flowing out. Then when her nineteenth birthday came and passed without redemption, she was heartsick. Blind and heartless tradition told her that if she reached her twentieth birthday without being married, she was doomed to be an old maid. Her one consolation was that her friend Irene was the same age and not married either.

It was her friendship that ultimately saved her from despair. Her relationship with Irene Stein wasn't all encompassing in the sense that they had to be together all the time and share each other's deepest secrets. That kind of thing was for little girls who had time for such games. Both these young women were too busy for that. It was more of a feeling of mutual respect and empathy that they had for each other. Part of it stemmed from the admiration the two families felt for each other. Alwine's friend Irene was the granddaughter of Gunther Stein.

It was only once that Alwine's mother had ignored her husband's stern admonition and talked about her experiences on the death trains. She couldn't help herself. She had to tell Gunther Stein's son about his father's kindness and heroism on the train. It would have been a sin, Emilie told her husband, if the bravery of the old man was withheld from his own family. As a result, there were tender feelings between the Freys and the Steins that the girls quite naturally picked up on.

Irene would have liked the quiet Alwine for no other reason than the kind way she spoke about her grandfather. It made her proud to think of him as a hero. But that bond was not the only reason the two girls were friends. Irene saw in Alwine Frey a simple, honest sincerity that touched her. She did not see Alwine merely as a shy and awkward girl. She was the one person who saw what was underneath.

Alwine and Irene did not have a lot of time to spend with each other. Like Alwine, Irene was a busy woman, in some ways she was even busier than her friend. She ran her father's house now that her mother was dead, and took care of her father and two brothers. The two friends could only talk on Sundays at church or when their families socialized. Rarely did the two get together merely to pass the time, but on the few occasions when they did, there was always a third friend present.

Irene had two friends named Alwine. The second Alwine was a year younger and had only lately intruded on the relationship. The redheaded Alwine Bladt was mortified that by the time she was eighteen all her friends had preceded her to the altar. She had run out of unmarried friends and decided that Irene Stein should be her new closest friend. The timid Frey girl she only tolerated. Neither Irene nor Alwine Frey minded the intrusion much. Their friendship was not so closed or narrow that it could not allow another in.

So when Irene returned from Zeperow with her exciting news, both the Alwine's were there. But in the poignant silence that followed their initial happiness, Irene sensed disappointment and immediately understood their fear. She wanted desperately for them to be as happy as she was. The compassionate Irene had hoped to give a bit of hope she had brought back from Zeperow to only one of the Alwines, but it was hard for her to withhold it now from either one. Quietly she explained, "My fiancee has a friend. He is coming to the wedding and I have promised to introduce him to my friends."

Almost instantly there was a change in Alwine Bladt. Irene saw her expression come alive and her eyes brighten. Irene almost bit her lip, thinking that she had made a mistake.

Alwine Frey, in contrast, said nothing at all. She remained silent and apparently unmoved. For a moment Irene lost hope for her. It seemed as if she had already conceded this young man to the red head. Irene wanted to shake her good friend and wake her up. She wanted to tell her friend that she had done this for her and she should be more excited.

As the date in late October approached, however, Alwine was beginning to regret her promise to attend the reception. It wasn't because she had lost hope of attracting the attention of this new young man Irene wanted to introduce her to, Alwine hadn't even concerned herself with him. It was simply the feeling she had that this would be her induction into the world of anonymity which taunted girls her age when they were not married. There, she supposed she would officially become an old maid, which in her society was an awful stigma. But it was her best friend's wedding. She had to go.

On the morning of the church service in Vladimir she couldn't help being happy for her friend. It was the reception at the Stein household in the evening that she was apprehensive about. There would be dancing, but her Father did not allow his children to dance. There would be toasting with wine and she was not allowed to drink. There would joking and flirtations and her father would point out how frivolous and vain it all was. She was sure she would eventually be drawn into a corner with those women she was destined to join. This would be an initiation and she did not want to attend.

When Alwine's father and mother were about to leave for the reception they could not find their daughter. After only a few seconds of waiting Johann stomped out the front door to sit in the wagon. He was not accustomed to having his children keep him waiting. He had taught his family to be prompt. Emilie sent Adele to find her sister. "Be quick," she pleaded.

"She's sitting on her bed crying," the puzzled younger sister came back and whispered in her mother's ear.

Emilie would have liked to comfort her daughter but there was no time and she would not lie. She could not say, "Don't worry child, you will marry soon too," because she did not know that it was true. Instead, she bluntly said, "Don't waste your tears worrying about your future. You cannot possibly know what will or will not happen. Now come, Father is getting upset."

Alwine stayed close to her parents for the whole evening. Her friend Irene had been excited in greeting her and looked so happy that Alwine forgot her tears. But soon the bride had forgotten Alwine, there with so many other guests to attend to. So the shy nineteen-year-old sat with her parents, one eye warily watching a conversation going on in an isolated corner of the room. She needed to avoid that corner so Alwine clung to her parents like a little child who was afraid of strangers.

She had met Irene's husband August, and she felt a little disappointed when she first saw him. Irene, she had supposed, would be more concerned with character and intellect but August was good looking. She wanted to dislike him for that, but his warm smile and polite manners made it impossible. They were perfect together, two handsome people who were also nice people. For a moment, but only a moment, Alwine wished it was her wedding, but she felt so guilty about those thoughts that within a few minutes she was almost shaking. Silently, she begged for forgiveness and sought some other distraction.

Since she was not able to participate in any traditional on goings of a Volhynian wedding, Alwine watched the other guests as they passed the evening in lighthearted ways. She felt guilty drinking in the revelry vicariously as people engrossed themselves in the happiness of the evening. She hoped her father wasn't watching her. He did not approve of such frivolity, but out of respect for the Stein family he endured it on this evening.

Alwine could feel the rhythm of the dancing in her feet and fought hard to keep her feet from tapping. The music was so robust and happy that it seemed to float her away. Her heart swelled as she imagined herself magically floating across the floor to those rhythms. The more she watched and saw how happy the dancers were, the less she could understand why her father was so set against it. She found it exciting to watch, and enjoyed the laughter on the guests' faces. She was glad there was so much joy on Irene's day.

As the evening moved on, one couple in particular drew her eyes. Even though she tried to avoid it, she realized that her attention kept focusing on the redheaded Alwine and the young man who had been introduced as August's friend. There was something happening between the two that verged on being scandalous. Alwine Bladt was so bold that soon tongues were wagging about her conduct. It was her relentless pursuit of the boy that attracted so much attention. She was throwing herself at him. Alwine Frey could not comprehend such boldness. It was foreign to her sensibilities, but she was captivated by the phenomenon.

August Weiss's friend, whose name she had already forgotten, was a very outgoing and gregarious fellow. She would even concede that he was handsome, as Irene had said. Although she would have liked to believe that good looking boys were shallow she had to concede that she had already been wrong about August. It was puzzling. But the thing that set her head to whirling was how Alwine Bladt was pursuing him. If he left her side for just a minute she found him and was there at his arm whenever he turned around. It was shameful, yet it intrigued Alwine that he seemed to be enjoying it.

Alwine Frey was not dismayed at Alwine Bladt's apparent conquest. She suspected at first that both of them were equally irreverent as they made a spectacle of themselves dancing wildly and so closely that she could feel her face turning red just watching them. She was amazed that her friend's parents did not haul her away out of shame. Her own father would not have tolerated such behavior. Now she understood why he did not allow her to dance. By such a pair, the magic could easily be reduced to vulgarity. It was turned into something even more vulgar when Alwine Bladt's hair came undone and flung about the room like a reddish flame. Such immodesty would be talked about for days. Already embarrassed, Alwine Frey's face turned red and she turned away from the spectacle. She saw to her relief that her father wasn't watching. Yet Alwine continued to look on in fascination and made it her evening's diversion to watch the rowdy young couple.

In spite of the gaudy show, Alwine grudgingly admired the Bladt girl's audacity. Still it was incomprehensible to her how she could throw herself at a man so blatantly. Yet, she had to wonder what kind of nerve it took. She wished she had just a little of it.

Initially she thought that young man enjoyed the attention of the flamboyant Alwine Bladt, but then she noticed something she had failed to consider. When he was not with Alwine, he was different. He talked and joked with the men, and not in a loud way. He danced beautifully with Irene, without the wildness that embellished his dances with the red head. He held a wine glass and toasted the bride and her family and everyone applauded the appropriateness of the toast. She had to wonder, when he moved off, was he trying to get away from her? Was he only being gracious when she appeared at his side time and time again?

Slowly, her attitude toward him changed. He was full of life and fun, but was not without character as she had first suspected. It started to annoy her whenever the other Alwine forced herself on him and she thought she saw some annoyance on his part whenever she placed herself in his path. Alwine Frey came to the conviction that the young man deserved much better than Alwine Bladt. Yet she never considered herself as a candidate. No one would be interested in a dull girl with a grossly pointed nose. There were several girls at the dance she could think of as a better match and she even considered one or two of the older girls.

Alwine Frey was unaware that she was falling in love that day. The Bladt girl, on the other hand, was sure that she had her man and better still, she was sure, as were most other people that evening including Irene and August, that Albert Fischer was attracted to her. Alwine Frey was sure of nothing except that her eyes were constantly searching for him, but she felt it was only a point of curiosity. She blushed when she realized a few minutes later that her father had noticed her eyes following this man and his reproving glance made her start up a conversation with her mother. How silly she thought it was to be so concerned about a relationship that could not possibly matter to her. She was acting just like an old maid, living someone else's life, watching it unfold for someone else. She remembered the bitter tears she had shed earlier and the pain flooded back into her soul.

Her conversation with her mother broke off abruptly when her mother noticed that she wasn't even listening. Her eyes were searching for someone. Emilie Frey could not understand why her daughter was so distracted and turned away. When Alwine found Albert again, he was dancing with the other Alwine once again. On a turn of a slow waltz her eyes were fixed on him a second too long and he looked back. Embarrassed, she looked away to a picture on the wall. It was a photograph of the elderly Steins, long since dead, and while she looked she did not see Albert looking at her. All he saw was a profile, but it struck him profoundly. Perhaps it was the subtle smile she had for the portrait of the old man, whom she remembered so fondly. For a few seconds she looked not to be shy and withdrawn, but profoundly serene and radiant. Alwine could not look at the portrait for long without her eyes watering so she had to find something else to look at. Once more, her eyes turned in his direction but she was determined not to show any emotion and ordered the relentless pounding in her breast to stop. Another turn came, he seemed to be hurrying the turns now, and there were his eyes looking at her.

For a moment, until she found the composure to slow it down, her heart beat was all that she could hear. It was harder, however, to control the blood rushing to her face and she hung her head to hide her burning cheeks. With all the strength that her austere upbringing had given her she forced herself not to look his way again. It was as close to a flirtation as she had ever come in her life and although it thrilled her, it also scared her. Her entire upbringing told her that it was evil to dream of things you couldn't have and noble to accept the fate God had for you, no matter how dull.

When her father said it was time to leave she was relieved. She kept her eyes on the floor as they paid their respects to Irene and her father. But Irene insisted on hugging Alwine in her happiness, and asked if she could come back tomorrow. "Thank you, but tomorrow is Sunday and father would not allow it."

"But you must," Irene pleaded. "Couldn't you ask your father?"

"I'll see," Alwine answered, but she knew it was pointless. Her father would never allow it.

Albert was dancing with the redhead when the Freys left. The girl in his arms was becoming tedious. Too quickly Albert had seen what she was about and he was bored. She chattered endlessly and had told him everything about herself already. He would have liked to dance or at least talk with the Frey girl but he couldn't get away from this one for even a minute. Still, he couldn't be rude; he might just have to marry her after all.

When the second Alwine finally left with her parents, Albert felt free. He rushed to ask Irene about the shy girl with the slightly pointed nose. Irene was surprised and delighted that he had even noticed her, but she was excited to tell him all about her friend.

It was with determination that Albert prepared for church in the morning. There he could see and perhaps even speak to the quiet woman who had made an impression on him. Irene had told him that if he didn't talk to her there, there might not be another chance. Her stern father kept her much too busy to return to the wedding festivities. Even though he had no idea what he would say to her, he hoped for some indication that she liked him.

The truth was, he intended to leave Dombrowa engaged to be married. He had made himself a promise and sealed it by revealing his intentions to the ashen faced witch as he left the house. Now he needed to make good on that promise or face humiliation. He drew a deep breath thinking about the alternatives. How he hoped that she would be at church this morning.

He didn't usually care for girls who were awkward or hid in corners when everyone was enjoying themselves. But Alwine Frey was different, and when Irene talked about her he understood that it was her upbringing that made her so shy. His thoughts kept returning to that unforgettable moment last evening, when she had appeared absolutely serene and beautiful, with a wisp of a smile on her face. It had been more revealing than all the talking the other one had done. He was sure he had fallen in love at that moment.

But Albert knew that he needed more than just a dreamy-eyed girl for a wife. He was happy when Irene reassured him that Alwine was a very practical girl with talents and ambition. And when he heard that she was the one that Irene had intended for him all along, he knew all that he needed to know.

What he needed now was a chance to make a favorable impression. He had been warned about her austere father but that did not deter him. Albert really wanted to talk to the young woman. If he could do that, then he might find the courage to present himself at her home. How could he go back to Zeperow and face his brother and the witch without having accomplished that?

Albert sat in the pew with Irene and August and his host Wilhelm Stein. Although they arrived early, Alwine Frey was already there. Across the room, she sat quietly with her family, hardly looking up, or to the left or to the right. Her stone-faced father appeared even more intimidating than he had the night before and Albert's hope began to waver. He had just about lost heart when Alwine Frey looked up. She turned her head and this time caught his eyes without blushing. She nodded politely. It was only an indication of recognition but with that simple acknowledgment Albert's heart soared. He had an idea to cross the floor and sit closer to her but suddenly there was Alwine Bladt. Even before she sat down she was chattering.

After church, Albert told Irene what he intended to do. She was delighted but pointed out the one flaw in his plan. "You have no one to introduce you to her father and vouch for you. Without that...well, it's impossible!" But Irene wanted this match as much as Albert did, so she asked her father to take him to the Frey house. Wilhelm Stein protested that he didn't really know Albert well enough. "He's August's best friend," Irene said as if that was all he needed to know. "He cannot go over there without a proper introduction," she pleaded, "Alwine's father would not even allow him in the door." It was hard for Wilhelm Stein to refuse his daughter, even so, he tried once more to put her off. "Father," she finally cried while tears welled up in her eyes, "I'm moving to a place where I know no one. I would love to have Alwine close by." He had to give in.

Wilhelm Stein and Albert left just before Alwine Bladt arrived to spend the afternoon.

Irene's father felt uncomfortable in his role. He had to present Albert Fischer in the best light possible and yet he knew very little about the young man and felt a great obligation to the Frey family. Yet, his inclination was to believe Albert was a good man, level headed and prepared to work hard. His proof for that assumption was small but significant; only a serious young man would pick

Alwine Frey over the redheaded twit. If he could recognize the difference between those two then he had to believe that Albert was at least wise.

Johann Frey was surprised when he opened the door to his neighbor and the young man he remembered from the wedding. It took him only a few seconds to realize why Wilhelm was there with this boy and although Johann was always under control, he was flustered for a moment. He had been hoping for his daughter's sake that a young man would show up soon, yet it was a shock to see his friend there with this impious boy.

After polite greetings were exchanged, Wilhelm Stein got right down to the issue at hand. There was no sense in delaying this.

"Johann, my friend," Wilhelm began, hoping that he would still be his friend later, "this young man Albert Fischer of Zeperow is a good man and in need of a wife. Would you consider giving him your daughter Alwine?" There was a look of concern on Johann Frey's face so Wilhelm felt he had to reinforce Albert's position. "You know the respect I have for your family, and your daughter, and you know I wouldn't bring any man here that I didn't respect. I don't know this man well but he is a close friend of my new son-in-law whom I have come to trust. Albert is a hard worker and a Christian." Johann Frey remained cold and Wilhelm struggled for words to get past the impasse. Neither man knew how to continue.

Johann had considered many times what he might say at such a moment but now all his planning left him. The young man that stood before him had not impressed him the night before, he was loud and irreverent and his first impulse was to reject him. He would have done so except that he came recommended by Wilhelm Stein. But then he remembered too how his daughter's eyes had followed him around the room and how she had blushed at his behavior with the shameless Bladt girl. Why wasn't he at her house making this proposal? He was sure, however, that his daughter had taken note of this man. He decided to leave it up to her to reject him. That way, he would not have to dishonor his friend. It was a quick decision by a man who was used to patient thinking when faced with a problem. For a moment he even felt sorry for Albert.

"Ask Alwine to come here," he said to his wife, "we will ask her." Emilie stood at his side in shock and he had to repeat the request again before she moved. When his daughter came down the stairs he put the question to her immediately. "Alwine," Johann said deliberately and without emotion, "this man is looking for a wife. Do you wish to marry him?"

She did not see Albert standing behind her father and Wilhelm Stein so she was bewildered. Then her father stepped aside and she saw Albert. Alwine was overwhelmed by feelings she had never felt before. She stood there with her mouth gaping until she found the strength to whisper, "yes." Then fearing that her father had not heard, she said "yes" again, her voice quivering, while her head nodded vigorously. The word came out as a shriek. She repeated it again.

A chorus of giggles came from behind the kitchen door. The intrusion upset Johann Frey greatly, even though he was grateful that something distracted him from the shock of his daughter's answer. Emilie rushed to send the eavesdroppers away. But just then, as if she still wasn't sure that she had been understood, Alwine repeated her answer more vigorously, with her head bobbing repeatedly, "Yes father, I want to marry him." There was another chorus of giggles but Emilie returned swiftly to pull her daughter away before she totally embarrassed her family.

It was only then that a shaken Johann Frey invited the two men into his kitchen. He was a man of honor and could never allow himself to back out of a promise. He had allowed his daughter to make the decision, now he had to live with it. The eavesdroppers finally scrambled away as he opened the door for his guests.

Seven

While Albert was away, back in Zeperow the Fischer household was turned up-side down. Neither Johann nor Julianna knew what to do about Hedwig. She was so distracted that they feared she was mentally ill. She was always agitated and went from chore to chore only half finishing any work she started. Almost as soon as she began to cook a meal, do the wash, or bake bread, she would abruptly drop her work. Mostly she walked out the kitchen door and paced around the yard, or stood, blank-faced, silently staring into the empty fields. She looked anguished, almost in pain in those moments and no one could reach her. In truth, her husband hesitated to try. He was afraid of what he would find.

Julianna, had no understanding of how to help her either but she was a practical woman and did what was necessary. She just stepped in and finished the distraught woman's work, cooking the half-completed meal, getting the boys ready for school and keeping the house going. It was all she could do, just as her son could only hope that his wife would snap out of it. Though she knew Johann was concerned for his wife, his mother noticed that he had more meetings than ever that kept him busy late into the evening in the village. "Kantorrat business," he would explain.

Hedwig was not really aware that her behavior was strange. It seemed only logical to her that her mother-in-law finished chores that she had started because that was Julianna's function, to help her. When on occasion she remembered, hours later, that she had left her bread in the mixing bowl, and then found the loaves baking, she congratulated herself for having organized her house so well that it worked effortlessly, like one of those famous Swiss clocks. It all reinforced her opinion that she was in control, while her husband could not even handle his own family. It was hard for her to understand why Johann stood by and watched as his thieving brother conspired to take their farm and rob their sons of their inheritance. But having retreated into a world of brooding where her family could not reach her, she still found no comfort. The world was turning against her and she needed to do something drastic.

Since the day she and her husband had first come back to take over the farm, she had known that the boy was a threat. She could see it in his eyes that Albert hated her. Even so, she had tried to be warm, but he had rejected her even back then. He had rejected everything she had ever tried to do for him. "Get him an apprenticeship," she had told her husband, "find him something or he'll want the farm." But Johann had not listened and the boy was suspicious too. It wasn't with malice that she had withheld food, she could not be blamed if her husband did not earn enough to feed his own family and them too. No one could expect her to cheat her own family for their sakes. Besides, Albert's strength was proof that she fed him enough.

Now he was fulfilling her predictions. He was as stubborn and intractable as ever and bent on hurting her. He was looking for a wife. Hedwig was convinced that it was for no other reason than to take half the farm away. It was the one thing he could do to hurt her and his brother. The farm was too small to be divided; there was no way that two families could survive on this tiny plot of land. He ought to just let Johann have it. But he was much too greedy and selfish to see that. How her husband could just accept this was incomprehensible. It was up to her to find some way to stop him.

It was impossible for Hedwig to find any reasonable way to circumvent Albert from claiming his inheritance. No persuasion, no appeal, and certainly no pressure could be put on that stubborn boy. She had tried all that, and more. The pressure had finally unnerved her. During the time that Albert had been off to August's wedding, she brooded about his threat to return with a wife. She had been brooding and foaming until she couldn't function. But her frustration was close to boiling over now that Albert was due to return and she hadn't found a solution to her problem. She just wanted him to go away, to die, if need be. "Yes," she said to herself, while looking across those fields she so feared losing, "he ought to go away and die."

It didn't take a mother to understand the look of happiness on Albert's face when he returned home. But Julianna only acknowledged it with a kiss on the cheek, allowing Albert to make his revelation in his own way and in his own time. But Hedwig would not even look at him as he came in the front door. Johann was away. Only his nephews made a fuss, shouting, "Are you married now, Albert? Did you find a wife?"

"Where is Johann?" Albert asked. He wasn't thinking about the protocol of the situation that made it proper for him to tell the head of the household of his plans first, he just wanted to be sure that he was the one who told Johann. It was something he had been dreaming of.

"Papa went to a meeting at the Prayer-House," young Otto said. "He won't be back until late."

"Oh," said Albert. He was disappointed.

"Come and sit. Eat and tell me about August and Irene's wedding," Julianna smiled.

With the mention of food Hedwig tensed and abruptly declared, "There is nothing left." She was lying and she knew that her mother-in-law knew it. Quickly she ushered her sons to bed. Perhaps their protests would distract Julianna's attention from her lie.

Albert let her remark go. He was much too happy to let the witch spoil his day. Today he could let her say whatever she wanted since the time of her control was limited. But Julianna knew it was a lie. It was not just a mistake, but a despicable lie that was meant to injure and insult. She herself had prepared and set aside the food, expecting Albert to return at any moment.

For years Julianna had played the role of the subservient, widowed, mother-in-law, as custom required of her. She had endured her daughter-in-law's greed and her convenient oversights that somehow always worked to Albert's disadvantage. But this was too brazen. It was a slap in the face on a day that should have been happy. That was what Julianna resented the most about Hedwig, her capacity to take away joy. She stared at her daughter-in-law with cold eyes.

"What's the matter?" Hedwig asked, catching Julianna's glare. She had never been challenged by her mother-in-law before. It made her nervous.

"Hedwig, don't you remember, I cooked extra. There is plenty left over."

"I gave it to the dog," she said too quickly. Too late she realized she could have conceded that she had made a mistake. Now there was no retreat.

"No Hedwig, I put it away in the pantry."

"Oh Mother, you're getting so old," Hedwig said condescendingly, but with obvious nervousness, "that little bit that we put away is for Johann. A man who supports his family needs to eat. I gave the scraps to the dog."

Julianna scowled and bit her lip. She got up and went to the pantry. "What are you doing?" Hedwig screamed at her, "I said there was nothing left. You cannot give Johann's food to Albert!"

The scream shocked Julianna. She stopped and turned to see Hedwig with the cast iron frying pan in her hand. There was such a red rage in her eyes that she thought for one moment that the girl would attack her. She stared at her daughter-in-law, unable to comprehend the depth of her hatred. Had she gone mad?

It was Albert who calmed the situation. "Never mind Mother," he said, "I couldn't eat it anyway." The words sounded strange coming from Albert. They were almost conciliatory.

Hedwig was too involved with her own thoughts to hear what Albert was saying. She couldn't really understand why she had lied except that she wanted to hurt Albert. She never expected her mother-in-law to challenge her. That, she would never forgive. What she wanted to do was to hurt them both, but she was alone. Suddenly she realized how true that was. She was alone with two people who hated her. Hedwig trembled. Her husband was not there to protect her. Without a word she slunk off to bed, but had no intention to sleep. When her husband came home, she would tell him how his mother and brother had threatened her.

By seven in the morning the Fischer household was well into its daily routine. Even though Hedwig was the first to bed, she was the last to rise in the morning. She had tossed and turned most of the night. When Johann had come home she heard the chattering in the kitchen and cringed at the lies that Julianna and Albert were probably telling him. She had wanted to get up and put an end to it, but she was petrified. What if he believed them? When Johann finally came to bed, she pretended to be sleeping. She was too confused, too uncertain of what she should do, too unrehearsed in what she should say to him. Yet now in the morning she felt no better.

The house was empty when Hedwig got up. That annoyed her too, not because someone had done her work but because she had not been in control of the day's beginning. How could she possibly know what lies Julianna and Albert had told Johann about her?

Her children were off somewhere too, hopefully doing their chores before school. But where were Albert and Johann? Why was she alone in the house? Not even Julianna was there, and yet the milk pail was full and on the table with a cheesecloth over it, so she knew her mother-in-law was up and working. Still, things didn't seem right.

She took a crust of bread from the pantry and spread on a little churned butter. It was her breakfast. She ate, saying to herself, "I eat less than Albert, he has no reason to be upset." So that morning she ate less than usual to confirm to herself her martyrdom for her family even though there was no one there to witness it. That helped her to feel good about herself because during the night she had found no way of reconciling herself to what was about to happen. Rather, in the dark she had concluded that her mother-in-law was helping Albert in his conspiracy against her family. Julianna had betrayed her. Hedwig had tossed and turned all night. She was still awake even after everyone else had gone to bed and it disturbed her further to hear Albert in the dark, counting the miserable zlotys he had saved for this day. She hated him.

She still hated him in the morning as she gnawed at her crust of bread. As she ate, Hedwig began to hear voices outside. They were busy voices that shouted directions: 'left' and 'right,' then 'yes, no,' and 'forward' and they were mixed with the sound of heavy pounding. "What the devil is going on?" When she thought she heard Albert's voice her anxiety heightened. Was this his doing? It had to be something devious. Hedwig looked through the kitchen window but could not see anything there. She went out the door but the birch trees lining their lane blocked her view. But outside the voices were stronger and she recognized that they came from the grain field and panic struck her. She wanted to run out there and let him have a piece of her mind. How dare he? How dare he think that he was responsible enough to get married? How dare he think of taking away her sons' inheritance?

"Stop!" she shouted as she came through the trees. She found Albert and August on the other side of the birches in the grain field with shovels and stakes. "Stop digging in our best field. What do you think you are doing making holes in our grain field?"

"This is no longer your field," Albert told her as she ran right up to his face. "This is where I am going to build my house. It's my field!"

"Not this field!" Hedwig shouted at the top of her voice. "You cannot have this field, not this one! You can't ruin our best field like this!"

The shouting had stopped all the activity around them. August Weiss, who had come to help his friend measure for his new house stood there with his mouth gaping. Julianna, who had been doing chores with her grandsons in the barn came running. The boys following after her. Johann, hearing the shouting also peered out of the work shop door to see what was happening. When he heard his wife's voice, he knew he had to run. Even old Karl Weiss, August's father, heard the blaring as he scrambled over to see what Albert and his son were planning and was astonished.

"Johann and I agreed last night," Albert shouted back at her, making sure he shouted louder than she did, "this field is mine!"

"Liar! Liar," she screamed, her face twisted painfully, "Johann would never have agreed to give you this field. This is our best field. You thief, you good-for-nothing thief." She started to flail her arms striking at him about his head with a series of awkward, windmill-like blows before he could react. But Albert was strong and he just grabbed her arms and with a slight push she fell backward sharply.

"How dare you?" she continued yelling while she regained her feet. Tears welled up in her eyes but by now she noticed she had an audience. She saw Julianna and screamed at her frantically, "You see your son? You see what he is? He's a cowardly filthy little liar. He will never get this land! We have taken care of you all these years. It is ours!"

Johann was there now. He grabbed his wife and started to pull her to the house. "He attacked me!" she shouted at him. "Just ask them. They saw it. He pushed me to the ground! He tried to kill me! He wants all the land and he'll kill us all! You can't give him the land Johann, you can't ... you can't!"

Johann had no idea what to do about his wife once he was finally able to drag her away from Albert. So he did as he usually did when confronted with her temper, nothing. She sat at the kitchen table and alternately sobbed and then railed on him. All he could do was listen and cringe at her insane accusations but never once did he lose his temper. "It's your fault," she yelled at him now. "You should have bought more land. You should have taken back what Martin stole. But no, not you! All you worry about is church and politics. What about us, Johann? What do we have left now? Half this miserable farm, that's all! Will you divide that between your sons too?"

Johann could think of nothing to answer his wife. He liked to think that she had changed over the years. She was not the same person he had married. In fact, when he considered it, he knew that the change had come after the war. It was the separation and exile to Siberia that had changed her. The death of her parents had scarred her. But deep inside he knew that that wasn't all there was to Hedwig's outburst. Those things had only intensified tendencies that had disturbed him well before. He loved her but he had always known about her greed. He was ashamed of it, but powerless to do anything about it. Now in the crisis of their married life he had nothing to say. Perhaps she was right. Perhaps he had failed and given too much emphasis to other things instead of providing for his family. All he could say was, "God will provide, Hedwig."

She looked at him with unmasked contempt. It was something Johann had never seen before. There had been times when he had felt it, suspected it, but it was in the open now. He believed what he had said, but it was obvious she didn't really understand his faith. Her disbelief made him feel small.

"God will provide," Hedwig repeated mockingly, and with those words realized how really ineffectual her husband was. All her security was passing through her fingers and he wouldn't or couldn't do anything about it. For what he had allowed to happen she wanted to pound on him, but she thought of a better way. "When Albert leaves your mother has to go with him. Let him feed the old woman now." She emphasized the 'old' and watched Johann wince when she said it.

Johann nodded his head in agreement. He had consented to so many things already that one more couldn't make a difference, he was already numb. He would agree to almost anything to calm her down. But unfortunately there was one more thing his wife needed to know. Johann would have given anything to put it off, but he had already delayed it too long. He had been a coward this morning. He had left the house before telling his wife about Albert's other demands. Her being asleep was only an excuse. He was happy to be able to delay telling her, but her outburst had made him ashamed of what he had done. Now he had to tell her more news that would upset her, but if he didn't, he knew that further trouble would be on his head.

"Hedwig," he said softly. But she glowered at him to let him know that she loathed him. Johann hesitated and then realized he had no choice. "We have to take the house down."

"What? He wants the house!"

"Only half."

"I don't understand."

"Half the materials in the house are his, and half the barn, and the granary, and the implements."

"I suppose he wants half the animals too," Hedwig challenged. Her eyes were on fire again.

"Yes."

"Never! Never! Never! Never...!" she pounded the table as she spoke. "How can you let him do this? Where is your backbone, Johann? We have worked so hard!"

"Hedwig, the law is on his side."

"I don't care," she snorted, "I will not have all of our work come to nothing. We've taken care of them all these years. They should be grateful to us! The farm should be ours! But now they stab us in the back and you allow it."

Hedwig did not wait for a reply from her husband, she just ran into the bedroom. He remained at the kitchen table until he heard noises from the bedroom, pushing, grunting, scraping, breaking noises which quickly accelerated until he finally heard a crash. He hoped she wasn't hurting herself.

He found her beside Albert's bed frantically pounding on the floor. His brother's old mattress was on the floor and the bed was pushed over. The box that served as a night table for Albert was dumped out and the contents were scattered on the floor. Hedwig was looking for loose floorboards.

"What are you doing?"

"He's been saving money. I know he has. It's hidden here somewhere. If we find it then he'll have to stop."

"Hedwig, this is insane."

She scrambled out from under the bed and stared her husband in the face. What she said to him was full of contempt. "I'm insane? You let him do this to our family and you call me insane?"

"What is it that you think I can do?" Johann asked in desperation. "The law is on his side. This land belonged to our father. We knew when we came that it was only ours until he married. That was always understood."

"So you are content with being poor all of our lives?"

"What do you want me to do?"

"We should have killed him! We should kill him now!"

"Hedwig, what are you saying?"

"We should have killed him. Arranged an accident or payed some Cossack to slit his throat."

"Stop it, Hedwig!" Johann was incredulous, "to even speak of such things is sin. I will not listen to it."

"If you won't do it then maybe I will do it. It's not too late."

Hedwig began to sob uncontrollably. She put her head in her hands and refused to listen or even look at her husband. She was sure she knew what lay ahead and could not bear it. With half a tiny farm too small to sustain her family she could foresee only poverty. Her husband had proved to be too weak and ineffectual to make their land grow. He couldn't even hold onto this miserable piece of land. Johann would never make the difficult choices that she knew had to be made. Everything was on her shoulders.

Johann could not comprehend what was happening to him. Watching his irrational wife he wondered if he had failed his family? Was this all his fault? Maybe it was. But what could he do about it? What could anyone do? He could no more deny his brother his rightful share of the farm than his father was able to stop Hermann Martin from stealing his land. Johann could still remember how his father had suffered. What else could he have done?

Johann shook his head. He knew. He understood. His father had done everything he could do. In his fifties in 1919, his father had not wanted to start over again. So, not really knowing what conditions were like in Volhynia, and facing a horde of returning soldiers who wanted their jobs back, Joseph packed up his family again and returned to his home.

His first surprise was a pleasant one. The house, except for having been cleaned of everything useful, was still standing. It was in need of major repairs and the roof was leaking but there it stood, a shelter for his family.

The barns were in similar shape but all the machinery he had accumulated had disappeared. He had expected things to disappear, indeed, he had even hoped that someone would take the animals. The second surprise, however, was disconcerting. His neighbor, Karl Weiss, who had fought for the Russians in the Caucuses was totally surprised by Joseph's return. "You are the last one that we expected to come back!" Weiss had said, "Martin told us that you sold him the farm!"

There were no authorities to appeal to. Even the constable who could prove that Joseph had left too quickly to sell anything had disappeared. In fact, the western parts of Volhynia were still at war. With Germany defeated and Russia still in turmoil the Poles and the Ukrainians had renewed their age-old battle for control of this land. Joseph Fischer had brought his family home to a civil war.

As a consequence, neither Hermann Martin, who stubbornly maintained that Joseph Fischer had sold him the land, nor Joseph Fischer was able to establish legal claim to the land. Joseph went about his farming as if Hermann's bogus claim didn't even exist. He repaired his buildings as best he could and prepared to plant his crops while his former friend protested. But the war between the Poles and the Ukrainians put everything in doubt.

In the spring, with what equipment Joseph could buy and borrow, he ploughed his lands and began to farm again. Martin appealed to his German neighbors, however, they tended to believe Joseph Fischer. "A man does not return to the land he has sold," Karl Weiss told Martin. It was as close to calling him a liar as he dared to go. When the Germans would not listen to him, Martin complained to the Ukrainians and then to the Poles. They all laughed at him. Behind his back each group vowed, "When we win we will throw them both out."

For the time being the matter seemed settled. Fischer continued to farm his land. Martin, red-faced and fuming, continued to complain and the Poles and Ukrainians continued to fight. Then in 1921 the Treaty of Riga at least settled the war. The Western half of Volhynia was now part of the new Republic of Poland.

Johann could remember how happy he had been. He would never have dared to return to Russia. He came home to find his wife. Others returned also, not having found jobs in Germany, and lacking the means to buy passage to other parts of the world they came looking for their lives in Volhynia where they were born. They told themselves that things would be different under Polish rule.

The German-Volhynians learned quickly not to base their dreams on speculations. In Polish courts they found that Polish judges would not easily be persuaded to turn Polish and Ukrainian peasants out of their houses even if the deeds belonged to Germans. The legislature also, backed up the judges by declaring the lands that had been abandoned by the Germans had been forfeited. Even if this abandonment was at the point of a gun it made no difference. The Germans were stunned.

Those who had maintained their land by fighting in the Russian army, or those who returned early, or whose land had been laid to waste by the war so that no one wanted it, were lucky. They were allowed to keep their farms. But it was clear, Poland once again belonged to the Poles.

It was then that Martin ran to the courts and once again presented his bogus receipt to the magistrate as evidence of his claim. The magistrate turned to Count Viteranno's agents who confirmed that by their records Joseph Fischer had purchased half his property on terms, and inherited the lease on the other half. It was not a good day for Martin, but he would not be turned aside so easily.

With determination he went to the city of Lutzk and sought out a Polish lawyer to represent him. Soon, for reasons that made the Germans very suspicious, Martin had married again. The girl was half his age, very fat and very Polish. It was rumored too that Martin had converted again, to Roman Catholicism. Even the most naive in the community could see what Hermann was up to.

This time when the matter was laid before the magistrate, he was more sympathetic to Martin. A hearing was called and both sides made their claims. The judge, however, showed by his demeanor that he was favoring Martin and his scurrilous receipt.

He wanted to believe the German who was trying to be a good Polish citizen. But this time Joseph had a witness. The constable to whom Martin had presented his forgery in 1915 had returned from Siberia where the Russians had sent him for treasonable conduct. (It had been suspected that he had been too lenient with the Germans and the Jews.) He was convincing when he told how he had warned Joseph to leave Volhynia immediately, allowing him no time to sell his land. He remembered the receipt too. He had suspected from the beginning that it was forged and had refused to witness it.

The judge looked uncomfortable with his testimony but he found he could not entirely disregard it. Still, the road to success these days, especially for a judge with political ambitions, was not by ruling in favor of Germans. Yet Martin, despite his wife and Polish lawyer was really a German too. The magistrate's solution was a dubious compromise. It made no sense to either litigant. The land that Joseph Fischer had bought was returned to him, but the rented hectares were turned over to Martin, to continue with the lease. The magistrate smiled as he handed down the decision. It was a satisfying day for him when Germans left his court frustrated.

Johann could only shake his head. No piece of land was worth this kind of trouble. All he had ever wanted was to do the honorable thing, for his family, for his wife and for his brother. Yet when he listened to his wife, he felt like a failure. He could not understand what he had done wrong.

To his amazement, Albert had found no joy in finally wrenching his half of the farm from Johann. Strangely, the revenge he had anticipated so long had turned sour. Yet he could not take it back. His pride would not let him.

When Johann had returned home last night, Albert was still waiting for him. His mother had stayed up too, expecting to share in their joy. She had no idea, however, what Albert had in mind.

Quickly he had waded in with his demands. Johann had consented almost eagerly to giving him half the land. Even when Albert demanded the best field, his brother nodded. It was strangely unsatisfying so Albert felt compelled to press on. He asked for half the livestock, half the farm implements, and then finally asked for half the material in all the buildings, including the house. To each request Johann had quietly acquiesced, maintaining his dignity. It was Albert, rather than Johann, who became flustered. He had anticipated Johann's reaction incorrectly and yet he found it impossible to back off. It was only when Julianna began to feel sorry for the elder son and would not permit Albert to continue that he stopped. But although he made no more demands Albert wasn't finished. He would ask nothing more now, but he intended to count every board and every nail in every building on the farm. Somehow he had to exact some revenge and he wanted it to be painful.

It was the melee in the field that made Albert feel better. It was her reaction that finally made him feel like he got a measure of revenge and yet it was not satisfying at all. He felt sorry for Johann now. But Albert was also practical, all his sorrow could not change the fact that he deserved what he had bargained for.

Eight

To Johann Frey, his duties and responsibilities were clear. Although he trembled when he thought of the mistake he had made, he could do nothing but stand behind her choice now. He had only himself to blame. He had been so smug and arrogantly sure that she would reject that impudent young man. More than most men, he could appreciate the irony that resulted from his prideful decision. It was more obvious than it had ever been; God never let any act of pride go unpunished.

The wedding would be the best he could afford, without being ostentatious. Even though he had concerns about his daughter's fiancee, he was determined to send her into her marriage properly. That meant gifts and a dowry of sorts. Dowries in Volhynia were not as extravagant as they had been thirty years earlier but the tradition was still strong. They were considered to be a woman's contribution to her new home, an acknowledgment that their new life would consist of things that both parties brought to it. During these postwar years everyone had accepted that dowries had to be smaller. Johann was thankful for that.

Yet the giving of ritual presents was always complicated. Even in these poor times a groom could easily be insulted if the bride was not given enough by her parents. So it concerned Johann when Wilhelm Stein told him privately that Albert considered him to be a rich man. He would not disgrace his daughter, but he would not allow an impudent man's erroneous perception to prey upon his generosity. He and his wife would have to give it a great deal of thought.

Although Johann planned to fulfill every obligation placed on him by duty and tradition, he found greater satisfaction in what he did strictly out of love for his daughter. He had in mind a project and when he discussed it with his wife she was extremely happy. Emilie loved it when her husband allowed his softer side to show.

Johann also understood how little time he had. The wedding had been tentatively set for February. So on Monday, the day after the unexpected proposal, he told Edmund to get his sharp axe and bow-saw from the work shop. With Rudolf, they went into the orchard and selected a sturdy cherry tree with a mature and well-formed trunk. The one they selected had been a very productive tree, but for the purpose Johann had in mind, nothing was too good. Quickly they had it down and stripped the branches which were still laden with dying leaves. It produced a fine-looking log. Then Johann and his sons rigged a ramp and harnessed the horse to pull the log onto a wagon.

When they drove past the house, the younger children yelled out, "Papa, where are you going?" But Johann remained stone faced and Edmund and Rudolf only smiled and waved. Alwine, still flushed with happiness didn't think anything of it, but just shewed the children out of the way of the wagon saying, "Papa just wants some wood." She didn't care what for.

Emilie watching from an upstairs window smiled and felt warmly about her husband as he worked with his sons. She loved it that he was devoted to his family and had a tradition of faith. Tradition and faith had always played a great part in their life together. Had it not been a sin, Johann and Emilie could well have said that they were proud of their heritage. It was a heritage they felt an obligation to pass on to their children.

It was impossible to know Johann Frey without understanding his devotion to God. His neighbors used many terms to describe him; hardworking, dedicated, devout, pious, zealous, and Godfearing were most common. And even though Johann never indulged himself by listening to praise, there was one term that he would have objected to. That description was Godfearing. It was difficult for him to think of himself as a Godfearing man. That characterization might have been true when he was younger. Back then, fear had been the motivation for many of his actions. Now, however, the term was almost irrelevant, and it was only because the Bible spoke clearly that men should fear God that he even acknowledged the idea. But he and his wife were at a stage in their lives when God had touched them enough to make fear irrelevant. Fear did not seem right anymore. Fear was not what Johann wanted to teach his children. He would much rather have them be grateful.

He loved his children intensely. Try as he might Johann could not hide his true nature from them. No son or daughter of his, who had ever been held in his arms, could ever not know that he loved them. Enveloped in those arms they could feel both his strength and his warmth. So it was impossible for them not to love him too. Yet he knew love was not enough. Children needed discipline and rules and most of all they needed to understand that God was in control.

Johann was zealous but without being extreme. If he had failed to understand the trauma his family had suffered, it certainly wasn't out of indifference. Though his ways were stoic and demanding, he demanded nothing that he was not prepared to give himself. But he wanted his children to understand and to learn everything he had learned in his lifetime. He found, however, that some things were not transmittable from parent to child and had to be experienced personally. You could indicate to your children where God was, but they had to find Him themselves.

But that did not mean that he abdicated his responsibility. Rather, he steeled himself for those moments when he felt he had something important to say to his children. As a result of this stiff approach, what he said often came out more harshly than it was meant. Or sometimes in a moment of anger he rebuked openly what was better received in privacy. But even if he humiliated a child, he felt that inflicting shame was better than allowing them to develop pride.

There were some very basic principles that Johann diligently endeavored to teach his children. The foremost of these was that a man without God was a vain and vile creature. That principle, he was sure, would become self-evident to each of his offspring if they remained on the farm. But staying on the farm was the key.

Johann hoped that his children would stay on the farm because he had found that farmers discovered God more easily than other men. That seemed to be because they needed Him more. But why God loved farmers so much Johann had no idea. For all their supposed devotion, Johann suspected that most farmers were only beggars. They hounded God to regulate everything that they could not control: the seasons, the weather, the insects, the weeds, the rain and the sunshine, and even the Polish government. Johann wondered how He could tolerate such selfishness. Yet he was amazed how much God must love such men to allow them to pester Him so much. No one, he was sure talked to God more than farmers. Sometimes it seemed to Johann that God just loved men who would humble themselves enough to talk to Him. It didn't matter a whole lot what they said. And it seemed that the German farmers must have hounded God more than all the rest.

And that was why Johann was also adamant that his children remained in the German tradition. By that he meant they needed to speak German as their first language, married only Germans and retained their German or Lutheran faith.

To him it was only natural that the followers of Luther had the clearest communication with God. The Catholic Poles and the Orthodox Ukrainians followed mindless ritual, while the Jews were impossible to understand. It was simply a fact. The Germans had the best religion and the best language for communicating with God. Such truths were so plain that they did not even have to be explained. He was sure that deep down even the Poles and Ukrainians understood. It did not seem like vanity to Johann to think that way.

Johann ruled his home armed with the Bible in one hand and stoic tradition in the other. As a consequence it wasn't often that one of the Frey children would question their father openly. But on those rare occasions when it did happen and someone complained about the endless work, then Johann Frey would put on his emotionless face and remind his entire brood of all the blessings for which they had to be grateful. He would remind them that as far back as memory could reach, through stories handed down from generation to generation, the Freys had worked hard and sacrificed much. Their ancestors had been part of the great Lutheran reformation. Their family tradition was that during those turbulent times, now more than four centuries old, they had fought along side Martin Luther in order to free the German people from the Catholic heresy and tyranny. Work and sacrifice were a blessing.

The stoic believed strongly that the stories he told his children were the absolute truth. He had learned them kneeling at his parents feet during the long winter nights when he was a little boy. Mingled with the stories of Cain and Abel, David and Goliath, Samson and Delilah, were the stories of the Lutheran struggle for religious freedom. The context in which they were told made them as sacred as any bible story to Johann. He believed that his progenitors had fought at the side of the great reformer, Martin Luther, making war on the evil Holy Roman Emperor and against its Catholic religion. Johann Frey was loyal to these family traditions and to the faith that they told him had made him free and gave him his name. These were precious things and he felt strongly that his children should also know them.

It never occurred to Johann to question those old stories. Neither did it occur to him that Luther had fought his battles with the pen and printing press and not with the sword. What would have surprised Johann even more was that Martin Luther, despite being a descendant of peasants himself, actually took sides against Johann's ancestors in one of the monumental struggles of the sixteenth century.

The truth was that a direct ancestor of Johann Frey had taken part in the Peasant War of the 1520's that ravaged Southern Germany. Impoverished serfs and hopelessly indebted free peasants, stirred up by even more radical reformers than Martin Luther, rose against the oppression of their masters and their church. The rebels collected into mobs, roamed the countryside, destroying, murdering and plundering. The nobility and the church were terrorized.

Luther, whose reforms needed the support of the nobility to protect him from the Holy Roman Emperor, offered himself as a mediator. But he didn't even try to negotiate, instead he arrogantly told the peasants to go back to work and take their rightful, if lowly station in society, because it had been ordained unto them by God. It was a tactical error that only angered the mobs more. Luther barely escaped with his life. Many peasants now considered him a traitor and their leaders denounced him as a puppet of the nobility.

Luther could not accept his failure graciously. In a fit of temper that only euphemistically could be characterized as vengeful, he turned his pen on the peasants. Advocating their total destruction if they did not return to their duties he penned a pamphlet that was vile and bloodthirsty. Luther adhered to the concept generally accepted by the upper classes, that is, that God had ordained who would be master and who would be the servant, therefore the master ruled with the blessing and consent of God and the servant accepted his lot.

The German nobility did not need Martin Luther to tell them what to do with their rebellious peasants. When the bloody swords of the nobles were finally sheathed, the bodies of the peasants were piled high, higher than even Luther could have predicted. Luther's quasi-official sanction of the slaughter of the peasants, which afterwards made even those who participated sick with grief, might have been forgotten because he offered so much that was good. But unfortunately, he left behind him those pamphlets, printed so neatly and prolifically on the new Gutenberg presses. In them he had called for the cutting of the throats of the peasants who rebelled against God. Martin Luther had implored the people to rise up and stab at the hearts of the peasant rebels and if they did, God would surely bless them. In spite of Luther, this disastrous war, in which the ancestors of Johann Frey had participated, was the beginning of the end of feudalism in Germany.

One of Johann Frey's progenitors had escaped the final Armageddon, and running north to one of the free city states of Germany, he declared himself a free man. His name was Johann too, and in almost every generation thereafter, a child was named after him. For a generation he was known as Johann der Freie, (John the Free), and his descendants were known by the last name Frey. Yet freedom had its price too and for hundreds of years his descendants roamed northeast Europe, finally finding a permanent home in central Poland at the end of the eighteenth century.

Only a generation or two after the fiasco of the peasant rebellion, the descendants of Johann the Free began to follow the teachings of the Great Reformer again. They had forgotten any wrong that might have lingered to ruin the reputation of Martin Luther. They did not have his incriminating pamphlets to read, but rather his superior translation of the Bible, printed on the same Gutenberg Press. By now it seemed inconsistent anyway that such a good man could have any major character flaws. In subsequent generations and centuries the Freys defended their faith against the counter-reformation and in the thirty-years war, in which many more people lost their lives than in the peasant wars. They began to be Lutheran not only by faith but by the sacrifice of blood. Lutheran they were, and Lutheran they would remain. Freedom and faith, which had been earned by the blood they had spilled, was now their right and their heritage.

In spite of the oral tradition, in 1928, Johann Frey could not name one ancestor who had lost his life fighting for this religion. That did not diminish his belief in his family's ties to the reformer, because he felt strongly that Martin Luther was his family's benefactor and liberator. For that he gave him his loyalty and taught his children to be loyal also. He told them that their duty was to uphold the Lutheran reforms as the final reserve of religious truth, just as generations of Freys had done. It was a sacred trust.

As great as the influence of that heritage was on their lives and as much as tradition and religion ruled their hopes, there had been events that shaped the character of Johann's children that he had no control over. Alwine was old enough to remember the war and so was Edmund, though his memories were not as detailed. Johann's family had endured the greatest trauma ever experienced by the German-Volhynians. Their father had not been there to help them through it; he had gone to war. He remained firm that no child of his would wallow in self-pity.

The tree that Johann and his sons delivered to the mill would produce good lumber but it was too fresh to turn into anything as important as what he had in mind. He traded it with the mill owner for some cured cherry wood which he brought home. Very carefully his boys unloaded the boards into his work shed. They laid them on the floor and piled the wood so that every board lay flat and straight until needed for his project. There in the work shop, freed from prying eyes, he would build his tribute to his oldest daughter. His sons, Edmund and Rudolf would work with him as they had done in winters past while he taught them the intricacies of working with wood.

None of them would even let on that they were making something for their big sister Alwine. It would remain a surprise and Alwine didn't even become curious. It was normal for her father and the boys to spend their winters in the work shop, fixing implements that had broken in the summer, and crafting new things for the house. The girl knew that her father loved to teach the boys about wood work and each spring they would appear with something new for their rooms. Papa too had a new table or cabinet for her mother at the end of each winter. So Alwine didn't notice anything unusual now, she was happier than she had ever been.

Johann tried to teach his sons everything he knew about crafting with wood. Rudolf applied himself and showed signs of becoming an adequate craftsman. But the promise of excellence that a father hoped to find in at least one of his children, lay with Edmund. Whether it was in his school work, farming or woodworking, he was the one who had natural ability. Edmund was already working with finesse and innate ability while his brother was still mastering the basics.

Vain as it sounded, even his father had to admit that Edmund had a gift. But it was not vanity that Johann acceded to, he was simply acknowledging a truth. A gift was a talent or ability that could not be explained in any other way. No amount of teaching or practice could account for it. So it must come from God and it was never vain to acknowledge Him. And since it was a gift it was not to be trifled with, nor boasted about, nor hidden. But the amazing thing about Edmund was that his Gift was to do well in everything he put his hand to. And it was in his school work in particular he had excelled. That scared his father. For when Edmund was immersed in his books he seemed to carry the weight of the world on his shoulders. It seemed to his parents that he had been that way since they had brought him home from Siberia.

Edmund had only been four years old when the trains left for Siberia. That was much too young to have any concrete recollections of that horror, but he did have impressions. They were scattered fragments, some of bleakness, some of cheek-biting, finger-numbing cold, and the impression that his family had endured a period of desperation. Vaguely, he recalled a time when there was never enough to eat, when his mother cried inconsolably when she thought the children were asleep. But there were peaceful fragments too. Brilliantly white snow and vibrant green summers when he and his brother Rudolf played outside forever during long days when the sun never seemed to set. Edmund cherished them even if he didn't understand what they represented.

As he grew up the boy was never quite sure why no one would speak about the war. When he learned from an old photograph that his father had been a Russian soldier he asked about it and was rebuffed coldly. It was only when he began school again that his hunger was nourished. With books to feed him he ate everything he could lay his hands on. Before long he understood more than his family could ever guess. Yet he could never discuss these things at home because his father would never allow it. He was convinced his father would never allow him to be anything other than a farmer.

Now, several years after he had stopped attending the Kantor-School, he continued to read and to listen. But there were questions that no one seemed to be able to explain to his satisfaction. Only his natural curiosity kept him from despairing. It gave him hope that there were answers to his unpossable question.

Nine

In the fall of 1928, Edmund longed to be anywhere but this restricting farm. He had learned to appease his father with his hard work but secretly he wanted so much more. So when his mother and sister needed to go to Vladimir to shop for Alwine's wedding and his father was too busy, he gladly volunteered to drive them.

While his mother and sister shopped, Edmund found himself with time to do some exploring. His father had given him several errands and he finished them quickly and had more than an hour to spare before he had to meet his mother at the big red-brick Lutheran church. He had a few zlotys in his pocket and though he knew it was frivolous, what he wanted to do was go to a café where people bought real coffee and sat at tables discussing politics and philosophy. Near the church there was such a place where Edmund had seen Polish men sitting and talking.

It was from the German-educated Kantor Biberdorf of Dombrowa that he got the idea. His teacher was fond of reminiscing about days spent in philosophical discussions in cafes near his school. For Edmund he had painted a romantic picture of the great university cities: Berlin, Heidelberg, Vienna, Paris, Cambridge and even Krakow. There, students met in informal groups to develop ideas too radical for stuffy classrooms. But intrigued as he was,

Edmund could only imagine what it was like to discuss philosophy without the limitations of home, tradition and dogma.

Edmund had never done anything so frivolous as to use up a whole zloty for a cup of coffee, yet if it was the price of admission to a new world he was prepared to pay it. He knew that Vladimir was not Paris, nor Berlin, it was not Warsaw, nor even Lutzk, but it was the largest city close to his home. It was actually a backward place when compared to other old Polish cities with fine universities, but to Edmund it represented Poland. The café that he picked was also an unlikely spot to find enlightened discussion, except on this particular day. It was by sheer coincidence that in Vladimir that morning three university students had arrived from Krakow.

The three were seen sporadically in the region and used the café to rest their weary feet and relax. At a table near the front door they sat drinking coffee and talking about the problems their country faced. Although their world was Krakow, and the university there, their dedication was to Poland and to social justice. If that meant enduring the stagnancy that was Vladimir they could tolerate it for a few days.

Edmund ordered a coffee and paid with his precious zloty for a drink he had never developed a taste for. His parents rarely wasted good money on real coffee. With his cup in hand he spotted the three men engrossed in conversation. He chose a table close to them. He told himself that all he wanted to do was to listen. With his head down and his eyes fixed on the dark-brown liquid that he found bitter, he strained to listen to the table next to him. His heart jumped when he discovered that the three men, not much older than he, were looking for answers too. The Polish they spoke revealed that they were not locals but it didn't matter to Edmund.

Though he could not discern their political orientation, he soon knew that they all agreed that Poland was in trouble. One of them seemed to control the conversation by posing provocative questions.

Edmund enjoyed listening to him turn his comrades' comments back on them with questions that forced them to examine their viewpoints more closely. It was an effective tactic except that one of the group was so opinionated he never seemed to understand the point of the question. Edmund got the impression that that one cared only about his own opinions. The third was more quiet but when he spoke he revealed a keen sense of history and deep feeling for the peasants of Poland and their problems. Slowly Edmund figured out that the one with all the questions was the leader of the group and his name was Ivan. The obstinate fellow's name was Peter, but he never seemed to hear the name of the third.

It was when the belligerent fellow, Peter, began a diatribe about the minorities of Poland that it finally grabbed Edmund. He was listening to a man who hated him. Perhaps he hated all foreigners. It frightened Edmund and fascinated him at the same time.

"Do you intend to get rid of all foreigners?" Ivan asked. "How would do it? Do you mean to deport them, expel them, buy them out, or will you just shoot them?"

"Of course not, but if they want to be in Poland, they must become Poles. No more Ukrainian-Poles, German-Poles or Jewish-Poles. We shouldn't have to put up with this nonsense."

"What nonsense?" the quiet one asked.

"Trying to accommodate every group that claims special privileges because of language or religion."

"So what do you do about it?" Ivan pressed. His question seemed to have purpose.

"First of all you make them use the Polish language."

"That is amazing Peter," Ivan said. His tone was full of incredulity. "For a hundred years the Russians did the same thing to us. Are we Russians now? No. We kept our language alive in our homes and we learned to hate the Russians. If we do this we will be the same as the Russians and we will be hated just as they were."

Edmund savored the discussion. Almost immediately he realized that this was the same discussion he heard around German tables, but from the opposite viewpoint. It was even more surreal that the Poles demonstrated just as much passion as Germans. He would have liked to join them but he wondered how they would accept the opinions of a German. Peter would object, Edmund was reasonably sure of that.

Just then, he looked up from his drink and saw that one of the trio was watching him. Edmund nodded politely. He was ashamed of his prying and hoped that he didn't look too embarrassed. Quickly the youth turned his attention back to his coffee. But the conversation at the next table quieted for a second and when he looked up again all three of the Poles were looking at him.

"Has our conversation been interesting to you?" asked the opinionated one, Peter.

Because Edmund didn't like him he thought about making a lame denial. But he couldn't do it. His head told him to leave but his heart wanted to stay. "I am sorry to have been caught eavesdropping," he said red-faced, "but yes, I found it very interesting."

The Poles smiled.

"Are you from Vladimir?" Ivan asked.

"No," Edmund answered and hoped he would not have to tell them that he was from a little farming community. However, they looked at him expecting a more complete answer and he felt compelled to say, "I'm from Dombrowa. It's close by."

"That's a German village isn't it?" asked Peter, "full of German farmers."

Edmund was not sure whether it was said with as much contempt as he inferred, but he felt uncomfortable and was sure he had made a mistake. "Yes, I'm German," he said now, surprised at the defiance in his own voice. He hadn't meant it to come out like that but since he was preparing to leave he didn't think it mattered much.

"Come join our discussion." The invitation came from Ivan and it sounded sincere. "We three know each other so well it's becoming stale. We need some new viewpoints. I am Ivan and these are my friends Misha and Peter. We are students, discovering our country, you might say." Edmund made a note; Misha was the name of the quiet one.

"Yes," said Misha, stretching out his hand to Edmund, "here we are in this wonderful ancient city discussing it without the help of a local resident."

"He's a German," Peter said, not even bothering to look at Edmund, "he is hardly a local."

"There have been Germans in Vladimir for seven hundred years. My family has been here for almost a hundred years," Edmund replied. He was surprised how insulted he felt.

"Ah, yes," said Peter, "and in that time have you bothered to understand Poland at all. No, you are still Germans. You speak German, you marry German, you farm German. You do everything German."

"I speak Polish," Edmund answered in defense but he realized that his answer was insufficient. "But this region has been part of Poland for only a few years. Many Germans here speak Russian better than Polish. Thousands of people in Volhynia speak only Ukrainian. Who knows what language will be spoken here in another twenty years."

"Perhaps you are thinking it will be German," Peter said angrily.

Edmund did not answer.

"But it's true," Ivan offered, "many languages are spoken here. I wonder if there is a land in all the world that has changed hands more often. What reasons do these people have to be loyal to Poland? Except in the hearts of Poles, Poland has been dead for more than a hundred years. How can we expect other people to have the same feelings for her that we have?"

"As a German," Edmund ventured, "I find it hard to understand why it is so important for you to destroy our heritage? Why is it offensive to you that there is such a thing as a German-Pole?"

"I'll tell you why. If you are a Pole your loyalty is with Poland, but if you are a German-Pole where is your loyalty, with Germany or Poland?" Peter asked and sat back looking smug.

"I was born in Russia, so I am really a German-Russian-Pole. In a case like that how do you determine your loyalty, by birth, by heritage or by residence? I don't know, I feel German, particularly when I am around Poles, but I feel no more loyalty to Germany than to Poland."

"Absurd," said Peter.

"I wonder," Misha interjected, "do we consider loyalty to be so important that we find it hard to understand someone with divided loyalties? Do we assume that someone cannot be loyal to Poland if he insists on speaking German in his home?"

Ivan looked at Edmund, "You say that loyalty is more complicated than we Poles think, but Peter thinks it is simple. He believes you Germans are disloyal. Is it really possible to be loyal to two countries?"

"I don't know but I do have to leave," Edmund said, "someone is waiting for me." He realized that his hour was almost spent.

"Is she pretty?" Ivan asked smiling. "Better go then, lovers don't understand divided loyalties at all."

"It's my mother."

"Well then you must go," said Ivan, "Mothers understand many things, but they do not like to be kept waiting."

"But before you go tell us one thing German!" The request came from Peter and Edmund found himself on the defensive before the words even left his mouth. "Why do the Germans hang on so stubbornly to their language and traditions when it would be better for them to change?"

"That's a strange question for a Pole to ask," Edmund answered trying to sound incredulous. "I don't know the answer, but you as a Pole should."

"Ah, but you have thought about it," Ivan observed.

"Certainly, every German-Pole has considered it," Edmund answered, forgetting for a moment that he had to leave. "But when many Germans first came here during the last century, they were promised that they could keep their language, their religion and their schools."

"The famous promises of Catherine the Great, the German Queen of Russia," Peter scoffed. "Russia would not honor them but you expect Poland to?"

"But what has changed?" Ivan asked Peter, "These people are still on the same land they settled. Only the border has moved east. They did not move to Poland, Poland moved to them."

"How wonderful it must be," Peter said with great sarcasm, "to be able to hide behind hundred-year-old promises and use them as an excuse to ignore reality. The world has changed. No one but the Germans care about the old Tzarina anymore, and no one will honor the promises she made, not the Russians and not the Poles. To expect it is ludicrous."

"Peter has a point," Ivan said, looking at Edmund again.

Although he was becoming uncomfortable Edmund felt it necessary to respond. "If a man needs to realign his loyalty every time a treaty changes his borders then he will be a confused man, of little use to anyone. I understand your concerns but you must admit that it is a hard thing. Loyalty is a thing of the heart. It may be easier to change a border than a heart."

"Well said," Misha offered with a smile. "You should meet with us again, we have many other important questions to consider in this new country of ours."

Misha had given Edmund a perfect exit but as soon as Edmund had finished he thought of something else to say. "You Poles resisted the Russians, the Germans and the Austrians for more than a hundred years as they tried to erase everything that makes you Polish. Why would you now want to do the same thing to us?"

"It's different," said Peter curtly.

"How is it different?" Misha asked. "It seems that every time we want to repeat a mistake of history we say, 'This is different.' The only thing that's different is that this time we are doing it."

"This is our land. We are not the invaders here." Peter was getting annoyed. "Every country has a right to ensure its own survival and considering who our neighbors are, we need to do whatever is necessary."

"The Ukrainians would argue with you on that one," retorted Misha. "This place, this whole area around Vladimir Volhynski has been Ukrainian, Lithuanian, Polish, Russian. It has been run over by Cossacks, by Turks, by Tartars, Swedes, even Napoleon and who knows how many others. The Austrians and Germans occupied it during the war. It is as if this land was made to be fought over. We are all invaders here."

"Yes, yes," Peter repeated impatiently, becoming more annoyed at his comrade's historical journey. "But it is Poland now, and Poland it will remain. Our country only exists because Germany fell and Russia had a revolution. But those two wolves still sit on either side of us and if they ever agree on anything again, it will probably be to crush Poland. If we are divided they will tear us apart. Poland has been resurrected for the benefit of Poles, not for Germans and Russians. Whatever we do to survive will be justified."

"So Peter, your first act in unifying the peoples of Poland would be to destroy the language of the Germans and the Ukrainians. Ask this German how that will unite them with us?"

Now Edmund wanted to get away. He realized that it had been vanity that made him ask one more question and now he was stuck waiting for the answer. His mother would ask questions if he was late. Questions he did not want to answer. "I have to leave,"

Edmund said, pulling his coat tightly around him to emphasize the point.

"I am leaving too," Misha said, "may I walk with you?"

Once outside the café Misha asked which way Edmund was going. He pointed up the street in the direction of the Lutheran Church. "Good, I am going that way too." Then he held out his hand, "Misha Maczowiak."

Edmund took his hand hoping that he would not walk far with him. "I'm Edmund..." he didn't want to give his last name.

"Did Peter's comments bother you?"

"He hates Germans. It is uncomfortable to be hated."

"Yes, Peter has some very hard opinions."

"Do you really believe there will be another war?"

"There will always be another war."

"I mean between Germany and Poland."

"You can count on it," Misha said emphatically, "that is what worries Peter. Will you German-Poles fight with Poland or with Germany?"

"I was born Russian. Maybe I will fight with them."

Misha laughed uneasily. "Do you say that to be humorous or evasive, Edmund?"

"I'm sorry, I don't know the answer."

"My friends and I will be here for a few more days, come and talk with us again. If we are both Poles we should know each other better. I personally think there are many things more important to discuss than loyalty."

"It would be difficult for me to return."

"Think about it. Don't be put off by Peter, he talks as he thinks but really he's a reasonable fellow. We're all reasonable. We want what is best for Poland."

"What is best for Poland?"

"Poland may be a new country, some say reborn, but it is caught up in old ways. The Government protects the rich and despises its workers. Something must be done. I come from a small farming community myself. I'm a peasant and proud of it. I fight for the day that the peasants can stand proudly in Poland and live decently."

"Fight?"

"Politics Edmund. Our party fights for workers and farmers. It is for all Poles, Germans and Ukrainians included. But we need people like you."

"Peter doesn't think so."

"Even Peter will concede that the cause is more important than ethnic differences. This republic will soon be a dictatorship. Pilsudski will soon be running everything unless he is not strongly opposed and that will be bad for everyone. Nothing stands in his way right now."

Edmund smiled, "There are too many political parties in opposition."

"Yes, too many, you are right. There is the real danger. A fragmented opposition is like no opposition at all. Ultimately, it will justify the old general and that will be too bad."

But Edmund was staring across the street where his mother and sister were engaged in conversation with the pastor in front of the big red church. Misha couldn't help but notice his stare. "Is that your mother?" he asked.

"Yes," Edmund confirmed awkwardly, fearing that the Pole now expected to be introduced. He could only imagine what awkward questions that would evoke.

"The young woman who looks like you, is that your sister?"

"Yes," Edmund replied, feeling tense and nervous about Misha hanging around until he would have to introduce him to his family.

"Your sister is beautiful," Misha commented, "I would stay to be introduced but I have to leave. Excuse my rudeness."

The tension left Edmund's voice. "Good-bye," he said confidently.

"Come back to the café tomorrow if you can. Farewell, Edmund."

Edmund was relieved. His mother and sister were standing just across the street from the red brick church with the Pastor. He had not wanted to explain to his mother who this Pole was and how he had met him. Now, even if they saw him, he could explain him away. He was a stranger asking for directions. He caught himself, however, and felt a sinking feeling in his gut. He was preparing to lie.

But his mother had seen nothing and didn't even question that he was late. Instead she left him there with the pastor as she and Alwine went to pick up a package before they returned home. He was grateful that they were so preoccupied.

Pastor Schoen invited Edmund to come inside and wait in his office. Though Edmund hesitated, the Pastor was not a man to be refused. "I understand from your mother," he said as they walked, "that you are the thinker of the family." Edmund didn't know how to respond so he just smiled.

The pastor was the spiritual leader not just for this beautiful large church and its congregation but he was the minister for all the churches in the district including Dombrowa. He trained and directed the Kantors in his area, both in their duties as lay-ministers and as teachers. He had married Johann and Emilie Frey more than twenty years earlier in 1906, just after his beautiful church had been built. Now Emilie and Alwine had come to him to tell him of her impending wedding in February and he had been happy for them. But Pastor Schoen more than most men understood the dangers of the times. Today he was more interested in young men like Edmund Frey who might help their community to survive. He had grave concerns for the future of the Germans in Volhynia.

Once he had taken Edmund inside the Pastor asked how he had passed the afternoon but the teenager hesitated to tell him.

"Do you know the man you were speaking with across the street?" the Pastor asked.

Edmund was surprised. "Only that his name is Misha Maczowiak. We met in...in the town."

"He's not from Vladimir."

Edmund couldn't tell if that was a question or a statement. For a moment he though that it was silly of the Pastor to be so parochial in worrying about one of his flock speaking to a man who was not of his district, but he indulged him, "No, he's a student from Krakow."

"How did you meet him?"

Again Edmund hesitated on the answer, but the Pastor didn't press the issue.

"Edmund," he said, "it's not only your mother who talks about your intelligence. The Kantor of Dombrowa told me how sad he was that you could not continue your education. He said he had never had a student of your comprehension and thirst for understanding."

The words were more than flattery to Edmund and he answered a little wistfully, "Father says I need to prepare myself to be a farmer. I have more than enough education to do that. Any more would be a waste."

"Is that truly how you feel?"

"I wouldn't go against my father's wishes."

"I'm sure you wouldn't Edmund, but I'm also sure your father understands that farming isn't the only occupation approved by God. To be given the gift of learning and to disdain it is not what He intended."

Edmund was surprised how much he wanted to open up to Pastor Schoen. He thought it was the man's sincerity that made him feel like he could trust him but he had bottled his frustration for so long that he would have opened up to any invitation. His voice almost broke as he confessed, "I don't want to be a farmer. But what else is there? My family isn't rich. I just can't do whatever pleases me. I can't see any other path for me."

"Yes, I understand. I believe you should continue your education, Edmund. We have need of young people like you in Volhynia. I will talk to your father. I think I can make him understand."

"He won't understand."

"You must give your father some credit. I have known him longer that you and I'm sure I can reason with him. We must educate our finest young men."

"I don't think I could go back to the Kantor School."

"Certainly that would not be appropriate at your age. That is not what I was thinking of. What if I could arrange for you to be taught privately in your spare time."

"What would be the point?"

"Edmund, it may not mean much to you now but listen and think about what I'm going to tell you. Opportunities present themselves everyday for men who are prepared. I can promise you this. An education is never wasted. Apply yourself to your best talents and God will be pleased. God needs men like you and so does Volhynia."

"I want to be of service. I would like to do more than just farming."

"I will talk to your father on my next visit to Dombrowa, Edmund. But may I ask you one more time about your conversation with the Pole, Maczowiak?"

"I met him at the café down the street."

"Did he try to recruit you?"

"I don't know what you mean?"

"This Maczowiak is an enemy to Poland and he is your enemy too. He is a communist. If the police saw you with him...well, you do not need that kind of attention and neither does the German community"

Ten

After Hedwig's now infamous outburst Albert decided to build his house over the hill on the other side of the field, where it could not easily be seen from the old house. Though he would never admit it, it was for Johann's sake that he did it. His thinking was simple. If Hedwig couldn't see his house every time she looked out of her front door, she would probably be less angry with her husband. The truth was that Albert was embarrassed that the story had spread through Zeperow and down into Antonufka. It was one thing for Albert to struggle with his sister-in-law in private, but this kind of notoriety was not what he wanted. But despite his embarrassment, moving the location of his house was the only concession he would make freely. He was determined to get all that was rightfully his.

But before Albert could start building, he and Johann had to pay a visit to the Countess Viteranno. They needed to inform her of their intention to divide the land. The Countess always accepted these arrangements and it was necessary in order to legally divide their inheritance.

As they approached the mansion, the brothers saw two cars. One was the vehicle on which Albert had changed the tire and the other was a smaller, sleeker, grey machine that looked very attractive. Both cars were parked in front of the cottage behind the mansion. They concentrated so much on the automobiles that neither brother even noticed Martin's carriage.

They went to the back entrance and knocked for several minutes, but there was no response. Eventually they decided to try the cottage to see if anyone was there. After a few minutes the Countess herself opened the front door.

"There was no response," Johann explained while indicating the mansion, "so we came over here."

"That place is much too big for me to live in by myself," the countess explained. "I live here now." Her attitude was matter of fact and direct, just as Albert remembered she had been with her flat tire. There was no shame or emotion displayed in letting these men know she no longer had any servants and that she was poor. She was too dignified to play games like that. "What is it you want?" she asked.

"My brother Albert is getting married and we want to sever our land."

"Right now?" she asked. There was a hint of annoyance in her voice now and she looked around, almost as if she was looking for an excuse. "Oh, well," she finally conceded, "you Germans are so fastidious about these thing. We shall do it right now." She invited them into the foyer and excused herself.

As she entered a room at the other end of the hall Johann and Albert could hear other voices, men's voices. They were raised, almost shouting, but unintelligible. Johann and Albert looked at each other and shrugged their shoulders, whatever it was, it was none of their business. A while later the brothers heard horses and a wagon outside. Johann peered out of the window to make sure that no one was tampering with his horse and wagon. What he saw was someone else driving off. "Who is it?" asked Albert as he tried to peer over his brother's shoulder. "Martin."

A few minutes later another man appeared at the end of the hall. He was headed straight for the front door with a deliberate, almost angry gait. The countess was behind him; she almost had to run to keep up with him. There was a look of concern on her face that was unflattering and seemed out of character. The man was extremely thin and wore a crisp blue suit with shiny black shoes that clicked on the marble floor of the old guest house. There was a look of determination on his face that was intimidating. Johann and Albert stepped aside quickly. The man's face was frozen in a contemptuous glare. The brothers thought it was for them but as he passed by he ignored them totally, as if they didn't even exist. As the stranger opened the door he turned and waited for the countess. Albert and Johann were astounded that the usually unflappable countess seemed flustered. As she finally caught up to him at the front door, she seemed very vulnerable but the man's face stiffened even more.

"Next month then?" she asked, sounding hopeful, almost pleading.

Coldly he replied, "Perhaps."

Johann had seen it before and knew where this kind of cold arrogance came from. "Military," he whispered to Albert.

Ludmilla Viteranno was visibly shaken as she took Johann and Albert into the den. She fumbled with the papers and commented during an awkward moment that she should never have fired her clerk. It was a joke but no one laughed and so she fumbled some more with her papers. She mumbled constantly as she searched, all the while looking very uncomfortable. "So many of these contracts are in Russian," she said with obvious disgust. "My father banned Russian on the estate as soon as Poland was reestablished." Eventually she found the correct papers and made a notation that she initialed and made Johann and Albert initial it too. The unpleasant paperwork out of the way she hurried the farmers to the door.

As they reached the door she seemed sorry for her conduct and tried to make small talk. She was still nervous, however. "How have the crops been this year?" she said with a tremor in her voice. But even before they could reply, she responded to her own question, "You can count on the Germans to do well. I have given my own lands to the management of one of your fellow Germans."

"Martin?" Albert asked, with an inflection that betrayed his feelings.

"Albert!" Johann said sharply. He wanted to reprove his brother for the intrusion on the lady's privacy.

"You do not approve of Hermann Martin, Albert?"

"His family and ours have had some difficulties," Johann stated quickly, thinking to cut off Albert from answering in his blunt fashion.

"I am aware of your difficulties, but that matter was resolved in the courts years ago. It is time to let it go."

"He won't let go until he has all our land," Albert shot out. The Countess only stared at him, questioningly. "The day I changed your automobile tire, he tried to run me down."

"I'm sure you are mistaken," she answered, having regained some of the assertiveness the men had expected of the noblewoman. "You must admit he has been the most successful of all the German farmers in the area."

"That's because...." Albert wanted to say the man was a thief but Johann cut him off. "Yes, Madame," Johann said with force, "he does have success and I'm sure your fields are in good hands. Madame, we must leave. Thank-you."

After the door had closed, Johann remarked to his brother, "I hope she has not made a mistake by hiring Martin."

"Hope? I know she has." Albert was still annoyed that she hadn't believed him, and said, "Maybe they deserve each other. I can't believe she defended Martin!"

"She does not have the business sense her father had," Johann had to agree. "The estate was still in good shape when he died, but even she does not deserve to be swindled by Hermann Martin."

"Then why didn't you let me warn her."

"There is more going on than we understand. She was not upset because of Martin or because of us."

"Who do you think he was?"

"I don't know, at first I thought it was her husband. He looks a lot like him."

"I didn't know she was married."

"She was married right after the war to a rich German. But she got a divorce; there was a big scandal. But I don't think it is him. This one is military, an officer. Her husband was too rich and important for the military."

"How do you know he's military?"

"I've served in the Russian and Austrian armies. You get to know the officers by the arrogance. The way he stood, the way he walked, the way he pretended not to notice us. He was military!"

"I wonder what he was doing there?"

"It's really none of our business."

Mid-October was not a good time to start building, but Albert had no choice. His bride had to have her own home. It would be unthinkable to have her live under the same roof with the witch even if there had been room. Since it was not a large home that he planned to build, he hoped to finish it before the snow, or at least, he was anxious to finish the most important part before the freezing temperatures came.

He hired Ewald Hartenberger to construct the most unique part of his German style house. The brick wall that partitioned the kitchen from the sleeping quarters of Volhynian homes was not just a simple wall. It served several purposes that made its construction critical, and being the main support for the roof was only the first of these. The wall also served as the chimney for the smoke from the big cooking stove, and yet 'chimney' was too simple a description for it. The route the smoke took to get out at the top was what made the wall so special. The chimney tunnel snaked back and forth over the length of the wall, taking smoke and heat on a long, winding route of many meters. On its way the heat permeated the bricks, which in turn radiated heat to the house. This piece of engineering was clearly the key to the success of the construction. It was also the most intricate and skillful work that was required. Ewald Hartenberger was the local craftsman who was the best at this art. Even though he was reticent about beginning so late, Albert would not be dissuaded and insisted that the weather would hold.

After shrewdly bargaining his own help as a part of the fee and after purchasing the material on credit at the local cooperative, he and the master went to work. But Albert had more in mind than just helping. As they worked together he was very attentive and Ewald joked that he now had an apprentice. It was only half a joke, because the master-builder quickly guessed what his young employer was up to. He had noticed how Albert took an aggressive interest in every detail of the work and studied how the bricks, mortar and tiles were manipulated. This was more than just interest or fascination. It was not the first time someone had tried to steal his secrets. Ewald understood the motivation. A poor farmer in Volhynia needed to take advantage of every opportunity to acquire skills that might help him to feed his family. Unless he had a large farm, he needed to supplement his income. Even though Albert already had a trade, it did not have the earning power of Ewald's talent. But if he had any hopes of picking up this trade by observing just one project he soon gave them up. He realized that the kind of mastery that Ewald Hartenberger exhibited came only with much practice and took years to learn. Albert had to content himself with helping.

From then on it became his objective to help the construction to finish ahead of the cold weather. The 'chimney-wall' had to be airtight along its entire path, otherwise the dangerous smoke and gases could leak into the house. The risk of building the wall so late in the fall was that the frost could cause the mortar to cure too quickly. The resulting cracks would make the chimney useless. Each evening as Ewald Hartenberger and Albert finished, they piled straw and hay against the newly completed sections to insulate their work from the cold. But they were lucky and the bad weather held off until the end of October just as Albert had predicted.

When it was done, Albert could not stop expressing his admiration for the work of Ewald Hartenberger. He was motivated by the realization that if they had been unsuccessful and the wall had developed cracks, it would have to be taken down and there would not have been time to rebuild it before the really cold weather came. Then he would have had to move his bride in with Hedwig. He didn't even want to think of that possibility, so he counted himself really lucky that the wall was finished before a single snowflake fell that year. But now an unpleasant job waited for him.

Hedwig couldn't bear the ignominy of having her house torn down around her. Her discomfort was not because of any emotional attachment she had to her home, but partly because she had been so adamant that Albert would not get even one rusty nail. It was ironic too that so often in the past she had pleaded with her husband for a bigger house, and now that the house was finally coming down, it was only to be rebuilt even smaller.

She begged her husband to let her take the children to visit her sister while this humiliation was being forced on her. She was uncommonly contrite and Johann wanted desperately to spare her any more pain. But it was extravagant to take a trip when they needed money to rebuild their home, and it broke his heart to tell her no. He was more than a little amazed when she came back a while later and told him that she had enough money for the train fare. She had saved it from what he gave her to run the household. It seemed difficult to believe, but he wanted so much to spare her this additional disgrace that he asked no more questions. He allowed her to go.

The evening before the dismantling started, just hours after Johann's return from the train station in Lutzk, Albert went to his secret spot to recover his money. He needed to pay Ewald Hartenberger and wanted to make an installment on his debt to the cooperative before beginning the next phase of building. However, when he lifted the floor board, his money pouch was missing. He knew immediately what had happened. Hedwig had stolen it.

Albert ran out of the bedroom, into the farm yard and to the shed where his brother was working. "Your wife stole my money!" he cried out angrily, defying his brother to deny it.

"What?" Johann was startled by the accusation. But Albert thought there was something suspicious in Johann's reaction. He felt certain that Johann had recognized his wife's guilt.

For a moment Johann himself suspected Albert might be right. He recalled finding Hedwig frantically searching for the hiding place. Back then he had not taken her threat seriously. Johann was so sure her behavior that day had been an aberration, not likely to be repeated, he had not considered it again. He did not want to believe that she could have gone through with it. "Why would you say such a thing?" he asked, shaking his head.

"Don't deny it, you know she took it!"

"I don't know what you're talking about."

Albert took Johann back to the house and showed him the empty box and repeated his accusation. "She took it and she's run off with it. We'll never see her again."

"Don't be so quick to accuse Hedwig," Johann said angrily, "she's not even here to defend herself. Something else may have happened to your money." He wanted to believe what he said but found himself doubting his own wife's innocence. Had she continued her search and found it? Where did she really get the money for her train fare?

"She's gone, Johann. Face it."

"Nonsense!" He was becoming angry with Albert's posturing.

"The witch couldn't care less about you," Albert answered. "She cares about nothing but herself."

"Albert, don't say this. We don't know what happened."

Albert couldn't stop. Now he had the appropriate excuse and he wanted to spew everything out. Every humiliation, every insult and hurt that the witch had ever done to him or he had imagined, he wanted to throw them back into Johann's face. Now he could vent it all and redeem some of the frustration and revenge he had so far been denied.

"She has finally done what she has been trying to do all these years. She couldn't starve me to death and she couldn't work Mother to death, so she stole my money. See what kind of woman you married Johann. She's a witch! I suppose we should be grateful that she's gone."

"That's enough Albert!" Johann clenched his fist. His sympathy for his brother's loss was quickly disappearing.

Albert perceived Johann's clenched hand as a threat and braced himself for a fight. If his brother wanted a fight he was ready, but just then their mother burst in. "So you found it," she said to them, indicating the open floor board. "When I heard you shouting I thought that was what it was." Julianna walked past her sons and went to her section of the bedroom and retrieved the sack of coins from under her mattress and handed them to Albert.

"You took it?" Albert asked, still shaking with anger. "Why?"

"To keep it safe!" she answered him, then Julianna turned to Johann. There was compassion in her voice for her older son as she explained, "Johann, I found her one day searching for it. I was afraid she would find it. She wasn't thinking of the consequences."

"Why didn't you tell me?" Albert asked.

"I had hoped to put it back before you knew it was gone, but I gave Hedwig the train fare from it. I couldn't just put it back and pretend not to know." Julianna saw Albert's brow wrinkle in anger and was dismayed at her son's attitude. "You, the both of you could have put your heads together and made this less painful. Johann you should have sent her away and Albert could have easily helped. But both of you were only thinking about yourselves!"

"You're right mother," Johann conceded sheepishly. But it was relief that he really felt. He had hoped beyond hope that it was not his wife who had taken the money. A weight had been lifted off his shoulders when he learned that his wife was not guilty. But his brother was still red with anger.

"You gave her my money, after everything she's done to us!" Albert snapped.

"Don't speak to your mother like that!" Johann yelled back at him.

"No, it's alright," his mother said, "I shouldn't have done it. But don't you see Albert, that there was no reason she should have to be here while the house was being torn down. It was better for everyone that she got away."

"I'll repay you, Albert," Johann said. "I knew all along that I should have asked where she got the money."

Albert's rage subsided gradually. In his mind Hedwig was still guilty. It still made him angry to learn that she had intended to steal the money. He shuddered to think what would have happened if she had found it. Though he was relieved that his money was safe and he could go on building, he remained puzzled by his Mother's generosity with his money.

The tearing down of Joseph Fischer's house was big news in Zeperow. There were plenty of helping hands available when the work started. Of course August Weiss came to help his friend, as expected. Several of Johann's friends came too, and many of their neighbors came to help. Some of them the Fischer's knew only passingly. They even brought their wives. Ostensibly, they had come to see the house come down. But the intention was not to knock it down, but to dismantle it board by board, and nail by nail, saving as many of the costly materials as possible. It was slow, tedious work and boring to watch. It was Julianna, standing behind some of her neighbors as they whispered, who first understood their curiosity. They had come expecting to witness something more, something gossip-worthy. They were, however, disappointed that Hedwig was not there. Instead of conflict, all they could see was the stoic Johann Fischer trying to hang onto his dignity. Many of the wives soon went home.

An accountant would have been proud of how Albert sorted and inventoried the products of the old house. He spent hour after hour measuring, matching and making sure that two equal piles of lumber were neatly stacked on the ground. He spent an exorbitant amount of time pulling nails, straightening and sorting them. He was meticulous in his determination to sort every bit of salvageable building material, but his neighbors suspected there was more to it than frugality.

The men who had donated their time to the brothers and even August looked on incredulously. This was a side of Albert that even his closest friend had never seen. The men made a joke of his pettiness. One brought Albert the kitchen curtains and asked him which half he wanted, another picked up a rusted nail, broke it in two, and gave a piece to each brother. But as they laughed, Albert only shrugged his shoulders, they could never understand and he could not back off now. Revenge was what he had lived for. He would not cheat himself.

There was one person, however, who was able to make Albert see that he had gone too far. Surprisingly it was Hermann Martin. When he heard what was happening he drove by and stopped on the road to gawk. He laughed loudly and shouted insults at Johann and Albert in a booming voice. "You stole this land from me," he yelled for all to hear, "now you are trying to steal it from each other. God curse your thievery!" It was preposterous but effective, especially as he came by every day to harangue them. Martin's ridicule grated on Johann and Albert too. Even their helpers took the humiliation personally. Before long there were fewer hands to help.

But Hermann Martin didn't stop there. Everywhere he went, to the cooperative store, the tavern, and even in Lutzk, he made fun of his enemies. "Just like a couple of Jews," he rehearsed to anyone who would listen. "It makes sense too. Have you heard Albert speak Yiddish? It's like he was one of them."

Only when Albert heard what Martin was saying about him did he get the sinking feeling that his revenge was indeed hollow. So when it finally came to tearing up the floor boards, Albert relented and said it wasn't necessary, even though it meant that his own house would have only a dirt floor. The concession shocked Johann.

When the house lay in two piles, Johann judged that he had enough material and credit to rebuild his house almost as big as it had been. For his wife's sake he even decided to make one improvement, a partition in the bedroom that she had longed for. It was a conciliatory gesture, and one of faith, because he had a nagging doubt that she was not returning. He had not heard from his wife since she left. Johann was fighting hard to keep that hope alive amid his growing fear. But new hope came from a strange source. His brother shocked him for the second time by offering to help rebuild his home. It was a gesture that pleased not only Johann, but made Julianna proud. If it was possible to soften Albert, anything was possible.

Eleven

Albert made the trip to Dombrowa again in late November while his house was little more than an outline against the dark and sullen sky. For all practical purposes Johann's home was rebuilt and Albert had redeemed some of his self respect by helping his brother. Although his own house had to wait, he was glad for this break. Inside, he felt as dark as the sky. The revenge he had so yearned for had left him drained and empty. It had even obscured the good feelings he had felt when he had become engaged. Somehow, it just didn't seem real anymore that he was getting married. The emptiness was unbearable and he wanted to find some relief. The official reason that he gave for his visit, however, was that Alwine's Pastor wanted to meet with both of them before he married them. It was a reasonable excuse and if it wasn't enough, he had one more; Hedwig was coming home.

It was a very nervous Albert Fischer who appeared at the door step of the Frey household in Dombrowa. He could not explain why he was so much more nervous now than he had been in October when he came to ask for the hand of a girl he hardly knew from a man who had no reason to say yes. As he knocked on that door he knew where his fear came from. He hoped desperately that they hadn't changed their minds. To his relief, Albert knew that it was something that was just not done. A family did not agree to a marriage and then back out without serious reasons. A thing like that could make enemies and the Germans had enough enemies in Poland without making more among their own people. But then why was he so nervous? Perhaps it was because he was beginning to realize how audacious he had been.

It was Alwine's younger sister Adele who came to the door and invited him in. The young girl was carrying a toddler but Albert couldn't remember the baby's name. It didn't matter, she ran off as soon as Adele put her down and the teenager scurried after her. He hardly got a greeting out of his mouth before he realized he was standing inside the front door, abandoned. Now he was even more nervous. It wasn't a good start. Albert had hoped that Alwine would open the door and welcome him in or come rushing downstairs when she heard he was there. He had imagined holding her trembling hand and calming her, but she was nowhere to be seen. He stood there awkwardly until Adele returned, the toddler safely collected in her arms again, and took him into the kitchen.

As in most Volhynian homes, the Frey kitchen was the center of their living. However, unlike other households where the kitchen was the only place guests could be entertained, Emilie and Johann Frey also had a parlor. But it was into the warmth of the kitchen that they welcomed their closest friends and family. Albert began to relax as he felt their acceptance here in this intimate place where Emilie fed him and Johann chatted with him casually about last season's abundant crop and the length of the dreaded Volhynian winter. Still, Alwine was nowhere to be seen and he felt too self-conscious to ask where she might be.

Albert filled an awkward silence with a progress report on his house which prompted Johann to tell a story. He had heard about two feuding brothers. They hated each other so intensely that they had to tear down their father's house to the last board when dividing their inheritance. Every bit of lumber, every window pane, every nail, and even all the bricks in the chimney had to be counted so that they could be divided equally. Every building on the farm was to be torn down because of their enmity. "Have you ever heard of such a thing?" Johann Frey asked, almost stone-faced.

"Personally," interjected Emilie, "I don't believe it. It's ridiculous."

"I'm not so sure," Johann explained quite calmly, "when brothers are close then they give their lives for each other, but when they fight it isn't wise to stand in the way. Remember Cain and Able, Isaac and Ishmael, Jacob and Esau, and Joseph and his brothers. What do you think Albert?"

Albert saw Emilie smirk at her husband's statement and was relieved that at least she wasn't looking at his burning face. Panic gripped him as he thought that they might know who those brothers really were. Yet he felt such an impulse to correct them about the one glaring error in the story that he had to fight off the desire to set the record straight. Where did they get the idea that he had made Johann count every brick? Johann's chimney had been left intact. Albert hung on. The real question was whether they really knew? Was this their way of leading into telling him that they didn't want him for a son-in-law? Was that why Alwine was not there? He wanted to say something profound to them about brothers sometimes falling out, something to justify himself, but he suspected the best course was silence. When Johann Frey looked at Albert again for a response, he shrugged his shoulders.

Because Albert seemed uninterested, Johann changed the subject. "Tomorrow we will drive into Vladimir and you and Alwine can talk to the pastor. Then Alwine and her mother want to do some shopping for the wedding." Johann looked at Albert as he said this. He was disturbed that the boy might still be thinking he was rich. "I am not a wealthy man," he felt he had to explain, "but I will give my daughter what I can afford." Albert just sat quietly, trying not to show how relieved he was that his future father-in-law wasn't backing out.

He brightened up when Alwine finally came and sat beside him smiling warmly. It made him feel so good he wanted to tell her about the house he was building for her, but he was afraid to bring up the subject again. Instead he told her that Irene had sent her greetings and was looking forward to the day when she would have her best friend close by. It was the best news he could have given her and silently, under the table, she slipped her hand into his. Within a few minutes the whole atmosphere had changed and Albert found what he had come for.

In the morning they set out for Vladimir. At the last moment Alwine's younger brother Edmund asked to come along. When his father asked him what he intended to do there, he was evasive and mumbled something about seeing the sights. Though he thought it was just a waste of time, Johann Frey had only one more question, "Are your chores all done?" The young man nodded yes. "Then come on."

"I wondered why he got up so early to do his chores," Emilie whispered to her husband. "I wonder what he is up to?"

Her husband was puzzled too, Edmund had not been himself for weeks. He wouldn't call it strange behavior. It was just unusual. On Saturdays, Edmund would volunteer to go into Dombrowa and get the weekly German language newspaper for his father. When he gave it to his father it looked like it had already been read, even though it was neatly put back together. More than ever before, Edmund followed the local debates on the political problems of Poland. It was all he wanted to talk about. On Sundays, he usually came home late from church not because he wanted to be with his friends, but because be became involved in political conversations. His parents could see there was something going on, but they were sure he would tell them about it when he was ready.

Now as they drove to Vladimir, Edmund talked the entire time. To Albert he sounded like a younger version of his own brother. That annoyed him at first but it was hard not to feel the boy's energy. By the time they were in Vladimir, he had rehearsed to them the entire litany of grievances of the common man against oppressive governments, rich landlords and rich churches. When the wagon stopped at the red brick church in Vladimir, Edmund was away before the others even had a chance to stand up.

Albert couldn't help commenting, "He sounds like a Communist." But when he looked at Edmund's father he knew he had said the wrong thing.

The beautiful red brick church was the center of the Lutheran congregation. This was the same church that Johann Frey and Emilie Winkler had married in some twenty-two years earlier. It was comforting to them to think that Alwine would marry there too. That kind of continuity was rarely seen anymore among the Volhynians. Albert Schoen was the pastor who had married them and now he would marry Alwine and Albert. Johann and Emilie had confidence in him. He would start the couple off correctly, reminding them of their duties to God, Church and community.

Albert Schoen greeted the Frey family warmly. The man was respected, not just because he had endured everything with his church and congregation from Russian persecution to exile, but because he cared. People like Johann and Emilie were the reason he loved his work, and he was convinced that his mission was to secure their future. He knew what his church meant to his people. He also knew that it would take more than the inspiration of a brick building to save the German community. Yes, marriages strengthened the Germans, and he wanted to do whatever he could to get the couple started in the right way, but more was needed. It would take all the talents of all the young men like Edmund Frey, fully educated and developed, to save the German community. Pastor Schoen was determined to harness his enthusiasm for his cause. But when he asked about the bright teenager, he was disturbed to hear that he had gone on some mysterious sight seeing expedition into the city.

The future of the Germans in Poland and the future of all Poland was on Edmund's mind too as he made his way to the Café near the park. He had not been to Vladimir for a few weeks, yet he was certain that his new friends had returned from Krakow. Edmund was also keenly aware that he had told his parents a lie about his reason for coming. It wasn't the first time. After his initial meeting in the café, he had worked hard to find a reason to come back. He couldn't find a legitimate one. That was when his lying began. On the pretext of going to work for a neighbor for the day Edmund had walked all the way into the city. He regretted the lie, but he found that after the first time it became easier.

That day, he had spent several hours with Ivan and Misha. Fortunately, the hostile one, Peter, had returned to Krakow already. In the café and in the streets he accompanied the two men, feeling grown up and so very bold. Even though he now understood that his friends were communists, Edmund felt excitement in their presence. They were so full of ideas and so much of what they said rang true. He even wondered what it would be like to travel through Poland with them.

Today as he entered the café again he was disappointed not to find them there. He bought a cup of coffee and sat down and waited. Coffee, even black, was beginning to taste good to him. But his friends did not show up. When he eventually asked the clerk if she had seen the three young men from Krakow, she explained that they left shortly before he arrived. They had gone off to the market. Edmund left immediately.

The open air market was only a short walk from the café. As he walked he felt a strange sense of urgency to find them. Perhaps because he knew his time was limited today and his father would ask very specific questions if he was late.

The streets were crowded as Edmund walked around looking for a recognizable face. He saw none of his friends as he walked back and forth among that street stalls. Tiring, he stood against a wall while the crowds passed by. The din of the vendors grew wearisome and he had almost decided to go back to the church when he heard the shouting. This was more intense than merely a merchant arguing with a customer over the price of potatoes. The shouting was attracting a crowd, most of whom joined in the bickering back and forth. Edmund couldn't make out what the shouting was about so he asked a passer-by what was happening. "Communists," the man said through gritted teeth.

Edmund knew he ought to leave but his feet wouldn't carry him. He had to know if his friends were involved. It just seemed too much of a coincidence. He pushed his way through the crowd despite his better judgement. At the center of the contention he saw Peter and Ivan. Peter's face was red with anger as he seemed to have taken on the entire market. He was shouting foul language but the entire crowd was against him. Ivan stood beside Peter, trying to calm him down. But Peter refused to be calmed and traded blow for blow with the crowd in a verbal assault. If this was going to become physical, it was easy to see what would happen.

"Spy," they accused him, "you communists are nothing but spies for Russia!" But Peter couldn't let anything go unchallenged. "Puppets," he cried, "you are slaves and puppets of the rich, unable to think for yourselves."

Edmund backed off. He could only imagine how the argument got started, but with Peter's temper he knew where it was going. The hot-head, he was sure, would get what he deserved but he worried about Ivan.

Shortly, he heard the clatter of running boots and someone shouted "Police!" Without warning one of the vendors threw a punch at Peter and a one-sided melee began. The crowd wanted blood before the police dragged the communists away. Edmund wanted to get away but the crowd was pressing in as the brawl attracted more attention. Within seconds the police were shoving their way to the center. There were cheers as they arrested Peter and Ivan. It was, after all, illegal to be a communist in Poland.

"We're not traitors," Peter continued to protest, "we are more loyal to Poland than all of you."

Quickly the police pushed their prisoners through the crowd. They were shoving them right toward Edmund. He looked for a way out but the crowd was too thick. Edmund trembled as his friend Ivan brushed by him as he was led away. But his friend did not make eye contact. Edmund felt ashamed. It was then that he understood the difference between commitment and the game he was playing. If he truly felt as strongly as his friends then he ought to be willing to give up everything for his beliefs. The trouble was, he didn't know what he believed.

All of a sudden there was a hand on his shoulder and he tensed. He thought he was under arrest. He realized he must have been seen with them before. Edmund turned around. It was Misha. His friend motioned for Edmund to follow him.

"What happened?" Edmund finally asked when they were well away from the market.

"Peter got into an argument. He called Pilsudski a sadistic pig. Those men probably fought for the Old General. Ivan was trying to get him away, but nothing stops Peter when he gets going."

"What will happen to them?"

"They'll be questioned?"

"And then?"

"Who knows? It depends on the mood the police are in. They know he's a communist. He's been arrested before. Every time he's arrested he faces the possibility of just disappearing. But it's his own fault, he doesn't know when to shut his mouth."

"What about Ivan?"

"Ivan? It's a shame about Ivan, he's a good man but he knew what he was getting into."

"They can't just kill them, can they? Poland has laws!"

"This is Pilsudski's Poland. He is the worst kind of dictator, a war hero whom the people love. He believes he can do no wrong."

"They love Pilsudski, they hate communism. How can you win?"

"It's not easy. The important things never are. But someday Poland will wake up. It will be a long battle but we will win. You could be part of it, Edmund. We need people who can reach out to the German Poles. Join us!"

"I don't know. Why weren't you..." Albert couldn't finish the question.

"Why didn't I get involved? It doesn't further our cause to get arrested for brawling. Peter is a fool and Ivan is too soft-hearted. We need passion but we need reason too. We need men like you, Edmund. Communism is going to be the new order of the world. Everything else has failed. Some day everyone will see that it is the only way to freedom. Come with me!"

"Right now?"

"Yes."

Edmund felt strangely tempted. Misha's offer was exciting, but instantly he knew he could not go. The thought of his parents waiting for him at the church, and him failing to show up disturbed him. "I can't," he said, and then added, "not now."

"The train for Krakow leaves at four. Meet me if you change your mind."

Only an hour later, as Edmund shook Pastor Schoen's hand, he found himself looking at the floor nervously. He was still thinking about Misha's invitation. Edmund had hoped to avoid the Pastor, but his parents had insisted on meeting at the church. Then, to everyone's surprise, just as they were about to leave, the Pastor pulled the young man into his office where they talked for half an hour. Johann Frey grew more impatient with every minute's delay. Still, when the pastor came out it was only to ask Johann to come in.

"Johann, your son is a very bright young man," Albert Schoen began as he sat his old friend in a chair, ""

Johann nodded but did not smile. He did not believe in compliments even if they came from a man of God. Pastor Schoen understood and got to the point right away.

"I wonder what you would think of allowing the Kantor in Dombrowa to tutor your son privately?"

Johann had no idea what to make of the request so he could only ask, "How much education does a farmer need?"

"Volhynia, particularly German-Volhynia needs more educated men. We need them to fight for our futures in the courts and in the government of Poland. Some of our young people need to become more than farmers."

"You want Edmund to become a lawyer?"

"If that is his inclination. He is bright enough to become anything he wants."

"That would mean university. I can't afford that."

"Let's take it one step at a time. If he is bright enough and works hard enough then scholarships can be arranged. Opportunities come to hard working young men."

"Is this what you want Edmund?" Johann asked his son.

"If it's all right with you, Father."

"There will be no shirking of your chores at home?"

"No, father."

"I'm still not sure."

"Then be sure of this," Pastor Schoen explained, choosing words that were clear and forceful, "if we don't fight for our rights then Poland will take them away. Farmers are important but we must have young men like Edmund prepared to fight for us in the courts and in the civil service and even the government. Our language, our lands, our churches are all at risk. This means education, preferably in Polish universities."

Although Johann Frey understood and was impressed by the strong statement he was unconvinced. "Why my son?" he asked. Johann was waiting for a better reason.

"He's bright, he has personality, curiosity, leadership abilities." The Pastor was using every adjective he could think of to describe Edmund but his father's face remained passive, unmoved. Albert Schoen was puzzled and out of ideas when he looked at a painting of Christ on a cross that hung on the wall behind Johann. Only then did the minister understand what Johann required. "Johann, God has always required a sacrifice of those who love Him. I believe this may be yours."

"You think God wants this?"

"I'm sure of it."

"Then I can't object."

Edmund was quiet on the way home. It was such a contrast to his behavior earlier that his mother thought he was sick. Edmund explained that he had tired himself out.

Twelve

The morning of February 12, 1929, Emilie Frey got up early to prepare herself and her family for what she expected to be a long day. Though she and Johann had worked for weeks to organize everything for their daughter's wedding, Emilie faced the day with ambiguous feelings. Her daughter, who had entered this engagement with such anticipation, now seemed moody and withdrawn. Emilie thought she understood what was bothering Alwine but had been hoping the girl would come to her. Besides, Emilie was too busy to start seeing problems where none really existed. She was now preoccupied with making this day everything her daughter hoped for, keenly aware that reality often fell short of expectations. She couldn't help thinking that it was this kind of disappointment that Alwine was experiencing. If that was all, then it was best to let her get over it herself. All she could do, Emilie determined, was her best to make the day go as smoothly as possible.

As the older children did their chores, Emilie fed the younger ones and sent them off to get dressed in their best clothes for their sister's service. Everyone was cooperating except for Else. The usually vivacious six-year-old was dawdling, twirling a lock of her dark hair around her forefinger and ignoring her breakfast. Nothing her mother could say seemed to motivate her to go faster.

"Elselein," Emilie finally asked in frustration, "what is wrong with you? Don't you realize we have to hurry?"

Else looked up at her mother with large, brown, puzzled eyes and started to say something, "Mama, why...?"

"Because today your sister is getting married and we must travel all the way to Vladimir and back."

"No, Mama, not that, I mean..."

"What is it dear?"

"Mama, does it hurt when you get married?"

"Hurt? Why no, what a silly question."

"Oh," Else said, but she still sat playing with her oatmeal, looking unsatisfied.

"Is there something wrong, Else? Is it too hot?"

"Mama, are you sure it doesn't hurt when you get married?"

"What makes you ask such a thing?"

"Well, if it doesn't hurt then why does Alwine cry so much?"

Emilie let out a huge sigh. She could guess what the problem was but it was too late for this. She delayed going upstairs because she was unsure what to say to Alwine. Yet, as the minutes flew away, Emilie knew she had to deal with it before her husband found out. He would be upset, even angry, and that would only complicate the situation for her distraught daughter. Finally, Emilie couldn't put it off any longer. She took a deep breath and went up to see her daughter. Adele, who had been trying to comfort her sister, was sent down stairs to supervise the other children in the kitchen. Then Emilie put her arms around the red eyed young woman. "What is the matter, daughter?" Emilie asked gently.

"Why did father make me choose?" Alwine complained intensely through her tears. "Why didn't he say no? I know he wanted to."

"Are you telling me that you don't want to marry this man now?"

"What if I made a mistake Mother? What if I am unhappy for the rest of my life?"

Immediately Emilie imagined the fiasco of a canceled wedding at this late stage and struggled to control her temper. "Pull yourself together, daughter," Emilie said tersely, "it is too late to change your mind!" But she regretted those words as soon as she had said them because they were insensitive and she could see the pain they caused in her daughter's face. She changed her tone. She repeated Alwine's last question rhetorically, "What if you are unhappy in your marriage?" and then added, "but what if he is a good man? What if you are happy and you have a good life?"

Alwine looked at her mother strangely.

"Do you really think you have made a mistake Alwine," her mother asked, "or are you just afraid that you might have made a mistake?"

"I don't know, mother, how can you know something like that?"

Emilie knew that what her daughter was feeling was simple, old-fashioned fear. She remembered her own wedding. She had not known her husband at all, but she had to have faith that her parents had chosen well for her. At sixteen, she had supposed that her parents had selected a husband for her with great care and that had eased her mind. Later, as an adult, it had become evident that even such important decisions were made more as a matter of convenience and opportunity than careful selection. No wonder her daughter was now in fear for her future. Having participated in the selection process Alwine knew first hand how lightly the decision had been reached. How could she explain to Alwine that in spite of all this, everything would probably turn out well? Should she remind her that a few months ago she was in tears, thinking that this day would never come? She wanted to explain to Alwine that there was little chance of making a huge mistake. How could she explain such a concept without appearing callous?

"Think a little Alwine," Emilie finally began, "what are you really afraid of?"

"I don't know, Mama."

"Alwine," her mother began in a serious tone that made her daughter forget her tears for a moment, "if you expect a man to make you happy you will be sadly disappointed. We are simple farmers. We don't have the riches of the world to make us happy. God has not chosen to bless us with great wealth, but instead He gave us much work and the faith to endure. If you can't find happiness in simple things then there is probably not a man in all of Volhynia who can make you happy.

"Daughter, it makes little difference whom you marry. You have just as great a chance at being happy with Albert as anyone." Alwine looked up at her mother more perplexed than ever and Emilie struggled to find the right words to explain her statement. "You must decide what you want in life and work for it. If you want joy, be happy with whatever God chooses to bless you. If you want love, love your husband. Find a way to be grateful and you will be happy. Be sad and angry with your life and you will be miserable no matter whom you marry. You will probably never find what you are looking for if you depend on someone else to make you happy."

Alwine looked at her mother speechlessly. This was not consoling. Her mouth gaped and Emilie understood she was staring into the face of disbelief.

"Daughter, I love your father, but that is not all there is to life. Better than falling in love is learning to love. What I am saying is that you can learn to love as surely as you learned to walk and to talk, if you work at it. But don't expect a man to make you happy. You have to provide your own happiness. It doesn't matter whom you marry, you have an equal chance whoever you chose."

"But Mother, how can that be?"

"If you had your choice of all the men in Volhynia, who would you pick over Albert?" Alwine shook her head to indicate she had no idea. "Would he be Lutheran?"

"Of course," Alwine nodded.

"Would he be a farmer?"

"Probably."

"Would you want to work with him so you could have a home?"

"Certainly."

"Well then you have all the opportunity to do those things with Albert, and you certainly don't know any man whom you would rather have, or do you?" The question brought both a blush and smiling shake of Alwine's head as she acknowledged that no one interested her more than Albert. "So there is no reason for you to feel this way and no reason for you not to get married today."

"No, Mama."

"Good, because your father would never have allowed you to back out, his pride would have been offended."

"But Mama," Alwine began to protest until her mother cut her off.

"Yes dear, even your father has pride. Good men can have faults. Why do you think that he hates vanity so much? Because he knows it is one of his own weaknesses he despises it."

"How do you know so much, Mama?"

"Life teaches all lessons to those who would learn. You will learn all the things you need to know to be happy and keep your home functioning. If you have a good man it will add to your happiness but if not, then you will have to learn to be happy without his help."

Alwine did not understand everything her mother was saying to her but realized that what she said was full of hope despite the bluntness of it. When she thought about it, Alwine could see that it was true that it really didn't matter whom she married. Her choice in any case was limited to the German-Volhynian farm boys raised in the Lutheran faith. At least her fiancee was not fat or ugly and realistically there was no honorable way for her to get out of this. It would be particularly awkward since she had been allowed the choice. That decision brought with it a responsibility that she now had to accept.

But the feelings she had when she had blurted out 'yes,' so many months ago, were only a memory now. Alwine knew that a marriage based on romantic love was not really an option for young people of Volhynia. Yet by some miracle she had been able to see and develop an infatuation with the man she would marry and by an even greater miracle she had been given the choice of saying yes to his proposal. Nevertheless, she now faced the possibility of having chosen badly, with no other reason to think so than self doubt. Was it love she had felt that day now so long ago, or was it something else? She had nothing to compare her feelings with. Whatever it was it had abandoned her now and the feeling that had taken her breath away was choking her instead. Doubt stared her in the face, with only her mother's troubling assurance to comfort her.

She berated herself for being so fickle and wondered if it was really possible to fall in and out of love so quickly. Her mother had often explained to her, "I came to love your father as I understood that he loved and cared for me." But Alwine now feared that love was already over for her. Her brief time of infatuation was gone and she was sure it was the end of love. She had been so impatient and arrogant in thinking she could fall in love with a man of her own choosing. Perhaps this was God's punishment to her for her vanity. She could only repeat remorsefully, "Why didn't Papa say no?"

Her mother threw up her arms in frustration and returned to her work.

All of Alwine's fear flew away at the altar. Seeing Albert waiting there in his new suit, his face beaming, rekindled those first romantic ideas that had entered her mind at Irene's wedding. He was so good looking! She felt such relief at the return of those warm feelings that she floated through the ceremony, never acknowledging the duplicity that had tormented her only minutes before. How could she have even thought that this wasn't meant to be? More than ever Alwine was convinced that her mother was wrong, a man could make her happy.

Excitement and pride radiated from the groom's face as his bride came down the aisle of the big red church in Vladimir. He had wanted to marry for the most practical of reasons but was jubilant that he had found so much more. To him, her blush, which he could see even through her thin, flowered veil, made him feel tender emotions he had not expected. The traditional white dress she wore was a simple frock of cotton but he thought she made it look like a gown. Nothing could have been more beautiful. There wasn't a girl in all of Poland more lovely than she right now, and he felt grateful she had said yes to him.

The young couple was euphoric as they left the church with family and friends trailing behind them. But then, just an hour later, as the whole party and guests were on the road to Dombrowa a sudden February storm swept out of the north and hounded the party all the way home. By the time they reached the Frey farm, drifts were beginning to form across the roads as the snow was whipped by relentless winds. The German Volhynians had lived in that region long enough to quickly recognize that this was going to be a bad storm. Nevertheless, the wedding feast went on as planned. Johann and Emilie fed their guests in their home even as the wind beat down on the town and screamed as it exploded against its stout little houses.

When the wind rushed against the Frey home, it whistled shrilly and ominously. It swirled and eddied the snow into every crevice, dampening the spirts of the wedding guests. In fact, after the first few hours the affair was nothing less than depressing. Alwine was among the first to take note of how subdued the celebration was and her disappointment was overwhelming. As the cold evening went on her discomfort grew. At every opportunity she sought out her friend Irene, hoping her company would cheer her up, but it didn't help.

The typical Volhynian celebration lasted several days. Although most of the guests went home after the first day, family and close friends who had traveled far usually settled in for a longer visit. Today, it was evident that everyone was trapped at the Frey home. Only those guests who lived close by attempted to fight through the driving snow to get home that night. Since her father's house was close by, Irene and August left during a slight lull in the wind. Now Alwine felt abandoned.

She was shocked that her doubts had returned. Was she really that fickle? There was an uneasy feeling in the pit of her stomach. She wanted to blame it on the storm, but suspected that her own vacillation caused the problem. Certainly there was not the jovial atmosphere at her celebration that she had seen at her friend Irene's reception. In the midst of her own doubts and fears the storm created an atmosphere that seemed to foster coldness.

Alwine did not even think to look further than her own troubled heart for the reasons for this coldness. She did not even suspect that her own father, whose stern rules were not conducive to uninhibited partying, kept the festivities overly sober. He would not even hire the traditional brass band so that his guests could dance, and he permitted no alcohol, except for a little homemade cherry wine for toasting. Yet Alwine blamed herself for the pall cast on her party and was sure everyone knew of her discomfort. She hated being the center of attention.

For several days as the storm continued, the farm house almost became a prison. Waiting for a break in the storm, the men made it a ritual to gather around the kitchen table and talk politics and farming for hours on end, or until Emilie chased them out so she could bake bread for her guests. The women also gathered in the parlor and other corners of the house to talk, but Albert and Alwine were left awkwardly alone. However, went it was time to sleep there wasn't a place where they could be alone. That first night the women slept upstairs and the men downstairs. Whenever Alwine heard the women whispering, she thought they were feeling sorry for her, but she felt only relief.

In the morning her parents offered the couple the privacy of their bedroom, but all Alwine could think of was her embarrassment. She was sure that if she and Albert disappeared for a while everyone would know what they had been up to. Her face burned red just thinking about it. Emphatically, Alwine declined, to her new husband's disappointment. Instead, to pass the time Alwine tried to make friends with her new in-laws. She liked her mother-in-law but the woman kept trying to find a place for her son and his wife to be alone, while Johann, Albert's brother, was too preoccupied with politics to talk to her. He and her brother Edmund were getting along just fine.

Then there was the enigma of Hedwig. She tried to talk to her too, believing that they should have much in common being married to brothers, but the woman just glared at her with cold empty eyes. Even Alwine's mother was rebuffed by the woman when she tried to explain that there was something familiar about her. Emilie had only wanted to explore whether or not they had met before, but Hedwig was indifferent. There was no hint of interest in Hedwig's eyes nor the pretense of a smile.

Two days later, when the snow stopped, the drifts were up to two meters high on the roads. Nothing moved, not even snow ploughs. By now Alwine felt positively oppressed in the confinement of her parents' home where everything that happened convinced her that she had made a mistake. She told her equally frustrated husband that she had to get out. Almost defying the snow, the couple sneaked out of the house and struggled across the drifts to the Stein home to be with their friends, August and Irene. There, as Albert and August talked in the kitchen Alwine and Irene retreated to her old bedroom. For the first time Alwine felt she had someone to confide in.

"I keep thinking he made a mistake. She has the same name. Do you think he got us mixed up?" Alwine asked, "She's so much prettier than I am. I'm so awkward and I can't even dance. I wonder if Albert went to the wrong house to get a wife."

Irene laughed, "You think Albert wanted to marry Alwine Bladt? Impossible!"

"I just feel that if," Alwine could not form the words she wanted to say, "you know, if we...then it's too late."

"Alwine, Albert is a much more sensible man than people give him credit for. He doesn't want her. He never did. She just threw herself at him. The moment he saw you he came asking questions. He never even considered Alwine Bladt."

Alwine's look of surprise made Irene smile. "Alwine," she continued as if revealing a secret, "from the first time I met Albert I thought you and he would be perfect together. I admit I desperately wanted to have a friend living close by so that I would not be so lonely for Dombrowa, but it was always you and never Alwine Bladt that entered my mind."

"But she's your best friend," Alwine protested.

"Why, because she says so? Alwine you have always been my closest friend. We have been friends all of our lives. I was never happier than when Albert chose you."

With Irene's reassurance fresh in her mind it was only a short time after her return home that Alwine accepted her parents offer of the use of their bedroom. But later when Alwine found the courage to come back down, she made the mistake of making eye contact with Hedwig first. Thinking that Hedwig knew exactly what she had been doing, Alwine's face turned beet red and she had to turn away. Hedwig mistook her abrupt departure as something else.

After a week of being trapped the roads were finally cleared. Teams of draft horses attached to heavy ploughs fashioned from huge timbers fixed into triangles worked hard to clear the roads. No one was happier than the bride's parents that the ordeal was over. Johann Frey and his sons had already slaughtered an extra sow to feed their guests and his wife had baked countless loaves of bread and used much of their winter supply of food. It was a great expense.

Alwine's husband and brothers would have had the wagon loaded in no time if Alwine's father had not been there. Johann Frey paid special attention to the way the wagon was packed and imposed his opinion at every step. Unsure what his father-in-law was trying to accomplish, Albert became annoyed but said nothing. His father-in-law made sure everything was arranged on the wagon just the way he wanted it. It seemed pointless to Albert to keep rearranging the load. A job that should have taken fifteen minutes took an hour. When it was finally done there was wasted space at the back of the wagon and his father-in-law was still directing everything.

Finally, when everything else was on the wagon, Alwine's brothers brought out the item that their father had saved for the end. Although it was covered in a blanket Alwine smiled immediately when she saw it. Her father had obviously built something for her. He had always teased her that when she got married that he would make her a fine piece of furniture and she knew this was it. The pieces he had made in his work shed in the winter months had always fascinated her. She would run her fingers over the smooth wood, enjoying the grains and textures. "This came from that tree?" she would ask, always amazed how useful a tree could be in death as in life. Now her brothers were loading onto the wagon the piece that he had made for her and she beamed with delight.

It was just like her father to remain calm, as if it was nothing special. The object was loaded into the space Johann had reserved for it and as soon as it was safely aboard he put the end board of the wagon back in place and said without any sign of emotion, "Alright, now you can leave."

"Oh, Johann, don't be silly," Emilie chided. "Show it to us."

"It belongs to Alwine," Johann replied casually, "let her show it to you if she wants to."

Alwine kissed her father on his cheek and said, "Whatever it is, Papa, I know it's wonderful. Thank-you." Then she went to the wagon and had Edmund and Rudolf lift the end board off again. She removed the blanket from the treasure.

"Oh, Papa," Alwine cried, "it's beautiful. Just like you promised."

To Alwine, it was the most beautiful piece of cherry-wood furniture that she had ever seen. It was a four-drawer dresser that her father had made of the cheery tree that had grown in their own orchard. "Actually," Rudolf corrected, "it's made from the wood that we traded for the cherry tree." The design of it was rather plain, for it had none of the ornamentation that would make it costly in a store. The face of the drawers had no fancy symmetrical carvings, nor were there raised panels to enhance the design. The beauty was not in the design but in skill with which it was put together. The joints were flawless and almost invisible. The grain of the wood was matched from piece to piece, blending either one surface or contrasting or balancing on another. The drawers pulled open and closed as if gliding on ice. The stain on the wood brought out every grain and the coats of varnish and linseed oil made it glisten even in the dull winter sunlight. Alwine's fingers slid across the top of it like a caress. Her father had kept his promise. He always kept his promises.

Thirteen

Stroking that special gift created the few truly happy moments Alwine could remember when she looked back on those first months in her new home. For a long while she felt like a stranger there. It wasn't her husband's fault. He was gentle, very attentive and patient, at least for a while. But her brooding wore his new found patience down until he had no idea how to make her happy. He withdrew to his work, hoping his wife would warm to her new surroundings on her own. Alwine Fischer had to admit that her unhappiness was not her husband's problem. He tried hard to please her and so her discontent was all the more disturbing.

Alwine was bothered too that her friendship with Irene Weiss did not bring her the joy she had hoped for. She did not see her old friend as often as she had hoped, but when she did the contrast in their lives was too poignant for her to bear for long. Irene was happy. She and her husband August were very close and she got along well with her in-laws, whereas Alwine felt tension. Irene could not help her. Her happiness only added to Alwine's concerns.

Alwine had a plethora of complaints about her new life and why she was unhappy. Foremost among them was the house her husband Albert was so proud of. For a new house it seemed to have a lot of used materials in it and it was small. That annoyed her, but not as much as the disgusting dirt floors. She was self-conscious too about sharing a bedroom with her mother-in-law. Even though Alwine knew that these aggravations were minor and ought to have been tolerable, she couldn't help feeling sorry for herself. It was one thing to be aware that poverty was the lot of farmers in Volhynia and another to experience it so profoundly. Alwine knew that other brides had been brought home to cramped quarters and her parents had taught her that it was no disgrace to be poor. In spite of the warning there was so much that she was unprepared for. It all worked to make her miserable, more miserable than she could hide, and she was slow to realize what the real problem was.

However, Alwine was not raised to give in to self pity. Unable to figure out why she was not happier, she dismissed her feelings as homesickness and assumed that it would take her a while to become comfortable in her new situation. It had been built into her character that duty was more important than happiness. Although she despaired that duty by itself could not bring what she hoped for, she conceded it might be all she would ever have. Still, it was senseless to complain, and she believed she could never be happy until she changed herself.

Ironically it was her father's gift that sparked her change of attitude. Even though it pleased Alwine to see that piece of furniture as the center piece of the bedroom, she was initially angry that it sat on a floor of dirt. She had asked Albert to raise it off the ground and he obliged her by putting it on blocks of wood, but she knew it deserved better. The beauty of the finely finished cherry-wood reminded her that there was so much that was better in her father's house. The floors, the furniture, the bedrooms, and even the Hartenberger chimney that Albert was so proud of she considered inferior. She often caressed the drawer, her fingertips following the striking grain, its beauty contrasting so harshly with its surroundings. It made her think of her father and that is when she felt most ashamed. It occurred to her that she was being vain and selfish. It hit her like a brick and made her weep, but the hurt went even deeper. In the midst of a flood of tears everything her mother had said came back to her. "She was right," Alwine said in bewilderment, "I'm the one who's keeping me from being happy."

It was as if a light went on and Alwine realized what her responsibilities to her marriage were. She needed to bring more than pots and pans, sheets, curtains, and a piece of furniture. She needed to bring herself and all her energy, both emotional and physical. It was with the kind of determination that was worthy of the daughter of Johann and Emilie Frey that she resolved to change her attitude and do as her mother had advised. She would make herself happy.

Her new attitude ingratiated her to her mother-in-law who had been patiently waiting for her to adjust. Julianna had been doing the lion's share of the work and Alwine now rectified that. She had to admit that her mother-in-law had been so gracious that Alwine was sure they would easily become friends. Even now as Julianna let it be known that she was glad that Alwine was beginning to feel happier, she also revealed that she expected to continue sharing the work.

It was no real surprise to Alwine that her change in attitude coincided with the coming of spring. It was always her favorite time of the year and when the gardening season approached she became really excited. Gardens, teeming with vegetables, berries and flowers were an important part of any family's economy and Alwine knew this was where she excelled. Her husband and mother-in-law, seeing the joy with which she planned and anticipated the planting were glad to help, but Alwine led the way. She spent as much time as she could in the plot that Albert had set aside for her, never seeming to tire of working in the warm spring sun. She could almost believe she was happy.

Alwine did not consider her new resolve as a change but only an acceptance of her circumstances. While she had been brooding and sulking she had considered no one's feelings but her own. Now she wondered what tensions she had caused her husband's family while she was being so selfish, especially since relations between her husband and his brother's family were already strained. Even though Irene had told Alwine some of the history between Albert and Hedwig, it was hard for her not to feel responsible in some way. Alwine began to feel that she needed to make friends with Hedwig so that the coolness between them would ease.

On a warm spring day she decided to bake a specialty of her youth. It was called Streusel Kuchen, (Sprinkle Cake). On a layer of sweet dough about two centimeters thick she spread a layer of fruit. Fresh fruit was best but now she had to used canned fruit, and her mother-in-law gave her a jar of dark purple plums. They were her favorite for this treat. Over that she sprinkled a topping made of brown sugar, butter, flour and a touch of vanilla, then she baked it. When it was done, she disappointed her mother-in-law by telling her that it was for a neighbor. Julianna assumed it was for her friend Irene. If she had known it was intended as a peace offering for Hedwig she would have warned Alwine.

In the early evening, before Albert returned home, Alwine delivered it. Quietly and thoughtfully she walked down the tree lined road to her brother-in-law's house, idly speculating how someday the cake in her hand would be remembered as the peace offering that began to heal family wounds. She laughed at herself. Such thoughts were vain but making peace was never wrong so she could forgive herself a little vanity.

She was jolted from her day dreams when she came to the lane and could hear Hedwig screaming. She almost turned back. But it was quickly apparent that Hedwig was shouting for her boys, Gustav and Otto. Alwine looked around to see where the boys might be and heard their voices among trees in the orchard. They were playing. She smiled, remembering how her brothers had loved to play games in the orchard. It was evident that they had not heard their mother so Alwine thought she would collect them and bring them to the house with her. She would show them the treat and entice them home and they would all laugh about it. As she got closer to them, she was shocked. "Leck mir am arsh," she heard one of them yell, but with restraint so their mother could not hear. "The old cow can yell as loud as she wants, I'm not going," the other called to his brother. The language shocked Alwine. None of her brothers would have ever considered talking like that.

The boys didn't see Alwine and they continued their game which she now witnessed in full view. Their pants and underwear lay on the ground as Gustav and Otto were having a contest to see which one could urinate higher. The target was the overhanging branches in the orchard. Embarrassed and shocked Alwine quickly retreated behind some trees. The game continued and she could hear the rustling that sounded like water trickling on leaves followed by loud cheering. "How do they do that?" Alwine asked herself and was tempted to look but she could not. Several minutes later, after listening to their alternating claims of victory, she composed herself and began to walk down the lane to Johann's house.

When the boys noticed her, they hurried to pull on their clothes and came running. "Hello Alwine, what have you got there?"

"Something you'll like." She still felt the redness in her face but managed to control her voice.

"What is it?"

"I'll show you when we get to the house."

At the front door Hedwig came out screaming at her sons, "Where the hell have you been?" Then, only belatedly saw Alwine. "Oh, you! What do you want?"

The greeting was cold and Alwine had to find some courage to speak to the woman. "I brought you some baking," she was finally able to say, handing the tray to Hedwig, then turned to leave. She had only gone a few steps when Johann came out of the door, chastising his wife, "Hedwig, invite Alwine in!" But Hedwig only stared at her husband blankly. "Please Alwine, come and sit. It's so nice to see you."

Hedwig dropped the baking on the table and walked away from it. She didn't even pretend to be pleased. But when the tray was uncovered the boys jumped at the treat like vultures. "We don't bake much in this house," Johann said, in an inept attempt to excuse his sons' manners. At that his wife gave him a look that filled Alwine's with sorrow. What had she done?

"How is your brother Edmund?" Johann asked, awkwardly trying to change the subject. "I so much enjoyed talking with him. He is a very informed young man. Your parents must by proud of him."

Alwine hardly heard what Johann was saying. Rude as it was, her eyes were fixed on Hedwig. Cold contempt was quickly turning into malice. But even looking straight at her, Alwine could not anticipate what Hedwig did next. Quickly she was at the table again and swooped up the gift. "What the hell do you mean I don't bake much?" she demanded, and threw the tray against the opposite wall. "It don't want that 'scheis dreck' in my house. I wouldn't feed it to the pigs."

"Hedwig!"

Otto and Gustav were dumbfounded and visibly disappointed. But within seconds they were on the floor trying to salvage some of their treat.

"I'm so sorry Alwine," Johann began to apologize. His eyes were looking down on the table his head shaking.

I took Alwine several seconds that seemed like an eternity to find an excuse to leave. "I must return to make supper for my husband." She had to force the words out and still they were thin and shook her whole being. Her eyes were glazed as she turned and left through the front door.

"Vanity, vanity," she repeated to herself as she walked home. How could she have initiated such a travesty? Who was she to think that she could make peace where it wasn't wanted? Her father was right; God punishes vanity immediately and severely. Only when she reached her gate could she compose herself and even then she hoped that her mother-in-law would not notice her red eyes.

Alwine said nothing of her strange encounter to Albert or Julianna but the next day she baked another cake. When Julianna teased her that this time she expected a piece, Alwine just smiled. But she would not allow it to be eaten until later that day when she intercepted Gustav and Otto returning from school and invited them in. The boys beamed when Alwine showed them what she had made.

As Alwine watched her nephews joying her baking with their grandmother she wanted to tell them not to say anything to their mother. She didn't want to cause more trouble. Yet before she could put her thoughts into words that they could understand, Gustav said it for her, "Don't worry, we won't tell Mama." Julianna was tempted to ask what that exchange was about but she let it pass.

With her new attitude it was only a short time before Alwine felt better. She realized that it would take a while before she felt completely at ease and secure in her new world, but all that had happened confirmed that her happiness was in her own hands. She did, however, stay a healthy distance away from Hedwig.

It was several weeks later that Alwine asked her husband to plant some fruit trees at the edge of her garden. Albert liked the idea but explained that they didn't have the money. Still, his wife was adamant. "Make sure to plant some cherry trees," she said to him quietly, "when our daughter grows up you can cut one down and make her a wedding present."

Albert did not understand this cryptic message. "It's silly to plant a tree just to cut it down," he protested. Alwine could not get him to understand her subtle message and had to whisper it in his ear. The next day he took their wagon and came back with two cherry and two apple trees and planted them at the edge of the garden where they wouldn't block the sun.

Albert was flushed with a kind of happiness he had never experienced before when his wife told him he was to become a father. He trembled when she first told him and showed tender emotions that Alwine rarely saw. She had seen his humor, his charm and his amorous side, but she had also recognized that often he was self-absorbed. She had also seen his anger and knew that he could rage. But now Albert was so tender she almost fell in love with him again.

The boy was born prematurely in the bitter cold of January. The baby was small and the delivery was remarkably easy, or so the attending women commented, even though Alwine did not agree. It was fortunate that the delivery was easy because the midwife could not attend, so Julianna and Maria Weiss had helped Alwine through the birth. Alwine was grateful for their help. She was relieved too that they had recent experience helping Irene with her new daughter.

Albert and Alwine were both pleased to have a son. Like most Volhynian men, Albert thought he deserved a son and felt great pride that his first was a boy. Immediately following the birth he bought a round of beers for his friends at the tavern in Antonufka. He was so happy that he even bought one for Hermann Martin. Martin slapped Albert on the back with more force than a congratulatory pat needed, it almost knocked Albert down. Hermann laughed and said, "Hope he's not a runt like his father."

Alwine had a different reason for being grateful for a son. She had always felt that the role of the eldest child really belonged to a boy. As much as she had tried, she could not quite understand why God sometimes allowed daughters to be born first. After all, he had set the precedent by creating Adam before Eve, and Adam's first child was a son too. She had always felt that life for her would have been easier if she had been born second or third. Besides, it was obvious that men wanted sons first.

Albert and Alwine gave their first son only one name, Ewald (Eh-Valt). They were simple peasants and it was not their way to give children more than one name. The name they chose was very common but it surprised everyone. The tradition was to name children, especially first sons, after family members. No one could remember an Ewald on either side of the family.

The boy was small, however, and so fragile that he was three months old before his parents dared to take him out in unsteady April weather for his christening. With Irene and August Weiss, who had consented to be the child's godparents, they appeared before the Kantor. As the Kantor held the child in his arms and sprinkled the water on his forehead, coaxing a feeble whimper from him, his parents, grandmother and godparents looked on apprehensively. They only had to compare him with August and Irene's little daughter to understand he was not healthy. The smiles they gave each other were forced and cautious.

Almost as a confirmation of their worst expectation, a fever struck the boy as they returned home. It felt to both Alwine and Julianna like a very slight rise in temperature, but it was having a ravaging effect on the little body. By the time they reached home he seemed be in excruciating pain. The little nourishment that he took, he could not keep down and he was in constant pain. A bed was moved into the kitchen, the warmest part of the house, and Alwine slept with him there.

Albert, perhaps because there was nothing he could do to help, asked the questions no one wanted to hear, "How sick do you think he is? Will he live?" His mother, thinking he was being insensitive, rebuked him as she had never done before. Even Alwine, holding back her tears, cast an accusing stare his way. She didn't want to hear questions for which she had no answer, at least no answer that allowed any hope. All Alwine could really do was to pray, and she did that constantly.

Though little Ewald recovered it was clear that the baby had serious problems. Worst of all there were no doctors close by to diagnose his illness, or prescribe medicine when he was fighting his fevers. His parents didn't dare try to take him all the way into Lutzk for fear that he would not make it. They relied mainly on Maria Weiss, who was the closest thing to a nurse in Zeperow, for advice. Alwine and Julianna had to cope as best they could to keep the boy alive and hope he would outgrow whatever it was that held him back.

In May, when her baby seemed to be doing better, Alwine received a letter from her brother Edmund. She hadn't seen nor heard from him since her wedding the year before and so she was overjoyed to be opening this envelope. Edmund, she had to confess, was her favorite brother even though he and she were so different. Her brother had often been her only refuge. So many times as they were growing up, when in the quiet of a Sunday afternoon, or the blazing whiteness of a winter, she remembered disquieting things, she could look into Edmund's eyes and find quiet understanding. He had the most soothing eyes. Yes, to others, they were full of the fire of curiosity, but to Alwine they full of the balm of Gilead. He never had to say a word. She missed him terribly.

But lately in her mother's letters she had read that Edmund was not happy. Even though Mama hadn't elaborated, Alwine thought she knew why. Edmund wasn't meant to be a farmer.

As Alwine began to read she was overwhelmed. She looked at his chicken scratches on the paper and assured herself that it was Edmund's writing. The teachers at school had often ridiculed him for it. Edmund wrote too quickly. She supposed it was because his thoughts came too fast for his hand to catch up. Neatness just slowed him down. She read the excited scribbling again to make sure she had got it right.

Dombrowa
May 15, 1930

Dear Sister,

I have so much to tell you that I don't even know where to start. The only word to describe it is miracle. Pastor Stein has arranged a scholarship for me to attend the Polish University at Krakow. What is even more miraculous is that father has agreed that I can go. I am so happy I can hardly express how I feel. I would say it is like a dream coming true but if I had dreamed this I wouldn't have believed it.

One day it seems like God has nothing new in store for you and that you must accept the inevitable. But then the skies open up and you see to the ends of the earth. I am going to a university. A place where they can teach you anything and everything there is to know.

Dear Sister, I don't know if you will be able to come home before I leave in the fall but I promise to write to you.. I hope, Alwine, that you are as happy as I am and as excited.

Your Brother, Edmund

Alwine wanted to write back quickly. She cared about her brother and wanted to warn him. She wanted to warn him that the promise of a dream did not always resemble the reality. She wanted him to consider that he might be following a false dream. But the words wouldn't allow themselves to be written. It was a hard thing to ask a person to give up their dreams. Did she really have that right? So in the end she only congratulated him and asked him to write often.

As Edmund had anticipated, Alwine was not able to arrange a visit in Dombrowa before he left. So she waited anxiously for that first letter from Krakow. Was he alright? How did he like the big city? Was he lonely? Was this adventure too ambitious for a farmer's son? If she sensed that he did miss home how could she tell him gently that he ought to go home?

When the letter finally came she hesitated to open it. She was sure that he was sad and homesick just like she had been. Alwine waited until she was alone. But her wonderful brother had filled the paper with his enthusiasm and curiosity. He marveled at the immensity of the city. How it dwarfed Dombrowa and even Vladimir. He was immersed in the intricacies that made the city work; the university, the marketplace, the industry, the crowded streets and traffic, the thousands of roofs that spewed out coal smoke. Most of all he wrote about the people, the students, the professors and the ideas. There was not a hint of loneliness.

Tears flowed gently down Alwine's cheeks as she read but the emotion that set them off was not familiar to her. She was neither happy nor sad, neither worried nor relieved. Perhaps, she thought, she was jealous. Not jealous of Krakow nor the university, but of the abundance with which Edmund was able to fill his life. Alwine rebuked herself. If her precious brother could find happiness in the fulfillment of his dreams why couldn't she?

When his next letter came she was more prepared. He was still excited and rambled on about the wonders of Krakow. Alwine, who had always been able to sense her brother's moods, could not find any evidence that he was unhappy or lonely. All she could do was write back about mundane things; the inadequacy of her home, the strange behavior of her nephews and her sister-in-law. She even talked frankly about her husband, who at times was boorish and insensitive. She mentioned the progress of her baby, although she did not write about his many illnesses.

It all contrasted so sharply with what was going on in his life. Faced with her brother's happiness she understood that she was only pretending. Perhaps that was all that there would ever be in her life.

Eighteen months after the birth of Ewald, joy came again when a healthy boy was born to Alwine and Albert. This time they gave him a familiar name, Edmund. Julianna commented that with a good family name the boy should feel welcome and not wish to leave this life early. As his mother spoke, Albert looked at his older son playing in the corner of the room. He was half the size he should have been at almost two years of age. The boy couldn't even walk yet, showed no sign of talking, and he was sick so often that his death was expected with every new fever.

Albert had to wonder about his future, especially in a farming community where a man was judged by how he could work. It was not purposefully that Albert neglected his son, he just had no idea what he could teach a boy who would never work. He did not have his wife's faith and although he was not bitter, he was disappointed. But now he had a healthy son.

Unexpectedly, the most profound reaction to having another child in the family came from Ewald. As his younger brother grew, it was as if the older boy finally understood what was expected of him. When Edmund began to stand, Ewald copied him and even began to walk. It seemed to his family that he had been holding back. Now that Ewald caught on, he was even running while Edmund still wobbled. Later, as Edmund began to talk, Ewald copied that too. Alwine was beginning to think that she was raising twins and it looked that way too, especially during the period when Edmund caught up to Ewald in size. But Edmund soon outgrew his weaker brother. It was clear again to everyone that Ewald's physical abilities would always be limited.

Albert was now happier too. He did not say anything to the women, but deep down he felt that having a sick son was like having no son at all. He thought he loved Ewald but he couldn't do the things that a son ought to do, and fulfil the needs that a son ought to. It just wasn't the same. Even when Ewald was walking and talking Albert showed only a passing interest in him, patting him on the head occasionally more like a pet than a son, but when he saw Edmund he scooped him up and they laughed together.

Alwine noticed Albert's preference for Edmund and was hurt for Ewald's sake. She understood the importance of a healthy son to a farmer but she also knew that Ewald needed his father's love too. She tried to talk to her husband about it but he became defensive and rejected any idea that he was anything but a loving father to the boy.

However, it was his brother that changed Ewald's life. From the moment that Edmund could crawl, he was into everything, and Ewald, perhaps seeing the attention that his younger brother received, copied everything he did. It was no use Alwine telling the older boy that he ought to be more responsible. Ewald simply had not had the strength to explore his world earlier. The more active Ewald became the more attention he got, even from his father, and so he continued to follow Edmund, tenaciously striving to do everything he did, and building muscle tissue in the process.

As happy as Alwine was for the progress of her sons she was becoming concerned for her brother Edmund. In the second year at the university his letters were much more infrequent and the joy seemed to be muted. He was critical of the Government in every letter and even his life at the university was no longer satisfying. Alwine wrote and told him to come home if the was not happy but she felt sorry for that letter because he was a long time replying.

When Edmund finally did write it was depressing again. He was angry because a history professor whom he really liked had disappeared. Edmund was sure that the had been kidnapped by Pilsudski's henchmen and many who opposed the old General were disappearing. When Alwine wrote back, all she could think to say was, 'do nothing rash, brother, promise me that.'

Fourteen

The summer after Ewald turned five Alwine was pregnant again. She was more irritable and depressed than she had ever been but she didn't blame her pregnancy. She told herself that it was her husband's unkept promises that made her so angry. They had been married for almost six years and there was still no floor in her house. Things should have been better by now.

She blamed the acne that marred her face during this pregnancy on her filthy floor too. She hated to look in the mirror because the acne had reddened her face so much. No wonder she couldn't keep her face clean, she lamented. As long as she had to put up with these conditions the house would never be clean and neither could her face.

That summer, while she was so distressed, she spent as much time as she could working under the shade of the young fruit trees that her husband had planted for her. The house was much too hot and being pregnant amplified the heat as well as her emotions.

Even outside, however, she couldn't escape her demanding children. Edmund was old enough now to be both persistent and cunning. One blistering day he just couldn't leave his mother alone to relax in the shade with her mending. Even Omi could not coax him away though she could see he was headed for trouble. It was when his mother closed her eyes for a moment that he seized his chance to get at her sewing basket. He wanted only the basket. In seconds he had dumped the contents in the grass. As his mother opened her eyes she saw him shake the last of her precious needles and thread onto the ground. Alwine shrieked. Instantly Edmund looked to run away but she had him before he could turn around. "Edmund, Edmund!" she cried as she looked into her empty box. "What have you done?" But the boy only looked back at her with a blank, unrepentant stare. She lost control. Grabbing a thin branch lying on the ground and holding the boy by the wrist she began to apply the branch on his padded behind. The first stroke was not well aimed and totally ineffective, but as soon as she raised the stick the second time it was ripped out of her hand. There stood Ewald looking very stern with the stick clenched firmly in his hands. "There will be no beatings today!" he pronounced with great conviction, and then he explained with much seriousness, "It is hot enough today already!" Within seconds Alwine's rage and self-pity was transformed into laughter and gratitude. She grabbed both her boys and held them close. For such a boy there was hope. Her prayers had been answered.

A daughter was born in December of 1934. They gave the girl a traditional German name that Alwine had always admired, Hertha. Julianna, still not able to let go of some of her old superstitions, wanted them to pick a family name. But Alwine insisted on the one she had chosen. She had dreamed of calling her first daughter Hertha. It didn't even matter to her that it was also the name August and Irene, across the road, had given their oldest daughter.

The baby's hair was very light colored at birth but by the time she was one-year-old it had turned very dark, almost black, and was offset by penetrating blue eyes and an delightfully impish smile. More quickly than had happened with his sons, Albert learned what it meant to have a daughter. With a whimper she was able to soften his heart and he would indulge her more than his sons. He would, however, only admit much later that even though his sons made him proud, only his daughter made him happy.

This new creature made Edmund and Ewald happy too and she soon became the center of their play and attention. Little Hertha loved attention. Being even more precocious than either of her brothers, she gave excited squeals of delight to everything new that they tried. When she was barely able to walk she followed her brothers everywhere.

With three busy children to take care of, Alwine was beside herself. She had never been able to understand when people described her as a calm person. Perhaps, quiet, she could understand, and shy, but not calm. In reality, she was a very intense and nervous person. She did not believe that she was extremely meticulous nor particularly picky, but her house, and especially her kitchen had to be clean and orderly. Meals had to be ready when her husband was ready and chores left undone frustrated her. Her mother-in-law helped with the endless cleaning yet nothing was ever clean. Alwine knew that the only way she would ever be able to keep her house really clean was to get a wooden floor, the one her husband and promised years ago and had hastily forgotten.

She begged him for it. She teased him about it. She even ridiculed him for having broken his promise. Still it seemed that the more she wanted it, the more Albert resisted, blaming the depressed farm market for their lack of money, and there was the mortgage to pay. Alwine knew all the reasons but she needed that floor.

Certainly a floor would be expensive, and the first years of their marriage were a struggle for them financially. Alwine could see that not many young couples their age had it easier. They all had to struggle. Even Irene and August, who also had three children, found it a strain to make ends meet. Between his crops and the work he found off the farm, Albert earned as much as August did working full time on his farm. They paid their bills, and the mortgage to the Countess Viteranno, but could not find the money to make improvements on their home. But Alwine was adamant.

Alwine was not totally unsympathetic to Albert's concern about paying off their debt to the Countess. Soon after they were married the world wide depression had hit Polish farmers particularly hard. In recent years, a number of local farmers had lost their lands because they could not make their payments. Not in anyone's memory had the Countess, nor her father before her, behaved so vilely. They had always been understanding and lenient when payments were late. Some said it was because 'Her Highness' was in need of money. The rumors surfaced again about the inherited wealth she had squandered. But others were convinced that it was Hermann Martin who was behind this new policy. It was no secret that the countess had let Martin become much more than just the manager of her fields, and though most people did not know exactly what their relationship was, they were afraid. After all, Martin now managed all the repossessed farms. Albert was sure that nothing would give his old enemy more pleasure than seizing his land. There was no way that he would let that happen. All this Alwine understood, yet she needed that floor.

The children noticed the difference first. Alwine scrimped on the food budget and they complained about it. Ewald was the most outspoken. Having just returned from a visit to the Weiss house where he and Edmund had idled the afternoon in play with the Weiss children, Ewald took the opportunity to chastise his mother. "She gave us cake," the six-year-old said. "They always have cake. Everybody has cake but us. And why?" he asked with dramatic flair that almost sounded rehearsed, "Because you are too lazy to make us cake." He was bitingly sarcastic in his tone and full of indignation, but Alwine could only smile. Julianna too found it hard to keep from laughing. Alwine had to give up that route to her new floor.

It was Chaim, the Jew who lived just down the road that gave Alwine her best chance to earn money. He came looking for

Albert, who unlike his other neighbors did not find it offensive to work for a Jew occasionally. He wanted Albert to help spread the manure on his fields and was willing to pay well. But Albert was away with his nephews, digging a well for a farmer on the other side of Lutzk and would be gone several days. Alwine hesitated only briefly, and said, "Can I do it?"

Chaim looked at the little woman and not wishing to offend said, "It is hard work and it is dirty."

"I can do it!"

Chaim looked at her again tentatively and said, "You must do the whole field!"

"I'll do it."

Alwine worked hard fertilizing Chaim's field. Though at first she felt uneasy working for the Jew, what she saw there intrigued her. Alwine had been taught that Jews were not like other people, that they were different and contact with them was not good. But now, all she could see were the similarities. Chaim's house was no bigger than hers, his animals just as thin and his work was just as hard. At noon his wife served them a meal that could have been prepared in her own kitchen. She could see that like all farmers, the Jew, had little reward for all he did. Her neighbor suffered the farmers' lot. He was no different than a Christian farmer. As they worked, Alwine could feel his reverence for the land too. He was not unlike her father. All this was remarkable to her.

Chaim was satisfied, even pleased with the work that Alwine did. He was impressed to find a woman who could work all day as hard as a man. He asked her to come back the next day. Though Alwine noted that he only paid her a portion of what he had offered to pay Albert she was glad for the money. Alwine accepted it with thanks, but thought how this was just another similarity between Jews and Christians, their distain for a woman's work.

When Albert returned from the other side of Lutzk, he was in a good mood. Julianna suspected instantly that he and his nephews had stopped into the tavern on their way home and chided him for it. Gustav and Otto were old enough to earn their own way in the world now and enjoyed working with Albert when he had enough work. "The boys just wanted to spend some of their earnings before the witch takes it all," he said smiling, and pecked his mother on the cheek. Albert was much more affectionate when he was intoxicated. She pushed him away.

After supper, Alwine told him that she had worked for Chaim for three days and earned some money. She put the coins into his hand saying, "Here, put it toward the new floor." It was an attempt to embarrass him but he only laughed and Alwine felt she should have known better than to hand him money when he was drunk. He was so disarmingly charming and happy when he was drunk, not mean and ugly like some men. People loved to drink with him for that reason. Now she supposed he would shrug off her suggestion.

He surprised his wife when he kissed her full on the lips, something he would never do in front of the children when he was sober, and pulled a pouch of money out of his pants. "Here is the rest of the floor." Julianna and Alwine stared cautiously. His generosity always disappeared when he became sober. "It's all right," he said, sensing her uneasiness, "I only had one...no, two beers. I'm not drunk. When we finished the well they offered us a bonus if we dug out an old drainage ditch that was filling in. It couldn't have been easier."

The floor went in that fall during the time that Alwine went home for the marriage of her younger sister Adele. When she returned, she gently caressed the fir planks upon which she now walked in her kitchen and bedroom. There was some satisfaction that came with the accomplishment but on the whole Alwine could only think what a struggle it had been just to get a floor into her home.

But despite her joy over the floor, Alwine came home troubled. While she was home her mother revealed to her that she had not heard from Edmund in Krakow for many months. Alwine struggled to recall when she had last received a letter from her brother and decided that it had been almost a year. When she thought about it she recalled that she had been relieved that his letters had become less and less frequent. They were unfathomable and depressing. She would have suggested that he come home but she was sure it wouldn't have been received well.

Now that she was home, in a quiet moment, she pulled out Edmund's last letters to see if she could find a clue. They were full of lamentations. He was angry that Jozef Pilsudski, the warrior-hero, who had become the president of Poland had turned into a dictator. He was angrier still that the people of Poland loved the old man so much that they couldn't see what was going on. In front of their eyes the promise of freedom and democracy that had been the point of all Polish ambition for more than a century, had turned into ruthless autocratic rule. Opposition party leaders, labor leaders, and even liberal university professors were disappearing. More and more Edmund's letters were full anger and rage.

Only as she read the last letter from her brother, decrying Pilsudski the despot, did Alwine become concerned for Edmund. As dangerous as it was to write such things it was even more dangerous to speak them. Her brother Edmund was certainly not someone who could hold his opinions to himself. How could she not have understood what her brother was getting himself into?

Quickly Alwine wrote to her brother. Even though she suspected that she had left it much too late, she could think of nothing else to do. She begged him to write to his mother and tell her that he was alright. She warned him too of the danger of speaking his mind in such an environment as he described. With all the emotions she could transfer onto paper, she asked him to come home. But even as she wrote, she dreaded that her brother might never read her letter. She had left it too late! Alwine kept all these things in her heart, she did not want to tell anyone what she truly feared had happened to Edmund.

It was an early winter that year. Snow fell in late October and though it melted, it returned in early November to stay. Julianna caught a flu virus which she found hard to shake so she spent a lot of time in bed. Alwine nursed her as well as she could but without medicine, the virus persisted. It worried both Alwine and Albert because Julianna was sixty-nine years old and in Volhynia that was extreme old age. But Julianna was not yet ready to give up and die. She had survived other flu epidemics. Epidemics that had come in the late nineteenth century and early in this century before it had even been diagnosed, when there was little resistance to the virus and the very young and the elderly became violently ill. After a week she was still very tired but recovering.

The crisis over, Alwine looked to beautifying her home again. Now that she had a floor, everything else looked so drab and especially the windows with their old curtains. It was one of those projects that grabbed her attention and wouldn't let go until she finished it. Every corner of the house was searched for the right material for curtains but Alwine couldn't find anything she liked. She knew even before she started that there wasn't any. It was just that she needed to justify the expense and couldn't do that until she had proved to herself that there was nothing else to do the job. Julianna told her to go to the cooperative store in Antonufka and buy some material while she looked after the children. After some hesitation Alwine allowed her mother-in-law to convince her that she was well enough to look after the children. Besides, it was a mild day and the walk would not take long.

Ewald, Edmund and her little granddaughter, whom Julianna loved so much, behaved well for her. To them, she was Omi, a person of boundless love; unfortunately they could not understand that boundless energy did not go with that love. It was too much activity too soon and the old woman felt her breathing becoming labored and she was afraid that her fever was returning. She lay down on the sick bed that now had a permanent position in the kitchen. She proposed to rest for only a few minutes, but she fell deep into sleep.

The children played quietly for a while as Omi slept, until Edmund, now almost four, grew tired of playing in the house. All the pots and pans were on the floor by now, and the contents of the pantry were scattered everywhere. Eventually everything that they could reach or lift was on floor. Fortunately, the two women of the house had put everything breakable out of their reach. Edmund was tired of indoor games and wanted to go outside and play in the snow. Although Ewald knew that it wasn't quite right he had neither the strength nor the willpower to resist Edmund. Hertha, watching her brothers put on their coats, began to cry. She wanted to go out too. Ewald could not find her coat. All he could find was her diapers. He took one and tied it on over her black hair like a kerchief and took the excited little girl out to play.

From the tool shed they retrieved the sled that their father had made them and pulled each other over the snow. Edmund became upset that Hertha could not or would not pull the sled so he jostled it until she fell into the snow. But Hertha enjoyed rolling off the sled into the soft snow so much that she did it over and over, hardly noticing the cold.

That was how Alwine found them when she returned from shopping for her curtain material. She came down the lane screaming. Ewald and Edmund had never heard her like that but knew they were in trouble. In a flash they scampered inside the house, hiding under the bed they shared. Hertha stood in the snow smiling, her skin was blue from the cold but she was outrageously happy and cried only because she sensed her mother was angry.

Alwine wondered what her mother-in-law could be thinking to allow Hertha out in the cold without a coat. As she wrapped her daughter in her arms and rushed her inside she was flushed with anger. But as soon as Alwine entered the house and found her mother-in-law in her uneasy sleep she understood what had happened. She wrapped her daughter in blankets and put her into the bed that the girl usually shared with her Omi. In a few minutes the little girl was warm and asleep. Her brothers had managed to tire her out. Edmund and Ewald remained under their bed, as if pinned there. Alwine saw them there and was content to leave them. She knew that if they came out she would have to punish them and she hadn't quite figured out what was appropriate.

After assuring herself that both Hertha and Julianna were resting, Alwine hurried to clean the mess her children had made. Now that she had a floor that she could keep clean it was important for her to keep it that way. She was determined to clean up the mess before her husband came home. Almost precisely at the moment she was done the boys came out from under their self-imposed prison and behaved like nothing had happened. Alwine could not understand how they knew to come out of hiding just when she was too tired to punish them. She made an attempt to tell them what they had done wrong but they were profoundly uninterested. Their mother could only shake her head in frustration.

Julianna's relapse lasted several days. When she was fully better, she noticed the new curtains and commented on how lovely they were. Alwine called the bright yellow curtains her 'snow curtains' and Julianna assumed it was because she had trudged through the snow to go buy them. Her daughter-in-law could not bring herself to tell the old woman what had happened while she slept. After all, no harm was done. Besides, Alwine thought the real blame rested with her.

Everyone thought it was a miracle that Julianna recovered from her flu, especially since only the week before, old Maria Weiss had died after only a few days of fighting the same virus. Her husband who had always supposed that he would be the first to go, became deeply depressed. August and Irene tried to cheer him up but he would not be consoled. As long as his wife was alive, he had not felt like an invalid but now he considered himself a burden to his son's family. Within a few months he too had died. All of Zeperow and Antonufka said that he died of a broken heart, but Hermann Martin in the tavern at Zeperow spread the rumor that August and his wife had grown tired of having his useless body around and starved him to death. Of course no one believed it, not really.

Fifteen

In 1935, on an intensely brilliant summer Sunday morning that should have banished any excuse for feeling badly, Alwine went for a walk in the pasture because she was ill. She had to get out. Her stomach was churning from the smell of sausages and eggs that reached every corner of the house. She was pregnant again and had lost her breakfast so many times in the past few weeks that she didn't even bother eating that meal anymore. Unfortunately, that didn't mean that her family didn't want to eat. It was an ordeal for her to cook meals. The smell caused her head to swim and her stomach to revolt. After three pregnancies, Alwine had not expected that this one could have anything new to offer, yet it insisted on being different. It insisted on making her so sick she couldn't do her work.

As she came to the top of the rise that separated her home from her brother-in-law's, she caught a glimpse of her nephews quietly stalking toward their house. They were sneaking into the back by way of the barn, treading gingerly. It was still very early and they had obviously been out all night again and did not want to be caught.

The breeze blowing over the hill was cool and pleasant and made her feel so good that she sat down on the soft spring grass to enjoy the refreshing air for as long as she thought her family could spare her. She wasn't a naturally nosy person but her brother-in-law's house fascinated her. Whenever she went for a walk, she was drawn there, as if staring at their home could answer the many questions she had about her in-laws. The truth was that the household of Johann Fischer was such an enigma to her that their activities filled her with both fascination and dread. Especially where Gustav and Otto were concerned there was always the expectation of excitement. But when they were prowling as they were now, it was just prudent to be watchful. At least that was the excuse Alwine now used to convince herself that she wasn't held there because of morbid curiosity.

For six years she had been watching Gustav and Otto grow. From wild little boys they had developed into irreverent and raucous teenagers, with little respect for anything, not even their parents. Yet when they visited her, they behaved like gentlemen and she was troubled by that duplicity. She liked them, and even admired them in some ways, but heaven help her if her boys grew up to be like their cousins. They drank wildly, talked boorishly, scandalized the young women who were foolish enough to encourage their company, and went from one practical joke to another, usually with disastrous results.

Her first memory of their pranks was that harmless incident in their orchard and the bizarre competition. Now, after six years she still blushed to think about it, yet she knew that was mild compared to the other things they had done or were rumored to have done. There was the time they stole their father's horse during the night in the middle of the spring ploughing, to ride to Lutzk to party with a group of like-minded Ukrainian boys they had met. A fight broke out over the differences between Germans and Ukrainians, and Gustav and Otto landed in jail. They sold the horse to pay the fine and then told their father that it was stolen. As far as Alwine knew, Johann Fischer still thought it had been stolen but the boys had told their uncle the truth, knowing that he would never tell their father.

The list of their pranks and misdeeds went on and on. When a neighbor's dog annoyed them, they started on a campaign of vengeful taunting. They poked it with sticks and threw dirt and stones at it. The dog became such a nervous, whimpering wreck that the owner finally had to destroy it. They opened the farm gates of their neighbors, even their closest neighbors, leaving cows to wander the countryside. Some were never found again. They did all their work at night and even though they were suspected, they were never caught. When accused they were so incredibly aloof it was hard to believe they could be guilty.

It was natural, however, that they would develop a dislike for Hermann Martin. That particular hatred came naturally to them. They were incensed, however, that Martin had never been made to pay for his crimes. They decided it was time for justice, even if it was their own particular brand. Every year they seemed to find some new way to taunt their family enemy. Elaborating on old themes, they stole a team of horses from Martin's barn and ran them all night so that they were useless in the morning. They released his cows into his grainfield just before harvest. But most cruel of all, they captured his dog and sent it running through a field of dry hay with a burning rag tied to its tail. They worked their devilry so well that it was not possible to prove anything.

Nevertheless, Martin wasted no time in storming over to their farm to complain every time he was victimized. Johann Fischer was furious with his sons, but their mother protected them by lying about their whereabouts. Shocked and embarrassed, Johann could do nothing. "If you won't protect them," she said derisively, "I will!"

The boys always told Albert about their pranks because they knew he enjoyed a good laugh, especially when it was at Hermann Martin's expense. They found that vengeance was no fun when nobody knew about it and Albert was too blinded by his hatred to see the damage this course was having on his nephews. His wife blamed him in part for their hooliganism.

The more they got away with, the more they attempted. But their most bizarre prank almost turned into a fiasco. They were both drunk and had wandered over to the Martin farm with no particular intent, except doing whatever mischief was available for them in the middle of the night. Martin's new dog was so young that it was easily pacified. While they were considering what to do, Otto felt the need to relieve himself and so he urinated into the well. Gustav thought it was a great idea and followed his brother's lead. Their filthy prank would have ended there if Otto hadn't spotted a wagonload of manure by the side of the barn with a pitchfork sticking out of it. Carefully they rolled it closer to the well and proceeded to pitch one forkful after another until a good portion of the load was down in the well. They could hardly keep themselves from laughing, but it was not enough for Gustav. He perched himself on the rim of the well, lowered his pants and added a personal touch. However, as he started to pull up his pants again, he lost his balance and slipped backwards, toppling into the polluted water. He screamed for help as he splashed around in the filthy water while his brother shouted at him to shut up. Otto lowered the rope at the end of the counterweight and lifted Gustav out of the hole just as the door of the house opened. They ran as they had never run before because they knew they were in trouble if Martin recognized them, but Gustav's pants were still in the well.

In the dark, Martin did not realize what had been done to his well. He only heard voices but saw nothing. He supposed he had foiled Gustav and Otto in some mischief. He was even a little smug that he had scared them off. But in the morning when his wife went to draw water and a bucket of stinking slop came up, she shrieked. Martin rode to Johann's house immediately, his rage almost out of control, and Gustav's filthy pants in his hand. Johann had already left for the day and Hedwig would take none of Martin's accusations. He shouted even louder than he did in defense of her sons. She claimed her sons had been home all night.

The clothes, she told him, were not her son's. Gustav and Otto remained hidden in the house, laughing.

Alwine heard about it from Albert who could not control his delight and laughter. She looked at her husband as if he were mad. Where Martin was concerned he behaved like a child and she was concerned for both him and her nephews. Such maliciousness was beyond her understanding. If it wasn't for the fact that they hated each other so much, Alwine could have believed that Hedwig and Albert conspired to twist the boys.

Hedwig, she could almost forgive. It was natural for a mother to protect her sons. Yet, while she defended her sons' most outrageous behavior with the rage of a she-bear, she also railed on them mercilessly for the least little offence they gave to her. Alwine could not understand her, and lacking that understanding, reserved her judgement.

The boys were no more consistent than their mother. When she was not within earshot, they spoke about her in ways that made Alwine cringe. She often overheard them while they talked with Albert, using language right out of the gutter. And yet, there would be moments when they were so gentle and considerate that Alwine could only stand there and shrug her shoulders.

Eventually, Alwine knew, the boys would have to suffer the consequences of their actions. But right now it seemed that Johann was the only one who dealt with any consequences. How did he keep his sanity? It seemed to Alwine that he was the one hint of sanity in the Fischer family and yet his family had no respect for him. Neither his wife, nor his sons and certainly not his brother had anything good to say about him, while he cared deeply about all of them.

Johann was so highly regarded in their little community that even his sons' repeated misdeeds were often overlooked. Frequently people refused even to accuse either Otto or Gustav because they knew their father would work tirelessly to make it right. So often he had repaired the damage his sons caused with his own hard work and a sincere apology. It did not seem fair to people that such a father should have such sons, or even such a wife. But within his own house, Johann seemed totally ineffective.

For six years now Alwine had watched Otto and Gustav grow up, and strange enough, she had grown to love them. Their rude language, their irreverence, their constant pranks and near-criminal behavior were an enigma. It was as if the boys who were such a scourge to the community were not the boys who showed up at her door. Alwine did not have the insight to really understand what they felt but she knew that when they were in her home they were different. They eagerly helped with whatever they were asked to do and used no language that ever offended her, at least not when they knew she was listening. They behaved, in many respects, better than her husband. They were kind and loving toward their grandmother and were affectionate to their young cousins, especially little Ewald, in whom they found great humor. She could only hope that as they grew up they would find themselves, but right now, as they were sneaking back into the house she knew that they had been up to something.

Alwine stayed sitting on the grass up on the rise for some time. Her stomach had settled but she knew that it would revolt again if she went into the house before breakfast was over. A little while later Johann came out of the house dressed for Sunday and walked to his shed. She heard him bang the shed door closed and run back to the house. "Hedwig! The wheels have been stolen right off of our wagon!" he shouted as he opened the door.

"What do you mean?" his wife cried back. Her shrill voice carried right up the hill to Alwine.

"Someone stole all four wheels off the wagon. They must have done it in the night."

"Why wouldn't they just steal the wagon?" Hedwig asked.

Why indeed, Alwine had to agree. Now she understood. It was obvious to her that the boys had removed the wheels. But why? "Probably so they could sleep in on Sunday Morning," Alwine answered herself. Without the wagon, Johann would have to ride the horse to church. What had they done with the wheels? She looked around and saw them leaning against the back of the shed.

Alwine stood up and walked back to her house. She was happy that the boys had done nothing more terrible than hiding the wagon wheels. They would be found she reasoned. Johann would ride his horse to church and the boys would get their rest now, and their recompense later. The worst thing she could have done was get involved.

It saddened Alwine to think that her husband's family was so torn. The number of times that Hedwig had said something civil to her, Alwine could count on the fingers of one hand. The good words her husband had for his brother were even fewer. Unfortunately, she had no idea what to do about it, except to observe and watch the family disintegrate. She dreaded how it might affect her children someday.

Only a few minutes after Alwine walked through the front door Johann arrived on horseback, bringing a warning of thieves in the neighborhood. "Polaks," Albert said with disgust, implying that either all thieves were Polish or that all Poles were thieves. After her brother-in-law told Albert about the disappearance of his wheels Alwine felt the guilt of her secret and said, "I was up on the hill this morning and noticed a set of wagon wheels at the back of your shed."

Johann seemed puzzled for a second and then Alwine thought she saw his shoulders droop. He looked embarrassed now. "Did you see who put them there?" he asked hesitantly, perhaps knowing the truth already.

Alwine shook her head and was glad that it was the truth.

"I think I know," Johann said sadly, "I'll deal with it after church."

Whatever it was that Johann did, it didn't work. Later in the day the boys were seen in their orchard throwing stones at passing traffic, trying to scare the horses into bolting. This time they were caught red-handed. But it was their mother who went after them with a rod, yelling and swearing at them. They were too big and too fast so Hedwig only managed to add to the embarrassing spectacle.

During these depression years, Albert worked hard. He had no choice. He knew he was poor and understood that he could work all his life and not get ahead. He heard his brother talk about the great depression that had lowered the price of wheat from 23 zlotys for a sack in 1928, to only 8 zlotys in 1934, but never could understand the worldwide forces involved in the catastrophe. He was sure the blame for his poverty lay with the Polish government. Governments were responsible for all the bad in the world. That was simply the way it was.

Their poverty was so deep that it wasn't until the fall of 1935 that he kept a horse through the winter. Until then, Albert would sell the horse at the end of autumn so that he would not have to feed it through the cold months. But, he would have to buy another in the spring when the demand and the price was high. Then again, after the harvest, he would sell the horse and lose as much as 75 percent. Still, he figured the cost of the winter feed was worth the difference.

That was only an example of how Albert and Alwine kept themselves in poverty. And it spoke volumes on how the Polish government failed to help its farmers. The government couldn't even provide them with basic information that could change medieval farming habits. Had they lived in Germany, or England, or anywhere where stable governments cared about the productivity of their farmers, it might have been different. There, a department of agriculture could have told them that they were feeding their animals wrong.

A horse's nutritional needs changed in winter when it did little work. It was in the spring and summer when they pulled heavy implements and loaded wagons that they needed the high energy feeds, and then only to supplement the powerful fresh grasses that they ate. In the winter a horse could get by in a sheltered barn with a few oats and a little hay. But Volhynian farmers insisted on feeding their work horses high protein grains even in winter, while their poor cows were supposed to produce milk throughout those cold months on the cured hay that lost nutritional value every day. Of course Albert didn't have a horse through the winter, so the grain went to the pigs and the chickens who burned it off just to keep warm. By the end of the winter the cows' milk production was measured in cups rather than liters. Albert never learned what he was doing wrong.

Albert did have someone besides the government to blame for his poverty. He never failed to curse Hermann Martin whenever he saw him driving by, especially in the winter when Albert had to walk. Had he calculated the total loss of land because of Martin's swindle, he would have found that he was missing a mere two hectares. It was not enough to get him out of his cycle of poverty but he was sure that it would have changed everything. He fumed about it incessantly. In any case, Albert didn't need to add up his losses to hate the man. He could never be near him without feeling the rage grow in the pit of his stomach and his eyes glaze over. An opportunity to get even was his heartfelt wish.

In the spring of thirty-five, Albert bought a new horse for the season. He had little cash but he made the best deal he could with the money he had. He thought he had done well in his horse trading but after only a few days he knew he had been cheated. The horse was much older than it appeared and the coloring that had been applied to cover up the grey hair was rubbing off. He had bought the animal from a Jewish trader in the neighboring town of Tarnow, and though he had absorbed all the prejudices his religion and culture spewed out about the Jews, Albert felt he knew them well enough to get satisfaction without the help of the law. Other men would have raged or gone to the constable complaining about the thievery, but Albert had a plan of his own.

A week after he had purchased the horse, he hitched it up to the wagon and drove through Zeperow to Tarnow where most of the Jews lived in a community not unlike his German village. The trader claimed that the horse was not the one he had sold to Albert and told him to go away. It was the reaction Albert had expected but he had to try. He knew all along that he would probably have to go to the Rabbi and put his complaint before him. In his dealings he had learned that most Jewish men found it hard to lie to their Rabbi. When he brought the religious man back with him to the horse trader, they began to talk in Yiddish.

"Have you made a mistake?" the Rabbi asked. Reluctantly the man conceded that he might have been fooled. But then he protested, "He should have brought the animal back right away!" Both men were startled to hear Albert answer in Yiddish, "The coloring did not come off until two days ago." The Rabbi and the horse trader stared at Albert. They both knew Gentiles who could understand a little Yiddish, but few could speak it with the facility of this man."If there has been a mistake then let's correct the mistake," Albert continued, "that's all I want."

"I see you are a reasonable man Fischer," the horse trader replied, embarrassed and relieved. "I am sorry for my mistake. I was fooled too. I bought the horse only a few days before I sold him to you." He pointed to his pens and after mumbling something to himself he said with resolution, "Choose from any of the horses I have left."

Albert was not a fool. No longer limited by the lack of cash he selected the best horse in the paddock and knew that he got an animal much better than he had paid for. As he finished harnessing the black gelding, Albert shook the hand of the Rabbi and the trader to make sure they knew he was satisfied and had no ill feelings. But only after he was out of the village did he start to laugh out loud. This would make a good story.

On the way home, Albert dropped into the tavern in Zeperow to buy himself a congratulatory beer. He felt in no way ashamed for having claimed a much better horse than the original price he had paid. In fact he felt good about it. There had been so few occasions lately that had brought him a profit that he believed he had earned it. The beer would help him to celebrate a good outcome to a good day, as well as afford him the chance to boast. A good trading story was always enjoyed and when it involved the Jews, who had an almost mystical reputation in that art, the story was received even better.

He had begun to relate the tale to several acquaintances at a table when he noticed that Martin was in the tavern. Albert pretended not to see him. He would have rather walked out, not wishing to share his story of good fortune while his enemy was there, but didn't want people to think he was intimidated. So he stayed to finish his beer. It didn't matter what Albert felt, because Hermann swaggered over to their table with a beer in his hand and a leer on his face. He had watched as his neighbors sat rapt, listening to Albert, and felt a compulsion to interrupt. It was another chance to get Albert's goat.

"So what lies has this Fischer been telling you today?" he asked.

Albert looked away and held his tongue.

"Albert's been telling us about his new horse," one of his companions said. "He got the best of the horse trader in Tarnow."

Martin laughed brusquely, "I'll bet it's dead in a week! Albert against that Jew, not a chance in the world!"

Everyone laughed except Albert. He had no intention of finishing his tale with Martin standing there ready to ridicule every word. Albert was disappointed. The fire of enthusiasm had been stolen. So he sat, feeling cheated once again by Martin. People would have talked about it for days. "Did you hear how Albert Fischer got the best of that Jewish horse trader down in

Tarnow? He got the best horse in his stable for practically nothing. The old Jew had tried to sell him an old nag but Albert outsmarted him." Of course he would not mention how long it had taken him to figure out that he had been sold a bag of old bones, nor that it was the Rabbi's presence that actually convinced the horse trader to tell the truth. That would not add to his image. As he drank the beer, Albert brooded. Hermann Martin was at fault again. Now, even the beer didn't taste so good. Martin spoiled everything.

Albert finished his beer and left, unaware that Martin was only a few minutes behind him. He had traveled only a short distance when he heard a wagon approaching him from the rear. It was Martin. Had it been anyone else, Albert would have started to pull over to allow a safe passing, but he wasn't inclined to do that for Martin right now. The closer the other wagon drew, the more determined Albert was to not look back and just ignore him.

He could hear Hermann now, his loud acerbic voice driving his horse to go faster. Martin loved good horses. It was his pride and joy to own the best animals and pass his neighbors on the road. He could not tolerate anyone being in front of him. Neither was he used to people blocking his way.

Most days, he could have intimidated even Albert to move aside, except today. Martin's enemy was feeling good about himself and he was angrier than usual. He didn't flinch and never looked back, never made a move to the left or the right and didn't speed up. Martin was yelling again, "Move over! You don't own the road!" He tried to bring his rig beside Albert's, but he would not budge, even though for an instant he feared they were going to crash. Luckily, Martin reigned back his horse just in time. Still, Albert stayed his path driving his horse down the center of the road.

Hermann began to yell obscenities. He used every foul idiom in German, Polish, and Ukrainian that he knew. Albert understood them all as most Volhynian men did. It was almost a victory in itself to have produced such anger. Albert wanted to turn around and laugh in his face but he didn't dare. "Are you as deaf as you are stupid?" Martin shouted, "you ignorant lodrak."

As they got closer to Zeperow, their neighbors, working in their fields, heard the yelling and stopped to look up. When they saw it was Hermann Martin and Albert Fischer they dropped their work. The racing wagons were kicking up the dust and it was evident that something exciting was going on. They ran to the road side to see the race develop.

There was a cross road just fifty meters ahead and when Albert saw it he knew he had to beat Martin to it. He was afraid that Hermann would try to pass him there, and if he did, he could cut Albert off and drive him over the edge of the road. He waited until he got closer and then urged his black horse on, thinking, "Let's see what kind of a horse trader I am." To his gratification the horse jumped into a trot and caught the surprised Hermann off guard. They reached the road first and were across before the wagon behind could react.

Now it was a race. Martin whipped his horse to catch up to the despicable Fischer. Albert finally turned around and saw his enemy bearing down on him. There was a glare in his eyes that matched his own hatred. Albert urged his new horse on, he lashed the reigns and was pleased with the instantaneous and powerful reaction. However, as he looked back again, Martin was still gaining on him.

The race lasted for less than a kilometer. There was a turn ahead that neither wagon could have negotiated at their current speed, but with Martin sitting right behind him it was also too dangerous to slow down. Albert knew what he had to do. To avoid a catastrophe he would exit at Ernst Thann's lane and stop there. That farm lane bent too, though not as severely as the road and it looked infinitely less dangerous than flying around the corner with this insane traitor on his heels.

Martin was still whipping his horse furiously. Albert wanted to slow down so he could make his planned escape safely, but

Hermann was pressing him so much that slowing down was impossible. He was too obsessed with overtaking Albert to worry about the sharp curve ahead. Albert thought of abandoning his escape plan but he knew the alternative was even worse. He'd fly off the edge of the road and probably kill himself. But unless Albert was able to stay clear of Martin until he got to Thann's lane his route to safety could turn ugly too. Left without an alternative he shouted at his new horse, desperately hoping it would respond to his voice. It did, and Albert gained a few meters on his pursuer.

He planted his feet squarely against the foot board to brace himself for the jolt he expected as the wagon jumped from the road to the farm lane. The lane had a slight down grade for several meters and he hoped the horse wouldn't stumble in the transition. The gelding reacted magnificently once again and the wagon flew off the road and onto the lane. Albert bounced high off the seat. He had visions of flying under the wheels of his wagon, but felt only relief when his rear hit the wagon seat again. The pain was irrelevant. Now he pulled back hard on the reigns hoping the horse could stop before smashing into the gate. For a split second, it looked like the horse was going to smash right through. He thought of jumping from the wagon but the horse stopped just inches from the gate and Albert was able to hang onto the seat and avoid falling under his horse.

Behind him there was a clamor like nothing he had ever heard before. It was over before he had a chance to look around. A timber snapped and there was a tearing sound, followed by a piercing inhuman whine. Albert shuddered.

When he did turn around, he saw that Martin had followed him onto Thann's lane, but something had gone wrong. His horse was on the ground, kicking his forelegs and writhing in pain. Albert bit his lip as he recognized the problem. Hermann had driven his wagon onto Thann's newly ploughed field to avoid driving right into the back of Albert's wagon. The horse could not negotiate the transition from the hard gravel to the soft footings and went down heavily and awkwardly. Albert's heart sank.

In the time it took for Albert and Hermann to understand what had happened, their neighbors, including a very bewildered Ernst Thann, were on the farm lane with them. Martin jumped from his wagon, the rage had turned into concern for his horse. Albert came over to help too. He'd never intended for anything like this to happen, but he knew before he got out of his wagon that Hermann's horse was finished.

"Don't touch my horse!" Martin barked out. "You murdered him!"

Albert drew back. He watched Martin detach the harness from his wagon, wishing he could help. But by now there were enough of their neighbors to assist him. They pushed the wagon off the horse carefully but quickly. Instantly it was clear the horse was lost. Both hind legs were mangled. They were almost torn off by the oaken shaft of the wagon that had broken when the horse went down and there was a deep gash on the horse's withers from which the blood gushed out. The women gasped and turned away, even Albert had trouble looking at it. As much as he might have wished some catastrophe on Martin, so that his enemy could feel the same pain of loss he felt, even he knew this was wrong.

More neighbors came to witness the spectacle. Even Johann came running, reaching the lane out of breath, but he stood back when he saw that Albert was safe and Martin was tending to his shattered animal.

When Martin had accepted his horse's fate, he turned away and found himself staring into Albert's face. A piece of the broken shaft from his wagon lay at his side and he picked it up. Ernst Thann, mistaking his intentions, said to him, "That's no way to do it. I'll get my rifle." But Martin was staring at Albert and growled, "It's not for the horse! I'm going to break your leg!"

Johann Fischer stepped in front of Martin. "There must be a better way to settle this," he said with his hands raised to stop Martin.

Hermann drew back, but only for an instant. He was not going to let Johann protect his brother. "Don't try to protect your brother," he cried as he swung the lumber. Johann was able to deflect the blow with his forearm but it still glanced off the side of his head. He staggered back several feet and landed in Ernst Thann's arms. In a flash Albert gripped the lumber, ripped it out of Martin's hands and brought it down full force on his head. Martin dodged, but not in time to come away unhurt. The blow made his feet wobble and his knees give out. He lay on the ground bleeding from a gash on the side of his head.

Johann Fischer and Martin recovered. Both men had headaches for several days. Hedwig ridiculed her husband as he lay in bed for having been wounded in what should have been his brother's fight. She was angry because, as usual, Albert had come away unscathed. But Johann was working again quickly, escaping his bed much faster than expected. His boys joked that their mother's tongue was their father's cure.

Martin recovered altogether differently. His head rang from the pain for several days, but his pride was injured even more and his anger was out of control. When his children made too much noise, he kicked them and his Polish wife out of the house and sent them to live in the barn. "Stay there until you learn to be quiet!" he screamed. He had his rage to nurse him back to health, and it seemed to be an efficient cure.

It was a month or so later, as the notoriety of it all was fading and Albert began to feel silly about the whole event, when the feud flared up again. It happened in the cooperative store in Antonufka. Albert had taken Edmund and Ewald into town to register them for school in the fall. On the way back he stopped at the tavern for a beer. The boys waited outside. It was Ewald's idea and Edmund thought it was wonderful. They gave their father time to drink a couple of beers and then went in. Papa was always in a better mood after a drink. It was then that the timing was right for Ewald to ask him for money to get some candy. Albert cheerfully handed him a coin, but as the boys were leaving, their father turned and said, "I want the change." Ewald turned to Edmund outside and sighed, "He's happy."

In the co-op the brothers ogled all the candy. There were only a few jars but everything looked so delicious and sweet. "How much can we have for half of this?" Ewald asked holding up the coin. The clerk smiled, "That coin will get you three pieces each."

Edmund looked at Ewald while wetting his lips in anticipation. He wanted three pieces. Ewald shook his head, "Papa expects change. We'll take one piece each, and one for Hertha."

"Give me the money!" a familiar voice behind them said.

They turned to see Jozef Martin, Hermann's son, and Ewald clenched his fist around the coin to protect it.

"Give me that coin," the boy who was half again as tall and twice as wide as Ewald, insisted. Jozef's large body had Ewald pinned up against the counter, but the stubborn boy refused to budge. The clerk was getting nervous but he did nothing. He was hoping that Jozef's mother, who was off in another part of the store would stop her son. But she never did see what her son was doing.

Jozef's insistence became stronger and he put all his weight against Ewald.The clerk became worried and feared that the smaller boy would be smothered. He was coming around the counter to step in as the boys' father came through the door. Albert Fischer grabbed the Martin boy by the neck and jerked him back so that he fell on the floor. He pulled the boy up and took him to his mother, telling her to keep her filthy boy at home if she couldn't control him and repeated what he had said in Polish just in case she hadn't understood. Then he added, "Tell your husband to teach this boy some manners. He can't behave like a Pole for the rest of his life." She turned red and hurried out of the store.

"Buy your candy and let's go home," he barked at his boys. His voice was full of anger but there was a smile on his face. The brothers didn't know what to think. "Get a whole bunch for the family," their father added. Edmund gasped as their father gave Ewald another coin. It was hard not to like him when he was full of beer and flushed with excitement.

The law suit came shortly thereafter. Martin was seeking compensation for the loss of his horse, the pain from the gash on his head, and he wanted an end to the harassment of his wife and children. For compensation Hermann Martin wanted all the Fischer lands, both Albert and Johann's. Johann, he claimed had assisted Albert in the brutal attack against him.

With the witnesses available there should have been no worry as to the outcome of this preposterous action but it wasn't all that clear to the Fischers. Martin had established himself as a quasi-Pole with a Polish wife. A Polish judge might just take offence at a German throwing a Polish woman out of a store. He might just use that pretext to give Martin everything he asked for. It wouldn't be the first time that a German was discriminated against in a Polish court.

Albert's nervousness was augmented by the presence of the Countess Viteranno in the Lutzk courtroom. It was supposed she was there to support Hermann Martin, the man who managed her lands. When he saw her, Albert was sure he had lost. She sat by herself, her face obscured by the outlandishly broad rim of her yellow hat and the court officials waited on her as if she were a queen. But as the day progressed and she sat silently and alone, it was apparent that she was not there to testify. She never acknowledged Albert with so much as a nod, but he would have been less nervous if he had known that she was equally aloof to Martin.

The case was finished in a matter of minutes. In the end, it was not the many witnesses that Albert had that turned the day for him, but it was the lack of any witnesses for Martin that made the judge dismiss the case.

Martin protested strongly, "They're all German. They're lying to save one of their own. They're all lying."

Bluntly, the judge explained it to the astonished Martin. "It wouldn't matter if all the Germans in Poland had come to testify. The point is that you have no one to testify for you."

There was a celebration that night in Antonufka. Albert Fischer was the hero and Martin was officially declared the villain. Otto and Gustav Fischer carried their uncle around the tavern on their shoulders. For an evening he was Albert the Giant Killer, and everyone loved him. The jokes were all at Martin's expense. The spirit of the revelry belied the devoutness these farmers professed. Johann Fischer left after the second bad joke. Some drunkard asked, "How does Martin call his Polish wife to bed? - He goes, suey, suey!" The celebration had gone too far in Johann's opinion.

Albert Fischer was a changed man after that. The flush of excitement over the victory lasted only a few days but there was a deeper change, the kind of change that comes when a man knows he has the respect of his community, when he knows his neighbors no longer regard him as a victim. No one needed to pity Albert Fischer any more and that made him feel good. It didn't matter so much anymore that Martin still held the piece of land that he had swindled away from his father. When the courts dispensed justice fairly it didn't matter that Martin was rich, and that he managed all of the Countess's land. It only mattered that you were willing to stand up for your rights. It could make a man proud.

Edmund and Ewald started school in the fall of that year. It was not because Alwine didn't love Ewald that she hadn't sent him to school earlier, but it was just the German-Volhynian-Lutheran brand of pragmatic thinking that told her not to push the boy. From time to time fevers and pains racked Ewald's little body and he would be in bed for days. Alwine was sure that if his Omi wasn't around to spend so much time with him that the boy would have been dead already. Under those conditions no one could expect Ewald to concentrate on school. So why send him? Even now she hesitated to let him go, fearing how the extra stress would tax him. But the boy insisted on going with his brother who was already taller and much stronger. Ewald could not accept that it was important for Edmund go to school and not for him.

Ewald's determination and enthusiasm were a combination that Alwine could not resist. It seemed so unfair to give up on his life when he refused to give in. "If he survives this," she said to herself, "then it will do him a lot of good. If he doesn't..." She bit her lip. Alwine couldn't bring herself to say what her husband and others had been saying, that the walk to school would kill him.

It was hard for Alwine to describe the heartache she felt about her oldest son Ewald. The worst part was reconciling the fact that he faced a life of difficulty and possibly early death, despite his great love of life and even greater determination. Her heart told her to prepare herself for the worst and pamper and love him while she had him, but her head said that he needed the challenge of life for his heart and mind to grow strong. She hoped with all her being that the boy would prove everyone wrong and live a long and happy life, but that meant surviving to adulthood and acquiring the skills an adult needed. She allowed him to go to school, even encouraged him when she saw his determination.

It was a five-kilometer walk to the Bet-Haus in Antonufka where the school was held. Alwine's eyes were wet the first few days when she saw Ewald struggling home. The walk back and forth and the hours of concentration wore him down. The whole evening he was in pain. Julianna massaged his legs every night and Alwine wrapped him warmly. In the morning Alwine would ask him if he really wanted to go back and he would reply with determination, "I need to go, Mama, it's an important lesson today." In the evening Edmund would arrive well before Ewald and Alwine would go out to the yard gate to watch for him.

Sometimes she would walk out to the road and scoop him up in her arms saying, "I missed you so much," and carry him into the house. As soon as she picked him up his body would melt into hers. By the time she reached the front door he was asleep.

When the snow began to fall, Alwine's concern deepened for him. She gave Edmund instructions never to walk ahead of Ewald. She begged her husband to drive the children to school in the morning. That way Ewald would only have to walk one way. This was going to be the first year that they could afford to keep a horse through the winter and she thought that was more than coincidence. But Albert became upset. "Why are you sending him to school anyway?" he asked angrily. "It's just a waste of time! He can't learn!" She wanted to take his head off for his insensitivity, but it was more important to get him to agree. Patiently she answered him, "Because he wants to go. Because he thinks it is important. There's not much we can do for him but this much we can do."

Albert started to grumble again but stopped abruptly. Alwine looked up and caught Julianna's eyes staring down her son. "All right," he said, "but only for the winter."

She understood that Albert had acquiesced to his mother and not to her. At least her mother-in-law had begun to see how important this was for Ewald, Alwine was grateful for that. Yet she could not help reflecting that it was always that way. Alwine would ask Albert to do something and he would be reticent, but then a look from his mother, more often than not, brought compliance. It did not upset Alwine. She thought a son ought to be loyal to his mother. Still, it annoyed her.

It made a world of difference to Ewald when his father began to deliver him and his brother to school. There were fewer nights when he just lay in bed suffering, and sometimes he could even help Edmund do their homework, which up to now, the younger boy had been doing for the both of them. As Ewald was less tired and began to study at night he made better progress in school. It seemed there was hope for him.

In December, Alwine gave birth to another boy whom they called Alfred, but he lived for only one short week. They buried him in the cemetery by the little prayer house in Antonufka. After a few days, Hertha wondered where the baby was. She didn't understand when Oma tried to explain what death was, but accepted it when she was told that he was with Jesus. She was only two years old and forgot her baby brother quickly. However, Alwine couldn't forget so easily. She cried whenever she found herself alone for a few moments, hiding her tears because even in the face of such tragedy she was expected to be strong and deny her emotions. She worked hard at forgetting but the only thing that really distracted Alwine from her grief was her determination to help Ewald succeed.

The Volhynian schools of the 1930's were boring places. There were few text books and the community was too poor to buy reams of paper for the children to practice their skills, so the emphasis in school was on tedious repetition and boring lectures. It took great concentration for the children to really learn their letters and numbers. The teachers did the best they could with the resources they had, but there was little help for those who were slow.

For a while, Ewald was able to pay more attention, but when his pains and fevers came back that winter, his work in class suffered. Even the time his mother spent with him in the evenings couldn't help Ewald to keep up. As his fragile health caused him to miss more and more school, he fell hopelessly behind. Ewald felt terrible enough that he couldn't keep up, but when the other boys came to the conclusion that he was stupid, as well as weak, they teased him mercilessly.

It was Jozef Martin who was the ringleader. Jozef was two years older than Ewald and yet he was only a year ahead in school. He was larger than most children his age and terribly overweight. His father had brought him to the Lutheran school in Antonufka because it was so much closer than any Catholic school. "Teach him to read and add," he told the Kantor, "that's all he needs."

Jozeph, however, spent all of his time picking on the younger and weaker boys.

At first, Edmund tried to defend his brother, but the frustration of the endless harassment wore him down too. He got tired of fighting his brother's battles, especially when he lost so many of them. Now during breaks, Edmund would search out a friend and run to the opposite end of the schoolyard to play. Sooner or later one of the girls, quite often Hertha Weiss, would come shouting at him that the ruffians were hurting Ewald. It was too much for Edmund. He couldn't cope with it. Jozef was much too big. "So go tell the teacher," he yelled at her, and averted his eyes from Hertha's accusing stare.

Yet one day, Edmund's anger overcame his fear. He was eating lunch with Ewald when Jozef and his friends began to tease him. "Dummy, dummy, dummy ... dummy," they called out as they circled around the brothers. Ewald ignored them and that bothered Edmund even more. After only a few seconds he was seething. He jumped up quickly, hoping to surprise one of them and knock him over. He didn't have a target in mind but the one he caught by the tip of his foot was the Martin boy. He came crashing down, his face grinding into the grass. Seeing Jozef prone gave Edmund courage. "Polak, Polak, Polak," he cried derisively, "your mother is a stupid Polak, and your father is a thief." It was what his father said all the time, so he knew it to be true. Jozef's face turned deep red and he charged at Edmund, but the smaller boy was too agile and swift, he dodged easily.

Now several other boys, including some who only minutes ago were teasing Ewald, turned on Jozef. The cry of "Polak, Polak, Polak," was one they responded to eagerly and soon it rang across the playground. Incensed at the betrayal, Jozef lunged at Edmund, who had turned them against him. Over and over again the over-weight boy tried to grab Edmund but he missed every time. Edmund was laughing as the bell rang, but even he had to realize this wasn't over.

That afternoon as they walked home, Edmund grew pale when he saw a group of boys running after them. Even from a distance the unmistakable hulk of Jozef Martin was recognizable. Edmund wanted to run. He knew he was faster than all of them and he resented it that his brother couldn't keep up. He was shaking with fear and fought the urge to bolt, but his mother had told him never to leave Ewald. The boys stopped a few meters short, almost as if to savor the moment. Jozef Martin, glowed with delight as he began to torment them. "We are going to kill one of you," he said with vengeful delight. "Which one will it be?"

Edmund felt his knees begin to weaken and buckle. His voice quivered as he pointed to Ewald and said, "Him."

Ewald, was steadier. He faced Jozef with a defiant stare. "No one," he answered confidently. Then he turned and walked away. The ruffians simply knocked the two of them down and threw dirt in their faces. Just before leaving, Jozef tried to kick Edmund but he sidestepped him. Spitefully, Jozef kicked at Ewald and caught him hard on his right thigh. The boy leaned on his brother in order to walk and cried all the way home.

It became Jozef Martin's favorite game. Whenever he and his friends felt the urge, they followed the Fischer brothers as they left the school and roughed them up. Alwine got tired of them coming home in pain, with torn shirts and pants, but her husband would not go to Martin and talk to him about his son. She had to do it. Hermann yelled at her, "If your sons won't stop teasing him then he's just going to have to protect himself. Now get out of here!" Alwine couldn't understood it.

She grew afraid for Ewald so after another bout of fever kept him home in the spring, Alwine would not let him return to school. In the fall he begged to go back and his mother relented. He attended sporadically for a few months, but it went from bad to worse. The school system was unsympathetic to those who needed extra help and by Christmas even Ewald had lost hope. The humiliation of sitting with a lower grade while his younger brother moved forward was too hard for him to bear. Now, even he didn't want to go any more. Alwine and Julianna found useful but non taxing things for him to do around the house, and helped him to learn to read from the Bible. Yet when the enthusiasm vanished from his voice and his eyes, Alwine could only wonder what would become of him. This seemed more tragic than the death of her baby.

Sixteen

Albert had never been so proud. All his life his brother had told him that revenge was self-destructive and better left to God. If that was so, then he ought not to be feeling so good. Obviously his brother was wrong again.

Even better than that, he was now famous. His fame, dubious as it was, was strangely exhilarating. A horse race that was never really fair, a blow with a heavy timber, and a court case that was no case at all, were the consequences of rage and anger. They were by no means achievements to be lauded. Yet most people thought that Martin deserved all he got and the person who did it to him deserved to be a local hero. Albert agreed.

The only detractors were his wife and mother. Alwine was the first to notice his new swagger and warned him sternly with the old proverb she had learned at her father's side, "Pride goes before the fall." Albert resented it. What he wanted was his wife's support, not her criticism. He couldn't understand why she wouldn't be happy for him nor why even his mother disapproved. It mystified him. He was a hero everywhere but at home. In his house and in his fields he was still the same old Albert Fischer, struggling to make a living and fumbling like much of German-Volhynia. It was no wonder that he spent so much time in the tavern, where for him, beer was quite often free.

As a new spring approached in 1936, Alwine and Julianna became concerned. Albert wasn't making his usual preparations for the spring planting. It was a time that he usually looked forward to, and anticipated with a flurry of work, cleaning and repairing his implements and ordering the new grain seed. But this year Albert languished in the tavern and Alwine feared that her warning was about to be realized. Disaster was not far away when providence, in the form of Kantor Himmel, saved him.

Almost a year after the horse race that started all the uproar, Albert was offered the position of town constable. The Kantorrat, the village council led by the Kantor, offered him the position. Herr Himmel, aware of his own negative image, nominated Albert simply because of his immense popularity. Perhaps he hoped that the appointment would reflect favorably on him. Ironically, Albert detested the man who was his biggest support for this position. The choice, nevertheless, was made nearly unanimous by the council, except for Johann Fischer, who abstained from the vote, citing a conflict of interest. The other members of the council were impressed by Johann's integrity, making them believe even more that their choice was correct.

Albert accepted the appointment even though the pay was minimal. He was to receive a horse, a pistol and a hundred kilos of wheat annually. But it was the honor of the position that he found irresistible. It meant the community respected his judgement. There was no way his ego would let him turn this down.

Albert loved it. From day one he knew that it was what he wanted. Not that he had any illusions of having innate abilities to do police work, nor any great interest in the law; he just enjoyed the incidental benefits of his office. It made him feel even better about himself. The position had come at just the right time in his life. As a farmer he had been unable to prove himself and he was partially justified in his complaint that he had too little land to be a real farmer. This job fitted him like a glove and now he began to feel that he had a chance to prove his worth.

With no clear instructions, Albert was left pretty much on his own. His duties were set out by nebulous tradition rather than by any civic statutes. He would have to rely on a lot of common sense to pull him through, even though he knew that there were a number of people, including his brother, who doubted he had any sense at all. But he thought he had as much ability as any man and he was confident.

The first test of that ability came in his first week. While he was riding into Antonufka, sitting proudly and straight-backed on his official horse, he heard his name being called. There in the center of the village, Anna Kludt, a young widow he was passingly acquainted with from church, came running across the street calling to him, "Herr Fischer, Herr Fischer!" He liked the ring of it, "Herr Fischer." No one had ever addressed him so formally. His head was too full of self-importance to notice the urgency in her voice until she was standing beside him out of breath. Frantically she gestured to him to follow her. It was only then that he began to understand that this job was not given to him just for his own gratification.

Half way back to her house the woman regained her power to speak but she was running and talking at the same time so that Albert couldn't understand everything she was trying to say. "A big dog bit my little boy," was all he could hear. Albert was slightly indignant.

A dog bite was a minor thing, requiring a reprimand for the owner and a mother's loving touch. He was all set to be sympathetic and comforting but he was sure she was over-reacting like women who did not have a man around usually did. Coming into the house he envisioned the imprint of a few teeth on the boy's leg, or perhaps a scratch and a little blood. From what he knew of Frau Kludt, he thought she tended to be an overprotective mother, as widows often were. She needed to understand that it was unreasonable for her to try to protect her son from every childhood experience. A little dog bite, after all, was a good lesson.

The child, a boy of seven or eight was whining, but when his mother undid his bandage to show Albert the bite, he winced and the boy began to cry uncontrollably. Albert blanched at the sight of the torn flesh. There was a gash almost six inches long and all around the wound, the boy's leg looked like ground-up meat.

Shaken in his naivety, it took Albert a few minutes to collect himself. In those few moments he lost his arrogance as he realized that there was nothing anywhere to tell him how to proceed to rectify this wrong. He felt inadequate. It was obvious that the dog would have to be destroyed but was he supposed to do it? He had no idea. All he could think to do was to ask the woman how it had happened. Right now all he wanted to do was mask his uncertainty.

"It was bound to happen sooner or later," the widow sobbed, in response to Albert's question. "Every Wednesday that Cossack and his beast come into town. They frighten me to death. I've watched him teasing the children with his wild dog. He just laughs at them when they run away. I knew that sooner or later it would break loose and hurt someone. If I had known he was in town I would never have sent Peter out."

"So you know who the owner is?" Albert asked.

"Yes, he belongs to that filthy Ukrainian! I don't know his name. You must have seen him and his big red mongrel. Perhaps the clerk at the cooperative can tell you his name. I sent Peter there for a few eggs. As he came out the dog jumped on him and tore up his leg." She was crying now and angry. "He must be destroyed, Herr Fischer! You must make sure he is shot!"

Albert bit his lip. He didn't really know how to respond to her demand right now. He knew that a dog like that ought not to be allowed to live, but with one word of her explanation the matter had become more complicated. That the owner was Ukrainian made everything much more difficult. Albert was even more confused than he was a few minutes ago about how to proceed so he excused himself. He decided to find out more about this Ukrainian and his dog at the cooperative.

In general, the Germans had good relations with the Ukrainians since both communities considered the Poles to be their oppressors. But when it came to civil matters, the Ukrainians, even those who lived close to the German communities, did not want to be subject to German officials and German rules. Most Ukrainians considered Germans to be visitors in their country. And visitors do not make rules in your home.

At the store, the clerk told Albert that the boy had not provoked the dog, unless being frightened and running away was a provocation. The old Ukrainian had a hard time pulling the dog off the boy and then he just left him lying there. So the clerk had carried him home. The old man was more worried about getting his dog away than about the child. It was that shiftless Trepenko.

Albert had seen the both of them in Antonufka several times and hadn't taken much interest except to notice that the dog was always angry and the man seemed to enjoy being a nuisance. Their visits to town were barely tolerated. Even though he was kept at the end of a heavy rope the dog was always snarling and the old man insisted on taking him everywhere, even into the store. Right now that was all incidental to Albert. The most concerning fact was that Trepenko was Ukrainian. It would have been much simpler if he were German. Knowing that sooner or later he would have to confront him, Albert wanted to know where he lived.

A customer in the store knew about him. He was a recluse. Trepenko lived on a farm a few kilometers south of the town. The local Germans still called it the Arndt farm, after the family that had originally cleared the land but had been sent to Siberia by the Tzar. Trepenko had claimed the land in 1915 and because the Arndts all died on the death trains, his claim went uncontested. But Trepenko was apparently still suspicious that the Germans wanted to take his land away. Some of the villagers thought it strange that he came to Antonufka to shop when he felt like that, but when they asked him why, he laughed and said, "I don't want to buy from the Pole."

Albert did not look forward to talking to Trepenko but he couldn't think what else he should do. A dog that tore flesh should be put to death. Normally, the owner of such an animal did that himself without any intervention. But Albert suspected that Trepenko was not likely to do that. Perhaps the Ukrainian might respond to a request to leave the dog at home. He was sure that the man would not react kindly to an order from a German so he would have to choose his words carefully. It was worth a chance. Still, as he rode off to the Ukrainian's home, Albert reassured himself several times that his pistol was loaded.

Five kilometers to the south of Antonufka lay the old Arndt farm. More than twenty years after its original owner had left it, it was in desperate need of repair. "That's what happens," Albert told himself, "when these people get something for nothing." He had only a slightly higher opinion of Ukrainians than Poles. Even the fields lay fallow and that was unforgivable in Albert's opinion. He would have given anything for such a piece of land. Properly maintained and cultivated, it was enough to be a real farm. But only the land looked like it was worth saving.

It was obvious that the man lived alone. There were no curtains and the windows were dirty where the glass was still intact, and where it wasn't, the openings weren't even boarded up. The roof sagged and probably leaked. Even the counter weight of the well had rotted and broken. There was nothing to put Albert's mind at ease that he would get an easy reception, just the nagging feeling that Trepenko's attitude would match his decaying surroundings.

The large red mongrel was tied to the front of the house. He was already barking wildly, straining at the end of his rope as Albert came up the short lane. His teeth were huge and Albert had seen what damage they could do. He placed his hand on the butt of the gun. Trepenko, hearing the racket came and stood on the stoop. Albert felt disgust at his dirty appearance, thinking he was a perfect match for his fierce dog. It was easy for him to let his prejudices take over. "Lodrak," was the apt description. It meant slob, and it was all he could think of to describe the man. It was going to be hard for him to hide his contempt.

The man had a big grin on his face but it was definitely not friendly. It was more of a smirk than a grin, as if to say, I know what you are here for but I don't have to listen to you. He kicked his dog aside and sat down, perhaps to show how casually he treated the German constable's visit.

"What do you want German?" Trepenko asked in Ukrainian, still smiling through his dirty teeth.

"Your dog mauled a boy in Antonufka," Albert answered in Polish. He understood Ukrainian but in difficult situations he was more confident speaking in Polish.

"A little bite," Trepenko replied mockingly.

It annoyed Albert that there wasn't a hint of remorse in the man's voice.

"Your dog didn't just bite the boy, he almost took off his leg," Albert replied sharply.

"It's nothing. A small scratch."

Albert shook his head. It irritated him that the man was mocking the injury to the child. It grated on him so much that all his affectations of diplomacy vanished. "You ought to get rid of the dog, he's dangerous."

Trepenko's face muscles tightened. "It wasn't his fault," he spat. He meant to defend his dog at all costs. "The boy teased him. He threw stones."

"That's not true. There were witnesses. The boy did nothing."

"Germans," Trepenko spat between his dirty teeth. "Liars.'

"Don't bring your dog to town again!" Albert found himself shouting. His plans to request a favor from the old man had flown as soon as he lost his temper. "If it happens again, you'll pay."

"You don't scare me, German. You don't make the laws here. I'll take my dog where I want."

"You don't need to bring your dog to Antonufka."

"I need him for protection."

The answer caught Albert off guard. "Protection? From what? From little boys?"

"From Germans who want to steal my farm!"

It took Albert a few seconds to understand the man's answer. "You want me to believe that someone would hurt you for this?" There was contempt in his voice and Trepenko understood it immediately. The Ukrainian's face grew red with anger at the insult and he grabbed his dog's rope. That was the signal for the mongrel to start lurching and growling at Albert.

Albert jumped back, almost falling over. That made Trepenko laugh again. "Are you afraid of my puppy?" he ridiculed. He patted the dog's head which made him settle down, then he turned and shouted, "Get out of here German before I let him have you for supper."

Albert retreated. When he was safely on his horse he called out one more time to Trepenko, "Don't bring the dog to town."

He knew he had missed his chance. If he had controlled his anger he might have been able to convince the man not to bring his dog to town again. But he knew Ukrainians were fiercely independent people who recognized no authority but their own. He already knew the probable outcome of this impasse.

Back in Antonufka, he only stopped off at the cooperative before he returned home.The next week Albert was in town early on Wednesday morning. He sat quietly in a chair in the corner of the store and waited. It was about eleven o'clock when the clerk alerted him that Trepenko was coming. His red dog was tugging at his leash and panting as he brought him right up the center of the road. It was an act of defiance. A challenge that Albert knew he had to meet.

Quietly, Albert came out and stood at the door. Trepenko saw him and began to laugh. "Oh see Antonufka," he shouted mockingly, "Trepenko is coming with his big bad dog. You better hide before he gets you." The town's people were stopping to stare at the absurd figure in the middle of the road. They had all heard about the boy and they knew their constable was waiting.

Albert was sure the Cossack was drunk. He was baiting the dog with the kind of abandon that only a drunkard would attempt. Repeatedly, he ordered him to attack and then jerked the rope back hard. But the dog didn't know it was a game, he became angrier with every jerk of the rope. A couple of times it looked like the big red would break loose. It was dangerous. The dog was seething and foaming with anger.

The commotion in the street was attracting more and more people. Frightened women chased their children indoors but most people couldn't take their eyes off the mesmerizing scene. They wanted to see what their new constable would do.

With a crowd building, Albert felt he was under scrutiny too. He could see them out of the corner of his eye and thought he knew what they were thinking. Should he take the initiative or should he wait and react to whatever Trepenko did next. He decided that it was foolish to wait. Something was going to happen and it was clear to Albert that the onus was on him to avert a disaster. There was only one way to do it. As Trepenko yanked on his dog's rope once more, Albert drew his gun and held it to the back of his leg, out of sight. He needed to end this stupidity.

The dog grew even more furious as he saw the man approaching. He snarled and lurched like a demon, practically strangling himself on the rope. It was all that old Trepenko could do to hold him. Albert prayed that his owner could hold onto him a little longer. "Come to play with my dog?" Trepenko asked. "Want me to let him go, German? He'll rip you a-..."

The threat was all Albert needed to hear. Trepenko had his words cut short. Three shots rang out and the crowd gasped. His nerves were quivering. He expected to have to empty his pistol into the creature, but it dropped so quickly he stopped after three shots. The crowd was silent. It was almost anticlimactic. When the astonished Ukrainian looked up, Albert had the gun pointed right at his head.

It was hard for him to feel any sympathy for Trepenko. "Get your dog out of here and do your shopping somewhere else from now on. We don't want your business any more," Albert told him, and walked away. Quickly, however, he scrambled onto his horse and rode home. He wanted to leave before anyone saw how he was shaking.

Riding past his meager little grainfield on his way home, Albert stopped and looked at all the work he had neglected. Without saying a word to his wife and mother he went into his fields and began to plow. He was only a week behind the season and his farm was so small it would be easy to catch up. He couldn't tell his family why it had become so urgent. It just seemed important to get to the things he had been avoiding. It was several days before Albert returned to Antonufka.

It was a contradiction that Albert had no idea how to resolve. After the incident with Trepenko, he felt at the same time less adequate and more confident. His dilemma was that on the one hand he was not sure he liked making such decisions, especially when they required him to use his gun. But he had also learned that he was very capable of making them and accepting their consequences. It was a curious sensation for Albert to have such odd and complicated feelings. On the other hand, the experience had not affected him so deeply that he spent a lot of time dwelling on his feelings. Feelings, after all, were just that. They come and go.

In Zeperow-Antonufka, it was remembered as the day that the constable shot the mad dog. Trepenko's dog wasn't really rabid but people remembered how frenzied it was and how it foamed at the mouth when it died. It was mad enough for them. They were proud of their new constable and it proved that their council had chosen correctly. Kantor Himmel gloated about the selection, explaining it was the best decision he had ever made. Even Johann Fischer withdrew his unvoiced objections.

As Albert resumed his duties, with the renewed understanding that his primary responsibility lay with his farm and family, he also found his status as local hero had grown. Consequently, people came to him to solve all kinds of problems, few of which logically came under the purview of the village constable. Besides trying to keep the peace, negotiating between feuding neighbors, chasing strange dogs and stranger strangers out of town, people asked him to assist in their dealing with the countess and help them in their livestock trading. Young men in particular came to him to introduce them to the parents of prospective brides. It stretched the traditional role of the constable almost to the point that he was more of a magistrate and advisor than a policeman. Strangely enough, only one person began to feel that Albert was beginning to usurp his responsibilities. That was Kantor Himmel.

In the fall the strangest request of all for his services came from the Countess Viteranno. She sent him a note and Albert reacted as if he had been summoned by the Tzar. In the midst of his harvest he dropped everything, washed, and rode to her estate. The note was a complete surprise. In the past he had always brought issues to her attention and so he assumed that it was an urgent problem if she felt the need to summon him. He only hoped that Hermann Martin would not be there.

The countess was very agitated. She sat in a chair beside him looking very nervous. Then she stood up again and paced about the room. She was struggling for words. Albert couldn't guess what she wanted, but it wasn't his place to question her.

"Herr Fischer," she finally started, and that perked him up, she usually called him Albert. She had never been so formal with him. Now he knew this was serious. But she let that beginning drop almost as soon as she said it. A deep breath followed and she began again, less formally, “Albert, let me be direct. I know how you detest Hermann Martin.”

Albert was puzzled. It was no secret he hated Martin.

“I used to believe it was just jealousy but I know better now,” she continued. “Hermann is trying to steal my land.”

It was the easiest thing in the world for Albert to believe, but he couldn’t understand why she was telling him. There were more powerful officials than he, and the Countess had better access to them. “I believe you,” he said, “but the Polish police have more authority than I do.”

“I cannot go to the police,” she blurted out impatiently. Then she explained quickly, “It’s too complicated to explain. I asked you here because I believe you are the one person who can understand how dangerous the man is, and you are not afraid of him.”

He nodded. He hardly noticed the flattery. What she said was true and he was glad someone else had finally acknowledged it.

“If I do not find a way to destroy him, I will lose everything.” The countess was trembling.

“What do you intend to do?” Albert asked.

“I don’t know how else to say it. I have to find some way to kill Martin.” She put her hands on his hands in a most tender way, as if she were comforting him in a time of difficult decision. “My only hope is that you will do it for me.”

Albert had a hard time responding. He was unprepared for her request. “I don’t like Martin,” he was finally able to say, “but I can’t kill him.”

“You don’t understand how desperate I am,” she said, squeezing his hands more tightly. Her voice was filled with an unusual tremor. “I have no other way out. Don’t you see? With him out of the way I could arrange to have your lost property restored.”

Albert was startled. When he compared it to what she was asking him to do, he finally understood how small that parcel of land really was that Hermann had taken. He shook his head. “That piece of land is hardly worth going to jail for.”

"There are other things I can do for you. I can cancel your mortgage. With Martin gone I will need someone to manage my lands. Albert, I would be forever grateful."

"There is no one I'd rather see dead. I've dreamed of killing him. But no, I won't murder him. The risk is too great. Everyone knows how I hate him. I would be the first one suspected."

"Albert, it wouldn't have to be murder. In your duties there are times when you have to use your gun. If Martin were to attack me you would be perfectly justified. It would be your obligation to defend me."

He wondered how far she had planned this.

"It's still murder, even if we got away with it we would know that. I don't think I can."

"Well then, if it is on moral grounds that you refuse, then there is nothing more to say. I'd forgotten that you peasants actually believe in God. But what will you do if he gains title to my property. What will he do to your little community then?"

Albert left, but he had to find his own way out. She seemed more distraught than ever when he left her. All the way home he thought and rethought what he had just passed up. He almost rationalized his objections away. It would hardly be a loss. No one liked him anyway, there wasn't anyone he hadn't offended. It was only justice that he get his land back. But in the end, it was still murder and he knew it.

In the summer of 1937 Kantor Himmel left the position he had held in Zeperow-Antonufka for fifteen years. Albert was happy to see the officious and unimaginative man go back to his beloved Germany. He had been pompous and arrogant, but worst of all, condescending. He had been born and educated in Germany, and in his opinion, if it wasn't German it was inferior. That label was also applied to Germans born outside of Germany. Still, it was with mixed feelings that Albert found himself at the train station in Lutzk in his official capacity to pick up the new Kantor/teacher.

Generally this position had been eliminated by the Polish government in Volhynia. When the Poles required instruction in Polish in all schools, and that teachers be certified by the government, they ended the traditional Kantor/teacher position throughout most of Volhynia. When a community was lucky enough to find a certified teacher, who also qualified to serve as Kantor, they grabbed him. This new one was not from Germany. That was no longer allowed, but he was from Silesia, which as all Germans knew, was German territory temporarily under the Polish flag. Albert expected no more from him than the old one and he was not excited to be in his company for the ride home from Lutzk. He was further dismayed when he saw the youth of the man he was picking up. He looked like he was barely in his twenties. The only thing worse than an old arrogant German was a snotty-nosed, young, arrogant German and he was set not to like the young teacher at all.

However, on the way to Antonufka, Albert found that Erich Winkler was nothing like Himmel. He did not talk about himself, nor his education, rather he was full of questions. He wanted to know about the town, the children and the school and he was very interested in where the best fishing was. When Albert passed a stream that he knew was particularly good for trout, the young Kantor asked him to stop. It amused Albert at first as they walked along the bank examining likely fishing holes and he looked on in amazement when the young fellow rolled up his pant legs and waded in. He was beginning to like him. They laughed the rest of the way into town and Albert brought him straight home for dinner.

It was not stretching the point to say that his new position had a profound effect on Albert, but the change was limited to certain areas of his life, while Julianna and Alwine were still faced with the superficial side of him. At home he barked out orders as if they were all his servants. His wife became annoyed at her husband's new found arrogance and told him so. She was also disturbed because God had neglected to provide the fall that he deserved. She feared that the longer God waited, the greater the fall would have to be to shake him loose from his overbearing attitude. But there was nothing she could do.

One warm afternoon, Albert came riding home sitting high in his saddle looking ever so proud of himself. Julianna was standing outside the door getting some fresh air. She could see him coming down the road. It bothered her no end to see him treating his family so lightly. As he rode up to the gate he shouted to her. "Give me a drink, old woman," he bawled without even the common courtesy he would use in the tavern to order a beer. Julianna was insulted. "What is it that you want from this Old Woman?" she asked. "Water! I'm thirsty!" Julianna retrieved the bucket of drinking water from the house and held it for Albert. "It's too heavy for an old woman to lift any higher," she said. As Albert leaned down to take the dipper, Julianna grabbed his arm and pulled him out of his saddle. With a yelp he tumbled from his perch. He reached out to his mother to break his fall, but she only backed away.

"Why did you do that?" he yelled, holding onto his wrist. He hoped it was not broken.

"For calling your mother an old woman, you pompous ass."

His wife gave Albert no more pity than his mother had as she wrapped his sprained hand. "You've been walking around with your head in the air. What do you expect? No one can stand you anymore."

Albert still couldn't comprehend why his wife and mother complained. He was working again, harder than ever, and if he had found something that allowed him a little pride he couldn't see anything wrong with it. In fact, he believed he had changed. Spending time with August Weiss and Erich Winkler and listening to their conversations had caused him to think more deeply about his community, and its problems. It was not the kind of change Alwine and Julianna were looking for, but there were others who were astounded.

Johann Fischer was more amazed that anyone about his brother. He was flabbergasted when Albert came asking questions about the effects of Government policy on the Germans. Johann was more than happy to explain and was pleased when he saw his brother working to understand. August and Irene Weiss saw the change too. A friendship that seemed to be dying was saved as Albert delved into the issues they thought he was oblivious to. He went to meetings with them and stayed long into the night, talking.

As Albert stayed away from home longer and longer his wife found the burden of raising the family resting on her shoulders. She had another baby coming and she worked long hours. Julianna helped as much as she could but her worn out body required a lot of rest. Alwine couldn't understand her husband's neglect of his family, especially since they were so poor. Albert's work as the village constable did little to advance the family's welfare. Her own garden added much more. She spent a lot of time there. It was her hobby, her therapy and her salvation.

But the only way that Alwine had to get any personal money was to raise chickens. Usually it was easy. All she had to do was allow a brood hen to hide her eggs in a corner of the yard and hatch them at her content. However, once in a while, for some unknown reason a hen would abandon the nest she had been incubating. When Alwine discovered this, she gathered the eggs and collected them in the kitchen. She wrapped the eggs in warm towels but was careful to let them cool for small periods and turned them constantly. Despite the work involved her success rate was very high so she continued at it. The money bought her fabric for dresses and window curtains and hairbrushes, all the incidentals that men fail to budget for.

Hertha loved the little fuzzy feathered chicks. One day as they were hatching, her mother was out in the garden and Julianna was sleeping, but this didn't bother Hertha at all. She had the experience needed to take care of those little new lives. As they hatched in their little box in the warmest part of the kitchen, she watched them dry off and become fluffy little chirpers. There wasn't room for them all in the box as they dried out and Hertha became afraid that they would trample the newer hatchlings to death. Knowing that the chicks' primary need was warmth, she carefully placed them in her apron, one by one.

When Alwine came in from the field, Hertha proudly opened the cradle of her apron to show her mother what she had done. The shock hit her as one by one the chicks tumbled onto the floor. They had suffocated. Alwine, already tired and upset with her absent husband, was ready to come apart. By the door there was a willow switch that the boys used to herd the cows out of the pasture. She grabbed it. It wasn't just a swat, it was a blow, but it was meant for her soft behind. However, Hertha twisted so quickly that the full force of the blow came across her face like a whip. She ran out of the house screaming.

Alwine sat down and cried. She didn't realize how hard she had hit her daughter so her remorse went elsewhere. Her first thought was about the zlotys she had lost, and the second was for the carelessness that her husband would accuse her of in the loss of the chicks. Frustrated, she set to work cleaning up the dead chicks, but as she picked up the downy balls she noticed that some of them were reviving. Within minutes, seven previously dead chicks were running across her kitchen floor. She had acted too hastily.

She went out to look for her daughter and heard Hertha crying somewhere in the garden and her heart sank. It had been half an hour. Hertha never cried unless she was really in pain. "Hertha, come inside," she called. The wailing continued and a lump got stuck in Alwine's throat. How seriously had she hurt the girl?

Alwine searched the garden for her precious daughter. The wailing came from behind the currant bushes and Alwine ran to her. She picked her up and saw a huge red welt across her face running across her forehead and continuing down her cheek. She had to pry the little girl's hand away to look at it properly and when she did, Alwine began to cry herself. With Hertha cradled in her arms she ran into the house and laid the girl on her own bed. There she washed the sore with a cold wet cloth and literally bathed the surprised little girl in her own tears.

When she had done everything possible to comfort her daughter, Alwine cooked her favorite treat, pudding. But Alwine could not wash away her remorse so quickly. The next day she asked the little girl again if there was anything she wanted. Hertha pursed her lips and put her index finger on her chin, she was seriously thinking. "Well, another one of those puddings would be nice," she said so sweetly that her mother almost laughed.

For three days Hertha got everything she asked of her mother. She enjoyed her mother's remorse very much, but the only thing she could think of was more pudding. To her surprise, she found that pudding every day was too much of a good thing. Besides, she was beginning to feel guilty of taking advantage of her mother.

It had taken him years to develop an interest, but now Albert Fischer quickly came to the realization of something his neighbors and friends had known for a long time; German culture in Volhynia was under assault as it was in all parts of Poland. The Polish government was not about to accept anything less than complete assimilation. Polish language, Polish education and Polish commerce was to supplant all German institutions. If possible, they even wanted to make Germans worship in the Polish language. War had been declared on all things German.

Unlike the Poles of the last century, who had to endure their persecutions alone, the Germans of Poland had an ally to the west. Their fatherland, although humbled in the Great War and humiliated by the Treaty of Versailles, was determined to be a power again. It had already recovered enough to flex its muscles, making noises about a primarily German part of Czechoslovakia called Sudetenland. That, of course, made the Poles nervous. But it was the belligerent leader of that resurgent country who concerned them most. He presented himself not just as the leader of his nation, but as the leader of all German speaking peoples and particularly the oppressed minorities of eastern Europe. In exchange for his support he appealed to them to arouse their feelings for their native land. As Adolf Hitler made his overtures to these people, the Poles had already assumed their German citizens were just waiting to betray them.

In response, the Poles intensified their attempts to assimilate the Germans. The Germans interpreted the Polish reaction as blatant persecution. The effect was that they were driven both emotionally and philosophically into the waiting arms of Adolf Hitler, feeling that only the German government had the willpower and the strength to protect them. Many Germans living in Poland joined Hitler's party. To them the term "Nazi" had no negative connotation. It was only the abbreviation of the name of a political party.

Many of the men in Zeperow and Antonufka joined. August Weiss was one of the first, as also was Ewald Hartenberger. Erich Winkler signed up and convinced Albert to join too. Even Johann Fischer felt it was the best thing to do. They had no idea that the man who presented himself as their savior was a madman.

Throughout the latter part of the decade the Volhynian-Germans considered themselves to be under siege. It was an unthinkable affront to be expected to become Polish and they fought against it any way they could. The ties they had to their German heritage were reinforced, sometimes subconsciously. Alwine was pleased that her husband attended Sunday services at the Bet-Haus more regularly, but did not associate it with his need to feel more German. The women, though forbidden to conduct their church auxiliary meetings in the German language, carried on anyway, and were more intense in their attention to duty. More time was given in elementary schools to the study of the German language especially since it was forbidden in the higher schools. Babies born in the era were given distinctively German names. Albert and Alwine named their third son, born in the fall of 1937, Einhardt. The Vohlynians became some of the most staunch Germans in the world.

Since the Volhynian-Germans associated themselves with Germany more than ever, it was with awe that they comprehended the German annexation of the Sudetenland in 1938. With that event, the Germans of Volhynia allowed their own expectations of a German rescue to crystallize. Despite the cautions of more sober people, many in Volhynia talked openly of their hope. Hearts raced at the prospect of a German invasion, even though Germany had never had any claims to this territory in the far east of Poland.

Now the Polish and German communities in Poland were truly galvanized in their hatred and suspicion. The Polish became fearful of Nazi aggression and distrustful of the indigenous German population, while more and more Polish Germans listened to the speeches of Adolf Hitler. Albert came with his friends to the Bet-Haus, where Erich Winkler set up a radio. They listened, entranced as the German Chancellor spoke of the great destiny of the German people, yet what interested them most was his offer of help to the Germans living under oppression. They could not understand then, that in his hands they were only pawns in an ageless European game.

Seventeen

In 1939, even the Volhynians knew that war was inevitable. Few of them knew anything of the shuttling back and forth of diplomats and cabinet ministers in those final months that did nothing to prevent the war. Neither did they know of the meeting in Moscow between Hitler's minister and the Russian leader, Joseph Stalin, which sealed the fate of not only Poland but also the Germans of Volhynia. In fact, many Vohlynians looked on the coming war as one of liberation for them. Little did they suspect that their savior was coming to do what neither the Tzar nor Pilsudski had been able to do.

That September, as the tanks rolled across the western border of Poland and up from the Sudetenland, Poland immediately lashed out at its traitorous German population. Two policemen came to the home of Albert Fischer in the night. They pounded on the latched door but did not wait for an answer before kicking it in. "Albert Fischer, you are under arrest for treason," one yelled, while the other held a gun to his head. They grilled him for a half an hour about his anti-Polish activities as he sat in a kitchen chair, frightened. Their questions were accusations and all his answers were wrong, but it didn't help him that he began with a lie.

"Are you a Nazi?"

"No," he answered out of fear.

"That's a lie. We know you are!"

"You are a spy!"

"No."

"Another lie!"

"No, I'm not a spy."

"We know very well that you're a spy. One of your traitorous relations was apprehended nearby. He confessed everything."

"No, it's a lie. I don't understand."

"Who are your comrades in the Nazi party? Whom do you report to? Have you used your position to gain information for the Germans?"

"No! No! No!"

"You are lying!"

"No!"

"Why should we believe you? You've lied to us already. We know you are a Nazi."

"I was afraid."

"You might as well confess. We know all about you. You have been working with a convicted traitor."

"I don't know what you are talking about. I don't know any such person."

"Does the name Edmund Frey mean anything to you?"

"My brother!" Alwine gasped, "we haven't heard from him in years."

"Shut up woman!"

"We've been watching you Fischer. You passed information to your brother-in-law about Polish defenses."

"No!" Albert was dumbfounded. He had no idea where they got such information. "I don't know anything. I have no information."

"Don't lie to us again! Where did you get the information? Who is your contact? What is your source?"

"I don't know," Albert was sweating, "I never did anything like that."

Alwine watched from the door of the bedroom paralyzed with fear. In her arms she clutched her six week old daughter Else while Hertha buried her face in her dress, terrified. Edmund and Ewald watched motionlessly from under the kitchen table where they had crept to hide. They sat with their eyes riveted on their father; they had never seen him afraid before. "Please don't let them shoot him," Edmund whispered to God, hardly hearing his own words.

Julianna put down her precious little two-year-old grandson, Einhardt, and left him screaming as she kneeled before the interrogators, pleading for her son. "Please don't hurt my son. He would not do such a thing! He's a simple farmer."

They ignored her pleading, bound up Albert's hands and dragged him out of the door. It was the beginning of terror for Albert and his family, as they wondered if they would ever see their father again. He was hauled off to Antonufka and thrown into the Bet-Haus. There were several German men already there, Kantor Winkler, most of the Kantorrat, and other prominent men of the community. They looked at each other with stone-cold faces trying to hide the fear they could not speak. There were memories of 1915.

"It's Russia all over again," one of them finally found the courage to say, and they all agreed. "If I get out of this, I'm going to take my family back to Germany, I wish we had never come here," said another. He nor his parents had ever seen Germany.

Before long, every male leader of the community was in the room. Johann Fischer was dragged in only a few minutes after Albert and he was followed by August Weiss. Even Ewald Hartenberger whose only political adventure ever, was joining the Nazi party to be with his friends, was arrested. In all there were twenty men. A few of them showed signs of bruising, they were the ones who had resisted. The police made them sit down in the center of the hall with their hands tied behind their backs.

It was Ewald Hartenberger who spotted him in the doorway. At first he thought that he had been arrested too, but that didn't make sense, and then he noticed that his hands were untied and that he was laughing and joking with the Polish policemen. Ewald nudged Albert with his shoulder and nodded his head in the direction of the front door. It was no surprise to Albert that Hermann Martin was with the Poles; it was where he would have expected to find him. Whatever he was telling the policemen, it was not likely to be good for the prisoners.

The men were left tied up all night. Albert tried to sleep but he was too uncomfortable or too scared to even doze. Several of the men lamented that they had been accused of treason and feared that they would be shot as traitors. Johann Fischer tried to assure them that the Poles intended only to throw them into jail. "There will have to be a trial before they could shoot us; this is Poland, not Russia." No one was comforted.

In the morning the men were loaded onto a truck and hauled away. Martin was there again, mocking and ridiculing. "Well how proud are you now of Germany," he called, and "Shall I tell your wives to write you at Bereza Kartuska? What do you think of your Nazi party now?" Many of the prisoners including Albert vowed not to forget this day. As Albert looked around, he saw that every one of his comrades had his eyes on Martin. "How do you suppose they knew who the members of the party were?" August Weiss asked, looking at Hermann.

"It's not like we kept it a secret," Johann answered. "We did it openly." He was always the voice of reason, even when one wasn't wanted.

As they passed out of sight of the Bet-Haus Albert asked August, "What is Bereza Kartuska?"

August gave his friend a painful look and shook his head, Albert wasn't sure if he didn't know or didn't want to answer. Johann Fischer, however, did not hesitate to explain. "It's a prison camp. Pilsudski built it to house his political enemies and Ukrainian terrorists."

"I heard they torture people there." Ewald Hartenberger said, looking a little pale.

"Those are just rumors," Johann interjected, "there is no need to believe them."

"I believe them," one of the other prisoners said. "I heard you don't ever get out of Bereza Kartuska."

"Johann is right," August agreed, "those are only rumors. Besides, we are not terrorists or political prisoners. There is no reason to torture us."

Albert was not so optimistic. "The Poles think we are traitors."

But the truck did not take them north. They headed down the road to Lutzk and there were thrown into the largest prison in the city. Every cell was crowded with Germans and Ukrainians.

In the prison the interrogators continued their attempts to terrorize the prisoners into making confessions of treason. Albert was questioned several times over the course of the two days they were there. Always they began by saying they knew everything and he soon realized that they said it because they knew nothing. There was nothing to know. He was more careful now to tell the truth whatever they asked. Whenever he was tempted, all he had to do was think of his wife. She was always quoting the Bible, "The truth will make you free." He was punched several times but he had nothing to tell them. He could not tell if they believed him.

Soon the Poles realized that they had cast their net too wide, but they did not want to release the German men, believing they would run to help the invading army. They would send their prisoners to camps that were being hastily thrown up to hold them. However, four of them were considered dangerous enough to be sent to Bereza Kartuska: Erich Winkler, August Weiss and Johann and Albert Fischer.

Two hundred kilometers north of Volhynia the truck stopped inside the marshaling yard of the infamous prison camp, Bereza Kartuska. It was a stark place with austere wooden barracks that until now had housed only a few suspected Ukrainian terrorists. But its numbers were about to swell and the activity of the place was more indicative of a busy construction project than a prison camp. The Volhynian men, however, had only to look around at the intimidating machine-gun towers and high fences of tightly strung barbed wire to know where they were.

As the farmers stepped off the truck they were lined up and a guard yelled out the rules of the camp. He had an irritating, squeaky voice and his tone was full of anger. Yet through the anger and shouting he kept a twisted smile on his face, and pounded a rubber truncheon into the palm of his left hand as he talked. Albert's eyes were fixed on that instrument as the soldier slammed it over and over again with every point he made. Soon the guard's hand was beginning to turn red. Yet he continued on, seemingly oblivious to the pain.

There was one rule he was intent on teaching the new inmates. It seemed to delight him to drive home the point, twisting his wry smile even more, while pounding the hard rubber into his hand. "Prisoners have no rights!" he blared. When he finished, the palm of his hand was blazing red. Albert wondered what a man who could inflict such pain on himself was willing to do to others. As if he had heard what Albert was thinking, the guard walked up to Erich Winkler, and without warning slammed the truncheon into his mid-section, doubling him over. Erich fell to the ground struggling for air. The guard stepped back, waiting for some sign of protest and seeing none, he smiled. Now he knew he had explained his most important rule well. His assault on Erich Winkler was only a demonstration of the pain he could inflict, but for now he was satisfied that it had reinforced his lecture.

"Pick him up!" he shouted, indicating August and Albert who stood right beside their friend. They were ordered to carry Erich into Barrack No. 3. Each man was issued a blanket and assigned a bunk, but within a few minutes they were all hauled out again. It was the same guard again who had assaulted Erich that herded them out to start work. He set himself at the door and glared as each of the new men came out. Though he had caught his breath, Erich was wary as he passed the guard with his insidious smile, hoping he would leave him alone. There was no need to worry. The man was looking for a new victim. He enjoyed spreading the pain around. He tripped Albert as he stepped out of the door and then kicked him in the ribs. "That's for being clumsy," he said. Albert shuffled off to work, holding his side.

That night, a handful of bread and a cup of water was their supper. One man from Lutzk commented, "It could be worse. We could all be fighting in the Polish army against the Germans." Then he added as an afterthought, "They'll be slaughtered you know. The Germans will beat them into the dust." But Johann cautioned his group, "Be careful, talk like that will only get you into trouble. Don't give him a reason." He smacked his right fist into his left palm to indicate whom he meant.

"Be careful of Smiley," Erich Winkler winced. From that time on, barrack No. 3 had a name for the guard with the twisted smile.

There was plenty of work in those first few days as the Poles were in a hurry to erect more housing for the German traitors they were collecting. And when trucks started arriving half way through the morning the urgency of the construction was evident. Each new load of prisoners was indoctrinated by Smiley in the same manner that the men from Zeperow had experienced. However, not all of the new prisoners were set to work. There were not enough materials to keep them all busy. Those who were unlucky enough not to have work were assembled in the yard and marched. Hour after hour they marched in a circle, several men abreast. Those who were working on the barracks were warned not to look at them unless they wanted to join the relentless march.

It was on his third day at the camp while he was working on a roof that Albert spotted a prisoner who looked familiar. The gaunt man was working at nailing siding onto the building right next to his. There was something familiar in the profile but the short glimpse that Albert caught wasn't enough to identify him. He was terribly thin and it appeared as if he had been in prison for a long time. Initially, Albert shrugged it off thinking that it was only the haunting look of starvation that attracted his attention. Twice during the day Albert caught a rubber truncheon across his back because a guard thought he was idling while he was staring at the willowy figure. The third time, Smiley caught him staring when he was supposed to be working and he showed no mercy. With a bleeding lip and aching head Albert joined the march around the compound.

That night he asked his friends if they had recognized the man who he supposed was some long lost member of their community. No one else from the Zeperow contingent had noticed him. Despite a hard day's work Albert slept uneasily. His mind kept struggling to put into focus the face that was so mysterious and yet halfway familiar. He began to think it must have been an illusion and hoped it was not some eerie view of the future that he was seeing.

It was a relief when he saw the prisoner again the next day. Now he at least knew that he wasn't going insane. Albert pointed the man out to several of his comrades, but they only glanced at the stranger and shook their heads. No one remembered him. Later in the day Albert was working beside his brother and when no guard was watching, Johann whispered, "I saw him."

"Then you know him?" Albert blurted, unable to control his excitement. "Who is he?"

"Shh," Johann cautioned, "the guards." He looked around and whispered, "It's your wife's brother, Edmund."

Albert was stunned, but immediately he knew that Johann was right, it was Edmund. It had been several years since Albert had seen his wife's favorite brother. He knew that there had been some falling out between him and his parents. He had supposed it regarded the boy's failure at school but even Alwine seemed to be in the dark about the details. Albert had laughed insensitively when he heard that Edmund had left the university. He told his wife, "I knew it would happen. Farm boys don't belong in a university." The statement had made Alwine angry. She missed her brother and couldn't bear it when her husband belittled him. It had all been mysterious but Albert had remained unconcerned. Edmund was too much like his own brother. One of him in his life was enough. Yet now the boy was at Bereza Kartuska, looking very much like he had been there for a long time.

When the new barracks were finished there were several thousand Germans and hundreds of Ukrainians interred in the camp. The guards kept them busy with the march. From sun up to sun down they marched on the parade ground with only short rest periods and little sustenance. On particularly hot days they were given water, but only a spoonful at a time. There was only one meal all day. They ate it in their barracks at night. Usually it was bread, but sometimes there was a watered-down soup that tasted slightly of chicken and potato. It was a monotonous routine and many of them prayed that the German army would soon be there.

Early, while the men were still in good spirits, they joked about the conditions, but they did so in the relative safety of their barracks. Still feeling pain in his belly after eating, Albert complained contemptuously, "We should ask them to leave the chicken in the pot a minute longer tomorrow!"

"Impossible!" Erich replied, "That chicken has to last for the whole war."

"When the German army gets here, I'm going to find that chicken and stuff it down the cook's throat," Albert shot back, "Let him choke on it all the way to hell." It felt good to laugh but the feeling that the German army would soon set them free felt even better. Spirits remained high through the first week.

Several days later, while Albert was marching, he caught sight of Edmund again. He seemed even thinner now, if that was possible. But when he saw his brother-in-law going to the latrines Albert raised his hand and asked to go relieve himself. The guard shook his head. He wasn't interested in walking all the way across the compound to the latrines, but Smiley said, "I'll take you."

It had become a game for some of the soldiers to take men to the latrine. It was an amusement many relished as a means of breaking the boring routine of their guard duty. The latrines were merely trenches dug on the far side of the parade ground away from the barracks. Simple wooden planks, only about twenty centimeters wide were laid across the trenches as precarious perches for the prisoners. The game was simple. In the time it took the guard to count to ten the inmate had to finish. If he wasn't off the plank by then, he took the risk of being knocked into the pit. The whole garrison would break out in laughter when that happened. Consequently, the men of Bereza Kartuska waited until the last minute, and learned to finish quickly. Unfortunately, no matter how fast they were, the guards only had to count faster in order to have their fun.

Albert ran across the parade ground as fast as he could with Smiley following, arriving at the latrines just behind Edmund. There was a furtive look of recognition in Edmund's eyes but no time to say anything. Edmund perched on a plank and Albert squatted facing him. Several times, Albert put his hand down on the plank to balance himself, putting out three fingers where Edmund could see them. Then quickly Albert stood up and jumped off the plank and said loudly in Polish, "False alarm." The cheated guard smacked him over his head. Distracted by Smiley and Albert, the guard watching Edmund failed to catch him before he was off the plank. A chorus of boos came from the machine gun towers.

Albert hadn't thought about Smiley's reaction when he shot off the plank so lightheartedly, but the pain in his head let him know he had disappointed the most hated and feared of the guards. He hadn't recovered from that blow when Smiley punched him in the face. "You think you can cheat me?" he yelled and shoved Albert backward toward the pits. "You can't play games with me, you swine." Another push and Albert would have been in the putrid mess, but just as he was resigned to the fall, the air raid siren began to shriek. German planes were overhead and all the prisoners were shoved into their barracks while the Bereza Kartuska guards aimed their rifles and machine guns uselessly at the sky. The planes did not attack.

Back in his bunk that night Albert was relieved to have escaped a close call. He couldn't understand what had made him take the risk. Nevertheless his main concern now, was whether Edmund had understood. It was impossible to know if he had even seen it, never mind understood it. All Albert was sure of was that Edmund had recognized him, so he forced himself to stay awake for a long time that night, just in case. He didn't come and Albert knew he couldn't. It was ridiculous, to expect a man in Edmund's condition to risk crossing the compound after curfew. It was not just ridiculous, it was impossible.

Smiley now watched Albert like a hawk. Several times each day, as the prisoners were marched around the compound, the guard would ask Albert if he wanted to relieve himself. Albert declined but the soldier persisted, "I'll get you yet." He smiled his crooked smile as if he were teasing a school mate.

Albert understood what the guards were trying to do when they offered him water as he marched with his comrades. He shook his head but they insisted. "Drink it all," they warned, "you can't waste water." Again and again they made him drink. While others were limited to a spoonful at a time, he got more than he wanted. He hoped to hold on until the night when he could relieve himself through a crack in the floor. He had listened as other men had done it, refusing to accept the humiliation of being knocked into the latrine. However, he couldn't control his muscles for as long as he hoped, and if he wet himself he knew that they would beat him. He raised his arm. The guard took him across the compound and even though he knew it would be hard to escape the pit, he was glad that Smiley would not get to see it.

After only a few seconds on the plank, however, his ears caught the familiar sound of a truncheon smacking into a bare hand. Albert bit his lower lip as Smiley took over and finished the count. But the guard gloated for a second too long before he raised his stick. Albert, facing the inevitable simply gave in. Abruptly he jumped into the pit and stood facing Smiley. He had wanted merely to show his resignation to the inescapable outcome, but to everyone else it seemed like a whimsical gesture of defiance. A huge roar of laughter came from the other guards and set Smiley's face on fire. He had been cheated again.

Angrier than ever, he swung his stick at Albert's head as he stood waist-high in the muck. Albert dodged and surprised himself by avoiding the blow. The humiliated guard, however, had stepped onto a plank to get at his victim and lost his balance when he swung so wildly. The board tilted and launched him sideways. He attempted to break his fall by stretching for another plank but it gave way too and he fell in, splashing the contents over the edge. Albert jumped out quickly and ran back across the compound. The guards couldn't control their laughter.

As soon as Smiley was cleaned up, he marched over to the parade ground and grabbed Albert. The crooked grin was gone. He was finished being easy on these Germans and dragged Albert away to play a different game, one that would teach him a lesson. "Time for you to earn your supper," Smiley said. Albert could only guess what he meant to do.

A hundred men were packed elbow to elbow in a very small room in the main building of the compound. Ostensibly, their reason for being there was to get their daily meal. They waited for hours, however. When the door was finally opened, tempers were already thin. One by one, three loaves of round bread were thrown into the room. Those willing to grab and claw, indiscriminately and quickly, got a little. The result was sickening. Eyes were gouged, punches were thrown, arms and legs were broken, hair pulled out and teeth lost. Frequently lives were lost too. The soldiers watching from the high windows cheered.

Albert had no idea what to expect. None of his group had ever been subjected to this form of torture, even though it was a daily event. After a few minutes' Albert asked what it was about. "It's about entertainment," he was told as the man pointed to the windows, "The guards like to laugh. If you put on a good show you get to come back, but if you don't, you don't eat."

Albert resolved to go hungry when he saw the slashing and flaying that erupted when the first and second loaf of bread were thrown in. The guards, their faces pressed into the glass, were laughing. He did not want to be their entertainment. But the third loaf came right at him as it ricocheted off outstretched arms and landed right in his hands. He was able to tear off a small piece before more desperate hands tore it away. He tried to shove the morsel into his mouth but before he clamped his teeth together a big Ukrainian had him by the throat and shoved his fingers into Albert's mouth. He pulled the bread out and almost took Albert's teeth with it.

The men remained cramped in the room all night. It had been intended as a lesson for Albert and it was. Yet the experience had a strange effect on him. He could never really explain it but for the rest of his time at Bereza Kartuska he was contemptuous of the Polish guards and Smiley in particular. It was almost as if he had determined that if this was the worst they could do, he could take it. He no longer feared the truncheon, the latrine, nor the room. He was, however, more determined to find and talk to Edmund.

When the Luftwaffe flew over the camp again panicking the garrison at Bereza Kartuska, Albert took advantage of the confusion. "All prisoners to their barracks," the guards were screaming. They were more afraid than the inmates of the menacing planes. Experience had shown the Germans below that the planes only toyed with the prison camp guards. They had no intention of dropping any bombs on the camp or strafing it with bullets. Still, the Poles made everyone take refuge, and prisoners were glad for the break; it was a welcome rest from the marching. Now, as Albert realized that the guards were more concerned about what was happening in the air, he knew his chance had come to look for Edmund. He ran from barrack to barrack trying to find his sister's brother. "Edmund Frey," he kept calling, but no one responded. Finally a Ukrainian said, "That's his bunk, but he's not here. He told me there was someone he had to find."

It hit Albert immediately. Edmund had gone looking for him at Barrack #3. He had understood. It frustrated him that only now, as he tried to get back to his own building, the guards tried to stop him. "But I'm in the wrong barrack!" Albert protested. "Never mind, just stay there!" they shouted, but they were more concerned about several stragglers than him. Albert pushed his way out again. "Hey you, get inside!" they ordered as he ran off. He paid no attention but dodged the confused guards who soon gave up chasing him.

"He's quick like a rabbit, that one," the soldiers laughed. Only Smiley took any real note of his insolence, saying, "I'll slow him down."

He reached the building out of breath and panting, yet his only thought was to look around for Edmund. He was sitting on his bunk talking to Johann. Albert embraced his brother-in-law and sat beside him, relieved and so out of breath he couldn't even ask the questions he had considered since he first noticed him. While he caught his breath, Johann and Edmund continued their discussion of the war and its likely outcome. "If I were to find you two in hell, you'd still be talking politics," Albert finally was able to say, shaking his head.

Edmund turned to him. "I'm sorry," he said, "seeing your brother brought back so many memories. How is my sister? How many children do you two have now?"

While the machine guns wailed vainly at the sky, the three of them remembered a cold February, now more than ten years old. Those days seemed so good now and they found themselves laughing aloud about the snow storm that had imprisoned them. Edmund recalled how upset his father was about the sow he had to slaughter to feed the wedding guests. But once that reminiscence was over, Albert sat back and watched as his brother and Edmund began their debate again. They seemed to have so much in common. They talked as if they were still sitting at his father-in-law's table at his wedding and the world had not changed, except that Edmund was sick and weak. But not even that could prevent the young man from exploring the reasons for this war and its ramifications with Johann.

Albert sat by and watched. He was a little annoyed. His own brief dalliance with politics was over. He was no longer interested in such things since he blamed his association with the Nazi party for his current predicament. He didn't care any more what Pilsudski, the long dead tyrant, had done to the Germans. Even Hitler, with his advancing army didn't impress him. In the last two weeks he had done a lot of thinking and although he could not express himself as well as these two, he knew what he felt. He had realized that war put peoples' lives at risk. Nothing was worth that and he hated the people who did this to him, his family and friends. They were all politicians. To Albert, politicians and politics were not worth discussing as long as he and his friends were in prison and his family was unprotected in Zeperow. He said little as the two talked. He wasn't even listening. He was watching Edmund.

It was not reassuring to look at his brother-in-law. Now that he sat beside him, his physical condition looked even worse than he had imagined. Despite his interest in events, his eyes were dull and tired, and he was so pale. His every gesture showed how infirm he was. Even as he talked, he was getting discernibly more tired, forcing words out of his mouth with pain. It was so deliberate, like someone constantly trying to catch his breath. Looking into Edmund's hollow face, Albert wondered how he had ever been able to recognize him. Where once there had been muscle and sinew, skin hung loosely. How could this have happened to such a strong young man?

Slowly, the horrifying fact that Edmund was dying forced itself on Albert. He felt such a profound sorrow that he was almost shaking. It was obvious that Edmund had been starved. He must have been at the camp so much longer than the Zeperow men. Sitting so close to him he couldn't understand how he had even been able to recognize him at a distance. What was it that had attracted his attention? Was his wife right?

His wife would have said it was fate that God had put her husband there to find her brother. Usually Albert scoffed at such speculations about divine intervention. As he saw it, in his life there had been a distinct lack of Godly interference and he could not understand why God would care about one man more than another. Besides, what did God think that he could do for Edmund here where he couldn't even help himself. It was hard for him to accept such things, but he had to wonder.

"How long have you been here?" Albert finally asked. He remembered the question of his interrogators. They always came back to Edmund. He wanted to know why they had said he was a traitor and a spy.

Edmund stared at his brother-in-law as if he was trying to remember. "Years, I think," he finally replied, "I have trouble remembering what year it is."

Johann and Albert glanced at each other. "It's September 1939," Johann said.

"I think I came here in 1937, maybe '36."

"What happened?" Johann asked. "What did you do?"

Edmund hesitated. "I was accused of spying," he said slowly, then added, "I've never been formally charged or had a trial."

"Are you a spy?" Albert asked. Johann stared at his brother but Albert shook it off. "Every time they questioned me they asked if I was working with my wife's brother. I think I have a right to know. I might be here because of you."

Edmund's eyes closed for a second. Almost wistfully he said, "It's true. It doesn't seem possible but it is true. It must be true, I'm here."

"For heaven's sake, what were you thinking? You've condemned your whole family!"

"It's not what I set out to do. It seemed so natural then, so simple and uncomplicated, but now I can't believe I could be so stupid. I went off to Krakow to help my people. But in Krakow I could see that it would never work. The Poles didn't want us unless we were willing to become Poles. A friend told me that there was another way to help. I believed him."

It was a sketchy explanation and neither Johann nor Albert really understood it. Perhaps it was because Edmund struggled so much as he talked that they found it hard to follow. Every word was forced. His strength was drained and he closed his eyes so often that Albert and Johann had to fight back the tears. When the planes were gone it was painful to watch Edmund trying to get up.

Both the brothers sprang to their feet to help the emaciated prisoner to the door. "No," Edmund said emphatically, raising his hand to signal stop, "if the guards see that you can't help yourself then they find a way to finish you." But then he turned to Albert as if something had triggered a thought. "I am probably going to die here. When you get out, please tell my parents how sorry I am. Ask them to forgive me."

The request stunned Albert who had no idea how to reply. As fond as he was of thinking that life had made him hard he was moved by Edmund's acceptance of his own death. How could he possibly respond to his brother-in-law without first encouraging him to fight? And yet, how much more fight could there be in him? He couldn't imagine what he would tell his wife and her parents.

"The German army will be here soon," Johann felt compelled to interject, "and we'll be free."

"I'm afraid they won't get here soon enough," Edmund replied, his voice shaking.

Johann put a hand on Edmund's shoulder and assured him quietly, "Albert will do this for you. He's a good man."

But before Edmund reached the door Albert jumped up and put his arms around him. "I will do what you ask, but you must promise me you will not give up. Just imagine the smile on Alwine's face when she sees you walking through our door beside me." Edmund smiled.

The next day, with a small stone he had picked up, Albert scratched the corner post of his bunk, one line for each of the fifteen days he had spent at the prison camp. After his talk with Edmund it haunted him to think of losing track of time and he was no longer so sure that the German army would come very soon. It disturbed him to think he might fade slowly and painfully like his brother-in-law. Every day on the parade ground he looked for Edmund and was always relieved to see him still alive. But the boy looked so weak and weary that it almost brought tears to his eyes. He smiled encouragement whenever their eyes met, but it seemed a futile gesture. Still, he thought it was at least as helpful as his brother Johann's prayers.

If Albert had not been so distracted by his concern for Edmund, he might have noticed that many of the guards were becoming more and more nervous. Some of them, perhaps with hidden motives, confided to prisoners that the Germans were close. The war was finished. But Albert gave no credence to such rumors. He couldn't chance the disappointment of them being untrue. Had he been aware of the truth he might have kept a lower profile and avoided the resentful glare of Smiley, who watched him like a hawk. But Albert felt a duty now toward his sister's beloved Edmund. Even if all he could do was keep watch, that was what he needed to do.

Smiley sensed that Albert had lost his fear of him and resented it. He didn't realize Albert's energy was all directed to saving his brother-in-law; he just hated the fact that he had not been able to ruin his spirit. He had starved, beaten, kicked, prodded and humiliated the man and still he showed no fear. He was determined to teach Albert one final lesson. This time he wanted to do more than just humiliate him.

"Leave it, Jan," some of the other guards told him, when he told them his plan, "What does it matter now?" Another warned him, "The Germans are coming, be careful."

"It matters to me, and I don't care about the Germans," Smiley yelled back.

At the main building he had organized his favorite amusement, one more time. Smiley turned to Albert and ordered him to follow. "Tonight you fight for your supper. Let's see how quick you are." In Albert's opinion it was the best he could hope for, he knew how to survive that game.

When they reached the building, the rest of the unfortunates were inside already. Smiley called out, "Don't close that door, I've got one more." He shoved Albert through.

As soon as Albert stepped into the room he sensed a change. The first man he touched threw a punch that sent him reeling. But the room was too crowded for him to fall. Carefully he made his way to the back wall. Whatever had changed, his strategy was still the same. If he sank away into the background and didn't participate he would survive.

Besides, he had learned to do without. The blessed witch had taught him how. The game was more dangerous than the hunger in his belly so he sated himself with the idea of not giving Smiley the satisfaction of seeing him fight like a desperate animal. He made his way to the back wall, carefully making it clear that he was no threat to anyone.

It took him a few minutes to understand this new tension that he felt. Then he remembered what he had heard. The guards had added a new twist to the game since Albert had played last. They were no longer content just to watch the violence develop on its own. Now they bribed several prisoners with promises of extra food and privileges to start trouble. With splinters of wood hidden up their sleeves they were told that, the better the show, the greater the reward.

Quickly, the panic took over. Had Smiley targeted him to die? He searched the room frantically for a place to hide, some hole he could crawl into to survive. But as he scanned the room he saw him against the back wall. It was Edmund. Albert closed his eyes and hoped the vision would go away, but it wasn't a dream. Edmund's eyes were glazed and he looked dead already leaning against the wall. Albert pushed his way to his side no longer worried about himself. His brother-in-law could barely stand but he smiled weakly as he recognized Albert.

"Are they crazy?" he asked, "Can't they see you are sick?"

"It doesn't matter," Edmund replied, in a voice so thin that Albert could hardly hear. "I'm going to die soon anyway. It might as well be tonight."

Now Albert forgot about himself and Smiley. The only thing that mattered was making sure that Edmund survived. That meant getting him some food. He began to jostle for position and realized quickly that he had more strength than many of the men there. It amused him to think that while the witch was trying to kill him she had actually made him stronger. He took a position only centimeters behind an enormous Ukrainian who had taken up his position early and kept everyone else away. Albert hoped somehow to get a handful of food, without getting killed.

The door opened. The first loaf flew to the left. The bread floated like a disc just above outstretched arms until it was grabbed and there was a melee in that corner. Albert could see that the next loaf was coming right at the big Ukrainian. Without thinking he ducked under the big man's outstretched arm. Leaping like a jackrabbit in front of the big fellow, who had not expected to have to move to catch his food, he caught the loaf. More swiftly than even he could have anticipated, he ripped into the bread and tore off a chunk. Instantly, he threw the rest of the loaf at the Ukrainian who fumbled it onto the floor. But he stomped on the bread with his big foot and dared anyone to challenge him for it. Within seconds a group of desperate men were on him.

Albert clamped his hands around the morsel of bread like a vice and pushed his way back to Edmund. Someone tried to grab his hands but Albert brought them up like a hammer and caught him on the jaw. He made it back to Edmund with the bread still intact.

While the rest of the room was in an uproar, he stood beside his dying brother feeding him bit by bit. With all is strength he intended to protect the bread in his hands until Edmund could eat it all. But the boy ate so painfully slowly.

"Why are you wasting food on him, can't you see he's dying?" someone finally asked. Albert paid no attention. It was his job to keep Edmund alive. It was his mission. It was what God had sent him here for. In his mind he could see himself carrying Edmund home and laying him on his bed, for his sister to care for and nurse back to health. No one could stop him.

The din of fighting stopped now. The big fellow had managed to rescue only a mouthful of food. He blamed Albert and demanded the bread that Albert was feeding to Edmund. Albert saw him coming and stepped in front of his brother-in-law. "Give it to me," the man demanded as he towered over Albert. His fist was massive and looking at it, Albert almost gave in. As he held out what was left of the bread the man undid his fist to grab the food. Just then Albert pulled it back and kicked him in the crotch as hard as he could. He dropped like a rock screaming while the guards watched at the window laughing with glee, all except one.

As Albert turned, he saw someone choking Edmund, trying to pull the bread right out of his mouth. Albert punched him in the side of the head. He was still staring at the man when someone else attacked him. Edmund tried to warn Albert but the words wouldn't come fast enough. Summoning all the energy his frail arms could produce, he pushed Albert aside. A sharpened stick plunged into the wall beside Edmund's head, splintering into useless particles. Lying on the floor Albert looked up and saw Smiley looking through the window. His crooked grin was bigger than ever. But now the man lunged at him and was on top of him, his hands reaching for Albert's throat. Albert pushed his hands away easily. He smashed his fist into the man's face, knocking him over. Then he drew back and stood beside Edmund to protect the both of them, but it was all over. The tension was broken. Everyone was too tired. The faces in the window quickly disappeared.

In the morning there was an eerie silence throughout the camp. The men still locked up in the room were puzzled. No one came to let them out. They were really puzzled when they heard cheering outside and few minutes later there was banging on the door. It flew open and someone shouted, "The guards are all gone. They have fled. The German army is coming."

The room emptied quickly but Albert stayed with Edmund. All night Albert had stayed awake to make sure Edmund was alive. In truth, he had been afraid to sleep. But now, Edmund, though he had survived the night, was too weak to walk. So Albert waited. He knew that soon Johann, August and Erich would come looking for him.

Eighteen

Alwine and Julianna Fischer were in a state of bewilderment after Albert was dragged away. They had no idea where to go to inquire about him or to protest his arrest. Even if they had known where to go, they knew that their cries would fall on indifferent or even hostile ears. With German panzers advancing rapidly in the west, the Polish government was not going to listen to protests of German innocence. Alwine blamed Adolf Hitler. With his declarations of support for the oppressed ethnic Germans all across eastern Europe he made it appear as if the invasion was happening on their behalf. No wonder the Poles were convinced of their treason. The German chancellor had practically announced it to them. The only thing that Alwine and Julianna could do was to pray and hope that Albert was not already dead and hold tight to each other while the war took its course.

With the men gone there was no communication within the community because families cowered in fear in their little houses. Despair weighed heavily on the two Fischer women, casting a gloom about everything they tried to do. The children were not even allowed outside to play lest they attracted some unwanted attention. Even when Alwine went out to her vegetable garden she kept a wary eye on the road. At any time she expected that the Poles would come and drag the rest of the family away. She was painfully aware that this had been the course of events twenty-four years earlier. Now, as then, survival was all that counted and she was almost comforted that the situation was familiar. At least she had first hand knowledge that it was possible to survive.

On a misty September morning the women became painfully aware that one German man was not gone. He still rode up and down the road to Antonufka with a carefree attitude carrying on his business. For him, even the war did not seem to exist. He was an annoying man at the best of times and now he was positively gloating. Hermann Martin stopped to taunt the women while they worked to harvest their garden under the cover of the light morning mist. "How is your husband?" he called mockingly and eerily through the fog. "I bet he'd sell me the farm now, but I'll just wait until the Poles burn you out!" He drove away laughing, and Alwine cringed. More than ever the women were insecure.

Alwine Fischer fought her fear and suspicion that the Poles would soon be back to haul away the rest of the Germans with the only resource she had left. Prayer was not a tool of last resort for Alwine. She had always remembered her mother's prayers during their exile in Western Siberia. Consequently, she did not question the power of her God to answer them as she already had proof that He would. As she looked back now, it did not seem possible for a woman and four little children to survive that journey without God's help. She didn't question why many who prayed equally fervently had not survived because she did not think in those terms. She only knew that she needed Him and He was there. Only now she prayed more frequently, not only on her knees but in her heart she prayed constantly. She was glad that she did not have to apologize for having forgotten Him in the intervening years.

Several days after the start of the war, Alwine knew she had to overpower her fear of leaving the house in order to go check on Irene. Irene was alone with her children and Alwine worried about her friend. Julianna encouraged her to go. "At least we have each other to rely on," she said, "Go let Irene know that she is not alone. I will manage here. I'll send Ewald and Edmund across if I need you."

Alwine waited and made sure that no one was on the Zeperow road and hurried to the Weiss house. Irene saw her coming up her lane and ran out and flung her arms around Alwine. "Oh, Alwine!" she cried, "I'm just so glad to see you. I've been so afraid just sitting in my house and waiting for news of August. Have you heard anything?"

"No," Alwine said with considerable disappointment.

"Do you think they will hurt them?"

"I don't think so, but we do have to face the possibility."

Irene cried throughout their commiseration and Alwine was surprised. She had always thought of Irene as the strong partner in their friendship.

"What shall we do if they kill our men?" Irene cried.

"There is not much that we can do Irene. But we must be strong for our children. We must look to their safety."

"But what if they kill us all."

"Talk like that is useless," Alwine said with conviction. "If that is all we think about then we might as well lie down and die. We are alive, God will help us Irene, He will help our men and we will help our children to survive. I pray for it constantly."

"Pray!" Irene cried softly as if a light had come on. "Yes, I will pray. You're right Alwine, only God can help us now."

Alwine stayed with Irene for several hours. She was sure that with a little reassurance that the strong Irene, the one who knew about so many things, would emerge again. But as the time stretched on Alwine began to be worried about Julianna and her own family. She was afraid that Omi might send the boys to fetch her and that they would run into some danger. They could be such reckless boys. She finally tore herself away from Irene's tears, gave her a reassuring kiss on the cheek and started home.

She was barely out the door when she heard the sound of a horse and carriage rolling up the lane. There was fear for a moment but when she saw who it was she was relieved and curiosity took over. It was Chaim, their Jewish neighbor. Alwine opened the door and called for Irene. There must have been too much surprise in her voice because Irene came rushing to the door in fearful anticipation, calling, "What is it, Alwine? What is it?"

"The Jew, Chaim, is coming."

He stepped down from the carriage and doffed his hat to the two women and started to speak. "Your mother-in-law told me that you were here Frau Fischer. I'm afraid I gave her a bad scare when I drove up to your door. I am sorry about that."

"We all have much to fear right now Herr Chaim," Alwine said. She wondered what he had come for. She suspected for a minute that he had come to buy their livestock in some devious plan to swindle the stupid women while their husbands were gone. It was the way she had been taught to think about Jews.

"I come with some bad news," he said.

"About our husbands?" Irene asked excitedly.

"No, I am so sorry. I have no news about them, except that I have heard that most of your men are in detention."

"That is good news," Alwine said, "We did not even know that."

"I'm glad to help, but I have just come from Lutzk and there is a rumor that many of the German farmers are being burned out of their homes. In the middle of the night angry Poles set German houses on fire while everyone is sleeping. I am sorry to bring you such news but I thought it was the least I could do."

"Oh my God," Irene cried, "What shall we do, Alwine. They are coming to kill us."

"I am sorry to upset you," Chaim restated, sorry for the reaction that he elicited from the two women. "It is happening near Lutzk. It may never reach out here, but I only wanted to warn you."

"Thank-you, Herr Chaim," Alwine said sincerely as she stepped forward and shook his hand. Tradition had taught her to be uncomfortable around Jews but she knew her neighbor had been thoughtful and she wanted to show her gratitude. "I want you to know that we are both grateful for your warning. You were very kind to come."

"Frau Fischer, it was my duty as your neighbor. We Jews are no strangers to this type of violence. Inevitably, when this trouble begins, these cowards discover that Jewish houses burn as easily as others."

"Oh, I hope not," Alwine said with genuine sincerity.

Before the neighbor left Irene was crying again. Alwine could understand why. She suspected that she herself had come to Irene's home to be comforted by her but instead had found her friend distraught. In the face of Irene's need, her own need seemed less important. Still, now she had to go home, Julianna would be getting worried and she didn't want her to send Edmund to look for her. She was especially worried about Chaim's news, now that she recalled what Hermann Martin had said the other day. It was easy to believe that he would spearhead the Polish vigilantes.

"Listen, Irene," Alwine said, trying to think on her feet and still puzzled about where all of Irene's strength had flown. The truth was that she didn't know what to do, but that just wasn't acceptable now. She needed to leave her friend with something tangible to hold onto. "Bring your family to our house and we will take turns keeping watch at night."

"I don't think I could stand it if I wasn't here to keep watch on my house," Irene answered.

"Well then, stay here. Sleep in the fields." That was a good idea, Alwine thought. She couldn't understand how she had come up with it. "That's what we are going to do. We will sleep in the potato fields where no one can see us."

Alwine ran most of the way home to tell her mother-in-law what she had learned. Julianna agreed it was a good idea to sleep in the potato field but as she rushed to help Alwine prepare, she realized that Hedwig was unaware of this new terror. Both women concurred that Julianna should go warn Hedwig and her grandsons. They had not seen the boys nor Hedwig since the day they had come racing across the field when their father was hauled away, only to find that their uncle was gone too and could not help them. "Go home and take care of your mother," Julianna had told the strapping teenagers, "You must be men now."

Julianna was glad that Hedwig had two such strong young men to protect her, even if they could be wild and unpredictable at times. She and Alwine only had each other. She wondered if one of them would be willing to stay with her and Alwine. It would be comforting. Yet Julianna knew she would have to gauge Hedwig's mood before she asked. She could be so volatile.

She knocked hard on the door. There was no answer so she called out for Hedwig and her grandsons. Where could they be? She knocked again, harder. Finally Hedwig came to the door, frantic and terrified. She would not open the door until she was sure it was Julianna on the other side. Fear had made the woman even more angry and suspicious than usual.

"The cowards have run off," she blurted out immediately as she opened the door, yelling at the top of her voice as if Julianna were deaf.

"What do you mean?"

"Otto and Gustav, they ran off the day after their father left."

"The police took them?" Julianna was puzzled.

"No, don't you understand? They ran off and left me here alone. They went to join the German army!"

"No!"

"Yes. Do you think I am lying? They left me here alone, just like their father!"

"Johann didn't leave you."

"He might as well have," Hedwig ranted. "Politics, Nazis, religion, it's all he's interested in. He should have known it would get him arrested! Now I'm alone and those swine, Otto and Gustav have left me to be killed by the Poles!"

It was bad timing for the news that she bore, but Julianna felt she had to let her know about the burnings. Hedwig screamed and threw a kitchen pot against the wall. "I have no one to protect me," she wailed.

Julianna understood how much more intense fear could be when you were alone. She felt sorry for the miserable woman. "Come stay with us," she said hesitantly, but as soon as she said it she knew it was the right thing to do. "Yes, come stay with Alwine and me, we will protect each other."

A look of disbelief came on Hedwig's face. "Why ..." she started to ask but did not finish. Like a shadow crossing her face, fear was replaced with something else, something Julianna couldn't understand. "No. I won't leave my home. The Poles will come and take it if I leave. Hermann Martin will come and claim it. That's what he did before."

"Hedwig, what are a few hectares compared with your life?"

"I have to save the farm for the boys. They'll want it some day." She turned and stared at Julianna again as another mood came over her. With anger she began to explain, "I won't stay with her. Alwine and Albert want this farm. They're not satisfied with their share. They want it all. She tried to poison us, you know. I stopped her but I won't give her another chance."

Julianna wanted to shake her oldest son's wife and force her to think about what she was saying but instead she hurried back home. "I won't stay with her," she explained to Alwine, "she'd drive me crazy." Then she scooped up her grandson and added, "and I would miss my Einhardt so."

That night Alwine took her family into the potato fields to sleep, while across the road, Irene did the same. Luckily these September nights were mostly warm and dry. The children thought it was great fun. In the morning she waved her handkerchief to let Irene know that they were well and Irene waved back.

When after several nights they had seen no sign of mobs or torches Alwine convinced herself that sleeping in the fields was unnecessary. But two nights later hundreds of motorized vehicles were rolling over their small country road. For hours the motors hummed, moving without lights under the clear sky. Though Alwine and Julianna supposed it was the military, they were still frightened. What if they were coming to pick up the rest of the German population? The rumbling on the road lasted for hours and the women were afraid for their lives. Nervous that the house could be set ablaze at any moment, they gathered up the children and led them out the back way, through the barn. Only Einhardt and the baby slept that night. Alwine was afraid to sleep in the house again.

As the days passed the Fischer women had no idea how the war was progressing. Besides fearing for their safety, the only thing that concerned them about the war was the return of their men. But Ewald and Edmund were excited about the war. Their prejudices against the Poles had grown into hatred. They were sure now that the Poles were as stupid and cruel as everyone said. They were so young they could not understand that their opinions were the product of years of subtle influence, at school, at church and at home. Whether it was the jokes and the laughter, or the blatant contempt that was displayed for the Polish people, it all taught the boys that whatever was German was superior. They learned it all as easily as they learned simple addition, and believed it was just as true.

When they saw their father being taken away and heard the cries of their mother and grandmother their contempt turned into hatred. Now they longed for German victory because to them it meant that their father would return and that the Poles could be finished, whatever that meant. They had no real concept of war but imagined it was much like a soccer game, only with guns. In this contest between Germany and Poland they expected the Germans to win, and win big. Unfortunately, they were missing the game.

It was after the boys heard their Omi say that she wished they had a radio so they could understand what was going on that they got the idea. In the morning, after their chores, they snuck out the back way and started to walk toward Antonufka. Ewald was sure that the radio in the cooperative store would tell them what was happening in the war. They had strolled almost to the Antonufka turn off when they were accosted. It was Jozef Martin and several boys that Ewald and Edmund didn't recognize. They were Jozef's cousins, his mother's nephews, who had been sent for safety into the country as soon as the war started.

The Martin boy renewed the question he had asked of Edmund and Ewald several years before. "Which one of you shall we kill first?" he demanded. Edmund remembered how he had answered then, but now he was ashamed to repeat it. He kept quiet. Ewald was also afraid, but too stubborn to show it. He knew he could not fight but refused to give them the satisfaction of showing fear.

His father had told him that bullies never carry out their threats when challenged. Ewald put this theory to the test by defying these cowardly Poles by glaring at them. His Father was wrong. But even bullies had to work up the nerve to do their dirty work. The ruffians shoved the boys around, ridiculed them, called them traitors, enemy spies, and German weaklings. Finally, they shoved them to the ground and kicked at them, striking solidly on their legs and backs. Edmund and Ewald put their arms up to protect their heads and cried out in pain. Their agony only spurred the bullies on.

"Stop, stop," Alwine cried. They heard her shouting but it was so faint that no one even turned to look at her. "Stop, I tell you, don't make me shoot!"

The Martin boy turned and saw Alwine Fischer waving her husband's police pistol at them. "Run, she's got a gun!"

They didn't know that she hadn't the slightest idea how to use it. She grabbed it on impulse when she found her sons missing and then went looking for them.

Jozef Martin and his cousins didn't stop running until they were far off. When they did stop, they were shaking and indignant about this further proof of German treachery, and fully intended to tell Jozef's father how that crazy woman had threatened them with a gun, for no reason. They expected that he would go right over and shoot that stupid woman.

It was dusk when they heard him thundering down their lane. Julianna raced to a window and saw Martin reign his horse to a stop. He stood up and yelled for Alwine, "Come out, woman. Come threaten me with your gun!"

Alwine opened the door. She had known this would happen and had resolved to face him when he came. What she wanted was to put herself between him and her children. She had no confidence that she could convince Martin that her only intent had been to protect her children. Nevertheless, she was prepared to let him rant and rave and even threaten, but then she hoped he would just leave. But Julianna was more suspicious and offered her daughter-in-law the gun again. Alwine waved it off, "I have no idea how to use it."

"How dare you threaten my boy with a gun?" he raged at her when she stood outside, her back to the door. His face was red and his fists were clenched so tightly that his knuckles turned white. Alwine was afraid that he was going to jump down and beat her.

"Herr Martin," she said, trying to achieve a conciliatory tone but her voice only squeaked with fear, "Your son and his friends were beating Ewald and Edmund."

"Liar!" he screamed.

"No, I'm not lying," Alwine said, shaking. She desperately wanted to reason with him. "They are much bigger than my sons, and I only waved the gun at them to ..."

"There is the truth," Martin yelled as he jumped down from his wagon. "No one threatens my son with a gun without having to deal with me. Not even a woman."

"I did not threaten them, I only wanted to chase them away. They were kicking the boys." She could feel her voice quivering.

Alwine was afraid. He was face to face with her now, his voice screaming terror. Alwine's head was spinning. She was afraid she would faint.

"It's time you Germans learned a lesson. You just can't do whatever you want in this country."

"Herr Martin, I don't even know how to use a gun. I wouldn't ... I couldn't ..." She knew her protests were pointless.Seeing her so vulnerable he raised his hand and slapped her across the face. Alwine fell backwards with a burning sting on her left cheek and jaw. She was dazed. His fist was clenched to strike her again but the door opened and Julianna was there with the gun, aimed right at his head.

"Stop right there," the old woman said.

"You wouldn't dare!"

"I will not let you hurt my family," Julianna yelled at him sternly. "Alwine does not know how to use a gun but I do. My husband taught me to shoot when we ran from the Russians in the last war. I haven't forgotten."

Martin could see the barrel of the gun moving left or right as he moved. At first he thought she was bluffing but the more he thought about it, the more he actually believed she knew what she was doing. He had to believe she would not be sad about killing him.

"Get out of here Martin," she said strongly, and when he didn't move she said it even more forcefully. "Get out of here! I swear to you that I would gladly give my life to rid my family of you. To see you dead would be the highlight of my old age."

Martin began to shake. He backed up slowly with his hands raised to show Julianna that he was not about to do anything stupid. He retreated but his face was still red, and his eyes were fixed on the old woman. Not for a moment did either Alwine or Julianna believe that Martin would not be back, but at least he was gone for now.

With the dark coming on quickly and their encounter with Hermann Martin still foremost in their thoughts, the women took their family once again to sleep in the potato fields. There were no clouds in the sky that unusually warm September night. That made it easier to sleep outside in the fields but also made it easier for groups of vigilante Poles to do their works of terror. Tonight, however, it was their fear of Martin that prompted Julianna to take the pistol with her into the potato field.

It was after midnight when Alwine woke up. Neither she nor Julianna had slept soundly, stirring to any faint noise. There was something happening on the road. The women peeked timidly over the tops of the potato plants to see what was going on. But the moonlight only revealed shadows. Soon, however, a tiny light flared like a wooden match and soon after another larger light began to grow. It was a torch.

"They're going to burn our house," Alwine whispered, almost resigned to it happening.

"I see only one torch and one shadow, Alwine. I bet it is that coward Martin."

Julianna raised the gun into the air and was about to shoot a warning shot, but then thought better of it. She lowered it and took careful aim at the shadow. "No," Alwine whispered, "what if you shoot him, what if you kill him?"

"With this gun, at that distance, in the dark it would be a miracle if I hit him. You might call it the will of God if I did hit him."

"Oh, Oma don't tempt God."

"Alwine, have courage. If our Albert does not return, we are at the mercy of men like Martin. It is better that he understands that we will not easily be trampled on."

The torch was burning brightly now. The flame outlined the perpetrator. It looked very much like Hermann Martin. Julianna fired at him. The flame stopped moving toward the house. It just stood there in the open seemingly startled. Julianna raised the gun and fired again, she wanted him to run away. Even the women could hear the second bullet as it thudded into the side of their house. It had the opposite effect that Julianna had wanted. Martin now rushed to finish his diabolical work. Quickly she fired again and she knew she hit him just as he was about to throw the torch. There was a cry of pain but the torch had an altered trajectory. It thudded against the side of the house and fell at it's base. Alwine ran through the potatoes not knowing what waited for her there and grabbed the torch and threw it away from the house. Only then did she think that he might still be there and began looking frantically into the dark to find him. She was much relieved when she heard the scurrying of feet up her lane to the road.

Julianna followed Alwine to the house. Incredibly, the children had slept through the whole thing.

"What have we done, Oma?" Alwine asked when Julianna stood beside her.

"We have saved our house, daughter."

"For now," Alwine agreed reluctantly. "But what will he do now? The Poles believe everything he says."

"I'm not sure that man would want it to be known that he was shot by an old woman while trying to burn down a house full of children. Besides Alwine, if Germany loses this war and our men don't return it won't matter what we did tonight. The Germans will be finished in Poland." Alwine could not have known how right her mother-in-law was.

In the morning Alwine slept in. She realized too late that she had failed to give her morning signal to Irene. Her neighbor, she was sure, would be frantic with fear by now, perhaps she had even heard the shots as she slept in her fields. She went inside to let her mother-in-law know she was going across the road. But when she came outside again, Irene's oldest daughter, Hertha, came running down the lane.

When she saw her mother's friend the girl yelled, "Frau Fischer, Frau Fischer, please come, something is wrong with Mama." As Alwine opened the gate to her yard, she could see there were blood stains on the gate, but that did not concern her now. She caught her friend's daughter in her arms and they rushed back up the lane hand in hand.

Alwine found Irene in her bed where she had dragged herself. There were bruises on her face, dried blood about her mouth and bewilderment and fear on her face. "Oh, Irene, what is wrong?" Alwine cried as she came to her side.

Irene struggled to say something but nothing came out of her mouth. She swallowed and tried again, "Please, Hertha, tea." Her voice was raspy and weak. The distraught daughter did not seem to understand so Alwine gently took her hand and said, "It will help your mother to feel better if you could brew some tea, sweetheart." Hertha Weiss ran to the kitchen, anxious to do whatever was right.

"Alwine, please help me to clean up," Irene pleaded in obvious pain. Alwine got water and a wet cloth and gently wiped the blood from her face and tried to clean her up, all the time terrified of learning what had happened.

Irene's daughter brought in a cup of tea and Alwine held it to her mother's lips. The warmth seemed to help her voice to return. "Thank-you daughter," she said, "you're such a good young lady. You've been so brave with your father gone. Would you go take care of your sisters and brother? Find them something to eat. I'll be all right now."

"Yes, Mama," the girl said obediently but it was obvious to Alwine that she really didn't want to leave her mother.

When the girl left the room Irene began to cry, big stifling sobs came from her and all that Alwine could do was to hold her. "What happened?" Alwine asked already knowing the answer. "Who did this?"

"It was Martin," Irene said controlling her tears. "There were shots last night, Alwine. I thought maybe they came from your house. We were sleeping in the fields and I thought for sure that the Poles were coming for us too. A few minutes later a wagon was coming up our lane. Oh Alwine, I thought it might be you but it was Martin. He said that some Poles had shot him because he was German. I don't know why I believed him. Why would they shoot him, he's on their side? He was bleeding from his arm and he asked me to bandage it. I couldn't leave him bleeding Alwine.

"While I put on the bandage, he started saying how this was all Germany's fault and how stupid our men had been to join the Nazi party. He said some awful things about Albert, Alwine. And about Albert's brother and father. I told him that you were my friend and I didn't like him talking like that, would he please stop. He became angry and said that you had threatened to shoot his son with a gun. What idiocy. That's when I began to suspect that maybe it wasn't Poles who had shot him. I asked him to leave but he became angry. He said he was going to teach you a lesson and then he began to hit me. Oh Alwine, did you shoot him?"

"No, but Julianna did. I don't know how to shoot a gun. I wish now that I did, I wish that Omi had killed him."

"Oh, Alwine, I wish she had."

"When our men get back Irene, they will take care of him."

"Oh, Alwine, no. We can't tell them. Promise me that August will never know."

"But Irene, why?"

"Alwine, please promise," Irene cried, "that Albert won't know either. What Albert knows August finds out."

"Why Irene?"

Irene pulled her friend closer and whispered, "He raped me!"

The blood drained from Alwine's face. She felt awful. She knew too well the stigma attached to any woman who was raped. Since her actions had contributed to this disaster she could do no less than promise Irene what she asked.

"I promise, Irene. But I must tell Omi, so that she will tell no one about last night."

"Alwine, there's one more thing you should know. He said he was coming back for you and your family."

That afternoon Alwine returned to her house, gathered her family and they moved into the Weiss house. To the children she merely said it was to help take care of her friend who was sick. She told only Julianna the truth.

Nineteen

The entire world reeled at the shock of Poland's quick defeat, but the prisoners at Bereza Kartuska were ecstatic. When they realized that the guards had abandoned the camp, many rioted, releasing their pent up frustrations by smashing their reeking barracks and ripping down the loathsome barbed-wire fences. But ultimately, most were just glad to be free to return to their frightened families. Even the Ukrainian terrorists shouted for joy that Poland had fallen. Had they known that Russia was quickly advancing from the east they might all have behaved more soberly.

Albert Fischer and the Zeperow contingent were as happy as the rest of the inmates about the early victory, but right now they were more worried about how to get Edmund Frey home alive. When they looked at Alwine's brother after that last night of incarceration they shuddered. Their captivity had only lasted about eighteen days in total, and though they were all thinner, none of the Zeperow men were nearly as bad off as the young rebel. Edmund was so feeble that his friends agonized whether taking him with them would kill him. Yet they knew they couldn't just leave him to die alone. The problem was they had no transport and they could not expect him to walk.

It was a rationalization and Johann Fischer and Erich Winkler knew it. They had to find a way to transport their ill friend home and that meant a horse and a wagon. The rationalization came when they told themselves that the Poles owed it to them. After dark, while August and Albert cared for Edmund, they ventured off awkwardly to steal a horse from some unwary farmer. Albert shook his head as they left, the two unseemly robbers looked so uncertain and ill prepared for this kind of work. Yet surprisingly, they returned only a short time later with an old sway-back farm horse and a creaking, weather-beaten old wagon that hadn't seen axle-grease in years.

Albert took one look at the horse and complained, "I knew it was a mistake to send you two to do this. Couldn't you find a horse that had a chance of making it to Zeperow?"

"We took that one on purpose," Johann explained, flustered by Albert's criticism. "We thought it wouldn't be much of a loss."

"You mean you had a choice?" Albert was amazed.

"I'm happy to admit that I am not good at this," Erich conceded.

"Albert, please don't joke about this," Johann requested, "we only did this for Edmund's sake. We're not thieves."

"You didn't steal it," August offered, "you just liberated it."

"Liberated!" Albert laughed, "I think you liberated his owner. He's probably rolling on his floor laughing at you."

"Just the same, I hate being a thief," Erich declared. "As soon as we reach home, I'm going to bring the horse back. I don't care what you think." No one doubted that Erich would do it and Johann Fischer would not let him assume the responsibility alone. "I will have to come with you," he added, "I stood guard."

"Be careful," Albert couldn't help jabbing one more time, "the farmer will probably shoot you for returning that bag of bones."

But getting Edmund to Zeperow alive meant they needed more than just transportation. Having criticized his friends for their poor attempt at burglary, Albert took it upon himself to find a meal. "I'm afraid you might come back with something else that wouldn't be missed," he said, shaking his head. After being gone for an hour he came back with a chicken. "I liberated something too," he said, proudly holding up the dead foul.

"I don't think that the bird would agree that it had been freed," August joked.

That night, as they plucked Albert's catch by the roadside, they felt good, almost giddy, about their freedom. While the bird was roasting over their small fire, August remarked in jest how skinny the chicken was, it reminded him of the phantom chicken at Bereza. "We never did find that bird," he pointed out. "If I didn't know better I'd swear you went back and got that chicken of a thousand soups?" Having berated the horse, Albert felt he had to defend his prize. "Compared to that one this is as fat as a Christmas goose. With this bird they could have fed the entire camp, for a year," he protested. "The Polish had no idea such a prize was right under their noses. Imagine, if their army could have had such a chicken, who knows how long the war would have gone on. Of course it took a German to find it!"

It was not much of a joke but they were all so relieved to be away from that awful prison camp it didn't take much to make them laugh. Even the stoic Johann could not resist. Pretty soon August was holding his sides as he rolled in the grass in front of the fire. Even Edmund, wrapped in prison blankets, could not contain himself, but when he started to cough his friends grew concerned. They stopped. After the laughter died and most of the chicken was devoured, August looked at the leftovers and grinned. "It could still feed the whole camp," he said with a smile. The laughter started all over. Soon, however, the bones were picked clean and Albert couldn't resist, "It could still feed barrack #1." They all looked at Edmund who smiled weakly and explained in his feeble voice, "You know why there were no rats at Bereza Kartuska? Long before you came, we ate them all." It wasn't a joke.

It happened faster than Albert could have foreseen. His wife had rushed into his arms to welcome him home while the children cheered to see their father again. Albert had rehearsed a hundred ways to prepare her and now he still did not know what to say. So without a word to buoy her for the shock, he told her that her brother Edmund was lying in the wagon. The happiness on her face quickly turned into a look of horror that she could not disguise but she held back her tears. There was nothing he could have said to prepare his wife for this shock, but at least he was relieved to have brought the boy home alive.

Alwine wasted no time turning her nursing skills on Edmund. She had the men put him in the warm bed in the kitchen and fussed over him like she knew her mother would do if she were there. Yet nothing, not her love, nor her attentions and not even her good cooking could undo years of deprivation as quickly as she wanted it to disappear. But nevertheless, her efforts made an amazing difference. At first only his voice indicated to Alwine that his health was improving. It had been a mere whisper when Albert and Johann had carried him into the house, but two days later it was much more clear and strong. She could only hope that other signs of recovery would follow more rapidly.

Alwine's concern was Edmund's physical health, yet it disturbed her that Edmund was so uncharacteristically quiet. The enthusiasm he was so famous for had drained out of him along with his energy. "Be glad," Albert told her, "if he starts to talk politics again I'm going to throw him out." The humor didn't cheer her.

The Volhynians had no time to gloat over the German victory which should have meant an end of their problems with Poland. Even the joy they felt over their men's safe return from prison was muted by the shock of the involvement of the Russians in this new partition of Poland. The gloom settled not only on the Germans but on the Ukrainian and Jewish populations too as they anticipated what the communists would do to their communities. They had all heard the stories of their relatives who had remained in Russia after the first war. Now they asked themselves how this could have happened to them. In very quick order, Adolf Hitler, the man who had appealed to their loyalty, seemed to have betrayed them. He had called on the Volhynian-Germans to remember their heritage and then sold them to the communists.

In those short autumn days right after the war the mood in Volhynia was almost funereal. No one felt the tension and anxiety as tangibly as August Weiss. His family had smothered him with affection when he returned and he was overjoyed to be back with them, yet he soon sensed that something else was wrong. His usually calm and cheerful wife behaved almost neurotically whenever he left the house for even a few minutes. She never wanted him to be gone and rarely even left the house herself. At first August attributed it to the fear and confusion his whole community felt as they realized that they had not been saved by Germany but had actually been cast aside. Yet there was more to his wife's erratic behavior, he was sure, and he hoped she would let him know what it was. But August would not pry, deep down he was afraid to hear what was troubling his beautiful wife.

August wasn't the only husband to come home to a distressed wife. Albert and Johann Fischer found that their wives had endured threats of burning and murder too. But whereas Albert was greeted in a rush of tears and excitement, Johann found his reception cold. Hedwig screamed and flailed at her husband with her fists when he came through the door. She had endured three weeks of intense loneliness in her house with almost no human contact and she blamed her husband for it. According to her, even their sons' desertion was his fault. The loneliness was suffocating and yet it was not as great as her fear of losing the farm. Hedwig still remembered the Russian terror, and fearing a return of those days, she had sat in her house, enduring heart-wrenching loneliness, as if that could stop it from happening again. In her mind she had saved the farm, no thanks to Johann.

Johann endured his wife's tirades because as a good Christian he had no alternative. Yet even his patience had its limits. When Erich Winkler left to return the miserable horse and wagon they had liberated together, Johann went with him despite his wife's objections. Hedwig's ire was full when that happened. "If you leave me again Johann, don't bother coming back at all," she shouted at the top of her voice as they drove off.

Johann almost turned back, but he had made a promise. Besides he had accepted over the years that his wife was full of anger and fear and he believed that for the most part she said and did things on impulse. She would settle down. He knew she was in pain about the boys, so was he, and yet they could not talk about their grief together without her shouting accusations at him.

And then too, there was the secret he was hiding from her. Her obsession with holding onto their tiny plot of land was about to suffer a severe blow. Johann, better than anyone, knew the implication of the Russian invasion of Volhynia. However, he said nothing to his overwrought wife. He had no idea how to tell her that the land was as good as lost. Johann just shrugged his shoulders and went with Erich. Perhaps while he was gone, he would think of a way to tell her.

Left once again to stew all alone, Hedwig's heart turned to rage as her constant companion. In her mind she fomented plan after plan. She had to protect the land, the house and herself, not only from the Russians and Poles but from her own family. When she listed the people she counted as her enemies, her husband now found a prominent spot; there was Albert who schemed to get her land, Alwine because she was Albert's wife, Julianna who had betrayed her kindness, Erich Winkler who had taken her husband away when she needed him, Otto and Gustav who had abandoned her, and Johann who had wasted her life. But at the top of the list in her mind was Hermann Martin. And yet, after all was said and done, he was smarter than the rest. It was a great puzzlement for her that such a man seemed to come through every disaster unscathed and usually richer. Why wasn't her husband like him.

When Johann came back in a few days, having returned the worthless horse and wagon to a very astonished Polish farmer, he was even more surprised to have his wife rush into his arms and shower him with tears. He assumed that she had convinced herself in his absence that he had left her and the loneliness that descended on her then had almost broken her. "Never leave me again," she pleaded.

In the midst of the uncertainty about the destiny of the German-Volhynians, another more immediate problem bothered the men of Zeperow and Antonufka. Whenever two men met, the conversation was sure to turn to Hermann Martin. Some men talked openly about killing him. They were serious. They ranted about justice, but Erich Winkler and Johann Fischer called it by its real name, revenge. Enlisting Albert's help, they were able to prevail on the hotheads to be more patient. The logic was irrefutable, if Albert could wait, so could they. All except one agreed.

What surprised everyone was the intransigence of August Weiss. Even Albert was astounded that his friend pressed so hard for action against Hermann Martin. There seemed to be little justification for it. August was not hurt any more than anyone else by Martin's actions so his friends scratched their heads. It was out of character for an otherwise malleable personality. Yet, only because Albert asked, would August listen to the Kantorrat's request for restraint. "Wait and see," they told him, "wait until we understand what the Germans and Russians have in mind. Don't act hastily." August conceded grudgingly.

While the towns of Zeperow and Antonufka waited to see what their futures held for them they were relieved to see one thing return to normal. Albert Fischer resumed his duties astride his horse, with his pistol hanging at his side. While cleaning the gun he had discovered that there were three bullets missing. He asked his wife about them. He feared that the boys might have been playing with the weapon. Alwine became flustered and turned red. She found it difficult to lie, so Julianna quickly jumped in, explaining that in their fear, while he was gone, she had shot at an imaginary intruder. Albert laughed, as he imagined his mother shooting at shadows and went on with his cleaning. He was happy to be working again. It was something to do while everyone waited.

Albert didn't resume his office purely out of a sense of duty. He had listened as Johann and Erich explained that there was a greater threat to the community than Hermann Martin. What they said convinced him that German-Volhynia was finished. Even if the communists were to make some sort of overture to the Germans to indicate that they were welcome to stay, his heart could not conceive of life under Russian rule again. The only thing left was just to find the most propitious way of leaving, while salvaging the best of their lives here. Albert was not at all clear what he could accomplish as he took up the gun again, he only knew that he could do nothing for anyone while sitting in his kitchen.

It was early in November when the radio announced that Hitler's foreign minister, Von Ribbentrop, had come to an agreement with Stalin on the disposition of the ethnic Germans in his newly acquired territories. To the great relief of the Volhynians they were to be resettled in Germany. In fact, all Germans living in Russian occupied territories from the Baltics to Romania, and of course eastern Poland, were to be returned 'home.' It became painfully obvious that this was what the Fuhrer had intended all along. The German Reich was ready to forgive its expatriates and welcome them home like long lost children. The Volhynians could only shrug their shoulders. The alternative was unthinkable.

It was a complex game that the Russians and Germans were playing. As the two powers annexed Polish territory they also wanted to end a long history of problems. Russia wanted to rid itself of their troublesome Germans with their divided loyalties, while Germany wanted to replace the Polish majority in their new territory with a friendlier people. Centuries of problems had taught both nations that the Poles and the Germans were just too loyal to their heritage to be assimilated. This was to be a massive undertaking, involving millions of people.

The Volhynian Germans were to be resettled in the newly renamed territory called the Wartheland. This former part of Poland that stretched from the old border, east to the Warthe River was now incorporated into Germany. The plan was presented to the Volhynians as a fair exchange. It appeared to be so simple. You gave up your land in Volhynia and received land in Wartheland as compensation. Nothing could be more fair.

In their naivety the Volhynian Germans thought they understood that this compensation was to be reciprocal. The Poles who gave up their land in the Wartheland, the Volhynians supposed, would also be compensated. To them it was a gigantic swap. Many Germans assumed that the Poles would actually prefer to live in Russia, rather than under German rule. They were wrong. And nowhere did any such commitment for the resettlement of the Polish people appear in writing. Where did the mysterious promise come from? Not even the Volhynians could remember where they heard it. Whatever its source, it was untrue. Perhaps they just imagined it.

Nothing in their history had prepared the Volhynians for the full impact of this repatriation. There was nothing comparable in their collective memory that could ever disturb their conscience more than what they participated in during the spring of 1940. Under ordinary circumstances it was unconscionable. It was the thing for which the Polish people would never forgive them, and yet the Volhynians could only understand that all they had done was to clutch desperately to the only hope offered them.

The beginning of their sin was in finally recognizing the futility of remaining in Volhynia. To be bounced back and forth between Tzarist Russia, fragmented Poland, and now Communist Russia held no future. Here they would always be mistrusted foreigners. Nevertheless, there was no joy in the prospect of leaving their land, their homes and villages, the churches and the graveyards of their ancestors, but it was more than clear that they had to leave now. No other opportunity seemed forthcoming. "Home to the Fatherland," was not a slogan that inspired them. There was no age-old longing that enticed the Volhynian Germans, like the cry "Next year in Jerusalem," did for the Jews. It was merely that this was the only offer of a rescue they had, and so they consented to return to the land of their ancestors. The modern Volhynians were as pragmatic as their grandparents when it became necessary to leave their homes.

Although the Volhynians never rallied to the cry, "Home to the Fatherland," in Germany it was tantalizing and irresistibly romantic. The propaganda machine of Adolf Hitler made it seem like the Volhynians and the other ethnic-Germans were returning after years of captivity in a foreign land. They were regarded as prodigal sons, tired of wallowing in the mire, pining to return to the fatherland. Of course, the articles that appeared in German newspapers and magazines made it seem to the public that only the magnanimous intervention of Adolf Hitler had made their return possible. It was wonderful propaganda.

One article released to the German news service during late 1939 reported an interview with a hundred-year-old grandmother. "Our leader calls and we must go," she was quoted to have reverently declared. In interview after interview, similarly patriotic families spoke of their age-old desire to come 'home.' No mention was ever made of why their fathers had left Germany in the first place, only that they ached to return. The Volhynians were shocked when they read such inventions. There was no mention of the heartbreak of leaving the lands their parents and grandparents had broken their backs to claim from the forest and swamp. There was no hint of the betrayal they felt that a German leader, hundreds of kilometers away in Berlin, could accomplish what the Russians and Poles had not been able to do.

Yes, there was some relief among the Volhynians that they had been spared from communist rule. The rumors about what happened to German farmers who found themselves behind communist borders after the Great War shook them deeply. Even the memory of the Siberian exile was still strong and few Volhynians doubted that it would happen again. The prison camps in Siberia, the collectivization of farmland, the ruthless terror of the man called Stalin, all these things contributed to the sigh of relief that the Germans felt. Under these circumstances the Volhynians did not ask many questions about the morality of their rescue. It was like being pulled from a burning house. The joy and pain were inseparable.

As with many religious people, the Volhynians reacted to disaster by reaffirming their faith. Giving little thought to such abstract concepts as hypocrisy, they flocked to church. In their final weeks and months in Volhynia, the Bet-Haus in Antonufka swelled with worshipers every Sunday. Some came to lament their loss, other to give thanks for their rescue, most could not differentiate the two feelings.

Finally strong enough, even Edmund Frey came to church with Albert and Alwine. His sister was excited to have him come, even though she supposed that he was there only for her sake. She didn't realize that it was soothing for him to hear the soft words of the religion of his childhood once again. Still frail, Edmund, came seeking things he thought were long dead, hoping to find strength in the ritual his father had taught him to honor in his youth.

With Erich Winkler at the pulpit it was easy to listen to the preaching. The words Edmund heard were familiar but the tone was different. As he listened, he began to understand that this was a more gentle preaching than he had ever heard. The reasons became very clear the more he thought about it. The Germans no longer needed to do any political posturing, at least not from their pulpits. The church was no longer the last line of defense against the Polish regime. Stripped of these political concerns, the Lutheran religion could afford to be less abrasive and demanding. Edmund sat in the back of the prayer-house, Albert and Alwine on either side, and drank it in.

It was during his second Sunday that Edmund's quiet reflection was disturbed. His attention was aroused when a murmur, distinct and compelling, spread through the congregation. All eyes in the room were turned to watch a large man and his teenage son as they came down the aisle of the Bet-Haus. Edmund was more shocked than anyone to realize he recognized the man. He stared so hard that it was several minutes before he understood that the whole community was as dumbfounded as he was to see them there. But why? They couldn't possibly know what he knew? Edmund leaned over and whispered into Albert's ear, "Who is he?"

"That's Hermann Martin," Albert said with undisguised disgust. "Yesterday he was a Pole, today, he wants to be German again. He no longer needs his Polish wife and his Polish religion. He has kicked them both out."

Edmund couldn't take his eyes off Hermann Martin. His calm enjoyment of the Sunday Service was gone as he fixated on the man responsible for his incarceration. His heart beat faster and he wanted to hide but nothing could move him to take his eyes off Martin. The feeling was familiar, it was fear, and he had felt it before in the presence of this man. "He's a swine," he mumbled thinking he was speaking under his breath.

"I know," Albert confirmed, not at all startled by Edmund's pronouncement.

Hermann Martin didn't care about the whispering of his neighbors, he was just determined to reestablish himself as a German. Even he had no illusions about coping with this communism that the Russians were about to impose, and if it upset his neighbors to see him at church he couldn't care less. When they glared at him, he glared back, unintimidated. He even gave his old enemy Albert Fischer a taunting half smile. But the smile left him when he caught sight of the thin, young man sitting beside him. Edmund lowered his eyes quickly. He did not want to be recognized by this man. He would not have been relieved to know that Martin would spend the rest of the day struggling to recall who he was.

In December, the Reich sent out its resettlement committee to expedite the agreement between Stalin and Hitler. One adjunct of that committee was assigned to the insignificant communities of Zeperow and Antonufka. Ludwig Dreger arrived without announcement driving a black sedan and wearing a grey, military overcoat that didn't look quite right on him. Perhaps it was because it looked like part of a uniform and yet lacked military insignias or markings of any kind. It was a condition that the Russian government had imposed on the resettlement workers before allowing them into their territory. Not even inadvertently did they want to give the German military any status within their borders. It was a statement of sovereignty.

But Stalin was not just interested in making a statement of ownership. He wanted observers wherever the resettlement committee was working, making sure that the terms of the agreement were strictly adhered to. The man they were sending to that insignificant community in backward Volhynia was a junior officer, a native Pole. He had even spent some time in the district. A dedicated member of the party, he had left Poland years earlier after a tumultuous career as an outspoken student organizer. Harassed by Pilsudski's police and arrested so often that he feared his next arrest would be his last, he escaped to Russia. But he knew he would return someday. Lieutenant Peter Kuczinski was scheduled to arrive in Antonufka the day after Dreger.

When Dreger stopped his sedan in the middle of the road, Albert guessed who it was immediately. He tried to introduce himself but the aloof and arrogant German practically ignored his greeting. Even without the chevrons and brass stars, the man's clothes looked military to Albert and now there was no doubt. It was the arrogance that gave him away. This was a classic example of the attitude his brother had told Albert about so often. Working with this man was not going to be fun.

Despite taking an instant dislike to this fellow, Albert introduced himself again, this time making sure the man knew he was the constable. He wanted to offer his assistance, supposing it would be eagerly accepted once the man knew he had authority. Albert's persistence didn't come entirely out of a desire to serve, he hoped that his work would put him in a favorable light with the committee. However, Dreger said nothing in response to his offer. Instead, he pulled a paper out of his pocket and handed it to him.

"That's the man I'm looking for," he said, "the schoolmaster. Can you tell me where to find him?"

Albert led him to the Bet-Haus where Erich was packing books. Dreger wasted little time on introductions and small talk before he took control like a general. Immediately he began to give instructions. "You are assigned to assist me. As the leader of this community and schoolmaster your knowledge of the area and the residents will help my work. I will expect your full cooperation during the registration for resettlement."

"Of course," Erich responded, "but you should know I have only been in this community for a few years. Albert Fischer here, our constable, knows the district and the people better than anyone."

"Very well then, if you wish, he will assist you."

Within an hour, Ludwig Dreger had laid before the two men a comprehensive plan for the registration of all German residents of the area. The plan was explicit in every detail, and it was exceptionally demanding when it came to the verification of German ancestry. Every applicant would be required to prove that they were German. Dreger beamed with pride at the efficiency of the scheme he displayed. Erich and Albert were awed but Albert couldn't understand the reasons for the ponderous paper work.

"We know who is German and who is not," he said, "yet you are going to make us all prove it to you?"

As far as Dreger was concerned, Albert was a slow-witted local. He had a dossier on the village and had selected Erich Winkler as the only man worthy of assisting him. Erich was more German than all the rest put together. But now that he had accepted Albert as a member of the team he was prepared to be indulgent for a while. He explained, "Those who are permitted to return to the Fatherland will immediately be granted citizenship in the greatest country in the world." Dreger looked directly at Albert as he talked, but even the uneducated Volhynian could feel the condescension in his voice. It sounded as if he were talking to a child who didn't know the answer to a simple question. "It is our responsibility to make sure that those who attain this privilege truly deserve it. They must be able to demonstrate clearly that they are German, not just by name and language, but by blood."

"I don't understand," Albert said, reacting more to Dreger's demeanor than the explanation.

Now Dreger's condescension was mixed with annoyance and indignation. He spoke tersely as if Albert was an idiot, incapable of grasping the lofty idea he was explaining, and was therefore wasting his time. "Of course you don't understand. You have lived here too long! It is not surprising that you no longer know what it means to be truly German. You have become polluted living among these foreigners." Then he turned to Erich, "But you, Schoolmaster, I'm sure you understand."

"I believe you are trying to keep the German people pure," Erich answered.

"Exactly!"

But Albert still didn't comprehend the concept of racial purity. He looked blankly at his friend Erich for an answer. The explanation, however, continued to come from Ludwig Dreger whose voice was now high and crackled with contempt. "You people have been living in this backward country for more than a hundred years. Do you expect us to believe you kept your blood pure in all that time? Even in your small community I promise you we will find people who are more Polish and Ukrainian than German, or perhaps even worse. It is amazing the lengths people will go to in order to hide impure blood."

"Do you propose to keep everyone out of Germany who has any foreign blood in them?" Erich asked, astounded at the magnitude of such an undertaking.

"No, not at all. We expect that most of the East-European Germans have been somewhat polluted by these eastern races. What matters is to what degree. These measures are meant to insure that those accepted for resettlement are not just trying to pass themselves off as Germans. Who knows how many of these Slavic types will attempt to gain entry into Germany in this way? If someone cannot prove that they are more German than Polish they will have to stay here."

"Who decides that?" Erich asked.

"The committee decides. We have been given certain criteria to follow and we will also rely heavily on church records and local leaders like yourselves. But I have the final say.

"And there is one other reason for us to be thorough. A Russian officer will be coming to observe all we do. It is likely that they will try to foist on us all their criminals and other degenerates, but we will not oblige them. We must be vigilant. However, let me be clear, we want the Germans to come home, but only the Germans. We will not deny those who have a Ukrainian or Polish grandmother here or there, but if they are hiding Jewish blood, well you see my point. Let me assure you, there won't be any of them sneaking into Germany by way of this resettlement."

Now Albert understood. It even sounded reasonable.

At home, the quickly recovering Edmund Frey couldn't ask enough questions about Martin. Once prompted, Albert volunteered substantial information about his lifelong enemy. "I only hope," he finally said to Edmund, after explaining his long history with the man, "that he tries to register for resettlement so that I can tell the committee everything he's done."

"Albert, be careful," Edmund said seriously, "he could make things dangerous for you."

"Martin is finished," he simply replied, not understanding Edmund's warning.

Albert's statement seemed to be confirmed the next day when he saw and heard Dreger and Martin shouting at each other in the Bet-Haus office that Dreger had taken over. Albert was too late to hear the substance of the argument but he was pleased with the result. Martin stormed out.

"He's been rejected," Albert thought to himself smugly. His face beamed satisfaction. Right now Dreger didn't seem so bad.

When Albert was called into the office right after Martin left, he felt secure that the man's attempt to regain status as a German was finished. He hoped desperately that Dreger was going to ask his opinion so that he could seal the rejection. It made no sense to him that Martin could qualify to return to Germany after spending his life stabbing his German neighbors in the back. He just wanted to make sure Dreger had no second thoughts about rejecting him.

To his surprise, however, Dreger made no comment about Martin. Instead, he asked Albert about his brother-in-law Edmund. Why was he living with him? Why hadn't he registered for resettlement? Albert was disappointed and hesitated to answer.

Dreger looked at him impatiently and Albert was afraid that he thought he was hiding something. Quickly he told the man that he had rescued Edmund from Bereza Kartuska, where he had spent more than two years in prison.

"Then he wasn't detained just because of the war?"

"No," Albert explained, "they thought he was a spy."

"Was he?"

Albert thought it a strange question for an official of the Nazi government to ask. He shrugged it off as bureaucratic curiosity, the need to know everything about everyone, and answered coyly. "I don't know. He was dying at the camp so we brought him back here. He leaves for Vladimir tomorrow and he will apply there for resettlement with his parents."

"I see," Dreger said, never explaining his interest, and then dismissed Albert.

"One more thing Herr Dreger, if I may."

"What's that, Fischer?"

"Did Martin apply for resettlement?"

"Yes."

"You have rejected him?" It was more of a statement than a question.

"No," Dreger said. He was annoyed by Albert's impudence.

"He's not much of a German."

"I have heard of your problems with Martin. You shouldn't let your personal feelings interfere with your duties."

"Did you know he betrayed us to the Poles? He laughed while they dragged us off to prison."

"I know it all. There is nothing about Martin that I don't know Fischer. I will take it all into consideration," Dreger countered tersely.

Albert left in a state of confusion. He couldn't see how Dreger could dismiss him so easily or how he could think he knew Hermann Martin better than his own neighbors knew him.

Alwine Fischer would have loved to accompany her brother home all the way to Dombrowa, where she could visit with her parents one last time before this resettlement, but it was impractical. The resettlement was too close and Ewald was sick so she could not leave him. Nevertheless, she cried to think of the tearful reunion Edmund would have with their parents. She had never resented that Edmund was her father's favorite, he was hers too. A trip to Lutzk was all that she would allow herself and only because Julianna insisted that she go.

Albert was still struggling with what had happened in Dreger's office as he drove Alwine and Edmund in his old farm wagon. He could not understand Dreger's reasoning. He fumed about it, talking about nothing else as they drove to Lutzk in the early morning, wrapped tightly in blankets against the December cold.

Seeing his brother-in-law so agitated, Edmund couldn't help but warn him again about Martin. But Albert waived it off once again, saying, "Martin can't hurt me."

"He has powerful friends," Edmund replied, but Albert still refused to listen.

He laughed, "The only friends he had were Poles and he has betrayed them too."

"He's good at betrayal," Edmund shocked them by saying, "Martin was the man who betrayed me to the Poles!"

Albert and Alwine could not believe what they heard. They made Edmund say it again. "Why haven't you told anyone before now?" Albert asked.

"I'm not sure he wasn't working for the Germans when he did it. For years I have been thinking about it. It's only in the last few days that I figured it out myself. There was no reason for anything to go wrong with the assignment. They gave it to me because I was new and it was not dangerous. They didn't even provide me with a cover story. I was only there to pick up some papers.

"I was to meet a man in Lutzk and he was to give me a packet to take to Krakow. It was Martin. But I was arrested as soon as I took it from him. He stood there grinning.

"I have thought about it so often in the last few years. How I hated him and his awful grin. I wondered if he did it out of pure pleasure. Only recently I finally understood that the only thing he had to gain was the trust of the Poles. That had been the goal all along. They sacrificed someone unimportant, someone who knew nothing for this man to win the confidence of the Poles.

"If the Germans want him back then one thing is certain, he has information that they do not want the Russians to have. They will protect him. That's why you must be careful Albert!"

The trains of Poland which never ran on time under the best of circumstances had even greater problems in this transitional time. After waiting on the platform for several hours Albert was finally able to tear his wife away. Albert had duties and he couldn't be away all day. For the last time, Alwine kissed and embraced Edmund who smiled the wan smile of someone not quite well. Alwine sobbed as Albert gave Edmund a goodbye hug and turned away to blow her nose. She caught a glimpse of a man who looked like Dreger inside the station.

As they walked to the wagon, Alwine kept looking back, cheerfully waving, inwardly crying. Her brother was still so thin and wrapped up in one of Albert's old coats he looked so forlorn that she sobbed. "He's like a lost child," she commented to her husband, "I hope he'll be alright."

"With all the food you gave him," Albert spoke wryly, "he'll be better off than we are." It was meant as a joke but Alwine took it seriously.

"Do you want him to starve?" she retorted, "who knows how long that train will be getting to Vladimir? He looks so weak. Mama and Papa will be so shocked when they see him."

Alwine went on talking about her brother as they drove off, but Albert was distracted. He saw what looked like Hermann

Martin's horse and carriage, the fancy one he used on Sundays. He looked around for the man but did not see him. That made him even more nervous. However, at that moment the train whistle blew as it pulled into the Lutzk station. They smiled at each other confidently. Edmund would soon be home.

"Did you know Dreger would be at the station today?" Alwine asked after they were away from the station.

"Dreger was there?"

"I think so. I only caught a glimpse of him through the door."

"Are you sure it was Dreger?"

"It looked like him. He had the same coat, but I can't be sure."

Albert stopped. He looked over his shoulder. The train was pulling out. Edmund was gone.

Twenty

Ludwig Dreger and the resettlement committee had one clear mandate, making sure that no undesirables got into Germany. The screening of these eastern Germans had to be so thorough that no Poles, no Ukrainians and especially no Jews got past. Those Poles, Lithuanians, Latvians, Estonians and others, who because of Nazi collusion with the communist leader Joseph Stalin, were unfortunate enough to find themselves under communist rule were out of luck. There was no rescue for them. On the other hand people who could prove their German heritage even though they had lost their German names and perhaps even their language could be repatriated if they had proof that they were German.

It was the proving, however, that could be lengthy and with the approaching deadlines it became urgent for those who wanted to escape to prove their family history. Even though the committee had hired men like Erich Winkler and Albert Fischer, men who knew their communities, to help with the resettlement registration, they still wanted proof that people with names like Nabrotzky, Grudzinski and Luczinski really were Germans. So if the Germans had changed their names to make life in Poland more easy, or had acquired their names by intermarriage, the onus was on them to prove it. Ludwig Dreger in particular could not imagine that people with Polish last names and horrible foreign accents could be called Germans. In doubtful cases only an appeal to church records of marriages and births could satisfy the committee.

But the records were only available for a short time. The Russians had stipulated that all church records be left behind as state property. If someone couldn't prove they were German now, no appeal was possible after January 2, 1940, when the resettlement was to be carried out. That edict not only made the registration process more frustrating, but it caused a great deal of paranoia in the ranks of the Germans. The paranoia came from the belief that the Russians had sinister motives. The Germans were afraid that the Russians intended to foist upon them undesirables, infiltrating Germany with spies, agitators and Jews. Dreger himself exemplified that fear by pouring over the lists and noting incomplete and unacceptable information.

It was this unfailingly intense scrutiny by Ludwig Dreger that made Erich Winkler so surprised at his reaction one day as he showed him a name that he could not recognize. He had discovered it as he pecked out the rapidly growing list on an old typewriter. Erich amazed himself that he could put so many names and faces together. In two years he had become familiar with most of the congregation except with a few recalcitrant ones who never came to church. Once in a while he came across an unfamiliar name and was happy that Albert was there to make him aware who the man was, so that Ernst Thann's cousin and Ewald Hartenberger's brother-in-law did not get left behind. The only name that neither he nor Albert could identify was that of Maria Schmidt, a widow, aged 40, who lived alone out on the Zeperow road. Even Albert shrugged his shoulders as he tried to recall what widows lived so close to the Viteranno lands. He didn't know any widows on the Zeperow Road filling that description.

When Erich pointed out the name to Ludwig Dreger, he was at first enigmatic, dismissing it as a thing of insignificance. That was not like the usually precise and thorough Dreger, which astounded Erich. But then Ludwig, even as he was walking away, did a sharp about-face, almost as if he realized the inconsistency of his behavior, and set out to correct it. He revealed to Erich that this Widow Schmidt was a 'special case,' and he had been asked to put her on the list. He ordered Erich not to mention it to anyone and then again, uncharacteristically, he softened his tone and requested that the Schoolmaster keep that confidence.

But Erich Winkler, was more concerned about the effects of the lost records on the German-Lutherans than about one enigmatic widow that was somehow important to an odd man like Dreger. Like most of the thinking men in Volhynia, he knew that the loss of these documents would have far reaching effects. It was presumed that the Russians wanted the papers in order to destroy them, thereby changing history and denying that the Germans had even been there. Of all the terms of the resettlement, this one was the most onerous to the Germans. To leave the records behind, perhaps to destroy them and rob their ancestors of their achievements seemed immoral and unforgivable. Erich could not justify the Russian action and therefore tried hard to save as many of the records as possible but it was not easy under the scrutiny of the Russian observer, Peter Kuczinski.

Erich Winkler was not alone. Men like Pastor Schoen in Vladimir were even more suspicious about what the Russians intended. He had realized that without civil records of any kind it would be difficult in the future for Germans to make any legal claims. Clandestinely, he encouraged the rescuing of church records and even set his secretaries to work making duplicates by hand. He and his staff saved only a fraction of the records. Erich Winkler didn't have the time nor the resources to accomplish much, especially since most of the papers were kept in Lutzk, but he had to try.

Albert sympathized with Erich's concern for the loss of so much valuable information but he was too busy to help with the work of saving them. He had his hands full making sure that the other terms of the resettlement agreement were understood by the farmers of the region. Letting the emigrants know what the Russians would permit them to take and what had to remain behind was his main concern now and occupied all his time.

Since the Russians did not want this exodus to destroy the agriculture of the region, the emigrant families were allowed to take with them only a horse and a wagon, which they could load with their personal belongings, household articles, food and pets. They had to leave behind all their livestock, farm machinery and even their small hand tools. The simple rule, Albert had to tell them, was that if you were in doubt about taking it, then you shouldn't. Still, almost everyone had questions about specific items. It was Albert's job to ride from farm to farm and advise people on what they could and couldn't bring with them and help them to dispose of the things they couldn't take. Since the Russians would not compensate them for what they left behind, the Germans had at least bargained the right to sell their possessions.

So many farmers were trying to sell off their livestock and machinery that prices dropped quickly. The haggling was ferocious. Many a farmer became dismayed as the purchaser of a cow returned the next day to pick it up and presented only half the money they had agreed on. Disputes flared up everywhere as Germans argued with potential buyers over the price of their life's work.

Every day Albert was called on to mediate when deals went awry. With his knowledge of Polish, Ukrainian and Yiddish his time was not spared. He had to reason with the Germans who were upset at what they thought was robbery. Albert took one man after another aside and said to him, "Take the money, tomorrow you'll be even more desperate and sell the cow for even less." To the occasional Pole and Ukrainian, if he knew them to be reasonable men, he would pose the question, "Has he been a good neighbor?" If the answer was yes, which it was for the most part, he would say, "Don't do this to a good neighbor, add a little for the sake of your friendship?" They usually did.

Where Albert was in real demand was in negotiating with the Jews who also came looking for bargains. The Germans had been taught to be mistrustful of these people. They believed that the Jews, by trickery and subtleness, were able to get the better of any Gentile in a business deal. Albert's reputation was that he was the only member of the community who could deal with them on equal terms. When he explained that the main principle of his bargaining was to be fair and expect fairness in return, the farmers were sure that he was only being coy, preferring to keep his secret to himself. His friends were sure that Albert's knowledge of their language prevented the Jews from deceiving him. He knew that he negotiated no better or worse than the other farmers with their Jewish neighbors, nevertheless, his reputation spoke more loudly than his success justified. The Germans happily testified, "That Fischer must be part Jew, he can bargain like the best of them."

Unfortunately, this praise was repeated too often and eventually came to the ears of Ludwig Dreger. From then on, the resettlement official kept a closer eye on Albert, studying everything the constable did with suspicion.

Erich Winkler noticed Dreger's increasing interest in Albert and confronted him about it. Ludwig shrugged it off and even denied any prejudice, but the Schoolmaster pressed the issue. "What do you have against Albert Fischer?" he asked so sincerely that Ludwig felt he could confide.

"The man speaks Polish and Ukrainian and this Jew language like he was born to it. Can he really be German?"

Erich defended his friend, "He's as German as I am." Still, Dreger was not persuaded and intensified his observation of the man. Now as Albert excelled in his work, and more of his neighbors praised him, the more it counted against him in Dreger's book. Unwittingly, Albert was getting himself into trouble.

A week after Alwine and Albert had left Edmund at the train station they got a desperate telegram from Dombrowa. WHY

WASN'T EDMUND ON THE TRAIN? IS HE WELL? STOP. JOHANN FREY. Alwine broke down in a flood of tears. Edmund had never reached Dombrowa. She blamed herself for not going with him. Neither Julianna nor Albert could comfort her.

Albert tried to convince her that he was just fine. "He's gone back to Krakow or Berlin," he said to calm her down. He tried to convince her of something that he didn't believe himself, that Edmund had changed his mind about going home.

"No, he wouldn't do that," Alwine protested, "he promised me that he would go to Dombrowa and be with mother and father for the move."

"It's like being in the military," Albert tried to explain, "once they have you, you have to do what they want. You obey orders. Alwine, he's disappeared before because of them and turned up. I'm sure he'll turn up again."

In spite of her better judgement Alwine let herself hope. Albert, after all, had brought him home. Perhaps he was right. She desperately wanted to believe him. She owed him that much for saving Edmund in the prison camp. Yet as desperately as she wanted to believe, still her anxiety was not relieved. She wished that she could the feel as secure as Albert that she would see Edmund again.

Alwine didn't know that Albert didn't believe his own words either. He was sure that something sinister had befallen his brother-in-law. Perhaps the people he was involved with were even more dangerous than he imagined. They had betrayed him before, they could have again. It was more suspicious than ever that Martin had been in Lutzk that day. And Alwine had seen Ludwig Dreger there too. Hadn't Dreger been curious about Edmund and hadn't he told Dreger that Edmund was taking the train to Vladimir? Albert shook off his thoughts. They were confusing and they lead nowhere, except to the guilt he would feel if he had somehow contributed to the boy's disappearance.

But the thoughts would not leave him alone. Shirking more pressing duties, Albert rode into Lutzk the next morning. He hoped Dreger would not notice. With no idea what he was looking for, he determined to go to the train station again. The image of Edmund standing there that day, wrapped up in an old coat, looking so thin and so vulnerable would not leave his mind. It angered him to think that his work in rescuing the boy ... 'boy' why did he always think of him as a boy when he was almost thirty years old ... had been rendered pointless. He wanted to find something to indicate what had happened to that pathetic ... that's why he always referred to him as a boy, because he looked so vulnerable ... a pathetic young man, a boy.

Albert accomplished little in Lutzk that day. Questions of the station master and ticket sellers produced not a single clue about Edmund. No one had noticed the sickly looking German. Neither had they seen a man fitting the description Albert gave of Hermann Martin. The only remarkable thing about that day was that one of the ticket agents had seen the Countess Viteranno arguing with a stranger. He had become concerned for the lady, but then he saw them leave together.

"What was the argument about?" Albert asked.

"I have no idea. She had wanted to buy a first class ticket to Krakow but I had to tell her that the new border was closed to all but official traffic. She was upset and the man she was with didn't want her to make a scene. Like I said, they walked out of the train station together. I assumed everything was alright."

Albert wondered. "Was he about my height, maybe a little taller, dark hair, grey military-style overcoat?"

"That sounds like him. He had a German accent."

Albert returned home with nothing to add to his suspicions. He knew he had to confront Hermann Martin. He would do it in the morning before he reported to Antonufka.

The next day, as the Fischers ate breakfast Julianna opened the door to an insistent knock. It was the Martin boy, tall and fat as ever, but his face was red and he panted for breath as he asked for the constable. Albert's first impulse was to throw the boy off the property but there was an urgent and pleading tone in his voice that Albert had never heard from any member of that family. It made him curious.

"What is it?" Albert asked gruffly as he came to the door.

The blood drained from the boy's face as he caught his breath. "My father is dead," he managed to say, "he's been shot."

The body lay on the floor of his shed. Albert's first thought was suicide. "Farmers," he said to himself, "kill themselves in their barns or sheds." He didn't understand why, but any farmer he had ever heard of had killed himself in the barn or the shed where he worked. But the first problem with that easy conclusion was that it was not consistent with Hermann's character, he was not that obliging. The second was that the bullet was in Martin's back. The way the body lay, face down, with the head pointing to the door, it looked as if he was shot as he walked away from his murderer.

This was more than Albert had ever expected to deal with as a constable; he was out of his element and knew it. "Even in dying," Albert thought disrespectfully, "Martin can't do anything without causing me problems." He was not sure who could investigate this but he knew it wasn't him. All he could do was to put the body in a wagon and take it into Antonufka for burial.

The villagers, despite their hatred for the victim, were horrified at the murder, yet no one was really surprised to hear about it. Albert, whose mandate as constable did not include the investigation of murder, nevertheless, found it impossible to divest himself of this nuisance. The Kantorrat shrugged its collective shoulders, they had no more authority than he did in this matter. Dreger deferred any official police capacities to his Russian counterpart. Lieutenant Kuczinski, the Russian authority said, "You look after it, it's a

German matter. I can't be bothered." The consensus was to call it a random murder by some person or persons unknown and let it be. Good riddance!

The only one who cared at all was Erich Winkler, who had to bury the man. His problem was that he didn't know where to bury him. Some said that he was Lutheran but others swore that Martin had converted to Catholicism so that he could marry his Polish wife whom he had recently thrown out of the house. Erich rode to see the Catholic priests and to ask the whereabouts of the widow Martin. The wife and the priest agreed that it would be a desecration for him to be buried on the hallowed grounds of the catholic cemetery and that the Germans should dispose of him as they wished. But, nevertheless, that day, the newly widowed Frau Martin returned to her home to claim her son and all of her husband's property.

There was no undertaker in the village so it was up to the Kantor to prepare Hermann Martin for burial. He had wanted to do the body the dignity of burying it washed and in a clean shirt when he noticed the scar on the left arm. He called the only other man who seemed to take an interest to come take a look. "To me," he confided to Albert, "that looks like a bullet wound."

"How do you know?"

"I'm a hunter Albert, I've seen what bullets do to flesh! It's not very old."

"And so? It's not what killed him."

"No," the Kantor replied, "but think, Albert. What if someone tried to murder him before and came back to finish the job?"

Albert thought for a moment. He looked at the newly discovered wound and then at the lethal hole in Martin's back. It didn't make any difference what he thought. Martin was dead and nobody cared.

In a ceremony, as short on words of hope as Martin was devout, the Kantor and Albert buried him in a section of the cemetery reserved for strangers. Only the two men attended. His wife was not there and would not allow her son to come to the funeral of the man who had used and betrayed her. For the first time in his life Albert felt sorry for Martin. He had served only himself and now no one mourned him.

After the burial, Albert sensed a strange mood in the community. It was not fear that a murderer was among them, nor even relief that an enemy from within had been silenced. It wasn't even apprehension about the pending resettlement. This feeling followed Albert wherever he went. He noticed it in the quick turning of heads when he met people, the sudden change of conversation when he entered the tavern, and the whispers of shoppers in the cooperative. No one had to explain it to Albert. The talk was that he had killed Hermann Martin.

The fact became more apparent as too many of the village men slapped him on the back while he was trying to drink his beer in the tavern. No one said it directly and no one congratulated or thanked him either. As sure as they were that he had done it, they also realized that it was murder. To Albert it was disturbing to think that people suspected him of murder, no matter who the victim was. If he allowed that suspicion to stick, it would taint him for the rest of his life.

He told Dreger that he wanted to take a few days to investigate the Martin matter. Ludwig Dreger laughed at the absurd request and then objected strongly. "You think you're a real policeman? You're nothing Fischer, in Germany you couldn't even be the dog catcher. There is too much work to be done and only two weeks in which to do it. I can't spare even you."

"What if I just did it on my own time?" Albert asked.

"No, that's not acceptable! The committee needs all your time. What does it matter anyway," Dreger said coldly, "From what I understand you should be as happy as anyone to be rid of him!" He smiled as he finished saying it, but it was not a warm smile. It made Albert angry.

"He was my enemy, yes, but I didn't murder him even if it is what people believe."

"You won't accept the credit even though it would make you a hero?" Dreger's tone sounded more like derision than an inquiry.

Albert answered tersely, "He was shot in the back. The person who shot him was a coward not a hero."

Dreger would not relent, however. He told Albert to get back to his job. "Let's get these people out of Russia," he said, "this Martin was insignificant. As you once said yourself, he was hardly German."

Albert was no investigator. By all rights he should have let the whole thing drop. There were enough people who were thankful that Martin was dead that it seemed a crime to try and find out who murdered him. Besides, what would he do if he found him? Shake his hand? Pat him on the back and say, "Don't do that again, but oh yes, thank-you!" And where could he begin to look? Albert had solid reasons to forget about Martin. But faced with the gut-wrenching feeling he had, knowing that he was the chief suspect, he knew he had to ignore them all. He was not a murderer.

It also nagged at him that Dreger and Countess Viteranno, and Martin too, had been at the train station the day that his brother-in-law had disappeared. But what really disturbed him was the memory of a strange request that the Countess had made of him several years earlier.

Ignoring Dreger's order, he rode out to the estate in the early evening. He had hardly seen the noble lady in the years between and he really didn't know what he would ask her. He imagined the conversation starting, "Well, did you ever find anyone to kill Martin for you?" He laughed at the ludicrous situation he found himself in and when he finished chuckling he began to feel disheartened. What right did he have to be asking questions of the Countess? With the cold wind blowing the drifting snow across the road and the dark coming, it was easy to talk himself out of this pretentious venture.

As he turned his horse toward home, however, he looked down and noticed the impressions of an automobile in the snow. The tire tracks were so new the wind hadn't had time yet to fill them in. His first thought was how nice it would be to have an automobile and drive through the wind and snow in the warmth, on cushioned seats. That would make a winter's ride to the Viteranno estate less discouraging. Albert looked at the tracks again. There were more cars on the road all the time but he only knew of three people who possessed one, the Countess, Ludwig Dreger and the Russian Kuczinski with his military machine. He hadn't seen the Countess driving her car in a long time. Most likely these imprints were one of the two others, probably Dreger. Where was he going on this road if not to the Viteranno Estate? This was no time to be fainthearted, if it was evidence he wanted he had to be bold and it had to be now.

When he was only a few meters from the long lane to the manor house, he saw the lights of a vehicle speeding toward the road. Afraid that it might be Dreger, he pulled his horse down the steep embankment and hid behind a stand of pine trees. While he watched the car plowing through the snow, Albert felt a sense of familiarity, as if he had watched this scene before. It was, of course, Dreger's automobile. It turned sharply onto the road and as it disappeared into the blowing snow, Albert was still watching, wondering what Dreger's business was with the Countess.

As he made his way up her lane, Albert remembered the time, years ago, when he and Johann had come to the farm to divide their inheritance. A man had shot past them in the hallway. Johann had commented on his military bearing. He had sped off just like Dreger had a few minutes ago. It seemed so clear now! The face was the same. It had been a younger but just as arrogant Ludwig Dreger. Albert could only shake his head. There were so many more questions than answers.

As surprised as she was to see Albert, the countess invited him in anyway. She led him to the same room where she had made the desperate plea that Albert had only recently remembered, only today she seemed more relaxed, almost resigned.

Albert began awkwardly. “I suppose you heard about Martin?” he asked, still feeling uncomfortable, but relieved that he had found a better beginning than what he had rehearsed on the road.

“Yes,” she replied, and then added, “poor man!” The comment was almost an afterthought.

“I remember a conversation we had some years ago.”

“That was a long time ago. I hope you aren’t here hoping to collect a reward now.” Her last remark was made flippantly, but Albert thought he detected that she had suddenly become nervous.

“I didn’t kill him,” Albert replied quickly.

“Oh! But then I don’t have any more money anyway so it doesn’t matter. The few things I still possess will soon be taken from me. Perhaps the Bolsheviks will take me too. It’s very kind of you to come but as you can see, I just don’t care any more.”

“Then you didn’t have Martin killed?”

Through a pitiful, nervous laugh she said, “I had reason to back then, but no longer. Martin wanted my land, which I’m about to lose anyway. Hitler has betrayed us all, Germans and Poles alike. He has sold us to the communists and rendered the matter mute. What reason would I have to kill him now?” Then she turned and faced Albert and said teasingly, “I have heard that most people think it was you who shot him?”

“I didn’t!”

“And neither did I. He made so many enemies.”

Albert almost turned to leave but there was a question on his tongue that he really wanted to ask. It was no good trying to leave while it plagued him. “About Martin’s enemies, Madame, was Ludwig Dreger one of them?”

The countess blanched. “What? Ludwig? Why would you think I knew anything about...? Oh yes, you must have seen him drive off.”

"I saw him here ten years ago too."

"What?"

"You, he and Martin were arguing."

"Herr Fischer," she only called him Herr when she was upset, "I did not kill Martin over a ten-year-old argument, that is ridiculous!"

"Why was Dreger here tonight?"

"Dreger is an old friend. He was paying his respects. He is a gentleman and you are not to ask me such questions. Now I must insist that you leave!"

"Is he helping to get you into Germany?"

He could see a look of concern as it flashed in her eyes but her voice managed to disguise her shock. "If I could, I would certainly go. There is no future for me here, but even if the Germans allowed it, Kuczinski has informed me that I am not free to leave."

"Not even under a false name, like Maria Schmidt?"

Her face turned to stone for a second. "Preposterous," she finally blurted out, "even if I considered such a plan it would be too dangerous." Her voice was full of anger and bewilderment. "Your questions are becoming ridiculous. I want you to leave!"

Albert had one more idea. Early in the morning he showed up at the Martin farm to ask the dead man's wife some questions. Martin's wife had as much reason to shoot him as anyone. Unfortunately, the woman was hostile at first and refused to open the door to Albert. She mumbled something in mixed Polish-German about not allowing her son to go to Germany. Albert had to use all of his patience and persuasion to convince her that he hadn't come to take her son away. She calmed down.

"Why are you here then?" she asked, puzzled.

"I want to ask you and the boy if you know who shot your husband?"

"He was your enemy, why do you care? If I were to guess at who killed him, I would guess that it was you."

"I had nothing to do with your husband's death." He was beginning to get tired of saying that.

"Don't get me wrong," the woman explained. She was very willing to talk now and did not even attempt to hide her venom for her dead husband. "I ought to thank whoever did it. He was going to take my son to Germany and I would never have seen him again. The man was a pig."

"You were very angry with him?"

"If he wasn't my son's father I would have killed him myself, but I didn't."

"Do you know who might have shot him?" Albert asked again.

"Every German in the area and half the Poles. Take your pick."

"Can I speak to your son? Did he see or hear anything that night?"

"No," she said forcefully. "He can't tell you anything. The boy is confused. First his father teaches him to hate everything German and then he wants to take him there."

She was so straightforward that Albert had to believe she was telling the truth. He decided to try another approach. "Has anyone ever tried to kill your husband before?"

She laughed,"You hit him over the head. Don't you remember?"

"I mean recently."

"No, why?" she shook her head.

"Are you sure? We found a bullet wound on his left arm." He pointed to the place where he had seen the scar and drew his finger across the area to show her the precise point of the wound. "It had almost healed."

A strange look came across her face as she realized she knew something he didn't. "For that you should ask your wife."

"My wife?"

"You really don't know?" she asked.

"What should I know?" Albert asked, bewildered.

"My brother's boys stayed with us during the invasion because their parents thought they would be safer in the country. I had to beg Hermann to allow it! But he couldn't stand the noise so he sent them out and told them to go bother the Germans. They came running home crying that the crazy German, Fischerova, was chasing them with a gun."

"You mean my wife?" he asked, hardly believing his ears.

"Yes! My husband worked up such a rage even I was afraid when he left. I didn't see him again until almost morning. His arm was bandaged up and his clothes were bloody. When I asked him about it he just hit me. He never told me what happened."

As Albert rode home he recalled the missing bullets. He had accepted his wife's explanation, but now he felt like a fool. He was furious and wanted to know why she had lied.

Julianna confessed right away. "I shot Martin," she said, resolved to accept the consequences of her lie, "we didn't tell you that the coward came to burn down our house. From the potato field I shot at him three times. I only wanted to scare him, I never expected to hit him. In the morning we saw the blood on the ground."

"Why didn't you tell me?"

There was a guarded look between Alwine and Julianna and then Albert's mother said, "We were afraid of what you might do. We thought you might try to kill him and get yourself into trouble."

"That's only partly true," Alwine interjected. She hated lies and she felt that this one had run its course. Her husband needed to know. "We promised Irene Weiss that we would tell no one, but now I think we should."

"What does Irene have to do with this?" Albert asked.

Alwine found it hard to explain the conclusion of that painful night. If she was going to get through it, she had to make it short and simple. "Martin ran across the road to Irene's house and told her that he had been shot by irate Poles. She bandaged him up but she didn't believe him. He beat her and then he ... he raped her."

Julianna continued as her daughter-in-law became too emotional to finish, "We promised her that we would never tell. Now we have broken our promise."

"Why would you make such a promise?" Albert asked with genuine incredulity. "We would have had him arrested."

"And what about Irene?" Julianna took an indignant tone with her son. "Do you know what happens to a woman when everyone knows she has been raped? She is never able to look anyone in the face again."

"Oh, that's ridiculous!" Albert exclaimed. "Everyone knows what Martin was."

"Just the same," Alwine confirmed, "it is what every woman fears and it is real. It is hard to know what is worse, being raped or having everyone know it."

It was a concept that Albert had trouble coping with and he tried to exit the conversation before he became too entangled. "Maybe you have a point," he conceded. It was no use arguing when women stuck together like this, he thought, but he knew one thing for sure. If a man had raped his wife he would want to kill him and he knew August well enough to know he felt the same way.

"I'm going to speak to August," Albert announced.

"Why?" asked Julianna, "you can't tell him!"

"Rape is a very good reason to shoot someone. If he did it, I want to know."

"He's your best friend," Julianna chided him, "how can you do something like this to him. What if she never told him? What will that do to them?"

"She told him," Alwine said softly, "she couldn't keep it from him."

Alwine's revelation triggered a memory in Albert. After they had returned, it was August who had been most vocal in condemning the man they all considered to be a traitor. Albert had thought nothing of it then because there were a dozen or more men who felt the same. But now he knew where August's anger came from and suspected that he had not given up his quest for revenge. Albert had to find out.

Alwine would not let Albert go alone. She could not betray her friend and not face her, their friendship demanded that. Her husband was happy to have her along, he thought it would make it easier to talk to their friends.

Alwine did not want her husband to blurt out what he knew to their unsuspecting friends, so she took Irene aside and told her that she had broken her promise. There was a moment of pain in Irene's face that made Alwine feel guilty. It seemed to her that she was watching the unfolding of a moment that would change their friendship forever. How relieved Alwine was when Irene turned her head and nodded her acknowledgment as if to accept what she knew was inevitable.

Alwine could only imagine the pain. "Irene, I'm sorry."

The four friends sat around the kitchen table where their friendship had begun, but only August didn't know what was coming. He didn't understand the awkward silence that followed because Albert found it hard to word the questions he had. It was not the way their evenings usually began.

"Did you kill Martin?" Albert eventually asked his friend, trying hard not to sound accusatory.

August laughed lightly, as if it was a joke. "Why? Because of Bereza?"

"You were the one who persisted..."

August cut him off, "I don't believe it, you're serious! You're asking me? You're the one they're blaming and you want to put it on me. You're supposed to be my best friend."

"I didn't kill him!" Albert protested. He was just as offended that August, his best friend, had accused him.

"Neither did I, and after all we have been through together ... Bereza Kartuska. Why would you ask me? There are a hundred men with better reasons."

Irene gently touched her husband's hand, "He knows!"

August's eyes flashed at Albert and his face flushed with anger. "If a man ever deserved to die, he did. I have never been so glad that anyone died, but as God is my witness, I didn't kill him. I wanted to, I even thought of several plans but I never could bring myself to do it. I'm ashamed of my cowardice!"

"If you ask me," Irene interrupted, "the man you should be asking is that Dreger fellow."

"Why do you say that?" Albert asked.

"Often I can't sleep. I have nightmares. So I stand at my door late into the night watching the road. The night before Martin died he and Dreger met on the road and argued. They didn't fight but their voices were raised and both men were very angry."

"How did you know who it was?"

"I would know Martin's voice anywhere and I recognized Dreger's car."

"Did you hear what they said?"

"No. It wasn't clear but they were shouting at each other. They were threatening each other."

Albert looked at his wife, "That was the day we put Edmund on the train. It seems obvious that the two of them were involved with something but I don't know what and I have no idea what to do about it."

Frustrated, Albert decided to drop the issue. Finding out who murdered Martin was as hopeless as trying to find out what happened to Edmund and just as depressing. All that was left to him was to confront Dreger and he could only guess at the reaction. He had nothing as evidence, only suspicions, even he knew that. If he accused his boss he knew he would never leave this territory. He decided to drop it.

But when he saw Dreger again in the morning, the man was furious. "Don't you ever question the Countess again," he yelled right into his face. "You have no authority to question her and no right to make accusations. You will stop this little investigation immediately, I order it!"

He should have said that he already stopped, that he had produced nothing of significance, but he was angry. "It's easy for you to say but I'm the one that everyone thinks of as a murderer."

"Accept it. You could have been a hero," Dreger said with obvious scorn.

It sounded contemptible coming from Dreger and Albert gritted his teeth. "I can't accept it. I didn't kill him and I don't want that kind of reputation."

"I'd be careful Fischer," Dreger said. His eyes were still full of anger that made what he said seem like a warning, "you will find that the more you deny something the more people want to believe it."

"What do you mean?"

"Of course you wouldn't understand. I'm telling you if you try too hard to prove that you didn't do it people will begin to believe that you are only trying to hide the truth."

He was right, Albert didn't understand. It sounded like an insult, or worse, a threat. He knew he should have kept his mouth shut but he found it hard to do when he was so angry, still he knew he had to be careful. "I don't have anything to hide. Everyone knows about my feud with Martin but it's the man he met with secretly on the road to Zeperow, he has something to hide."

"What are you talking about?" Dreger queried with a sudden increase of stress in his voice. The anger in him caused his voice to quiver as he tried to ascertain what Albert knew. "What are you talking about?" he insisted.

"Martin was seen arguing with someone on the road the night before he died. Someone with an automobile much like yours. Maybe he was his killer."

"Where did you come up with that preposterous story? Did you dream it or did you just make it up?"

"They were seen on the Zeperow road. There are a lot of people who live on that road, like the Countess Viteranno, and that widow Maria Schmidt," he said and knew right away that he shouldn't have. He just wanted to see Dreger's reaction.

Dreger's voice was just a loud scream now. "You're a liar Fischer and a stupid backward Pole. You are dismissed from your duties for the resettlement committee."

Now Albert was sure that Irene had at least told the truth. He was almost sure that Dreger had killed Martin, perhaps he had done it for the Countess. The dilemma for Albert, however, was not how to prove it, but how to survive if he did prove it.

More convinced than ever of Ludwig Dreger's involvement in Martin's death, Albert rode out to the Viteranno estate again. Perhaps he could reason with the Countess and she would tell him the truth. But she was gone and while he was leaving the Russian liaison, Kuczinski, drove up the lane and was equally distressed that the lady was gone.

"She's run off," Kuczinski said.

"Because of Martin?" Albert asked.

"You think she killed him? If she did no one cares but you," the Lieutenant replied. "No, she ran because she knew we were coming for her sooner or later. She is a spy, a traitor to her country."

"Which country, Poland or Russia."

Kuczinski smirked, "What does it matter?"

As the days to the resettlement came closer Albert was relieved that people forgot about Martin's death. No one slapped him on the back any more without reason or bought him unsolicited rounds of beer at the Tavern. Perhaps they had accepted that he had not done it or were satisfied to leave him alone even if they thought he was a murderer. Whatever their reasons, people finally seemed to have something more important to occupy their anxiety. Albert was grateful.

Two days before Christmas, Erich Winkler found something that explained a lot. He had been watching the sparring between Ludwig Dreger and Albert Fischer with both fascination and alarm. He had become frightened when he saw Dreger's condescension turning into fear and then into anger. He tried to warn Albert but by then it had gone too far. Each day that passed Ludwig was more critical of Albert and everything that he did. It made no difference whether he did his work well or badly, it was commented on contemptuously by Dreger. Even after he had fired Albert, Dreger would not stop his ranting. He seemed more intent than ever on defaming him.

"Do you think," Dreger tauntingly speculated in front of Erich, "that Fischer is really German? I've heard it said that he speaks Yiddish and Polish better than he speaks German."

Erich couldn't understand why Dreger was doing it. It was as if simply firing him hadn't been enough. Sometimes it seemed that Dreger had no specific reason for harassing Albert and only got some kind of perverse pleasure from it. Still Erich couldn't help but feel that it was leading to something, something unthinkable for Albert and his family. He watched his boss carefully, hoping to discover what he was up to.

Another day Dreger said to Erich, "I understand that Fischer dealt well with the Jews. How do you think a simple farmer developed such a talent? My God, I heard his father was mistaken for a Jew and was almost hung. Do you think it is in their blood?"

"If you had been with us at Bereza Kartuska, Herr Dreger, you couldn't say such things," Erich said in defense of his friend, but Dreger just ignored him and went on talking. There was nothing he could do.

"You shouldn't be so naive, Erich. The man's a fool," Dreger raged again and again, "a stupid fool. He's concerned over the death of one traitorous German while we are preparing to unite these people with their Fatherland. He must be a fool, what do you think Erich? Never mind you're a fool too! It's hard to believe he's really German. I wonder what we would find if we rattled his family tree, Poles and filthy Jews probably. The man doesn't belong in Germany. He's trying to hide something with all these questions about Martin, don't you think. A guilty conscience perhaps? Do we really want men like him in Germany?"

The day before Christmas-Eve the Kantor cleaned the chapel area of all the paper work that Dreger had assigned him. It was the last Christmas for the Germans in Volhynia and he expected the Bet-Haus to be packed. He had not had time to prepare a sermon. The Christmas story, simple and full of hope would be more relevant than ever, he thought. Combined with all the favorite carols it would be a memorable and nostalgic evening. To finish the service he would have the congregation sing the most favorite of all German language carols, Silent Night. The last 'Silent Night' in Volhynia he thought, and liked the phrase and wondered how he might work it into the service without sounding too trite. He looked for a piece of paper to write it down and grabbed a blank sheet off a pile on Dreger's desk. When he turned it over, however, it wasn't blank.

It was a draft of the resettlement list. Erich picked up another sheet. It was more of the list. Since he had typed most of the names, he was familiar with it. But this copy was different from the one he saw last. There was a black line made with a straight edge through some of the names, not many, but one or two on each page. He had picked up the last page first and with his pulse beating fast he looked first for his own name, Winkler. It was there without a line through it. Quickly, he thumbed through the loose pages to the F's. The names of Albert and Johann Fischer and their families were stroked through and a simple three letter indictment was written beside them with a question mark. JEW? He put the papers back and noted the empty file folder under them with the label, 'Resettlement Master List.'

On New Years day, while the community awaited the next morning much as the children of Israel must have waited their exodus, the Kantor went to the Bet-Haus early to clean up his own papers. He found the sealed envelope with the master list. He removed the list that Ludwig Dreger had edited so neatly and inserted his own copy. At first he had thought to put a line through a name or two to make it look like Dreger's list. As he read the names, however, his conscience could not allow him to do it. It was all or nothing. He only hoped that Dreger didn't check the list one more time before it was too late.

Twenty-One

The day after New Year, Erich Winkler stood dumbfounded and shaking his head as Ludwig Dreger told him he was leaving immediately. Erich wanted to ask him how he could leave at such a critical point, but instead he found himself in a panic to write down the instructions which Ludwig blurted out so casually at the last minute. "Well, the real work is already done," he said half apologetically when he saw the flustered look on Erich's face, "just a few things for you to clean up." Last of all, Ludwig pulled a large brown envelope from his case. "This is for the Russian Kuczinski," he said, "I'd give it to him myself but he's probably off getting drunk and I need to leave. Make sure you give it to him or they won't let any of your people across the border."

Erich took the envelope and tucked it under the notes he was taking. He was thinking as fast as he was writing. It was incredible that Dreger would leave now on the eve of the completion of his work. If Erich needed any more proof, he had it now, that the man didn't care about the people he was supposed to be helping and must have had some ulterior motive for being here. Why else was he leaving now? Erich was still asking questions when Ludwig Dreger turned on his engine and drove off without even an attempt at an explanation.

Dreger's abrupt departure appeared even more mysterious when Erich looked at the envelope that had so unceremoniously been handed to him. His eyes widened as he read the label on the envelope, 'Resettlement List - Zeperow-Antonufka.' His first impulse was to tear it open, but contrary to what Dreger had so casually observed, there was a lot left to do and less than twenty-four hours to finish it. Laying the envelope on his desk, he rushed to find his friends Albert, Johann and August to help him with the last great task that needed to be finished. At precisely 5:00 a.m. the next morning every German was to leave his home. Erich and his friends had less than twenty-four hours to get that information out to every corner of the district.

Hours later, when he was sure that every resident had been contacted, Erich Winkler relaxed and then he realized he hadn't given the envelope to the Russian yet. He turned it over repeatedly, wondering if he should or shouldn't, when he noticed that the envelope wasn't even sealed. This was too easy. It was obvious, Dreger had wanted to rub it in that he had found Erich's substitution. He wanted him to find out when it was too late to do anything about it. All the other lists and paper work were gone. But even in his defeat Erich couldn't resist another look and to his total amazement found that his unedited copy was still inside. It was hard to believe that Dreger hadn't noticed the switch. Instead of being pleased the Schoolteacher had to wonder why. But unfortunately there was no time to think it through, he had to get the envelope to Kuczinski, who was at the tavern as Dreger had suspected.

The envelope jarred the soldier's memory, "Yes, I have to get this to the border."

As the Lieutenant turned to leave Erich asked him, "Do you know why Dreger left so suddenly?"

Kuczinski turned and smiled. "He left before I decided to shoot him. He was trying to sneak that Viteranno woman out of the country and I'm sure he helped her to escape. He knew I couldn't arrest him, but he wasn't at all sure that I wouldn't shoot him." He was about to walk away when he turned again and asked, "Albert Fischer is your friend isn't he?"

"Yes?"

"Warn him to be careful when he gets to Germany."

"I don't understand."

Peter Kuczinski just smiled and walked away from Erich without responding. His departure seemed as enigmatic as the German's.

On January 3, 1940, the world changed for the Volhynians as it did for most East European Germans. Almost a million Germans were coming home; from Volhynia in Russia, from Romania, Latvia, Estonia and the Government General and all across eastern Europe. Agreement for resettlement had been reached earlier in Latvia and Estonia than in Volhynia and other agreements would follow. The resultant displacements would affect millions of lives and take years to complete, but during this cold winter it was the Volhynians who would have to move. The propaganda agency of the Third Reich reported to the world that these people were jubilant to be returning to the Fatherland, but on the faces of the Volhynian-Germans there was only resolution. They hoped that what was ahead was better than what they were leaving behind, and better than what the Russians were bringing.

Alwine Fischer said good bye to her house with no ceremony and certainly no tears. She had no special fondness for her cluttered little house, with its crowded bedroom and dingy walls. Giving it up was the least of her worries. Still, she dreaded leaving for some very practical reasons. She hated uncertainty and no one could tell them exactly where they were going and what they would find when they got there. Just as troubling was this January weather that was already giving the promise of being bitterly cold. She dreaded this journey for her little ones, for her old mother-in-law, for herself and the ordeal her husband would have to face. Alwine was extraordinarily nervous when she climbed onto the wagon.

Her hands were shaking and her mind raced through a million reasons why this was wrong. Yet in the back of her mind she knew there was something waiting for her that she didn't want to face.

As they drove past the garden that Alwine had tended so carefully and saw the fruit trees her husband had planted, she felt a sinking feeling in her heart. Yet in that instant she felt relief too. She was grateful that she was not devoid of any feeling for the loss of this land that had sustained her family. She looked at the trees in her garden again. It was ironic that they were only beginning to produce abundantly now as they were leaving. Her garden had been her refuge. There she found both solitude and relief, a place to be alone with her thoughts, a place to pray, a place to hope. There, what was drudgery to others was joy for her. It was a point of great concern, whether or not her new home would have such a place for her.

The trees reminded her of the wedding gift she carried on the wagon. As she looked behind, she saw the dresser her father had made for her covered by a blanket. Alwine regretted that her daughters would not receive such a wonderful treasure, made from the wood of a tree planted and harvested especially for them. Nothing else could ever be that special.

Before long, the Zeperow road was full of wagons, all of them headed to the train station in Lutzk. Albert and his wife rode up front and huddled behind them were the children and Grandmother Julianna. They were all wrapped in blankets against the cold. Sheltering the huddled family on one side from the biting wind was Alwine's cherry-wood dresser. It had been the first thing she had made her husband load up. The rest of the wagon was filled with household items, many of which had little worth, but they had refused to leave anything behind that they were allowed to take. They were headed to Germany on a promise, just as generations ago their progenitors had gone east on another promise. But there was not the same joy of expectation now. This seemed like rejection rather than a new beginning and it was bitter.

As the long line of farmers drove through Zeperow-Antonufka the Germans were shocked to see how many of their Ukrainian neighbors had come to see them off. Overcome with emotion they cried and threw themselves on their friends' necks, kissing them liberally to the point of embarrassment. The Volhynians smiled politely but they knew that the sentiment was overstated, the Ukrainians were only expressing their desire to be free. They too wanted to be rescued.

In the middle of Antonufka, Albert almost wished he still had his gun when a hulking man ran out of the darkness and started to shout at him. It was Trepenko, the man whose dog he had shot. It took a few second for Albert to realize he was not angry, but just the same he didn't want to stop to make out what the man was shouting through his dirty teeth. Frustrated, Trepenko jumped and ripped the reigns out of Albert's hands, wrapping his massive fingers around them. Then he stopped the horse and shouted at Albert in broken German. It was an instruction he had obviously rehearsed. "You, German, you tell Hitler not to forget about us. You tell him to come back, we Nazi too."

"But Trepenko, you hate Germans."

"I hate Russians more. You tell Hitler, come help us!"

Albert nodded and that satisfied the huge man. He gave the reigns back, patted his old enemy on the back and stumbled away in the dark. Albert looked at his wife and shook his head, "He thinks I'm going to have a conversation with Adolf Hitler." For a moment, however, he was flattered that Trepenko had chosen him to deliver his message. Yet he laughed as he looked back and saw that the huge Ukrainian was taking no chances. He stopped every wagon that could not find a way to avoid him.

In Lutzk, Albert kissed his family good bye. He left them at a warehouse close to the train station that had been set up for the Germans so they could wait comfortably for the train which was coming shortly. The women, children and a few elderly men were to be spared the ordeal of the overland trek. They would take a Russian train to the border. Only the men had to drive their wagons all the way to the city of Lodz deep within Poland, or what the Nazis called the Government General. In the midst of winter the Volhynian men would have to travel more than 350 kilometers of frozen road in their farm wagons.

The scene was repeated over and over across the breadth of Polish Volhynia as German families collected at train stations. For too many people it was reminiscent of the summer of 1915. Just as then, the men were gone, leaving the women defenseless. What if the Russians changed their minds? Any moment now Alwine expected the same train to appear on the tracks that had come when she was only six years old to haul them away to Siberia. She tried to stay optimistic but her fear that the Russians would betray them again was overwhelming. As the anxiety mounted, she quietly resolved that under no condition would she allow her family to be put aboard one of those terrible metal freight cars. She didn't know how she knew, but she was sure it meant death.

Albert, Johann and August formed their own little caravan to travel across the frozen Volhynian roads to the Bug River. When they saw how some of their countrymen had built gypsy-style wooden canopies over their wagons where they could take refuge from the wind and cold they wished they had been as smart. It was too late, however, and on the second day out, a snow storm caught them and drove them off the road. Fortunately, they found a house, most likely abandoned by some other German family, and passed the worst of the storm in warmth. In the morning the wind and snow had stopped but there were high snow drifts across the road. They could not allow themselves the luxury of hiding in their refuge till the roads were clear. They had to keep going, they were expected at the border. By pushing and pulling their wagons through the drifts, they made only a few kilometers by noon. By then the roads were more passable as the lines of wagons ahead of them had already broken down the high drifts.

But there were casualties everywhere, wagons with broken wheels and axles sat idle while men worked feverishly to repair them. They had succumbed to the extra strain off pushing through heavy snow and high drifts. Tragically, some foolish men had stayed on the road during the blizzard and suffered the consequences, tumbling over the edge. They came across one that had fallen off a steep bank and was lying half-submerged in a small tributary of the Bug River. Frantically its owner and his friends were trying to rescue it from the ice with ropes and pulleys. The three Zeperow men stopped to help pull on the ropes, but minutes later the wagon had broken completely through the ice. Everything was lost.

Adding to the problem of the snow and clogged roads was the intense cold. It was colder than normal even for a Volhynian January and the men were thankful not to be on the road alone but in the safety of friends. How they wished they could have traveled on the trains with their families. Yet, in spite of the freezing temperatures and snow-covered roads the men reached the border before the trains ever arrived at Lutzk to collect their families.

Erich Winkler had not told either of the brothers what he had found in Dreger's list so they were not nervous when they approached the border. The Russian border guards examined their wagons and checked their names off a list and waved them across the bridge. There wasn't even a hint of a problem.

But none of the men thought to ask the Russians if the train with their wives had reached the border yet, they just took for granted that they were well ahead of them. They crossed the bridge not knowing that their families were still huddled in the cold warehouses of Lutzk.

Once they were on the other side of the river there was rest in an old army barrack that had been converted for these trekkers. The sleep was sorely needed. The Volhynian caravan had pushed hard and the temperature had gone so far below zero that the men could feel the cold wind biting at the marrow of their bones. It didn't matter how many layers of clothes they put on, the wind found a way through and many of the men suffered from frostbite. They were all exhausted after this first stage of their trek.

Whatever satisfaction the weary travelers felt at having come so far was quickly forestalled when the astonished men learned that their wives and children had not yet even reached the border. "Don't worry," the German officials said with smiles, "they are coming, there has been some trouble with the trains." But they could not say what the problem was. When the Volhynian men wanted to stay and wait, at least until it was confirmed that the trains were coming, they were emphatically refused. Every day more wagons were expected and there was not room enough or food enough for them all. "One day of rest and then you move on. No more!" they were told. Neither were they permitted to go back. "If you return, you will not be allowed to cross the border again. The Russians won't let you leave twice." Reluctantly they moved on, but they were more troubled than ever and still had the bulk of the road ahead of them.

There were other rest stops along the way but for the most part the men had to fend for themselves. The temperatures kept dropping. Sometimes they traveled through the freezing night because they couldn't find shelter. Anxiously they looked for the government rest-stops, but their concern was not rest, rather they wanted to know about their families. No where was there any news of the trains and each day the men wondered how far behind they were falling. Yet, if they complained, the soldiers shouted at them, "If you Poles ever expect to be German you will have to learn to listen and obey. That is the German way. Now shut up and stop grumbling!"

While the men worried, their families waiting at the Lutzk station had almost lost hope. The train that was supposed to move the women and children to the west was a week late. The warehouses where the refugees were supposed to sit and wait for a few hours had become their living quarters. They were grossly inadequate. The floor was cold and hard and the walls were hardly adequate to keep out the cold. The facilities were unhygienic or did not even exist. Sleeping was almost impossible in the cold. Understandably, many people ate up the food they had brought for the train trip in the first few days. There wasn't even any food to be bought. They had forgotten how the Russian trains worked. Every moment spent there was full of the threat of disaster.

The weather was just as bitter in Lutzk as it was out on the road where their men traveled. Julianna shivered and complained that it was colder than it had been in years. The only warmth came from the fires set in the steel barrels in front of the warehouse doors. The heat hardly warmed the people standing around those fires but there was nothing else to do, no way to make things better, except to huddle in blankets on the cold warehouse floor and wait. The only amusement the children could find was to scrounge for wood to keep the fires alive. Even the promised help of the Red-Cross did not materialize.

Wrapped in a blanket with her baby in her arms, Alwine was determined not to let her children sense her fear, not as long as she had even a little hope. But that did not free her from the internal panic that was prompted by old memories. What was happening was all too familiar. Even walking outside offered her no relief as it only offered a view of the railroad platform where she had left Edmund to meet his fate. She kept visualizing him there, thin, forlorn and wrapped in that tattered coat. It brought tears to her eyes. In her life she had not had good luck with train stations.

By the end of the week she began to suspect that the trains were never coming. She wanted to scream out, "They have betrayed us again!" but she couldn't do that to the children. For them she had to be strong and hopeful as her mother had been strong for her when she was young. Courage, she now understood, is something you pretend. But at least she had Julianna to lean on and to listen to her fears in the night. Alwine cried only when the children were asleep. In the morning she had to fight her tears back and present a picture of calmness. She had all but resigned herself to their betrayal when finally a train whistle blew and hundreds of people collectively cried, "It's here, it's here." No one was more relieved than Alwine to see a long line of passenger cars waiting for them and not one of them was a freight car. There were seats and there was heat.

Again, Alwine fought back the tears. In her heart she felt she had failed. Under similar circumstances her mother had been so much stronger, so much more in control. Where had her strength come from? Faith? Alwine wiped her tears as she realized her mistake. She had forgotten to pray throughout this ordeal. She would not make that mistake again.

But the train did not move smoothly to its destination. The volume of traffic that this mass migration created caused multiple problems for the Russian rail system. The cars had to be continually shifted and sidetracked, causing long delays for reasons the passengers could only guess. The frequent stops evoked even more anxieties and created other problems for the train. While the cars were stopped, the steam in the heating hoses condensed and the collecting water froze. Consequently, shortly after the trains started again, they had to stop so that teams of workers could thaw the hoses. While they worked the passengers wrapped themselves tightly in blankets and huddled for warmth and continued what seemed to be a life of waiting. After each delay, Alwine looked out of the window to judge carefully that they were still moving west.

January was almost over by the time Albert, Johann and August reached the city of Lodz on the eastern corner of the newly organized German district of Warthegau. Despite the delays, their families had reached the city well ahead of them. In makeshift accommodations all over this city, as in other cities across Poland, Eastern-German arrivals were being temporarily housed. The new accommodations were barely better than the warehouses in Lutzk.

In fact they were warehouses and factories too, converted into temporary barracks with the minimal essentials.

Whatever vision the new arrivals had about being welcomed home quickly dissipated. This was no paradise that they had come to. The food was sparingly given out and they had to listen to their children cry for hunger. In front of their parents' eyes young men were quickly inducted into the German army. The pressure on them to join was insistent. If they didn't volunteer they were made to feel guilty. Yet everyone waited patiently for the promises to be fulfilled that everything they had given up would be replaced. Even the skeptical Alwine made no loud complaint.

Shortly after they arrived, the wagons that the men had practically sacrificed their lives to drive through the harsh winter, were unloaded and the contents were put into storage. All their household goods, from the precious to the mundane, were put away with such haphazard organization that the Volhynians wondered where the vaunted German efficiency had gone. With minimal cataloguing and identification the Volhynians could not understand how the Germans could keep the promise that their things would be forwarded to them in their new homes. "How is it possible?" they asked and were brutally rebuffed. "This is Germany and you are not used to German ways!" They were told that everything that they needed, the benevolent Reich would provide. The government, after all, had only the best interest of these people in mind in everything they did.

Even Albert began to doubt. When he returned from surrendering his load, including the wagon and horse, he shook his head. He told his wife that she would probably never see her dresser again. Alwine simply replied, "At least we're not in Siberia." Her reaction surprised him but he had to agree.

There in the drafty old factory where the Fischers ate and slept, Ewald became sick. It was what Alwine and Albert had dreaded and expected. But the boy had been to the brink so many times before and recovered that his parents thought it was just another episode. Cheerfully, he said, "Mama, I'll get better." True to form, in a few days he was well on the way to recovery, with only a slight fever lingering. It seemed like his indomitable spirit would always carry him through.

It was at the end of January that almost the whole camp was transferred further west to the city of Zwickau, ostensibly to make room for more Germans from Romania. By now, everything they had brought out of Russia, except the clothes on their backs and a few items of luggage were gone. Only the most optimistic people still expected to see their household goods again. The promise that all would be compensated became a joke among the Volhynians, but it was a joke they kept to themselves. They had learned that the Germans charged with their care did not have a sense of humor. Any jest was taken as criticism and an affront to the whole German nation. It was not tolerated from these foreigners.

Zwickau was just another refugee camp, bleak and barren. The promise that this was to be their final stop before they were to be returned to the land seemed hollow. The only thing that made it any better was the work of the Red Cross as they struggled to keep the refugees warm and fed and the children happy.

Albert and Alwine got to know several of the workers who seemed genuinely interested in the welfare of these resettled refugees. One woman in particular came to see them often, taking time to hold the baby and learning the names of each of the children. It wasn't long before the Fischer children would rush to her whenever they saw her coming and wait patiently as she teasingly searched her pockets for the treats she had hidden there. Her name was Anna Sebastian. She was a native of Zwickau and a young widow, slightly older than Alwine.

Anna was determined to do what she could for the children of the camp and took an instant liking to the vivacious Fischer children and their unassuming mother. She gave Alwine some insight into what was happening in Germany but her outlook was not positive. She pointed to the harshness with which the resettlement was being conducted and said, "Why would a government that cared about these people subject them to such deprivation knowingly. And make no mistake, they knew people would die. They knew children would die. They care little for their own people, and not at all for the Poles and even less for the Jews."

Almost as if to make Anna's point for her, Ewald relapsed and even the continuous nursing of Alwine and Julianna was not enough. He continued to decline so that even his parents, who had witnessed a score of reversals, began to worry.

Anna Sebastian felt the boy's forehead and hurried to find the camp doctor but came back in tears. "He's too busy," she cried, biting her lip to keep from yelling out her anger. Alwine was too concerned for her son to see the pain etched on the Red Cross worker's face or to catch the hesitation in her voice. "It's not true," the distraught woman confessed, no longer able to contain herself.

"What's not true?" Albert asked.

"The Doctor said he can't come, but really he won't come! Sick children are of no value to the Nazi's. A waste of resources!"

Albert backed off, his instinct for self-preservation was strong. Anna's words were treasonous but his worst fear was that someone might have heard them. She was being irrational and that was dangerous. He did not know how to respond to her and her ridiculous accusations. Fortunately, with every breath she became even more upset and finally left weeping.

Weakened by the cold and oppressed by the lack of food, Ewald's little body, so full of character and wit, gave up at the end of February, just five days after his tenth birthday. Up to the moment of his death his whole family had hoped for one more recovery. He had overcome so much, returning from the brink so often that it was unimaginable that he would die even now. Edmund and Hertha sat in a corner crying, not really understanding but feeling abandoned. Ewald's parents and grandmother were stunned.

It mattered little to Alwine that many healthier children had already died in the ordeal of the resettlement, nor that Ewald had never been expected to live this long. She turned away from the doctor who came to confirm the death but had been too busy to see the boy when he was sick. Now when he said, "Isn't this better, he was not healthy anyway," Alwine closed her ears and her heart. She cried bitterly for her oldest son and began to believe what Anna had said was true. They had to have known that people would die.

The camp officials were indifferent to the tragedy of the family except to grant them a simple casket, a burial plot and a shovel to dig a grave. Death, after all, was now a daily occurrence in Zwickau. Albert himself dug the grave. He held back his tears as he made the sides of the grave straight and corners sharp. Though he wished all the while that he was still in Volhynia digging wells, he wanted to do this for his son. It had to be done right.

Alwine was grateful for the comfort of her new friend Anna, who came to the funeral. She was more composed now. Still, Alwine missed Irene who was in the camp and had sick children of her own to look after. But Alwine knew that somehow a wall had gone up between them. They had hardly talked on the train. Alwine blamed herself for the loss.

As they walked back to the camp together after the short funeral Anna Sebastian made it clear that she still believed it was murder. "This need not have happened," the Red Cross volunteer said to Alwine, pointing to the crosses, most of them for children. "He hates whatever is weak and fragile."

"Whom do you mean?" asked Alwine.

"Adolf Hitler, of course. There are things going on in this country that are unspeakable, Alwine. If you can avoid it don't take anything from them. Don't take the land they offer. Go somewhere else, go to America. Whatever Hitler gives you, it will not be free. You will never be able to pay him all that he wants."

Alwine did not understand what her new friend meant, but she didn't like the sound of it. She was already suspicious of the Government. From what she could see those who had called them out of exile didn't care much about the people. Unfortunately, she had no idea what to do about it.

Twenty-Two

As the German Reich made plans to recall its expatriate populations from eastern Europe, it envisioned no problem in making room for these people. In their newly annexed territories like Warthegau all they had to do was to expel the Polish majority and the logical place to move them was into the Government General. Starting in the fall of 1939 they displaced hundreds of thousands of Poles and Jews, but by the end of January the German appointed governor of that area requested a stay on more transferals. Warsaw, Lublin, Krakow and the areas between were saturated well before there was enough room in Warthegau for all the new Germans. The stay was granted, effectively slowing down the resettlement process.

For reasons that even his closest advisors couldn't understand Adolf Hitler vacillated in his opinion of the Poles. Though he always considered them to be subhuman, only slightly better than Jews, he and Himmler, his chief organizer of this migration, were not always consistent in their ideas about what to do with them. Some they shipped to Germany to replace factory workers lost to the Wehrmacht (war-machine), others they sent to the Government General area of Poland to face starvation while working there on less than adequate rations. However, when it was pointed out that some of the Poles had for centuries intermarried with Germans, they reconsidered. Many had blonde hair, blue eyes and by Nazi standards were culturally more German than Polish. Perhaps these were worthy of redemption. Hitler, after all, was fascinated with racial types. He toyed with the idea of reclaiming the 'German blood' in these people for the good of the German nation but he changed his mind so often that subordinates got mixed signals. No one ever knew exactly what his ultimate goal was, and so finding a way to achieve it was impossible.

The only thing that the Fuhrer never vacillated about was that sooner or later, those Poles who could not be redeemed, had to give way to the new German population that was now crowded in the camps. It only became a matter of concern how long it would take. Neither was he concerned about compensation, for the Poles who were ripped out of their houses and off their lands. Contrary to what the Volhynians had been told, or hoped, or imagined, this was not an exchange, it was a confiscation. The stance of the Reich was that the Poles were a vanquished people and had no rights.

As the pace of the resettlement slowed the government was also able to do a better job of evaluating its prospective citizens. In early March Albert first heard about the strange examinations that some members of the camp had undergone. Previously there had been forms to fill out, innumerable forms that contained questions of German heritage and genealogy. There were also questions of how much land, livestock and equipment they had left behind. But this was different. It was strangely invasive. "Perhaps," the Volhynians thought, "the examination had to do with a medical problem. Perhaps they were looking for diseases." They were given no specifics.

Albert and his family did not have to wait long to see what the talk was about. Only a few days after he first heard about it, each member of his family, from Julianna right down to the baby were examined. They had no idea that the examiners were from the SS Race and Resettlement Office, attached to the Central Office of Immigration, or that most of these men had undergone crash courses in anthropology, biology and eugenics, specifically to prepare them to be able to differentiate between the races.

They concentrated on the head and face, making measurements and jotting evaluations that were never explained. They checked eye color, eye spacing, nose width, head circumference, face shape, lip shape, hair color, hair type and every conceivable characteristic. When they finished with the face, they checked the physical formation of the rest of the body: hands, fingers, feet, toes, bone structure, muscle development, body proportions, etc. They even made the whole family stand together and evaluated them like a lot of cattle in an auction pen, but they rarely commented on anything. When it was over there was relief but no explanation.

During March and April of 1940 the German refugees started to trickle out of the camps to take possession of their new farms. Slowly the evictions of the Poles started again. Some few went as workers to Germany and some movement began again to the Government General, but many just became workers on the lands they had forfeited. Landowners became slaves.

Albert and his family were not among these lucky first to be resettled. He had more papers to fill out. It mattered little to protest that this information had already been given. This project was too big and there were bound to be numerous duplications and cartons of information gone astray. All that the camp office had on Albert Fischer was one thin dossier. It seemed that practically no information about him that had been gathered in Zeperow had survived the transport west. But Albert wasn't the only one who lacked sufficient documentation and had to fill out form after form for the second and third time, although he was one of the very few from his community who ran into so many problems. He could not understand why this had to happen to him.

When the first bus left there was genuine joy in the whole camp because all could now anticipate the end of their incarceration. Albert was disappointed that his family was not among the first groups to take possession of their new farms. Yet he and his family were buoyed by the fact that August and Irene Weiss and even Johann and Hedwig had come to that final step out of this ordeal. For Albert it meant that they would not be far behind. He went to the bus to bid them farewell and they all spoke of how they expected to be reunited soon. Even Hedwig kissed him good bye.

Buses transported the fortunate Volhynians to their new homes. As Johann Fischer and August Weiss caught sight of the land where they were to live, their eyes grew wide and their mouths fell open. These were wonderful farms with large houses and neat barns that were about to fall into their hands. This was much more than just compensation for the meager farms they had left behind. They were awed and their hearts soared with gratitude as all their hardships had now proved profitable. It was too good to be true.

Then in a sudden and unexpected encounter they were brought back down to earth. As the Volhynians stepped out of the buses, they looked into the terror stricken eyes of the farmers whom they were displacing. Those same buses that had brought them were also there to take away the families who had built up these farms. Polish and German families stared at each other in bewilderment.

The Germans, who had been willing, if sorrowful to leave Russia, now had to consider that these people did not want to leave their homes. To them this was not a German province called Warthegau, it was still Poznan or Lodz and it had been their home for as long or longer than the Germans had been in Volhynia. The sight of these terrified people was sobering, but it was too late.

Albert and Alwine hoped desperately to be reunited with their old neighbors from Zeperow. Their hope was not without reason. One of the better provisions of the resettlement was the emphasis on maintaining the integrity of Volhynian communities. As long as the Committee, working with criteria that was handed to it, was of the opinion that a village was strong and viable and not polluted by too much inbreeding, they attempted to keep its residents together. It helped the morale and increased the stability of the new communities they were building. Albert and Alwine were not yet disturbed that they had been omitted from the first group of Zeperow refugees to be resettled on their own land because they felt sure that they would be reunited with their friends.

Yet, only a few days after Johann had stepped off the bus Albert received a disturbing letter from his brother. He did not know what to make of it but Alwine read it over and over again. She and Anna Sebastian both stained it with their tears.

Belschewo, Warthegau,

April 4, 1940

Dear Mama, Albert, & Family,

I hope this letter finds you all well and happy. Hedwig and I are fine, but I must confess that as I sit in this house, which is much bigger than the one I left behind in Volhynia, I have an overwhelming feeling of shame. My wife laughs at me and calls me foolish because I am so tormented, but I just don't know what to do.

Somehow I had the impression that the people who gave up these farms were as willing as we were to be resettled elsewhere. I had thought that they did not want to be German as we did not want to be Russian or Polish. But as I stepped down from the bus I saw their accusing faces, I was shamed into realizing the truth. These people did not give up their homes willingly as we did, but had to be ripped out of their houses. I doubt that there was ever any intent to give them anything in exchange for this land. Nothing is as we supposed.

The land is good and I have much more of it than I could have imagined. To help me raise the grain I have contracted to supply to the German army, I have been given farmhands. They are good, hardworking young men. When I asked them where they came from they told me that their parents once owned these farms.

The other day I saw August Weiss. He does not seem to feel the same way. He says it is a matter decided between governments and makes the point that if we did not take the land it would be given to someone else. He thinks we earned it with our suffering. I wonder, however, if what we suffered at the hands of the Russians and Poles justifies this or makes it more contemptible?

Nevertheless, I wish you all well. I do not like to think of you languishing at the camp. Unfortunately, I have to wonder if coming here will be better for you.

Yours son and brother,

Johann

Albert did not know what to make of the letter. Johann, he was sure had not lied, but he was an alarmist. He was sure that the Poles would receive the land and the houses that they had been promised. He still did not yet understand that they had been promised nothing. In his mind he imagined the same family whose land he was to receive walking into the house he had left behind in Zeperow, as inequitable as that might be. He was positive they would receive their just reward and he was equally sure that if the situation were reversed the Poles would not be that generous to the Germans.

Alwine, however, fretted over the letter because she understood its moral implications. Yet she could not afford to suggest to her husband that they refuse resettlement. She looked at her family already suffering the effects of this cold winter in surroundings that seemed worse than Siberia and wondered where they would be next year if they weren't away from here. Einhardt was now sick, Ewald had already died, and even as she consoled herself with the rationalization that he was never meant to live long, she was so afraid that the rest of her children would meet the same end. The mere thought made her cry. Yet it was true, in this camp even healthy children were dying. For her children's sake she had to take the one option that was left to them no matter what the moral consequences were.

The resettlement of the Ethnic-German populations of eastern Europe, including Volhynia, into the German-annexed lands of Poland produced a moral dilemma not only for the Fischers, but for all the newcomers. For years afterwards they sought to understand exactly what had happened. The argument they confronted most often was whether they had come home willingly when called by the German Government or whether they were refugees in the true sense of the word, displaced or chased out of their homelands. If they were refugees then they were as much victims as the Poles were, but if not, then they had collaborated in the displacement and robbery of thousands of Poles. The Poles no longer had a government of their own to look out for their interests and were easy prey.

In later years, while academics discussed, fretted, apologized, accused and excused, those peasants who lived through it rarely spoke of it. They found it hard to talk about. Most of these peasants never really understood what had happened, but their situation made them uncomfortable. They felt like they had made the wrong choice in a game that had given them only one option. They believed they had been lied to about the fate of the displaced Polish farmers. The Poles, however, never accepted that the Volhynians did not know the truth.

For the Volhynian-Germans there had been no practical alternative. With a decree, they had lost everything. Their lands, their houses, their businesses were now within the borders of communist Russia. They knew what the communists were, having lived beside them now for twenty years. What they hated most was their avowed atheism and what they feared the most was the communist policy of disallowing private ownership of land, even small farms. The communists were totally opposed to exactly those things that the German-Volhynians held most precious. No

Volhynian-German had to sit down and weigh the pros and cons of leaving Volhynia. There was no decision to be made.

When the door to the west opened the Germans felt relief, even though they had been betrayed by Germany. If by some twist of semantics they were not to be considered refugees, such sophistry was beyond their comprehension. If Adolf Hitler had not sent an invitation they would have left clandestinely because their aims and the communist's goals were incompatible. Left in the east, it would not have been long before they were marching to Siberia and too many of them, like Alwine Fischer, could still remember.

When they left Volhynia, the German farmers truly believed that they were part of a huge exchange. Although, they did not investigate the mechanics of the swap, they assumed that the Poles would participate in it as full and equal partners. How they came to the conclusion that the Russians were eager to give land to the Poles, even they could not say. There were some vague assumptions that since the Poles and Russians were both Slavic peoples it was somehow a better fit. Of course they were wrong. Some swore that it had been explained to them just that way, but many more of them could not remember how they came to this understanding. It may just have been, considering their lack of sophistication, that it was easier to believe that the Poles would be compensated. What they forgot was that the Poles no longer had a government to fight for their rights.

Robbed and persecuted, the Poles would find it hard to forgive the Volhynians and harder still to believe that the German farmers had not known from the beginning that their land had been stolen. But as Johann Fischer had discovered, the truth could not be hidden forever. Even the most thick headed farmer could no longer deny it, the land they had been given was stolen land. During the war years the Volhynians would have ample opportunity to prove some measure of good will, but too many showed instead that they believed the Nazi propaganda about subhuman Slavics.

In mid-April, Albert was becoming more and more anxious. He began to suspect that he had been forgotten. Every day he went to the camp headquarters to remind them that he was still waiting. Day after day they told him to be patient. Then very suddenly, Einhardt, just three years old, came down with a fever and even Albert's priorities changed. Julianna cradled him constantly. Alwine prayed and begged for help as his condition worsened.

Fortunately, Anna Sebastian happened to come by when the boy was the sickest. This time she refused to allow the Doctor to say no.

Einhardt had bronchitis and it was close to turning into pneumonia. He had to be taken to the hospital. The little boy whimpered and cried as he was taken from his grandmothers arms and sped away in a car, leaving his family stunned. Not even his mother was allowed to come along.

Alwine had begged the doctor, "Please, for the boy's sake, let me come with him? He's so afraid!"

"Don't worry," the Doctor said without emotion, "when he is well, we will return him. Be strong! You are German now!" Alwine hated those words by now. If being German meant you are not allowed to feel then she didn't want it. She could only cry as she watched her little boy being hauled away.

Anna Sebastian went to see the child every day even though Alwine was not allowed outside the camp fences. She kept Alwine informed but struggled to find anything hopeful to say. She found herself repeating the same thing every day, "It's too soon to tell!" She could see the hope in Alwine's eyes and became painfully aware of her inability to report any progress.

A week later, the words were cold and ugly even when they were delivered by a friend. "Your son is dead," Anna said, but the tears streaking down her face and her quivering voice had already given it away. "He died today in the hospital. Pneumonia."

Alwine could not be consoled. "How shameful it is," she cried to her husband and mother-in-law, "that Einhardt had to die alone without the comfort of his family."

Julianna hardly heard Alwine through her sobbing. Einhardt had been her joy. Hertha, only six years old, tried to comfort her grandmother and the two sobbed together. Edmund cried by himself where no one could see him. Alwine's heart turned cold with the shock. She thought for a short while that she would never forgive God for this evil which followed so closely the death of Ewald, but she knew who was really to blame.

Albert quietly reported to the camp offices and requested that they return the body of his son for burial. The secretary looked at him blankly. "Why?" she asked, "they will bury him." Albert could not believe her unfeeling words. He opened his mouth to protest but had no idea what to say. He needed help.

"For heaven's sake woman," from the other side of the room a voice booming with authority seemed to rush to his defense, "even here a family has the right to bury their own children!" It seemed to echo his very thoughts.

Albert recognized the voice and when he looked to the side he saw his friend Erich Winkler. He had just arrived in Zwickau. His work in filling in for Ludwig Dreger had been appreciated by the Committee so that now he worked full-time for them. Assigned to Zwickau after having served in several camps, he had recognized Albert across the room, but was shaken when he heard his conversation with the secretary.

The two men dug Einhardt's grave together. It pleased Albert and Alwine to have their Kantor at the grave side, even if he had no more official church office. They asked him to say a prayer over the grave and then showed him where Ewald lay. Erich offered a prayer there too. Alwine cried with every word.

There was nothing that could console Alwine. She even rejected the sympathy of the women who came around to comfort her because she wanted to feel the pain. She wanted to feel angry and cold. She did not want anything to diminish the horror of her son's death. The cost of repatriation had become too great to bear.

She wrote a letter to her friend Irene, mainly because she could think of no one else to write to, in which she accused the Nazis of letting her little son die. She was convinced that he had either died of their neglect or they had done something to hasten it. No one died of pneumonia anymore! The doctor had been too quick to snatch him away from her and would not even allow her to come to the hospital. "Why else had they hesitated to give them the body? They think of us more as Poles and Ukrainians than Germans," she wrote. "We are like livestock to them and not human at all, they rip our sick children from our arms like they were culling animals." She wrote and sent the letter off before she told her husband what she had done.

"Are you crazy?" he screamed when she told him what she had done. "What do you think is going to happen if they read that letter? We'll be stuck here forever! They'll shoot us all!"

"I don't care. They killed Einhardt and Ewald too!"

"And now you want them to kill us all one by one. They are in control. We can't fight them."

It was only when Alwine realized that the rest of her children were vulnerable that she began to regret her words. Her husband shocked her into understanding that her living children needed her. She found in the quiet of night that she could pray again and that she loved Edmund, Hertha and the baby Else as much as she loved the ones she lost.

Twenty-Three

Erich Winkler was shaken by the circumstances that his friends had fallen into. It was natural that he felt pain for a friend in trouble, but his pain was mixed with guilt. He had rescued Albert and his family once and now he had to question if they would have been better off without his help. It seemed to him that having helped once had made him responsible for the consequences too. "What does it all mean," he asked himself, "if you don't see it through to the end?" It brought to his mind a Bible story he had preached more than once in the Bet-Haus in Antonufka. What would Christ have said about the good-Samaritan if he had given the wounded man water, bandaged his wound, and then left him in the road? Would it have changed the definition of what a friend and neighbor was? For Erich the answer was yes. He had to help again even if it meant taking a risk.

He had to be careful. Erich had little more authority than the camp secretaries. Any real power within the resettlement commission was reserved for the military. Yet his good service and his skill with people were appreciated and needed, and so he was tolerated by men like Camp Commander Wiesner. Nevertheless, he had to be sure not to overstep his authority. It wasn't wise to question policy nor to come to the aid of individual families who were under scrutiny. It was easy for civilian employees to fall out of favor quickly with men used to military efficiency and instant, unquestioning obedience.

Shortly after the heart-wrenching funeral for the little boy, Einhardt, Erich went to the camp files and retrieved the dossier on Albert Fischer. He took it to his desk and studied it from top to bottom trying to understand why he and his family were still in Zwickau when his friends had all been resettled. He found out that Albert's papers, which the family had filed in Volhynia, had disappeared. But he also found four sets of the documents that Albert had been forced to fill out at the camp. This was a committee ploy used to delay an application for resettlement almost indefinitely. They pretended that the process was meant to weed out liars, following the theory that it was hard to keep the details of a lie consistent. Somewhere in the process those who had invented German ancestry would trip themselves up by changing or forgetting a detail. The question Erich asked himself was what they thought that Albert was hiding.

When he came across the reports of the race examinations, he flipped through those pages quickly. He knew what this was about but could not understand the details. There were measurements and comments that meant little to him. It was the section at the end, the overall assessment of the whole examination, neatly typed in captial letters, that caught his attention.

THE PRIMARY QUESTION, WHETHER ALBERT FISCHER IS A JEW, CANNOT BE CONCLUSIVELY ANSWERED. HOWEVER, WE CAN SAY CONCLUSIVELY THAT THERE IS A MIXING WITH INFERIOR RACES. THE INDICATIONS ARE VERY EVIDENT. BODY PROPORTIONS INDICATE POLLUTION FROM INTERIOR RACES, IN THEIR CASE PROBABLY POLISH OR EVEN POLISH-MONGOL. SECOND, A MENTALLY AND PHYSICALLY RETARDED SON (THE CHILD DIED IN FEBRUARY BEFORE WE COULD EXAMINE

HIM) SHOWS POSSIBLE HEREDIATRY PROBLEMS. THIRD, THE OLDEST DAUGHTER, HERTHA, HAS VERY DARK TO BLACK HAIR, WHILE THE REST OF THE FAMILY HAS MEDIUM BROWN HAIR COLOR EXCEPT FOT THE INFANT WHO HAS BLOND HAIR. CLEARLY THIS IS A THROW BACK TO NON-NORDIC BLOOD.

ON THE POSITIVE SIDE, NONE OF THE FAMILY NOW LIVING IS DEFICIENT MENTALLY. ALL MEMBERS OF THE FAMILY ARE BRIGHT AND ALERT AND THE BOY, EDMUND, IS ESPECIALLY ACTIVE. IT IS OBVIOUS THAT GERMAN HAS BEEN THE PRIMARY LANGUAGE OF THE HOME AND THEY ALL SPEAK IT PROFICIENTLY. THE FATHER AND SON ALSO SPEAK POLISH WELL BUT THIS IS TO BE EXPECTED. CURIOUSLY THE FATHER ALSO SPEAKS UKTRAINIAN AND YIDDISH, WHICH HE CLAIMS HE LEARNED THROUGH COMMERCIAL CONTACT.

RECOMMENDATION: CLASSIFY AS 'BARELY SUITABLE' SUBJECT TO FURTHER EXAMINATION.

Erich cringed as he read that pronouncement, 'barely suitable.' It was a travesty to have superficially trained SS functionaries conducting examinations and writing quasi-scientific assessments about race. Besides being amateurish this was the science of haste and prejudice.

Erich was only slightly familiar with the criteria they were using to condemn these people. Months ago he had been asked to take the four-week course to qualify him to conduct this questionable research. He had refused, saying that it was beyond his scope. Now after reading report after report he knew what they were doing was immoral. But he could do nothing. He had seen what they did to people who had done nothing wrong and wondered how he would fare if he questioned instructions that came from Himmler himself.

There were six classifications that the displaced Germans could fall into: very suitable, suitable, in general suitable, barely suitable, unsuitable and ethnically or biologically unsuitable. At the top was the Fuhrer's Nordic ideal and at the bottom was what he considered to be the degenerate races. The characteristics that they claimed constituted the ideal Nordic type would disqualify most of the population of Germany. He doubted that even Adolf Hitler himself could qualify. 'Barely suitable' was right on the borderline. It was a judgment that was easily downgraded but was rarely reversed. The same people who only a month or two ago had been accepted with compassion, were now only a step away from being classified as unworthy and degenerate. Why the change? No one really knew. Perhaps as Hitler and Himmler saw more and more foreign-looking Germans they questioned the wisdom of accepting them without investigation. Or as the dislocation of the Poles slowed down and they saw that some of them resembled Germans more closely than did these easterners, they had to question their standards. But the new criteria depended much on impressions and interpretations of ill-trained investigators who could be brutally unfair.

Erich had seen it before in other files. The assessment report, for all of its duplicity was a condemnation. Once a negative comment was entered into a file, these so-called 'Scientists' would find more and more negative indicators. In the end mere suspicion inspired evidence to grow out of every conceivable physical or cultural difference they discovered.

Erich had a good idea who had started the accusation and when he saw the final item at the end of the file it was confirmed. There was a letter from Ludwig Dreger to the committee. It was a torrid denunciation. He charged that Albert was a stupid, inefficient, lazy oaf, whom he had been forced by circumstance to work with when he was an agent in the resettlement. Dreger dwelt long on Albert's neglect of duty and his unauthorized investigation of Martin's murder. But curiously, Dreger didn't mention Martin by name; he said it was an insignificant Pole who had been shot. Ludwig represented the search into the murder by Fischer as self serving but never explained how. He wrote that Albert was a degenerate, polluted not just by associations with non-Germans, but most likely by degenerate blood also, either Slavic or Jewish or both. He wrapped his evidence up in one small incident. Albert's father had been hung during a Ukrainian pogrom against the Jews. Erich was astounded. Albert had told him that his father died as the result of an accident in his fields.

Nevertheless, Erich now understood why Dreger had not switched the list back. In Russia, Albert might have survived but with this letter of condemnation he had hoped to finish him off once and for all. He had signed it with a flourish, emphasizing his rank, Captain Ludwig Dreger. The military listened to its own.

As more and more Volhynians were resettled they were replaced in the camp by other east Europeans. Many of these new arrivals were from Romania and Albert noticed that a lot of them didn't even speak German, or spoke it so badly they could hardly be understood. He looked at them and wondered if he would still be in Zwickau when they were gone.

Albert grew so frustrated with the number of times he was told to be patient that most days he refused even to walk to the office to check on the status of his papers. In mid-May he threw up his arms and shook his head when they made him repeat the whole process again. Having to do this one more time taxed his understanding of what was reasonable. Not until his wife and Erich Winkler sat down and argued with him would he begin the meaningless paperwork again, and then only with Erich's promise of assistance.

But as soon as Albert had finished signing the last document he and his family were ordered to report for examinations again. It was the same invasive battery of prods and probes that they had undergone already. He and Alwine could not understand why. Surely they hadn't lost these papers too?

"What are they trying to find out?" Albert complained to Erich Winkler. "They measure, touch and poke, they ask questions and make notes but never tell us anything. Let them do what they want with us, we won't go through this again!"

Erich bit his lip. He knew what was happening but found it hard to explain to his friends. Besides being against camp policy to release the contents of confidential files, even to the parties involved, he was afraid of their reaction. But Erich knew that there was no possibility that his friends could survive without knowing what they were up against. It was like being judged without even being told you were on trial.

"Come walk with me Albert and Alwine," Erich said quietly, "I need to tell you something."

As they walked behind the old factory, out of sight of the camp offices, Erich put it to his friends plainly, telling them what Ludwig Dreger had done. He had barely started when a look of horror came over them, and they comprehended the seriousness of the situation. He didn't want them to give up but he had so much more to tell them and had to make it plain and clear. "If you cannot prove you are German you will be sent to the ghettos of Warsaw or Krakow. But you will not return."

"What can we do?" Alwine asked, her husband was too stunned to speak.

"Submit to every test they have. Let them touch and probe so they can't say you're trying to hide something. Show no frustration, give them any and every piece of evidence you have that you are German. Speak the best German you can, that will put you in a good light. Albert, don't use any of the Yiddish or other foreign words and phrases that you usually use to color your language.

Don't criticize Germany, the Reich or Hitler. Tell them how stupid your ancestors were to ever have left Germany. Do everything you must to change their impression of you."

"What are all these examinations about?" Albert asked. He had suspected all along that they were more than everyone suspected.

"It's about race," Erich answered, but the look on Albert's face told him he didn't understand and neither did Alwine. He didn't have time to go into long detail. "What you should know is that I have asked for you to be examined this time. You need to impress them with your attitude. If I have to, I will go the camp commander and tell him about Dreger's lies, but I'm not sure they would believe me. They are military and so is Dreger. The best thing will be if you prove to them that you are German, not Jewish. I won't lie to you, there is not much chance that they will change their minds. They don't like to admit mistakes. You will still be classified as barely suitable, but there is a difference between being barely suitable and being accepted for resettlement and being barely suitable and living in a ghetto in Krakow."

"Oh, my God," Albert exclaimed, "we are finished!"

"No. That's not the attitude to take! Show them that you can be an asset."

Albert and Alwine did everything Erich asked them to do yet two weeks later the end of May was fast approaching and they were still in the camp. Now it seemed that even Erich had failed them, and Anna Sebastian came to the camp less and less frequently. Zwickau had truly become a prison.

Albert felt betrayed. Everyone and every circumstance was working against him. Even in the quiet of a warm spring night, while his family slept in their dirty blankets on the warehouse floor, he could find no solution and no solace. Instead, tears welled up in his eyes. The little bit of the manhood he had left made him muffle his sobbing as best he could. It embarrassed him that he had brought his family to the point where they had nothing to do but die, especially when he had given so much trust to the promises of the Nazi party.

Despite his attempt to be quiet, his wife woke from her restless sleep. But he did not see her get up and when she came and sat beside him he was startled. Ashamed of his tears, he immediately turned away to hide them, forgetting it was dark. But Alwine knew her husband well and did not mention the sobbing when she began to talk. The sound of her voice in the dark annoyed him at first because he wanted to be alone in his misery and because he was apprehensive. If she asked him a question, he would not be able to answer without revealing that he had been crying. Then she would know he was a failure and he couldn't face that.

But Alwine spoke quietly and reassuringly, she did not want to invade his dignity.

"Maybe it's my fault," she said, "I couldn't say all the things Erich told us to say and so I said nothing. I'm sure I did not impress them."

Albert shook his head, "You would not even lie to save our lives!" Alwine had given him a target for his anger. "What can we do now? Even Erich avoids me now. He said he would follow our paper work through and nothing has happened. Now, even he tells me to be patient."

"We have to find out what they intend to do with us," Alwine said softly, but with determination, "we have to ask Erich!"

But Albert was not listening, he was wondering if his wife was right. Was she to blame? "What if they found the letter you wrote to Irene?" he asked. "We will be stuck here forever because of you," he snapped, and became more angry when she did not defend herself. "She never answered your letter, did she? It probably never left the camp."

"If it is my fault then at least you can denounce me and perhaps they will let you and the children and Oma go."

Her admission disarmed Albert. She would make the sacrifice for her family that he was not prepared to make. It had been

Johann, his brother, who had told him that he had a better wife than he deserved. He was right. Albert took back the words he had spoken in anger. Together, they determined that in the morning they would do something to force the issue. If Erich could not help them, they would demand to see the camp commander. Whatever happened would be better than not knowing, but it frightened them just the same.

But in the morning they received a letter from Alwine's parents. They had been resettled in a village just fifty kilometers away and though they had some reservations about how they had obtained the farm, they were happy with it. However, it was sad and puzzling news that had prompted them to write. They had received a telegram from the War Department that Edmund had died in Poland fighting the resistance. They had not even known that he had joined the army and had not heard from him since he left Lutzk. They wondered if Albert and Alwine knew anything that could help them to understand this mystery.

"It's not true," Alwine said adamantly to her husband.

"They may have made a mistake," Albert conceded, "lots of men thought dead returned from the Great War."

"Oh, I believe he's dead," Alwine explained, "but I don't believe he died like they say. He didn't leave us to go join the army. You know what that prison camp did to him? He was in no condition to go to war. He would never have done it, especially just before he went to see Mama and Papa, and they expect us to believe he didn't even write home once."

"Maybe he didn't know where to write," Julianna offered.

"No, Mama," Albert shook his head. He had to agree with his wife. "Alwine is right. He was going home when he left us. This just proves what we suspected all along."

For Albert, the confusing events of those last days in Volhynia came to the front again, but this time they came almost as relief from the troubles that plagued him in Zwickau. For the moment, he forgot about his more pressing problems. It was as if Edmund,

Martin, and the Countess reappeared in his memory like they had never really left. Old suspicions were aroused and now there was another piece to the puzzle that added to both the confusion and the suspicions. Albert cursed himself for not having done more in Volhynia when he at least had the freedom to ask questions.

But Alwine became so distraught that she was in no condition to go with her husband to the camp offices as they had planned. So without informing his wife, Albert went to see Erich to talk to him privately. His friend seemed evasive until Albert reassured him that he had not come to badger him about getting out of the camp. Erich's recent tendency to avoid him bothered Albert, but right now he wasn't worried about himself and so he ignored it. This time he asked his friend to go for a walk around the camp and Albert told him of the letter his wife had received.

"My wife doesn't believe her brother just joined the army and neither do I. I believe that if we find the reason for Edmund's disappearance we will also find Martin's murderer. And I believe we will find Dreger in the midst of the whole thing."

Erich thought for a minute. He had been afraid to tell Albert that all his advice had failed to change anybody's mind. Neither had he found the courage to go to the camp commander and tell him of the injustice being perpetrated. So he felt anxious now, even obligated to listen to Albert. But the strange thing was that what Albert said almost made sense. In light of the critical letter he had found in his file, Albert's information was almost revelatory. If this was some plan of Dreger's to cover up something that had gone wrong in Volhynia then even Albert's predicament made sense. It could be a coverup or it could be revenge. Maybe more than Edmund Frey's mysterious disappearance could be resolved by pursuing this. "What if we got a copy of Edmund's military record," he ventured with new enthusiasm, "that would tell us where and when he joined and how he died."

"Can you do that?"

"I have to be careful. We are not supposed to requisition information except for official purposes and if they catch me I'm in for it," Erich said hesitantly, "but yes, I can."

Erich had not felt so anxious since Zeperow, when he had switched the documents on Dreger. With trepidation he filled out the request form and slipped it in with other forms to be signed by camp commander Wiesner. It went out in a regular communique packet and then all he had to do was wait and intercept the return mail.

He did not want to have to explain the requisition to Wiesner so Erich placed himself by the door each morning to intercept the courier and sign for the day's dispatches. He would skim through the stack before handing it to the secretary who's responsibility it was to open the mail. He did not expect an answer for several days, but he hoped that when it came, he would somehow be able to snatch the letter he wanted without causing suspicion. On the fourth day the courier arrived early and the secretary received the documents. Erich waited all day for the Commandant to ask who had requested the document. He rehearsed a hundred answers but the question never came. The piece he was looking for hadn't yet arrived.

The next day he made sure that he was waiting early and a quick scan told him the document he wanted was there. Casually he laid the packet on his desk but the secretary came over and scooped up the pile saying, "This is my job, Erich, you shouldn't concern yourself."

It happened so quickly that Erich's head was spinning. It shouldn't have been so easy. Only a few minutes after the secretary took the mail into the office, Commandant Wiesner came out holding the questionable paper in his hand. "Who requested this?" he blustered, but he didn't wait for a response. "Another errant dispatch," he concluded and laid it down right in front of Erich, "Find out where this belongs."

During his noon lunch break Erich took the letter to Albert. "I don't understand what this means," Erich said as he handed him the paper. It was a short and simple response to their inquiry.

THERE IS NO RECORD OF ANY EDMUND FREY, BORN AUGUST 21, 1911, DOMBROWA, VOLHYNIA, ENLISTED IN ANY BRANCH OF THE MILITARY.

Albert did not tell his wife about the response because he feared that it would only add to her anxiety, especially since it only increased the mystery and confusion surrounding Edmund's disappearance. However, now he had no idea how to determine the truth about his brother-in-law's fate. If there was no record of him joining the army how could they send out a death notice? "What do we do now?" he asked Erich. This time his friend had nothing to offer.

For Albert the worst thing about this dead end was that it abruptly put him back into the middle of his own problems. But whatever direction he looked, there stood Ludwig Dreger. It was too coincidental that his name kept popping up whenever trouble appeared. Ironically, it seemed as if he had traded his life long enemy, Martin, for Dreger. Albert would have rather had Martin back again; he had no idea how to fight Dreger. He had known from the beginning how to fight his way through Bereza, but he had no skill in this kind of fight.

In June even the Romanian-Germans were beginning to leave the camp, having been accepted for resettlement. There were only a handful of Volhynians left now and even Erich was no longer needed. He was to be transferred to teach school at one of the new German communities in Warthegau. But before he left, he had one more camp document to deal with. It was the list for the next busload to leave the Zwickau camp, and his friend Albert's name was on it. Erich should have been ecstatic except that the destination was that part of Poland that Hitler had renamed the

Government General. He had hoped that somehow their problem would go away but it was becoming evident that without his direct intervention a family that deserved better would be doomed. He got up his courage and went to see the camp commander and told him of his friend's plight and the false accusations made against him. He tried everything short of denouncing Ludwig Dreger.

Commandant Wiesner seemed unimpressed. He was a military man forced to work with a lot of civilians and he didn't like it. He would much rather work with soldiers; they were more efficient and less emotional. As Erich told him of the dilemma faced by Albert and Alwine the Commandant wondered what this motives were. It seemed to Erich that he wasn't listening.

When Erich told Albert and Alwine goodbye, he could only tell them what he had tried to do, but he could not give them much hope. He had failed with the commandant. He did not know that his seemingly hopeless intervention had saved Albert and his family from a trip to Krakow. Commandant Wiesner was impressed enough to look over their file one more time and temporarily remove their names from that list, at least until he had returned in a few days from a meeting of the resettlement commission in Berlin.

As Erich left, Alwine had to pull her husband from the depths one more time. If there had been liquor available, he would have gotten drunk. He felt useless. She put her arms around him and tried to reassure him saying, "In Zeperow, no one did more for the resettlement than you, Albert. This is not fair."

"There is no one to help us now," he said, shaking from fear.

"We have to see the Commandant ourselves. What have we to lose?" she asked. "What worse can happen to us?"

"What if they deport us?"

"If that's what they intend to do then they'll do it anyway. We must convince the commander that we have been treated unjustly. That is the only way we can stay in Germany." They went to the office to ask for an appointment but the commander was away.

While they were waiting for Commandant Wiesner's return, Alwine received another letter from her mother. Emilie wrote that she had asked the army if they had any personal effects of her son to return. She had hoped that this might in some way help her family to accept his death. The answer that the army gave her couldn't have confused her more; they had never heard of Edmund Frey. In her confusion Emilie wrote to them again and asked why they had sent her a telegram advising them of Edmund's death if they had no record of him. How could they know he was dead?

Within a few days a young lieutenant had come to her door asking questions. He was genuinely concerned about the mysterious telegram. It was a crime to send out such false information. He took the paper with him to continue his investigation. Emilie's tone was hopeful. Perhaps it had been a case of mistaken identity and Edmund was really alive.

As he handed the letter back to his wife, Albert could no longer hold back the information that he and Erich had already discovered. It all seemed so senseless.

Twenty-Four

Neither Albert nor Alwine had ever met Commandant Wiesner before, yet as they walked into his office his size alone intimidated them. He was much taller than Albert, taller even than Erich Winkler, and the man stood so straight and rigid that he seemed immoveable. He was thin for his height, but muscular, with a receding hairline that he made no attempt to hide. But it was his cold unsmiling face that made them feel uneasy. The soldier did not even bother greeting them nor to shake their hands. Erich had told them that he was a stern, but fair man. They weren't so sure,

Because he did not like to prolong unpleasantness, Commandant Wiesner made no pretense of liking these people. What he had to do was best done on a totally impersonal level. It was rare that he met directly with camp inmates, but because Erich Winkler had been an adequate employee, he had decided to give these people a chance to state their case. Yet, when he looked over their file he found nothing to justify any change in their status and he regretted his decision to meet with them. What he dreaded now was an emotional outburst of the type that weak people relied on when they lacked the discipline for rational behavior. He had already determined to cut them off as soon as he saw any sign of an emotional outburst.

Once they were in his office looking timid and scared Wiesner was sure that his assessment was correct. He determined to end this unpleasantness quickly. He allowed them to sit down but before they were comfortable he said, without any emotion, "I have reviewed your case. You are not to be resettled. Instead you are being sent to Krakow in the Government General." Then he stared at them and dared them to start whining.

Alwine looked at him directly and without fear or trembling, asked, "Why?"

The commander had expected shock and tears. He was so relieved that he gave them the courtesy of an explanation. "The indication in your file is that you have lied," he said, and then added, "You seem to be more Jewish than German."

"We have always been German," Albert protested.

"Perhaps that is what you have been told. However, there is evidence of racial pollution. Apparently, over the course of a century you have become more like them than German."

"We have given you the information about our families over and over again, Herr Commandant," Albert now jumped in, "there was nothing to deny my brother German citizenship. I don't understand how you can say that."

"I'm not a scientist," he answered truthfully. It was better that way, he really didn't want to understand. "I don't pretend to understand how these things work. But I am told that it is not just ancestry that is assessed, Herr Fischer, we also have reports about your activities in Volhynia."

"Dreger," Alwine said with disgust.

"I beg your pardon?" the surprised commander reacted.

"These reports are all from Ludwig Dreger, aren't they?" Alwine challenged him.

"I'm not at liberty to say who wrote them," the soldier answered, but as he said it, he looked and confirmed to himself that the name at the bottom of the condemning report was Ludwig Dreger's. He looked at the couple who were staring back intently. They were scared, but calm. He continued, "the fact is ..."

"Those are not facts," Alwine interrupted, "my husband worked as hard as anyone for the resettlement committee and because one man writes lies we are condemned."

The commander became cold. He didn't like being cut off in mid-sentence and he also sensed that this woman would soon be crying and pleading just as he had imagined. "Frau Fischer, the man who wrote this report is an official of the German Reich and I would caution you before you make any false accusations. The fact is that while your husband should have been working for the resettlement committee he busied himself with the investigation of the murder of some insignificant Pole. He neglected his duties and spent an inordinate amount of time drinking beer instead of attending to his work."

"So it was Dreger," Albert said.

"It hardly matters who wrote the report," the commander said angrily. They were refusing to accept the truth.

"Believe what you will," Alwine said, "but they are all lies. I bet he doesn't write of the time my husband spent in Bereza Kartuska being starved to death because of the Nazi party. He doesn't write of the miles he rode for the resettlement committee. No one worked harder than my husband to get our village out of Volhynia, not even Dreger!"

It surprised Commander Wiesner that she did not burst into tears. He liked the defense this woman gave of her husband and especially that it did not include whining. He detested groveling and that was what he had prepared himself for. Nevertheless, he had not changed his mind about them, there had to be more than this to negate an official report. "What reason would he have to lie?" he asked, thinking that they could not give one, or else they would use the usual limp excuse, 'I don't know, he just doesn't like us.'

"Herr Commandant," Albert now took over, "I know why he lied."

Wiesner looked at Albert. He said nothing. He didn't like civilians who grumbled about the military. The commandant sat back waiting for Albert to say more. He would not invite the man to make his accusations. His intention was to let this farmer condemn himself.

Albert took a few seconds to understand that the Commandant's silence was an invitation to continue. "Dreger wanted to smuggle a Polish woman out of Volhynia and I spoiled his plan."

Wiesner continued to stare at Albert saying nothing.

"She was a Polish noblewoman, the Countess Viteranno. I understand that she was once married to Dreger's brother, but the Russians thought she was a spy. Dreger was desperate to get her out before the Russians found her. When Martin was found shot, I uncovered their plan to sneak the countess out of Poland with a false German name. Then she disappeared. The Russians were still looking for her when we left in January."

Wiesner still said nothing. This was not what he expected. It sounded almost plausible and it was definitely too contorted for a simple peasant to invent. But most of all, there was something that struck him as the names Dreger and Viteranno were put together. But the commander couldn't put his finger on the connection so he asked a question, mostly with the intent to distract himself. "Do you believe Dreger killed this Martin fellow?"

"Perhaps," Albert said, both relieved and pleased that the commander was considering his story. "There wasn't a man in Zeperow or Antonufka who didn't hate Martin. When Ludwig Dreger placed him on the list, people were angry. So there were many men who could have done it."

"You say men, so I take it you never considered that the Viteranno woman could have done it?"

"No," Albert said quickly. "But years ago she asked me to do it for her." Both the Commandant and Alwine looked at Albert in surprise. "I said no!" he added quickly.

"It says in Dreger's report that the man was a Pole. Why would he expect to be resettled?"

"Martin was whatever it suited him to be at the time, German, Pole, Catholic, Protestant," Albert explained, shaking his head. "He had no loyalty. He betrayed us all. He gave the Poles the names of all the members of the Nazi party and four of us were sent to Bereza Kartuska. Then, when the Germans won, he threw his Polish wife out of the house."

"Why was it so important for you to investigate this man's death?"

As quickly as he could, Albert explained about Edmund and the circumstanced leading up to Edmund's disappearance and Martin's death. He was almost out of breath when he finished.

"And you took it upon yourself to investigate his death hoping to find your brother-in-law?"

Albert looked at the floor. "No, I didn't think of that. Everyone thought that I had killed Martin and even I admit that no one had more reason to hate him than I did."

"So you wanted to prove your innocence."

"Yes, but instead I made an enemy out of Dreger."

"Do you have any proof of your story?"

"What kind of proof?"

"Anything tangible..." he stopped. Their faces told him they did not understand what he was talking about, and so he rephrased his explanation, "some evidence that supports your story."

Albert looked at his wife for support. He had thought he was getting somewhere but now he was at a dead end. He had done everything he could.

The commander shuffled uneasily in his chair. They had started well but without proof this interview would soon turn the way he had first suspected. They were peasants and had no idea what constituted proof. He was not prepared to have his time wasted any longer. "I need proof," he said forcefully.

"Would this be proof?" Alwine finally asked. She handed him two sheets of paper, one of which was a letter. "A few weeks ago my mother got a telegram from the army saying that Edmund had been killed in action."

"So he reappeared?" the commander commented. But with the letter was the report from the army that Albert and Erich had requested. He read them attentively. "One telegram reports him as dead in action, another claims he has no military record? A clerical error?"

"Someone is lying," Alwine pointed out, "and it is not my husband. Someone is trying to hide how he died. My mother had a visit from the military asking about the telegram."

"This, if it is true, it is the beginning of evidence," the commander said, indicating the paper that Alwine had handed him. Wiesner sat back and looked at the couple again. They looked different now, not like peasants anymore, but stronger, more confident, like real Germans. The one thing, the only thing, that they had given him that he could follow up on was the telegram. It should be easy enough to find out if there was an investigation going on. That would lend some credibility to the couple's story. He looked at the reports he had on his desk about Albert Fischer again and let his eyes linger on the imperious signature of Ludwig Dreger. It surprised him how much more that signature stood out now, its arrogant flourish putting everything into doubt. He had the feeling that the report was not true, at least not the whole truth, which left the question, why? "If you will be patient a few more days, I will try to get some answers."

This time Albert was reassured by the request to be patient. As they left the office, the Commander opened the door for them and even shook their hands. Finally someone saw them as people.

Later, Wiesner annoyed his secretary by making her place a series of phone calls trying to ascertain if any office was investigating the telegram. When the frustrated secretary was finally connected, she put the Commandant on the line but even he was shuffled between departments. But, he persisted with the kind of military tenacity that caused him to win promotion after promotion, until finally a busy staff officer put him off by telling him that he would make some inquiries and get back to him. But Wiesner would not let him go until the promise was firm and he had the man's name and rank, and knew who his superior officer was.

Within hours a call came back. A Lieutenant Hohensee was very anxious to talk to him. He had the telegram in question but had been unable to get anywhere with it and wanted to know what the commander's interest in it was. It disturbed the lieutenant that someone was sending false telegrams to the parents of boys who were fighting for the Reich and he wanted to find out why. The puzzle, however, was complicated by the fact that the subject of the telegram, Edmund Frey, was never enlisted in the military.

Wiesner's experience, however, told him not to volunteer any information without first eliciting something in exchange. "Lieutenant, I have a proposal," he said, waiting long enough to assess the lieutenant's level of interest. "If you promise to phone me immediately with the results of your investigation, I can tell you where to look next."

The lieutenant hesitated, "I'm not sure I can do that."

The commander was not going to be brushed off. "I need this information to do my job Lieutenant and if I go through official channels it will take too long. I merely want to expedite this matter."

"Before I agree, I ought to know exactly how you are involved?" the Lieutenant asked cautiously.

"What you find may have some serious consequences for a family applying for resettlement," the commander said. "Innocent people may have been accused falsely. What you find could clear them."

"All right, I agree."

"Good. First, tell me, is the telegram official?"

"Yes, but no one seems to remember it or will admit to having sent it. It wasn't logged."

"Lieutenant, perhaps someone in the telegram office will flinch if you mention the name Ludwig Dreger. He is a Captain in the SS. If you can tie the telegram to him, you will probably also find a connection between him and this Edmund Frey. I suggest you confide in his superiors. I suspect that they know nothing about this, but if they do, you will have to back off."

"Thank-you for your help," the Lieutenant said.

"I don't want just your thanks. I want to know that you will keep your word."

"Of course, on my honor."

"That's good enough."

The call back came much sooner than Wiesner had anticipated. The phone rang in his home early the next morning, about three o'clock. "I'm sorry to wake you but I thought you should know that the lead you gave me has brought some remarkable and unexpected results."

"This could have waited until morning, Lieutenant."

"Yes sir, except that Ludwig Dreger is headed to your camp in Zwickau right now to arrest someone called Albert Fischer for treason. I'm afraid I was not discreet enough and someone warned him of our investigation before I could talk to him. I will say no more right now commander, I am also on my way to Zwickau but I believe I am well behind Dreger. You must stall him until I get there."

It was just after nine o'clock in the morning when Dreger, in the uniform of an SS Captain, arrived with papers to arrest Albert Fischer. The commander had asked his staff to stall him but they were not equal to the task. Dreger stormed into Wiesner's office. He handed the commander the papers and demanded Albert Fischer, immediately.

"And who are you?" the commander asked.

Dreger reached into his pocket and pulled out his identification and shoved it toward him. He stared directly at Wiesner while the Commandant looked them over, but the veteran had been around too long to be intimidated so easily. "You will, of course, give me time to read these documents, Captain Dreger?" the commander asked.

Ludwig Dreger scoffed, "Is that really necessary?"

"I'm sure you realize the importance of procedure, that's why you brought these documents, isn't it?" Wiesner said calmly. The charges listed were vague. They were also written in longhand with obvious haste. It gave the Commandant a reason to go slowly. The handwriting matched the signature at the bottom of the page. It was all Ludwig Dreger's. The more he read the more suspicious he became of the haste with which this warrant was prepared. He realized that if he turned Albert Fischer over to this Captain, the poor farmer would not be alive much longer. He looked desperately to find something technically wrong with the document, something more than its vagueness. He was desperate to find something.

"How can you accuse this man of treason when he isn't even a citizen of the Reich?" the Commandant finally asked, knowing it was irrelevant.

Dreger looked at him incredulously. "What does that have to do with you? If the document is in order, surrender the man!"

"You are the signing authority on the papers and the man's chief accuser. Isn't that unusual?"

"This is a special case, Commander. The man is an enemy of the state, a dangerous enemy."

"I notice that you didn't bring any guards with you. Do you intend to transport this dangerous man alone?"

Dreger was becoming suspicious. "Commander," he said tersely, without trying to hide his irritation, "are you trying purposefully to delay me? You have the papers, filled out in every detail. You are now authorized to turn Fischer over to me."

"Are you going to execute him here or do you intend to dump his body on the road back to Berlin?" He hoped to shock Dreger into realizing that his plan was known. That would deter a reasonable man.

"What are you talking about?" Dreger demanded, his face turning red with anger.

"Isn't it strange that we have been denying this prisoner German citizenship because of your report to the resettlement committee, Captain Dreger? Now you show up with documents that you have drawn up and signed yourself, to arrest this poor farmer. You bring no guards to assist you. Tell me, does anyone besides you have any accusations to make against him."

"None of this is your concern. You are delving into a dangerous area, commander. If you aid this man to escape, I will be coming back with papers for your arrest." The tone of Dreger's threat gradually heightened and soon he was shouting at the commander, "I demand that you bring the prisoner right now, or I will find someone here who is loyal enough to do it!"

"No, I don't think so. You are not going to ..."

"Then I will find him myself," the red-faced Dreger yelled as he stormed out of the office, but the Commander was close behind him, hesitating only long enough to retrieve the pistol he kept in his desk drawer. With determined strides Dreger was heading toward the warehouse that housed the remaining refugees and had almost reached the door when a black sedan pulled in front of the office. The Commander came out of the office just as Lieutenant Hohensee stopped his car.

"Hohensee?" Wiesner asked quickly.

"Yes," the lieutenant said, nodding.

"That's him," the Commandant pointed.

"Captain Dreger," Lieutenant Hohensee called. But the man either didn't hear him or didn't want to. He just kept walking toward the warehouse as if no earthly distraction could keep him from his purpose.

"We need to stop him," the Commander shouted, "he intends to kill Fischer!"

They ran after Dreger who had reached the warehouse and was busy looking for the man he hated so. He was like a bulldog whose bone had been stolen, looking behind draped blankets and into every corner of the building. The prospective settlers hardly knew what to make of him, but they were wary of the gun and the look of rage in his eyes.

All Dreger wanted was to get rid of Albert Fischer; later he could make up excuses. He rehearsed the excuses frantically as he walked. Fischer pulled a gun! No, implausible. He was dangerous! He was trying to escape! That was it. Once the man was dead, who would care? Then he would take care of that commander who had the audacity to question him. He heard the footsteps behind him, but arrogantly he paid them no attention, except to say to himself that no one had better interfere.

"Captain Dreger," a new voice kept calling, probably some low-level assistant to the Commandant. He didn't recognize it so he felt no obligation to acknowledge it. He was looking for the traitor, just doing his job.

"Captain, Dreger. I am Lieutenant Hohensee and this paper gives me the authority to ask you some questions. Sir, you have to answer!"

Hohensee and Wiesner had caught up with him now and strode beside him as he urgently surveyed the warehouse for his enemy. He turned and shouted, "I'll answer your questions later. I have an assignment to fulfil now."

"Who gave you this assignment?" the Lieutenant asked.

"Irrelevant!" Dreger blurted out forcefully, but refusing to be distracted.

"No Sir," Hohensee said, half out of breath. "My orders come from your direct superior and unless yours come from a higher source, you will come with me now!"

Dreger turned to face the Lieutenant and the Commander. "Show me your orders!" The Lieutenant gave him his papers and Dreger tossed them away. "You don't know what you're interfering with. An enemy of the Reich will get away and you will be responsible."

"He won't get away Captain," the Commander assured him, "he has been here for months. Let's return to the office."

Ludwig Dreger reluctantly accompanied these two men back to the offices. When he was seated, he still avoided the questions that the Lieutenant asked. To him this interrogation was at worst an inconvenience, a distraction while he waited to finish his job. He needed to destroy Fischer. After that he would tell them why.

But when he was confronted with the confession of an office functionary in assisting Dreger to send out an unauthorized telegram, he flinched. He had to say something. "That telegram was necessary for the security of a covert operation. Highly secret!"

"So secret your superiors don't even know about it?" the Lieutenant shot back. "You can answer these questions truthfully to me or you can answer them to your superiors."

"That is what I would prefer," Dreger said, "let me finish my job here and I will report to them myself."

"Captain Dreger," the Commander smiled, "you're fooling no one. I know the office for which you work. I know how they react to the suspicious behavior of subordinates. How do you think your career will go if they feel you are hiding something from them? Perhaps the three of us can clear this up now and you can persuade the Lieutenant to write a more favorable report to your commanding officer."

"All right, what do you want to know?"

"The truth," the Lieutenant said.

"We suspect Albert Fischer in the deaths of two, or even three of our agents in Poland. He is dangerous and devious. The Russians may even have planted him. It would be just like them to plant a Jewish spy in our midst. The telegram was a plan to flush him out so he would reveal himself. But your interference," Dreger indicated the Lieutenant, "spoiled that."

The commander didn't believe him. "No, Captain, all I did was to point the Lieutenant in your direction. You have some vendetta against this peasant Albert Fischer and that's what this is about."

"He murdered three people," Dreger shouted as he jumped up and pounded Wiesner's desk. But Hohensee was there to make sure he sat down again.

"What evidence do you have of these murders?" Wiesner asked calmly.

"I don't need to give you my evidence. This is not a trial. It ought to be sufficient that I say it."

"Captain Dreger," the Lieutenant interrupted, "I don't think that you realize that you are the one required to give answers here. There are some serious breaches of protocol here. If I report that you are hiding something then you ought to think how your superiors will view it."

"What is the evidence that you have?" the Commander asked again. "Who were these people that Albert Fischer is supposed to have murdered? Is one of them Hermann Martin?"

"Yes."

"And Edmund Frey?" the Lieutenant asked.

"Probably," Dreger responded coyly.

"You are suggesting that he killed his own brother-in-law?" Hohensee asked.

"When he found out he was working for us, yes."

"You are aware, Captain," the Commandant interjected, "that Albert Fischer was the one who rescued Edmund Frey from the prison camp?"

"He was also the last one to see him alive!" Dreger responded belligerently.

"The man's own sister was there too. Do you suppose she helped him to murder her own brother?" Wiesner asked cynically.

"He was there, that ought to be enough," Dreger insisted.

"Who was the third?" Hohensee asked.

"Another agent," Dreger responded impatiently.

"The Viteranno woman?" Wiesner asked.

"How do you.......of course Fischer told you."

"In your report you stated that Albert Fischer was spending too much time investigating the death of Martin and you do not even mention the disappearance of Edmund Frey or Countess Viteranno."

"I could not write a full report in Volhynia; what if the Russians had got hold of it? I had to wait until he was in Germany to make the charge."

"Why wait all these months then?"

"When you bait a trap it is sometimes necessary to wait!"

"I take it that since you say you have evidence against Fischer that you wanted to trap someone else?" the Lieutenant asked.

"Yes."

"Who would that be?" Hohensee asked.

"If you think I'm going to answer that," Dreger said contemptuously, "then you can't understand anything!"

"Captain Dreger, your contempt is an unacceptable alternative to the truth. You may intimidate others with your references to plots and secrets but we believe you less and less with each lie." The Commandant turned to the Lieutenant and said, "May I suggest that since the Captain won't explain himself, that we ask Albert Fischer to help us. Perhaps he can shed some light on the Captain's motives."

When Albert came in the Commander told him that Ludwig Dreger had accused him of the murder of his brother-in-law, Hermann Martin and the Countess. Albert stood there like a frightened child. His first thought was that the commander believed Dreger and wondered what his wife had gotten him into by suggesting they go to the Commandant.

"Look at him sweat," Dreger cried, "he's guilty."

"Sweat," Wiesner said, "is not evidence of guilt, only of nervousness."

"I didn't kill anyone," Albert finally blurted out. "I had no reason to kill Edmund and I have no idea what happened to the Countess. But I'm sure that I spoiled the plan Dreger had to sneak her into Germany. They were lovers."

It was the word 'lovers' that sparked an old memory in Commandant Wiesner's head. "So, is that what this is all about Captain Dreger?" the Commandant asked. "You blame Fischer for her death. You want vengeance?"

"That's preposterous," Ludwig shouted.

"Is it?" the Commandant continued, "Some of us are old enough to remember a scandal that occurred some fifteen years ago, or maybe more. You are the brother of Conrad Dreger, the industrialist, aren't you?" Ludwig Dreger sat quietly and stone-faced. "Your brother divorced his beautiful aristocratic Polish wife because she had an affair with his younger brother. Isn't that the way the story went. She went back to Poland and the younger brother was shuffled off to the military.

"But your affair didn't end. Did you get yourself assigned to the secret service so you could see her or was that just a benefit? Perhaps you told them that you could get her to betray her country."

"This is ridiculous," Dreger finally exploded.

"It wouldn't have been difficult for you to get yourself assigned to the resettlement committee when you found out she was in trouble. Unfortunately, Fischer here spoiled your plan."

"You have no idea what this is about!"

"You are right Captain, we don't have the whole picture," the Commandant replied, "but we have the part we need. We know why you are trying to destroy an innocent farmer. Even if this is a legitimate operation..."

"It is!" Dreger protested.

"Even if it is you may have put it at risk with your desire for revenge on a peasant. Doesn't that make a pretty picture for your home office?

"I'm positive we don't know everything, but we know Albert Fischer is innocent. May I suggest Lieutenant Hohensee that you turn the Captain over to his superiors and they will get the rest out of him."

"Or they may just sweep it under the rug," Hohensee added with a little regret in his voice.

"Yes, but that is their prerogative, and I'm sure they would appreciate our discretion if that is the case. I have what I need. It is obvious that the charges against Albert Fischer are false. And you Lieutenant have what you need for your report."

"The telegram is a hoax."

"Yes, and you know who sent it. Since Captain Dreger is not cooperating it would be prudent to turn everything we know over to his superiors. I don't believe they know what he has been up to but they will certainly appreciate our discretion. You can be sure that they will not be as gentle with his evasions as we have been."

The Lieutenant did not arrest Dreger but he made him return to Berlin with him. There would be some explaining to do but Wiesner wondered what kind of story he would tell. He decided to prepare his own report, just to cover himself.

Twenty-Five

Jerzy Finkowski, who still preferred to go by his American alias, Jerry Fink, had watched helplessly as his neighbors and friends disappeared from their Belschewo farms. Still, every time a group was gathered up by the Germans, and he and his wife were not among them, Jerzy let out a sizeable sigh of relief. The relief was neither satisfying nor comforting. It was more a reminder that the terror was always at the door. But each day as Jerry contemplated his neighbors' fate and his own luck, it was hard for him not to imagine that there was a reason he was being spared.

Two reasons that he could think of seemed logical enough to be true. The first was that the Germans were impressed with him as a farmer. After all he had one of the most efficient operations around, with immaculate buildings and a well-groomed herd of milk cows that grazed on rich, green pastures. Everyone acknowledged that Jerzy, his neighbors called him by his Polish name, had the best kept farm in the surrounding kilometers. It was easy, therefore, for him to imagine that respect was the reason that he had been spared the humiliation his friends suffered and that it would continue to spare him. But in his heart he knew it was improbable. The more realistic reason was that he had an American passport.

What Jerry considered to be his good fortune, however, did not mitigate his feelings for his Polish neighbors who were being ripped out of their homes one by one. It was hard to control his anger at the Nazis and the invading easterners who farmed land they had no right to. The feeling of impending doom was thick, like a fist closing tightly around Jerry. What a time he had picked to come back to Poland!

Thirty years earlier he had left Poland headed to America to find the legendary streets of gold. Eventually, he found work in the farms of Minnesota at dismal wages, and then drifted down to Chicago, where a man willing to work hard could earn a decent wage and even save money, if he could deny himself the bars and other entertainments that were so profuse in the city. For Jerry that was easy. He had come out of Minnesota with a goal. He wanted to save enough money to return to Poland and buy a farm.

When he first came to America, he found lots of work in the coal mines of Pennsylvania, but that was what he had run from in Poland. Even the steel mills of Pittsburgh could not entice him. It was only when he saw an advertisement for farm laborers in the Midwest that he found something that sparked his interest. It was as if a boyhood dream of open spaces had returned to him. When he reached Minnesota, he fell in love with the beautiful farms and the work in the sunshine. In a short space of time the young Pole realized that the country life was what he wanted. He saw it as a dream not just for himself, but for his family in Poland. Someday he would buy a farm and his whole family would live with him there. However, he learned quickly that on farm wages he would never be able to buy a piece of land of his own. That was when he made the sacrifice and migrated to the big city, and worked in Chicago's huge stockyards at rail's end. He could not imagine that it would take twenty-five years to save the money he needed.

In 1937, at the age of forty-five, having forgone marriage and almost any other worldly possession in order to save for his dream, he left America. Fortunately, the year before, as he was getting close to his goal, he had the foresight to become an American citizen.

He packed everything he thought he might need or what he thought his family might need, even buying a 'New York' treadle sewing machine. He was sure his mother would love it even though he couldn't remember whether or not she sewed. It didn't matter, she would learn.

Back in Poland, when Jerzy saw the piece of land he wanted, he purchased it immediately, even before he returned to his home. To his dismay, his mother had gotten old and was not interested in a farm life. She had indulged his dreams, which he wrote about in his letters, because she liked the money he sent her. His little sisters and brothers had also grown up and had lives of their own. Disappointed, Jerzy returned alone to the farm he had purchased. But he was desperately lonely and so he married a widow who was happy to find a man to support her into her old age. She loved the sewing machine.

The Germans had looked twice when he presented an American passport so that now he assumed it was the thing that had protected him from them. But as more and more of his neighbors were dispossessed he became unsure how long the passport would protect him. The Germans did not leave him alone. They surveyed his holdings, counted his cattle and told him how much grain and milk he had to produce. They took away his farm hands and replaced them. But he was still there when his neighbors were all gone and so in July he relaxed. Then his world came crashing down.

The seizure of his farm was all the more bitter for Jerry because it came so late. He had supposed that he had been passed over, if not accepted, and now his hopes were dashed and the bitterness was intense. Not even his American citizenship had saved him. Instead, a soldier tore up his passport in his face, declaring it a fraud. They dragged him and his tearful wife off only hours before the Fischers arrived to take possession of this land.

It was mid-July when Albert Fischer jumped off the back of the military truck that had been assigned to take his family to their new home. There was no bus for the last Volhynian family from Zeperow to arrive in Belschewo. Albert and Alwine were overcome with emotion at being reunited with their neighbors, Thann, Neuman, Hartenberger and not too far away were Johann and Hedwig Fischer. Even August and Irene were close by. It was a comfort to be so close to friends.

Commander Wiesner had been true to his word and worked diligently to find a place for the Fischers near the village of Belschewo, close to where the rest of his neighbors from Zeperow had been located. What was the displacement of one more Pole when a deserving German family needed a farm?

There were only three children now. Edmund was almost nine and Hertha was now seven. Alwine cried to see them running in the fields freed from the stifling atmosphere of the camp. And today, the fourteenth of July, was little Else's first birthday. It was a birthday present for her, they all said, and a good omen that she could start the second year of her life in this place.

Their new home was more than they had been promised. In Volhynia, Albert had possessed a mere four hectares, and only if he exaggerated the size. But now he had a full twenty hectares of land. The two-story white stucco house, with three bedrooms was much superior to the one he had left behind. There was a large, well-kept barn and an implement shed. It was wonderful, and after what they had endured in the last year it would take no time at all to call this place home. It was a good feeling but Albert repeatedly patted the envelope of papers in his breast pocket that was the final confirmation that this was their home. The documents proved they were finally German citizens, when in their hearts they had never been anything else.

To greet them at the farm were four Polish farmhands, two men and two women. They introduced themselves and carried the luggage, now only one old suitcase, into the house. This was a totally new experience for both Albert and Alwine to have servants, men to work the fields and girls to milk the cows and do the house work. It was something else they would find easy to get used to.

The lead hand was called Stefan, a young man in his late twenties, Alwine guessed, or maybe in his early thirties. She was too polite to ask. It was easy to like this man. The way he directed the others without appearing aggressive or pushy, and the way he obeyed without condescension when orders were given to him, was unusual. That kind of confidence, Alwine understood, came from deep understanding and so immediately she felt she would be able to trust Stefan. She only hoped it would not cause any problem for Albert.

After a tour of the farm Albert was excited. Everything was better than he had hoped. Even his lead hand described the farm in glowing terms and Albert could see with his own eyes that he was not exaggerating. The cows were of that very productive breed called Holstein-Frisian, and Stefan said it was the best herd in the area. The equipment and implements on the farm were almost all new. The buildings were in excellent condition and newly renovated with modern technology like electricity and indoor running water. The crops had all been planted and were now growing profusely in the well-kept fields. Things could not have been better.

It was Alwine who brought him down to earth and though he resented it a little, he had to acknowledge that she was right. The first thing she reminded him of was the awful price they had paid already. Einhardt and Ewald were dead. The loss of those children continued to pain her and colored everything they had gained through the resettlement. The second thing was that the farm had not been given to them without strings attached. They were required to give a large portion of their produce in milk and grain every year for the support of the German military. This was not objectionable to either Albert or Alwine, since, as they saw it, the compensation that Germany had given them for their farm in Volhynia was more than generous. Still it was an obligation they had to take seriously since the failure to produce could mean the loss of the farm. Nevertheless, with a farm such as this Albert and Alwine could face the future without fear. The quotas would surely be met.

Right away Albert took charge. His first thought was to impress upon the farm hands the superiority of the German agriculture. To him the irony of the situation was totally lost, he just took for granted that anything German was superior to everything Polish. But since he could find no major flaws with the way the farm was being handled Albert found only little things to change. First he altered the milking times, making the girls get up even earlier in the morning. Then he changed the routine of the chores for the men, taking time to criticize even the way the men held the shovels and pitch forks in their hands. All this Stefan and the others took in stride with inward amusement, but being careful never to show any impatience or ridicule. In all this Albert assumed that he was making great changes in efficiency and productivity.

When he was finished fine-tuning the farm, Albert thought he had won the confidence and trust of his employees, when in fact they had won his by passively adhering to all he said. Stefan, he almost considered a friend and as such he asked him about the former owner. "After all," Albert confided to his foreman, "he built not a bad little place." He was shocked when Stefan informed him that he was an American, who was mad as hell when they took away his farm. "I think he believed they were going to leave him alone, but I watched as they tore up his passport. He swore vengeance." He was even more surprised when Stefan told him that Jerzy Finkowski had not been sent to the Government General but that he lived in Osziency, which the Germans called Ossenholz, a larger village not far from Belschewo and he had a work permit.

As Alwine inspected her new house, she caught a glimpse of the garden from the window of an upstairs bedroom. She wanted to run downstairs and look at it, but something held her back. It didn't seem right to enjoy the garden that someone else had obviously cared for so tenderly. But Alwine could not stay away forever. After a few days she finally walked around it. It was as well kept as any garden she had ever seen and teemed with healthy vegetables and flowers. She wanted to run her hands through the dirt, but she could not bring herself to work in it. She sent the girls out to tend it just because it was a crime to let it go to waste. In the spring she would plant one of her own.

Julianna and Alwine Fischer enjoyed getting back to the everyday routines that had stabilized their lives for so many years. It was easy after the confinement and restrictions of camp life to again enjoy the preparing of meals, the baking of bread and other work that after many repetitions had seemed so boring and onerous. Now they were a pleasure, a sign of returning to that highly underrated condition, normalcy. The women were content.

It was doubly nice, however, to have two young Polish women to help with the heavier chores like milking the cows, feeding and watering the animals, butchering the chickens and helping in the fields. But nicest of all were the amenities of their new home. What Alwine appreciated the most was that the stable was not attached to the house in the traditional Volhynian style, banishing both germs and smell. The electric lights were wonderful in the dark hours. The switch that turned them on and off fascinated the children. When they wouldn't stop flicking the lights on and off Alwine had to make up the lie that more electricity was wasted by turning them on and off than by leaving them on. There were many things to learn.

Yet it was hard to ignore that the owners of their farm had been forced to leave their most precious possessions behind. Looking at their furniture reminded Alwine that her possessions, especially the cherrywood dresser was still in a warehouse. She did not expect to see it again. Even so, that was not as concerning as the proof she now held in her hands that the Poles were not going to be resettled. No woman, headed for a new home, would have willingly left behind that wonderful sewing machine.

Overall, life was promising to be easier here and it made it hard to believe that their country was at war. While the fighting did not seem to bother Albert, it concerned Alwine greatly, even though this time the war wasn't at her own doorstep. Nevertheless, she realized that these were things she could not change. Governments controlled war and it had been well demonstrated in her life that governments were more fickle than the weather. The elements were controlled by God and though He often seemed arbitrary, you knew that ultimately He loved his children. With governments it was not the same. They loved the people only for their ability to produce taxes, food and sons for their armies. It was this ultimate product that the Nazis coveted and that worried Alwine.

Her fears were realized when she received another letter from her mother toward the end of August. Her father was in great distress beacause her brother Arnold had been drafted. This came just as they had finally accepted that Edmund was dead. Now as they worried about Rudolf, who was already serving, they had to cope with Arnold leaving. He was only nineteen. Alwine, with Albert's consent and encouragement, took the bus to visit her parents and brought her three children along.

Her father spoke with anguish about his sons. Repeatedly, Johann spoke about Otto being his last son. That distressed Emilie. She didn't want him to speak as if Rudolf and Arnold were already dead. But her husband could not seem to understand and kept repeating, "I don't want them to take Otto too."

Alwine tried to talk to him but when she saw him sitting alone outside his front door so deep in his own thoughts, she could only cry. This was not the strong, unemotional man she had grown up with. This was not the man who had taught her to block every impulse to self-pity and indulgence. It was almost as if this was a betrayal of everything he had taught her and yet she could not be angry. She wanted to ease his pain and yet could not find the words. She remembered the deaths of her own children. The pain was still intense and yet, even her reflections couldn't help her to understand what he was feeling. There seemed to be some mysterious element to her father's grieving which she could not comprehend. Alwine quickly saw that she was no help to him or to her mother. She returned home after only two days.

As she departed, Alwine tried to say something cheerful about the large new farm that her father had. Instantly she realized her mistake. Her father's eyes grew misty and he said, "They have given me this cursed land and have taken away my sons. I don't know what I will do if they don't return." Alwine couldn't leave on that note. She laid her head gently on his arm as he sat rocking and said, "Rudolf and Arnold will come back Father, don't worry." But the words sank deep into the pit of her stomach and made her feel nauseated. She thought it was because of her pregnancy.

When the bus returned to the village of Ossenholz, Alwine and the children could tell from some distance away that there was some commotion going on in the streets. There were army trucks and soldiers running about with rifles. Alwine's immediate fear was that the war had somehow reached their little corner of Germany but quickly she realized that it was not true. Something else was going on. She hoped it would not delay them too long.

As the bus reached the village Alwine understood what was happening. The soldiers were collecting Jews from the town. She wanted to remain on the bus and hide. She kept telling herself that she wanted to spare the children from witnessing the brutality of their own soldiers, but she did not want to see it either. Finally she had to force herself to go. Holding the baby in one arm and dragging Hertha and Edmund by the other, she tried to hurry through the streets to the far side of the town.

Since the day she had read Johann's letter in Zwickau, Alwine had dreaded that someday she would have to come face to face with the Poles who were displaced for their sakes. Thankfully she had missed it, and yet the guilt was always there just the same. She knew of the ongoing displacement of both Poles and Jews and knew what it meant. By the closest of margins her family avoided the Government General ghettos. How could she explain to her children what their country was doing?

Edmund was fascinated by the soldier and the guns. The soldiers smiled and winked at him as he passed by and waved at them. His dawdling made it hard for his mother to keep moving. Her heart was pounding and she was afraid to stop. But even Hertha was asking what the soldiers were doing as Alwine struggled to push by.

As they passed a line of people being forced into the back of a truck, an elderly man with greying hair and slow reflexes dropped his hat. As he stooped slowly to pick it up, a soldier objected to him getting out of line and brought the butt of his rifle down on the man's hand. The sound of cracking bones reverberated through the street. Edmund looked at his mother and understood that she had seen it too. "Why did he do that?" he asked, "he was only reaching for his hat!"

The soldier heard the question that to him seemed more like criticism. He turned quickly to face his accuser. When he saw that it was just a little boy, his anger turned into a wry little smile. He walked over to Edmund and patted him on the head in a forgiving gesture and said, "These are Jews. They are our enemies. You don't need to feel sorry for them."

Alwine grabbed Edmund's hand and led him away. She doubled her pace to get away. Hertha protested that she had to run to keep up and finally her mother stopped. "Someday we will have to pay for this," she said out loud. But when Edmund asked what she meant, she only said, "How can God look down and bless us in this land. It isn't even ours." Edmund didn't understand that either. Then she tightened her hold on little Else who was slumping over her shoulder, sleeping, and walked away without looking back.

On that day Alwine Fischer did not understand what was to become of those Jews, except she supposed that they would wind up in the Government General Zone. She remembered that Erich Winkler had warned them that they couldn't get out alive if they wound up there. She wasn't sure if that was really true; maybe it was an exaggeration. Yet, Alwine knew what it meant to be an exile. It had been twenty-five years since she and her mother and brothers had been on trains to Siberia. That, she had accepted, was what happened to enemies of the state. They declare you an enemy and that is their excuse to take away everything you have and send you away to die. If you fight, they shoot you and if you don't fight they find some other way to kill you. She was not anybody's enemy and she doubted these people were her enemies.

Alwine was convinced that nothing good would come from this. She couldn't even have defined what 'this' was. Perhaps it was the war, or the resettlement. Maybe it was the brutal way the government dealt with people and the treatment of the Jews and Poles. Whatever it was, it was infecting everything, killing the joy of living. The Tzar had done similar things and he was dead. Poland had been vengeful against its Germans and Ukrainians and it was gone. She was sure, too, that God would punish the Germans. How and when, she had no idea. She was afraid.

As they continued on their way home, Alwine noticed that a man was following them down the dusty road. She felt no fear at first but when he seemed to be mimicking their every turn she became concerned. She kept herself between the man and the children and only Edmund realized someone was behind them. "Who is he?" he asked, but his mother could only shake her head. "Let's hurry home," she said as sweetly as she could.

When they reached the lane to their home, the man was only a few paces behind. Within shouting distance of her house Alwine found the courage to turn and ask, "What are you looking for?"

"Work," he answered in Polish.

"You'll have to ask my husband," she answered much relieved.

Albert was watching his wife from the door of the shed. Besides wondering why she had come home so soon he noticed the Pole who was following her up the lane. Every day he had to deal with men looking for work but he was suspicious of them all. He had no work, but no matter how he said it, they could not seem to understand. "I'm hungry," they would plead, "my children are starving." He knew right away that Alwine would wind up giving him a loaf of bread, and in truth, her generosity made him feel better.

Albert was still thinking about how to say no when Stefan came out of the shed and a look of astonishment came over his face. Quickly he whispered into Albert's ear, "That's Jerzy Finkowski."

Albert crossed the lane quickly. "What do you want?" he asked, with more seriousness than Alwine thought the occasion called for.

"I'm ..." the man started to answer, but Albert cut him off.

"I know who you are. What do you want?"

"I want work."

Albert shook his head. "I don't need any more workers."

There was added strain in the voice of the stranger now. "No one knows this farm better than I. I can help."

"No, I have enough help."

The man was turning red. "I need to work. This is my farm! You have no right to keep me off of it!" There was anger and frustration in his voice.

Now Albert felt threatened. "Show me your work permit!"

"Why?"

"Never mind why. I said, give it to me!"

Hesitantly, the man pulled a card out of his pocket and handed it to Albert. "Now get out of here!" Albert ordered.

"But my card?"

"Never mind your card. Get out of here or I'll have you arrested."

The man walked away, his face still red with anger and his fists clenched. Albert watched him until he had completely disappeared. When he was gone Albert turned to his wife, "That was the Pole who owned this farm. He would probably have killed us in our sleep."

The next day Albert rode into Ossenholz and presented the man's card to the resettlement committee and demanded that he be deported. Jerzy Finkowski and his wife were sent to Warsaw to work in a factory.

When Alwine heard what her husband had done, she wanted to cry, but she was torn too. What if he was right? What if he had intended to kill them all? Hate made things so complicated.

The harvests were good in those years, making it easy for the farmers to reach their quotas. For a while, things went so well that even Alwine discarded her fears for the future. To her it appeared, as the memory and heartache of Zwickau dulled, that Adolf Hitler had done the right thing after all, at least for the farmers of Volhynia.

Those first couple of years, Albert really enjoyed running his new farm and working beside his Polish boys, as he liked to call them. Stefan was an exceptional worker and totally dependable. The other fellow, who went only by his last name, Urbanski, was a good worker too, but not as capable as Stefan. The hard work of the three men, combined with the demand for food created by the war, made their farm prosperous. In a time when so many people were desperate, Albert and Alwine finally had enough to meet their needs. It was the first time in their married life that they could say that.

Considering that the Poles had no choice about where they worked, there was almost a congenial rapport between the farm hands and the Fischers. When the work was done at the end of the day, they all ate the same food at the same table. It never occurred to Alwine and Albert that it should be any other way. Stefan, Urbanski and the two girls shared one of the bedrooms. It did not seem to be an inconvenience. As they now had three bedrooms, the house did not seem very crowded. They knew others had less room and had to make other arrangements but for them there was no excuse.

The difference between their attitude and some others came into focus when they invited August and Irene for dinner. Although Alwine saw little of Irene Weiss anymore, she still regretted the loss of the friendship. She took every opportunity to rekindle it and invited the pair to her home often. They rarely accepted. However, one Sunday evening when August and Irene did accept a dinner invitation, even Alwine had to admit it was over. To her surprise the couple was offended when the Polish farmhands were invited to eat with them.

"Really Alwine, we're not in Poland anymore, there is no reason to pretend you like them," Irene said loudly enough for all to hear. Alwine was so embarrassed she could not speak. "They are not German, they are Poles," Irene explained, "it's not good to treat them this way. It only gives them hope."

"What are you saying?" Alwine later found the strength to ask. "What is so wrong?"

"They eat at your table and there is a rumor that they sleep in your house."

"Where should they eat and sleep? In the stables?"

"That's where ours sleep!"

Alwine became so flustered that the tears welled up in her eyes. She had to run up to her bedroom and August and Irene left without saying goodbye.

Alwine could not understand the change in Irene but it was obvious that their friendship was different. She never bothered to invite them again. Neither were she and Albert invited to visit the Weiss farm. Even their children did not play together anymore.

For the Fischer children their release from the confines of the Zwickau camp was the signal to start the process of growing up again. Alwine and Albert were astounded how quickly they recovered from the hardships of the camp and were grateful for their resilience. But they were lonely for friendship and could not understand why the Weiss children could not play with them anymore. Both Edmund and Hertha realized how much they missed Ewald, who had been so full of ideas and fun.

For a while they found new friendship from an unusual source. When additional hands were needed Albert hired a man from the town of Belschewo named Ivan Maczowiak who proved to be hard working and dependable. When his wife became ill, he asked if he could bring his two sons. Alwine was happy for Edmund and Hertha to have new friends to play with. The two boys played with her children all day but Alwine noted that they were incredibly hungry. When Maczowiak returned home, she gave him a loaf of bread and a few vegetables in a bag. While their mother was ill, the boys came each day but Ivan's work ended in a few days.

Hertha was happy to get back to school after the long absence. She was grateful too, to see old friends again and make new ones. Her joy was short lived. Very quickly school became boring again. She had to admit that her favorite time was the summer when she could play outside all day.

On the farm she found a rusty old bicycle that was kept in the shed. It enthralled her and she determined to learn how to ride it. It was a boy's bike and it was much too big for her but that could not deter her. She tipped over time and time again trying to mount it until Stefan showed how she could ride a boy's bicycle. He told her to put her leg under the bar rather than trying to straddle over it. That meant she had to ride the bike while it was tipped at an awkward angle and she could not sit on the seat, but at least she reached the pedals. Stefan held the bike as she awkwardly made a turn around the farm yard and then he returned to his work. Without his help Hertha crashed over and over again, but she would not give up.

Soon she was racing around the farm yard on the bicycle with the most triumphant grin on her face radiating from under her wind-blown black hair. But she found it hard to make tight turns.

If she wanted to ride to the end of the lane she had to dismount and turn around. She needed to practice making tight turns. After several unsuccessful attempts she swerved right into the path of a mother hen leading her chicks to the farm pond for a drink of water. The hen squawked wildly, calling her chicks to run away. The warning came too late. The bicycle and Hertha landed on several of her fluffy, white and brown chicks and crushed them.

When Hertha saw what she had done a terrible memory clicked. The tears were on the verge of bursting through her tough exterior, but she held on and would not allow herself to be overcome. Coolly, after looking around to assure herself that no one was looking, she scooped up the dead chicks and tossed them into the pond. Then she picked up the bike and put it away for another day. Later, she stood beside her mother at the edge of the pond and heard her exclaim with disappointment, "Look at what that stupid hen has done! She's led her chicks into the water and drowned them." Hertha willingly agreed that the hen was demented. "Ts, ts," she said very seriously, "what a dumb hen!"

The vitality of Hertha's personality endeared her to everyone. Else on the other hand became a charming little girl in a completely contrasting way. The two girls proved to be so dissimilar that it was hard to believe that they were sisters. Although one was dark and the other had blonde hair, and one had her father's nose while the other had her mother's pointed nose, it was in personality that the two contrasted the most. Else was shy and tender whereas Hertha was open and often blunt.

All the little animals of the farm yard were part of Else's world and she was protective of them all. She wanted to cuddle every little creature, whether they were willing or not. The dog, the cats, the chickens and chicks, the duckling, piglets and calves were her concern. Anything that was small or was a baby she cared for intensely.

When her mother put duck eggs into a hen's nest Else was right there to help the hatchlings. Later, when the hen went wild as the ducklings just slipped into the water when she took them for a drink, it was Else who came to the rescue. The noise of the distressed cackling brought the little girl running across the yard to see what was the matter. Her reassurances to the hen that everything was all right went unheeded so she waded into the pond to recover the strange chicks in order to put the hen at ease. Almost immediately Else sank up to her knees in the mud and was crying for help herself. Urbanski heard her. He reached her by stretching out and grabbing a handful of her blonde hair and pulling. Her scalp hurt for days.

Quickly, Alwine learned that nothing could be slaughtered when Else was around. She would put up such a fuss at even the mention of dispatching a chicken to be eaten for dinner that Alwine could not do it. But the slaughter of livestock on a farm was inevitable so they had to send Else down the road to the Thann farm until the butchering was done. The little girl came back none the wiser. As long as she did not see the animal being killed, she would even eat the meat.

As for Edmund, he missed Ewald the most. The void that was created in Edmund's life when his older brother died was tremendous, and eased only gradually. It took a while for Edmund to find that he could find lots of interesting things to do without his brother. He was the only one of the family who concerned himself with what was going on daily at the front. Soon his favorite pastime was playing soldier and gaining victory after victory for the Reich and much glory for himself. His sister was not interested in war so he played by himself or whenever possible with friends from neighboring farms or at school.

In school Edmund adjusted to his new situation easily. During lunch a boy from the town offered to trade a toy gun for his sandwich, which was only bread with a little butter. Edmund eagerly accepted and learned how easy it was to trade food for almost anything he wanted. He was too young to understand that war often caused food shortages in the towns and cities. The morality of what he was doing was something he never thought about.

When Edmund brought home a disappointing report card, a friend pointed out that all he had to do to improve was to bring food to the teacher. He started to bring fruit or half of a loaf of bread and then cheese, a couple of eggs or a piece of butter. The teacher barely acknowledged these gifts but when Edmund brought home his next report card his parents were pleased as they had never been before.

The family was so content in those days that Alwine had almost forgotten about the curse. Then in March of 1943 Rudolf died in action in Russia. Emilie wrote to tell Alwine that the shock had caused her father to become ill. How glad they both were that Arnold had escaped front line duty because of a foot condition. He was working in relative safety behind the lines. But her father's unrelenting concern was for his youngest son, Otto, who was a healthy and robust seventeen-year-old. He would soon be eligible for the army and everyone was sure that the wehrmacht would not pass him by. Johann fretted continually. Emilie wrote that she thought it would be good for her husband if his daughter and grandchildren came for a visit. It might distract him from his worries.

Alwine would have gone but she was pregnant again so she promised to send the children as soon as school was out. It would be good for everyone. It would give her a rest and Julianna too, as she was not feeling well either. She sent along a note for her mother not to be afraid to send the children back if they became too much work.

Nevertheless, it was surprising when the three returned after only a few days. With her husband's disturbing illness it was too much for Emilie to look after the grandchildren, even with the help of her teenage daughters. Now even his memory was failing him. She had put four-year-old Else on his lap and he had played and teased her and been delighted. But then he had asked his wife,

"Whose child is this?" She answered, "Why Alwine's. Don't you know your granddaughter?" He had turned aside and cried and for the first time consented to see a doctor.

In August the child Alwine carried was stillborn. As she buried yet another child, she fought hard to feel the pain. But for some reason she was numb. It seemed there was no more room in her for grieving. That made her feel guilty. Guilty, because the child at least deserved to be mourned. Guilty, because she was tired of the pain and mourning. Guilty, because she hated living on this 'borrowed' land. She wanted to be free of it all. If she could have, she would have run away.

Twenty-Six

Alwine woke up with a shock. The numbness she had felt since she had buried her stillborn child moved away like a curtain on a window. Pride and arrogance, she discovered, were more subtle than even her father had taught, but they were no more dangerous than apathy. If it was true that the whole community had fallen into the trap of vanity and pride, it was just as true that she had allowed herself to escape into quiet resignation. It had taken a shock to make her wake up to the fact.

The awakening had come at the home of Alma Neuman, when her neighbor invited Alwine for an afternoon cup of tea. To Alwine, it was just a friendly cup of tea, a time to relax and chat. But to Alma it was much more. It seemed to Alwine that her friend wanted to be a grand lady and was no longer content with the simple life of a farmer. Now that she had more land and a larger house than she had ever imagined, and even had servants, Alma had fallen in love with ostentation. It was a pitiful scene.

Alma called her fourteen-year-old house girl away from her chores to serve the two women. But Alma wanted more than the girl was capable of. She barked at the young girl continually. "Bring more hot water, Katja. Another spoon. More sugar, Katja. Don't run girl! Don't be so slow!" The youngster, a farm girl, had not been trained to be delicate like Alma thought she should be. The girl's discomfort was obvious. Alwine felt for her.

The girl was upset and flustered. Her fingers were thick and strong, more suited to milking cows than pouring tea. Clumsily she bounced around the kitchen upsetting herself and Alma more and more with every awkward movement. She was so nervous that it was inevitable that something should go wrong. Unfortunately, it was the sugar bowl that dropped and smashed on the floor. Sugar was expensive and hard to find during wartime. Alma was furious at the incompetence. She slapped the girl across her cheek. It was so hard that Alwine almost cringed. But Katja could deal with this better than she could deal with delicate sugar bowls. She refused to cry and screamed at her mistress and called her a thieving German. Alma Neuman grabbed a wooden spoon and beat the girl, eliciting screams that sent shivers down Alwine's spine.

"Enough, enough!" Alwine pleaded.

Alma turned sharply to her friend, her eyes still on fire, "We don't pamper Poles here like you do, Alwine, they have to be taught their place!"

Alwine walked home slowly, berating herself. How could she have forgotten so quickly? How could she have ignored the signs? It was simple, she had wanted to. She had denied the truth. The arrogance she had observed even from the beginning of the resettlement had infected them all. Even these Volhynians who had suffered so much that they ought to have known better were infected with false pride. They ought to have known it was wrong. There was no excuse for them and there was no excuse for her. She too had fallen in love with this new way of life that was not really hers. Worst of all, she had ignored everything.

She believed in divine retribution and knew that nothing could prosper for long that continually misused, abused and denigrated people. It was as if only Germany counted in the minds and hearts of the people. Germany had become like the Russia of her youth, intolerant of everything non-German. It was just another sign of national pride gone wrong and now the curse she had ignored was more evident than ever before. She was sure it would grow to engulf everything she loved.

But a curse had to have a consequence and slowly Alwine realized that Germany had already created its own consequence. It was the war. Whatever else Alwine feared, she feared the war most. War exacted its price from the guilty and the innocent and her family had already begun to pay and yet, the payments were only beginning.

Rudolf had paid the price and so had Edmund, she told herself. With two brothers dead, one drafted and a third quickly approaching the age of conscription Alwine wondered where it would end. Her husband, thank goodness, was still at home but she had to wonder how long that would last. Many men in the Belschewo district had either volunteered or been drafted. August Weiss had gone off to the army without even dropping by to say goodbye to Albert. Ernst Thann, Ewald Hartenberger and many others were off fighting and even her younger sister, Adele, was alone while her husband fought in the east. The price was too high.

The worst thing was that there was nothing that she could do about it. But did that mean that she should stop feeling? She could see that the ultimate end would be disastrous, yet she felt as helpless as she was on that train to Siberia. All she could do was cry. Often now, Alwine retreated to her garden. There the truth was much more simple. Do the work, reap the harvest. It was honest. It was the way all things should be.

For her husband, Albert, who never intended to volunteer, the shortage of German men in Belschewo created a unique problem. In the fall of 1942 he had been appointed 'Ort's Bauern Fuhrer,' (District Citizen's Leader). It was a position he was not allowed to refuse. Though he was proud of the title at first, he soon realized that it was more work than ceremony, and not at all like his position as constable in Volhynia. His job was to coordinate all the farm work in his area while the other men were absent. The planting, the care of the crops and the harvesting, along with all the machinery that had to be moved from farm to farm were all under his direction. He also had to direct and motivate the Polish farmhands to work without supervision.

The demands on his time frustrated Albert. He wished there was a Stefan for every farm. Usually, however, he came home cursing and bemoaning the laziness of the Poles, and he did it within earshot of young Edmund. It had escaped Albert that these people worked only to prevent their expulsion to the other side of the Warthe River. He could not understand why they should not want to do their best. He had no sympathy for them and used threats of deportation to the Government General to get them to do what he wanted. He barely understood what that threat implied.

If that had been the worst of his problems, Albert would have been content. However, in addition to the work load, the wives of the farmers complained to him constantly. They complained that the crews that he sent were not productive and demanded that he oversee them every minute. Each day a new problem arose: the seed potatoes were late, fields were not cultivated in time, barns needed repair, farm hands were not working. The complaints never ended; the machinery was not scheduled correctly, the harvesting was going too slow.

It didn't take long for Albert to feel really harassed. "It's like I'm married to every woman in the district," he complained to his brother Johann, "but I get all the work and none of the benefits." Johann rebuked him for his irreverent words and as Johann walked away Albert shouted after him, "I should join the army and leave this job to you!"

The reason for their complaining soon became clear to Albert. The women weren't interested in the harvest, they wanted to know why he was not in the army with their husbands. Few of them were subtle about it. "My husband is fighting," they asked, "how come you're not?" Irene Weiss was the most critical of all, especially after it was reported that her husband had gone missing in Russia in the summer of '43.

Albert was soon exhausted. He found himself in the beer hall of Belschewo almost everyday trying to escape the wagging tongues of the complainant wives and the ever increasing work load. His work suffered, his farm suffered and his family suffered. Before the harvest of 1943, he escaped the only way that was acceptable, he enlisted in the army. Within weeks he found himself in Minsk, close to his old home province of Volhynia, fighting the Russians, and feeling sorry for himself.

The week after Albert left, Erich Winkler was transferred to Belschewo to teach school. His predecessor had joined the army too.

With her husband gone, Alwine turned to Stefan for help in running the farm, she knew better than to rely on the new District Leader. Julianna, her main support for so many years, was old and tired and Alwine felt she could place no more burdens on her. Yet, she found that the respect she felt for Stefan deepened and turned into friendship as they worked together. He did everything he could to make the farm run smoothly, including keeping everyone else motivated. The result was that the farm never ran more smoothly or more productively. Even Jerzy Finkowski would have been astounded. Stefan proved to be a demanding but fair taskmaster for the other workers and an innovative problem solver.

When Albert left, the newly appointed District Citizen's Leader, (Albert had decided not to recommend his brother Johann for this onerous position), was resentful of the burden imposed on him and refused to schedule the threshing machine for Stefan until the very end of the season. But Stefan and Albert had been so efficient that their grain had been the first planted and the farm stood to lose a major part of the crop because of the delay. Alwine pleaded with the man but he remained indifferent and from the smell of him, drunk. She threw up her arms in frustration until Stefan made a suggestion.

"I understand that the man can be bribed," Stefan whispered.

"I don't know what I can do!" Alwine continued, not understanding what Stefan was driving at. He smiled. It was refreshing; she couldn't even conceive of the idea of a bribe.

"We need liquor to bribe the man," he said bluntly.

"I have no liquor," Alwine said as she shrugged her shoulders.

"Fischerova," Stefan explained carefully, "I know a man who will give us the use of a still for a portion of the product. We could even sell the excess."

"I don't want to sell liquor," Alwine shuddered as she answered. Her father had taught her about the evils of liquor. She found the idea repugnant. But Stefan explained that the crops had to be saved. The words almost stuck in her throat. "Make just enough to get us the equipment," she instructed, hoping somehow that her father would understand.

"Fischerova," Stefan pleaded, "we appreciate the way you treat us here, but some of us have families that are starving. Liquor is the only way we can get money. It would mean so much."

The request shocked Alwine and she hesitated to answer. It was the moral implications and the duplicity of it that caused her to flinch. Yet as she looked at Stefan she understood he was telling the truth, he was unswervingly loyal, and meticulously honest. He was not only loyal to her but to his family too. She could not say no. Just as Stefan was starting to explain the need again, Alwine cut him off. "No, no, Stefan, there is no need to explain. Do what you need to do. Just make sure you keep it out of sight. Don't let Edmund see."

Very quickly Alwine found that all the farm's needs were being met on time. Stefan made sure that Alwine never had to see the liquor that he used to bribe the District Leader or that he and Urbanski sold to send money to their families.

Alwine hated deceiving her own son but she thought she had no choice. His attitude was another symptom of all that she saw wrong in the Reich. Lately he had started yelling at the Polish girls and insulting them as they went about their chores. "They're only Poles," he sneered when his mother asked him to stop. Then he announced that he was no longer going to eat dinner with Poles and took his plate to his room. Neither could she help but notice the resentment in his eyes whenever she and Stefan discussed farm business. He didn't like it when his mother allowed Stefan to make decisions.

"Where did you learn such behavior?" she finally asked him. "Why do you say such awful things? Why do you hate Stefan, who has been so kind to us?"

Edmund shot a contemptuous smirk at his mother. "Don't you know anything? Did you never go to school? The Germans are the smartest and strongest people of all. We are destined to rule over all the inferior people. The Slavic people are almost as useless as the Jews and Black people. It has been scientifically proven."

"Scientifically proven," Alwine repeated to herself. She had no idea what it meant, she had no education, but she suspected that it was just something you say to justify a lie. But she couldn't leave it alone.

Alwine sought out Erich Winkler after church and asked what it was that her children were learning. He was ashamed, but had to confess that he had no choice but to teach the official line. He whispered to Alwine, "The last thing they want is for these children to think for themselves."

That fall and winter Edmund became more and more difficult to live with. With all that was falling on her shoulders Alwine found it easiest just to leave him alone. She regretted that decision.

In the midst of the harvest Julianna died. Alwine had known it was coming and had tried to brace herself. But with the loss she was afraid that she would turn stone cold again. She was glad she had Stefan to take care of the farm-work while she busied her herself with the preparations for the funeral. As long as she kept busy then everything would be alright and she would have no time to be concerned with her feelings, or lack of them.

Albert got leave to come back to the funeral. He was so weepy that he could not see that there was something wrong, which was fortunate. How would she be able to explain that she had no tears for her friend and support of so many years? But then at the grave side, as the casket was lowered into the ground, Alwine felt a warmth on her cold cheek. They were tears. They turned into a torrent, and then a well of gratitude.

In February of 1944 Alwine got a scare. Stefan became ill with the flu. With the shortages of medicine and doctors it was always worrisome when someone fell ill, but Alwine had special cause to worry about Stefan. The prevailing attitude was not to worry about the health of the Poles entrusted to German care. As important as Stefan was to the operation of the farm, Alwine felt that his loyalty and friendship were more important. She made him stay in bed and nursed him as best she could. He failed to recover and was even getting worse. She had to get him to a doctor but the nearest one was thirty-five kilometers away. They would have to go by train.

Alwine did not hesitate to make the decision. She would have to accompany Stefan to ensure his safety. There were traveling restrictions imposed on Poles within the Reich and Alwine was sure that he would be arrested if she did not go with him.

Leaving very early in the morning, she had the girls wrap Stefan in blankets. Only Edmund was upset that his breakfast was delayed. Urbanski drove them to the train station in Ossenholz. The train trip of thirty-five kilometers to the village of Brunow took almost four hours.

By ten o'clock in the morning when Alwine got Stefan to the doctor's waiting room, it was packed full. After a six-hour wait, it was finally their turn to see the doctor.

When Alwine first saw him, she felt relief. He was an elderly man with well-greyed hair. Experience, she felt, was the best asset of any doctor. But what she really hoped for was that he was of the old school and not full of the new thinking about races.

She was wrong. When he found out that Stefan was Polish he ordered them out of his office. "How dare you expect me to treat a Pole?" he said sternly. Alwine couldn't believe it. She was horrified and her reaction shocked even her. The usually timid woman became aggressive. "Four hours we rode in the train! Six hours we waited and you will not see him. I am just a farmer but I have always understood that doctors took a sacred oath not to turn away from anyone who was sick. Is there no decency left in Germany?"

"I am not a veterinarian," the old man said defensively. He did not want to be lectured by a peasant woman.

Alwine had no answer for the absurd remark. "Please," she finally said, "for God's sake he's a human being."

The doctor remained adamant about not treating Poles, but now he seemed compelled to justify himself. "You should know Frau Fischer how these people are. They will do anything to get out of work. They are always feigning illness."

"Herr Doctor, I know this man. He is a hard worker. With my husband gone off to war my farm would be lost without him. Believe me, he is sick. I would not have risked coming all this way with him if he was just pretending."

She didn't know what changed his mind, she was just glad that he did. He prescribed some pills to reduce the fever and sent him home. As they left the office the Doctor offered a weak apology, saying, "I'm sorry about this but I have to be careful. You never know who is in your office these days, it might have been a trap." She did not understand what he meant until she thought about it on the train ride home. It made her cry.

Stefan recovered, albeit slowly. When the spring came and the planting was at hand he was strong again and eager to get at the work again. Now he felt he owed Alwine a debt.

Albert regretted joining the army almost as soon as he was inducted. As soon as they put a rifle in his hand he realized that the enemy had guns too. Somehow he suspected that they wanted to kill him more than he wanted to kill them. He would have given anything to get out but he knew that was out of the question. He observed very quickly, however, that those soldiers who had something worthwhile to offer were able to go on leave much more often. Food was the number one bribe, and Albert knew where to get plenty of it. Before long he was coming home regularly and taking back bags packed with food stuffs.

While he was at home he observed that the farm was running well and he had some ambiguous feelings about that. He was glad to see that when other farms were having a difficult time, his obligations were being met. Still he was somewhat embarrassed that productivity had gone up without his supervision. Albert sought out Stefan and gave him some very specific instructions about things he wanted changed by his next visit. He wanted Stefan to change the milking times again and the feeding schedule. Albert even ordered renovations in the stalls, and somewhat ambiguously he asked Stefan not to hire extra help so often. Stefan listened attentively but said nothing.

After Albert left again, Stefan went to Alwine and told her the reasons why they should not make the changes that Albert had ordered. Cleverly he described how they would create more work than he and Urbanski could cope with. Alwine appreciated his frankness and took upon herself the responsibility of changing her husband's orders. Her admiration of Stefan grew as she realized how savvy he was. He knew better than to confront her husband.

But neither she nor Stefan had counted on Edmund overhearing their conversation. The boy didn't like this Polish servant changing his father's orders. He protested loudly, "Mama, no, they have to do what papa says!" His mother brushed him aside with the tired old rebuke, "This is grownup business, Edmund." Doubly insulted, Edmund took it upon himself to rescue his father's plans. He got up early in the morning and banged on the farmhands' door. He wanted the girls out of bed to do the milking as his father had ordered. Urbanski came to the door, grinning from ear to ear. For a long time he had wanted to put the boy in his place. He shouted through the door, "Go back to bed little boy!" Edmund was furious.

What Edmund hated most was that no one would listen to him. His mother's trust of Stefan was contrary to everything he was being taught. She insisted on allowing the Poles to run the farm as they pleased. Was his mother not able to think clearly? Had she missed what was so obvious to the whole world, that the Poles were stupid and lazy? Edmund wanted no part of this traitorous treatment of the Poles. It was as if his family was collaborating with the enemy.

Alwine was happy when Edmund joined the Hitler Youth. It kept him busy and out of everybody's hair. The boys marched, sang songs and worked hard. Alwine thought it was all harmless. What she should have understood was that the leader of this imitation Boy Scout organization wanted to turn her son into a Nazi. Instead she was just happy to have him out of her hair.

The local leaders soon found in Edmund a willing and zealous follower and praised him for his desire to do the right thing. "Someday the fatherland will be proud of you, Edmund," they promised.

Since his mother persisted in her attitude, Edmund determined to wait until the next time his father came home and let him know how Stefan was taking over. He was sure that his father would agree with him and do something about it right away. However, after waiting patiently for weeks, Edmund was unable to clearly explain Stefan's terrible behavior to his father. He had wanted to say that Stefan was subverting his directions, but could only say that Stefan had changed everything. When he tried to tell his father that Stefan was unduly influencing his mother, all that came out was that Stefan was lying. Ideas that seemed so clear in his mind turned to mush coming out of his mouth. His father didn't understand what he was talking about and dismissed everything the boy said.

To add to the insult, his father was not even upset that Stefan had not made one of the changes he had requested. Instead, he praised Stefan's foresight and conceded that his wife was a better manager than he. Albert would not argue with success even when it violated every principle of German superiority. Edmund ran off to his father's workshop and cried.

It was at one of his youth meetings that Edmund learned what to do about this blatant disregard for standards. A guest speaker in an impressive grey uniform, brightened by colorful ribbons and medals, informed the boys that it was their duty to report to their leaders when they saw traitorous acts being committed or planned. He cited several cases where young boys just their age had been awarded medals for thwarting the plans of traitors and spies. "Great Glory," he explained with the kind of patriotic emphasis that the boys could not resist, "comes to young men who put loyalty above all else, even family." He listed the things that they should be watching for: speaking of defeat, secret communications, listening to foreign radio broadcasts, speaking disloyally of the Fuhrer, and collaborating with the enemy, especially with the communists. Edmund determined that he would expose Stefan.

Night after night, after everyone else retired, Edmund sneaked across the hall way to listen at Stefan's door. He wanted to hear what the traitors were planning so he could report them and teach his mother a lesson. He wasn't even interested in the glory, he told himself.

But not until Stefan hired Maczowiak during the haying did Edmund hear anything remotely incriminating. Still, it took him several nights to put it all together. It was exactly what the boy had been waiting for. Late at night, Maczowiak, was telling the others what they were waiting eagerly to hear, that Germany was losing the war. He was explaining that the Germans were retreating in the west, and in the east the Russians would soon be coming to liberate their Polish brothers.

Edmund's blood ran cold at the lies he heard. He knew they were lies, Germany could not lose, not to those inferior Russians. He knew Maczowiak must be communist to say such things, and so were Stefan and the others to believe him.

Edmund could not sleep that night. The thought of reporting Stefan and Maczowiak excited him. His imagination went wild. Each time, as he rehearsed exposing the traitors, the rage in his heart grew. Each time he imagined them being dragged away their crimes were greater, earning him even more praise. In his mind he repeated the words, "I told you so," to his mother a hundred times. But no matter how he tried, he couldn't imagine her pain away. She would not be happy. Still, he was right to do this. He knew he was right and if it hurt his mother then it was too bad. She would soon realize that he was right, and if she didn't ... no, she had to realize the truth! He hid his face in his pillow and cried, his mother had to understand the truth. He had no choice but to do it.

Edmund got up early in the morning with the intent to rush to Belschewo to report the traitors. But as soon as his mother saw him she sat him down to have a heart to heart talk. She had meant to do this for some time now. Alwine spoke softly and that annoyed him too. It was hard for him to feel anger when she spoke so softly, especially when he needed to be angry to carry out his plan. She told him how worried she was about him and how mean he was to the farmhands. "Don't you know how hard they work? Without them we would lose this farm." Edmund bolted, he ran out of the kitchen door yelling, "No, they're traitors, how can you trust them?"

Edmund ran down the road as far as his anger could carry him. He intended to report everything to the police, even his mother. He saw her in his imagination, being dragged off with the others, Else and Hertha tugging at her apron, crying. Else and Hertha ... he hadn't considered them. What would he say to his sisters? Even though he was right, they would hate him. It brought a tear to his eye and then a torrent. It was not something he could do. His mother's words came to him clearly again, "Without them we would lose the farm!" Did she care more about them than him?

Defeated, he returned home but was unable to go into the house. Instead he hid in his father's work shop. There he found that working with tools he was able to find some diversion from his worries. He stayed there for the rest of the day and every day that he could. In that shop, Edmund put to use all the techniques he had picked up watching his father and everything his grandfather had taught him. It became his world and most people were content to leave him there.

Alwine didn't know what to do. She was sure that she had lost Edmund's heart now. He was still a child but he was confused and so was she. She was losing him to the war as surely as she had lost her brothers Edmund and Rudolf. This land was cursed.

Twenty-Seven

While Alwine was still in a quandary over her eldest, she received another letter from her mother. It was the one she had been dreading. Otto had been drafted. This catastrophe, following so closely the death of Rudolf, was more than her father could handle. He had collapsed.

Alwine quickly put one of the Polish girls in charge of the children and reinforced Stefan's charge of the farm. Early in the morning she had Urbanski drive her into Ossenholz to catch the bus.

Alwine did not get there in time to kiss her brother goodbye.

She had missed him by only a few hours. But that didn't bother her half as much as seeing her father bedridden and struggling to hold on to reality. When she asked her mother what was wrong, Emilie shook her head. "The doctors don't know. They think it may have been a stroke. Twice they have given him electrical shocks but it hasn't done any good. They want to do more but I'm not sure it's a good idea."

When Alwine sat beside her father's bed and began to talk with him she was surprised that he recognized her. Her mother had warned her that he might not, but as they continued to talk she found herself constantly correcting him. "No Papa, we're not in Dombrowa any longer, don't you remember the resettlement?

Papa, I'm married now, I have children of my own. No Papa, Edmund is not coming home and neither is Rudolf. Don't you remember Papa, this is Germany, not Volhynia?" After a few hours of this she couldn't bear it any longer. She had to leave the room and wanted to crawl into her mother's arms to cry. Emilie, however, frowned on such self-indulgence.

The next day Alwine's sister Adele arrived. The two married daughters, along with their younger sisters, Else and Klara, took turns sitting and reading to their father. He loved to hear the Bible and in particular he enjoyed the New Testament. The girls were amazed how he seemed to know every word and anticipated upcoming passages, mouthing them as the girls read. "How could he remember things so clearly and not know what happened just yesterday?" they wondered, shaking their heads. When Adele and Alwine compared notes, they couldn't help remarking how clearly their father remembered things that had happened in their youth. It brought tears to their eyes. Emilie would have none of that.

"You didn't come here to cry," she scolded them after a couple of days. "I think you should both go home. Both your husbands are off to war. You have your own families to take care of." Adele began to protest but her mother remained firm. "Else, Klara and I can manage. I'm sure your father appreciates your visits but enough is enough. Your families need you."

When Alwine returned home, she found her household in an agitated state. Hertha came running down the lane shouting something about her father. At first Alwine thought that he might have gotten a leave and come home unexpectedly. When the little girl clutched onto her mother with tears in her eyes, she knew something was wrong. "What is the matter, Hertha?"

"Mama," she said, still not in control of her voice, "we got a telegram while you were gone. Papa has been hurt." Alwine ran the rest of the way up the lane to her house. She had not listened to all that Hertha had said. Her mind was stuck on the word 'telegram.'

Edmund handed her the paper explaining, "He's not dead Mama. He's wounded, but he's not dead."

Alwine didn't know what to say so she read the telegram that unfortunately gave few details, except to say that he had been evacuated to a hospital. She read it several times and then could only repeat Edmund's words, "he's not dead, at least he's not dead!"

As Albert lay on the hospital bed so far from the front lines, it was hard for him to keep from smiling. Despite the pain that racked the left side of his body he was feeling lucky. Not a leg, nor an arm, nor even a finger was missing or mangled and he was beginning to walk again. All that was wonderful enough, but today the doctors had told him that he would not have to return to active service. As soon as he was well enough, he could go home with an honorable discharge. He would have to live with a few bomb fragments in his leg that could not be removed and would have to use a cane for a long time. But he was free.

The doctors could not have given him better news. Albert had no idea how he would have been able to summon up enough courage to return to the front. Without tears, or regret or even guilt he had accepted that he was a coward. The last six months had been a hell for him, a hell that had only been exacerbated by having been reunited with his nephew Gustav. Albert knew he was a coward, afraid to fight, afraid to die, afraid to kill and if he now rationalized that nine out of ten of his comrades were cowards too, it was only because he had witnessed it. Not everyone could be a Gustav Fischer.

It had been after his last leave that his luck ran out. He had been transferred to the front and into a new platoon. To his surprise and even delight his corporal was his own nephew, whom he had not seen since the German invasion of Poland. Gustav was no longer a skinny teenager but a fully grown man, who at twenty-two was a leader and a veteran. There was authority in his voice, and that silly teenage swagger he had once exhibited was replaced with the disciplined, deliberate gait of a soldier. Albert could recall thinking how his wife would have loved to see this. She had always liked his nephews Gustav and Otto, even when their parents had given up on them.

Albert was impressed with how much Gustav had grown and with the obvious respect that his men had for him. But when his nephew spoke to his platoon Albert could see some of the old habits were still there. The corporal spared his men no obscene language and no bad joke, but if that bothered anyone it was offset by the obvious confidence his men had in him. Gustav took the lead in every foray. In the thickest of battles Gustav always went to the front and never sent a man where he would not go. He was their leader, not their teacher nor their nurse.

Despite the unexpected surprise, Albert was extremely nervous that night. Nothing could take away the knowledge he was at the front and that men died here. Later, when the other soldiers slept, Gustav took Albert aside. "Don't worry, Albert," he said, "if I shout and yell at you. I don't mean you any ill by it. I just can't show any favoritism. But I promise you if you stay close by me in battle, I will protect you, just stay behind me." Gustav was so positive in his promise that Albert believed him.

In the next few months, when all that the German army in the east seemed to be doing was retreating, Albert stayed close to Gustav. The only drawback to this was that Gustav had the uncanny ability to find the thick of any skirmish and he never flinched in putting himself and his men into the heart of the fighting. Each time Albert was sure that he was going to die, yet he always came out without a scratch. As tough as Gustav appeared when barking orders, he was even tougher under pressure, fighting harder and smarter, shooting faster, dodging more quickly and running faster. As long as Albert stayed close to his nephew he was all right.

But even with Gustav's help, Albert did not get over his fear. The drawback to being with this rough and ready corporal was that his platoon got all the tough assignments. His willingness to tackle the difficult was well known to the officers and his ability to accomplish the impossible was becoming legend in the division. Every dangerous assault, every well protected bunker that needed to be taken out, every house that needed to be searched, and every dangerous patrol seemed to come Gustav's way. He never turned down any opportunity to fight. Albert dreaded these assignments but he always stuck close to his nephew, and he never let him down.

But it was when they were caught behind enemy lines that Gustav showed his greatest prowess, his determination to survive. During a hasty retreat caused by incessant mortar fire, Gustav and Albert were cut off while running through a boggy wood east of Warsaw. How they got lost neither one knew but when their army was in retreat Albert was right behind Gustav even though it seemed like he would never stop running. They weaved through the trees and underbrush and never stopped until they were blinded by the night. It was then that Gustav had to admit that he was lost and they might very well be cut off from their own army. Still he showed no fear.

They heard the heavy artillery throughout the night and slept uneasily in the hollow of a thicket, covered in rotting leaves. In the morning Albert was confused and disoriented but Gustav set off immediately in the direction of his lines without flinching or second guessing his decision. With empty rifles they went looking for the German army.

For hours on end Albert followed Gustav who never seemed to tire. For all Albert knew they could be walking straight into enemy lines. By the afternoon, their bellies retching with hunger, they began to see where the shells from the previous night had fallen in the forest. Broken and mangled trees littered the ground and bomb craters marred the terrain.

"Our army must have been here," Gustav commented and led on.

It was Gustav who heard them first. The voices were muffled but growing louder with every inch they advanced. Albert soon heard them too but they were too low to be made out. Were they German or Russian? They had to be careful.

Gustav moved in with the stealth of a fox. He pointed to a crater. The voices were clearer now. There were laughs interspersed with the talking. The fools had let down their guard and now for the first time the two Germans could clearly hear that they were Russian. Gustav and Albert raised their empty guns and in a quick dash burst onto the crater's edge. Gustav shouted in Russian, "Drop your weapons!"

There were four very surprised Russian soldiers in the crater, sharing a cigarette. They dropped their weapons and crawled out. They were young, Albert thought, he doubted that even one of them was twenty.

Gustav asked them where their lines were. There was fear on their faces but none of them spoke. While Albert pointed his empty rifle at them Gustav went behind and put his rifle to the head of one of the frightened young soldiers and demanded an answer. The boy hesitated and with a move as quick as lightning Gustav shattered his skull with the butt of his rifle. He fell like a stone. The others tensed and Albert tried hard not to show his shock at the brutal murder. The others quickly told Gustav everything he wanted to know. It made no difference, however, before Albert could say a word the other three were dead.

It had happened so quickly that Albert could only stare at their lifeless bodies while he groped to understand what had just happened. His blood ran from his face and he wanted to be sick. Nothing he had ever seen, not all his experiences at Bereza Kartuska, or in the camp at Zwickau had prepared him to be a party to such a grizzly slaughter. He could not understand what it took to kill so coldly.

Gustav noticed Albert's reaction, "You know I had to do it."

"Had to?"

"Yes, had to," Gustav said sternly looking directly into his uncle's eyes. "They were dead as soon as they gave up their rifles. We're behind enemy lines. We're not in a position to take prisoners. If we had let them go, they would have had their comrades here in minutes and we would be the ones lying there. I just saved our lives."

"We could have tied them up."

"Grow up, Albert," Gustav said to his uncle, "there lie four Russians who will never reach Germany!"

"I understand," Albert said, "I was just ..." He couldn't finish. He didn't know what he felt.

"They said their lines were a kilometer ahead. We'll have a better chance getting through at night."

"How do you know they didn't lie?" Albert asked.

"They were too scared to lie."

At dusk they began to move forward again. They progressed painfully slowly, watching their flanks and rear so that no enemy could surprise them. It was dark in the woods and they soon found themselves stumbling over roots and rocks. It was inevitable that they should be detected. It was pitch black when Albert talked about giving up but Gustav was unwilling to listen.

"If they found those bodies back there, they would shoot us anyway," Gustav answered angrily, "you surrender if you want to, I'm going through the lines right now. You can come with me or stay here and wait for them to find you." With that he stood up and boldly walked forward. After a few seconds of hesitation Albert followed.

They had only gone a short distance when a voice in the dark called out in Russian, "Halt, who goes there!" Gustav took no time to respond. "A friend," he blurted out in Russian. There was a deeper shadow in between some trees ahead and a dim light that barely outlined a human figure. The guard asked for a password but without betraying any fear nor nervousness Gustav responded that he was lost and didn't know the password. He talked so frankly and plainly about having been separated from his company that the guard let him approach. Albert was mesmerized by the bold move and the folly of the Russian. There was not a hint of deceit in Gustav's voice and by the time the shocked guard recognized his enemy's uniform, Gustav's bayonet was in his heart.

It was almost too easy. Gustav and Albert crossed over to the German lines without even seeing another Russian soldier.

But the faces of those dead young boys never left Albert. He couldn't think or sleep and especially he couldn't look into Gustav's face without seeing them. If this was bravery, he knew he had none. He could no longer follow Gustav into battle.

A week later, while facing a line of Russian tanks with nothing but rifles and a few bazookas, the platoon was pinned down. Desperately, Gustav was calling his men to follow the general retreat. Albert heard him but he didn't follow and he never could explain why. He held his bazooka in place while he and his partner got off one more shell. It was too late. A tank had zeroed in on them and a shell landed only a few yards away. Albert couldn't even remember hearing it. He couldn't remember the death of his partner nor being buried alive, with bits of shrapnel riddling the left side of his body. He never saw or heard Gustav come running back and frantically digging him out.

Two days later he woke up in a hospital far to the west. For him, the doctors reassured, the war was over. No words could have been sweeter. The thought of returning home was almost as dear as hearing that he would not have to fight again. He could forget the faces of those little boys lying dead in that crater. He could forget it all. He could even forget what his wife said about living in a cursed land. Anything was better than the front.

Twenty-Eight

Six weeks after his injury Albert came home. Though his wife fussed over him in a way that he had never before been pampered, he could tell that something else was distracting her. It was not like Albert to notice these things, but then it was not the same Albert that had come back from the war. In the quiet moments he sensed and saw the sadness and the tears glistening in his wife's eyes. It wasn't difficult for him to get her to tell him what was wrong. Otto was missing in action but that was only one problem. Sobbing, she showed him a letter from her mother. The paper looked like she had read it a hundred times but she had not wanted to bother her husband with bad news so soon after his return.

September 15, 1944

Dear Alwine,

It was good to get your last letter and hear that Albert is recovering from his wounds and will soon be home. What a blessing it is. It is so nice to have something to be grateful for. Unfortunately, now there is more bad news. Only yesterday we received a telegram that Otto is missing in action in Romania.

I have a terrible fear that he is dead, but I try hard to hope for the best.

Oh, Alwine, I'm afraid that I have done an evil thing. I read the telegram to your father. Else and Klara pleaded with me not to, knowing how much he adored Otto, but I was sure he would want to know the truth, at least the man he used to be would have demanded it. He didn't say a word but just stared out of his window so I was sure he had not understood. But later poor Else came running to tell me that Papa was outside going down the lane. He was determined to go to find Otto. We had to have a farmhand help us get him back into the house.

If there is a chance that Otto is alive I pray he will be found soon. I fear your Papa will not be able to accept it, if he is dead.

I write you this so that you hear it first from me but please do not feel that have to come. I have Else and Klara to help me while your family needs you. The girls have grown up so much in the past year. It is a great comfort.

Please give my love to the children and tell them I miss them.

With much love,
Your Mother

Emilie Frey was right, Alwine could not leave her family right now though she ached to be with her parents. She was torn between being a daughter and a wife and mother. She felt like she was abandoning one family, yet she had a husband and children of her own that needed her.

Alwine received another letter only two weeks later. It was not from her mother but from her younger sister Else. She had written surreptitiously looking for either help or comfort. She explained that her mother was weakening quickly because of the time and energy she spent looking after and worrying about father. She was neglecting her own health. Else hoped that somehow Alwine might be able to tear herself from her family. Perhaps she could talk to her mother.

Albert told her to go. He showed her his leg and how he hardly needed the cane anymore. He only used it for fear of being returned to the front. Alwine's mouth dropped and she screamed with all the power her lungs and heart could provide. "My brothers are dying and you pretend to be injured to stay out of the war. How could you do such a thing? It's disgraceful!"

"Shut up, woman!" her shocked husband shot back angrily, "I've come as close to death as I ever want to be. Do you want me dead too?"

"It's not right!"

"What is right? Is dying right? I'm not going back. I've had enough."

Alwine calmed down. She had been so absorbed in her parents problems that she never considered her husband's feelings. "I'm sorry," she said, deeply ashamed. "I'm sick over my brothers and my father. Forgive me."

"Go," he said, abruptly, "perhaps it will make you feel better. But don't stay too long," he warned her, "I don't think it will be long before the Russians reach us."

Alwine found that conditions were as her sister had said. Their mother was worn out and looked like she never slept. Yet weak as she was Emilie struggled to be there for her husband. It was only because of the visit of her daughter that she took a few minutes to sit and talk.

Alwine saw a dimness in her mother's eyes and a pallor on her face that worried her. All her life Emilie had been a very vital woman, full of energy and always hopeful. Now she sat, barely making conversation, just listening to her daughter with eyes whose fire seemed to be waning and a body grown old in a few short months. She was only fifty-five.

For a few short minutes Alwine was able to make her happy as she talked about what her grandchildren were doing. How Edmund's attitude was changing and she could actually talk to the boy now and how Hertha was becoming such a help around the home. She described little Else's last adventure, chasing a goose that she presumed was persecuting a hen and her chicks by chasing them away from the pond. It provided Emilie with the only laughter she had in a long time but it lasted only a few minutes and the smile drifted from Emilie's face almost as soon as Alwine stopped talking about her grandchildren. Struggling to avoid talking about her father and the gloomy path that conversation would take, Alwine instead talked about her sister Adele's loss of her husband. Emilie's eyes filled with tears for her daughter, but it was the term 'fallen' that brought energy to her voice.

"They make it so innocuous don't they?" she said with a sarcastically bitter edge that Alwine recognized. It revealed a hint of her mother's former strength. "They send a telegram to say that your son or husband has 'fallen' like he tripped and stubbed his toe. Why don't they just say he's dead? Why don't they just tell us that Otto is dead in Romania? Our son and our daughter's husband. Poor Adele, what will she do without a husband?"

"Mama," Alwine said, "everything will be all right." But she herself didn't know what she meant, and when her mother gave her an incredulous stare she felt silly.

"God knows, all will someday be fine again," Emilie said, "but not for us. When your parents teach you that you must trust in God they don't tell you how much that trust can hurt."

"It's not like you to be so bitter Mama. On the train to Siberia it was your hope that kept us alive. It was your strength that brought us through, Mama."

"Mama, you can't give up," her daughter Else now interjected.

"Don't tell an old woman what she can or can't do. I have no intention of giving up. If I wanted to give up I would not work and pray as I do. Sleeping and moping, that's giving up."

Alwine and her sisters, Else and Klara were sure that their mother was wearing herself out in caring for her husband. But during her visit Alwine could not find anything to cheer up either of her parents. Her father barely recognized her and when he did, he talked and acted as if she were still a child. Emilie lost her patience once with him when he spoke to Alwine as if she were only ten years old, "For heaven's sake," she yelled, "can't you see she's a grown woman!" But Johann Frey just continued as if he hadn't heard a thing. It was as if only the past existed for him.

Not even able to accomplish the task of comforting her mother Alwine returned to her family. She was proud, nevertheless, of her sisters Else and Klara who had taken over the management of the house and the farm. Else, now a woman in her early twenties, who certainly would have been married and running a household of her own were it not for the war, seemed very pragmatic about the whole thing. In fact she wound up comforting her older sister as they said goodbye. "Thank-you for coming," she said, "I'm sure it has helped." Klara seemed equally positive. "Whatever comes," she declared, "we will manage it."

That fall the whole community was depressed. Though young boys like Edmund still believed what was being broadcast on the radio and taught in the school, that the forces of the Third Reich were winning, no one else did. There was a terrible lack of sincerity in those broadcasts, for the details of the victories were very sparse, and the term 'strategic withdrawal' was being used more and more often. It was, however, considered traitorous to speak of defeat and Albert's secret preparation of a wagon in the shed for a hurried flight west was, strictly speaking, illegal.

A fear arose among the transplanted Volhynians that they had kept repressed for more than four years now. It stemmed from the fact that all around them in the towns and even on the farms lived thousands of the Poles who were the true owners of the lands that the Volhynians now farmed. With the impending defeat of the German army it was reasonable to assume that these people would, with the help of the Russian army, reclaim their lost lands. What was unknown, and what the German-Volhynians feared most was how much anger the Poles held for those who had taken the land that Adolf Hitler had offered them. Already now a number of the farmhands were deserting, leaving in the middle of the night perhaps to join the resistance. The Germans expected them to return with vengeance.

Alwine regretted her earlier criticism of her husband, particularly when everywhere in the district men were being recalled to the army even if they had been declared unfit. It was further evidence of what went unspoken, that the defeat of the eastern army was imminent. Alwine was glad that Albert was still home, even grateful that he pretended that his injuries would not heal in order to be with them.

Edmund still refused steadfastly to believe that Germany could lose the war. The wagon waiting in the shed, at the ready, was an affront to his loyalty. Neither did he let the talk of Polish revenge impress him. He knew that the Poles were a weak, ineffectual people, destined to be ruled by others and unable to think for themselves. He tried to tell his parents but they didn't listen to him. They regarded his protestation as childish and pigheaded.

He told himself that he worried too much about Else and Hertha to report his parents to the authorities. Unsure what to do he discussed it with his schoolmates. To his surprise they were neither shocked nor interested. Almost every one of them could report that his parents had similar plans and could list down to the last item the things they had prepared for their eventual escape. It only served to confuse Edmund even more.

However, it was when his mother asked Edmund to take some blankets she had packed out to the escape-wagon that he vented his frustration. He flatly refused to do it and his mother was about to shrug it off as another in a series of events in a turbulent year for the boy. But his father had overheard him. "Do as your mother asked," he yelled at the boy. His wife had talked to him about Edmund's behavior and he felt that what was required was a strong hand.

"No!"

The refusal caught Albert by surprise but only served to make him angrier. "Take them out unless you want to feel the back of my hand!" he raged. He could barely conceive that a thirteen-year-old could be so insolent.

"No! I won't do it! You're a traitor. The Reich cannot lose."

"You're just a boy, what do you know?" his father yelled.

"We are winning! Every day the radio talks about our victories. It will not be long before the Russians are turned back."

"You're a stupid boy," his father said turning away, and this was the insult that Edmund found most demoralizing. He was telling the truth as he heard it and his father refused to listen. But his mother had remained silent and now saw the disappointment in his eyes. She came over and put her hand on his shoulder but he shrugged it off.

"Why does everyone believe we are losing the war when we are winning?" he finally asked, breaking out in tears.

"Your father was at the front son," his mother tried to calm him down by saying, "he knows what is going on. Every day the Russians get closer."

"But they wouldn't lie to us, Mother. Would they?"

"Son, it's a hard thing sometimes to learn the truth," Alwine explained, "but governments lie to people all the time, especially in war. If the Reich allowed people to spread the idea that they were losing the war then there would be panic among the people, so they lie. But people are not stupid, they can read the signs."

"But Mother, they promised that we would not lose the war," Edmund protested just as the tears were welling up in his eyes.

"The Germans can never lose a war against the Russians! The Russians and the Poles don't know how to fight! We shouldn't be afraid of them!"

Alwine didn't know how to make him understand. She put her hands gently on his shoulders but he drew away as if her touch was repulsive to him. As she struggled to find words to make him understand, he ran out of the house.

Edmund was sitting on the front step of the Belschewo school house when Erich Winkler saw him from the two rooms he occupied in a house across the street. The teacher could see that something was wrong and strolled across to find out what it was. "What are you doing here so late Edmund?" he asked.

Edmund's face tightened and he sternly replied, "I'm a coward."

Erich invited Edmund back to his home. In his little kitchen he offered the boy a tea and 'butterbrot.' He didn't want to press the boy about his problems if he didn't want to talk, but he couldn't help asking, "What makes you think you're a coward?"

"My group leader said we had to report traitors but I couldn't do it."

"Who are the traitors you want to report?"

"Mama and Papa," Edmund cried, "they are preparing a wagon. They say that Russia is going to win the war."

"Oh," was all that Erich could think to say. He knew that only the blind and the very young could still believe that Germany could win. Nevertheless, this was serious business for the boy and he wanted to be gentle.

"I couldn't do it. I was going to my group leader to tell him but I couldn't."

"That's not cowardice Edmund, that's loyalty," Erich told him reassuringly. "Besides, your group leader has gone back to Germany. You see he believes too that Germany is going to lose."

Edmund looked up from his tea with the incredulous look that Erich had anticipated. Erich knew it was time to tell this boy the whole truth.

"What makes you think you have to report your parents?"

"They taught us in Hitler Youth to report suspicious and traitorous activities. It's my duty."

"Yes, I'm sure they taught you well. In the past few years I have often been forced to teach things in school that I did not believe. The choice was between teaching what they told me to and not teaching at all. Perhaps I made the wrong choice."

"I don't understand."

"War is a bad thing, Edmund, not just for the killing that goes on but for what it does to men's minds too. Wars need to be justified, that means governments have to be able to tell their people that they are fighting for a just cause. They tell them that the enemy can't be trusted, or they are evil. It makes it easier to kill when you believe the enemy is evil. They build up their soldiers by telling them that the enemy can't win, that they don't know how to fight or are too lazy and stupid. Do you know what I'm talking about, Edmund?"

Edmund shook his head.

"Germany is losing the war. Your parents are not disloyal, in fact, they are being really loyal to what really matters, you. They tell you the truth. Everyone else has been lying to you. I have been lying to you. Your parents are good people and they know, like everyone else, that when the Russians liberate the Poles they will be very angry with us. All the Germans are preparing to leave. I'm sure all your neighbors are and even I am ready to leave."

The boy was totally unprepared to hear what his teacher was saying and thought that the whole world was turning against him. But was it true? Could Germany lose the war? "Herr Lehrer," he asked with a whimper, his voice shaking with uncertainty, "how can the Russians be winning? We are so much stronger?"

The teacher looked at Edmund as if he hadn't understood a word he had been saying. For a second he just wanted to remind him that he was the student and that he should just accept what the teacher had said; that was the German way. However, he became bitterly aware of the fact that he was part of the problem. That was not easy for him to admit. A teacher in Germany was an autocrat within a society that worshiped authority. How could he tell a young boy that the obvious truths that he had been taught were manufactured propaganda, unbridled bigotry and self-righteous arrogance?

"Edmund," he began, "how do you like the house you live in?"

"House?" Edmund questioned.

"Yes, is it better than the one you had in Volhynia?"

"Yes, it's much bigger."

"Does it have electric lights?"

"Yes."

"Running water in the house?"

"Yes."

"And how many cows does your father have?"

"Twenty."

"Was your house in Volhynia as good?"

"No. It was much smaller. We had no electricity or running water."

"How many cows did you have in Volhynia?"

"Two."

"The Poles who owned your farm before you, they built the house, bred the animals and cleared and tilled the fields. How could the Poles have accomplished all this if they were stupid and lazy?"

Edmund almost saw where the teacher was going and felt the need to defend his heritage. "It wasn't always like that."

"Yes, I'm sure that's true. But do you see that the Poles might not be as stupid and backward as you have been taught."

Edmund couldn't or wouldn't acknowledge this statement. It was too much to think about. The war, Germany losing, Russians winning, everything he had been taught said it was wrong and that it couldn't happen. He couldn't say anything, it hurt too much to see his whole world fall apart. He could not bring himself to thank Erich as he left to go home, he could only walk and kick at the stones.

By November the Reich was in desperate trouble. Exhausted from fighting on too many fronts against too many enemies, the armed forces were taking heavy losses. The Russians were ramming at the eastern line time and time again. Each charge cost lives and each time the Germans were able to repulse them even more lives were lost. The armies were so depleted that men who had been declared unfit were now called up again. It was even rumored that boys as young as fifteen years had been called up to fight.

In Wartheland the people were tense. The harvest had been dutifully gathered but the feeling of joy and security that usually accompanied the threshing of the last wagonload of grain was missing that year. People recalled the last harvest in Volhynia. It was eerily similar. It was an uncomfortable season.

In their sheds the instruments of their escape stood at the ready, loaded and overloaded for the dash west. With each day that passed, however, people found more and more items that they considered absolutely necessary to take with them, or just could not leave behind. At first they had prepared food and clothing to help them survive, but now they packed items of worth, both intrinsic and emotional; the silverware, the china dishes so faithfully saved for, and the New York sewing machine that was so wonderful. Slowly, but surely they overloaded their wagons.

No one knew why they waited so long, much too long in retrospect. It was as if they were waiting for a signal or for someone to shout the order to leave, and then they would all begin together. No one wanted to risk being first. One wagon loaded to the hilt with a family's worldly goods could be easily stopped and turned back or even made an example of, as traitors and cowards. But had they all moved together no one could not have stopped them. Instead, they were all waiting to panic together.

In mid-November Albert got a letter from the army asking him to report for a medical examination. They wanted to determine if he was fit to return to duty. He smashed his fist into the wall when he read it. He had gone to great lengths to make sure he kept his cane with him and walked with a limp everywhere. It embarrassed his wife that he had a slightly more exaggerated limp on Sundays. It had worked to the point of making him one of the very last to be recalled. Either Germany was so desperate that it needed everyone, or someone had told on him. He supposed that the truth was that the German war machine was desperate.

Albert cursed and swore, in both Russian and Ukrainian. When his wife rebuked him for it, he merely shrugged it off and said, "The Russians have the best swear words." He did not want to return to the army. He thought about running away but knew immediately that it was not a path open to him. That was the worst thing he could do for his family and he eliminated that option quickly. The only thing left was to convince the German doctors that he was still unfit for duty.

Were it not for the seriousness of their situation Alwine would have laughed out loud. In the few days that he had left before he was to report, Albert practiced using his cane, exaggerating the limp of the left leg and wincing ever so convincingly with each step. Yet, when he had his performance perfected, he began to fear that it was not enough to fool the doctors. He had to find something else. He remembered that the explosion that had buried him had caused a concussion. And there was the rheumatic fever he had suffered as a child. The convulsions from that disease all of a sudden reappeared, probably as a result of the trauma to his head.

It all raced through Albert's mind like a whirlwind. There was so little time for him to put it all together and it all seemed so desperate and perhaps futile. Yet his discomfort with the thought of returning to the front was even greater. Germany was losing and more men than ever were dying. A letter came that last day from Alwine's mother, Otto was now confirmed dead and she could not bring herself to tell her husband. It convinced Albert that he was doing the right thing. He said to his wife, "If it keeps me off the front for even one more day it's worth it!" To which she replied, "Just be careful that these Nazis don't shoot you!" With those words everything became ambiguous again and Albert vacillated. Should he report for duty and take the consequences or pretend to be just a little worse than he was.

It was while the doctor was examining his leg that Albert knew what to do. With the doctor's first remarks on how improved the leg was, Albert realized that he would soon be at the front if he did not put his whole plan into action. When the doctor asked him to put his weight on the leg, Albert winced bravely, lost his balance and fell over. He answered questions with vagueness and pretended to not understand them. He pointed to his head and said that he still had dizzy spells because of the blow it had received when he was wounded. Finally the doctor examining him said, "We will be sending you to the Hospital at Berlin for further examination and evaluation." It was not what Albert had hoped to hear, but it was better than the front.

Twenty-Nine

As winter approached in December of 1944, the gloom of the Germans in Warthegau was so pervasive that even Edmund became convinced of the inevitability of defeat. His mother, like most others, hoped desperately that the Russian army could be turned back. Not since the day Albert had been recalled had Alwine heard from him. Yet, as long as no telegram came she could just assume he was alright, and that was one thing less to worry about. Her priority now was to keep her family ready to flee to the west. She wasn't quite sure why she hadn't left already except that it seemed ludicrous to leave a warm home for an uncertain destination in the middle of winter. And then there was the problem of timing too. Later she might curse herself for it, but Alwine could not be the first to go.

For her, the problem of when to leave had lately been complicated by one more thing. Only recently she had discovered that she was pregnant again. With trouble coming, and the probability of another winter flight, she could not believe that the pregnancy could go full term. She remembered painfully that the three children she had carried on this cursed ground had not survived, two of them had lived barely a month and one was still born. Her eyes watered too when she thought of Einhardt and Ewald who had died on the way here. She would be happy to leave immediately if it wasn't for winter. It had been the largest, most productive piece of land she and her husband had ever owned, but it was not really theirs.

"It's better that we leave," Alwine explained to her son Edmund. "This place is cursed. We were never meant to possess it." But Edmund, who was still struggling to stay loyal to Germany, scoffed at her suggestion. He would do nothing to help her.

Stefan was a source of strength to Alwine in those days. He encouraged her to make preparations to leave and though he was not optimistic about a journey to the west undertaken in haste in winter, he was also aware of the consequences of her staying. He knew she had reason to fear the resurgence of the Poles. It would be better for Alwine and her children to suffer the hardships of the road than to wait for the wrath of his countrymen. His admiration and loyalty for his mistress were total and he felt an obligation to see her away safely.

But Stefan, loyal and faithful as he was, knew that the impending change also brought opportunity. He had already determined what his course of action should be once Alwine and her children were away. As soon as the Germans were gone, he would reclaim his own property. The farm on which he had been raised was only a few kilometers away.

He had been happy there growing up and he was terribly insulted that some German interlopers occupied it now. It made him grateful that his parents had died shortly before the German invasion. They would have found it unbearable to be removed from their land. His parents had lived their lives in hope of seeing Poland free and at least at the end of their lives they had seen it free. It seemed only just that he should claim the land they had preserved all their lives for him.

Stefan's parents had taught him well. Though they were poor farmers, they had an intense loyalty to the land. They even understood the value of an education so they made sure that Stefan learned to read and write. But most practical of all was what they taught Stefan about survival. "The way we Polish endured the brutal giants," his father had told him, "was by being accommodating, and by being exactly what they expected us to be. They thought we were stupid and needed their guidance, so we acted that way and as long as we did, they did not feel threatened and left us alone. We worked hard and gave everything our best effort and in the end we outlasted them. They wanted us to become Russian and German but we waited them out." But when Stefan saw the invasion coming he said to himself, "Unfortunately, we did not kill them!"

Stefan had listened well to his father. He had made all the accommodations that the Germans had required of him and he was glad that they were leaving, but he was still uncertain of the future. While the Germans moved west again the other giant that lived beside Poland was coming from the east. During the last century the Russians had been even more cruel than the Germans and now with the communists coming, who knew what would happen. Maczowiak, the part-time worker from Belschewo, a confessed communist, had told them that the Russians were coming to free the Polish people. Maczowiak might believe that, but Stefan knew that when the Russians came to Poland they always came as conquerors. "They may rescue us from the Germans, but will they ever leave again?" Stefan had asked. But another of the workers had pointed out, "If they give us our farms back then I will be happy to have them here." It really didn't matter to Stefan, he had survived the Germans and he was sure that he could survive the Russians too. His father had given him the formula. Don't be too smart, don't be too stupid and work so hard that they think they can't do without you.

When he had first been sent to this farm as a laborer, he was astounded that one of the best farms in the district was still in Polish hands. Yet Stefan didn't care for Jerzy Finkowski. The man seemed to be consumed by passions that Stefan couldn't understand, sometimes speaking as if he were a Pole and sometimes as an

American, but really not being interested in anything or anyone but himself. That had lasted only a month until the Fischers came. He had no better understanding of these Germans who called themselves Volhynians either. That they were Germans who used to be Poles or Poles who were Germans at heart didn't affect him at all. They were the enemy who had to be tolerated until things changed and he was prepared to survive them.

Now, almost four and a half years later, Stefan was not thinking of revenge like many of his countrymen. His primary objective was to get his own land back and he didn't want to be concerned about things like vengeance and retribution that only stopped you from thinking clearly. Yet, he had been so unprepared for what had happened in the past four years that now made him anxious about Alwine's safety. He wanted Alwine Fischer and her children to go quickly, before it was too late.

He had been put totally off guard by this woman. They had become friends and she had made the last four years more than just bearable. Her husband Albert was a passable fellow, although he thought that without his wife he had the potential of being a really arrogant German. It must have been she who made him into a real man. She was that good, and Stefan could do nothing until he felt that she and her children had a reasonable chance of escaping.

The children, he had grown accustomed to. Hertha made him laugh, and little Else who was so gentle and yet so determined made him feel protective. Edmund, was a concern, but he understood that he was confused. "Let them all go to Germany and be safe," he thought to himself, "she saved my life, I'll help save hers."

Almost constantly he thought about what would surely be a grueling journey and even weighed the possibility of going with her. He would drive the wagon and not stop until she was safe. But what about his farm? Would it still be there when he returned? It was likely that someone else would be squatting on it and then how would he prove that it was his? If they asked him where he had been and he told them that he was rescuing his German master's family, would they laugh at him or would they kill him? In the end Stefan knew he had to choose the land. He would send Urbanski to drive them.

It was so disturbing to him that he couldn't help speculating on scenarios that seemed only remotely possible. What if she didn't leave? What if her husband didn't come back this time? What if she didn't get away on time and the Russians captured her? He saw himself taking her in to protect her. What would that lead to? When he stepped back and looked at his emotions and the wild ideas that kept racing through his head he had to admit that he loved her. That had been obvious to him for some time, but amazingly he was now beginning to think that it might actually be possible for them to be together, if everything fell into place.

It was thrilling to entertain such thoughts, but agonizing too, since he could not really bring himself to believe that she could be interested in him. It was part of her nature to be faithful and loyal. She had character, that was what he respected more than anything. It was a paradox; the reason that she could not love him was exactly the reason he loved her. So his only way to show how he felt was to help her to leave. Urbanski would be glad to go, he was a good man who was more afraid of the Russians than the Germans. Stefan's one remaining duty was to convince her to leave quickly and it was there that he most often encountered the stubborn young Edmund. Did the boy sense what his feelings really were?

Christmas passed in gloom, and New Years day went by uncelebrated. Then on the evening of the third of January the eastern sky was lit up as if as by a gigantic thunderstorm, but there were no clouds. The lights were amazing to watch and the giant cannons, heard from a great distance, sounded like muffled thunder. It was the final alarm, the signal for the Germans to leave. Survival was more important now than loyalty.

Stefan stayed up all night. He gave the horses an extra ration of grain, it might be the last they'd see for a while, and then he greased the axles and wheels. Alwine couldn't sleep at all. She came to the shed in the middle of the night to make sure the provisions were secure on the wagon and there was adequate space for three children to sleep. She was surprised but not shocked to find Stefan there making sure everything was ready.

There was nothing in Stefan's loyalty that shocked Alwine anymore. He thought things out one step ahead of everyone else. It was comforting for Alwine to be relieved at least of the responsibility of worrying about him, he could certainly take care of himself. She did not completely understand his loyalty, but she attributed it to his nature, which was to be totally trustworthy. Alwine never even conceived of any other reasons for his generosity and did not imagine that he might still be grateful to her for having saved his life. Stefan was a good person not because of anything she had done but because that was who he was. Now in the quiet of predawn, before the others woke, she wanted to thank him, but she didn't know what to say. Nothing she could think of could be adequate.

"Stefan, I cannot thank you enough. I don't know how I can repay you for your faithful service, I ..." It was a stumbling beginning, the words were like stones while what she was wanting to express felt like flowers.

Stefan shook his head, "No, thank-you," he said, "you have made these years bearable."

"We're not as different as we think, we Germans and you Poles."

"Don't let Herr Hitler hear you saying that."

"I don't know how to adequately thank you, and it is unlikely that we will ever see each other again, but I will pray for your safety."

"And I yours," he said, and immediately felt the blood rushing to his face. He feared the tone was a little too personal so he quickly added, "and for the little ones." Stefan was tempted to say something further but as he wrestled with the impropriety of it all he heard a disturbance in the farmyard. The sound of horses and wagon dismayed him and Alwine. They thought the worst. Stefan rushed out to the barn door with Alwine right behind him. In the barn yard stood was a wagon pulled by two horses. It wasn't the Russians. In front of the wagon a man stood holding a lamp. It was Johann, her brother-in-law, and Hedwig.

"Alwine, we saw the light in your barn and I thought perhaps if you were ready you would want to travel with us," Johann said anxiously. "If we get a head start, we can be kilometers away before dawn."

"How can you travel in the dark?" Stefan questioned.

"I will carry a lamp ahead and guide the horses," Johann answered, "we will be well ahead of the others. At dawn the roads will be packed."

"I didn't know you were coming. I'm not ready. The children are still sleeping."

"We must leave now!" Hedwig insisted.

"I can't leave my brother's family."

"Johann, go ahead. I am not alone. Urbanski will be with me. I'll be all right."

"We can wait a few minutes," Johann offered.

Alwine looked at Stefan, who nodded to confirm that she should do it. "Go now if you can," he said as he rushed off to wake Urbanski.

It was Edmund who protested the most about being woken so early. When his mother informed him that they were fleeing from the Russians he began to wail out loud. Johann rushed into the house to help his sister-in-law but neither could reason with the boy. Frustrated, Alwine slapped him across his cheek with her open hand but it only provoked him to scream louder.

From the barnyard they heard Hedwig screaming now. "Leave the brat behind! Johann we must leave! Leave them all behind they will only slow us down." It was the old Hedwig again, the one they hadn't seen in several years.

"Go on, Johann," Alwine instructed him. "I'll be all right."

"I'm sorry Alwine," Johann apologized, "I'll try to reason with her."

"No, Johann. You go on ahead. Perhaps we can catch up. She's right you know, the children will only hold you up." Johann shook his head, reluctant to leave her behind, but Alwine insisted, "Please Johann, the more we argue the more time we both lose."

But now Alwine felt the urgency of leaving more than ever before. The children all protested being woken so early but their mother bundled the girls up in their warmest boots and coats. Edmund adamantly refused to move but sat on the edge of his bed locked in protest. Alwine promised them a treat of hot cocoa and the girls livened up but Edmund held fast.

When Stefan and Urbanski pulled the wagon up in front of the house, they were dismayed that the family was not ready. Stefan knew how to handle Edmund. He wrapped the boy in a blanket, picked him up like a sack of potatoes and set him in the wagon, even though what he really wanted to do was to throw him in.

It was a mild morning for January but that could change any moment and who knew how long they would have to travel or how far they had to go. Alwine gathered up Edmund's clothes and last of all put on her fleece coat, styled so that the fleece was inside like a lining. It had been an early Christmas present from Albert. When she climbed on the front seat beside an anxious looking Urbanski she turned to say goodbye to Stefan but was surprised that he was nowhere to be seen. As she looked for him, however, she saw a paleness on the eastern horizon that was more than the light of a hundred big guns. It was the coming sunrise and she told Urbanski to hurry. If only she could have gone with Johann.

It was somehow appropriate that she was leaving this cursed land in January, the same time of year that she left Volhynia. She did not care to say goodbye to the house or the garden, they had never really been hers. She had no illusions either that this January escape would be easy and could only hope that the weather would be bearable and that they would all be safe.

Edmund continued to protest but the chill made him pull on his clothes quickly. He had overcome the intense loyalty that blinded him to the possibility of a German defeat, yet he still had hoped that the Russian advance could be stopped. He thought it shameful to show so little faith. Beside his two sisters he knelt with wool blankets wrapped around them against the weather, but there was nothing as cold as the contempt he felt for Stefan. To Edmund, even the loss of the war was now Stefan's fault.

Edmund had supposed all along that it would be Stefan who would drive the wagon. There was something wrong with the man. He feigned loyalty but disobeyed his father's orders. Yet by far the worst thing he had done, was to convince his mother to betray the Reich. It always nagged Edmund that his mother seemed to trust Stefan so much and allowed him to run the farm as he wished. He did not enjoy the prospect of spending days on the road with him but when he realized that it would be Urbanski driving, instead of being happy, he found further reason to resent Stefan. It was a sign of cowardice that Stefan, a single man, would make a married man do what was obviously his duty.

As they started away Edmund said, "You see now Mama, he's a coward. He's staying behind to steal everything he can get his hands on."

Alwine became angry. "Shut up," she yelled at her son, "you have no idea what you're talking about." Edmund shrank beneath his blanket, humiliated, but not willing to give up his feelings.

The light in the east was slowly spreading, but it was still dark when they headed down the lane. Sounds wafting up from the road hinted that more people than just Johann Fischer had gotten an early start and the closer they got the louder the noises became, almost turning into a din. And then came the realization that the road was already swelling with her fleeing neighbors. Nevertheless, it was somehow comforting to Alwine that she would not be alone on the road, but it didn't overcome the sinking feeling that they were too late. They were all too late.

As the last of the cover of darkness was removed, it became clear that the road was overflowing. Both Germans and Poles were fleeing the communist horde. Ahead of them and behind them was an unbroken line of wagons and there were more refugees joining the flow at every junction. Alwine almost cried at the sight. If only she had listened to Stefan.

The line moved slowly but steadily and by noon they had traveled enough distance that Alwine was beginning to feel encouraged. If they could keep this pace, she felt that there was a chance of escape, for it seemed that most of those who wanted to join the escape were already on the road. Here and there a straggler appeared, perhaps someone who had made no previous preparations but was panicked by the sight of his neighbors leaving and so joined them like a lemming. But these were few so there was hope of escaping. Several times, small groups of German soldiers passed them going the other way. That was reassuring too, perhaps they could delay the Russians enough to allow their countrymen time to escape.

But if Alwine had been encouraged by the speed they had made in the morning, what she saw in the afternoon scared her. At a side road that became visible only as they came around a bend there was another line of wagons as long as the eye could see waiting to join the flight west. Such a mass could only clog the road and slow everyone down. But the wagons on the main road showed no signs of easing up and letting this file merge. She and Urbanski could see that the wagons were tightening up their formation, leaving no gaps. Today there was no room for courtesy. Without a prompt from Alwine, Urbanski closed the gap with the wagon in front so that the horses were tight against it. It was everyone for himself.

As they approached the intersection and Alwine looked at the wagons on the side road standing so expectantly she began to feel uncomfortable. Those people had just as much right as anyone to escape. She wondered how desperate she might be if she were waiting there with her children. It would not be so bad, she thought, just to let a few wagons in ahead of her. The people behind her might be angry but they would just have to wait.

She put her hand on Urbanski's arm and said, "Slow down, we will let a few of them in."

"Oh, no," Urbanski warned, "you let a few in and the whole line will go. We'll be here for hours!"

Alwine had to agree but it was too late. As she listened to her farmhand, a small gap had developed in front of them and a man with a rifle had jumped at the opportunity. He waved his hands frantically scaring the horses and then grabbed the harness as they stopped. He waved the rifle to make sure that it was seen but did not point it at them. "This line will pass now," he shouted.

"A few wagons maybe," Alwine said with force, "but only a few."

The man clutched his rifle more deliberately and spoke directly to Alwine, "We have been waiting for hours, we are going to pass now, and you will not stop us." He turned around and signaled for the line to start.

Faced with such a long delay Alwine had no choice. In her broken Polish she ordered Urbanski to drive on, and drive over him if he must. The wagon lurched forward and the horse bumped the man, knocking him and his rifle to the ground. Alwine stood up and craned her neck to see if he was alright. The man was getting up but the wagons on the main road showed no signs of stopping to let the others in. He was angry now frantically waving his arms and threatening with his rifle. "I hope he doesn't shoot someone," Alwine commented to Urbanski.

"If he wanted to shoot someone he would have done it by now," Urbanski replied. Then he added, "But if he's not careful someone will shoot him."

The prediction came true almost immediately. A shot rang out behind them and as Alwine turned she saw the man lying on the street. "Someone shot him," Edmund cried, "he pointed his rifle and someone shot him."

Alwine strained to see what was happening but there was already a crowd of people surrounding the body, while the main line of refugees kept passing by, indifferent to what had happened. When she sat down again there were tears in Alwine's eyes. She tried to dry them but they were back in force before very long. He just wanted to save his family and neighbors. She was angry and disappointed with herself. At the crossroad she had been ready to kill him herself.

Thirty

The incident at the crossroad stayed with Alwine all day. She felt responsible for the man's death. It was a terrible thing to value your own life above that of someone else, yet that is what she had done. And still, the more she thought about it, he had done the same thing and that had cost him his life. It only added to the irony that he wasn't trying to save himself alone, but there were all those wagons on the side road with families and children hoping to escape. It was not a matter of right or wrong, it was a matter of survival. Sadder yet, survival was still very uncertain and escape was even less sure.

At the end of the day they had not gone far. The names of the towns and villages they passed were familiar to Alwine, which was how she knew that they had only come a few kilometers. The painfully slow pace at which they traveled made the children so cranky that Alwine had no choice but to stop for the night. She chided herself for giving in to their pleading. She had hoped to catch up with her brother-in-law but now that was unrealistic. It distressed her to be so weak, especially when she remembered how strong her mother had been under similar circumstances. That was what she envied about her mother, the iron-will and determination to go on, even when others gave up. But Alwine allowed her children to push her into stopping prematurely so they pulled off the road and slept in an abandoned farm house and let their horses eat hay in the barn. The owners of this place, she supposed, were up ahead on the road but she felt like a thief just the same.

As she tried to sleep, the events of the day raced through her mind. Her flight with the children reminded Alwine so much of what happened thirty years earlier that she began to think about her parents. That brought more pain. How could her parents cope with this turn of events? How could her mother possibly have joined the exodus with her father being so ill?

Even as Alwine worried about her parents they were days ahead of her. With an ailing husband, Emilie was not willing to wait until the last minute to leave. She and her daughters, Else and Klara, bundled up their father and laid him on a mattress in a wagon. They did not try to rescue many of their possessions, just what was necessary. Emilie felt the urgency to be gone and was more interested in the comfort of her ailing husband than saving her possessions.

All the care Emilie took to make her husband comfortable did nothing for him. The cold and the bouncing wagon made him more and more sick. He complained constantly and so the wagon stopped frequently to allow Johann to recover. It was no use. Nothing they did made him comfortable. Emilie had a hard choice to make. It was no use asking her daughters, they would certainly stay if she wavered even the slightest bit. She told the girls that they would have to leave their father behind. The girls were inconsolable.

In a German village Emilie found a boarding house willing to look after her husband while she and her daughters continued west. But at the last possible moment she told Else and Klara that they were to go on alone. It had been her plan all along. The girls begged and pleaded, but with the same determination that had saved her family before she ordered them to go. With her heart broken she sent her two precious daughters, now themselves incredibly strong young women, on alone.

With tears in their eyes, Else and Klara drove their wagon toward Germany on the insistence of their mother. "Arnold or Alwine or Adele will find you there, I promise you will not be alone," Emilie told them forcefully, but the girls realized their true situation. They left their mother in tears, standing in the doorway of the boarding house. They knew they were unlikely to ever see each other again.

In the morning Alwine was up well before dawn. As she came out of the door the wagon was nowhere to be seen and she became alarmed. Instantly she thought that Urbanski had taken off with it and left them stranded. "Where's the wagon," she cried, "has someone stolen it?"

"Urbanski took it," Edmund blurted out with bitterness.

"We don't know that," Alwine said, not letting on that her son's words echoed her thoughts. Urbanski was nowhere to be seen. She fought back the tears. Alwine was well aware that if she broke down now her family was lost. She regained control of her emotions by asking herself what her mother would do. Almost immediately, as if that thought had taken control, she ran to the barn to find her servant. He wasn't there.

Just then two horses appeared from behind the barn pulling their wagon. They couldn't recognize it at first in the dark but then they heard the familiar voice of their farmhand, "Are you ready to go," he asked, "it's a good time to get on the road, we will be alone."

"Where were you?" Edmund demanded.

"What did you think little boy," he asked in a condescending tone he had learned by experience annoyed Edmund, "that I stole the horses?"

Edmund did not reply. He just stared at Urbanski.

"I hid them behind the barn so that none of these Germans would steal us blind."

"Germans don't steal horses," Edmund retorted.

Urbanski shrugged his shoulder and grumbled under his breath, "Why steal horses when you can take the whole country?"

They got onto the road early and were able to make good speed for a few kilometers before the road filled again. Then the progress was even slower than the day before. Now there were twice as many wagons as more and more refugees joined the flight. Alwine would have given up but for the memory of her mother's strength.

There were constant stops as refugees merged onto the narrow country road. Traffic was no longer content to wait on the side roads for openings. About midday an old wagon broke down in the middle of the road blocking all traffic. Alwine was surprised how quickly a group of a dozen men gathered around and assessed that the broken axle was not repairable and with one overpowering shove hurled it over the embankment with all its contents. The small family that was left stranded was divided between some other wagons and the line started again. The whole incident could not have taken more than twenty minutes, but even that delay was begrudged. Every time the line stalled people turned and looked nervously to the east.

At the end of that second day the territory and the names of the villages were no longer familiar to Alwine. It made her feel that they were making some distance, but when she asked a man how far it was to Belschewo, he said forty or fifty kilometers. "It can't be," she said to her children, "we made that much distance the first day, he must be wrong." But she could get no more reliable information from anyone and so she remained disappointed and toyed with the idea of traveling through the night. Then she changed her mind and decided with Urbanski that they would stop early and get a good rest and begin even earlier in the morning, making time when there were fewer wagons on the road. However,

Alwine found it difficult to stop while there was daylight. Every kilometer was precious.

At dusk, they approached a large building that caught the children's imagination. Many of the fleeing wagons were pulling into the place to stay the night and on Urbanski's advice, so did they.

"Is it a palace?" Hertha asked, "Does a princess live there?" Edmund was impressed too. "It's bigger than the Countess Viteranno's," he blurted out in surprise. Urbanski smiled, he was glad the boy was impressed. "It is a palace," he explained, "It's called Kovalevo, but I think you Germans renamed it Schwiedenau. It was built by a fabulously wealthy Polish Baron. He imported workers from France to build it for him."

"Where is he now?" Edmund asked.

"The one who built this is long dead but the present baron ran to England when the Germans invaded."

Edmund and Hertha were awe struck at the beauty of the mansion. It was like a palace from a book of fairytales. There were arched hall ways and marble floors running for great distances, gigantic windows consisting of what seemed like hundreds of pieces of colored glass, and huge chandeliers. Most of the furniture was gone and so were many of the paintings. That was obvious from the fading wallpaper around the areas where the pictures had once hung. Edmund and Hertha roamed the halls imagining that it was their home. Alwine would rather have kept them close but it was hard to deny them this diversion after the monotony of the road. It took a long time for the two to settle down.

Early in the morning Urbanski got up to check on the wagon and horses. He was at first pleased with the mild breeze that greeted him when he went outside. It barely felt like January at all. But when he stepped into a puddle and the mud clung to his boots he began to wince. He realized that today was going to bring real trouble if this thaw continued. He stooped down and felt the ground, it was hard but the top few centimeters were no longer frozen.

"What are you doing?" Edmund asked, startling Urbanski, who nearly fell over.

The farmhand stood up and smiled at the boy. "I'm not stealing horses if that's what you think. Are you following me?"

"No! Well . . . yes, but only because I couldn't sleep. When I saw you get up I thought maybe it was time to leave so I woke up mother."

"Good. You're right. It is time to leave. Feel the ground."

"Why?"

"It's not frozen. It's so mild the ground is thawing."

"So?"

"So we'll be traveling in mud today. That means slow progress and hard work for the horses. We need to get started before thousands of wheels turn the road into mud."

Their early start gave them only a few extra kilometers. By daybreak the mud was five centimeters deep and by mid morning it was more than twenty centimeters. The horses visibly strained to pull the wagon and every stop and start strained them even harder. Alwine was glad that Stefan had harnessed the strongest horses to her wagon.

Edmund was impressed with the way Urbanski had assessed the situation. He had been skeptical about the Pole's predictions at first but as the day progressed and everything he had predicted came true, Edmund's attitude began to change. For him at least the morning went by quickly as he studied the softening of the roadbed, watching as the wheels of the wagon in front sank deeper and deeper into the road. As the morning progressed, he made comments about it to Urbanski and began to ask questions.

Alwine was relieved by the change in her son but said nothing. If Edmund didn't know what was happening she didn't want to alert him for fear he might feel obligated to revert to his old obstinacy. They had enough problems without her son adding to it.

Near noon a patrol of seven German soldiers came marching by while the line of wagons was stopped for some snag up ahead. Their uniforms were dirty and mud was splattered up their boots and pants but they seemed to be in a cheerful mood. Edmund waved at them as they went by. He was proud of the uniform they wore and their smiles were the first he had seen in days. Jokingly he called out to them, "Why are you going that way? The Russians are behind us." One of the soldiers responded by waving his hand and yelling, "Come here boy, I've got something for you."

Before his mother could stop him, Edmund jumped off the wagon splattering mud all over himself and ran after the soldiers. "Come back, Edmund," his mother shouted, "come back."

"I'll be right back," he shouted and ran off to talk to the soldiers. They gave him three pieces of candy, enough for him and his sisters, tussled his hair and reassured him that Germany was winning the war. The reassurances seemed hollow even to the adamant loyalist that Edmund was, but he returned their smiles anyway. They had taken the time to make him feel good.

Edmund accepted the candy gleefully and popped one into his mouth quickly before running back to his mother. He was almost there when the thick, sucking mud grabbed his boot and he fell face down into it. "Edmund," his mother yelled, "now look what you've done." He was covered with mud from his boots to his face, and worse he had spit out the candy. Ignoring his mother's shouting he searched around in the mud for the precious sweet and finding it, spat on it and cleaned it off by wiping it on his dirty coat. Once it was safely inside his mouth again, he climbed onto the wagon and gave the other pieces to his sisters.

The soldiers and Urbanski had a good laugh. Only his mother seemed to be distressed by the whole thing. "Are you wet," she asked, "or only muddy?"

"It's just dirt," the boy replied.

"Clean off the mud the best you can."

It was while he was standing up in the wagon, scraping mud off his clothes, and flinging it at his defenseless sisters that Edmund spotted the armored vehicle approaching. It was coming from the west, almost knocking over the wagons that were straining to pull to the edge of the road to make room as it zoomed past. At first Edmund thought it was a tank but then he identified it from his schooling as a "Speewagon," a German armored personnel carrier. The markings were German but it was rushing up the road with little regard for the safety of the people there. Perhaps it was heading to the front. Hertha saw it too and shouted, "Look, Mama, a tank."

The German soldiers who had been momentarily distracted by Edmund were now marching again, headed in the direction of the armored vehicle. It stunned Edmund when they raised their rifles and started shooting at it. For a long time it didn't register with him that this wasn't a game but an actual skirmish. Then he understood that the soldiers jumping out of the armored vehicle were Russian.

While Edmund watched, the rest of the road panicked. Horses reared at the shattering noise of the gunfire and women and children screamed as if they had been shot. Wagons close to the fighting tried to get away but wound up toppling off the edge of the road and scattering their contents all over. Most families abandoned their wagons and headed for the muddy fields or hid behind their wheels. For a few minutes the fighting was so violent that all the sounds melded into one great din.

Alwine grabbed Else while Urbanski took Hertha and jumped to relative safety, hiding behind a bush at the side of the road, but when Alwine looked around, Edmund was nowhere to be seen. "Edmund, where's Edmund?" she pleaded hysterically, her eyes searching everywhere for the boy. "There he is," little Else pointed.

Edmund was still on the road. He had jumped off the wagon but now appeared to be oblivious to the gunfire. He was searching through the mud for the candy he had dropped again. He found it, cleaned it again and put it in his mouth, but then instead of running for safety he found a coin someone had dropped during the melee, put it in his pocket and rummaged for more. As the bullets flew, he hopped through the mud looking for loot.

His mother called to him frantically to come to safety but either he didn't hear her, or paid no attention. "That boy just will not listen," she raged, so infuriated that there was nothing but tension in her voice. Yet she was unwilling to run into the gunfire to get him. She turned and looked at Urbanski but he only shook his head, not prepared to risk his life for the fool. Alwine could not blame him.

The fighting was over almost as quickly as it started. The Russians were all dead but only two of the German soldiers were still alive. The one who had given Edmund the candy lay face down in the mud.

As the scattered refugees came out of their hiding places, they were jubilant with victory. They congratulated the two soldiers who had survived and acted almost as if the war had just been won. In their euphoria they were indifferent to the death that had occurred right in front of them and now lay on the ground beneath their feet.

Alwine was not in a mood to celebrate. She ran from her hiding place and grabbed her son shaking him with all the emotion her fear had produced. She tried to tell him of her fear and anger but her voice failed her. It squeaked and melted into tears. "But Mama," he said, so naively that she could not argue with him, "I'm all right. They weren't shooting at me!" Alwine could only stare him in the face. She failed to impress on him the danger he had put himself in.

The fleeing Germans paid no more attention to the bodies of the heroes who had rescued them than to their Russian enemies, they just dragged them out of the way and continued on. With equal haste, wagons that had been turned over were righted again and reloaded. The victory, small as it was, made everyone more cheerful and willing to help each other, yet as the line moved on, people no longer just looked behind them for the enemy, for in the back of everyone's mind remained the fact that the Speewagon had come from the West.

In the Fischer's wagon the old Edmund was back. He beamed triumphantly through his muddy face believing that the patrol had not let him down. His friends were heroes. He went on and on about how brave they were and how well they fought, and ignored the remark Urbanski made about them being dead. He bragged that any group of Germans could whip those Russians and speculated that with a little more time the war would certainly go in Germany's favor. That was certainly self-evident now. When he got too carried away, his mother asked him if all the blood and death he had seen hadn't meant anything to him. It puzzled her that he could not see their desperate situation and the terrible toll this war had taken. But Edmund just seemed to ignore everything she said and kept on babbling about the Reich.

When the boy refused to listen to his mother, Urbanski became annoyed. "Tell me then, if the German army is so great why are they running back to Germany? Why are we running away? If the Germans are so smart why are they running right into the Russians or didn't you notice the direction they came from?" It was a question that Edmund could not answer. Now he was angry with Urbanski again.

By noon it was all over. The whole road came to a stop as they ran right into the Russian army. Vehicle after vehicle came up the road until there was no possibility of moving forward again. The two German soldiers that had survived the skirmish threw down their guns and were dragged off. No one knew what to expect now. Alwine looked at her children huddled in the back of the wagon, fearing for their lives. Even Edmund's words could not extinguish the fear in his eyes.

"Go back to your homes," the uniformed men kept repeating in German and Polish, "turn around, everyone go back to the village you came from. Go back, go back."

Urbanski started to turn the horses but the soldier grabbed the reigns and held them. "No" he shouted, "not these horses, we'll take these. Get down from the wagon."

When neither Urbanski nor Alwine moved quickly enough he shouted at them, "Come down here or I'll shoot you where you sit! Are you German or Polish?"

"Polish," Urbanski shouted out proudly as he stood in front of the soldier. But then quietly, almost in a whisper he said "but they're not," indicating Alwine and the children.

"Get out of here, go home!" he said dismissing Urbanski. He left without looking back at Alwine or the children.

"Do you understand Polish?" the soldier asked Alwine.

She nodded her head.

"Are you German?" he asked again in Polish, and Alwine nodded again. She was sure that the answer had earned her a bullet and the tears welled up in her eyes. She wanted to plead for her children's lives but before she could form a word in Polish the man began to speak again. "You are to return to your homes."

Quickly she gathered Edmund, Hertha and Else close to her and started away. "What about the wagon?" Hertha asked.

"Take nothing from the wagons," the soldier warned them.

Thirty-One

Alwine grabbed her daughters' hands, sternly ordered her son to stay close, then turned and headed back down the road. There was no time to think about what was happening. There was only the prudence of obeying the men with the rifles. She did not even consider protesting the seizure of her wagon, clothes, food and horses. Why would she do anything that could earn her a bullet? The soldiers just kept repeating, "Go home, go home!" Home was Belschewo, but who knew what she might find there. "Go home, go home!" Those words had never before seemed so ambiguous, and yet, where else could she go?

She urged her children to walk quickly. "We need to do exactly what the soldiers say," she said forcefully, particularly for Edmund's benefit. Alwine was afraid that he would do something to provoke them and get himself into trouble. Just then, as if it were a test of her own words, a Russian soldier put a rifle in her face and made her take off her new sheepskin coat. Alwine did not protest. She undid the belt and gave it to him and turned away, glad to still have her life.

Where before wagons had pushed through the mud, hundreds of people were now trudging in the opposite direction. The unusually warm weather continued, making the mud on the road difficult to avoid, yet everyone knew that if the temperature tumbled to their usual January averages they would be in worse trouble. Even though it was mild for January, Alwine was chilled without her coat. Thankfully she had worn a shawl under it that now kept her from freezing. She prayed that the mild weather would continue.

More quickly than they had thought possible they came to the Schwiedenau Palace again. "We would have been better off walking to Germany," Edmund marveled. Had their progress really been that slow? Hertha pleaded with her mother to stop at the palace again, so she could enjoy the wonders of the place, but it was now occupied by the Russians. But as the daylight faded and the temperature dropped Alwine knew they needed to find shelter. Once they passed the opulent estate they found a small village where Edmund located a small house, more like a shack, that looked long abandoned. It was cold and damp but it had a roof and a dilapidated fireplace that, nevertheless, looked like it could still hold a fire.

Right away Edmund jumped into the job of making a fire. This was not the same Edmund who had fought his mother at every step and Alwine was not about to discourage his new cooperation, but she had to remind him that they had no matches. He remained undaunted. He took out his little penknife and whittled some shavings to use as kindling. He had learned well in Hitler Youth how to start a fire with the bare essentials. Alwine was relieved when she saw how his project distracted his sisters. For a few minutes they weren't thinking about their hunger.

When the pile of kindling was just right Edmund told his mother that he was going out to ask for matches. "No," his mother said, "it's too dangerous. Someone will grab you." Edmund grew serious, "It will take forever to start a fire without matches, Mama. I'll tell them I'm a Pole and some Germans chased us out of our home." Alwine's face flushed and she pleaded, "No Edmund, don't lie. Lies always lead to bigger trouble."

He knocked at a door close by and asked for matches or a hot coal to start a fire for his mother. "Are you refugees?" the woman asked, and Edmund nodded. As long as she didn't ask him if he was German he wasn't going to tell her. "Where are you from?"

"Belczewo."

"How many are in your family? Where are you staying?"

"Just my mother and two sisters," he pointed to the shack.

"Wait here."

She closed the door and a few minutes later returned with two wooden matches and a chunk of rye bread. Edmund took the matches but when the woman handed him the bread he hung his head and wouldn't take it. "We're German," he confessed.

"Are Germans too proud to eat Polish bread now?"

"No," he answered, "my mother said not to lie to you."

"Keep the bread," she said coldly as she closed the door. From a window she watched as Edmund returned to the little shack. She wondered whether or not to tell her husband. He hated Germans.

Alwine and the girls were grateful for the bread. Plain bread had never tasted so good but it was gone much too quickly. Then Edmund turned his attention again to the fire. He had prepared his kindling so meticulously that he only needed one match to start the fire. The kindling burned smartly and long enough for larger pieces of wood to catch fire as he judiciously placed them on the flames, being careful not to smother them. The flame had only begun to warm them when he realized that he didn't have enough fuel to keep the fire alive for long. His mother shuddered as he told her he was going out again to find more fuel, but he insisted and scavenged throughout the little village to find only a few pieces of wood.

With a small armful he returned to the little hovel, thinking he would have to come out again to look for more. But when he went inside the fire was blazing. Hertha, refreshed by the little bit of bread and the warmth had explored the other room of the house where she discovered a broken chair and small table. With the addition of the wood that Edmund laid beside the fire they had enough to warm them for at least a few hours. Else had already fallen asleep. Her tired little body had hardly been able to finish the small chunk of food. She now clutched the remnant protectively in her hand as she lay on her mother's lap in front of the fire.

"We should stay here," Edmund proposed to his mother, "and not go back to Belschewo. Maybe we could find another road to Germany in the morning."

Alwine was too tired to discuss the matter. It was tempting, but she did not feel right about it and she was too tired to explain her thinking clearly. Her last thought before she fell asleep was that in Belschewo people knew who she was. In times of trouble it seemed prudent to be among people who knew you, even if they weren't your friends.

A few hours later, when the fire had died down to just a few embers, Alwine woke with a start. The door flung wide open, nearly coming off its fragile, rusted hinges. As the draft rushed in, Alwine shuddered. Two men staggered into the doorway talking loudly and swaggering as if they were drunk. Outlined against the sky she could see that one of the men had a rifle in his hand. She froze, hoping that if she stayed still they would not see her. The cold air, however, woke the children and Else began to cry.

"Hear that? I told you there are Germans hiding in here."

"Good," said his comrade with the rifle, "I need to kill one."

They located Alwine by the dim light and put the gun in her face. "Where is your man?" they demanded.

"He's not with us. He's in the army."

"Lucky for him. If he were here, I'd shoot him," one of the drunks explained. "Lucky for you I don't shoot women."

Just then the other one pulled Edmund to his feet. "He'll do, let's shoot him."

"No," Alwine cried, "he's just a boy, a little boy."

Edmund twisted out of the man's grasp but then he had nowhere to run. The man with the rifle blocked the door. "Go ahead shoot him," the other called out. "No, not in front of his mother. Grab him, we'll take him outside." But Edmund was quicker than either of the drunks and bolted into the other room where there was a small window he thought he could break. He looked for something with which to smash it and found a board in a corner that Hertha had overlooked. As he grabbed it, he saw that his mother was standing in the doorway pleading with the drunks. "Please, he's just a boy."

"He's too little, let him go," the one with the rifle said.

"So what? He's German!"

"We'll catch one that's bigger, let's go."

Alwine rushed to the door as they left and shut it quickly leaning on it just in case they changed their minds. Edmund hurried to her side but the men had gone off looking for other prey. Relieved and frightened, the two of them found it impossible to fall asleep again. For a long time they listened to hear the telltale gunfire which would let them know that the two assassins had found a victim, but they heard nothing. They hoped that the drunks had given up.

Even when Edmund went over to the fire to stir up the last remnants of warmth his mother remained at the door barring it against the return of the drunkards. There in the dark she found herself looking at their dilemma in a new way. She knew now that they had to return to Belschewo. There, at least people knew who she was, and if by chance their own house was empty she would feel even safer. It was strangely comforting to have a choice to make. It made her feel more in control. It also made her feel less trapped and allowed her to remember her mother and the three years they had spent in Siberia. It had seemed hopeless there too and yet her mother had gone on making choices. Who would have believed that a revolution would have freed them? Who knows how God will answer prayers? It became very clear to her that it would be possible to pull her family through this ordeal as long as she had faith.

In the morning, Alwine braced her children for the day. Food and beds, she told them, were waiting for them at the end of a long walk, a walk she knew would take several days.

The roads were still full of refugees. The Russian military was there too, still yelling out their instruction from their vehicles. "Go home," they cried nonstop, "go back to your villages. There is nothing to be afraid of." At one point they even handed out bread which made Alwine so grateful that she almost believed what they said about not having to worry.

The freezing temperatures of the night soon gave way to the sun and the thaw began again. If you kept walking you did not get cold but felt the sun on your face during the morning and on your back in the afternoon. The warm temperatures, however, did not make the walking any more bearable for five year old Else. She protested loudly whenever her mother put her down and made her walk. Edmund was not able to carry her for long either. After several hours of her complaints Alwine finally worked up the courage to ask a Polish family if her little daughter might ride with them. Their wagon was pulled by one scrawny horse that the Russians had no use for. Safely tucked in the back corner of the wagon, with the sun shining on her, she fell asleep.

During the day, Edmund's pace put him well ahead of his mother and Hertha. Usually he was able to keep up to the scrawny horse and so he was there whenever Else woke up. When she saw him she would feel safe. For two days the little girl rode while her family walked behind, but in between they spent a night on the roadside, huddled around a fire to keep them warm, but barely able to sleep.

The next day, near noon, when they reached a larger town, Edmund was well ahead of his mother. She had instructed him to keep a close eye on Else so he paced right behind the wagon where she was again sleeping. But there was a road block in the center of the town. Polish policemen were there questioning the refugees as they returned to their homes. Edmund moved closer to try to understand what they were looking for. A policeman shouted for Germans to go left and Poles to go to the right. It took Edmund only a few seconds to figure out that it would be safer to be in the right line. He wanted to wait until his mother and sister were closer so he could lead them to safety but he didn't want to lose contact with his sister. Before he even saw his mother and Hertha he was standing in front of the policeman at the road block.

"Are you Polish, boy?" the man asked Edmund.

"Yes," he replied, without a hint of an accent.

"Move on then."

He was through. It had been so easy and now he looked for his mother. But her actions should have been totally predictable even for him. As soon as she heard the instruction she dutifully moved to the left. When Edmund finally caught a glimpse of her and Hertha in that line he wanted to shout at them, "No, don't just do what they tell you!" He shook his head. Either his mother was too obedient or too stupid. Just beyond the checkpoint he waited, hoping that his mother would look in his direction. The minutes passed and he became anxious. Soon he would lose track of Else. Even now the wagon with his little sister was pulling away. He would have to go after it but first he wanted to find out what was to happen to his mother and sister.

Many Germans coming through the road block were allowed to continue on their way. Others were being lead away by the police. Edmund hoped desperately that his mother and Hertha would not be detained but he was disappointed. Several women, including his mother and sister were soon led off into the town by two policemen. He had to decide quickly between following Else and following his mother. He chose his mother.

Keeping his distance, he watched as they were lead into a brick building only half a kilometer from the main road. It was the town jail and as the big front door closed behind them Edmund had a sickening feeling that they were gone. He could not imagine what was happening in there or how he could help them. Up and down he paced in front of the building hoping to get a glimpse inside but the windows were too high. Finally, too tired to pace anymore, he leaned on a building across the road and waited, feeling helpless and alone. He had never felt such loneliness before, nor realized the kind of fear it produced.

Alwine sat on the floor of a cell that was full of women and children with Hertha glued to her side. What she focused on intensely, rather than her own plight, was the hope that her son might have enough sense to stay with his little sister. She kept thinking of poor little Else waking up and finding herself alone. At least if Edmund was with her, she would not feel abandoned. Meanwhile, she held Hertha close to her side, it was all she could do for her.

The women in the cell hardly spoke to each other. They sat silently, expecting that Poland would now extract from them the price of losing the war.

After a while a guard came in. He studied the group as if he was looking for someone. Alwine was afraid that she knew what he was prowling for. He took a few steps toward her. His black shoes were all she saw. She kept her eyes on the floor trying not to attract his attention. All the while she was thinking of her friend Irene and the pain and humiliation she had gone through. Now as he approached, she feared it was her turn. To Alwine's shock the man knelt beside Hertha, stroking her dark hair. It was a gentle, almost fatherly gesture and Alwine smiled until she realized that what he wanted was more perverse than she had imagined.

In a flash, before Alwine could react, he lifted up the girl's dress and put his hand into her underwear. "She's only a girl," Alwine protested, but he slapped her across the face with his free hand and shouted, "Shut up!" He withdrew his hand and set the little girl down again, disappointed. But now the other women were alerted and shielded their daughters by sliding in front of them.

That's when Alwine first noticed that there were only women and young girls in the cell.

When the man had moved on, Hertha clung to her mother's arm even tighter. Puzzled and frightened, she asked her mother, "Why did he do that?" But Alwine's eyes were on the policeman as he moved around the cell. There was a palpable change of mood in the cell however, as women braced themselves to protect their daughters. His intention seemed to wilt under their glare. When he was gone Alwine turned to her daughter and explained, "He wanted to know if you were old enough." Hertha thought she understood.

But the women were defenseless. Other, more determined men came and several women were dragged out. One man grabbed Alwine by the arms and pulled her to her feet. Instantly, Hertha clutched onto her mother's leg and held on with all her might. At the top of her lungs she screamed, "No, no, don't take my mother away!" Her little fingers dug into her mother's leg and Alwine found herself hoping that she could hang on despite the pain. The officer tried to pry her hands away but the harder he pulled the more the girl screamed, "No, no, I want my Mama!" Her deafening pitch hurt his ears. Frustrated, he pushed Alwine to the ground again and moved on.

Alwine cried with her daughter as they held each other tightly. She had never been so thankful for her daughter's tenacity and persistence, qualities that until now had only gotten her into trouble. Yet, as she watched her assailant drag another screaming woman away, Alwine began to feel guilty. The guilt only lasted a moment, until she realized that she was a long way from being out of danger herself. Who could know what these men intended to do? Did they plan to use them and shoot them? She had witnessed vengeance before. It could be brutal.

The women were powerless to protect themselves and there seemed no earthly way for them to extract themselves from their captivity. Alwine could only pray. Silently, in the depth of her heart she struggled to express her desires. Words like help and rescue passed through her mind but she could not put them into coherent thoughts. Yes, she wanted to be rescued but she could not think why she was more worthy than the other women for God to single her out. She wanted help for Edmund and her baby daughter out there on the cold road too, but she wondered how many children were cold and homeless because of the war. It seemed such a selfish thing to want God to help you to rescue your own when there were so many suffering. Yet the praying comforted her. So many times in her life she had felt the warmth of her faith as she struggled with problems that seemed to have no solution. Whatever the fate was that had been prepared for her family she would find a way to accept it, but her feelings told her that death was not what she should fear.

Edmund waited outside the prison for hours. He vacillated between rage and self-pity. In his desperation he fantasized about rushing into the building. But in his fantasy he had a machine gun and annihilated the men who were holding his family. He saw himself shooting and shooting until all of his rage was gone. But there were no bullets, no guns and there were not even stones to throw. As he leaned against the wall, he cried to think his mother and sister might die in there. It felt awful.

Cold and weary he began to pace up and down the road again and even thought about going to find his little sister, knowing that that was probably what his mother would want him to do. But his feet would not take him in that direction. Every time he tried he was inexplicably held back, as if he had forgotten something important. Edmund couldn't leave. His greatest desire was to rescue his mother, but how could a boy of twelve storm that building? It was getting dark and the temperature was falling. He was shaking. The hunger was tremendous and he was desperate.

It was the desperation that finally won out. He had no idea where he got the nerve. Boldly, he walked up the steps of the prison. He beat his fist hard on the front door where all day he had seen women go in but never come out. His hands hurt by the time the door finally opened and someone shouted, "What do you want?"

In Polish, Edmund forcefully replied, "I want my mother!"

"Go home boy," the man who answered the door told him.

"I want my mother," Edmund repeated, while pointing inside, "she's in there."

"We don't hold Polish women here."

"You have my mother here, I saw you bring her in here."

He was allowed inside and another uniform, one with stripes, took over the questioning.

"You say we have your mother here?"

"And my sister."

"Are you German?"

"No, I'm Polish."

"Then we don't have your mother here. We only have Germans here. You know, the enemy."

"My mother was brought here with my sister. I just want them back."

"Is your mother Polish?"

"Yes."

"I tell you we don't have any Polish women here boy. What is your name?"

"Edmund Fischer."

"That's a German name, boy. You are German, aren't you?"

Edmund nodded to confirm the truth, and yet he began to protest. "I am Polish! I was born in Poland. I just want my mother back. My little sister is with her. I just wanted to get them out."

"How old are you?"

"Twelve."

"And your sister, how old is she?"

"Hertha is ten."

He turned and asked, "Do we have women here with children under twelve?" The question wasn't directed at anyone specific and no one responded. "We were told no women with children less than twelve!"

"Oh, what's the difference," one of his subordinates replied, "why don't we just take the little German runt out and shoot him?"

The officer put his hand on Edmund's shoulder reassuringly and looked into his eyes. "Wait outside," he said, "you've got guts."

"Fischerova," the officer called out as he went back into the cells, "Fischerova and daughter!"

Alwine hesitated to answer the summons. "What did they want now? What are they going to do with us?" she asked herself, fearing the worst. But slowly, almost unwillingly she found herself rising and acknowledging with a nod that she was Fischerova. Her daughter tugged tightly at her arm afraid that her mother was about to be taken away.

The cell door opened and they were led out. She could not remember the front door and wondered what waited for her and Hertha on the other side. Her faith wavered and silent tears filled her eyes. It was over. The door opened and as she stepped out into the darkness the rush of cold air seemed ominous. Alwine didn't think she heard the words properly, "You can go," but she obeyed the order and was surprised that the door shut behind her.

Edmund rushed up the steps to hug his mother. He had done it. He had rescued them!

But Alwine was confused. She did not understand the role that her son had played in her rescue and it took a few minutes for it to sink in that they had actually been freed. Then, as it did take hold, she realized that Else was not with Edmund and what should have been joy was turned into anger.

"Where's your sister?" she demanded, shaking Edmund, "where is Else?"

"I don't know."

"You should have stayed with your sister!" Alwine screamed.

Edmund was wounded. The disappointment was overwhelming. He had rescued his Mother and sister and now somehow he was in the doghouse again. It seemed like gross ingratitude. He fell silent with bitter resentment.

Alwine did not have time to think about what she had just done to him. She took the hands of her children and started to lead them back to the road to follow her little daughter. Edmund pulled away from his mother and followed behind, sulking.

Without stopping they walked for kilometers along the road in the dark. There was great urgency in Alwine's gait. She would not let herself slow down even though Hertha protested that she could not keep up. There was no thought of stopping now but wherever they found fires they asked if anyone had seen the wagon with a little blonde German girl. Everyone had the same answer. There had been many wagons but no one remembered the little girl.

They were tired and weary and it didn't seem possible that so much had happened in one day. And yet as they entered another little village Alwine was determined to keep searching. Tiny square houses lined the main road and from one of them came the raucous singing of reveling Russian soldiers. They sounded happy and were obviously drinking. Alwine crossed to the other side of the street. She did not want to be stopped again. Doubling her pace, she wanted to get away from that place, so great was her dread that they might stop her and she would not find her tender daughter who by now must be frantic with fear.

It was Edmund who heard it as he followed well behind his mother, brooding and cursing at every step. He heard the gate with its steady creaking as it swung back and forth on its old hinges, but that wasn't what attracted him. It was the faint and familiar sound of someone humming. It was intermittent and usually drowned out by the more boisterous singing of the soldiers. Edmund stopped to listen and recognized an old nursery rhyme. One clear note was all he needed to recognize the voice. Passing by on the other side of the road Alwine and Hertha had gone ahead in the dark, not noticing and not being noticed, but Edmund began to see a familiar shadow in the dark as it hung onto the creaky gate, swinging back and forth.

"Else?" he called quietly.

"Edmund, Edmund," her little voice came out of the dark and the girl ran into his arms. "Where is Mama?" she asked.

"Mama," Edmund called out loudly, "I found Else!"

Alwine came running back to pick up her little girl and squealed in delight. The singing in the house stopped suddenly. Edmund heard one of the soldiers calling in Polish, "Hey, someone is taking the little doll!" and several of the soldiers scrambled out of the door to prevent the abduction.

"What are you doing?" they demanded as they reached the gate.

"She's my daughter," Alwine said in her broken Polish, holding on even more tightly to the little girl. "We've been looking for her all night."

"Ah," one remarked, "the Mama." A group of five or six soldiers all repeated in an approving chorus, "the Mama."

"German?" one asked.

Edmund answered with a defiant yes, but the soldier ignored the boy's sneer.

"A Polish family gave her to us and said her family had disappeared." The soldier spoke good German, almost as if it were his native tongue. "They didn't want to be stuck with a little German girl so they just left her. She's a doll."

"Thank you, thank you for taking care of my little girl."

As Alwine turned to continue up the road the soldier called after her again. "Do you have any food?" Alwine turned and quietly said, "No." Within minutes they had a loaf of bread, some cured garlic sausage and several potatoes in their pockets. It was more than they could have hoped for. "Keep the potatoes warm in your pocket," Alwine told her daughter, "if they freeze they will be ruined." But as Alwine tried to thank the soldier he shook his head and said, "We wouldn't want our little doll to starve."

They found shelter in a warehouse at the edge of town where several German families had gathered. Before Edmund was asleep, his mother came and kissed him on the cheek. "I was wrong to be angry with you today." she said, "If you hadn't done what you did who knows where we would be." Edmund was too tired to acknowledge her communication, but he remembered it.

Alwine was more optimistic the next morning. The weather remained unseasonably mild and showed no sign of changing. But it was not a good idea to rely on midwinter mild spells too long. Should they be caught in a winter storm or even if the temperatures were just to drop to the seasonal norm, she and her family would be lost. She explained the urgency of their situation to the children and the need for them to walk all day with little food. While their stomachs were still full, they accepted the challenge eagerly, because they too wanted to get home. But within hours they tired of their walking and no reasoning could persuade them to stop complaining. Else would cry until her mother broke down and carried her or else she would let the children rest. Alwine had no other choice. So when she found a place for her family to sleep at night, she prayed that the weather would remain mild for her children's sake just a few days longer.

The next night the only shelter they could find was under some pine trees beside the road. There were other campfires there already so they felt safe. As methodically as he had built that fire the first night, Edmund built another and borrowed a flame from the other fires. Alwine was able to beg a pot from another campsite, then melting snow in it, she threw in the remaining potatoes they had been given for little Else's sake.

The fires, however, attracted the attention of a patrol of Russian soldiers who proceeded to move from campsite to campsite eating the food of the refugees. It happened so quickly that it seemed unreal. One giant stooped over their small pot, scooped the potatoes out with his bare hands and began to eat. The shocking sight of him with the scalding hot potatoes in his hands transfixed Edmund and Hertha. They could not understand why he didn't scream with pain from the heat and they watched as he gulped down their supper. When he had finished, he wiped his hand on his coat and smiled. Gently he picked up Else, holding her in his lap while he sang a simple song to her in Russian. Edmund wondered if that was supposed to make up for eating their supper.

It was only then, after the soldier had left, that the children realized that they had nothing left to eat and they cried. Alwine scraped the pot for the tiny pieces the soldier had left and fed them to Hertha and Else. Edmund tried to rescue bits of potato that had dropped from the huge paws but they were so dirty that he could only throw them away. To compensate for their hunger Edmund gathered wood and built the fire up strong and warm.

Not even Alwine woke until well into the morning and found the road already full when they started out. They felt their empty bellies but had no particular pain, just a little discomfort. Alwine begged some scraps of food from some soldiers that they passed and that was all they were to have that day. It seemed to be enough. "Perhaps our bellies are shrinking," Hertha said with a smile.

It took two more days for Alwine and her children to reach Belschewo. Alwine herself was almost hopelessly lost and just followed the crowd praying to find her little village and farm along the way. She had found that Edmund had an uncanny sense of direction. It was one of many talents she had discovered in him during this ordeal and now he used it to lead his family back to their home.

As they approached their home, only Alwine felt any uneasiness. The Russians had said, "Return to your homes." They did not say where to go if they no longer had homes to return to. Alwine did not trouble her children with her thoughts, however, but now during the last few meters she couldn't help but wonder.

Jerzy Finkowski, had already returned from the Government General to reclaim his property. The gate was closed and there he stood in front his house shouting at them as they returned, "Go away, you filthy German thieves. You are not welcome here." Alwine had no idea what to do next but Edmund yelled at the farmer in Polish, "Where shall we go?" The answer was instantaneous, "Go to Hell!"

They stood there for a few minutes at the gate of the farm where they had worked for more than four years not knowing where to turn next. Jerzy kept an ever vigilant eye on them for fear that they would do something evil. He could not understand that they waited at the gate because they didn't know where to go next, but he was sure that they were planning something devious. He intended to watch them until they were gone.

However, when Alwine had finally decided to take her family into Belschewo, they saw a man coming down the road. He was just a shadow at first but as he came closer, Alwine recognized him.

"Urbanski told me that they had turned you back. I nearly killed him when he told me he left you alone on the road. Every day I've come looking for you. Come with me to my farm. It isn't large but I have food and it is warm." Stefan picked up Else in his arms and started to walk. Not even Edmund protested.

Thirty-Two

Poland had been restored for the second time in the century. With the consent of their Russian liberators, the Communist-backed Polish Committee of National Liberation began to run the country. By February of 1945 the committee was setting up camps all over the former German-annexed lands where displaced Germans, like the Volhynians, were to be gathered. One such camp was set up on a farm on the outskirts of Ossenholz, now again called by its Polish name Osciency. An old barn was converted into sleeping quarters and an office was set up in the house. When it was ready, all the Germans now scattered throughout the area were ordered to report.

Even those who had not tried to run away were now forced out of their homes, as were the few refugees that had been lucky enough to find their homes still empty when they returned from their ordeal on the road. Most of the Germans were now homeless and were only able to find shelter in their former school houses and churches. Wherever they hid, however, all were ordered to report. This was no longer Germany and there were few places for Germans to hide. It was rare to be able to count on the friendship and protection of a Pole.

Alwine counted herself lucky to have a friend like Stefan. In his home, although she and her three children had to share a small room that was barely big enough to hold them, she felt safe. But now even she knew she had to report to the new camp. She had no choice but to leave the safety of Stefan's protection. Alwine was not convinced that it was hospitality that the provisional government meant to offer them in Osciency, but to stay with Stefan meant putting him in danger. She was terrified to leave even the meager comfort of his small house, but it was the law.

Stefan feared for them too. He knew that many of his countrymen were intent upon revenge and some of them talked openly about murder. Since he understood that many of his countrymen had used that hatred to keep them alive through the ordeals of the war, he feared what the camp held for his friend. In his home Alwine and her children had at least been safe.

In taking them in Stefan had no other intention than to repay the kindness of a woman who had treated him well. Sometimes he imagined that there could be more between them but he did not torture himself by dwelling on it. It became evident to him during their stay with him that whatever fantasy his mind might conjure up for himself and Alwine, was just that. He was as pragmatic in this as he was in everything else he did and accepted the obvious. But still he was concerned when he realized that Alwine had to report to the internment camp. He wondered if she had the skills to help her family survive. So days before they had to leave, he began to explain to her how he had survived.

When Alwine marveled at his understanding he laughed and said that the Polish people were professional survivors. They had survived the whole of the last century as Russian, German and Austrian underlings and so the whole nation was well prepared for the Nazis and now for the Russians.

"Everyone," he explained, "has his own way of surviving. Some pretend they are stupid and witless and so their masters leave them alone because they can't do any better. But my father told me the best way to survive well is to make yourself useful. You get up in the morning before your master and try to anticipate all his needs, and you are meticulously honest with him. Soon he trusts you more than he trusts himself. That way you survive and while you are surviving you are also learning. It is important to keep learning so that you know what to do with freedom when you have it.

It was close to the end of February when Alwine reported at the gates of the camp. She had seen enough of these places in her life not to be shocked by the conditions there. Still she and the children soon wished they could have stayed with Stefan. They were assigned to a corner of the barn where hastily constructed bunk-beds stood. They were hard and cold. Everything about the place was cold and comfortless. Worst of all, Alwine had no idea what the Poles intended for them.

Although Alwine did not recognize all the faces, many of the women were familiar. One of the Hartenberger women was there with her small son, the daughter-in-law and grandson of the man who had built their hearth in Volhynia. Alma Neuman was there, as was Irmagard Thann and so many of her neighbors. They all looked like they were in shock and Alwine knew she looked the same to them. It seemed like few people from the community of Belschewo had escaped. Of those who were missing there were terrible rumors. Alwine was shocked when she heard that Erich Winkler had been executed by the Russians. If they shot good men like him then what hope was there for the rest? There was a rumor too that thousands of German soldiers had been shipped off to Siberia and speculation was rampant that the Russians intended to do the same with the rest of the Germans.

It frightened Alwine when she heard such things. She knew the underlying cause of this disaster. She had understood it from the moment she had first set foot on this land. But knowing was no comfort, it did not make it any less painful. It hadn't even saved her from the consequences. She sat on her bed and remembered her father's teachings on pride and wept. The fault was hers too. She reviewed all the prideful and hurtful things she had done over the years. Her mind kept coming back to Irene Weiss. Alwine was sure it was guilt that moved her to continually think of her old friend. It pained her to remember that she had not even gone to comfort Irene when her husband died. How prideful had she been then? If only she could find Irene and make it right.

The morning after their arrival Alwine recognized a little girl as she warmed herself by a fire in an oil-drum. It was Irene's Hertha. Alwine started to look around for the mother but could not find her. For a moment she feared that the little girl was alone and took a few steps toward her. She wanted to comfort her. But then she saw Irene coming to collect her daughter. Alwine felt relieved. She wanted desperately to embrace her old friend and let bygones be bygones. But Irene led her daughter right by Alwine without even acknowledging her presence.

The National Committee had named a local man to run the camp, but he was rarely seen in the first weeks of its operation. Nevertheless, his staff made it quite plain that it was time for the Germans to pay for what they had done to Poland. They gathered the inmates together to let them know what would be expected of them. "You will work to earn your keep," they said. "You work where and when we tell you to work, sleep where we tell you to and eat what we give you. Complain and you will get nothing. If you don't work, you won't eat." Alwine didn't complain, but she remembered what her neighbors had said about the Poles in their service, "They get what they deserve."

After the truncated lecture the camp staff gave out work assignments. The masters were now the farmhands. Some would be sent out on daily work assignments and return each night to the camp. Others would be sent to live on the farms where they would work. There was no choice.

Alwine was prepared to work but she was not prepared for what the Poles wanted to do to her family. Edmund and Hertha were considered old enough to be taken from their mother and sent out to work on their own. Alwine's heart sank as she learned about it, but she was afraid to protest. With only a short farewell to sustain them the children were taken away and Alwine was given her assignment. Thankfully, she was allowed to take Else with her.

Gzelak was an old man who didn't care about his appearance. He wore dirty clothes and had dirty yellow teeth. Even his hair was a mess. His wife was dead and his children had moved on and so there was no one to care how he took care of himself. His small house was as dirty and smelly as he was. He had told the camp officials to send him a woman who would not be afraid to work.

For the first few days he shouted at Alwine as she cooked and cleaned. He complained too about the expense of feeding the little girl though she barely ate anything. Alwine worked hard in spite of the criticism. When his house was cleaner than it had been in years she worked every bit as hard in the barn with Gzelak. Soon the old man realized what a prize he had and softened. Overnight, his attitude changed and he began to treat Alwine and Else with tenderness. He became almost too kind.

Alwine was shocked when the old man appeared in the kitchen one day washed, shaven and with his hair wetted down and combed. He had on his best clothes. They were almost clean. Alwine knew something was up. Within minutes he proposed to her. "If you marry me," he lied, "you won't have to work so hard." Alwine laughed awkwardly, hoping to avoid embarrassment for both of them by making a joke of it. But he repeated the offer. This time he came so close that he could smell his foul breath. She thought she would faint. Bracing herself, she pointed out that she was already married, but it didn't seem to bother the old man. "Forget him, he's dead," he said, tugging at her dress as she pulled away. "We don't even need a priest," he laughed as if they were playing a game. She fended him off with her arms. But he became even more aggressive. When she told him, she had other children he told her to forget them. But then she cried even more and told him that she was pregnant. He didn't believe her. He tried to kiss her, but Alwine began to sob uncontrollably. Finally she found the courage to shove him away forcefully and his face turned red. She could not be sure if it was anger or embarrassment but he left her alone.

The filthy man reverted quickly to his old ways. Now he expected even the little girl to work for her food. He loaded the chores on Alwine and her daughter. Gzelak thought his tactics would change Alwine's mind. To his consternation Alwine did all the chores he required of her, working from dawn until well into the night and never complained. He gave up. Unable to convince her that her life would be much better if she were to sleep with him, he took her back to the Osciency camp. "Take her back," he said, "she's much too lazy. Send me one willing to work."

Edmund was shocked when he found himself back on his own farm. He might have been glad to be in the place he knew so well except for the prospect of working for Jerzy Finkowski. The man who was known among the Poles as 'the American', was glad to have the boy. As he explained to his neighbors, "If I can't get my hands on the father I can at least make his son pay. The bastard had me sent to the Ghetto in Warsaw. By the time I'm through with the boy he'll curse his father."

For four years Edmund had watched the Polish girls do the milking and never learned how himself. His father had told him that it was women's work and he was content to leave it to them. Now Jerzy made him learn. He was pitifully slow. Muscles in his fingers and hands that he never even knew he had, began to hurt. Jerzy chided him for his slowness and cuffed and threatened him if he didn't get any faster. At night his fingers and hands would swell and he cried from the pain. But in the morning he found that as soon as he was working the swelling went down.

Once, while he was under the threat of a beating for being so slow, he tried to cheat. He realized that by not quite emptying some of the cows' udders he could reduce his time considerably. Finkowski noticed immediately that the volume of milk was down. He checked every udder and came back in a rage spewing filthy language at Edmund. He slapped the boy to the ground and threw a pail at him, demanding that he finish the milking. "Try that again and I'll break your fingers."

When Edmund was not milking, he was cleaning stalls. With a wooden wheelbarrow his father had built he cleaned every stall and pen and found to his dismay that once he was finished, he had to start from the beginning again. Farm work, after all, was endless. He spent the whole day in the barn, milking, cleaning and feeding the animals. It was drudgery and Finkowski made sure it was painful; if Edmund took even a minute to rest, he hit him.

Each morning, after the milking was done, Edmund was allowed to eat. He received a dry piece of bread and a glass of milk. Edmund's life revolved around milk now and soon just the smell of it nauseated him. He requested water instead, denying himself the most nourishing part of his meals. In the evening there was a bowl of hot soup which he took to his quarters. It was thin but it was hot and he held the bowl in his hands and let the heat comfort him long after he finished eating the contents.

His bed was an old blanket laid over flea-infested straw in a converted chicken coop. With only one blanket he was cold in the drafty shed and that made it hard to sleep. He would curl up in a ball and then cover himself in straw to try to keep warm. Eventually he stopped worrying about the fleas even as they crawled through his hair and bit all night. Warmth was more important. It was hard for him to get up even to go to the bathroom. Often he woke up wet. He was afraid that he would be punished and tried to cover it up until he realized that neither Jerzy nor his wife cared how clean he kept himself.

When spring finally came, Jerzy Finkowski was not yet satisfied that he had tormented his enemy's son enough. He called at the camp and requested some day laborers. The camp sent out two women to do the milking and clean the stalls, leaving Edmund and his master free to do the field work. It was work that the boy's father had done with the help of two strong men, but Jerzy intended to do it with only the help of a twelve-year-old boy.

When it came time to plough the land, the farmer took the one horse that the farm was left with, and began to plough his fields. He set Edmund behind the plough and began to teach him. However, Edmund was too small and too inexperienced to do the kind of job Jerzy wanted. They ploughed several furrows as the vengeful man screamed and berated him for stupidity and laziness.

"You stupid German," he yelled as he grabbed him by the collar and dragged him away, "you lived all these years on the work of others and learned nothing. Your father taught you nothing but I'm going to teach you to work."

He pulled the boy back to the barn where he harnessed an old milk cow. "You will plough the old pasture by the road with this cow and then you will know what it means to work."

The pasture that Jerzy Finkowski wanted the boy to plough was a field that his father and Stefan had considered so infested with stones that it was useless as anything else. This stony land was to be the boy's training ground and his punishment. They made two passes down the center of the field with Finkowski leading the cow and Edmund trying to insert the blade into the rock-hard soil. After the two passes Finkowski left him alone, "You plough this field and do a good job or your life won't be worth living," he threatened convincingly. "I'm going back to the grain field but don't you dare think that you can bag off," Jerzy warned as he walked away.

Edmund had played in this field many times. He thought he knew every corner of it and each stone, but now he looked on it with new eyes. He kicked at the hard ground and looked at the two furrows he and the farmer had made. They hardly pierced the turf and the ground would never be softer than it was now in the spring. He looked at the cow and shrugged his shoulders. He knew the old cow, she was the one his father had called Strumpf, 'Stockings,' for her long black legs, but Finkowski called her Olga. She was the largest cow in the herd but she was also the most ornery. Together he and Finkowski had not accomplished much, how could he handle her alone?

"Hai," Edmund yelled, "hai, hai, hai!" The cow didn't move. Again and again he yelled the command he had heard his father use so often but the cow just turned her head and rolled her dark eyes as if to ask, "Who are you yelling at?" It was then that the boy realized that 'Hai' was a command for horses and the cow probably didn't understand 'horse language.' He yelled every conceivable call he had ever heard in German or Polish but Strumpf remained completely stationary. Finally he walked over and stared her in the face, pleading with her to understand what he wanted. Yet when she shook off a fly trying to land on her eye Edmund took it as a flat out refusal. He hit her over the head and winced painfully when his fist smacked against her hard skull. She shook him off as easily as the fly.

He would have given up right then if he wasn't so afraid of Finkowski, but he was determined to avoid a beating. Edmund took another approach. He tried tugging at the harness and giving the beast a gentle whip to let it know that it was time to move. She ignored it. Angered by her uncaring attitude, Edmund then used his father's favorite Russian swearwords to convey his contempt for her. No effect. He then grabbed her by the bridle and tried to pull her along, but he didn't have the strength of a grown man and she seemed determined not to move. She ignored his tugging until he gave up and sat on the ground. It was while he sat brooding that she started to walk. As soon as she took a few steps, the plough, which was only anchored by a few inches of the tough soil, fell over and dragged uselessly behind her. Edmund sprang up and chased after it trying to right the implement, but the plough was too heavy and too awkward to lift while it dragged behind the cow.

Still, he persisted, and just as he thought he might turn it up, she stopped. Strumpf looked back at him and gave a bawl as if to say, "I did what you wanted."

Once he righted the implement Edmund tried again to get the old bovine to move but he couldn't shout loud enough or whip the reins hard enough to bother her. In desperation, with tears streaming down his face, he tried planting the plough as firmly as his aching muscles would allow and then going to the front to give her a pulling start. When finally she began to walk, he raced to the rear hoping to reach the plough before it upended. His first attempt was not successful. The second was the same. So were the third, fourth and fifth. He lost track of how many times he had run back and forth. Now he was so angry that he picked up a sharp stone and whipped it into the cow's hind section so forcefully that she bellowed a loud protest and started to run wildly across the field dragging the plough and Edmund behind her. Edmund was so pleased that he hardly noticed the plough only made a scratch in the crusted soil. When he finally did look down, he tried with all the force he could muster to direct the tip deeper into the ground and saw with great relief that a deeper, wider furrow was being created. However, he had gone only ten short paces like that when the shearing tip caught on a large rock, giving him such a jolt that he lost hold of the handles and fell. When he looked up, Strumpf was strolling about the field again with the end-for-end plough trailing casually behind her. Yet even now as Edmund looked at the few meters of furrowed earth he felt like a burden had fallen from his shoulders. He had been successful. Buoyed by this he patiently brought her into position again and started all over. Things were working just fine when the tip caught again, but this time Edmund didn't let go, but held on tightly. He felt himself being lifted off the ground and was catapulted into the air, landing right at the cow's rear legs entwining him in the harness. Strumpf stopped and looked at him balefully as he scrambled to extract himself.

With all his heart he wanted to give up, but now the scratch in the earth mocked him. That furrow, imperfect and meandering as it was, would reveal to Jerzy Finkowski that what he had asked was possible and he would want to know why Edmund hadn't done more. He would accuse him of laziness. Edmund got up and went at it again.

The longest day of Edmund's life was not over until the sky was darkening and Finkowski came to collect him and the cow. On the field Edmund had been able to scrape only three of the most shameful furrows that any farm had ever seen. The disgraceful scratches were neither straight nor deep but weaved superficially over the field. In his great relief at having made the cow pull the wretched machine Edmund had not cared to correct her course. He knew he was in trouble. "The cow wouldn't work," he cried. Jerzy grabbed Edmund's hand and looked at the bleeding blisters, "Well at least you were trying. She always was a stupid cow. A couple of days more and you will both learn."

Never in his life had Edmund felt such contradictory emotions. He was so relieved that he had not earned the punishment he expected that he sobbed. But his greatest anxiety was about having to come back in the morning for more of the same. He was too sore and tired to go to the farm house to get his supper. Edmund was astonished when Jerzy delivered his food himself. More surprising was that it included a large chunk of bread and a piece of cheese along with the usual bowl of soup. But because of the pain that afflicted every part of his body he slept fitfully. Edmund had nightmares about that miserable animal, so waking and realizing he had to face her again brought no relief. Even more than Jerzy Finkowski she had become his enemy.

With all his heart Edmund wanted to be too sick to work the next day. His hands were sore, his muscles ached and his heart cried to be with his mother and sister. But no combination of pains was sufficient to win him a release. After breakfast it was back to the field with that cow.

As he renewed his struggle with the obstinate animal, his hands were wrapped in cloth that he had begged from Jerzy's wife. But a new pain was waiting for him in the field. Several young boys caught sight of his torment as they walked to school on the road beside the pasture. They sat on the fence enjoying his anguish, mocking and jeering at him as the uncaring cow toyed with him again. He refused to add to their enjoyment of the spectacle by screaming or running around after the cow as he had done the other day. Without the intimidation, however, Strumpf refused to pull. That brought more laughter. Edmund found a stick and beat her on the rump and she jumped and began to run bringing shouts of delight as the plough tumbled over again. The boys laughed so hard that they fell off the fence and rolled in the field. "Dumb German," they called, "don't you know you're supposed to use a horse?" They watched for hours until they tired of the laughing and teasing and decided to do something else. Even after they left Edmund accomplished little except that he reached a compromise with the cow. All he had to do to get her to pull the plough was to call her by her Polish name, Olga, and show her his prodding stick. Even she knows that this is Poland again, he thought.

That night as he washed himself beside the well in cold water he cried from the pain. His hands, his head, his shoulders and his legs all throbbed together. He wanted his mother and his sisters. He wanted someone to tell him everything would be all right and to hold him. Later, in his bed he prayed like he had heard his mother pray, there was no question of believing or not believing. He fell asleep before he finished.

Hertha was sent to look after the twin babies of a young woman who lived with her parents. It was the kind of situation a ten-year-old girl dreamed about without having any real idea what she was in for. The boys were less than a year old and required constant attention, but resourceful Hertha met the challenge head on. She loved children.

Even to Hertha's young eyes the girl, Tania, seemed very young to be a mother. Tania was a nervous and excitable individual and it didn't help that her parents were always yelling and swearing at her. Not that Tania was incapable of fighting back; the young woman gave back everything her parents threw at her and more, and it was not long before the new baby sitter got caught in the crossfire.

But Hertha had a warm bed, food and so much work that there was little time to miss her mother. If she stayed bright and alert, and she was very capable, she found that she was treated well, or at least she could avoid situations that could cause her problems. She rarely repeated a mistake.

She was, however, on duty at all times of the day and night. Her little girl's dream turned into a nightmare and she got only broken sleep. She changed and fed the babies, bathed them, played with them and did not have one minute of the day to herself. She was expected to respond to their every peep and the more she did, the more the boys learned to cry for attention. It was always her mealtimes and her sleep that were interrupted to care for them. When they were sick, she was expected to stay up and attend to their needs. Very quickly she became tired and weary.

One day, after a long night, Hertha was sitting by the kitchen table feeding one of the boys his bottle. The grandmother was baking bread while the young mother slept. Hertha longed to be in her bed. She felt like she had only slept a few minutes. As the boy reached for his bottle, it was knocked from her tired grip and fell to the floor. Hertha bent over to pick it up but she bend over awkwardly and the baby slid out of her arm. With a loud bang he landed on the floor. He screamed and wailed as Hertha hurried to gather him up and sooth him. Tania woke immediately and came running. She ripped her son out of the girl's arms. "You stupid, careless girl," she screeched into Hertha's face as she grabbed the baby, "you could have killed him."

The grandmother came running behind the daughter. In her hand she held a wooden cooking spoon. As she hovered over Hertha she was shaking with rage. But it wasn't until the girl tried to say that it was an accident that the Grandmother began to hit her. Over and over she struck at her with the spoon and when Hertha had the audacity to put her arms up to fend off the blows the grandmother became even more enraged. Screaming terror into the girl's face she dropped the spoon and started slapping with her open hand.

Finally, as the grandmother tired and then turned her attention to the infant, Hertha was finally able to tear herself away. She ran out of the house and hid in the garden. It was not much of a hiding place, however, and her crying gave her location away but it was all she had. For hours the terrified girl stayed there listening to the two women shout threats and obscenities at her from the house. She contemplated running away. But where could she run? She didn't even know where her mother was.

In the late afternoon the grandfather finally came to haul Hertha out of the garden. As soon as he dragged her through the door, the grandmother slapped her across the face again and sent her straight to bed without supper. She was so weary now that she fell asleep in spite of her pain.

In the middle of the night, however, she woke up. The throbbing in her head had increased. The pain was more intense than ever, yet she couldn't cry for fear of waking the others. With the kind of tenacity that had frustrated even her mother, Hertha bit her lip and transformed the pain into anger and indignation. She would not endure this injustice.

In the dark, crying silent tears, Hertha determined that she needed her mother. She stole out of the house making sure that she did not wake the twins. If they didn't wake, neither would the others.

It was a chilly April night and it was a long way for a little girl to walk with a thin coat and only her pain and indignation to keep her warm. If she had known where her mother was she would have gone there, but all she knew was that down the road was the Osciency camp. It was the only thing familiar to her and more important it was the last place she had seen her mother.

Close to morning the twins woke. They cried a long time before their mother realized that Hertha was not getting up. "You lazy thing," she shouted at Hertha, "get up!" Still the girl did not stir. The grandfather rose and found the girl's bed empty. He yelled at his daughter to come take care of her children. The disgruntled old man pulled on his trousers and went out to the garden where he thought the impudent girl had hidden herself again. He was not in the mood to search the whole garden so he called out for her. There was no response. He supposed she would return before too long. Where could she go? When she came back he would teach her to run off.

Hertha walked for what seemed like hours. She was so happy to see the sun come up that she ran the rest of the way to the camp. But her thin hope of seeing her mother there was dashed when she came through the gate. One of the matrons grabbed her before she could even explain what had happened. "You've run away, haven't you?" the woman accused as she grabbed the girl by the arm. She pulled hard. Hertha screamed. She hurt so much already that she couldn't bear any more.

"Shut up! You're going to get what you deserve," the matron shouted at her.

"What do you think you are doing?" Hertha heard a man ask. "What's all this screaming about?"

"Commissar Maczowiak!" the startled women explained, "this one's run away from her work. She needs to be taught a lesson."

The screaming had brought the man out of the camp office. As he came a little closer, Hertha thought she recognized him.

The man looked down, right into Hertha's eyes. "You're Fischerova, aren't you? Hertha Fischer. Why did you run away?"

"They beat me," Hertha cried, letting the anger finally give way to tears as she found someone to listen to her. Without thinking, she just rushed into Maczowiak's arms. He had no choice but to hold her and when the astonished woman tried to save him from the girl the Commissar waved her away.

"Do you know who I am?" he asked the little girl.

"You used to work on our farm."

"Yes, Hertha," he said, "now tell me how you got all those bruises."

As he carried her into the office Hertha forgot all the embellishments she had built up in her mind and told him the truth. She cried. She knew that she had been careless when she dropped the child but could not believe that she had deserved such a beating.

"No," Maczowiak said to her, in the privacy of his office, "such things ought not to be. What would you like me to do about it?"

"Well, you could arrest them," she said sincerely and then she remembered what her mother had given her years ago, "and if I could get some pudding I would feel better."

He laughed loudly. This was the precocious little girl he had known and she delighted him. "Well, what if I just make sure that you don't go back there? Would that be fine?"

Hertha thought about it and agreed. It was, after all, what she really wanted, not to have to go back.

"Then I will take you home and see if my wife has some pudding she can make for you and the boys."

"Could Mama, Edmund and Else come too?"

"No. But I promise you Hertha I will make sure they are well."

When they realized that Hertha was not coming back on her own, the grandfather and Tania came to the camp to report the run away. They hoped to be able to pick another girl and to bring her back with them. Maczowiak had suspected they would come after her and told his staff to send them to his office. The two were full of anger and accusation as they reported to the Commissar that the lazy and oafish girl, Hertha Fischer, had run away. They needed another to replace her.

"Did you do anything to make her run away?" Maczowiak asked. "You didn't beat her did you?"

"Who knows why she ran away?" the grandfather said, "she was a bad one. She stole food and miss-treated the children. Why yesterday she almost killed my grandson."

"Did that make you angry?"

"Of course," the daughter replied.

"Angry enough to hit her?"

"All right," the grandfather admitted, "my wife hit her a few times on her bottom. She was angry but she didn't really hurt her."

"Then why did she come back here all black and blue?"

"She came here?" the old man questioned, the tone of his voice changing to reflect the tension he felt all of a sudden. "So what lies did she tell you? I'll bet she never told you about trying to kill the baby?"

"She told me she dropped the child. It was an accident."

"She's a liar," the daughter interjected, "she lies all the time, and she's lazy. She should be punished."

"I think I know who has lied. You won't be getting another girl, not from this camp. We send them out to work and earn their keep, not to be abused."

"You can't do that," the grandfather raised his voice at the Commissar, "these are German dogs. We treat them no different from the way they treated us."

"We'll go to the authorities," Tania threatened, "you can't believe this girl over us!"

"I can," Maczowiak explained, "you lied, she didn't. I could put you in jail for this!" It was a bluff but it was a winning one.

Maczowiak thought it prudent not to tell anyone what he was doing. He felt no personal obligation to the Fischer family yet he remembered that Alwine Fischer in particular had been kind. She had not behaved like many other Germans. Just the same he had to be careful. It was not a popular thing for a Commissar to be doing, helping these people. He could easily be replaced.

Before he left camp, he found out where Edmund and Alwine were and then rode off with the little girl holding onto his waist. After he had put her safely into his wife's care he rode to Finkowski's farm and asked to see Edmund. Jerzy was puzzled that the Commissar should interest himself personally in the boy, but led him to the field anyway. There, after three days, Edmund was still struggling to plough with that obstinate cow. Maczowiak looked on in amazement and turned to the farmer as if to ask what he thought he was doing. Jerzy offered no explanation. He just shrugged his shoulders and walked away.

The field was still a disgrace and Edmund knew it. He was tired and almost numb to pain. Worst of all he no longer cared. When he saw the Commissar coming, he recognized him. He was not at all surprised that the communist had prospered under the Russians. Still, he didn't care what Finkowski thought of his work, nor did he care that Maczowiak had come to yell at him.

"Do you know who I am?" Maczowiak asked the boy.

Edmund nodded.

"Show me your hands. Take off those rags."

Carefully Edmund unwrapped them. His hands were raw with blisters, some freshly broken and others half healed or torn open again. Blood oozed from the dirty sores but the boy bit his lips to keep from crying.

The Commissar didn't flinch. This is what he had wanted the Germans to feel, the pain and humiliation of working like slaves. Yet now Maczowiak couldn't help thinking that they were teaching the wrong people. Women and children and a few elderly men were learning what their leaders should be learning.

"Do they beat you here?"

"No," Edmund shook his head but kept staring at his own hands.

"The work is hard, isn't it?"

"Yes," the boy confirmed but did not complain.

"Yes, I know it is, Maczowiak replied looking at the pitiful boy. It occurred to the Commissar that he should have been glad to witness the humiliation of the arrogant boy. He could remember him strutting around his father's farm sneering at the Polish help. It would be easy to leave him here and never bother him again. But it was his promise to his sister that he considered now. "Come with me," he said.

Maczowiak simply told Jerzy Finkowski that the boy was needed somewhere else. In a few days he would get another to take his place, one fit to do a man's work. The farmer protested, "Don't take him. He's only now beginning to be worth something." But when Maczowiak ignored him, Jerzy called him back. "The truth is," Finkowski blurted out, "my wife has become attached to the boy and we were wondering about adopting him."

"He has a family," Maczowiak sneered to the ridiculous suggestion. Edmund was greatly relieved.

After the obnoxious creature Gzelak had returned her to the camp, Alwine had experienced things that almost made her sorry that she had not accepted the dirty man's offer. The camp officials, believing the story he told them, that Alwine was lazy and rebellious, were determined to teach her a lesson.

She and Else were immediately sent to the farm of a bitter woman named Anna Pilusj. The woman had suffered much at the hands of the Germans during the war and had only one goal left in life, to make every German she met pay for that suffering. Her husband and all her children, except a teenage son, were dead. All Germans shared the blame. She told her painful story often, along with her desire for revenge. Now with her one remaining child, a dull-witted and overweight boy of sixteen, she was determined to repay the Germans every ounce of misery she had suffered.

From the beginning, Anna found in Alwine Fischer someone she particularly despised. Onto her, she projected all the venom she held for the German woman whom she had been forced to serve during the occupation. The verbal abuse was unrelenting and if that had been all, Alwine could have suffered through it. But while she and two other women worked, Anna and her son physically abused them. Anna especially loved to kick. The milking was done too slowly and that deserved a kick. The kitchen floor was not clean enough and so she kicked. The stable was not tidy enough so Anna kicked at anyone close. If anyone complained, she screamed, "You are treated better than the Germans treated me."

Slowly, Alwine began to think that it was because of Else that Anna picked on her. Somehow the little girl triggered something in her. "Do you think your little daughter will survive?" she would ask in Polish. "Many, many Polish children were killed by the Germans." Alwine could not refute her accusation. She remembered how she had felt when her son Einhardt had died. Nevertheless, it sounded like a threat. Alwine kept Else close to her side whenever possible.

Alwine did everything she could to avoid drawing Anna's attention but she couldn't avoid getting sick. She fought off the pain and fever of the flu for several days with nothing but willpower, but she only got worse. Anna saw her moving sluggishly and used it as an opportunity to pick on her. "Faster," she cried as she supervised the milking. Alwine tried to work more quickly. It wasn't enough. The bitter woman knocked the milk stool out from under her. Alwine slipped under the cow spilling the milk pail. The startled cow kicked her in the side. Quickly, Irma Thann, her old neighbor, hauled her out from under the animal. Alwine could barely stand.

Anna stood in her face screaming about the spilt milk. "You lazy dog," she yelled, "no food or rest for you until you've cleaned up this mess!" With that she slapped her again, hard.

Alwine could take no more. She thought she would die if she didn't lie down. Without saying another word she stumbled out of the stable, her little daughter helping to hold her up. Anna was livid, and shouted for Alwine to return to work. "I'm sick," Alwine managed to squeak out weakly, "leave me alone!"

She lay down in her bed in the straw but Anna would not leave her alone. She flew into a rage. "You are not sick! If you don't get up right now, you will be sorry." With that she kicked at Alwine but missed, lost her balance and fell herself, landing painfully on her hip. She screeched but quickly pulled herself up and limped toward the house. "My son will take care of you," she said as she left the barn.

However, when she got to the barn door and looked out she saw something that was even better. "Look who is coming!" she shot back through the door, "You'll soon regret what you did. It's the Commissar!" With that she disappeared for a few minutes. When the door reopened she had Commissar Maczowiak with her. Anna drooled with the anticipation of witnessing the punishment she thought the man was about to dispense to her disobedient servant.

"Well how are you feeling Fischerova?" the Commissar asked.

Anna was prepared to let this cordial greeting pass. Personally, she never even pretended to like these people but she could understand how it could be effective. It pleased her to think that the Commissar was baiting the woman.

"Not well," came the answer, and with it a smile that surprised Anna. "I have a fever and I feel weak."

"She's not sick," Anna objected, "she's just lazy."

"How do they treat you here?" the Commissar asked Alwine.

"I think you know!" Alwine responded.

"We treat our Germans as well as they treated us," Anna spat out.

"You're a good person Fischerova," Maczowiak said with a smile.

"What is going on here?" Anna asked. She could no longer contain herself. "You treat her like an old friend. You are supposed to punish her!"

"I know this woman. If she says she is sick then she is sick. She is not a lazy person and she never mistreated anyone."

Anna groaned. The Commissar was coddling the woman and she could not accept it. She began raving about the injustice. Finally Maczowiak ordered her to shut up. "I want you to take care of this woman," he ordered. "Give her more blankets and warm food."

"I will not be a servant to any German," Anna protested.

"Then have the other women do it. You enjoy having these women here to work this farm for you don't you? Well if you want it to continue then take care of this woman or you and your lazy son will be working this farm by yourselves. Now get out!"

Anna hesitated, her face twisted with anger and fear. "Get out," Maczowiak yelled again and she scrambled away.

"Do you know where my children are?" Alwine asked after Anna left.

"Don't worry about your children I am watching out for them."

"Oh, thank you," Alwine cried. They were tears of relief. "If I die, can you see that they find their way to Germany? That's where their father is."

"I can't make any promises like that, but you are not going to die Fischerova. The woman is too frightened to hurt you any more. I will let her know that I'm coming back in a few days to see if you are better."

Alwine was able to rest a few days. Else was assigned to bring her mother extra blankets and hot soup, but Alwine allowed her daughter to eat more of it than she ate. Nevertheless, in a few days Alwine was much stronger and the fever was gone. She was still weak but forced herself to work again. The other women had to work harder while she was sick and Alwine couldn't let that continue.

Perhaps because the Commissar had threatened her, Anna eased up on Alwine. It was not that she totally abandoned her ways, only that the edge was off her abuse. The screaming and swearing continued but there was less kicking.

Shortly after her recovery Anna watched as Alwine applied the advice that Stefan had given her. When the other women had left the stalls she stayed to clean and straighten up. Without knowing that she was being watched she cleaned and stacked the milk pails and made sure that the cows had fresh straw for bedding. Then finally she went for her supper.

Anna stopped her. She gave her a grudging compliment. "I heard about you, Fischerova," for the first time attempting to speak to Alwine in her broken German. "You let Poles make 'schnapps'." It took Alwine a minute to realize what she was saying. She was referring to the fact that she let Stefan distill liquor. "My woman, no schnapps, no schnapps. Nothing she give us, nothing but work." She spat on the ground to show her contempt.

Thirty-Three

Edmund and Hertha remained with Maczowiak's wife for only a few days. Besides the impropriety of a commissar harboring German refugees, his wife quickly grew tired of the extra work and insisted that they be sent elsewhere. Both Edmund and Hertha begged to be reunited with their mother, but the Commissar could not arrange that. Maczowiak was able to find positions for them where they would not be abused and delivered them there himself.

In their new situations Edmund and Hertha began to fear that they would never see the rest of their family again and that they would all be slaves forever. It all seemed like the end of the world and an unbearable load. Yet Edmund wanted to survive, and he found that as he changed his attitude, even this life was liveable. Wherever he was sent, he worked hard to make himself useful. But it was Hertha who had the best tools to deal with her captivity, a sense of humor and an intense attitude of self-righteous indignation. The combination made it impossible for people not to like her.

Else, on the other hand, was too small to have developed the means to cope with her situation. The screaming Anna Pilusj frightened her but her overweight son, Jan, terrified her. Even though lately, Anna, had stopped kicking, she could not control her teenage son. He stalked Else, jumping out at her when she least expected it. Usually he grabbed her and threw her around like a sack of potatoes. Hoisting her high above his shoulders he pretended to drop her and threatened to choke her if she screamed. Only at the last second would he catch her, but often he would miss. Alwine had to spend her nights comforting the little girl and bandaging her cuts and scrapes.

After eating and drinking beer, Jan's greatest pleasure was teasing Else. Whenever he was close, she clung to her mother so tightly that she could barely work.

One day, as Jan caught her unaware, he locked Else in a dark, dank basement used for storing potatoes. She screamed to be allowed out and cried that she couldn't stand the smell of the musty potatoes. He laughed and told the bewildered little girl that she would not be allowed out until she had picked the sprouts off all the potatoes. Promising to cut her into pieces if she didn't do as she was told, Jan went off and quickly forgot about her. Only a thorough search, prompted by her mother's frantic refusal to work until the girl was found, revealed where she was. Eventually, she had cried herself to sleep.

But as Jan realized that she was particularly sensitive to bad odors he went wild. He delighted in finding new places to lock her up. Whether it was the chicken coop, a pig pen or even the out house, he threw her in and threatened to leave her there forever. Now the girl became almost hysterical whenever she saw him.

Luckily for Else, he was lazy. Most of the day he spent either sleeping or drinking beer. But when he had excess energy to burn, he always looked for his favorite target. Whenever Alwine noticed him prowling, she told Else to run and hide in the barn, high in the haystack. If she was lucky she would even fall asleep there until his short attention span made him give up. But if she made a mistake and he saw her, there was no stopping him.

Often, when he was drunk, he would take his dead father's gun and run around the farm shooting and yelling like the Indians he loved to watch in American movies. Even his mother was afraid of him then. The rest of the women would scurry to find a place to hide when they saw him waving the pistol at them. Alwine grabbed her daughter and laid down in the hay field until it was all over. Luckily, there were plenty of places to hide.

One warm June day, however, Else was not careful enough and he caught her. Grabbing her long blonde hair as she came running out of the barn, he dragged her across the farm yard. He drooled with delight at having her in his power. In the middle of the yard he dropped her and handed her a barn broom. "You lazy pest, you have to work," he barked, "sweep the yard!" He handed her a heavy stable broom.

Else was so frightened all she could do was stand there with the big clumsy broom in her hands. "Sweep," Jan shouted, "sweep, sweep, sweep!" The broom was much too large for her little hands to operate properly. He became angry and kicked at the hills of loose dirt that she had managed to create. "Do it right, or I'll have to shoot you." He produced a gun in his right hand and laughed. But Else still could not handle the broom properly and now fear paralyzed her as he pointed the gun at her head. She began to cry. "Stop crying," he shouted, "get back to work!"

Alwine was in the field mowing hay with a scythe when she heard the shouting. She wanted to run to her daughter but Anna stopped her. "He won't hurt her," Anna said, "he's only having fun." Irma Thann pulled Alwine aside and whispered, "He may not hurt her, but he'll kill you for sure if you interfere. What will she do without a mother?"

Jan grew angry that Else wouldn't cooperate with his broom-game. The boy was sweating profusely in the hot sun and wasn't enjoying himself. He told her that she was useless and didn't deserve to live. Clutching her arm he swung her round and round. "Run if you want to live," he teased her and shot his gun into the air. "Mama, mama!" Else screamed as he made her run faster and faster. He swept her around until her hand slipped out of his sweaty grasp. He was panting hard but even then he wouldn't let up. "Keep running," he shouted at her. Then he fired his pistol into the ground close to her feet.

Else could no longer control herself and wet her pants. The boy looked at the puddle that she was standing in, cursed and berated her. He picked her up and flung her over his shoulder. She could smell the sweat on his fat body now and it made her sick. The tears streamed down her cheeks as she screamed and kicked. While he was wondering what to do with her he spotted the old well. He put her feet in the bucket and said, "You need a bath." While she clung to the rope crying, he lowered her to the bottom. It was a dry well but she was so frightened that she passed out anyway.

The girl was no more fun now and so Jan went away leaving her at the bottom of the musty hole. Anna could not stop Alwine now. She ran to her daughter. With Irma Thann's help she dragged Else from the well. Relieved to find out she was still alive she carried her to her bed and stayed with her until she revived.

After that Else could hardly be persuaded to come out of the barn and would not leave her mother's side at all. If she even saw the boy she grabbed onto her mother and wouldn't let go. Not even Anna's cussing and threats could tear the little girl away. That made the mother almost useless to Anna.

"You've done this to her, now leave her alone," Alwine chided as Anna tried to tear Else away. From the barn the girl had seen Jan as he stalked across the barnyard.

"You can't talk to me in this way. I don't care if the Commissar is your friend." She grabbed a broom and came at Alwine with it. "I'll teach you."

But Alwine just stood there, her little girl still clinging tightly to her leg. The first blow she fended off with her forearm but it glanced down her side almost hitting Else. As the next blow came, Alwine grabbed the end of the broom and tore it away. It was so incredibly easy that Alwine was amazed. Perhaps Anna had just lost her grip. But a strange look came over the woman as she stared at Alwine with the broom in her hand and saw that the two other German women were coming to her aid. She panicked and ran out of the barn toward the house shouting, "They're going to kill me, they're going to kill me." The house door slammed behind her.

"Now we've done it," Irma said, "he'll be out here with his gun soon. Should we run away?"

"Where would we go?" Alwine asked.

"Perhaps we could go to your friend the Commissar and explain what happened."

The women looked at Alwine as if it was her decision to make. Going to Maczowiak seemed logical, however, the more she thought about it, the less convinced she was that it was the right thing to do. The women decided to wait to see what Anna and Jan would do.

Strangely, nothing happened. Fifteen minutes passed ... half an hour ... and there was no sign of Anna or fat Jan. They expected that by now the teenager would have stormed out of the house brandishing his pistol. He had threatened to shoot them so often that it seemed it was only an excuse that he lacked. But there was no sign of him, nor of Anna.

"What do you think they are doing?" Jutta, the oldest of the three women asked Alwine. She had no idea. As they looked out the stable door, they could see that the front door of the house was shut tight. It was unusual on such a bright, warm day. "Do you think they've run off to get the police?"

"I don't think so," Irma responded, "there is someone in the house. I think they're frightened."

"The little twerp is a coward," Jutta said with a twisted smile. "I should have known, the loud ones always are." Alwine's two comrades began to laugh.

It was Alwine who brought a note of soberness to the situation. "This is not good. You never know what frightened people will do."

Someone had to do something. Alwine, feeling responsible for having created the situation made the first move. Quietly she gathered her courage and walked toward the house, intent on apologizing. If accepting the blame would ease the tension then it was worth the humiliation. Otherwise the frightened pair might go to the police and tell them some outrageous story. Alwine had no doubt that they would be believed. That was the last thing she wanted to happen.

Alwine fumbled for the correct words in Polish. She had never been good at speaking the language although she understood it well enough. Still, it was important for her to be truthful and sincere. She was not sorry for having protected her daughter and herself, what she was really sorry for was that the boy had so traumatized Else that it had provoked this situation. But she couldn't very well say, "I'm sorry you're so stupid." She was sorry, however, for the war and for the way the Germans had provoked the Poles in the same way that Anna and her son had provoked them. She was sorry. Sorry that Anna and her son were now as frightened of retribution as the Germans had been. It seemed there was nothing left now in the world but sorrow.

She could hear shouting as she came closer to the door. At first she thought it was directed at her and she almost ran back to the barn, but then she recognized the tone. It was Anna, yelling at Jan, belittling him. She called him a lazy, good-for-nothing, drunken coward. How right she was. When Alwine came close to the house, she could see them through the window, faces red with anger, arguing in deafening screams. They didn't even hear Alwine knocking on the door. She had to bang on it with her fist until they heard.

It was Anna who came to the window and peeked out of the corner like a frightened child. Alwine kept her hands in front of her to show that she had no weapon and was harmless, nevertheless, when Anna opened the door the width of a crack she had the gun. It was pointed at Alwine's head. Her hand shook nervously but it was up to Alwine to make the first gesture. "I came to assure you that I ... none of us mean you any harm."

"You were going to kill me."

"No Anna, I only took the broom from you. I thought you were going to harm my daughter. You're a mother too, you know that a mother will do anything to protect her child. I am sorry for what has happened."

"You say that because you are frightened."

"Yes, we are frightened and that's why we would never hurt you or your son."

"Shoot her," Jan said. The fat boy had come to the door to see who his mother was talking to. Anna turned her head and with a flick of her wrist struck him across the nose with the barrel of the pistol. "Shut up," she growled at him, "this is all your fault." He squealed in pain and Alwine could see the blood running through his fingers as he covered his nose. But Anna just turned to Alwine and said, "Go back to work."

After the incident, Anna was much calmer. The three women who worked on her farm could only speculate why. Perhaps the incident had given her a new perspective on fear. She became almost friendly, especially toward Alwine. She stopped kicking and best of all she even controlled her son's sadistic games. Before long she was even asking Alwine's opinion on the running of the farm. The venom was gone.

Thirty-Four

When summer came, Anna was sorry to see Alwine return to the camp. The pregnancy was well advanced and she could not do her fair share of the work. Alwine was upset too, but not because she had to leave. She didn't know why she cried and considered it a waste of tears. Until now there had hardly been time to think about her pregnancy and Alwine suspected that her tears were for the unborn child. To be having a baby under these conditions seemed ludicrous, if not disastrous. She couldn't imagine that the child might live. Looking back at the pregnancies she had survived in this cursed land was disheartening. There was not one baby to show for it. How could God torment her so? How could He have made the mistake of letting her get pregnant now? It was fear, more than anything, that made her cry as she returned to the camp to await the birth.

It was the first week of July when Alwine found herself at Osciency again. She hadn't seen the place in months but there was little difference. There were forms to be filled out for the Red Cross and then she went back to the barn. There were only a few sick women in the barn but before sunset others started to arrive from their assigned work. To her surprise and delight, Hertha and Edmund walked through the doors just after sunset. They were now day laborers, sent out to one farm or another to do chores.

Each evening they returned to the camp. It was almost too good to be true. Alwine wrapped her arms around her children and savored the time they had together. How good it felt, even though they were all still prisoners and subject to the whims of the Poles.

During the day, Alwine was one of the few women left at the camp. Most of those left behind during working hours were sick or too old to work. Since she was only pregnant, Alwine almost felt guilty for being there. But she was not content just to sit around and do nothing. She didn't feel sick, she just needed to rest more often. She tried to help by tending to the women who were ill, bringing them water and trying to make them more comfortable. But when Irene Weiss was returned to camp with a fever, she refused even to allow Alwine to wipe her brow. The bitter woman would not leave Alwine alone. Whatever Alwine tried to do, Irene was there to criticize and even taunt her.

To escape, Alwine walked around the grounds. Beside the old summer kitchen she found a garden where someone had planted vegetables. She had a hard time recognizing what was planted there. It was overgrown with weeds and did not look healthy. When she asked who had planted it, she was told about a woman who had begged or stolen seeds from the farms where she worked. But as soon as her garden was planted, she was sent away.

To Alwine there were few things more shameful than leaving a garden to go to weed. She began to care for it, spending the cool mornings weeding and digging with her fingers or a stick. Generally, Alwine did not like tending gardens she had not planted, but this one was different. It was like an orphan. Being careful not to disturb the roots of the stunted vegetables, Alwine began to pull the weeds. The carrots and the beets were a fraction of the size they should have been by this time of year. The potato tops were a little taller and more hearty and she could dig around them more aggressively to loosen the soil. There wasn't much else that she could rescue except for a patch of radishes. Yet when she was finished the vegetable patch looked like it had been saved. Perhaps there would be some sort of harvest from it.

The work felt so good that Alwine couldn't believe how much she had missed her garden. When her children asked why she worked when she didn't have to, Alwine looked at them in amazement. "You should all have had gardens of your own to take care of, then you would know."

"Know what Mama?" Hertha asked.

"In a garden you plant vegetables and flowers, but the garden plants hope in your heart. It's like a prayer that you plant. God blesses gardeners because they spend a lot of time on their knees."

One evening, as Alwine put her children to bed, she was totally shocked to see Hedwig Fischer coming through the barn door. As if drawn by a magnet, Alwine rose from her bunk and walked over to her with her heart racing. Her immediate reaction on seeing Hedwig was to wonder where Johann was. Had he escaped? She wanted to ask but couldn't bring herself to pose the question. "Hedwig," she called out tentatively as she got closer.

As Hedwig turned, Alwine saw the perspiration running down her face. It was the fever. But when Hedwig laid her eyes upon Alwine, she flew into a rage. She ran at her, flailing her fists and shouting, "It's your fault! It's your fault! He's dead because of you!" The other women had to restrain Hedwig and pull her away, but Alwine stood there white as a sheet. She turned her face away but saw only the accusing eyes of Irene Weiss. She cried.

During the day, however, only Alwine was there to take care of the sick. Without asking her permission, Alwine sat by Hedwig's side and used a wet cloth to wipe the perspiration from her forehead. There were no medicines or doctors and the cause of the fevers that afflicted so many was a mystery. Perhaps it was a combination of too little food and too much work. With rest and a minimum of care it almost always passed in a few days. Alwine only wanted to make her comfortable.

But Hedwig's health continued to falter. As she became weaker, she did not protest when Alwine offered to feed her some warm broth and washed her with a wet cloth. When she finished, Hedwig laid her head down and mumbled something. "What did you say, Hedwig?" Alwine asked as she put her ear close to the woman's mouth. She repeated it. The words were weak but discernable, "I killed him." Alwine blanched; she supposed she was talking about her husband. It was the fever. It could only be the fever but then Hedwig opened her eyes and said it plainly. "I killed him so they would blame Albert." Then she fell asleep. It didn't make sense. Fever makes people say strange things.

She wiped Hedwig's face again and heard someone ask from behind, "Why do you do that? You know she hates you."

Alwine turned and saw Irene Weiss sitting up on her bunk. It was such a relief to hear her friend talking to her again. "There is no one else to take care of her," Alwine replied.

"You're always taking care of things," Irene said with a sarcastic tone. "Do me a favor. Don't take care of me. Did you think that maybe she doesn't want your help? She blames you for her husband's death ..." Her hateful words were cut off by a cough.

"You're ill, Irene."

"Yes, but don't help me, Alwine. Your friendship has been nothing but a curse to me."

Alwine gasped. She couldn't believe what Irene was saying. She turned her back on her former friend and wiped Hedwig's brow again. She was hiding her tears.

"Leave her alone," Irene tried to yell but her words got caught on another cough. "She doesn't want your help. Her husband stopped on the road to wait for you. That's why they were caught. The Russians shot him. He was waiting for you, that's why he died."

Alwine's eyes flowed but she didn't know if it was for Johann or because of Irene's hateful words. She couldn't take any more of her accusations and laid down on her bunk. But such hatred was not easily forgotten. She soon found herself on her knees beside her bed. Of all the things that God had asked her to endure this torment was the worst she could have faced.

But Alwine was up again the next day feeling better. The first thing she did was tend to the garden. There she could think clearly and pray. Prayer eased the mind. Refortified, Alwine went to take care of Hedwig. The woman seemed eager for the attention.

Buoyed by Hedwig's reaction, Alwine risked asking her sister-in-law about her strange confession, on the chance that it was not out of delirium that she had spoken. "Hedwig, do you remember what you said yesterday?" she asked quietly. Hedwig shook her head ever so slightly, and stared off into the distance. "You said you killed him so that Albert would be blamed." Hedwig said nothing, her eyes were glassy and her face was blank. Alwine was sure now that it had been the fever talking.

As Alwine turned to leave, she saw Irene sleeping fitfully. Perhaps she was cold. Her blanket lay beside her on the floor. Timidly Alwine approached her. All she wanted to do was to pull the blanket over her, but then she saw the sweat on her face. She couldn't help herself. She found another cloth and wet it to cool Irene's fever. Irene woke.

"I don't want your help," she said weakly.

"Why are you so angry with me?" Alwine asked so directly and sincerely that Irene could not turn away.

Irene took the wet cloth off her forehead and threw it lamely at Alwine. "Why should you understand?" she asked with contempt. "I don't even understand. I just know that I hate you."

"What did I do?" Alwine pleaded.

"What did you do?" Irene replied angrily through labored breathing and coughing, but even though she was weak, her anger came through clearly. "What did I do to deserve this? It was you that Martin wanted to hurt, not me! He hated you, not me! Your husband was his enemy and I paid the price! I've suffered too much for your friendship!"

"You think I'm to blame?"

"It's obvious. You are my curse Alwine. My life wasn't meant to be like this. Now my husband is dead and my children will die here. When August died I wanted to pay you back your curse. I told them Albert wasn't really injured. I wanted him to die too."

It was irrational. Alwine wasn't at all sure that Irene meant everything she said, but she had conveyed her feelings clearly. It was puzzling. How long had her friend felt such hostile thoughts? Such anger was not consistent with the nature of the girl she had grown up with. Yet Alwine remembered all too clearly what Hermann Martin had done to her. If Irene had changed, she had a reason.

For a long time Alwine couldn't get her mind off what Irene had said. Words could hurt. They clawed at her insides and tore up her confidence. Was she really a curse? Could her friend really trace all her trouble to their friendship?

It was impossible to leave it alone. She had to work it out. Reflecting again on those dark months in Zwickau and the disturbing years in Warthegau under the Reich, Alwine wanted to understand how that curse had entered her life. She considered when she, herself, had first used that ominous word. It had probably started when Ewald, and then little Einhardt had died as a consequence of the resettlement. Later, her feelings had been renewed when she had realized what the Germans were doing to the Poles and Jews. It had become clear that something was seriously wrong.

Perhaps by accepting land they had no right to, she and Albert had brought this curse upon their family. But there had been no other alternative for them. Or had there? Hadn't they been warned not to take the land?

Though Alwine believed that curses were real, she saw them differently now. She believed in them, not in a magical or superstitious way, as some people believed, but in a very tangible way. It was actually simple to understand. Sooner or later people had to live with the consequences of their actions. So in effect, they cursed or blessed themselves. It wasn't at all mysterious, it was very logical. If you set a higher moral code for yourself, God expected you to abide by it. Alwine was sure that this is what the Volhynians had done in their arrogance. They had called themselves Christian and behaved like thieves. How could they now expect God to bless them? What she, Irene and all of Germany were experiencing were the consequences of their actions. The consequences effected the innocent as well as the guilty, and that was the real curse.

As the days passed, however, it was Alwine's concern for her unborn child that made her forget about Irene's anger. She dreaded the idea of burying another child.

But when she tried to think about something else, she only found other worries to occupy her mind. Was her husband dead? Was he with the thousands of German soldiers that had been dragged off to Siberia? Or what about her parents and her sisters Else and Klara? How could they have escaped with her father so ill? Where were her brother Arnold, or sister Adele and her family? There were so many things to concern her but there was nothing that she could do about any of it. Even the child getting ready to come into the world could count on little help from her and that ought not to be. She cried about it day and night but was careful not to let her children see her fear. They too had enough to cope with.

Edmund woke one night and caught her crying. He pressed her to tell him why. Alwine was weary of keeping her problems to herself. In a moment of weakness that helped to relieve some of her anxiety, she shared her deepest concerns with her oldest.

Edmund took his mother's worries seriously, more seriously than Alwine had ever suspected he could. They were problems that no twelve-year-old should have to deal with and certainly he had no ability to solve them. But Edmund had learned at least one thing in the last few months. Now he concluded that the only way he had to deal with problems that were too big for him was to ask for help. And if God could rescue him from Jerzy Finkowski, then he could certainly help his mother.

It was when Alwine was at her lowest point that Stefan showed up at the Osciency camp. He brought gifts of fresh vegetables and a container of fresh milk. He also brought Alwine two featherbeds, which essentially were two sheets sewn together and filled with down. He had rescued them from Alwine's farm after her escape. Alwine protested that it was too much. She could never justify sleeping in such comfort while others around them slept on straw with thin blankets. She told him to take them away. Stefan refused. Instead he went to the Commissar and convinced his old friend that it was time for Alwine to have some privacy as she was getting ready to give birth. Within hours she and Else were moved to a very small but private room, off to the side of the barn. There, in privacy, Alwine could finish the days of her pregnancy.

When Edmund and Hertha came back that night they found a pot of vegetables cooking and lay down on the thick blankets. For a few minutes they played and laughed like children ought to. Alwine was happy to see her children eat so vigorously, especially the picky little Else. It was wonderful to see them all smiling and enjoying life. Such a sight could keep hope alive.

"Mama," Edmund began. He wanted to make a special night even more special by sharing something important but found it hard to explain. "We're going to be all right," he finally said.

"I hope so Edmund."

"I know it Mama," he said forcefully.

"How can you know such a thing?"

"Papa is all right and we're going to be together again, and the baby will be fine too."

"Edmund, I'm not sure that..."

"No Mama," he interrupted, "we'll be fine. We're going to get out of here. I know it."

"I hope so."

That night Alwine woke up with a start. It was as if something shook her from her sleep. But it was not a frightening nor even an unsettling feeling that she had, even though it made her tears flow in a torrent. The words were quiet as a whisper and yet as clear as if they had been spoken by the angels themselves. It was reassuring and peaceful rather than heavy and foreboding. Her parents were dead. There was no need for Alwine to worry about her parents any longer. At that moment she realized too what Edmund was trying to tell her.

On a hot August day, while Alwine worked in her adopted garden she spotted storks flying over the camp. She pointed them out to Else who was terribly bored watching her mother work. "Run, Else, run and tell them that you want them to bring you a baby." Else was so thrilled that she immediately chased after the birds shouting loudly into the sky, "Bring me a baby! Bring me a baby!" Excitedly she came bouncing back to her mother. "Do you think they heard, do you think they will bring a baby?" she asked.

"Of course they heard."

The next day, August 6, 1945, Else was sent to play in the big barn. She didn't really want to go. She still felt safest with her mother, but with some coaxing she finally went with one of the other women. Hours later when she returned she found a little baby brother in her mother's arms. For days the baby totally consumed her attention as she watched him even when he was sleeping. She pointed out to her mother how determined he was to have his index and middle finger together in his mouth. She laughed at how he worked until he had them safely tucked away. The little girl couldn't believe her luck in having received such a gift.

"Did the storks bring him, Mama?" she asked, her face aglow and full of wonder. "Yes dear, they must have heard you." Else kissed the baby and turned to her mother again, "Are all babies so small?" Her mother didn't answer, but changed the subject. "What shall we call him?"

"I think we should call him Kurt."

It wasn't a family name but Alwine approved anyway.

Thirty-Five

Within hours of when he first began to perpetrate his hoax Albert regretted having hatched this desperate plan. It wasn't the immorality of his lie that pricked his conscience but the ever growing terror of being caught. The consequences of this deception were something he never wanted to face.

It had all taken on a life of its own. He had become bogged down by the lies so incredibly quickly that it seemed like it had happened without his consent. One lie was never enough, it always needed another to reinforce it. Soon Albert had rewritten his life. He invented a childhood riddled with disease, fevers and pneumonia. Even the story of a minor tumble became a concussion with lingering side effects. The trauma of his wounding, which had been serious enough physically, was not just a bad memory anymore but emotionally debilitating. There was too much to remember and keep straight. Yet Albert soon discovered that the more he rewrote his life, the more difficult it was to extricate himself from that invented life. He was trapped.

The pressure to keep his lies from unraveling under the constant questioning of the doctors was staggering. He dreaded the doctors now and wanted to be finished with the whole thing. It became apparent to Albert that it was just a matter of time before he was caught. Yet at times it seemed as if he himself couldn't tell the difference between truth and lie any more. He had to find a way to stop. He was sure that the penalty for confession was as just as bitter as the penalty for getting caught.

What Albert didn't realize was that he never really got them to believe his symptoms. They were laughable; a leg that shook violently without warning, like teeth chattering in the cold, nightmares left over from childhood fevers, headaches that exploded into strange visions. Luckily, the German doctors needed little convincing that there was something inherently wrong with Russian born Germans. They wrote on his report, 'feebleminded.' It was enough to keep Albert out of the war for months. They sent him to a hospital in northern Germany for further prolonged examination.

Albert thought he was going to go crazy. He couldn't even trust the other patients. He was afraid to talk to them lest he let something slip that would give him away. He lived in fear, not only for his life, but for his sanity. Never had he suffered this kind of loneliness before, not in the resettlement camp at Zwickau and not even in the prison at Beresza Kartuska. It was not just that he was away from his family, although that was heart wrenching enough, but now he was without even a friend. Albert had always had friends. Wherever he had found himself, even if they were only drinking partners, he knew how to make friends. But now even that superficial intimacy was closed to him because of his fear of giving up his mask.

He came closest to giving it all up when he heard that the Russians had overrun the Wartheland. When he hadn't received a reply to any of his letters home in more than two months he wanted to go find his family. However, he couldn't just get up and leave. There were two punishments for what he had done, prison and the firing squad.

His vindication didn't come until the spring. On May 7, the news was broadcast that the Reich had unconditionally surrendered and the rumor was that Hitler was dead. The doctors and nurses in the hospital were somber in defeat but relieved that it was over. One doctor who had interviewed Albert several times came and whispered into his ear, “No need to pretend any longer, the war is over.” It was so good to be alive.

Within days of the announcement the British were there to take over the military hospital. They questioned the doctors and nurses and then sent the patients, including Albert, to a civilian hospital.

He left his cane behind leaning on the wall beside his bed. With it, he left the last affectation of a limp, the uncontrollable shaking of his limb, the concussion and his memory loss. He was not proud of what he had done and when the British doctor gave him his hospital record with the report that his doctor had written he wanted to tear it up. There was nothing in that report that resembled the real Albert. He only thought better of it when another patient told him that it was proof of where he had been for the last six months. In times of uncertainty it was always good to be able to prove where you had been, so he folded it up and put it in the pocket of his uniform.

Albert couldn’t believe his luck. In the new hospital he had no reason to lie and therefore no reason to hide. He quickly made friends and found he had much in common with the man in the bed beside him. His name was Emil Heim and he was a farmer from southern Germany. A bullet in his spine had made his legs useless yet he and Albert both found solace by talking about farms, crops, cows and family. Often, however, Albert dominated the discussion and Emil thought he would never shut up. Neither did the other ten men in the ward and especially a young soldier whose bed was on the other side of Emil. But Albert didn’t care what he and the others thought. He was alive. The war was over. There was a great deal to talk about.

Albert told his friend about Volhynia with the soil so rich and wonderful that the Ukrainians had turned it with a wooden plough until the Germans came. The land was so fertile that a small plot was all you needed to feed your family and an acre of land was all you needed to pasture a cow. He told them too how Hitler had given that land to the communists and exchanged it for those cursed lands in Warthegau. It was the first time that Albert agreed with his wife that the land had been cursed. His wife was a smart one.

"It's remarkable," he said to Emil, "my brother always told me that I had a wonderful wife but I couldn't see it. Not until now." He missed his family more than he thought possible.

It was only when he was thinking about them that Albert became quiet. That's when Emil was able to talk and even though Albert only half listened, he began to understand how much they had in common. Emil spoke of his farm in the south, in the rolling hill district called Allgau, just before the Alps began. He spoke the same way Albert did about the land, with love and concern and pride. It pleased Albert to think there were men who loved the land as he did. In fact, Emil's love of the land was only exceeded by the love he had for his wife. There were tears in the man's eyes when he spoke about her; her gentleness, her healing touch, her understanding, her incomparable cooking. He spoke as if she were a saint. It was a little too much, and Albert was sure he was exaggerating, but a man who had sacrificed his legs in war was allowed to say whatever he wanted to, so Albert didn't question anything he said.

"Do you have children?" Albert asked his new friend. He missed his own so much.

"No," Emil said, "we've never been able to have children. It's the one thing we have always regretted."

"I have three children," Albert related, they were what he really wanted to talk about and he told Emil about his sturdy young son and his two pretty daughters. He related how desperately he wished to know where they were or whether they were dead or alive. He dreaded that even if they were alive they might be prisoners in the east.

"What will you do?" Emil asked him.

"I'll have to look for them."

In June, Albert was handed his release from the hospital. There was no apparent reason for him to be there and he was anxious to begin his search even though he had no idea where to start looking. His friends at the hospital wished him well and he had no trouble saying farewell to them until it came to Emil. There was a mist in Emil's eyes as they shook hands and Albert almost smiled thinking that the tears he was holding back were for him, that their friendship meant so much to Emil. It took him a few seconds to realize there was something else bothering his friend and Albert thought he knew what it was. "I wish I had a farm to go home to," he said as he was searching for something reassuring to say. He realized his mistake right away. He had wanted to say that he would trade his legs to know that his family was safe, but even that now had the ring of insincerity so he was smart enough not to make a bad comment worse by explaining it.

"I wish I had legs to walk home on," Emil replied instead. "I watch men leave and I know I never will. I'm not going to get better and I'm not getting worse, but they won't let me go." But Emil didn't want to wallow in self pity either. "What about you?" he asked to change the subject, "where will you go?"

"I don't know. I'm so anxious to find my wife and I don't even know where to start looking. Maybe I will have to go back to Poland to get them. Life is strange, isn't it? I can leave and yet I have no place to go. You have a home and can't leave."

As Albert picked up his bag, which contained a change of clothes and a coat for the bad weather, he hesitated. It felt awkward to be leaving. He didn't know which was worse, his own predicament or Emil's, but he began to suspect they could help each other. He had and absurd idea, but it felt right. It was as if his feet were stuck to the floor as the idea refused to leave. The more he thought about it the more plausible it sounded.

"To tell you the truth Emil," Albert explained, trying to make it sound as if he were asking Emil to do him a favor, "I have no idea where to start looking for my family. Why don't I help you to get home first and then I'll look for them?"

"How? I can't even walk."

"I'll carry you."

"It's impossible. It's hundreds of kilometers."

"Emil, you'd be doing me a favor. I have nowhere to go. I don't even know where to start looking for my wife. At least you have some place to go and how else are you going to get there?"

"But they won't let me go home."

"Who cares? Do you see any bars? The doors aren't locked."

"I can't even get out of my bed."

"We'll get a wheelchair for you," the offer came from the young man on the other side of Emil, the one they all called the boy. The whole ward joined in with enthusiasm. "Go with him, Emil," another voice across the way added and then others of their roommates joined in. "Go home, it's not doing you any good to be here."

Two of their ward-mates eagerly went off to search the halls for a wheelchair while Albert packed Emil's scanty things into a bag and two more men helped the paralyzed man to get dressed. Within minutes the two who had gone searching came back running behind a chair. "Hurry," they said, "we don't have much time. They've sent for the head-sister to find out what we're up to."

They picked up Emil and put him in the chair just as the stern nurse came into the ward. All eleven men stood in front of Emil to hide him and the chair. "So what are you boys up to?" she asked, condescendingly. She was tall and broad shouldered, more like an army sergeant than a nurse. "What did you do with the wheelchair you took?" The imposing nurse was not to be toyed with. She had been a head nurse for a long time. It was no use trying to hide it.

"Our friend Emil Heim is going home," one of them confessed, "and Albert is going to take him."

"Not under my nose you're not. Emil has not been released by a doctor and that wheelchair is hospital property."

"Sister, what does it really matter. He wants to go home to his wife."

"No, no, no!" she waved her finger. "Not on my shift. Patients don't leave without permission on my shift and hospital property does not disappear while I am on duty!"

"He took a bullet in the back for his country, at least it can spare him a wheelchair!" the boy pleaded.

"You men wait here and don't move. I'm going to get a doctor!" She called two nurses to stand guard at the door while she went to get an administrator.

"Damn it! What do we do now?" Albert asked.

It was the boy who came up with a solution. He opened the huge window to the street and said, "It's only a five-meter drop. We'll lower Emil and the chair. Get your bed sheets."

Tying their sheets together they lowered Albert down to the street first as passers-by gawked at the unexpected sight. Then the wheelchair came down and finally Emil dangled awkwardly in the air at the mercy of his friends above.

A crowd gathered quickly on the sidewalk below. The fastidious Germans demanded to know what was going on. One man in particular demanded to know if Albert was stealing from the hospital. He had to think quickly.

"No, no," Albert reassured him, "we were just seeing how fast we can evacuate the patients in case of a fire."

The man remained unconvinced. "Why did you lower the wheel chair first? Shouldn't your first priority be the injured man?"

"Well, what do you think costs more, the man or the wheelchair?" Albert asked.

The man hadn't even had time to digest Albert's ridiculous response when he heard screaming above. It was the head-nurse.

She was screaming, "Stop, stop!" Just as Emil was half way down. She had barged to the window and grabbed hold of the improvised rope. The woman was surprisingly strong. "Help, help," she kept yelling, "you can't do this. Stop them!"

"What is she complaining about?" the fastidious man asked Albert. He was immaculately dressed in a dark suit and tie. A typical German stuffed-shirt.

"She's afraid. She doesn't want to be next," Albert responded quickly. The crowd chuckled.

With the struggle going on above him, Emil had begun to swing and he was crying for help. Without the use of his legs it was hard for him to balance. He had to hold tightly onto the sheet. His feet were dangling only a few feet above the heads below. Albert began to jump, trying to grab Emil's feet and pull him down.

The nurse screamed more loudly. "Stop them! Stop them! They are stealing hospital property!"

Albert jumped and almost caught Emil by his left foot but as he came down Albert was grabbed from the rear. Both his arms were in a lock. He tried to break free but the man was strong. "Do not struggle," he said, and Albert recognized that it was the nosey man. "I'm holding you for the authorities. You are attempting to steal this wheel chair."

"For heaven's sake," Albert responded, "he's a cripple. How is he going to get home without it?"

"You can't just steal it. What would happen to law and order if everyone just took what he wanted?"

"My friend lost the use of his legs fighting for Germany. Don't tell me we don't owe him anything," Albert was angry. He thought he saw a sympathetic face or two in the crowd. "Help me," he cried as he tried to pull free, "my friend only wants to go home."

Emil was crying anxiously for help now. He had bumped into the wall several times already and the knot that was holding him was unraveling. His appeal was swaying the crowd. "Drop down," two men called up to him, "we'll catch you."

"Let me go," Albert demanded.

Finally, their comrades above had pried away the head-nurse's tenacious and sturdy fingers. Emil was being lowered again. He was almost down when the knot fully unraveled and he fell. The two men caught him awkwardly and fell back against Albert, who rolled over his captor. They all went to the ground. Albert jumped up quickly to see if Emil was hurt. He wasn't. With more help from the crowd Albert put Emil into his wheelchair and he started to run.

"Stop them, stop them!" the nurse was still yelling from the window. But the crowd was cheering the two escapees and drowning her out, while Albert's two assistants were sitting on the man who had restrained Albert.

Even out of breath, Albert and Emil laughed as they made their getaway. They were pleased with themselves, albeit surprised at their daring. It felt good to have taken the chance to be in control of their own lives. Unfortunately, they met their first disappointment almost immediately when they were informed that the trains were not running because of track repairs. The setback didn't destroy their optimism, however. They searched for the roads leading south and headed out enthusiastically. But by night fall they had traveled only a dozen or so kilometers and slept by the road side.

The next few days proved more interesting than either one of the veterans had imagined. In every town they passed through, they were stopped and questioned. They found that people were moved and inspired by the sight. Everyone assumed that the comradeship of the battlefield had been transformed into loyalty and brotherhood. It was one of the few good feelings left over from the war and it made people optimistic. More important, trucks and cars stopped and gave them lifts. They were given food, shelter and encouragement and occasionally even money. Everyone admired their courage.

On the fifth day, however, early in the morning, the wheelchair broke. A wheel got caught in a rut and the chair tipped over, spilling Emil onto the ground. Emil wasn't hurt but the wheel was hopelessly twisted. There was no way to repair it. Although they joked about telephoning the hospital for a replacement, the breakdown promised to make things considerably more difficult.

When they stopped laughing at their preposterous predicament, they were still left with the decision of how they should proceed. Emil was very self-conscious of the burden he was to Albert. He apologized again and again and insisted that Albert go on alone.

"That would be just fine," Albert joked, "but without you, I have nowhere to go. I know you believe your wife is a saint but what would she do to me if I came knocking on her door and told her that I left you on the road?"

"I can only imagine," Emil responded with a deep laugh like Albert hadn't seen from him before, "but it wouldn't be nice."

"We've come too far to give up. We'll just have to go as far as we can each day and make the best of it. I'll carry you as much as possible and when I can't carry you, we'll rest."

It proved more difficult than either man had imagined. Albert couldn't just swing Emil onto his back like one of his children, and neither could Emil jump up like his son Edmund. Albert had to squat and allow Emil to wrap his arms around his neck and then slowly lift him. But there was no way that Emil could wrap his legs around Albert and balance himself properly. It was a chore for Albert just to lift his friend into position and then get a hold on his legs. It was obvious that they had come to the most difficult part of their journey home.

They had only gone a few awkward feet when the rain started. Their fortune had been so good to this point that neither one could believe their luck had run out. The rain came down heavier and heavier and they were on the open road. And as if to accentuate their misery, on this day the cars just passed them by as if they couldn't even see them. They traveled like that for several hours.

Albert's back ached so they had to rest frequently even with the rain drenching them. Often, all that Albert had the strength to do was to let Emil cling to his shoulders as he dragged his friend along the roadside, stooping from the weight. As they struggled, they didn't hear the truck that approached them from the rear. The vehicle startled Albert and he slipped on the wet roadside and fell over, with his friend on top of him.

The truck stopped right beside them and they could see it was American. A soldier leaned out of the passenger's window and shouted through the rain, "Why do you carry him?" Albert and Emil found it hard to understand the strange pronunciation but when the soldier repeated it more slowly it was understandable.

"My legs are paralyzed," Emil responded, as he sat in the rain. Then looking into the man's uncomprehending face he said, "Kaput, kaput," and touched his leg. The soldier knocked on his rear window and yelled something foreign. In a flash, several soldiers jumped out the back. For a moment Albert and Emil were afraid, but one of the soldiers spoke understandable German and asked again about Emil's legs and translated it for his comrades. Then he asked, "Which way are you going?"

"South," Albert answered, already hopeful.

"Okay. The Lieutenant," the soldier said, pointing to the man who had originally spoken to them, "says we can give you a lift if you are headed in our direction."

Two of the American soldiers lifted Emil onto the back of their truck and Albert climbed in and sat beside him. As they drove south in the rain, they shivered under army blankets, but were so grateful that their smiles beamed at the American soldiers.

"Are you German," Emil asked hesitantly of the soldier who had spoken to him in German.

"No, I'm American. My parents were born in Germany!"

"Where are you headed?" Emil asked, determined to let them know where to let them off.

"One of our planes crashed in a river by some small town down south," the young man answered. "It's causing trouble. We have to get it out."

"Which river?" Emil asked.

He turned and spoke to his comrades in English and one answered, "Iller River."

Emil grew excited. "The Iller! It runs very close to my home, Reicholzried!"

"That's it," the German-American said, "that's the name of the town where the plane went down, Reicholzried."

"It's my home ... that's my home ...!" Emil said excitedly. He couldn't believe his ears.

The coincidence was a wonderful surprise, Albert being the most grateful for it, though he never said so. He smiled at Emil who beamed with joy, but Albert was so relieved that he just relaxed in the back of the truck eating the chocolate bar one of the Americans offered him. He watched Emil as he looked across the landscape, anticipating his home coming. There was a joy on his face that Albert envied and it made him sad to think that this wasn't his own reunion he was rushing to. The truth was that he was relieved to be going with Emil. But now he had to face the possibility of never finding his family. How relieved he was when he finally felt himself drifting into sleep.

As Emil kept an anxious watch on the road, he was too excited to sleep. The countryside became more and more familiar and his face beamed as he recognized landmarks. Indulgently the American listened as the happy man pointed out every familiar thing they passed. But after a while even Emil realized he was boring the soldiers to death and stopped.

"Why did you help us?" Emil asked the American. "We are your enemies."

"You were our enemy."

"Yes, it's over. But just the same for years we were shooting at each other."

"The lieutenant," the soldier said, indicating the man up front, "thought that you looked like you needed help. When you see a soldier carrying his wounded buddy you have to say to yourself, I would like a friend like that."

Emil nodded his understanding and looked out again at the beautiful green countryside of his home. It looked magnificent even in the rain. Only days ago he had thought he would never see it again, and now he had trouble controlling his emotions. He had a home and he had a friend. While he told the American that until a few weeks before he had not even known the man who was carrying him home, Emil cried. And when he explained how Albert had sacrificed going to look for his own family, the Americans seemed impressed.

"So your friend has no home to go to?" they asked.

"He has my home for as long as he needs it."

The rain stopped at dusk and Emil grew very excited. He began not just to recognize the landscape but the specific villages they drove through and after a while he knew the names of the people who lived on the farms they passed. He wanted to point out to Albert the landmarks that they had talked about for days but his companion just slept through his excitement. Soon they were crossing the railroad tracks outside the small town of Reicholzried. Shortly thereafter, where a country road joined the main road into town, Emil asked the Americans to stop.

He woke Albert. "We're home, Albert. We made it. It's just a few kilometers up that road," he pointed out.

"The lieutenant says that if it wasn't so late we would take you there," the American explained, "but we have to find the Burgermeister of this place and get ready for tomorrow."

"Thank the lieutenant and all your comrades for their kindness," Emil said. "We've come a long way and there's not much further to go."

It was dark when Albert carried Emil up the lane of the Heim farm. At the front door Emil insisted on standing when his wife saw him for the first time. She knew of his crippled condition but he did not want to greet her while being carried. So Albert put him down and let him lean against the door frame while they tried to straighten his badly wrinkled uniform. Then Albert supported him and knocked. Seconds later the door opened, slowly at first, and then it flung wide. "Emil, Emil!"

Thirty-Six

The longer Albert stayed with the Heims the more at home he felt. The trouble was that he felt so good that it was hard to think of leaving. It was almost as if Emil's wife, Marta, had used magic to soothe his body and to revive his spirit. It just wasn't right to feel that good, at least not while Alwine was still missing. He should have been out looking for her, but Marta made it so easy to stay.

That very first night Albert could already feel it. The way she fussed over her returning husband may not have looked unusual but it made Emil light up like Albert had not seen him before. Within minutes, maybe it only seemed like minutes, she had a hot meal in front of them and was listening as they talked about their ordeal on the road. They should have been weary but with Marta encouraging them they talked on into the night and it felt like the burden of the road just fell away. Somehow, as they related it to her, their ordeal seemed to wash away as if had been nothing at all. The important thing was that they were home. When they finally went to bed even Albert felt warm and at peace.

It continued like that for days. Not only was she a good listener, but Marta was as magnificent a cook, as Emil had promised. Nothing that came out of her kitchen was ordinary or mundane and it seemed that she never prepared anything the same way twice. When Albert commented that she must have a thick recipe book, Emil explained that she had no book at all, it all came out of her imagination. Delectable things to eat just appeared each day. Emil referred to it as a gift, one of many his wife had. In short order Albert had gained a kilo or two and did extra chores around the farm to work off the weight.

Marta was like a sponge when it came to listening and that made it so easy to talk to her. Somehow she was able to listen even while she worked. No matter what she was doing it seemed as if she was giving her full attention when you talked and was always urging you to get out your feelings. Not that she was intrusive or prying, no one could ever accuse her of that, and she was never harsh or even judgmental. Her brown eyes did not penetrate, but elicited trust, they were soft and clear and understanding. Albert found himself talking to her for hours on end and yet she showed no hint of boredom but absorbed it all. He never failed to feel better after talking to her.

When Albert talked about his wife, Marta said to him, "I like her. We will be good friends." With that prophetic statement despair and concern turned to hope and that hope allowed him to relax a little. It was so heartfelt and sincere that Albert could think of nothing else but bringing Alwine there to meet Marta. He could have sworn that a voice had whispered to him that his wife and children were fine. He knew he would have to go looking for them soon.

Marta especially enjoyed hearing Albert talk about his children. She loved children so much that she would ask Albert about his night after night. She laughed when Albert described their antics, especially his favorite, the vivacious Hertha. "How I would love to meet her," Marta would sigh.

Yet even when he told her about his son's rebellious side she would smile and say something sagacious. "Sometimes boys struggle to find themselves. They test their strength against their parents," she told him, "he'll be fine." Albert had to believe it.

It was difficult not to believe what she said and she appeared to understand so well.

She was so motherly that it was hard to believe that she and Emil had no children of their own. Albert was sure that if there was a perfect description of what a mother is, Marta would fit it. She looked like a mother, with soft features and those wonderfully tender eyes. It seemed she cared more for other people than she cared for herself. This was reinforced by the way she looked. Marta was slightly plump and always wore a plain dress and had her hair pulled back in a tight bun. She was much too busy to pamper herself with such vanities as hairdos and makeup. Yet everyone thought she was beautiful, especially the children that visited.

Sometimes Albert thought that Marta did more work than was humanly possible. He knew well that the work on a farm never waited for anyone and yet she accomplished it all. During the war she had hired a neighbor boy to do chores and now even with Albert's help there was a great deal of work. It seemed much easier working beside her. She handled it all and the housework too, cooking for three of them, caring for Emil and still she had time to listen. She was always listening. She was a saint. That was the way her husband described her and Albert was beginning to believe it too. Yet it was she who said to Albert, "I prayed for a Saint like you to come along and help my Emil. You are an answer to prayer."

The woman doted over her invalid husband. It was amazing how cheerful he was when she was near. She rubbed his legs and exercised them with her hands so that the muscles would not atrophy. Then she would have Albert help her to carry him into the kitchen or onto a couch, or to sit outside in the warm summer sun beside the house. And yet she hesitated to do anything for him that he could do for himself. Sometimes when Emil was struggling to reach for something on the table Albert would want to help him. Then he would see her quietly shaking her head. He understood.

In spite of her apparent sainthood, there was one thing about Marta that Albert treated with skepticism. It was a talent she had that Albert only learned about gradually as people appeared at their door day after day. At first he thought that all the visitors were Emil's friends, come to welcome him home. Mostly, Albert left them to their private moments and took a walk outside but after a while it was apparent that they came to see Marta, not Emil. They told her about their aches and pains, and talked about remedies. He could understand why people wanted to talk to her. She had a soothing way. However, he smiled to himself the first time he heard her recommend one of her home remedies. He remembered how his wife was always discussing cures with her friends and neighbors. It seemed that women all over the world talked about home remedies for illness. There was nothing strange in that. It was harmless. But when a teenage girl with a distressingly prominent wart on her nose came by with her mother, he almost couldn't control himself. Marta took an old black rotting potato from her cupboard and rubbed it on the wart and then told the girl to bury it in her garden. She promised that in a few days the wart would be gone. Albert was sure it was a joke but said nothing.

Nevertheless, day after day Albert heard parts of such conversations. Rashes, fevers, headaches, sores, bruises all showed up at Marta's door. She treated them all and Albert's curiosity got the better of him. During an evening meal he asked bluntly, "Do you consider yourself to be a doctor?"

"No, I'm not a doctor," Marta replied without offence.

"It's a gift," Emil eagerly explained, "she has the gift of healing."

Albert smiled, every talent Emil's wife had was a 'gift' as far as he was concerned.

"Some people call it faith healing," Marta explained, "some think it is a gift from God."

"So you heal people?"

"I don't heal. I don't understand how healing takes place but I get impressions about what people should do. Those who have faith in what I say heal."

"How did you learn to do this?"

"I didn't learn it. I can't remember when I didn't have the ability."

"Can you heal Emil's legs?"

Emil bit his lip. He was offended by the question and when Albert looked at his friend he felt sorry that he had asked such an insensitive question.

"Some things my gift cannot cure," Marta explained patiently.

"But she helps the pain to go away," Emil said firmly. He was his wife's biggest supporter.

"I can believe that," Albert said softly. He had not wanted to offend the couple but he knew that Emil didn't even feel any pain in his legs. He just assumed for friendship's sake that Emil was talking about his mental anguish.

Though religion was important to him, Albert never claimed to really understand the fine points of that inner power called faith. That was his wife's realm or his brother's, yet he could understand that people would want to believe Marta. Kindness and tenderness could make people feel better. He had seen it happen. But faith-healing was for others, not him. And yet he could remember how weary he had been when he arrived with Emil and how quickly Marta had made them both feel better. He shrugged it off.

Still, no matter how good he felt, Albert could not stay there forever. The mere impression that his wife was alive, even strong impressions like he had experienced, faded with time and were no substitute for having his family there with him. At Marta's suggestion he wrote to the Red Cross, giving the names of each member of his family, their ages and where he had last seen them. Answers were slow in coming, however, so it was time for him to go looking.

In early August, after the Allied leaders had their famous Potsdam conference there was encouraging news. Russia and the other eastern countries that the communists now controlled had agreed to expel their ethnic German populations. It was strongly felt that the presence of this minority had provided Hitler the excuse he wanted to invade them. Expelling the Germans would solve any future problem by taking away that excuse. No one knew exactly how many Germans lived in Russia, Czechoslovakia, Romania, etc. but it was millions and it was supposed that they would all want to come to the west. Germany accepted its responsibility to take them all back, even if they had been gone for centuries. The thing that excited Albert was that Poland had also agreed to expel its Germans. So Albert decided to explore the camps where the Germans were already arriving.

Marta embraced Albert with affection and instructed him emphatically. "You must bring your family back here." The offer was genuine and Albert felt no need to make any display of gratitude or even to make a polite protestation that it was too generous. He nodded and went off feeling good, and loaded with Marta's good food.

He explored the refugee camps, particularly Friedland, where the expellees were processed and granted German citizenship. His family was not there so he drifted, keeping close to the border, but did not have any particular plan. He knew he had to cross to the east but he was afraid of the Russians. He did not want to cross to the communist zone without being sure that he could return. When he reached a small city where the Elbe River was the border between east and west he got an idea.

On a warm night in late August, Albert took off his shoes and clothes, stuffed them into his backpack and started across the river. He used a piece of timber to float his pack across under the very bright light of the full moon. Slowly, with as little splashing as possible, he paddled in the placid river, clinging to the timber on which he had his life's possessions. As he approached the east bank he waded carefully onto solid ground and began to put his clothes on again. It had been easier than he thought.

But before he had his shoes on he heard the scrambling of booted feet across the pavement. They were on him before he could even get up. "Halt," a voice cried, "halt or we'll shoot."

Albert was taken to an old brick building only a few meters away and locked in a small room by himself. Looking through the tiny window, barely bigger than a crack, he could see the river and the lights on the other side. His bag and his shoes had been taken from him by the soldiers so he stood barefoot on a stone floor, shivering. Luckily his shirt and pants were dry.

The window was tall and narrow. At first glance it appeared to be much too narrow, but the more he stared at it, the wider it became. When he looked out, he was surprised that the ground was a mere two meters below. It was not a long drop. For a moment it puzzled him that they had locked him up so carelessly. At the door he listened for the guards and heard nothing; perhaps they were sleeping or had gone out on patrol again. When he opened the window the old hinges screamed. He waited to see if the guards had heard. "I just wanted some fresh air," he rehearsed, but no one came. It was a tight squeeze, one he could have made with ease if he hadn't put on so much weight at the Heim's. Still he managed to squeak through, ripping the buttons off his shirt and scratching his back till he felt the blood trickling down. He wanted to lower himself to the ground gently but the window ledge was too narrow for him to manoeuvre and twist. Bracing himself for the pain, he dropped to the cement below on his bare feet. It hurt but not as much as he had expected.

In a few minutes he was back in the water swimming for the lights on the other side, feeling the water stinging his scratched back. Half way across, when he thought he had made a clean escape, he heard the ringing of gun fire. He was never sure whether they were firing at him or some other German trying to cross the river. He got back to the west bank exhausted and frightened.

He passed out on the bank and woke up shivering. He had to find some warmth. He had no shoes, no food, and only a torn shirt and wrinkled pants. Crouching behind the corner of a building to get out of the breeze coming off the river he found some welcome warmth in the bricks that had been heated during the warm August day.

When morning finally come, a native, seeing Albert in this sad condition mistook him for a brave soul who had escaped from the communist zone. He congratulated him and pointed him to a soup kitchen where the homeless could get a free meal and shelter. He frequented the place for several nights. A worker there gave him an old pair of shoes and an old hat. But Albert still had to find his family so he got up early in the morning to walk on the river bank and study the other side. He spent his days roaming different parts of the riverbank, but the memory of the gunfire stopped him from trying to swim over again. There had to be a way to get to the other side safely. That was the key to finding his family.

He was so intent on his study of the other bank that he didn't see the woman approaching. When she called, "Hallo!" he ignored it, not believing that it was intended for him. He didn't know anyone here. But she persisted and when he finally turned to look, his mouth fell open. It was the faded yellow of her dress that he recognized first, and the familiar broad rimmed hat that shaded her face with its equally faded band of yellow ribbon. He stood there, staring as she waved to him from across the road.

"I knew it was you," she said as she came closer. "I saw you from my window yesterday and I thought there was something about you that was familiar. Today when I saw you again I was sure."

"Countess?" Albert asked, still not able to believe his eyes.

"Yes."

"I thought you were ..."

"Dead? I suppose there are a few people who would be surprised to hear that I'm still alive. But that's a long story. Like you, I am now here because Germany lost the war. Who would have ever believed that we could lose?"

"We?" Albert questioned. "Are you saying that you wanted the Germans to win?"

"You're surprised. I should understand how a person can be born in one country and have allegiance to another. When I was very young I married a German man. I fell in love with the country, but I couldn't live with the man. But that's another story. Over there," she pointed across the river, "if I am caught I shall certainly be executed. That's why we crossed the river ahead of the Russians. But it's much harder to cross now, the guards are making it more and more difficult. We've been watching you looking for a way across."

"My wife and children are still somewhere in Poland."

"Yes, many families are divided now. Getting across the river is difficult but not impossible. My friend and I have an idea you might be interested in. A sort of a business venture."

"I really don't think I have time. I have to find my family," Albert informed her again.

"Albert, look at yourself, your clothes are dirty and torn, your shoes are several sizes too big. You look like you have spent your last pfennig."

Albert looked down at his shoes. Up to now he hadn't even worried about having no money.

"Money makes everything easier," she continued, "money can open many doors for you. What my friend and I have in mind is an opportunity you cannot afford to forego."

"What is this business?"

"Come to the flat. We can sit down and be comfortable while we talk."

Ludmilla's flat was a small one bedroom apartment that overlooked the Elbe from across the waterfront street. On the second floor she opened a door and led Albert into a dingy apartment with a few pieces of old furniture. It didn't compare well even to her servants quarters on her old estate but she made no excuses.

"Darling," she called once they were inside, "I told you I recognized him. I brought him home."

The bedroom door opened and Albert blanched. It had never occurred to him that her friend was Ludwig Dredger. Albert looked in the direction of the door. He wanted to run and didn't know why he hesitated.

"Look at him," Ludwig laughed, "he looks like a rabbit ready to run for his hole." It was the same contemptuous Ludwig.

"The last time we met," Albert said rather nervously, "you were about to shoot me."

"Still afraid, Fischer?" Ludwig asked. As he turned to the countess there was a wry smile on his face. "I told you. We need someone with metal."

"Stop being so pompous, Ludwig," Ludmilla ordered. Her directness was a surprise to Albert but he was more amazed at the effect that her words had on Dredger. He was uncharacteristically quiet after her rebuke. Albert didn't have time to dwell on it, however. Ludmilla had turned to him now. "You must understand that at the time Ludwig thought that I was dead and that you were, well, responsible. But now it is different. You are the person we have been looking for."

Albert shook his head. He didn't understand.

"Why don't you just leave?" Ludwig scoffed. "Ludmilla saw a familiar face and thought it was a sign. How superstitious."

"He can do it," Ludmilla insisted.

"Do what?" Albert finally asked.

"Do you think you can get across the river?" Ludwig asked.

"I've already been."

"Oh, perfect," Ludmilla responded with renewed enthusiasm, "I knew you were the right man."

"Perhaps," Ludwig asked skeptically. "But what happened?" Albert hesitated to answer because he didn't want to respond to

Ludwig. "You were caught weren't you?" Dreger answered for Albert as he grew impatient.

"Yes," Albert responded a little sheepishly.

"We can help you get to the other side," Ludmilla said smiling.

"Why would you do that for me?"

"There is a price," Dreger shot back.

"I have no money," Albert replied, glad for the excuse not to have to listen to the arrogant Dreger anymore and turned to leave.

"You don't need money, Albert," Ludmilla explained, "we need you."

"Don't exaggerate Ludmilla. All we need is a body. One that can take orders."

"I'm not looking for work, I'm looking for my family."

"Your family is still in the east?" Ludmilla asked. She seemed genuinely concerned.

"Yes."

"We could help you get them out," Ludmilla offered and it sounded sincere to Albert.

"How?" he asked. Sincerity aside, he wasn't sure if he should trust her.

"Ludwig and I are returning to Berlin. We have friends there who can help."

"Why would you do this?"

"It's simple Fischer," Ludwig explained, "You help us and we help you."

"I don't understand."

"Of course you don't," Ludwig said contemptuously. "You don't need to understand. If you join us, your job will be to follow orders, not to understand."

"Ludwig," Ludmilla reproved him, "that is not fair and also not true." She turned to Albert, "We both know you are capable. I knew it the first time I met you and Ludwig knows it too."

"Preposterous," Ludwig blurted out.

"Stop it, Ludwig! It is true! In Volhynia Albert's boldness caught us both off guard."

"You mean his meddling."

"What do you want from me?" Albert asked again, not so much out of interest but to keep them on track.

Ludwig grunted. "Are you loyal to Germany, Fischer?" It was more of an accusation than a question.

Albert let out an involuntary little laugh. "You can ask me that after all that you accused me of?"

Dreger smiled, almost with delight. "You were surprised to see me, weren't you? You thought those two clowns in Zwickau had finished me. That was a minor inconvenience. I merely explained that I wanted to be certain that no Jews were allowed into Germany. I was almost promoted for what I did to you."

Albert wasn't sure whether to believe him. He was bragging.

"But that pea-brained Hohensee," Dreger continued, "he was at the front when I was through with him. And Wiesner, well, maybe someday, if he isn't dead already, I'll pay him back too."

"And me?" Albert asked.

"It doesn't really matter anymore. I was angry because I thought you exposed Ludmilla to the Russians. As you can see, she's safe. By God, Fischer, you may even have saved her life by making her run."

Albert relaxed as his old enemy continued. "The world has changed. Can you imagine, Russians occupying German territory, it's disgraceful. We have to endure it for now but it won't stay that way long. The German people won't tolerate it."

"What can they do?" Albert asked, wishing the man would get to the point.

"We work until Germany is strong again," Ludwig replied with conviction.

"We have a little scheme," Ludmilla explained. "But we need to get to Berlin. Just think, Albert, Berlin is where the East and

West meet now. They stare at each other across the border and wonder what the other is up to. That is where the opportunities will be."

"Opportunities?," Albert questioned.

"No clue, right?" Ludwig shot back with more contempt. "Peasants don't understand politics. We understand that this is beyond you but we need your feet and not your brains. We need a courier, with a certain, crude degree of savvy. It could be profitable."

Albert said nothing. He didn't like having his intelligence questioned but since he didn't believe Dreger, he didn't react. Whatever it was that Dreger had in mind was not likely to be profitable for anyone but him. In fact, Albert was looking for an opportunity to leave except that the Countess kept insisting that he stay. He wasn't at all sure what she was up to."Stay the night and think it over," she said several times, and when he started to leave again she brought out the Vodka.

Albert looked at her quizzically. Liquor was scarce.

"My last bottle. I brought it with me. At times it has been more helpful than money. I used it to bribe my way out of Poland, but this," she sighed wistfully, "is the last."

Albert decided to listen a little bit longer. He expected that they were going to elaborate on their plan but there was no more explanation offered. For a moment Albert supposed that they thought he had accepted their proposition, but he reminded himself that in spite of the liquor he had committed to nothing.

Now there was only talk of money, and at that prospect the Countess became positively gleeful. But Dreger drummed constantly about the intolerable occupation of Germany. Albert still didn't know what they had in mind and wasn't sure he wanted to know.

As they finished Ludmilla's last bottle of Vodka she was happy and started to speak in Russian. "Champagne is better," she said, "but Vodka is the drink of the proletariat. And I must become part of the proletariat."

Albert spoke Russian but had no idea what she was talking about. "What are you saying?" he asked, "and why are you speaking Russian?"

"Practice," she answered, smiling. "I had to speak Russian to get out. Now I will need it again to get back in."

It took a minute to click in Albert's brain. Perhaps the Vodka had slowed his thinking but he almost let the remark pass. Then it hit him. It was to be their same old game. They were talking of espionage and all Albert could remember was what happened to Edmund. Now he insisted on leaving, but at the suggestion, Ludwig flew into a rage.

"I told you it was an idiotic idea to get him involved," he shouted at Ludmilla. "You can't expect a peasant to have any vision. Look at him," he shouted into her face while pointing at Albert, "he's as frightened as a rabbit. I told you he couldn't handle it!"

"And of course you know everything, don't you," she shot back, in perfect control, her sarcasm bitting deeper because of it, "and what have you accomplished. You have nothing and without me you are nothing!"

Dreger's face turned red. Yet instead of flying into a rage he only grabbed his hat and stomped out of the flat slamming the door.

"Slam the door," she yelled after him, "that will show us how superior you are, how manly you are!"

She turned to Albert, smiled and sat down on the worn old sofa.

"He thinks he knows everything!" she finally said. "Everything has to be his way."

Albert struggled to change the subject. He was not interested in talking about Dreger. "How did you get out of Poland?"

"By the skin of my teeth!"

"You were lucky."

"Lucky," she said with contempt, "if a man had done it, you would praise his strength and cunning but because I am a woman it had to be luck!"

"I meant ..."

"Never mind," she cut him off, "no need to explain. Perhaps I was lucky, but I was smart too. I knew they expected me to run west so I went east, to the Ukraine. From there I made my way into Romania. It took me ten months to reach Berlin."

"We thought you were dead."

She laughed for an instant like a self-satisfied child who had played a huge joke on her elders. "Yes, even Ludwig thought so," she explained as she sank into the couch. "He was in anguish. But he deserved it. Do you know what he said when I told him you knew? He said, 'That bumpkin doesn't know anything!' Thank God I didn't believe him. Foolish Ludwig. He doesn't even like to think that I got out of Poland all by myself, because then he has to deal with the fact that he failed. He hates you, you know? You represent his failure."

As uncomfortable as Albert was with her sultry rambling, he thought he saw more closely what their argument was about. Ludwig had not flown into a rage at her derision of him because it was a game to them. They probably played it all the time and now they had him in the middle. The conclusion was inevitable for Albert, she had insisted on recruiting him because she knew it would disturb Ludwig.

Ludmilla smiled sheepishly at Albert. "He's such a baby," she said.

"Someday he'll hurt you," Albert observed.

"He loves me," she replied with a smugness that actually made Albert feel sorry for Ludwig.

"What will happen when he finds out you don't love him?"

Ludmilla looked at Albert with astonishment. "What makes you think I don't love him?"

"Ludwig may be blind but even I can see how you treat him. The only reason you insisted on including me in your plan was to annoy him."

She raised an eyebrow at his answer but did not protest. "I do love him," she finally said and then she hesitated before adding, "in my own way. He just wants more of me than I am willing to give. But, Ludwig won't hurt me. He thinks of himself as my protector."

"Is that why he killed Martin, to protect you?"

"You think Ludwig killed Hermann?"

"He said so himself."

"He did?" She was startled but soon she was shaking her head emphatically. "He told you that because he thinks I killed Hermann."

"He thinks you did it?"

"He thinks I killed Hermann and it injures him to think I had to do it myself."

Albert couldn't follow her reasoning and so he changed his question. "Why did you ask me to kill Martin?"

"Who better? You hated him even more than I."

"But I never asked anyone to kill him."

"From the minute I hired Martin to manage my lands he started to steal from me. He even found out that I was working for the Germans and demanded to be paid off. Fortunately, he was so absorbed in himself that it was easy to convince him that the Germans would reward him greatly for betraying Poland. For a while he was quiet, but then he began to make demands again. He even thought I should marry him. The pig wanted to move into my bed! He wanted to be a Count!"

"That's when you asked me to kill him?"

"Yes."

"I would have rather done it myself than ask Ludwig." She could see that Albert didn't follow her reasoning and explained. "Ludwig, in his own way is just like Martin. They both wanted to own me. If I had let him do that for me he would have been unbearable. That's the way it is with some men. Everything they do increases their claim on you. I would never have asked Ludwig to kill Martin."

"But he thinks you did it."

"Yes and I let him think it. It keeps him in his place. Ludwig is just like his brother. I was married to his brother when I was seventeen. He was worse than Ludwig. I hated him so much I had an affair with his brother. He divorced me, took my money, and threw Ludwig out too. I'll never let a man do that to me again."

Albert had no interest in her pathetic story so he asked again,"Do you know who killed Martin?"

"No. If you didn't do it I have no idea who. He had too many enemies."

"The Russians?"

"They wouldn't have shot him in the back. They would have executed him and made an example of him."

Albert had to agree.

"But when the Russians came he was angry. He said that Hitler and I had betrayed him, as if he knew anything about loyalty. He threatened me and when he demanded that Ludwig put him on the resettlement list everything unravelled. I didn't ask Ludwig to do it, I never even hinted at it. I couldn't stand the idea of being indebted to him like that. I just told him to get Martin out of the country and we could deal with him later."

"And you don't think Ludwig killed him on his own?"

"Why are you so obsessed with this still?" she asked, but didn't wait for an answer. "No, no. If Ludwig had done it, he would have told me and he would remind me of it every day."

"If you don't trust him why do you stay with him?"

"What should I do? I have no money and I am fond of him. I just don't want to be owned in the way he wants to own me."

"But you will leave him some day?"

"Perhaps, someday, when I get tired of him. Maybe when I find a man who will accept me on my terms." She sat beside Albert now and her tone changed. It was the way she talked to Dreger when they were in an amorous mood, in subdued tones, gentle and silky. He wasn't sure what she wanted. "What will you do if you don't find your family?" she asked.

"I don't know."

"I've always been impressed by you, Albert," she put her hand on his knee, "you're a very capable fellow." He took her hand off his knee. He was still holding her hand when the door opened.

"How cozy," Ludwig said.

"Oh, Ludwig, don't be ridiculous!"

"I heard you through the door. You think I don't know you don't love me? You think I don't know that you are only using me?" His voice rose higher with each utterance and finally he pulled out his gun and aimed it at Albert. "But I'm not going to be replaced by a farmer. Not a dirty Russian, Jew-loving farmer."

"No, Ludwig, no!," Ludmilla hurried to find words to appease her lover, "you misunderstood!"

Albert was sure he was dead. It felt so foolish not to have followed his first impulse to run away when he first saw Dreger again. Now as he looked into Dreger's eyes he saw again the same rage he had witnessed before, the rage he should have remembered. This time there was no one to protect him from the man except Ludmilla.

"Let me go," Albert pleaded, "I'll go away and you won't see me again."

"Too late. You keep turning up where you are not wanted, Fischer. You can't be trusted."

"Let him go, Ludwig," Ludmilla pleaded, "he's not interested in me. Let him go. I love you."

Ludwig stopped looking at Albert. His attention was focused on her now. He was like a child who had finally heard what he wanted to hear. Albert was too far from the door to make a dash for it and he didn't even want to risk trying to grab the gun. He had to stand there and wait.

Ludmilla was holding onto Ludwig now, tugging at the arm that was holding the gun but she couldn't budge it. She was speaking in those same seductive tones that moments earlier she had used on Albert. "Let him go," she pleaded, "I'll always be with you. You'll go to jail if you kill him. We can't be together in jail."

Ludwig turned to Albert again but the fire was out of his eyes. "Get out of here Fischer," he ordered. Albert didn't need a second invitation.

He was still scrambling down the stairs when he heard the shot. It stopped him in his tracks and he looked back. For a split second he thought that Ludwig had changed his mind and come after him. He let out a sigh of relief when he saw that there was no one behind him. A second shot followed quickly. Albert started back up the stairs but doors were opening and there was shouting. Soon a neighbor was knocking on the couple's door demanding to be let in.

Albert wanted to leave but he was torn between duty and fear. He knew he should stay and explain what happened to the police. But he was a stranger in the town with no one to vouch for him. They would keep him there forever and he had his family to find. Besides, sooner or later someone would discover that he had a history with Dreger and accuse him of murder. He couldn't risk it. Then the window of their flat flew open and a man appeared, yelling, "Police! Police! Murder! Murder!" Albert retreated to the river.

He had walked several blocks upstream by the time he heard the sirens. Looking across the Elbe he had the impression that he ought to cross now. Perhaps the patrols would be distracted by the commotion downstream. Quickly he took off his clothes and slipped into the river again. He told himself that he had to find his family. Nothing else mattered.

The only documentation that Albert carried was the German citizenship that had been granted by the Third Reich and his release from the German hospital. As much as he could, he avoided anyone in a uniform. But he was able to get directions to the nearest refugee camp, some twenty kilometers away. He walked there in less than half a day.

The camp officials, however, had no record of Alwine Fischer or any of the other members of his family. He left his name and the Heim's address on the camp bulletin board just in case. Then he hopped on a freight train to the next camp which was fifty kilometers to the south. There he got the same results. It was depressing but Albert would have gone on except that he was sick. He'd had little to eat and he was exhausted and broke. He didn't dare return the way he came, so he went further south. Soon he was on a train back to Reicholzried.

Marta Heim quickly brought Albert back to health. He may not have understood what power it was that made him well so quickly, but he was not about to question it either. After a few of Marta's meals and a few days of rest he felt good enough to return to his search. The only thing that prevented his leaving was Emil. Whatever his wife's gift was, it did not seem to help Emil. He was getting weaker but it cheered him to have his friend back, so Albert decided to stay a little longer.

But eventually Albert felt impelled to return to his search. He was off again in the last week of October with his friends' blessing and their renewed invitation to bring his family to the south. Even they recognized that he needed to try one more time before winter.

He checked the west side camps again but he did it without much hope. From the outset he knew that he would have to cross over to the east again. When he finally did it he hoped it would be for the last time.

He visited six different camps and found no trace of his family. Not even one soul from Belschewo appeared anywhere to give him any indication where his family might be. Were they all still trapped in Poland? He pinned his name and address on all the bulletin boards again and had almost decided to go home. He was so weary that all he could dream of was one of Marta's meals.

Albert was just about to give up for the season when he remembered there was someone in this east zone that his wife might contact if she escaped from Poland. He traveled to Zwickau, to the home of the woman who had taken compassion on them when they were in the relocation camp. Anna Sebastian was not at home but Albert left his name and address with her daughter and then turned around. It was now the middle of November and the days were growing not only shorter, they were also much colder. He was weak again and could feel himself wearing out. Perhaps in the spring he could try again and if he had to, he would even go back to Poland.

Thirty-Seven

For most of August and September, Alwine was allowed to stay at the Osciency camp to take care of her new baby. In the privacy of their small room she tenderly cared for the fragile boy, even though she could not nourish him adequately. Secretly, however, she resigned herself to his death. Her daughter Else loved him so much and yet Alwine did not know how to prepare her for the child's death. She cared so deeply that her mother could not disturb her joy. Gently the little girl held his tiny fingers and was content to be by his side whispering her love for hours on end. There was so much hope in Else that Alwine almost began to believe that her love might keep him alive.

During these days, Hertha and Edmund were sent out to work each day and came trudging back late in the evening. The children had to work the same long hours and just as hard as the grown ups. When they returned from the fields, they were just as tired and hungry.

Alwine felt sorry for all the workers. She wanted to make things a little more comfortable for them as they dragged themselves back to camp. In the afternoon she left little Kurt with the delighted Else and scrounged for wood for the cooking fire. But by fall the readily available supply of wood had been used up, so she had to range far outside the camp to collect enough. It took her hours as she had to bundle up the sticks she found and haul them to camp on her back. Then, in a large pot, she would cook whatever food the camp provided. Sometimes she was only given a little barley, sometimes a few beans and vegetables, but there was rarely any meat. Until it was depleted, she augmented the meals with fresh produce from the small garden she had rescued. It was a soupy concoction that she made. It barely served to fill the women's bellies and it wasn't very good, but it kept them alive.

Alwine's work was not assigned to her nor expected by her comrades. She did it because it was something that was needed and she assessed correctly that she was the only one capable of doing it. All the other women exempted from day labor were too sick to help. Men and women were only excused from the work in the fields if they could convince the camp officials that they were unable to get out of bed. Even Irene and Hedwig, as they finally struggled out of their beds, were immediately sent off to the fields again. If the camp officials got wind that anyone was feigning illness they dealt with them harshly. Sick as they were, Alwine did not expect them to help, but she did what she could for them too, when she wasn't caring for her own dying baby.

No one ever thanked Alwine for what she did. She didn't expect it. But it was noticed and respected. It was that respect, and the fact that it was generally known that Commissar Maczowiak was her friend, that soon made her the unofficial leader of the group. Yet if anyone mentioned it she became annoyed. She did not want to be a leader, she only wanted to get her family out of there.

One evening as the workers returned from the fields to eat the thin soup, one of the sick women now on the road to recovery, rose to eat with the others. Irene Weiss pounced on her, "We work in the fields all day! We get our share first!"

"Does that mean that only those who work can eat?" Alwine asked.

Irene looked at Alwine and turned red. She defended herself sharply, "It's only right that we eat first."

"She didn't mean you Alwine," Alma Neuman explained as though it ought to have been self-evident. "You work hard and you've got the baby to take care of too."

"Everyone does what they can," Alwine said quietly, "we have all been sick. We all know what it feels like."

"You are right, Alwine," Hedwig confirmed. "No one wants to get sick. Everyone has the right to eat." The women who knew Hedwig looked at her with astonishment as she defended her sister-in-law.

In the early fall, a rumor circulated that the Poles were going to release a number of the inmates. Several of the women came to Alwine and asked if the Commissar had told her anything about it. Alwine protested that she could not understand why they came looking for information from her. They became angry with her for feigning innocence. Since Maczowiak was her friend, they were sure that he would tell her first and make sure that she was one of the first to go. Alwine told them that she had not heard of anything like that and assured them that she did not expect any special consideration from Maczowiak.

Alma laughed, "Alwine, are you really that naive or do you just think we are stupid? We know that he gives your children the best placements. He even warns the Poles not to mistreat them."

"But he does that for all the children. Doesn't he?"

The women shook their heads. Alwine was embarrassed.

"It doesn't matter," Alma Neuman said, "we just want you to let us know what he tells you."

"If I learn anything, I promise to let you know," Alwine relented, shaking her head.

"Let's make a pact," Alma suggested, "we will all do everything we can to help each other to get out of here." It was a promise that no one had any trouble making. Alwine was sure that she would never be the first to know anything.

Somehow little Kurt hung onto life throughout the Fall, but he looked like death's shadow. It hurt just to look at him. His body consisted of a covering of skin over his bones. His face was hollow and his stomach distended. Alwine would not allow herself any hope, so when in October she was again farmed out she was sure that it meant the child's death. When she learned that she was to return to the old man Gzelak, she was sure her baby would not survive. But at least this time Edmund and Hertha were to be with her. Perhaps between the four of them they could do the work and take care of the child too.

Alwine was frightened that the old farmer Gzelak might still be angry with her so she determined from the beginning not to give him any reason to be unhappy about her work. For the first several days when Edmund woke up in the morning, he found that his mother had already been up for hours, working. The boy was astounded at the amount of work his mother accomplished, and yet she never complained.

"Why do you get up so early Mama?" Edmund finally asked, "Does the old man make you get up?"

"No, Edmund," she answered and thought it was a good teaching moment for her son. "If I do more than is expected then our chances of survival are better."

Edmund thought he had heard this kind of reasoning before. "Did Stefan teach you that?" he asked stone-faced.

"Yes, but he didn't need to. It is simply the truth. Our chances of surviving will be better if we make ourselves valuable to the Poles. If we do more than is expected then we will earn their trust and perhaps even their respect. Once we have their respect then they will help us to survive."

With his mother's sober but tender explanation, Edmund began to think differently. Determination began to take the place of bitterness. The next morning he rose with his mother and went to work with her.

Together they dug potato pits. A potato pit was a storage method that the Polish farmers used to preserve their harvest over the long, cold winter. It was familiar to the Volhynians farmers too and so Alwine had no problem doing it right. She taught Edmund to dig a pit about a meter square and a meter deep. The bottom was filled with the newly harvested potatoes and then they were covered with a thick layer of insulating straw. The rest of the hole was filled with earth and packed hard, creating a mound. In that way the potatoes were protected from the winter frost and were also easy to find in the spring.

The soil of Poland was not as soft as that in Volhynia. There was sand, clay and stones to be dug through. It was hard work but Edmund's experiences had already toughened him. He was no longer a sniveling, complaining boy, but a quickly maturing man of almost thirteen years. He had become determined in the last few months to do everything possible for his family's survival. Desperately he sought for a way for his family to escape. He was positive that a way out was going to present itself and he wanted to be ready to take advantage of it. He didn't know when or how, but he was sure it would come.

When the pits were all dug and filled and the harvest work lessened, Alwine and her family were sent back to the Osciency camp again. Miraculously, Kurt was still alive even though Alwine had been forced to neglect him. But now he screamed even to be touched, and so he had to be carried on a pillow to ease his pain. Hertha took care of him most of the time but Else was still his little guardian angel. Alwine, was warmed by her dedication and renewed in her conviction that it was her little daughter's intercession that persuaded the little boy that he should live. Yet it was a mystery how he hung onto life.

Irene Weiss was returned to camp in November too. She was sick again and badly discouraged. Even more sadly, she was now alone, and that, more than anything, accounted for her despair. Her two younger children had died and she did not know where her eldest daughter was. She feared the worst. Her daughter Hertha was now fifteen and extremely pretty, as her mother had been. Everywhere, the girl drew unwanted attention and now her mother could only imagine what was happening to her without her protection. The fate of her daughter tormented Irene. Everything in her life that was precious and important to her was now gone.

Alwine could remember the day everything began to change for her friend. It was hard for her not to feel some shame and guilt. After all, Martin had come that night to deal with her, not Irene. Since those days their friendship had altered until they hardly spoke to each other. Yet now, as she was defeated and sick, Irene allowed Alwine to help her. The rage was gone and there was the look of defeat in her eyes. Even the fires of hate had gone out, but so had her will to live. Alwine continued to nurse her and Irene did not object. She just looked at Alwine with cold eyes. "I'm going to die," she said without emotion.

"No. Don't speak like that."

"It's all right. I want to die. I have no one to live for any more."

"Don't talk Irene," Alwine told her, "save your strength."

"Why? I feel like the whole world has fallen on me!"

"You'll get better. We'll escape."

Irene shook her head. "Listen, Alwine, I was jealous of you."

"Jealous? Of me?"

"I was supposed to be the strong one, not you. When the war started, I fell apart but you stayed so calm."

"I was anything but calm, Irene."

"When August died I was so angry I hated you. I was so furious that Albert was still alive that I could have killed him with my bare hands."

"It wasn't your fault Irene. It was the war. We all said stupid things and made stupid decisions. We should never have taken the land Hitler offered us. It was cursed from the beginning."

"I was the one who reported Albert. He'd be here with you if it wasn't for me."

Alwine had suspected someone had reported her husband but was not prepared to hear this confession. She thought about it for a long time before it became clear to her. "Did you ever think," Alwine finally said, "that you probably saved his life? I'm glad he's not here. The Russians would have killed him just like they shot Johann."

The strength seemed to return to Irene's eyes as she realized that it might be true. She smiled and said, "I couldn't even do that right. I'm glad."

During the day Alwine was with Irene constantly, hoping her friend would hold onto life. She died, however, in mid-November as the weather began to turn cold.

After they returned from Gzelak's farm, Edmund's next assignment was easy. He was placed on a farm where there was little for him to do. No one cared that he idled half the day away, as long as he did his chores. Edmund didn't know that Maczowiak had put him there because he was worried about his friend Fischerova's oldest son. Luckily the boy was so small that he looked younger than his age. Equally fortunate, was the fact that no one but Maczowiak had bothered looking up the boy's age or the family's chances of escape would be limited.

Edmund noticed very quickly that Maczowiak spent a lot of time at this farm and that he was very friendly with the farmer's oldest daughter, a dark-haired beauty that even young Edmund was mesmerized by. The boy was familiar with the concept of infidelity and though he never saw them being intimate, he knew what was going on when they went into her bedroom. It surprised him that Maczowiak would betray his wife but he was not about to say anything.

In late November the Commissar rode out to the farm directly from Osciency not to see his pretty little mistress but to see Edmund. "I have some papers here that I need you to translate," he told the surprised boy, "they are in German."

Edmund became excited as he read the documents written on the letterhead of the Red Cross. "They're from the German Red Cross," he explained excitedly to the Commissar.

"I know that," Maczowiak laughed, "but what does the rest mean?"

"It says that those listed here have requested to go to Germany and should be released. Transportation arrangements will be made as soon as possible for them to go to Germany." Edmund scanned the list as fast as he could, hoping that his family was there. He found them on page two, Alwine Fischer and family. He held his breath because he wasn't quite sure how Maczowiak would take that news. He didn't know that the man knew exactly who was leaving and who was staying.

When Edmund came back to the camp that night he ran almost all the way. His side was splitting with pain and he could hardly catch his breath but he couldn't hold back his excitement. "We're going to be free, Mama!"

"What are you talking about, Edmund?" his mother asked tersely. She didn't like it when he raised false hopes and got everyone excited.

Still out of breath, all he could say was, "I saw the paper, Mama!" The boy was not able to explain the document he saw to his mother so both of them grew frustrated. "What are you talking about, Edmund? What paper?."

"But, Mama," he pleaded, "didn't you fill out some papers for the Red Cross?"

Alwine did remember the Red Cross papers filled out when she returned from Anna Pilusj's farm, but she had considered them insignificant and forgot them quickly. "Yes," she told her son, "there were some papers, months ago."

"Those are the papers," Edmund responded, now hopeful that his mother might believe him. "Commissar Maczowiak showed them to me. He wanted me to translate them from German. I saw our names, Alwine Fischer and family. We're going to Germany."

Now Alwine believed. But she was still prudent enough to keep it to herself and told Edmund to do the same. She did not know who else was on the list and so she preferred not to raise any false hopes. Edmund could not understand. He wanted to shout out the news to everyone, he was so happy. Only when Alwine explained how wrong it was to give hope and take it away again, would he listen.

Several days later, Maczowiak called Alwine to his office and asked her to bring Edmund along. He told her about the list but could give her no details about how and when they could leave. Instead he told her that there was a problem to resolve. Alwine knew by the way that he began that it was serious. He avoided stating the problem directly like she hoped he would.

"It's not likely that anyone will be leaving until the new year," he started, "and then it is mostly women and small children who will be leaving. The government, however, will not allow children older than thirteen to leave. They are too precious a resource." When he finished explaining this, he waited for a few minutes to let it sink in.

The confusion in Alwine's face was obvious to Maczowiak. He hoped she would understand, yet when she started to say, "But Edmund is almost thir ..." He put up his hand to stop her.

Edmund was quicker to understand. He stood up and declared, "I will be twelve years old in a few days."

"Good," Maczowiak smiled, "then there is no problem here. Of course it is easy to see by your size that you couldn't be any more than eleven or twelve-years-old. There must be some mistake on your documentation. These things happen."

December of 1945 passed and Alwine almost began to think that the whole thing might have been a hoax. But then on January 4 the list was posted. They had two days to get themselves to the village of Chelm, where on the morning of the sixth of January a train would arrive to take them to East Germany. There were only a dozen names from the Osciency camp on the list but for those who were on it there was great relief.

That night Alwine could not sleep. She remembered her pact with the other women of the camp and knew that there were two women on the list who were not present. Alma Neuman was one, the other was Hedwig Fischer. Early in the morning when the others were leaving for their daily work assignments, Alwine asked the whereabouts of Hedwig and the other woman. They were not far from each other. Alwine pulled a blanket, folded like a shawl, over her shoulders and started out to keep her promise.

It was cold that January, not at all like the previous year. It reminded her more of 1940 when the freezing temperatures and wild snow storms had made for a miserable ordeal during the resettlement to the Wartheland. But last year, thank God, January had turned mild as she walked for days with her children when their escape had been cut off. Now again a January flight was imminent with all the possibilities of hardship and sorrow that had been present in those other years. However, it was freedom that was at stake and that made the risk irrelevant.

As Alwine walked, wrapped in her blanket against the chill, her feet freezing in her worn out boots, she shivered and considered turning back. She told herself that it was the effort that counted, but then she wondered how she would feel if she were left behind. There were two farms she had to reach to leave her message of freedom but the cold was so discouraging and she had other obligations too. Somehow she had to arrange for her family to get to the train station in Chelm by the morning. She didn't even know where Chelm was, never mind how long it took to get there. It worried her but so did the thought of failing these women. How could she live with herself if they were left behind when a simple message could have told them that they were free? It was a matter of conscience, and she always lost arguments with her conscience.

She planned a circular route. First she would walk the five kilometers to the farm where Alma worked. Then, if she continued on she would reach the road where Hedwig was. That road curved around and eventually came back to the main road just half a kilometer from the camp. If everything went well, she would only be gone for the morning. She only worried about the reception she would receive from the Polish farmers. How would they receive the news that their workers were free? The best thing would be to get in and out quickly.

She reached the first farm fairly quickly but a big black dog went wild at the sight of her. Luckily he was chained up in the farmyard. Alwine hurried across the yard to the barn but it was so icy she could barely keep her footing. By the time she made it to the stall she had fallen several times and she was almost out of breath.

She hoped to find her friend quickly and luckily Alma was up already, hard at work milking. "Alma," she called softly and her friend popped out between two cows surprised to hear her name.

"Alwine? Is that you?"

"Alma, the Red Cross list is posted. Your name is on it. You have to be in Chelm tomorrow at 5:00 a.m. I don't know more. I have to leave right now."

Alma was almost overcome with excitement. She rushed toward Alwine insisting that she repeat her message, in case her ears had deceived her. But Alwine wanted to leave quickly. Her friend became agitated and cried. "Alwine, please stay and explain it to them. They won't believe me!"

She shook her head. "It's not possible."

Before Alwine could turn to leave, the farmer came through the door and shouted at her. "Who are you? What are you doing here?"

"Delivering a message," Alwine said, trying to stay calm.

"What kind of message do you have?" he came and bellowed in her face. "If you have a message for anyone on this farm you will come and deliver it to me first!"

Alwine tried to leave but the man grabbed her wrist and turned it painfully.

"Please don't hurt her," Alma pleaded, "she just came to give me the news. I have to leave to catch the train to Germany."

"It's a lie! You will never be allowed to leave! Get back to work." Then he turned to Alwine, "I'll teach you to bring such lies and upset the work here." He pulled her out of the door sharply.

"It's not a lie," Alwine protested over and over, but the man was not listening. He pulled her toward the house. When for a second she felt his grip loosen on her wrist she pulled it away. She began to run but in only a few steps the farmer caught her and started to pull her again. The agitation in the yard caused the dog to strain at his leash, barking and yelping like a hound being held back from the chase. "I'll feed you to my dog if you try that again," he threatened as he twisted her wrist a little more. It hurt so much that Alwine winced and stumbled. The farmer's feet slipped on the ice and he fell hard on his tail bone and he had to let go of Alwine again. She scrambled to her feet and began to run despite the ice. Somehow she made it to better footing without falling.

"Come back," he raged at her but Alwine just kept on running. The dog was barking even more wildly now. She was afraid he would break off his chain.

Alwine only looked back when she got to the road. She saw the man unchain the dog and point in her direction. She felt a lump rise in her throat and turned quickly to run. She never realized that once the dog was unchained, all he wanted was to play with his master and was no longer interested in a stranger he could not see. However, Alwine kept running until she had fallen so many times that she was wet and her sides ached. At any moment she expected to see the dog closing in on her.

Alwine no longer had any desire to finish the rest of her mission. She had turned the wrong way, back toward the camp, and could not chance turning back. She felt sick. This was a disaster. She was so close to having her family out of Poland that she did not want to risk missing that train for any reason. Some things were just too much to ask of a person. She felt that Hedwig would understand if she just knew the circumstances.

As she reached the point where the side road met with the main road again Alwine hesitated. She could go down that road and reach Hedwig but it was twice as long as the route she had planned. She had no idea when she would get home and there were arrangements to make. Fighting every step, she started down the road to the farm when she really wanted to go back to her family. Behind her there was no sign of the big black dog or the farmer and she began to say to herself, "Not all Poles are like that." She took a few more hesitant little steps down the road and looked back continually in the direction of the Osciency road. She didn't know why she was going this way but pretty soon she was too far along to think about turning back.

In less time than she had suspected she stood at the bottom of the farm lane. The white picket fence stood out against the snow. She stayed there a long time berating her lack of courage until someone finally came down the lane shouting in Polish, "Hey, you there, what do you want? Are you going to stand there all day?" It was too late to leave now.

"I want to see Hedwig Fischer. I have urgent news for her from the camp."

She was led to her sister-in-law without any more questioning. It was with dismay that Alwine realized that Hedwig was ill again with fever. She lay on a bed of straw, but smiled as Alwine came close. "You always come when I am sick," Hedwig said feebly but cheerfully. It was so strange to see Hedwig smile that Alwine almost forgot about her message.

"They are letting us go but we have to get to Chelm to take the train," she finally said.

"I'm glad for you, Alwine."

"Do you think you can make it, Hedwig? I'll help you!"

"I've known for a while I wouldn't make it. But I'm glad you came. I need to say something to you. You've been nothing but a friend to me and I treated you so badly. The world is different when you are dying. I need to apologize."

"It's in the past Hedwig. It's nothing."

"I was greedy. I wanted too much from Johann and from my sons. Now I have nothing. But I need to tell you something. I want you to know that I killed ..."

"Oh no, Hedwig," Alwine interrupted, "you didn't kill Johann. The Russians shot him at the roadside. It wasn't your fault at all."

"Not Johann. I shot Martin. I killed him. I'm not even sure anymore what I was thinking. I hated him even more than I hated Albert. I thought they would blame Albert and then somehow Johann and I would get our land back. I imagined that everything would be alright if they were just dead. I'm sorry."

"Oh, Hedwig."

"It's all right. I don't want you to forgive me. I spoiled everything in my life. I had a good man and I didn't appreciate him. I just wasted it all. Even my sons hate me."

Alwine had no idea what to say to Hedwig now. She couldn't offer forgiveness, not for murder, that wasn't her right. She turned to leave quietly but her conscience wouldn't allow it. She couldn't be that cold. There were a thousand words of comfort she could have given, all of them lies. Instead she stooped and kissed Hedwig on the forehead like a sister and said, "Get well and come to Germany when you can." Then she left.

Edmund and Hertha greeted their mother excitedly as she came into the camp. Hertha was speaking so quickly that her mother could not understand anything she was saying. "We don't have to worry about getting to the train, Mama," she was saying, and "We'll pay with the featherbeds."

"What are you talking about?" Alwine asked, but the girl was too agitated to explain it more clearly.

"Stefan was here while you were gone, Mama," Edmund broke in, "he has hired a farmer with a wagon to come to the camp and drive us to Chelm. When we get there, we will give him the featherbeds as payment."

Two things occupied Alwine's attention for the rest of the day. The first was trying to scrounge up enough food to sustain her family on the train. Under normal circumstances it was only a short distance to Germany but Alwine had no illusions about Polish trains or their efficiency, especially in winter. In a cloth sack she placed a bit of stale bread and tiny pieces of cooked potatoes. It wasn't much but it was all she could gather.

The second thing she worried about was her friend Alma Neuman and she kept looking for her, hoping that she would be able to escape the brutish farmer. But all day she did not appear, so toward evening Alwine asked to see Commissar Maczowiak. She told him of Alma's plight and her fear that she would not be allowed to leave but he could not or would not offer any solution to the dilemma.

"She must get there on her own," he said coldly, making Alwine wonder if she had done the right thing in coming to him. "There are many, Fischerova, who feel that it will take an eternity for the Germans to repay what they have done to Poland. Many feel that you Volhynians in particular should have no rights but should be treated as thieves and scoundrels. They feel that none of you ought to be allowed to leave."

"But the Red Cross ..."

"Where was the Red Cross when we Poles were being driven out of our homes? Where was the Red Cross when Alma Neuman beat a little Polish girl for dropping a tray of dishes? We are discovering death camps all over the country where Poles and Jews were systematically tortured and killed. Where was the Red Cross then? Be glad you are leaving but don't ask me to rescue every German you feel sorry for. It's just not possible, and I have no inclination to try!"

In the middle of the night the farmer came to the camp with his wagon to pick up his passengers. Wrapped up in their featherbeds the children kept themselves protected from the cold and Alwine kept the baby close to her and marveled all the time that the child had survived so far. The feeling of joy, however, that she often had anticipated when thinking about finally leaving Osciency did not come.

They left in silence as had all the others who were going home. The pain was so great for those who were left behind that they could not bring themselves to say any farewells. Somehow, joy did not seem to be the appropriate emotion for the time and the fact that Alma had never shown up at the Osciency camp only added to the muted feelings. Alwine did not say goodbye or thank Maczowiak either, it seemed inappropriate. Even Stefan did not come to say farewell.

Thirty-Eight

As Alwine stood on the platform of the train station watching her featherbeds drive away on the back of the farmer's wagon, it finally hit her. Those blankets were the last vestiges of her life in Volhynia and that false land they had called Warthegau. She was thirty-six years old and everything she had worked for was gone, disintegrated, like straw in a furnace. Soon there would be nothing left to indicate that she and her family had ever been there. How could so much work have come to nothing?

She wanted to cry but it wasn't the right time for that kind of selfish emotion. How could she let her children see her crying? Especially now when they were finally leaving this prison, she had to be strong for them. And yet she was so tired and hoped that they would swiftly reach a place where she could stop pretending to be strong, a place where she could mourn for herself and be selfish.

Right now, however, her children were with her, and she had to hold her emotions together. The children meant more than anything else. Who would not give up everything to save their children? She would! Without hesitation she would give up the world for their safety, for their freedom, for their futures and their happiness. They were the only heritage that was absolutely irreplaceable. They were worth more than featherbeds, furniture, farms and maybe even faith. What would her world be like without the vivacious Hertha, or Edmund, now so serious and determined? Life was unimaginable without the gentle little Else to hold and to comfort. They were the real treasures of her life and she was lucky to still have them.

As Alwine reflected on the last year, it amazed her that they had all made it when so many had died. She was overcome with emotion again at the realization that her family had come so close to oblivion, and yet her children were with her. The disappointment she had felt so intensely only a few minutes ago turned into relief. She whispered a prayer, the first one in a long time that was filled with gratitude and not selfish pleading.

Her baby cried just then and she was back to reality. She bit her lip as she looked at him, so small, bony and weak. There could be no illusion on this point. This train ride would not help his condition. The scraps of food she had, she intended for the children and not for herself. What she had eaten in the last few days would hardly sustain her, never mind produce milk for a baby. The train was a sentence of death for the child. She was sure of it. Yet what could she do? Osciency had worn them all down, now she had little nourishment for the child.

At that moment she remembered that Edmund remained positive, even now, that his little brother would live. Faith was a good thing and there was nothing wrong with borrowing a little from your children when your own ran out. Edmund had been right about their escape from the camp and maybe he was right about the baby too. Alwine put her arm on her son's shoulder and was grateful for the strength she felt there. It hadn't been there last year and he didn't pull away from her touch as he would have then, but he stood straight and strong as a pillar. The boy looked up and smiled at his mother, he was full of confidence now. How relieved Alwine was that he was with her. His strength made her feel as though she could go on.

But the train did not come. Alwine looked down at her little daughter, Else, six years old, and saw herself. She had been that age when they had been put on the train for Siberia more than thirty years earlier. She could not get over the feeling that her life had thus far been a series of escapes and train rides that had all ended in disappointment. She did not want this one to finish that way too.

The train had been promised for 5:OO a.m. No, she told herself, that was not right, they had not been promised that at all. The camp officials had merely told the Germans that they had to be here by 5:00 a.m. There was nothing magical, she convinced herself, about the time that she should be so worried when it passed without any sign of a train. When they had arrived, the platform was already full of Germans, most of whom had been here waiting for hours or even since the night before. Alwine could not believe they were all waiting in vain. They were from many different camps and they could not all have been misinformed.

The train was nowhere in sight even an hour after the sun was up. This disappointment brought back familiar feelings that reminded Alwine of why she refused to celebrate her family's release prematurely. It was impossible to know whether or not the Poles might change their minds at the last moment and stop them from leaving. Every second that the train did not arrive increased her anxiety that something like that had happened. It was as if the old superstitions rose up and muted Alwine's hopes. She feared that too great a show of happiness might doom their escape. It was what her father would have taught. Pride was still the great enemy.

The train was several hours late, but it did eventually come. As the engine screeched to a halt in front of the station, Alwine became nervous. A metal clad freight car stopped right in front of her. She had seen a train like this before and she looked anxiously up and down the length of it until she saw a wooden car. As her friends and neighbors climbed into the car in front of them she led her family to the next one. "Why are we going here?" Hertha asked, wondering why her mother wasn't joining with the people she knew. Alwine couldn't explain and just said, "I just feel better about this one." She realized then that she had never told her children about Siberia, not one word. But it was Edmund who supported her by saying, "It's a good idea Mama. Metal gets hot and cold much more quickly than wood. I learned that in Hitler Youth." Alwine nodded, she knew too.

There were only about a dozen people lying on the straw, but it was so reminiscent of her trip to Siberia that Alwine had to remind herself that this train was headed for freedom. Even the passengers who watched as Alwine brought her family aboard had the same blank stares and offered no hand to help them. Kurt whimpered as Alwine lifted him up to Hertha, and the girl heard a man say contemptuously, "Now we have to put up with a crying baby."

As Alwine sat her family down only a few feet from the drafty door, the cold stares made Hertha shudder. She tried smiling at an old man sitting close by but all she got back was a resentful glare that made her retreat to her mother's side. Else clung to her mother too and Alwine tried to reassure her children, "Everyone will feel better when we get to Germany. People will be much happier then."

"What do we have to be happy about?" a woman by the door shot back in German, but with an accent that Alwine could not place. "We have been expelled from our homeland. Because of our language we had to leave everything and go to Germany. My family hasn't lived in Germany for a hundred years. We didn't ask for this trouble, but now they punish us all, 'You speak German,' they point at you and say, 'you have to leave.' So why should we be happy?"

"We should be happy to go back to Germany," Edmund spoke up attempting to defend his mother.

"I was happy in Poland," a man said. "I had land and now I have nothing. You be happy, I want to be angry."

The train moved slowly, almost as if reflecting the somber attitude of its passengers. The car was cold and Alwine had her children huddled together against the freezing temperatures. Else snuggled as close to her mother's side as she could, both for warmth and safety, while Hertha and Edmund completed a semicircle around the baby. Almost from the beginning it seemed like they were not welcome in the car and the feeling was confirmed by the ignorant grumbling they could hear each time little Kurt cried.

Only an hour after they had left Chelm, the train stopped and the doors opened. Russian soldiers jumped up and walked slowly through the car looking each passenger in the face and asking to see their papers. Those who acted suspiciously were questioned at length and sometimes removed from the train. Edmund could see through the door that several men had been dragged off the train and were being hauled away.

But it was Kurt's crying that seemed to upset the other passengers the most. The baby was so fragile that he could not suffer being carried in anyone's arms, no matter how tenderly they held him. He would still only tolerate being carried on a pillow, but it was harder to keep him warm that way. When he was awake, he cried, but it was not the demanding cry of a healthy child, rather the whimper of a starving one. His annoying whine was the only noise that could be consistently heard in the car along with the rolling of the wheels. People didn't want to talk, they just wanted to complain. The anger became louder as the baby continued whimpering, but there was nothing that Alwine could do. She had no milk to feed him. She could only pray for quick arrival in Germany but the train moved so slowly that it seemed like it didn't want to arrive there. She apologized to the most vocal complainers. They wanted anything but an apology yet they were appeased temporarily. The whole thing caused Edmund and Hertha to become defensive. Without intending to, they placed themselves in front of their mother, blocking their family from the rest of the passengers.

There were more stops that day and at each one a few more passengers got on until Alwine feared it was going to be exactly like 1915. Fortunately, that did not happen and there was never any danger of the car being over crowded, but the train did move ever so slowly and cold winds began to blow through the boards chilling everyone. As they sought to protect themselves from the cold no one complained about the whining of a little child anymore.

In the morning, the train seemed to be creeping so slowly that it seemed to the passengers that they could have walked faster. One frustrated man opened the sliding door slightly to see what was going on. He only made a crack but immediately a bullet came crashing through the door, causing splinters to fly as it ripped through the dry wood. Quickly the door was closed but a volley of bullets followed, raking the side of the car.

Everyone scrambled to the floor. Alwine made her children lie flat but the jostling made the baby cry. "Shut that baby up!" a man screamed from the other side of the car. "Shut him up, he's drawing their attention," another accused. It was too absurd a charge for Alwine to answer and she didn't know what to say. She tried to pull Kurt closer to her but the movement only made him cry more.

"You shut him up, or I will!" the man raged again as he started to rise up. Immediately, Edmund jumped to his feet and placed himself squarely between the man and his mother, his fists clenched and eyes burning. He was small, but he had a look of determination that made the man think again. He waved at Edmund as if he were waving off some fly and lay down again. The lines were now clearly drawn; it was his family against the rest of the car. When Edmund finally sat down he placed himself between his family and these other Germans.

The rest of the day was no better for the baby. He was so hungry and thirsty that all he could do when he was awake was cry. His mother hadn't been able to breast-feed him in months and now there wasn't even a drop of water to feed him. When he slept, even Else was apprehensive that he would wake crying.

In the late afternoon, while the baby was sleeping, the train slowed down again for no apparent reason that the passengers could see and then it came to a dead stop. For over an hour it made no attempt to move. Finally someone got up the courage to look outside through a bullet hole and then started to open the door. "Don't open that door," a woman cried fearfully, "they'll shoot at us!" But there were no soldiers and there was no obvious reason why the train had stopped. The door was shoved all the way open and cold air rushed in. The cold draft woke Kurt and he started to cry.

Edmund noticed a well in an abandoned farm yard, only a few meters from the door and told his mother he was going to get some water for the baby. Before she could stop him, he retrieved a cup from their bag and jumped off the train. He hopped over an old fence and was at the well in a flash.

The well was shallow and there was water down there that had not frozen, but he couldn't reach it. There was no bucket and even the old rope was rotted away. Edmund looked around desperately but could find no way to bring the water up. Finally he undid his coat, pulled off his shirt and wrapped it around a stick which he lowered into the well and brought it up again, drenched. He had the wet shirt in his hands when the train lurched forward. "Edmund, hurry!" his mother shouted when she felt the movement. The train lurched a second time and kept rolling forward. Edmund stuck the cup in his coat pocket, bunched up the wet shirt and ran. The train was moving too slowly for him to really be worried but he felt his mother's anxiety and ran harder. With one hand he threw the shirt onto the train and started to grab hold. All of a sudden there was a hand in his face pushing him back and he fell down. Alwine moved so quickly that she even surprised herself. She handed the baby to Hertha and jumped to her feet in what seemed an instant. With a push that came from pure anger she shoved the man to the side. He went crashing to the floor and banged his face into the frame of the car door. His foot slipped and he was only saved from falling out by grabbing the frame of the door. Alwine was relieved that he held on, but only because he would have fallen right on top of Edmund as he ran beside the train. Quickly, Edmund grabbed hold of the edge of the car and vaulted himself onto the train while his mother pulled on his coat.

The culprit who had pushed Edmund was the same man who had threatened Kurt. Alwine wanted to say something to him, something evil and disgusting but she couldn't form the words. She had done enough. Her face was almost as red as the blood flowing from the vile creature's forehead. It was the sight of his blood that shocked her into a realization of what she had done but she didn't feel sorry. She was shaking at the realization that even she could be provoked to enough anger to kill.

Edmund retrieved his shirt and quickly squeezed out as much water as he could into the cup. There was more than enough left in the cloth to fill it full and Hertha dribbled drops of it onto the baby's lips. The boy sucked in the moisture. "Only a little bit at a time," his mother warned, "it's cold and he's not used to it. Warm it up in your hands first." Else thought it was great fun to let her brother suck the moisture off her finger tips and worked at it diligently until their mother said it was enough. It seemed to satisfy his immediate craving and in a few minutes the boy was asleep with his two fingers in his mouth. That was a good sign.

No one complained any more when Kurt cried. It seemed that the Fischers had paid their dues as passengers on this train and everyone acknowledged their determination to survive. Still, Edmund, kept a steady eye on the old man who had tried to push him off the train. He shivered whenever the man shot a glare back at him. The blood drying on his forehead made him look even meaner. "What's the matter Edmund?" his sister Hertha asked as she saw her brother's reaction. "It's cold without a shirt under my coat," he answered. He didn't want to admit his fear.

There was a collective sigh of relief when the train crossed the bridge over the Oder River into Germany. They were out of

Polish hands now but they learned quickly that they were not out of Russian hands. The familiar Russian uniforms were everywhere that the train rolled and it seemed like all of Germany was in Russian hands.

The refugees were deposited in a camp. It was not dissimilar to Ossenholz, except that it was a converted warehouse instead of a barn and the inmates were not sent out on daily work details.

What struck Alwine immediately was how impersonal it was. She had expected a warmer welcome. This was supposed to be her homeland. Even just being there should have made everyone feel better. But the staff talked indifferently about their plight and gave orders as if they were directing machines. At first Alwine thought it was only the contrast she was seeing to the deeply personal hate that the Poles had displayed for the Germans. Then with the passage of days she understood that it was much deeper than that. It was the look of defeat.

The first thing that the German officials had required of them on reaching the camp was that everyone be deloused. Their clothes were taken from them and they were required to shower with a harsh medicinal smelling soap that made the children cry. Later, when their clothes were returned to them, that same strong, soapy odor permeated every fibre. An attendant explained that for reasons of sanitation that all arrivals from the east had to endure this. The woman standing beside Alwine asked, "Do they think that there are no lice in Germany?" Alwine responded, "German lice must be cleaner than Polish lice."

The camp food was not much better than it had been in Poland and there seemed to be even less of it. Else refused to eat except when her mother coaxed her and even then she stomached only a few bites. For Kurt's sake, Alwine ate all she could.

No matter what his mother tried, it did little good for him. He neither gained weight nor lost it and Alwine still could not understand how he hung onto life. She had borne other children in both the lean years in Volhynia and also when there was plenty in Warthegau. So many had died. She had seen seemingly healthy children turn sick and die in days or even hours, but this baby, who had no help and no resources should have died and didn't. It just wasn't logical. Even the camp doctors just turned their heads away saying there was nothing they could do. Yet day after day the baby let it be known by his weak whining, protest that he was still alive.

Within days of their arrival the Fischers were moved to a different camp. It was to make room for more eastern refugees arriving almost daily. In a few short hours Alwine and her children were on another freight train and eighteen hours later they were unloaded at another camp within the Russian Zone. Once again they had to submit to the delousing and then settled into their new lodgings. The conditions were no better and the strange detachment of the camp workers was still evident. However, Alwine and her family were there for only a week and then they were delivered to a third camp, and forced to submit to another delousing.

Else still refused to eat the food and her mother began to worry about her. She was growing thinner each day. One morning the little girl came into possession of one small potato. Else had seen it roll off the back of a truck that carried food into the camp and very swiftly grabbed it, carefully protecting the precious tuber between her hands until she gave it proudly to her mother. It was a very small potato but Alwine boiled it for Else alone. She took her own ration of milk and made a small potato soup that Else gobbled down all by herself. It was such a relief for her mother to see her eat that she laughed out loud as the usually dainty little eater slurped down the soup and smiled at her mother.

While Alwine occupied herself with the day to day survival of her family, having given up trying to deal with the unsympathetic camp personnel, Edmund roamed the camp trying to understand what was going on. He was like a little spy on a mission, darting from place to place, reading all notices and listening to all the camp talk. He read the camp bulletin boards, having no way of knowing that his father had once pinned his address on those same boards. It had been removed long ago. Edmund tried to ask questions too, but he discovered that the adults only ignored him or shrugged him off. His only way of getting information was eavesdropping. Listening to the conversations, he began to understand that Germany was divided and that the west represented freedom.

He was actually returning to quarters frustrated when he heard several people talking about how to get over to the West. The key was to have relatives over there. They kept mentioning Rhineland and that name stuck in Edmund's mind as he ran home.

"You have to tell them that we have relatives in the Rhineland, Mama, and they will let us go."

"But that would be a lie. I don't even know where Rhineland is."

"You must do it, that's the only way we will ever leave this place!"

"Edmund, it scares me," she protested.

Edmund's face turned red with anger. He couldn't understand his mother's refusal to do as he asked, "You disgust me, you won't even lie to save our lives!" he shouted at her.

Alwine was shocked with her son's accusation. She looked at the intense hatred in his eyes and felt profound sorrow. Her every experience told her that lies caused more trouble than they fixed.

It was with apprehension that Alwine relented and entered the waiting lines. With her baby in her arms and her two daughters hanging onto her dress she waited for hours and rehearsed her words over and over again. There was no easy way for her to do this and she feared that if they began to ask her questions she wouldn't be able to answer them. She would not be able to explain where in Rhineland she wanted to go or even who waited for her there. Alwine was so nervous on that cold day in early February that she sweated and shivered.

It only added to her anxiety that Edmund had disappeared at this critical time. She had hoped that he would stay by her side lending her his strength. He had a kind of daring that she did not have and she desperately needed him near, but he was off somewhere again.

But Edmund was inching his way to the front of the line. No one paid him any notice as he weaved and dodged, squeezing to the front. There he listened as the interrogators asked questions; Where do you want to go? Why? Do you have relatives there? No, that train is full. By the time his mother made it near the interrogation desk, he already had a new plan.

He ran to her and whispered into her ear, "You must tell them we have friends in Westphalia."

"No," she said tersely. She had rehearsed Rhineland and could not change now.

"The trains to Rhineland are all full. They won't let us go there."

Alwine cringed at the thought of having to change her story so late. It was a bad omen to her, another confirmation that lies only led to trouble. "I can't do it, Edmund," she said shaking her head. "They'll never believe me."

"Then we're doomed. We'll die right here."

"Where should I say we want to go?"

"Westphalia."

The distraught woman said the name a hundred times as she approached the official. With her voice shaking, she said, "We have friends in the west. We would like to go there."

"Where in the West?"

When his mother hesitated, Edmund blurted out, "Westphalia."

The official looked up at the woman for confirmation and saw her red-faced and obviously flustered, but somehow she nodded her confirmation. In Alwine's mind she could see that it was over. They had been caught in a lie and she wondered what consequences would follow. The man looked down again and shuffled his papers until he found the one he wanted.

"Name?" he asked.

"Fischer, Alwine."

"The children and their ages?"

"Edmund, 12; Hertha, 11; Else, 6; and Kurt, six months."

"There is room on the train to Westphalia," the man said and made out a pass for them.

On February 5, 1946, a month after the Fischers left the Ossenholz camp, they finally saw the Germany they had dreamed of. On a heated train with real seats they crossed over to the West in such comfort that Alwine's eyes were wet with gratitude.

Thirty-Nine

Alwine couldn't believe the difference when she got to the West. The man who interviewed her was reassuring and even smiled as they talked. His friendliness made her feel so guilty that she confessed that she had lied to the East German officials and was sorry she had done it. The interviewer assured her that it was not the first time he had heard that story, and that she had made the right choice. But since she had no relatives or friends to turn to he decided to send her to the city of Westronfeld in the Renzburg District. He explained that the government needed to distribute the millions of refugees evenly. Otherwise, resources might be stretched too far in any one area. Alwine was relieved.

It was an easy ride to Westronfeld by train. They no longer saw the intimidating grey Russian uniforms. Instead, the soldiers they met were more likely to hand out chocolate bars to the children. It was wonderful for Alwine to see her children smile again and take an interest in the sights around them.

As the train stopped to take on passengers, the children became wide eyed, as for the first time in their lives they saw a black man. He came and sat on the bench opposite them and Hertha and Else couldn't stop staring at the man. He endured their mesmerized curiosity graciously. Both girls had heard of black people and had seen pictures in books but had never expected to see one. No matter what their mother said or did, neither Hertha nor Else could take their eyes off the dark-skinned man. Alwine smiled her embarrassment at the man who seemed to be the only one at ease with the scrutiny.

As she watched that man, it fascinated Hertha that he was chewing on something that he never seemed to finish eating. He just chewed and chewed and chewed and never swallowed nor did he put anything new into his mouth. It was a puzzle that intrigued the girl until she made a strange assumption. In a magazine at school she had read about ferocious black cannibals. So she assumed that the man in front of her was a cannibal and that what he was chewing was human flesh. Now her eyes were positively riveted as his jaws never stopped moving.

It was Else who finally whispered into her mother's ear, "What is he eating, Mama?" But her mother only shook her head. She did not know and was dismayed at her daughters' intrusive curiosity.

"Chewing gum," the man enunciated very carefully in a strange accent. Then perceiving that the girls did not understand, he pulled a package out of his pocket and held out two neatly wrapped sticks to Hertha and Else. Hertha drew back in revulsion, as if she were frightened to touch it. Else, however, took a piece and proceeded to eat it, swallowing the gum after only a few bites. "Candy," she said delightedly.

"No, no," the dark man laughed. "You have to chew it, not swallow it." He demonstrated by exaggerating his chewing and smacking his lips. Hertha's eyes nearly popped out as she saw the pink glob that she supposed was human flesh, roll between his teeth and squish like putty when he closed his teeth. This time she almost disappeared behind her mother as the man offered her another piece, but Else took it and chewed on it happily.

Hertha couldn't stand it any longer. She whispered quietly into her sister's ear, "You're a cannibal now."

"No," Else shook her head. She didn't even know what the term meant.

"You are too. I saw it in a magazine. Black people are cannibals. They eat people. Now you are one too."

"No!" Else said angrily.

"Quiet!" their mother said.

"Mama," Else cried, "Hertha said I'm a cannibal."

"That's silly, girls."

"It's true. I saw it in a magazine. Black men eat people."

The black man began to laugh out loud and the whole compartment joined in the amusement until Hertha realized that they were laughing at her. She was so embarrassed she turned red. It was a sight her mother had never expected to see.

"Little girl, I have never eaten anyone," the man explained still smiling. "This is gum. It comes from a tree and when it is flavored it tastes very good. Try a piece."

Hertha hesitated again but thinking that another refusal would cause more embarrassment she finally took it. It was different from anything she had ever tasted before and sweet too. She chewed the piece until all the flavor and sweetness were gone and finally lost interest in the nice man sitting across from her.

When they reached Westronfeld they were assigned housing. It was just one room in a house owned by a widow who lived alone. By decree it was required that every spare room and every house not fully occupied be made available to the refugees fleeing the east. Every empty den and attic was catalogued and assigned. The burden of the refugees displaced by the war was to be carried by everyone. But the woman, whom Alwine knew only as Frau Eberhard, did not need a government declaration to teach her her civic duty. She was glad to help.

Alwine and her family had hardly settled in when their hostess came by to see if they were comfortable. Seeing Else playing with a baby in the far corner of the room, she asked to see the child. Alwine hesitated. It hurt to see the shock on peoples faces when they looked at him, but she felt she could not refuse. "He's sick," she explained before she allowed the woman to see the baby, "we haven't had enough food."

Alwine could see the look of disbelief, but was grateful at how well Frau Eberhard controlled herself in front the children. "I can only imagine," she said with a voice full of incredulity, "what you have gone through."

"I think he's dying," Alwine said, unable to control her tears, "he barely has the strength to cry any more."

The woman came and put her arm around Alwine and comforted her. "We must get him help right away."

"The doctors at the camp just shrugged their shoulders," Alwine told her, "I don't think there is anything they can do."

"I'm going to get a nurse over here right away. You cannot always just accept the first thing they say," Frau Eberhard said emphatically, and went off in haste.

Alwine did not believe that anything could be done but she appreciated this charitable gesture. Human consideration was so much more than she had become accustomed to expect. Alwine acknowledged Frau Eberhard's kindness when she returned to tell her that a nurse was coming in the morning, but she refused to hope.

When she saw Kurt, the nurse said the obvious. "This child is seriously ill. He needs to be in the hospital."

The two women carried him to the hospital and Alwine stayed with him as the nurse laid him in an incubator and a doctor searched for a vein large enough to accept an intravenous needle. He shook his head all the while he was working. When the doctor had done all that he could, he said to Alwine, "Go home and come back in a few days but don't hold out too much hope. There is only so much we can do." Then he shook his head somberly, saying, "We cannot work miracles."

She looked in on her son one more time to kiss him before she went home to her other children. He was struggling to get his fingers into his mouth and that made Alwine smile. "Is that what keeps you going?" she asked him tenderly, and then she guided those two fingers that he loved so much into his mouth.

Alwine was certain that she had seen her son for the last time and it seemed ironic to her that just when the future began to hold some promise for the rest of her family the little boy should be deprived of his. He had held out so long against the bitterness of his existence and had been so brave in bearing cold and hunger that it hurt terribly to think he might die now. Worst of all, she now had to leave him there to die on his own. It hurt, but Alwine had borne pain before, and that knowledge made her fight through it. There were three children at home who now stood a chance of growing into adulthood but she had had to put this one in greater danger to accomplish the rescue. She wanted to be grateful but it was hard.

At home Alwine attended to her other children. She registered them in school. Even Else marched off with her hand firmly planted in Hertha's to attend her first class. Alwine was proud of her three brave children as she watched them walk down the road beside the Kaiser Wilhelm Canal to their new school. It seemed that their new life was already beginning with warm second hand coats from the Red Cross and packed lunches, consisting of bread and butter. How happy their mother was to see them laughing and joking. But best of all, Alwine was relieved that she did not have to be afraid that they might not return.

While the children were at school, Alwine got busy looking for other members of her family. She wrote to the Red Cross to ask if they had heard about her husband. She wrote to her uncles in America asking if her husband or any other member of her family had tried to contact them. In the next few days she wrote copiously, to everyone she thought could be of any help in locating either her husband, her sisters or her brother Arnold. She did not ask about her parents. She was sure that they had died.

Edmund came home from the second day of school distraught. "They called me a Polak," he cried. After all he had been through it did not seem fair to him. "In Zeperow I was German," he said in a rage, "in Belschewo they called me a Russian and now in Germany I'm a Polak." Alwine answered him gently, "You have endured so many things son, surely this is not so bad."

Alwine waited three full days before returning to the hospital. Before she went, she prepared herself for the worst by washing and packing Kurt's clothes; she was prepared to leave them at the hospital as a donation for some other child who might need them. She had forbidden herself any hope. It was too much to expect of God after all the blessings she had already received. It seemed so selfish to want one more.

But Alwine also didn't want to hear those final condescending words that would try to shelter her from pain. "We did our best but he was already too weak." Or perhaps the nurses would say, "It's for the best." They could not understand that she had been resigned to her son's death for so long that it did not come as a surprise, but it was still a heartbreaking tragedy, no matter how long it had been expected. She wanted to hide from the pain. She knew that the more people tried to console her the more she would cry. As Alwine stood in the hallway speaking to the nurse who had brought her son there in the first place, she had already accepted Kurt's death. "I would like to leave his clothes for some other child," Alwine said without emotion.

She made this statement with such calmness that the nurse was shocked. "Don't you want to see your baby?" she asked. It was the tone of the question that told Alwine that the nurse was not asking her if she wanted to see him for the last time. "Do you mean he's alive?"

"Yes, your son is alive."

The nurse took her to the boy. In just three days he had filled out from a malnourished, almost grotesque little figure to a healthy looking, normal child. He was actively moving his arms and legs and making noises with a volume that his mother had never heard before. Alwine shook her head, "This is not my child."

She concluded that her son had died and now they were trying to convince her that this little boy was her son so that she would take care of him. The nurse looked at her with a soft reassuring smile, "It is your baby, Frau Fischer. He is a fighter." Just then he put those same two fingers into his mouth with that same struggling motion that her son had always made. Those two fingers were like a life line for the little boy. Now Alwine was convinced that he was indeed her little Kurt.

She spent several hours with her baby and then in the afternoon when her children would be coming back from school she ran all the way home. She was so excited she shouted, as she came into the house, "He's alive, he's alive, Kurt is alive!"

It was another two weeks before the baby was released from the hospital. Else and Hertha were overjoyed to have their brother back and they too could only recognize him by the fingers tucked tightly into his mouth. But it was Edmund who reminded everyone that the only thing needed to complete their family was to have their father back.

The comment distressed Alwine since she had not had a positive response from any of her correspondence. Her uncles in America wrote that they had heard nothing about her husband, but that her sisters Else and Klara had written them from Iserlohn.

By the end of February, Alwine had written to every place where she logically thought Albert might have made contact. Her sisters were very happy to hear from her and wrote that they heard from her brother Arnold, but they had not heard anything of Albert nor from their sister Adele. Alwine got the impression, however, that there was one more place she should write. Because Zwickau was in the Russian Zone, Alwine had not supposed it worthwhile to write to her old friend Anna Sebastian, but since none of her other letters had generated any positive results she followed her impression and wrote. It couldn't hurt. She was not even sure that her letter would be delivered, much less answered.

Only two weeks later Alwine received a telegram. It was from Albert! Anna Sebastian had forwarded her letter to him in the south and he was coming by train to pick them up.

When Edmund, Hertha and Else returned home from school on a cold day at the end of March they opened the door and saw their father sitting in the middle of the room holding his new son. The girls screamed out their delight and ran to his side to receive hugs and kisses. Edmund was just as happy but he stood back to savor the moment. It had all come true. They were out of Poland, Kurt had lived and was doing well and their father had returned to them safely. All their hopes were fulfilled. When Hertha and Else were finished with their hugs and kisses Edmund came and hugged his father. It felt good.

Two days later they were on a train headed for the south. Alwine Fischer rested on the train. Watching Hertha and Else drinking in this new experience it seemed that they would quickly forget the last year and find joy in their new lives. Edmund was strong and in her eyes stood so much taller. Kurt was finally growing too. As she looked back on it, Alwine had surprised herself too. She could not quite figure out how she had survived. Perhaps there was more of her mother's strength in her than she had realized.

She drifted in and out of sleep thinking about her parents and the dreams of her youth. But when she reached her deepest sleep, she was planting a large garden full of tomatoes, carrots, peas, cucumbers, radishes and potatoes. She hadn't slept so peacefully in years and when she woke up, Alwine was happy. She looked at her husband and felt a warmth come over her. He had proved himself faithful and she knew she loved him, not in that girlish way she had felt when she had first seen him, but more deeply, with her entire soul. Her mother had been right and her dream had come true. She looked at her children and had to wonder if all their dreams would come true.

As she drifted to sleep again, she could not know that she had completed a circle begun more than four hundred years before, when a rebel peasant had declared himself 'frei' and left Allgau. Now his descendants were returning, free.

CPSIA information can be obtained
at www.ICGtesting.com
Printed in the USA
JSHW061349150722
28116JS00001B/4

9 781438 935591